THE BLADE HAD DISAPPEARED *BEFORE* IT ENTERED FLESH . . .

The clicking of heels stopped ahead, somewhere near the middle of the bridge. The fog was so dense here over the Thames that someone standing directly under a gas lamp could not be seen from fifteen feet away. Lord Darcy and Commander Lord Ashley also stopped. Then they heard a single sentence, "Now climb up on the balustrade."

"Good God!" said Darcy. The two men broke into a run. At the sound of footsteps the hooded man turned. He froze for a second as if deciding whether or not to run. Then his right hand dived beneath his cloak and came out again with a smallsword. Its needlelike blade gleamed in the foggy light. From the river below came the sound of a muffled splash.

"Take care of him!" Lord Darcy shouted. "I'll get the girl!" He vaulted to the top of the broad stone balustrade, stood for a moment, then took a long clean dive into the impenetrable blackness below.

Commander Lord Ashley's reaction was almost instinctive. His own narrow-bladed sword came from its scabbard and into position before the hooded man could attack. He did not see Lord Darcy's dive from the bridge. His eyes had not for a second left the hooded figure that faced him in the tiny area of mist-filled light beneath the gas lamp.

Then, as his opponent came in, he suddenly felt an odd surge of fear. The sword in the other man's hand seemed to flicker and vanish as it moved!

It was only by instinct and pure luck that he managed to avoid the point of the other's sword and parry the thrust with his own blade. And still his eyes could not find that slim, deadly shaft of steel. It was as if his eyes refused to focus on it.

Wherever he looked, it was always somewhere else. His own thrusts were parried again and again, for each time the other blade neared his own, his eyes would uncontrollably look away.

He did not need to be told that this was sorcery. It was all too apparent that he was faced with an enchanted blade in the hands of a deadly killer.

LORD DARCY

RANDALL GARRETT

COMPILED AND EDITED BY
ERIC FLINT & GUY GORDON

LORD DARCY

Copyright © 2002 by the Estate of Randall Garrett
"The Eyes Have It" was first published in *Analog*, January 1964. "A Case of Identity" was first published in *Analog*, September 1964. "The Muddle of the Woad" was first published in *Analog*, June 1965. "A Stretch of the Imagination" was first published in *Of Men and Malice* (Dean Dickensheet, ed.) Doubleday 1973. The four stories listed above were reissued under the title *Murder and Magic* by Ace Books in 1979. *Too Many Magicians* was first published in serialized form in *Analog*, August-November 1966, and then reissued as a novel by Doubleday in 1967. "The Ipswich Phial" was first published in *Analog*, December 1976. "A Matter of Gravity" was first published in *Analog*, October 1974. "The Napoli Express" was first published in *Asimov's SF*, April 1979. "The Sixteen Keys" was first published in *Fantastic*, May 1976. The four stories listed above were reissued under the title *Lord Darcy Investigates* by Ace Books in 1981. "The Bitter End" was first published in *Asimov's SF*, September–October 1978. "The Spell of War" was first published in *The Future At War* (R. Bretnor, ed.) Ace 1979.

A Baen Books Original

Baen Publishing Enterprises
P.O. Box 1403
Riverdale, NY 10471
www.baen.com

ISBN: 0-7434-3548-6

Cover art by Gary Ruddell

First printing, July 2002
Second printing, May 2003

Library of Congress Cataloging-in-Publication Data
Garrett, Randall.
    Lord Darcy / by Randall Garrett, ed. and compiled by Eric Flint & Guy Gordon.
        p. cm.
    "A Baen Books original"—T.p. verso.
    Contents: The eyes have it—A case of identity—The muddle of the woad—Too many magicians—A stretch of the imagination—A matter of gravity—The bitter end—The Ipswich phial—The sixteen keys—The Napoli Express—The spell of war.
    ISBN 0-7434-3548-6 (pbk.)
    1. Darcy, Lord (Fictitious character)—Fiction. 2. Richard I, King of England, 1157–1199—Fiction. 3. Detective and mystery stories, Amercan. 4. Fantasy fiction, American. I. Flint, Eric. II. Gordon, Guy, 1951– III. Title.
    PS3557.A7238 A6 2002
    813'.54—dc21

                                                                          2002018523

Distributed by Simon & Schuster
1230 Avenue of the Americas
New York, NY 10020

Production by Windhaven Press, Auburn, NH
Printed in the United States of America

10 9 8 7 6 5 4 3 2

CONTENTS

LORD DARCY

PREFACE

Randall Garrett's Lord Darcy is, without doubt, one of the best known and most popular detectives in science fiction and fantasy. The stories are set in an alternate universe where magic works and the Plantagenet dynasty of England never fell. (Yes, that's Richard the Lion-Hearted and the rest of the crew—say what else you will about them, the Plantagenets were the most colorful dynasty in English history.) This volume marks the first time that all eleven stories, including the full-length novel *Too Many Magicians*, have been collected between the covers of a single book.

With the exception of "The Spell of War," which we've placed as an appendix, all the stories are arranged in chronological order. An interesting facet of this series is that the date in the story corresponds closely to the year it was written. Garret wanted to give you the feel that this was taking place *now*—as our world would be with two "minor" changes.

Lord Darcy's career as the Chief Investigator for the Duke of Normandy (and Special Investigator for the High Court of Chivalry) spans a period of approximately a dozen years. The first story, "The Eyes Have It," begins with Darcy as a well-established detective, a man in his early forties. (We are never given his exact age, but since he is depicted as an 18-year-old lieutenant in the "War of '39," it is safe to assume that by the time "The Eyes Have It" opens—in the year 1963 of Garrett's alternate universe—he is approximately 42 years old.)

The stories contained in Part I, concluding with the novel

Too Many Magicians, all take place within a relatively brief period of about three years. From there, we leap forward several years. Part II contains three stories beginning in 1972 and ending two or three years later. The three stories in Part III take place shortly thereafter. We have placed them in their own section because they are closely connected. "The Napoli Express" is a direct sequel to "The Sixteen Keys," the basis for which, in turn, is set in "The Ipswich Phial."

Finally, we placed "The Spell of War" as the conclusion to the volume, even though in terms of internal chronology it is by far the earliest of the tales. The reason we did so is because this story is atypical. It is a war story, not a detective story. It was the last Darcy story which Garrett wrote, late in his career. It tells the tale of how Darcy first met Sean O Lochlainn—not, as they would become a quarter of a century later, as Chief Investigator and Master Sorcerer, but as a very young lieutenant and a young sergeant, fighting together with guns and magic in the trenches of the War of '39.

—Eric Flint & Guy Gordon, editors

P.S. Those of you who are also fans of the mystery genre—as Garrett was himself—will enjoy spotting the many clever allusions he tucked into the stories referring to famous detectives of fiction. Some of them, such as Rex Stout's Nero Wolfe, Archie Goodwin, and even the Pink Panther, are obvious enough. But our personal favorite is in danger of being lost in time. Not many will remember the once-popular 1960s TV show *The Man From U.N.C.L.E.* The pun, it is often said, is the lowest form of humor (which, needless to say, never stopped us from laughing at Garrett's superb display of the art). See if you can spot it three ways in his novel *Too Many Magicians.*

PART ONE

The Eyes Have It

Sir Pierre Morlaix, Chevalier of the Angevin Empire, Knight of the Golden Leopard, and secretary-in-private to my lord, the Count D'Evreux, pushed back the lace at his cuff for a glance at his wrist watch—three minutes of seven. The Angelus had rung at six, as always, and my lord D'Evreux had been awakened by it, as always. At least, Sir Pierre could not remember any time in the past seventeen years when my lord had not awakened at the Angelus. Once, he recalled, the sacristan had failed to ring the bell, and the Count had been furious for a week. Only the intercession of Father Bright, backed by the Bishop himself, had saved the sacristan from doing a turn in the dungeons of Castle D'Evreux.

Sir Pierre stepped out into the corridor, walked along the carpeted flagstones, and cast a practiced eye around him as he walked. These old castles were difficult to keep clean, and my lord the Count was fussy about nitre collecting in the seams between the stones of the walls. All appeared quite in order, which was a good thing. My lord the Count had been making a night of it last evening, and that always made him the more peevish in the morning. Though he always woke at the Angelus, he did not always wake up sober.

Sir Pierre stopped before a heavy, polished, carved oak door, selected a key from one of the many at his belt, and turned it in the lock. Then he went into the elevator and the door locked automatically behind him. He pressed the switch and waited in patient silence as he was lifted up four floors to the Count's personal suite.

By now, my lord the Count would have bathed, shaved,

5

and dressed. He would also have poured down an eye-opener consisting of half a water glass of fine Champagne brandy. He would not eat breakfast until eight. The Count had no valet in the strict sense of the term. Sir Reginald Beauvay held that title, but he was never called upon to exercise the more personal functions of his office. The Count did not like to be seen until he was thoroughly presentable.

The elevator stopped. Sir Pierre stepped out into the corridor and walked along it toward the door at the far end. At exactly seven o'clock, he rapped briskly on the great door which bore the gilt-and-polychrome arms of the House D'Evreux.

For the first time in seventeen years, there was no answer.

Sir Pierre waited for the growled command to enter for a full minute, unable to believe his ears. Then, almost timidly, he rapped again.

There was still no answer.

Then, bracing himself for the verbal onslaught that would follow if he had erred, Sir Pierre turned the handle and opened the door just as if he had heard the Count's voice telling him to come in.

"Good morning, my lord," he said, as he always had for seventeen years.

But the room was empty, and there was no answer.

He looked around the huge room. The morning sunlight streamed in through the high mullioned windows and spread a diamond-checkered pattern across the tapestry on the far wall, lighting up the brilliant hunting scene in a blaze of color.

"My lord?"

Nothing. Not a sound.

The bedroom door was open. Sir Pierre walked across to it and looked in.

He saw immediately why my lord the Count had not answered, and that, indeed, he would never answer again.

My lord the Count lay flat on his back, his arms spread wide, his eyes staring at the ceiling. He was still clad in his gold and scarlet evening clothes. But the great stain on the front of his coat was not the same shade of scarlet as the rest of the cloth, and the stain had a bullet hole in its center.

Sir Pierre looked at him without moving for a long

moment. Then he stepped over, knelt, and touched one of the Count's hands with the back of his own. It was quite cool. He had been dead for hours.

"I knew someone would do you in sooner or later, my lord," said Sir Pierre, almost regretfully.

Then he rose from his kneeling position and walked out without another look at his dead lord. He locked the door of the suite, pocketed the key, and went back downstairs in the elevator.

Mary, Lady Duncan stared out of the window at the morning sunlight and wondered what to do. The Angelus bell had awakened her from a fitful sleep in her chair, and she knew that, as a guest of Castle D'Evreux, she would be expected to appear at Mass again this morning. But how could she? How could she face the Sacramental Lord on the altar—to say nothing of taking the Blessed Sacrament itself?

Still, it would look all the more conspicuous if she did not show up this morning after having made it a point to attend every morning with Lady Alice during the first four days of this visit.

She turned and glanced at the locked and barred door of the bedroom. *He* would not be expected to come. Laird Duncan used his wheelchair as an excuse, but since he had taken up black magic as a hobby he had, she suspected, been actually afraid to go anywhere near a church.

If only she hadn't lied to him! But how could she have told the truth? That would have been worse—infinitely worse. And now, because of that lie, he was locked in his bedroom doing only God and the Devil knew what.

If only he would come out. If he would only stop whatever it was he had been doing for all these long hours—or at least finish it! Then they could leave Evreux, make some excuse—any excuse—to get away. One of them could feign sickness. Anything, anything to get them out of France, across the Channel, and back to Scotland, where they would be safe!

She looked back out of the window, across the courtyard, at the towering stone walls of the Great Keep and at the high window that opened into the suite of Edouard, Count D'Evreux.

Last night she had hated him, but no longer. Now there was only room in her heart for fear.

She buried her face in her hands and cursed herself for a fool. There were no tears left for weeping—not after the long night.

Behind her, she heard the sudden noise of the door being unlocked, and she turned.

Laird Duncan of Duncan opened the door and wheeled himself out. He was followed by a malodorous gust of vapor from the room he had just left. Lady Duncan stared at him.

He looked older than he had last night, more haggard and worn, and there was something in his eyes she did not like. For a moment he said nothing. Then he wet his lips with the tip of his tongue. When he spoke, his voice sounded dazed.

"There is nothing to fear any more," he said. "Nothing to fear at all."

The Reverend Father James Valois Bright, Vicar of the Chapel of Saint-Esprit, had as his flock the several hundred inhabitants of the Castle D'Evreux. As such, he was the ranking priest—socially, not hierarchically—in the County. Not counting the Bishop and the Chapter at the Cathedral, of course. But such knowledge did little good for the Father's peace of mind. The turnout of his flock was abominably small for its size—especially for weekday Masses. The Sunday Masses were well attended, of course; Count D'Evreux was there punctually at nine every Sunday, and he had a habit of counting the house. But he never showed up on weekdays, and his laxity had allowed a certain further laxity to filter down through the ranks.

The great consolation was Lady Alice D'Evreux. She was a plain, simple girl, nearly twenty years younger than her brother, the Count, and quite his opposite in every way. She was quiet where he was thundering, self-effacing where he was flamboyant, temperate where he was drunken, and chaste where he was—

Father Bright brought his thoughts to a full halt for a moment. He had, he reminded himself, no right to make judgments of that sort. He was not, after all, the Count's confessor; the Bishop was.

Besides, he should have his mind on his prayers just now.

He paused and was rather surprised to notice that he had already put on his alb, amice, and girdle, and he was aware that his lips had formed the words of the prayer as he had donned each of them.

Habit, he thought, *can be destructive to the contemplative faculty.*

He glanced around the sacristy. His server, the young son of the Count of Saint Brieuc, sent here to complete his education as a gentleman who would some day be the King's Governor of one of the most important counties in Brittany, was pulling his surplice down over his head. The clock said 7:11.

Father Bright forced his mind Heavenward and repeated silently the vesting prayers that his lips had formed meaninglessly, this time putting his full intentions behind them. Then he added a short mental prayer asking God to forgive him for allowing his thoughts to stray in such a manner.

He opened his eyes and reached for his chasuble just as the sacristy door opened and Sir Pierre, the Count's Privy Secretary, stepped in.

"I must speak to you, Father," he said in a low voice. And glancing at the young De Saint-Brieuc, he added: "Alone."

Normally, Father Bright would have reprimanded anyone who presumed to break into the sacristy as he was vesting for Mass, but he knew that Sir Pierre would never interrupt without good reason. He nodded and went outside in the corridor that led to the altar.

"What is it, Pierre?" he asked.

"My lord the Count is dead. Murdered."

After the first momentary shock, Father Bright realized that the news was not, after all, totally unexpected. Somewhere in the back of his mind, it seemed he had always known that the Count would die by violence long before debauchery ruined his health.

"Tell me about it," he said quietly.

Sir Pierre reported exactly what he had done and what he had seen.

"Then I locked the door and came straight here," he told the priest.

"Who else has the key to the Count's suite?" Father Bright asked.

"No one but my lord himself," Sir Pierre answered, "at least as far as I know."

"Where is his key?"

"Still in the ring at his belt. I noticed that particularly."

"Very good. We'll leave it locked. You're certain the body was cold?"

"Cold and waxy, Father."

"Then he's been dead many hours."

"Lady Alice will have to be told," Sir Pierre said.

Father Bright nodded. "Yes. The Countess D'Evreux must be informed of her succession to the County Seat." He could tell by the sudden momentary blank look that came over Sir Pierre's face that the Privy Secretary had not yet realized fully the implications of the Count's death. "I'll tell her, Pierre. She should be in her pew by now. Just step into the church and tell her quietly that I want to speak to her. Don't tell her anything else."

"I understand, Father," said Sir Pierre.

There were only twenty-five or thirty people in the pews—most of them women—but Alice, Countess D'Evreux was not one of them. Sir Pierre walked quietly and unobtrusively down the side aisle and out into the narthex. She was standing there, just inside the main door, adjusting the black lace mantilla about her head, as though she had just come in from outside. Suddenly, Sir Pierre was very glad he would not have to be the one to break the news.

She looked rather sad, as always, her plain face unsmiling. The jutting nose and square chin which had given her brother the Count a look of aggressive handsomeness only made her look very solemn and rather sexless, although she had a magnificent figure.

"My lady," Sir Pierre said, stepping toward her, "the Reverend Father would like to speak to you before Mass. He's waiting at the sacristy door."

She held her rosary clutched tightly to her breast and gasped. Then she said, "Oh. Sir Pierre. I'm sorry; you quite surprised me. I didn't see you."

"My apologies, my lady."

"It's all right. My thoughts were elsewhere. Will you take me to the good Father?"

Father Bright heard their footsteps coming down the

corridor before he saw them. He was a little fidgety because Mass was already a minute overdue. It should have started promptly at 7:15.

The new Countess D'Evreux took the news calmly, as he had known she would. After a pause, she crossed herself and said: "May his soul rest in peace. I will leave everything in your hands, Father, Sir Pierre. What are we to do?"

"Pierre must get on the teleson to Rouen immediately and report the matter to His Highness. I will announce your brother's death and ask for prayers for his soul—but I think I need say nothing about the manner of his death. There is no need to arouse any more speculation and fuss than necessary."

"Very well," said the Countess. "Come, Sir Pierre; I will speak to the Duke, my cousin, myself."

"Yes, my lady."

Father Bright returned to the sacristy, opened the missal, and changed the placement of the ribbons. Today was an ordinary Feria; a Votive Mass would not be forbidden by the rubrics. The clock said 7:17. He turned to young De Saint-Brieuc, who was waiting respectfully. "Quickly, my son—go and get the unbleached beeswax candles and put them on the altar. Be sure you light them before you put out the white ones. Hurry, now; I will be ready by the time you come back. Oh, yes—and change the altar frontal. Put on the black."

"Yes, Father." And the lad was gone.

Father Bright folded the green chasuble and returned it to the drawer, then took out the black one. He would say a Requiem for the Souls of All the Faithful Departed—and hope that the Count was among them.

His Royal Highness, the Duke of Normandy, looked over the official letter his secretary had just typed for him. It was addressed to *Serenissimo Domino Nostro Iohanni Quarto, Dei Gratia, Angliae, Franciae, Scotiae, Hiberniae, Novae Angliae et Novae Franciae, Rex, Imperatore, Fidei Defensor,* . . . "Our Most Serene Lord, John IV, by the Grace of God King and Emperor of England, France, Scotland, Ireland, New England and New France, Defender of the Faith, . . ."

It was a routine matter; simple notification to his brother, the King, that His Majesty's most faithful servant, Edouard, Count of Evreux, had departed this life, and asking His Majesty's confirmation of the Count's heir-at-law, Alice, Countess of Evreux as his lawful successor.

His Highness finished reading, nodded, and scrawled his signature at the bottom: *Ricardus Dux Normaniae.*

Then, on a separate piece of paper, he wrote: "Dear John, May I suggest you hold up on this for a while? Edouard was a lecher and a slob, and I have no doubt he got everything he deserved, but we have no notion who killed him. For any evidence I have to the contrary, it might have been Alice who pulled the trigger. I will send you full particulars as soon as I have them. With much love, Your brother and servant, Richard."

He put both papers into a prepared envelope and sealed it. He wished he could have called the King on the teleson, but no one had yet figured out how to get the wires across the Channel.

He looked absently at the sealed envelope, his handsome blond features thoughtful. The House of Plantagenet had endured for eight centuries, and the blood of Henry of Anjou ran thin in its veins, but the Norman strain was as strong as ever, having been replenished over the centuries by fresh infusions from Norwegian and Danish princesses. Richard's mother, Queen Helga, wife of His late Majesty, Charles III, spoke very few words of Anglo-French, and those with a heavy Norse accent.

Nevertheless, there was nothing Scandinavian in the language, manner, or bearing of Richard, Duke of Normandy. Not only was he a member of the oldest and most powerful ruling family of Europe, but he bore a Christian name that was distinguished even in that family. Seven Kings of the Empire had borne the name, and most of them had been good Kings—if not always "good" men in the nicey-nicey sense of the word. There was a chance that Duke Richard might be called upon to uphold the honor of that name as King. By law, Parliament must elect a Plantagenet as King in the event of the death of the present Sovereign, and while the election of one of the King's two sons, the Prince of Britain and the Duke of Lancaster, was more likely than the election of Richard, he was certainly not eliminated from the succession.

Meantime, he would uphold the honor of his name as Duke of Normandy.

Murder had been done; therefore justice must be done. The Count D'Evreux had been known for his stern but fair justice almost as well as he had been known for his profligacy. And, just as his pleasures had been without temperance, so his justice had been untempered by mercy. Whoever had killed him would find both justice and mercy—in so far as Richard had it within his power to give it.

Although he did not formulate it in so many words, even mentally, Richard was of the opinion that some debauched woman or cuckolded man had fired the fatal shot. Thus he found himself inclining toward mercy before he knew anything substantial about the case at all.

Richard dropped the letter he was holding into the special mail pouch that would be placed aboard the evening trans-Channel packet, and then turned in his chair to look at the lean, middle-aged man working at a desk across the room.

"My lord Marquis," he said thoughtfully.

"Yes, Your Highness?" said the Marquis of Rouen, looking up.

"How true are the stories one has heard about the late Count?"

"True, Your Highness?" the Marquis said thoughtfully. "I would hesitate to make any estimate of percentages. Once a man gets a reputation like that, the number of his reputed sins quickly surpasses the number of actual ones. Doubtless many of the stories one hears are of whole cloth; others may have only a slight basis in fact. On the other hand, it is highly likely that there are many of which we have never heard. It is absolutely certain, however, that he has acknowledged seven illegitimate sons, and I dare say he has ignored a few daughters—and these, mind you, with unmarried women. His adulteries would be rather more difficult to establish, but I think Your Highness can take it for granted that such escapades were far from uncommon."

He cleared his throat and then added, "If Your Highness is looking for motive, I fear there is a superabundance of persons with motive."

"I see," the Duke said. "Well, we will wait and see what sort of information Lord Darcy comes up with." He looked up at the clock. "They should be there by now."

Then, as if brushing further thoughts on that subject from his mind, he went back to work, picking up a new sheaf of state papers from his desk.

The Marquis watched him for a moment and smiled a little to himself. The young Duke took his work seriously, but was well-balanced about it. A little inclined to be romantic—but aren't we all at nineteen? There was no doubt of his ability, nor of his nobility. The Royal Blood of England always came through.

"My lady," said Sir Pierre gently, "the Duke's Investigators have arrived."

My Lady Alice, Countess D'Evreux, was seated in a gold-brocade upholstered chair in the small receiving room off the Great Hall. Standing near her, looking very grave, was Father Bright. Against the blaze of color on the walls of the room, the two of them stood out like ink blots. Father Bright wore his normal clerical black, unrelieved except for the pure white lace at collar and cuffs. The Countess wore unadorned black velvet, a dress which she had had to have altered hurriedly by her dressmaker; she had always hated black and owned only the mourning she had worn when her mother died eight years before. The somber looks on their faces seemed to make the black blacker.

"Show them in, Sir Pierre," the Countess said calmly.

Sir Pierre opened the door wider, and three men entered. One was dressed as one gently born; the other two wore the livery of the Duke of Normandy.

The gentleman bowed. "I am Lord Darcy, Chief Criminal Investigator for His Highness, the Duke, and your servant, my lady." He was a tall, brown-haired man with a rather handsome, lean face. He spoke Anglo-French with a definite English accent.

"My pleasure, Lord Darcy," said the Countess. "This is our vicar, Father Bright."

"Your servant, Reverend Sir." Then he presented the two men with him. The first was a scholarly-looking, graying man wearing pince-nez glasses with gold rims, Dr. Pateley, Chirurgeon. The second, a tubby, red-faced, smiling man, was Master Sean O Lochlainn, Sorcerer.

As soon as Master Sean was presented he removed a

small, leather-bound folder from his belt pouch and proffered it to the priest. "My license, Reverend Father."

Father Bright took it and glanced over it. It was the usual thing, signed and sealed by the Archbishop of Rouen. The law was rather strict on that point; no sorcerer could practice without the permission of the Church, and a license was given only after careful examination for orthodoxy of practice.

"It seems to be quite in order, Master Sean," said the priest, handing the folder back. The tubby little sorcerer bowed his thanks and returned the folder to his belt pouch.

Lord Darcy had a notebook in his hand. "Now, unpleasant as it may be, we shall have to check on a few facts." He consulted his notes, then looked up at Sir Pierre. "You, I believe, discovered the body?"

"That is correct, your lordship."

"How long ago was this?"

Sir Pierre glanced at his wrist watch. It was 9:55. "Not quite three hours ago, your lordship."

"At what time, precisely?"

"I rapped on the door precisely at seven, and went in a minute or two later—say 7:01 or 7:02."

"How do you know the time so exactly?"

"My lord the Count," said Sir Pierre with some stiffness, "insisted upon exact punctuality. I have formed the habit of referring to my watch regularly."

"I see. Very good. Now, what did you do then?"

Sir Pierre described his actions briefly.

"The door to his suite was not locked, then?" Lord Darcy asked.

"No, sir."

"You did not expect it to be locked?"

"No, sir. It has not been for seventeen years."

Lord Darcy raised one eyebrow in a polite query. "Never?"

"Not at seven o'clock, your lordship. My lord the Count always rose promptly at six and unlocked the door before seven."

"He did lock it at night, then?"

"Yes, sir."

Lord Darcy looked thoughtful and made a note, but he said nothing more on that subject. "When you left, you locked the door?"

"That is correct, your lordship."

"And it has remained locked ever since?"

Sir Pierre hesitated and glanced at Father Bright. The priest said: "At 8:15, Sir Pierre and I went in. I wished to view the body. We touched nothing. We left at 8:20."

Master Sean O Lochlainn looked agitated. "Er . . . excuse me, Reverend Sir. You didn't give him Holy Unction, I hope?"

"No," said Father Bright. "I thought it would be better to delay that until after the authorities had seen the . . . er . . . scene of the crime. I wouldn't want to make the gathering of evidence any more difficult than necessary."

"Quite right," murmured Lord Darcy.

"No blessings, I trust, Reverend Sir?" Master Sean persisted. "No exorcisms or—"

"Nothing," Father Bright interrupted somewhat testily. "I believe I crossed myself when I saw the body, but nothing more."

"Crossed *yourself*, sir. Nothing else?"

"No."

"Well, that's all right, then. Sorry to be so persistent, Reverend Sir, but any miasma of evil that may be left around is a very important clue, and it shouldn't be dispersed until it's been checked, you see."

"*Evil?*" My lady the Countess looked shocked.

"Sorry, my lady, but—" Master Sean began contritely.

But Father Bright interrupted by speaking to the Countess. "Don't distress yourself, my daughter; these men are only doing their duty."

"Of course. I understand. It's just that it's so—" She shuddered delicately.

Lord Darcy cast Master Sean a warning look, then asked politely, "Has my lady seen the deceased?"

"No," she said. "I will, however, if you wish."

"We'll see," said Lord Darcy. "Perhaps it won't be necessary. May we go up to the suite now?"

"Certainly," the Countess said. "Sir Pierre, if you will?"

"Yes, my lady."

As Sir Pierre unlocked the emblazoned door, Lord Darcy said: "Who else sleeps on this floor?"

"No one else, your lordship," Sir Pierre said. "The entire floor is . . . was . . . reserved for my lord the Count."

"Is there any way up besides that elevator?"

Sir Pierre turned and pointed toward the other end of the

short hallway. "That leads to the staircase," he said, pointing to a massive oaken door, "but it's kept locked at all times. And, as you can see, there is a heavy bar across it. Except for moving furniture in and out or something like that, it's never used."

"No other way up or down, then?"

Sir Pierre hesitated. "Well, yes, your lordship, there is. I'll show you."

"A secret stairway?"

"Yes, your lordship."

"Very well. We'll look at it after we've seen the body."

Lord Darcy, having spent an hour on the train down from Rouen, was anxious to see the cause of all the trouble at last.

He lay in the bedroom, just as Sir Pierre and Father Bright had left him.

"If you please, Dr. Pateley," said his lordship.

He knelt on one side of the corpse and watched carefully while Pateley knelt on the other side and looked at the face of the dead man. Then he touched one of the hands and tried to move an arm.

"Rigor has set in—even to the fingers. Single bullet hole. Rather small caliber—I should say a .28 or .34—hard to tell until I've probed out the bullet. Looks like it went right through the heart, though. Hard to tell about powder burns; the blood has soaked the clothing and dried. Still, these specks . . . hm-m-m. Yes. Hm-m-m."

Lord Darcy's eyes took in everything, but there was little enough to see on the body itself. Then his eye was caught by something that gave off a golden gleam. He stood up and walked over to the great canopied four-poster bed, then he was on his knees again, peering under it. A coin? No.

He picked it up carefully and looked at it. A button. Gold, intricately engraved in an Arabesque pattern, and set in the center with a single diamond. How long had it lain there? Where had it come from? Not from the Count's clothing, for his buttons were smaller, engraved with his arms, and had no gems. Had a man or a woman dropped it? There was no way of knowing at this stage of the game.

Darcy turned to Sir Pierre. "When was this room last cleaned?"

"Last evening, your lordship," the secretary said promptly.

"My lord was always particular about that. The suite was always to be swept and cleaned during the dinner hour."

"Then this must have rolled under the bed at some time after dinner. Do you recognize it? The design is distinctive."

The Privy Secretary looked carefully at the button in the palm of Lord Darcy's hand without touching it. "I . . . I hesitate to say," he said at last. "It looks like . . . but I'm not sure—"

"Come, come, Chevalier! Where do you think you *might* have seen it? Or one like it." There was a sharpness in the tone of his voice.

"I'm not trying to conceal anything, your lordship," Sir Pierre said with equal sharpness. "I said I was not sure. I still am not, but it can be checked easily enough. If your lordship will permit me—" He turned and spoke to Dr. Pateley, who was still kneeling by the body. "May I have my lord the Count's keys, doctor?"

Pateley glanced up at Lord Darcy, who nodded silently. The chirurgeon detached the keys from the belt and handed them to Sir Pierre.

The Privy Secretary looked at them for a moment, then selected a small gold key. "This is it," he said, separating it from the others on the ring. "Come with me, your lordship."

Darcy followed him across the room to a broad wall covered with a great tapestry that must have dated back to the sixteenth century. Sir Pierre reached behind it and pulled a cord. The entire tapestry slid aside like a panel, and Lord Darcy saw that it was supported on a track some ten feet from the floor. Behind it was what looked at first like ordinary oak paneling, but Sir Pierre fitted the small key into an inconspicuous hole and turned. Or, rather, tried to turn.

"That's odd," said Sir Pierre. "It's not locked!"

He took the key out and pressed on the panel, shoving sideways with his hand to move it aside. It slid open to reveal a closet.

The closet was filled with women's clothing of all kinds, and styles.

Lord Darcy whistled soundlessly.

"Try that blue robe, your lordship," the Privy Secretary said. "The one with the— Yes, that's the one."

Lord Darcy took it off its hanger. The same buttons. They matched. And there was one missing from the front! Torn off! "Master Sean!" he called without turning.

Master Sean came with a rolling walk. He was holding an oddly shaped bronze thing in his hand that Sir Pierre didn't quite recognize. The sorcerer was muttering. "Evil, that there is! Faith, and the vibrations are all over the place. Yes, me lord?"

"Check this dress and the button when you get round to it. I want to know when the two parted company."

"Yes, me lord." He draped the robe over one arm and dropped the button into a pouch at his belt. "I can tell you one thing, me lord. You talk about an evil miasma, this room has got it!" He held up the object in his hand. "There's an underlying background—something that has been here for years, just seeping in. But on top of that, there's a hellish big blast of it superimposed. Fresh it is, and very strong."

"I shouldn't be surprised, considering there was murder done here last night—or very early this morning," said Lord Darcy.

"Hm-m-m, yes. Yes, me lord, the death is there—but there's something else. Something I can't place."

"You can tell that just by holding that bronze cross in your hand?" Sir Pierre asked interestedly.

Master Sean gave him a friendly scowl. "'Tisn't quite a cross, sir. This is what is known as a *crux ansata*. The ancient Egyptians called it an *ankh*. Notice the loop at the top instead of the straight piece your true cross has. Now, your true cross—if it were properly energized, blessed, d'ye see—your true cross would tend to dissipate the evil. The *ankh* merely vibrates to evil because of the closed loop at the top, which makes a return circuit. And it's not energized by blessing, but by another . . . um . . . spell."

"Master Sean, we have a murder to investigate," said Lord Darcy.

The sorcerer caught the tone of his voice and nodded quickly. "Yes, me lord." And he walked rollingly away.

"Now, where's that secret stairway you mentioned, Sir Pierre?" Lord Darcy asked.

"This way, your lordship."

He led Lord Darcy to a wall at right angles to the outer wall and slid back another tapestry.

"Good Heavens," Darcy muttered, "does he have something concealed behind every arras in the place?" But he didn't say it loud enough for the Privy Secretary to hear.

This time, what greeted them was a solid-seeming stone wall. But Sir Pierre pressed in on one small stone, and a section of the wall swung back, exposing a stairway.

"Oh, yes," Darcy said. "I see what he did. This is the old spiral stairway that goes round the inside of the Keep. There are two doorways at the bottom. One opens into the courtyard, the other is a postern gate through the curtain wall to the outside—but that was closed up in the sixteenth century, so the only way out is into the courtyard."

"Your lordship knows Castle D'Evreux, then?" Sir Pierre said. Sir Pierre had no recollection of Darcy's having been in the Castle before.

"Only by the plans in the Royal Archives. But I have made it a point to—" He stopped. "Dear me," he interrupted himself mildly, "what is that?"

"That" was something that had been hidden by the arras until Sir Pierre had slid it aside, and was still showing only a part of itself. It lay on the floor a foot or so from the secret door.

Darcy knelt down and pulled the tapestry back from the object. "Well, well. A .28 two-shot pocket gun. Gold-chased, beautifully engraved, mother-of-pearl handle. A regular gem." He picked it up and examined it closely. "One shot fired."

He stood up and showed it to Sir Pierre. "Ever see it before?"

The Privy Secretary looked at the weapon closely. Then he shook his head. "Not that I recall, your lordship. It certainly isn't one of the Count's guns."

"You're certain?"

"Quite certain, your lordship. I'll show you the gun collection if you want. My lord the Count didn't like tiny guns like that; he preferred a larger caliber. He would never have owned what he considered a toy."

"Well, we'll have to look into it." He called over Master Sean again and gave the gun into his keeping. "And keep your eyes open for anything else of interest, Master Sean. So far, everything of interest besides the late Count himself has been hiding under beds or behind arrases. Check everything. Sir Pierre and I are going for a look down this stairway."

The stairway was gloomy, but enough light came in through the arrow slits spaced at intervals along the outer wall to illuminate the interior. It spiraled down between the inner and outer walls of the Great Keep, making four complete circuits before it reached ground level. Lord Darcy looked carefully at the steps, the walls, and even the low, arched overhead as he and Sir Pierre went down.

After the first circuit, on the floor beneath the Count's suite, he stopped. "There was a door here," he said, pointing to a rectangular area in the inner wall.

"Yes, your lordship. There used to be an opening at every floor, but they were all sealed off. It's quite solid, as you can see."

"Where would they lead if they were open?"

"The county offices. My own office, the clerk's offices, the constabulary on the first floor. Below are the dungeons. My lord the Count was the only one who lived in the Keep itself. The rest of the household live above the Great Hall."

"What about guests?"

"They're usually housed in the east wing. We only have two house guests at the moment. Laird and Lady Duncan have been with us for four days."

"I see." They went down perhaps four more steps before Lord Darcy asked quietly, "Tell me, Sir Pierre, were you privy to *all* of Count D'Evreux's business?"

Another four steps down before Sir Pierre answered. "I understand what your lordship means," he said. Another two steps. "No, I was not. I was aware that my lord the Count engaged in certain . . . er . . . shall we say, liaisons with members of the opposite sex. However—"

He paused, and in the gloom, Lord Darcy could see his lips tighten. "However," he continued, "I did not procure for my lord, if that is what you're driving at. I am not and never have been a pimp."

"I didn't intend to suggest that you had, good knight," said Lord Darcy in a tone that strongly implied that the thought had actually never crossed his mind. "Not at all. But certainly there is a difference between 'aiding and abetting' and simple knowledge of what is going on."

"Oh. Yes. Yes, of course. Well, one cannot, of course, be

the secretary-in-private of a gentleman such as my lord the Count for seventeen years without knowing something of what is going on, you're right. Yes. Yes. Hm-m-m."

Lord Darcy smiled to himself. Not until this moment had Sir Pierre realized how much he actually *did* know. In loyalty to his lord, he had literally kept his eyes shut for seventeen years.

"I realize," Lord Darcy said smoothly, "that a gentleman would never implicate a lady nor besmirch the reputation of another gentleman without due cause and careful consideration. However,"—like the knight, he paused a moment before going on—"although we are aware that he was not discreet, was he particular?"

"If you mean by that, did he confine his attentions to those of gentle birth, your lordship, then I can say, no he did not. If you mean did he confine his attentions to the gentler sex, then I can only say that, as far as I know, he did."

"I see. That explains the closet full of clothes."

"Beg pardon, your lordship?"

"I mean that if a girl or woman of the lower classes were to come here, he would have proper clothing for them to wear."

"Quite likely, your lordship. He was most particular about clothing. Couldn't stand a woman who was sloppily dressed or poorly dressed."

"In what way?"

"Well. Well, for instance, I recall once that he saw a very pretty peasant girl. She was dressed in the common style, of course, but she was dressed neatly and prettily. My lord took a fancy to her. He said, 'Now there's a lass who knows how to wear clothes. Put her in decent apparel, and she'd pass for a princess.' But a girl who had a pretty face and a fine figure made no impression on him unless she wore her clothing well, if you see what I mean, your lordship."

"Did you never know him to fancy a girl who dressed in an offhand manner?" Lord Darcy asked.

"Only among the gently born, your lordship. He'd say, 'Look at Lady So-and-so! Nice wench, if she'd let me teach her how to dress.' You might say, your lordship, that a woman could be dressed commonly or sloppily, but not both."

"Judging by the stuff in that closet," Lord Darcy said, "I should say that the late Count had excellent taste in feminine dress."

Sir Pierre considered. "Hm-m-m. Well, now, I wouldn't exactly say so, your lordship. He knew how clothes should be worn, yes. But he couldn't pick out a woman's gown of his accord. He could choose his own clothing with impeccable taste, but he'd not any real notion of how a woman's clothing should go, if you see what I mean. All he knew was how good clothing should be worn. But he knew nothing about design for women's clothing."

"Then how did he get that closet full of clothes?" Lord Darcy asked, puzzled.

Sir Pierre chuckled. "Very simply, your lordship. He knew that the Lady Alice had good taste, so he secretly instructed that each piece that Lady Alice ordered should be made in duplicate. With small variations, of course. I'm certain my lady wouldn't like it if she knew."

"I dare say not," said Lord Darcy thoughtfully.

"Here is the door to the courtyard," said Sir Pierre. "I doubt that it has been opened in broad daylight for many years." He selected a key from the ring of the late Count and inserted it into a keyhole. The door swung back, revealing a large crucifix attached to its outer surface. Lord Darcy crossed himself. "Lord in Heaven," he said softly, "what is this?"

He looked out into a small shrine. It was walled off from the courtyard and had a single small entrance some ten feet from the doorway. There were four prie-dieus—small kneeling benches—ranged in front of the doorway.

"If I may explain, your lordship—" Sir Pierre began.

"No need to," Lord Darcy said in a hard voice. "It's rather obvious. My lord the Count was quite ingenious. This is a relatively newly-built shrine. Four walls and a crucifix against the castle wall. Anyone could come in here, day or night, for prayer. No one who came in would be suspected." He stepped out into the small enclosure and swung around to look at the door. "And when that door is closed, there is no sign that there is a door behind the crucifix. If a woman came in here, it would be assumed that she came for prayer. But if she knew of that door—" His voice trailed off.

"Yes, your lordship," said Sir Pierre. "I did not approve, but I was in no position to disapprove."

"I understand." Lord Darcy stepped out to the doorway of the little shrine and took a quick glance about. "Then anyone within the castle walls could come in here," he said.

"Yes, your lordship."

"Very well. Let's go back up."

In the small office which Lord Darcy and his staff had been assigned while conducting the investigation, three men watched while a fourth conducted a demonstration on a table in the center of the room.

Master Sean O Lochlainn held up an intricately engraved gold button with an Arabesque pattern and a diamond set in the center.

He looked at the other three. "Now, me lord, your Reverence, and colleague Doctor, I call your attention to this button."

Dr. Pateley smiled and Father Bright looked stern. Lord Darcy merely stuffed tobacco—imported from the southern New England counties on the Gulf—into a German-made porcelain pipe. He allowed Master Sean a certain amount of flamboyance; good sorcerers were hard to come by.

"Will you hold the robe, Dr. Pateley? Thank you. Now, stand back. That's it. Thank you. Now, I place the button on the table, a good ten feet from the robe." Then he muttered something under his breath and dusted a bit of powder on the button. He made a few passes over it with his hands, paused, and looked up at Father Bright. "If you will, Reverend Sir?"

Father Bright solemnly raised his right hand, and, as he made the Sign of the Cross, said: "May this demonstration, O God, be in strict accord with the truth, and may the Evil One not in any way deceive us who are witnesses thereto. In the Name of the Father and of the Son and of the Holy Spirit. Amen."

"Amen," the other three chorused.

Master Sean crossed himself, then muttered something under his breath.

The button leaped from the table, slammed itself against the robe which Dr. Pateley held before him, and stuck there as though it had been sewed on by an expert.

"Ha!" said Master Sean. "As I thought!" He gave the other three men a broad, beaming smile. "The two were definitely connected!"

Lord Darcy looked bored. "Time?" he asked.

"In a moment, me lord," Master Sean said apologetically. "In a moment." While the other three watched, the sorcerer went through more spells with the button and the robe, although none were so spectacular as the first demonstration. Finally, Master Sean said: "About eleven thirty last night they were torn apart, me lord. But I shouldn't like to make it any more definite than to say between eleven and midnight. The speed with which it returned to its place shows that it was ripped off very rapidly, however."

"Very good," said Lord Darcy. "Now the bullet, if you please."

"Yes, me lord. This will have to be a bit different." He took more paraphernalia out of his large, symbol-decorated carpet bag. "The Law of Contagion, gently-born sirs, is a tricky thing to work with. If a man doesn't know how to handle it, he can get himself killed. We had an apprentice o' the Guild back in Cork who might have made a good sorcerer in time. He had the Talent—unfortunately, he didn't have the good sense to go with it. According to the Law of Contagion any two objects which have ever been in contact with each other have an affinity for each other which is directly proportional to the product of the degree of relevancy of the contact and the length of time they were in contact and inversely proportional to the length of time since they have ceased to be in contact." He gave a smiling glance to the priest. "That doesn't apply strictly to relics of the saints, Reverend Sir; there's another factor enters in there, as you know."

As he spoke, the sorcerer was carefully clamping the little handgun into a padded vise so that its barrel was parallel to the surface of the table.

"Anyhow," he went on, "this apprentice, all on his own, decided to get rid of the cockroaches in his house—a simple thing, if one knows how to go about it. So he collected dust from various cracks and crannies about the house, dust which contained, of course, the droppings of the pests. The dust, with the appropriate spells and ingredients, he boiled. It worked fine. The roaches all came down with a raging fever and died. Unfortunately, the clumsy lad had poor laboratory technique. He allowed three drops of his own perspiration to fall into the steaming pot over which he was working, and the resulting fever killed him, too."

By this time, he had put the bullet which Dr. Pateley had removed from the Count's body on a small pedestal so that it was exactly in line with the muzzle of the gun. "There, now," he said softly.

Then he repeated the incantation and the powdering that he had used on the button. As the last syllable was formed by his lips, the bullet vanished with a *ping*! In its vise, the little gun vibrated.

"Ah!" said Master Sean. "No question there, eh? That's the death weapon, all right, me lord. Yes. Time's almost exactly the same as that of the removal of the button. Not more than a few seconds later. Forms a picture, don't it, me lord? His lordship the Count jerks a button off the girl's gown, she outs with a gun and plugs him."

Lord Darcy's handsome face scowled. "Let's not jump to any hasty conclusions, my good Sean. There is no evidence whatever that he was killed by a woman."

"Would a man be wearing that gown, me lord?"

"Possibly," said Lord Darcy. "But who says that anyone was wearing it when the button was removed?"

"Oh." Master Sean subsided into silence. Using a small ramrod, he forced the bullet out of the chamber of the little pistol.

"Father Bright," said Lord Darcy, "will the Countess be serving tea this afternoon?"

The priest looked suddenly contrite. "Good heavens! None of you has eaten yet! I'll see that something is sent up right away, Lord Darcy. In the confusion—"

Lord Darcy held up a hand. "I beg your pardon, Father; that wasn't what I meant. I'm sure Master Sean and Dr. Pateley would appreciate a little something, but I can wait until tea time. What I was thinking was that perhaps the Countess would ask her guests to tea. Does she know Laird and Lady Duncan well enough to ask for their sympathetic presence on such an afternoon as this?"

Father Bright's eyes narrowed a trifle. "I dare say it could be arranged, Lord Darcy. You will be there?"

"Yes but I may be a trifle late. That will hardly matter at an informal tea."

The priest glanced at his watch. "Four o'clock?"

"I should think that would do it," said Lord Darcy.

Father Bright nodded wordlessly and left the room.

Dr. Pateley took off his pince-nez and polished the lenses carefully with a silk handkerchief. "How long will your spell keep the body incorrupt, Master Sean?" he asked.

"As long as it's relevant. As soon as the case is solved, or we have enough data to solve the case—as the case may be, heh heh—he'll start to go. I'm not a saint, you know; it takes powerful motivation to keep a body incorrupt for years and years."

Sir Pierre was eying the gown that Pateley had put on the table. The button was still in place, as if held there by magnetism. He didn't touch it. "Master Sean, I don't know much about magic," he said, "but can't you find out who was wearing this robe just as easily as you found out that the button matched?"

Master Sean wagged his head in a firm negative. "No, sir. 'Tisn't relevant, sir. The relevancy of the integrated dress-as-a-whole is quite strong. So is that of the seamstress or tailor who made the garment, and that of the weaver who made the cloth. But, except in certain circumstances, the person who wears or wore the garment has little actual relevancy to the garment itself."

"I'm afraid I don't understand," said Sir Pierre, looking puzzled.

"Look at it like this, sir: That gown wouldn't be what it is if the weaver hadn't made the cloth in that particular way. It wouldn't be what it is if the seamstress hadn't cut it in a particular way and sewed it in a specific manner. You follow, sir? Yes. Well, then, the connections between garment-and-weaver and garment-and-seamstress are strongly relevant. But this dress would still be pretty much what it is if it had stayed in the closet instead of being worn. No relevance—or very little. Now, if it were a well-worn garment, that would be different—that is, if it had always been worn by the same person. Then, you see, sir, the garment as-a-whole is what it is because of the wearing, and the wearer becomes relevant."

He pointed at the little handgun he was still holding in his hand. "Now you take your gun, here, sir. The—"

"It isn't *my* gun," Sir Pierre interrupted firmly.

"I was speaking rhetorically, sir," said Master Sean with infinite patience. "This gun or any other gun in general, if you see what I mean, sir. It's even harder to place the ownership of a gun. Most of the wear on a gun is purely mechanical. It don't matter *who* pulls the trigger, you see; the erosion by the gases produced in the chamber, and the wear caused by the bullet passing through the barrel will be the same. You see, sir, 'tisn't relevant *to the gun* who pulled its trigger or what it's fired at. The bullet's a slightly different matter. To the bullet, it is relevant which gun it was fired from and what it hit. All these things simply have to be taken into account, Sir Pierre."

"I see," said the knight. "Very interesting, Master Sean." Then he turned to Lord Darcy. "Is there anything else, your lordship? There's a great deal of county business to be attended to."

Lord Darcy waved a hand. "Not at the moment, Sir Pierre. I understand the pressures of government. Go right ahead."

"Thank you, your lordship. If anything further should be required, I shall be in my office."

As soon as Sir Pierre had closed the door, Lord Darcy held out his hand toward the sorcerer. "Master Sean; the gun."

Master Sean handed it to him. "Ever see one like it before?" he asked, turning it over in his hands.

"Not *exactly* like it, me lord."

"Come, come, Sean; don't be so cautious. I am no sorcerer, but I don't need to know the Laws of Similarity to be able to recognize an *obvious* similarity."

"Edinburgh," said Master Sean flatly.

"Exactly. Scottish work. The typical Scot gold work; remarkable beauty. And look at that lock. It has 'Scots' written all over it—and more, 'Edinburgh', as you said."

Dr. Pateley, having replaced his carefully-polished glasses, leaned over and peered at the weapon in Lord Darcy's hand. "Couldn't it be Italian, my lord? Or Moorish? In Moorish Spain, they do work like that."

"No Moorish gunsmith would put a hunting scene on the butt," Lord Darcy said flatly, "and the Italians wouldn't have put heather and thistles in the field surrounding the huntsman."

"But the *FdM* engraved on the barrel," said Dr. Pateley, "indicates the—"

"Ferrari of Milano," said Lord Darcy. "Exactly. But the barrel is of much newer work than the rest. So are the chambers. This is a fairly old gun—fifty years old, I'd say. The lock and the butt are still in excellent condition, indicating that it has been well cared for, but frequent usage—or a single accident—could ruin the barrel and require the owner to get a replacement. It was replaced by Ferrari."

"I see," said Dr. Pateley, somewhat humbled.

"If we open the lock . . . Master Sean, hand me your small screwdriver. Thank you. If we open the lock, we will find the name of one of the finest gunsmiths of half a century ago—a man whose name has not yet been forgotten—Hamish Graw of Edinburgh. Ah! There! You see?" They did.

Having satisfied himself on that point, Lord Darcy closed the lock again. "Now, men, we have the gun located. We also know that a guest in this very castle is Laird Duncan of Duncan. The Duncan of Duncan himself. A Scot laird who was, fifteen years ago, His Majesty's Minister Plenipotentiary to the Grand Duchy of Milano. That suggests to me that it would be indeed odd if there were not some connection between Laird Duncan and this gun. Eh?"

"Come, come, Master Sean," said Lord Darcy rather impatiently, "we haven't all the time in the world."

"Patience, me lord; patience," said the little sorcerer calmly. "Can't hurry these things, you know." He was kneeling in front of a large, heavy traveling chest in the bedroom of the guest apartment occupied temporarily by Laird and Lady Duncan, working with the lock. "One position of a lock is just as relevant as the other so you can't work with the bolt. But the pin-tumblers in the cylinder, now, that's a different matter. A lock's built so that the breaks in the tumblers are not related to the surface of the cylinder when the key is out, but there *is* a relation when the key's *in*, so by taking advantage of that relevancy— Ah!"

The lock clicked open.

Lord Darcy raised the lid gently.

"Carefully, me lord!" Master Sean said in a warning voice.

"He's got a spell on the thing! Let me do it." He made Lord Darcy stand back and then lifted the lid of the heavy trunk himself. When it was leaning back against the wall, gaping open widely on its hinges, Master Sean took a long look at the trunk and its lid without touching either of them. There was a second lid on the trunk, a thin one obviously operated by a simple bolt.

Master Sean took his sorcerer's staff, a five-foot, heavy rod made of the wood of the quicken tree or mountain ash, and touched the inner lid. Nothing happened. He touched the bolt. Nothing.

"Hm-m-m," Master Sean murmured thoughtfully. He glanced around the room, and his eyes fell on a heavy stone doorstop. "That ought to do it." He walked over, picked it up, and carried it back to the chest. Then he put it on the rim of the chest in such a position that if the lid were to fall it would be stopped by the doorstop.

Then he put his hand in as if to lift the inner lid.

The heavy outer lid swung forward and down of its own accord, moving with blurring speed, and slammed viciously against the doorstop.

Lord Darcy massaged his right wrist gently, as if he felt where the lid would have hit if he had tried to open the inner lid. "Triggered to slam if a human being sticks a hand in there, eh?"

"Or a head, me lord. Not very effectual if you know what to look for. There are better spells than that for guarding things. Now we'll see what his lordship wants to protect so badly that he practices sorcery without a license." He lifted the lid again, and then opened the inner lid. "It's safe now, me lord. *Look at this!*"

Lord Darcy had already seen. Both men looked in silence at the collection of paraphernalia on the first tray of the chest. Master Sean's busy fingers carefully opened the tissue paper packing of one after another of the objects. "A human skull," he said. "Bottles of graveyard earth. Hm-m-m—this one is labeled 'virgin's blood.' And this! A Hand of Glory!"

It was a mummified human hand, stiff and dry and brown, with the fingers partially curled, as though they were holding an invisible ball three inches or so in diameter. On each of the fingertips was a short candlestub. When the hand was placed on its back, it would act as a candelabra.

"That pretty much settles it, eh, Master Sean?" Lord Darcy said.

"Indeed, me lord. At the very least, we can get him for possession of materials. Black magic is a matter of symbolism and intent."

"Very well. I want a complete list of the contents of that chest. Be sure to replace everything as it was and relock the trunk." He tugged thoughtfully at an earlobe. "So Laird Duncan has the Talent, eh? Interesting."

"Aye. But not surprising, me lord," said Master Sean without looking up from his work. "It's in the blood. Some attribute it to the Dedannans, who passed through Scotland before they conquered Ireland three thousand years ago, but, however that may be, the Talent runs strong in the Sons of Gael. It makes me boil to see it misused."

While Master Sean talked, Lord Darcy was prowling around the room, reminding one of a lean tomcat who was certain that there was a mouse concealed somewhere.

"It'll make Laird Duncan boil if he isn't stopped," Lord Darcy murmured absently.

"Aye, me lord," said Master Sean. "The mental state necessary to use the Talent for black sorcery is such that it invariably destroys the user—but, if he knows what he's doing, a lot of other people are hurt before he finally gets his."

Lord Darcy opened the jewel box on the dresser. The usual traveling jewelry—enough, but not a great choice.

"A man's mind turns in on itself when he's taken up with hatred and thoughts of revenge," Master Sean droned on. "Or, if he's the type who *enjoys* watching others suffer, or the type who doesn't care but is willing to do anything for gain, then his mind is already warped and the misuse of the Talent just makes it worse."

Lord Darcy found what he was looking for in a drawer, just underneath some neatly folded lingerie. A small holster, beautifully made of Florentine leather, gilded and tooled. He didn't need Master Sean's sorcery to tell him that the little pistol fit it like a hand a glove.

Father Bright felt as though he had been walking a tight-rope for hours. Laird and Lady Duncan had been talking in low, controlled voices that betrayed an inner nervousness, but Father Bright realized that he and the Countess had been doing the same thing. The Duncan of Duncan had offered his condolences on the death of the late Count with the proper air of suppressed sorrow, as had Mary, Lady Duncan. The Countess had accepted them solemnly and with gratitude. But Father Bright was well aware that no one in the room—possibly, he thought, no one in the world—regretted the Count's passing.

Laird Duncan sat in his wheelchair, his sharp Scots features set in a sad smile that showed an intent to be affable even though great sorrow weighed heavily upon him. Father Bright noticed it and realized that his own face had the same sort of expression. No one was fooling anyone else, of that the priest was certain—but for anyone to admit it would be the most boorish breach of etiquette. But there was a haggardness, a look of increased age about the Laird's countenance that Father Bright did not like. His priestly intuition told him clearly that there was a turmoil of emotion in the Scotsman's mind that was . . . well, *evil* was the only word for it.

Lady Duncan was, for the most part, silent. In the past fifteen minutes, since she and her husband had came to the informal tea, she had spoken scarcely a dozen words. Her face was mask-like, but there was the same look of haggardness about her eyes as there was in her husband's face. But the priest's empathic sense told him that the emotion here was fear, simple and direct. His keen eyes had noticed that she wore a shade too much make-up. She had almost succeeded in covering up the faint bruise on her right cheek, but not completely.

My lady the Countess D'Evreux was all sadness and unhappiness, but there was neither fear nor evil there. She smiled politely and talked quietly. Father Bright would have been willing to bet that not one of the four of them would remember a word that had been spoken.

Father Bright had placed his chair so that he could keep an eye on the open doorway and the long hall that led in from the Great Keep. He hoped Lord Darcy would hurry. Neither of the guests had been told that the Duke's Investigator was here, and Father Bright was just a little apprehensive about the meeting. The Duncans had not even been told that the Count's death had been murder, but he was certain that they knew.

Father Bright saw Lord Darcy come in through the door at the far end of the hall. He murmured a polite excuse and rose. The other three accepted his excuses with the same politeness and went on with their talk. Father Bright met Lord Darcy in the hall.

"Did you find what you were looking for, Lord Darcy?" the priest asked in a low tone.

"Yes," Lord Darcy said. "I'm afraid we shall have to arrest Laird Duncan."

"Murder?"

"Perhaps. I'm not yet certain of that. But the charge will be black magic. He has all the paraphernalia in a chest in his room. Master Sean reports that a ritual was enacted in the bedroom last night. Of course, that's out of my jurisdiction. You, as a representative of the Church, will have to be the arresting officer." He paused. "You don't seem surprised, Reverence."

"I'm not," Father Bright admitted. "I felt it. You and Master Sean will have to make out a sworn deposition before I can act."

"I understand. Can you do me a favor?"

"If I can."

"Get my lady the Countess out of the room on some pretext or other. Leave me alone with her guests. I do not wish to upset my lady any more than absolutely necessary."

"I think I can do that. Shall we go in together?"

"Why not? But don't mention why I am here. Let them assume I am just another guest."

"Very well."

All three occupants of the room glanced up as Father Bright came in with Lord Darcy. The introductions were made: Lord Darcy humbly begged the pardon of his hostess for his lateness. Father Bright noticed the same sad smile on Lord Darcy's handsome face as the others were wearing.

Lord Darcy helped himself from the buffet table and allowed the Countess to pour him a large cup of hot tea. He mentioned nothing about the recent death. Instead, he turned the conversation toward the wild beauty of Scotland and the excellence of the grouse shooting there.

Father Bright had not sat down again. Instead, he left the

room once more. When he returned, he went directly to the
Countess and said, in a low, but clearly audible voice: "My
lady, Sir Pierre Morlaix has informed me that there are a
few matters that require your attention immediately. It will
require only a few moments."

My lady the Countess did not hesitate, but made her
excuses immediately. "Do finish your tea," she added. "I
don't think I shall be long."

Lord Darcy knew the priest would not lie, and he wondered what sort of arrangement had been made with Sir
Pierre. Not that it mattered except that Lord Darcy had hoped
it would be sufficiently involved for it to keep the Countess busy for at least ten minutes.

The conversation, interrupted but momentarily, returned
to grouse.

"I haven't done any shooting since my accident," said
Laird Duncan, "but I used to enjoy it immensely. I still have
friends up every year for the season."

"What sort of weapon do you prefer for grouse?" Lord
Darcy asked.

"A one-inch bore with a modified choke," said the Scot.
"I have a pair that I favor. Excellent weapons."

"Of Scottish make?"

"No, no. English. Your London gunsmiths can't be beat
for shotguns."

"Oh. I thought perhaps your lordship had had all your
guns made in Scotland." As he spoke, he took the little pistol
out of his coat pocket and put it carefully on the table.

There was a sudden silence, then Laird Duncan said in
an angry voice: "What is this? Where did you get that?"

Lord Darcy glanced at Lady Duncan, who had turned
suddenly pale. "Perhaps," he said coolly, "Lady Duncan can
tell us."

She shook her head and gasped. For a moment, she had
trouble in forming words or finding her voice. Finally: "No.
No. I know nothing. Nothing."

But Laird Duncan looked at her oddly.

"You do not deny that it is your gun, my lord?" Lord Darcy
asked. "Or your wife's, as the case may be."

"*Where did you get it?*" There was a dangerous quality
in the Scotsman's voice. He had once been a powerful man,
and Lord Darcy could see his shoulder muscles bunching.

"From the late Count D'Evreux's bedroom."

"What was it doing there?" There was a snarl in the Scot's voice, but Lord Darcy had the feeling that the question was as much directed toward Lady Duncan as it was to himself.

"One of the things it was doing there was shooting Count D'Evreux through the heart."

Lady Duncan slumped forward in a dead faint, overturning her teacup. Laird Duncan made a grab at the gun, ignoring his wife. Lord Darcy's hand snaked out and picked up the weapon before the Scot could touch it. "No, no, my lord," he said mildly. "This is evidence in a murder case. We mustn't tamper with King's Evidence."

He wasn't prepared for what happened next. Laird Duncan roared something obscene in Scots Gaelic, put his hands on the arms of his wheelchair, and, with a great thrust of his powerful arms and shoulders, shoved himself up and forward, toward Lord Darcy, across the table from him. His arms swung up toward Lord Darcy's throat as the momentum of his body carried him toward the investigator.

He might have made it, but the weakness of his legs betrayed him. His waist struck the edge of the massive oaken table, and most of his forward momentum was lost. He collapsed forward, his hands still grasping toward the surprised Englishman. His chin came down hard on the table top. Then he slid back, taking the tablecloth and the china and silverware with him. He lay unmoving on the floor. His wife did not even stir except when the tablecloth tugged at her head.

Lord Darcy had jumped back, overturning his chair. He stood on his feet, looking at the two unconscious forms. He hoped he didn't look too much like King MacBeth.

"I don't think there's any permanent damage done to either," said Dr. Pateley an hour later. "Lady Duncan was suffering from shock, of course, but Father Bright brought her round in a hurry. She's a devout woman, I think, even if a sinful one."

"What about Laird Duncan?" Lord Darcy asked.

"Well, that's a different matter. I'm afraid that his back injury was aggravated, and that crack on the chin didn't do him any good. I don't know whether Father Bright can help him or not. Healing takes the co-operation of the patient. I did all I could for him, but I'm just a chirurgeon, not a practitioner of the Healing Art. Father Bright has quite a good reputation in that line, however, and he may be able to do his lordship some good."

Master Sean shook his head dolefully. "His Reverence has the Talent, there's no doubt of that, but now he's pitted against another man who has it—a man whose mind is bent on self-destruction in the long run."

"Well, that's none of my affair," said Dr. Pateley. "I'm just a technician. I'll leave healing up to the Church, where it belongs."

"Master Sean," said Lord Darcy, "there is still a mystery here. We need more evidence. What about the eyes?"

Master Sean blinked. "You mean the picture test, me lord?"

"I do."

"It won't stand up in court, me lord," said the sorcerer.

"I'm aware of that," said Lord Darcy testily.

"Eye test?" Dr. Pateley asked blankly. "I don't believe I understand."

"It's not often used," said Master Sean. "It is a psychic phenomenon that sometimes occurs at the moment of death—especially a violent death. The violent emotional stress causes a sort of backfiring of the mind, if you see what I mean. As a result, the image in the mind of the dying person is returned to the retina. By using the proper sorcery, this image can be developed and the last thing the dead man saw can be brought out.

"But it's a difficult process even under the best of cir- cumstances, and usually the conditions aren't right. In the first place, it doesn't always occur. It never occurs, for instance, when the person is expecting the attack. A man who is killed in a duel, or who is shot after facing the gun for several seconds, has time to adjust to the situation. Also, death must occur almost instantly. If he lingers, even for a few minutes, the effect is lost. And, naturally if the person's eyes are closed at the instant of death, nothing shows up."

"Count D'Evreux's eyes were open," Dr. Pateley said. "They were still open when we found him. How long after death does the image remain?"

"Until the cells of the retina die and lose their identity. Rarely more than twenty-four hours, usually much less."

"It hasn't been twenty-four hours yet," said Lord Darcy, "and there is a chance that the Count was taken completely by surprise."

"I must admit, me lord," Master Sean said thoughtfully, "that the conditions seem favorable. I shall attempt it. But don't put any hopes on it, me lord."

"I shan't. Just do your best, Master Sean. If there is a sorcerer in practice who can do the job, it is you."

"Thank you, me lord. I'll get busy on it right away," said the sorcerer with a subdued glow of pride.

Two hours later, Lord Darcy was striding down the corridor of the Great Hall, Master Sean following up as best he could, his *caorthainn*-wood staff in one hand and his big carpetbag in the other. He had asked Father Bright and the Countess D'Evreux to meet him in one of the smaller guest rooms. But the Countess came to meet him.

"My Lord Darcy," she said, her plain face looking worried and unhappy, "is it true that you suspect Laird and Lady Duncan of this murder? Because, if so, I must—"

"No longer, my lady," Lord Darcy cut her off quickly. "I think we can show that neither is guilty of murder—although, of course, the black magic charge must still be held against Laird Duncan."

"I understand," she said, "but—"

"Please, my lady," Lord Darcy interrupted again, "let me explain everything. Come."

Without another word, she turned and led the way to the room where Father Bright was waiting.

The priest stood waiting, his face showing tenseness.

"Please," said Lord Darcy. "Sit down, both of you. This won't take long. My lady, may Master Sean make use of that table over there?"

"Certainly, my lord," the Countess said softly, "certainly."

"Thank you, my lady. Please, please—sit down. This won't take long. Please."

With apparent reluctance, Father Bright and my lady the Countess sat down in two chairs facing Lord Darcy. They paid little attention to what Master Sean O Lochlainn was doing; their eyes were on Lord Darcy.

"Conducting an investigation of this sort is not an easy thing," he began carefully. "Most murder cases could be easily solved by your Chief Man-at-Arms. We find that well-trained county Armsmen, in by far the majority of cases, can solve the mystery easily—and in most cases there is very little mystery. But, by His Imperial Majesty's law, the Chief Man-at-Arms *must* call in a Duke's Investigator if the crime is insoluble or if it involves a member of the aristocracy. For that reason, you were perfectly correct to call His Highness the Duke as soon as murder had been discovered." He leaned back in his chair. "And it has been clear from the first that my lord the late Count was murdered."

Father Bright started to say something, but Lord Darcy cut him off before he could speak. "By 'murder', Reverend Father, I mean that he did not die a natural death—by disease or heart trouble or accident or what-have-you. I should, perhaps, use the word 'homicide'.

"Now the question we have been called upon to answer is simply this: Who was responsible for the homicide?"

The priest and the Countess remained silent, looking at Lord Darcy as though he were some sort of divinely inspired oracle.

"As you know . . . pardon me, my lady, if I am blunt . . . the late Count was somewhat of a playboy. No. I will make that stronger. He was a satyr, a lecher; he was a man with a sexual obsession.

"For such a man, if he indulges in his passions—which the late Count most certainly did—there is usually but one end. Unless he is a man who has a winsome personality—which he did not—there will be someone who will hate him enough to kill him. Such a man inevitably leaves behind him a trail of wronged women and wronged men.

"One such person may kill him.

"One such person did.

"But we must find the person who did and determine the extent of his or her guilt. That is my purpose.

"Now, as to the facts. We know that Edouard had a secret stairway which led directly to his suite. Actually, the secret was poorly kept. There were many women—common and noble—who knew of the existence of that stairway and knew how to enter it. If Edouard left the lower door unlocked, anyone could come up that stairway. He had another lock in the door of his bedroom, so only someone who was invited could come in, even if she . . . or he . . . could get into the stairway. He was protected.

"Now here is what actually happened last night. I have evidence, by the way, and I have the confessions of both Laird and Lady Duncan. I will explain how I got those confessions in a moment.

"*Primus:* Lady Duncan had an assignation with Count D'Evreux last night. She went up the stairway to his room. She was carrying with her a small pistol. She had had an affair with Edouard, and she had been rebuffed. She was furious. But she went to his room.

"He was drunk when she arrived—in one of the nasty moods with which both of you are familiar. She pleaded with him to accept her again as his mistress. He refused. According to Lady Duncan, he said: 'I don't want you! You're not fit to be in the same room with *her!*'

"The emphasis is Lady Duncan's, not my own.

"Furious, she drew a gun—the little pistol which killed him."

The Countess gasped. "But Mary *couldn't* have—"

"*Please!*" Lord Darcy slammed the palm of his hand on the arm of his chair with an explosive sound. "My lady, you *will* listen to what I have to say!"

He was taking a devil of a chance, he knew. The Countess was his hostess and had every right to exercise her prerogatives. But Lord Darcy was counting on the fact that she had been under Count D'Evreux's influence so long that it would take her a little time to realize that she no longer had to knuckle under to the will of a man who shouted at her. He was right. She became silent.

Father Bright turned to her quickly and said: "Please, my daughter. Wait."

"Your pardon, my lady," Lord Darcy continued smoothly. "I was about to explain to you why I know Lady Duncan could not have killed your brother. There is the matter of the dress. We are certain that the gown that was found in Edouard's closet was worn by the killer. *And that gown could not possibly have fit Lady Duncan!* She's much too . . . er . . . hefty.

"She has told me her story, and, for reasons I will give you later, I believe it. When she pointed the gun at your brother, she really had no intention of killing him. She had no intention of pulling the trigger. Your brother knew this. He lashed out and slapped the side of her head. She dropped the pistol and fell, sobbing, to the floor. He took her roughly by the arm and 'escorted' her down the stairway. He threw her out.

"Lady Duncan, hysterical, ran to her husband.

"And then, when he had succeeded in calming her down a bit, she realized the position she was in. She knew that Laird Duncan was a violent, a warped man—very similar to Edouard, Count D'Evreux. She dared not tell him the truth, but she had to tell him something. So she lied.

"She told him that Edouard had asked her up in order to tell her something of importance; that that 'something of importance' concerned Laird Duncan's safety; that the Count told her that he knew of Laird Duncan's dabbling in black magic; that he threatened to inform Church authorities on Laird Duncan unless she submitted to his desires; that she had struggled with him and run away."

Lord Darcy spread his hands. "This was, of course, a tissue of lies. But Laird Duncan believed everything. So great was his ego that he could not believe in her infidelity, although he has been paralyzed for five years."

"How can you be certain that Lady Duncan told the truth?" Father Bright asked warily.

"Aside from the matter of the gown—which Count D'Evreux kept only for women of the common class, not the aristocracy—we have the testimony of the actions of Laird Duncan himself. We come then to—

"*Secundus:* Laird Duncan could not have committed the murder physically. *How could a man who was confined to a wheelchair go up that flight of stairs?* I submit to you that it would have been physically impossible.

"The possibility that he has been pretending all these years, and that he is actually capable of walking, was disproved three hours ago, when he actually injured himself by trying to throttle me. His legs are incapable of carrying him even one step—much less carrying him to the top of that stairway."

Lord Darcy folded his hands complacently.

"There remains," said Father Bright, "the possibility that Laird Duncan killed Count D'Evreux by psychical, by magical means."

Lord Darcy nodded. "That is indeed possible, Reverend Sir, as we both know. But not in this instance. Master Sean assures me, and I am certain that you will concur, that a man killed by sorcery, by black magic, dies of internal malfunction, not of a bullet through the heart.

"In effect, the Black Sorcerer induces his enemy to kill himself by psychosomatic means. He dies by what is technically known as psychic induction. Master Sean informs me that the commonest—and crudest—method of doing this is by the so-called 'simulacrum induction' method. That is, by the making of an image—usually, but not necessarily, of wax—and, using the Law of Similarity, inducing death. The Law of Contagion is also used, since the fingernails, hair, spittle, and so on, of the victim are usually incorporated into the image. Am I correct, Father?"

The priest nodded. "Yes. And, contrary to the heresies of certain materialists, it is not at all necessary that the victim be informed of the operation—although, admittedly, it can, in certain circumstances, aid the process."

"Exactly," said Lord Darcy. "But it is well known that material objects can be moved by a competent sorcerer— 'black' or 'white'. Would you explain to my lady the Countess why her brother could not have been killed in that manner?"

Father Bright touched his lips with the tip of his tongue and then turned to the girl sitting next to him. "There is a lack of relevancy. In this case, the bullet must have been relevant either to the heart or to the gun. To have traveled with a velocity great enough to penetrate, the relevancy to the heart must have been much greater than the relevancy to the gun. Yet the test, witnessed by myself, that was performed by Master Sean indicates that this was not so. The bullet returned to the gun, not to your brother's heart. The evidence, my dear, is conclusive that the bullet was propelled by purely physical means, and was propelled from the gun."

"Then what was it Laird Duncan did?" the Countess asked.

"*Tertius:*" said Lord Darcy. "Believing what his wife had told him, Laird Duncan flew into a rage. He determined to kill your brother. He used an induction spell. But the spell backfired and almost killed him.

"There are analogies on a material plane. If one adds mineral spirits and air to a fire, the fire will be increased. But if one adds ash, the fire will be put out.

"In a similar manner, if one attacks a living being psychically it will die—but if one attacks a dead thing in such a manner, the psychic energy will be absorbed, to the detriment of the person who has used it.

"In theory, we could charge Laird Duncan with attempted murder, for there is no doubt that he did attempt to kill your brother, my lady. *But your brother was already dead at the time!*

"The resultant dissipation of psychic energy rendered Laird Duncan unconscious for several hours, during which Lady Duncan waited in suspenseful fear.

"Finally, when Laird Duncan regained consciousness, he realized what had happened. He knew that your brother was already dead when he attempted the spell. He thought, therefore, that Lady Duncan had killed the Count.

"On the other hand, Lady Duncan was perfectly well aware that she had left Edouard alive and well. So she thought the black magic of her husband had killed her erstwhile lover."

"Each was trying to protect the other," Father Bright said. "Neither is completely evil, then. There may be something we can do for Laird Duncan."

"I wouldn't know about that, Father," Lord Darcy said. "The Healing Art is the Church's business, not mine." He realized with some amusement that he was paraphrasing Dr. Pateley. "What Laird Duncan had not known," he went on quickly, "was that his wife had taken a gun up to the Count's bedroom. That put a rather different light on her visit, you see. That's why he flew into such a towering rage at me— not because I was accusing him or his wife of murder, but because I had cast doubt on his wife's behavior."

He turned his head to look at the table where the Irish sorcerer was working. "Ready, Master Sean?"

"Aye, me lord. All I have to do is set up the screen and light the lantern in the projector."

"Go ahead, then." He looked back at Father Bright and the Countess. "Master Sean has a rather interesting lantern slide I want you to look at."

"The most successful development I've ever made, if I may say so, me lord," the sorcerer said.

"Proceed."

Master Sean opened the shutter on the projector, and a picture sprang into being on the screen.

There were gasps from Father Bright and the Countess.

It was a woman. She was wearing the gown that had hung in the Count's closet. A button had been torn off, and the gown gaped open. Her right hand was almost completely obscured by a dense cloud of smoke. Obviously she had just fired a pistol directly at the onlooker.

But that was not what had caused the gasps.

The girl was beautiful. Gloriously, ravishingly beautiful. It was not a delicate beauty. There was nothing flowerlike or peaceful in it. It was a beauty that could have but one effect on a normal human male. She was the most physically desirable woman one could imagine.

Retro me, Sathanas, Father Bright thought wryly. *She's almost obscenely beautiful.*

Only the Countess was unaffected by the desirability of the image. She saw only the startling beauty.

"Has neither of you seen that woman before? I thought not," said Lord Darcy. "Nor had Laird or Lady Duncan. Nor Sir Pierre.

"Who is she? We don't know. But we can make a few deductions. She must have come to the Count's room by appointment. This is quite obviously the woman Edouard mentioned to Lady Duncan—the woman, the 'she' that the Scots noblewoman could not compare with. It is almost certain she is a commoner; otherwise she would not be wearing a robe from the Count's collection. She must have changed right there in the bedroom. Then she and the Count quarreled—about what, we do not know. The Count had previously taken Lady Duncan's pistol away from her and had evidently carelessly let it lay on that table you see behind the girl. She grabbed it and shot him. Then she changed clothes again, hung up the robe, and ran away. No one saw her come or go. The Count had designed his stairway for just that purpose.

"Oh, we'll find her, never fear—now that we know what she looks like.

"At any rate," Lord Darcy concluded, "the mystery is now solved to my complete satisfaction, and I shall so report to His Highness."

Richard, Duke of Normandy, poured two liberal portions of excellent brandy into a pair of crystal goblets. There was a smile of satisfaction on his youthful face as he handed one of the goblets to Lord Darcy. "Very well done, my lord," he said, "very well done."

"I am gratified to hear Your Highness say so," said Lord Darcy, accepting the brandy.

"But how were you so certain that it was not someone from outside the castle? Anyone could have come in through the main gate. That's always open."

"True, Your Highness. But the door at the foot of the stairway was *locked*. Count D'Evreux locked it after he threw Lady Duncan out. There is no way of locking or unlocking it from the outside; the door had not been forced. No one could have come in that way, nor left that way, after Lady Duncan was so forcibly ejected. The only other way into the Count's suite was by the other door, and that door was unlocked."

"I see," said Duke Richard. "I wonder why she went up there in the first place?"

"Probably because he asked her to. Any other woman would have known what she was getting into if she accepted an invitation to Count D'Evreux's suite."

The Duke's handsome face darkened. "No. One would hardly expect that sort of thing from one's own brother. She was perfectly justified in shooting him."

"Perfectly, Your Highness. And had she been anyone but the heiress, she would undoubtedly have confessed immediately. Indeed, it was all I could do to keep her from confessing to me when she thought I was going to charge the Duncans with the killing. But she knew that it was necessary to preserve the reputations of her brother and herself. Not as private persons, but as Count and Countess, as officers of the Government of His Imperial Majesty the King. For a man to be known as a rake is one thing. Most people don't care about that sort of thing in a public official so long as he does his duty and does it well—which, as Your Highness knows, the Count did.

"But to be shot to death while attempting to assault his own sister—that is quite another thing. She was perfectly justified in attempting to cover it up. And she will remain silent unless someone else is accused of the crime."

"Which, of course, will not happen," said Duke Richard. He sipped at the brandy, then said: "She will make a good

Countess. She has judgment and she can keep cool under duress. After she had shot her own brother, she might have panicked, but she didn't. How many women would have thought of simply taking off the damaged gown and putting on its duplicate from the closet?"

"Very few," Lord Darcy agreed. "That's why I never mentioned that I knew the Count's wardrobe contained dresses identical to her own. By the way, Your Highness, if any good Healer, like Father Bright, had known of those duplicate dresses, he would have realized that the Count had a sexual obsession about his sister. He would have known that all the other women the Count went after were sister substitutes."

"Yes; of course. And none of them could measure up." He put his goblet on the table. "I shall inform the King my brother that I recommended the new Countess wholeheartedly. No word of this must be put down in writing, of course. You know and I know and the King must know. No one else must know."

"One other knows," said Lord Darcy.

"Who?" The Duke looked startled.

"Father Bright."

Duke Richard looked relieved. "Naturally. He won't tell her that *we* know, will he?"

"I think Father Bright's discretion can be relied upon."

In the dimness of the confessional, Alice, Countess D'Evreux knelt and listened to the voice of Father Bright.

"I shall not give you any penance, my child, for you have committed no sin—that is, in so far as the death of your brother is concerned. For the rest of your sins, you must read and memorize the third chapter of 'The Soul and The World,' by St. James Huntington."

He started to pronounce the absolution, but the Countess said:

"I don't understand one thing. That picture. That wasn't me. I never saw such a gorgeously beautiful girl in my life. And I'm so plain. I don't understand."

"Had you looked more closely, my child, you would have seen that the face did look like yours—only it was idealized. When a subjective reality is made objective, distortions invariably show up; that is why such things cannot be accepted as evidence of objective reality in court." He paused. "To put it another way, my child: Beauty is in the eye of the beholder."

A Case of Identity

The pair of Men-at-Arms strolled along the Rue King John II, near the waterfront of Cherbourg, and a hundred yards south of the sea. In this district, the Keepers of the King's Peace always traveled in pairs, each keeping one hand near the truncheon at his belt and the other near the hilt of his smallsword. The average commoner was not a swordsman, but sailors are not common commoners. A man armed only with a truncheon would be at a disadvantage with a man armed with a cutlass.

The frigid wind from the North Sea whipped the edges of the Men-at-Arms' cloaks, and the light from the mantled gas lamps glowed yellowly, casting multiple shadows that shifted queerly as the Armsmen walked.

There were not many people on the streets. Most of them were in the bistros, where there were coal fires to warm the outer man and fiery bottled goods to warm the inner. There had been crowds in the street on the Vigil of the Feast of the Circumcision, nine days before, but now the Twelfth Day of Christmas had passed and the Year of Our Lord 1964 was in its second week. Money had run short and few could still afford to drink.

The taller of the two officers stopped and pointed ahead. "Ey, Robert. Old Jean hasn't got his light on."

"Hm-m-m. Third time since Christmas. Hate to give the old man a summons."

"Aye. Let's just go in and scare the Hell out of him."

"Aye," said the shorter man. "But we'll promise him a summons next time and keep our promise, Jack."

The sign above the door was a weatherbeaten dolphin-shaped piece of wood, painted blue. The Blue Dolphin.

Armsman Robert pushed open the door and went in, his eyes alert for trouble. There was none. Four men were sitting around one end of the long table at the left, and Old Jean was talking to a fifth man at the bar. They all looked up as the Armsmen came in. Then the men at the table went on with their conversation. The fifth customer's eyes went to his drink. The barkeep smiled ingratiatingly and came toward the two Armsmen.

"Evening, Armsmen," he said with a snaggle-toothed smile. "A little something to warm the blood?" But he knew it was no social call.

Robert already had out his summons book, pencil poised. "Jean, we have warned you twice before," he said frigidly. "The law plainly states that every place of business must maintain a standard gas lamp and keep it lit from sunset to sunrise. You know this."

"Perhaps the wind—" the barkeep said defensively.

"The wind? I will go up with you and we will see if perhaps the wind has turned the gas cock, ey?"

Old Jean swallowed. "Perhaps I did forget. My memory—"

"Perhaps explaining your memory to my lord the Marquis next court day will help you to improve it, ey?"

"No, no! Please, Armsman! The fine would ruin me!"

Armsman Robert made motions with his pencil as though he were about to write. "I will say it is a first offense and the fine will be only half as much."

Old Jean closed his eyes helplessly. "Please, Armsman. It will not happen again. It is just that I have been so used to Paul—he did everything, all the hard work. I have no one to help me now."

"Paul Sarto has been gone for two weeks now," Robert said. "This is the third time you have given me that same excuse."

"Armsman," said the old man earnestly, "I will not forget again. I promise you."

Robert closed his summons book. "Very well. I have your word? Then you have my word that there will be no excuses next time. I will hand you the summons instantly. Understood?"

"Understood, Armsman! Yes, of course. Many thanks! I will not forget again!"

"See that you don't. Go and light it."

Old Jean scurried up the stairway and was back within minutes. "It's lit now, Armsman."

"Excellent. I expect it to be lit from now on. At sunset. Good night, Jean."

"Perhaps a little—?"

"No, Jean. Another time. Come, Jack."

The Armsmen left without taking the offered drink. It would be ungentlemanly to take it after threatening the man with the law. The Armsman's Manual said that, because of the sword he is privileged to wear, an Armsman must be a gentleman at all times.

"Wonder why Paul left?" Jack asked when they were on the street again. "He was well paid, and he was too simple to work elsewhere."

Robert shrugged. "You know how it is. Wharf rats come and go. No need to worry about him. A man with a strong back and a weak mind can always find a bistro that will take care of him. He'll get along."

Nothing further was said for the moment. The two Armsmen walked on to the corner, where the Quai Sainte Marie turned off to the south.

Robert glanced southwards and said: "Here's a happy one."

"Too happy, if you ask me," said Jack.

Down the Quai Sainte Marie came a man. He was hugging the side of the building, stumbling toward them, propping himself up by putting the flat of his palms on the brick wall one after the other as he moved his feet. He wore no hat, and, as the wind caught his cloak, the two Men-at-Arms saw something they had not expected. He was naked.

"Blind drunk and freezing," Jack said. "Better take him in."

They never got the chance. As they came toward him, the stumbling man stumbled for the last time. He dropped to his knees, looked up at them with blind eyes that stared past them into the darkness of the sky, then toppled to one side, his eyes still open, unblinking.

Robert knelt down. "Sound your whistle! I think he's dead!"

Jack took out his whistle and keened a note into the frigid air.

"Speak of the Devil," Robert said softly. "It's Paul! He doesn't smell drunk. I think . . . *God!*" He had tried to lift the head of the fallen man and found his palm covered with blood. "It's soft," he said wonderingly. "The whole side of his skull is crushed."

In the distance, they heard the clatter of hoofs as a mounted Sergeant-at-Arms came at a gallop toward the sound of the whistle.

Lord Darcy, tall, lean-faced, and handsome, strode down the hall to the door bearing the arms of Normandy and opened it.

"Your Highness sent for me?" He spoke Anglo-French with a definite English accent.

There were three men in the room. The youngest, tall, blond Richard, Duke of Normandy and brother to His Imperial Majesty, John IV, turned as the door opened. "Ah. Lord Darcy. Come in." He gestured toward the portly man wearing episcopal purple. "My Lord Bishop, may I present my Chief Investigator, Lord Darcy. Lord Darcy, this is his lordship, the Bishop of Guernsey and Sark."

"A pleasure, Lord Darcy," said the Bishop, extending his right hand.

Lord Darcy took the hand, bowed, kissed the ring. "My Lord Bishop." Then he turned and bowed to the third man, the lean, graying Marquis of Rouen. "My Lord Marquis."

Then Lord Darcy faced the Royal Duke again and waited expectantly.

The Duke of Normandy frowned slightly. "There appears to be some trouble with my lord the Marquis of Cherbourg. As you know, My Lord Bishop is the elder brother of the Marquis."

Lord Darcy knew the family history. The previous Marquis of Cherbourg had had three sons. At his death, the eldest had inherited the title and government. The second had taken Holy Orders, and the third had taken a commission in the Royal Navy. When the eldest had died without heirs, the Bishop could not succeed to the title, so the Marquisate went to the youngest son, Hugh, the present Marquis.

"Perhaps you had better explain, My Lord Bishop," said

the Duke. "I would rather Lord Darcy had the information firsthand."

"Certainly, Your Highness," said the Bishop. He looked worried, and his right hand kept fiddling with the pectoral cross at his breast.

The Duke gestured toward the chairs. "Please, my lords— sit down."

The four men settled themselves, and the Bishop began his story. "My brother the Marquis," he said after a deep breath, "is missing."

Lord Darcy raised an eyebrow. Normally, if one of His Majesty's Governors turned up missing, there would be a hue and cry from one end of the Empire to the other—from Duncansby Head in Scotland to the southernmost tip of Gascony—from the German border on the east to New England and New France, across the Atlantic. If my lord the Bishop of Guernsey and Sark wanted it kept quiet, then there was—there had *better* be!—a good reason.

"Have you met my brother, Lord Darcy?" the Bishop asked.

"Only briefly, my lord. Once, about a year ago. I hardly know him."

"I see."

The Bishop fiddled a bit more with his pectoral cross, then plunged into his story. Three days before, on the tenth of January, the Bishop's sister-in-law, Elaine, Marquise de Cherbourg, had sent a servant by boat to St. Peter Port, Guernsey, the site of the Cathedral Church of the Diocese of Guernsey and Sark. The sealed message which he was handed informed My Lord Bishop that his brother the Marquis had been missing since the evening of the eighth. Contrary to his custom, My Lord Marquis had not notified My Lady Marquise of any intention to leave the castle. Indeed, he implied that he had intended to retire when he had finished with certain Government papers. No one had seen him since he entered his study. My lady of Cherbourg had not missed him until next morning, when she found that his bed had not been slept in.

"This was on the morning of Thursday the ninth, my lord?" Lord Darcy asked.

"That is correct, my lord," said the Bishop.

"May I ask why we were not notified until now?" Lord Darcy asked gently.

My Lord Bishop fidgeted. "Well, my lord . . . you see . . . well, My Lady Elaine believes that . . . er . . . that his lordship, my brother, is not . . . er . . . may not be . . . er . . . quite right in his mind."

There! thought Lord Darcy. *He got it out! My Lord of Cherbourg is off his chump! Or, at least, his lady thinks so.*

"What behavior did he display?" Lord Darcy asked quietly.

The Bishop spoke rapidly and concisely. My Lord of Cherbourg had had his first attack on the eve of St. Stephen's Day, the 26th of December, 1963. His face had suddenly taken on a look of utter idiocy; it had gone slack, and the intelligence seemed to fade from his eyes. He had babbled meaninglessly and seemed not to know where he was—and, indeed, to be somewhat terrified of his surroundings.

"Was he violent in any way?" asked Lord Darcy.

"No. Quite the contrary. He was quite docile and easily led to bed. Lady Elaine called in a Healer immediately, suspecting that my brother may have had an apoplectic stroke. As you know, the Marquisate supports a chapter of the Benedictines within the walls of Castle Cherbourg, and Father Patrique saw my brother within minutes.

"But by that time the attack had passed. Father Patrique could detect nothing wrong, and my brother simply said it was a slight dizzy spell, nothing more. However, since then there have been three more attacks—on the evenings of the second, the fifth, and the seventh of this month. And now he is gone."

"You feel, then, My Lord Bishop, that his lordship has had another of these attacks and may be wandering around somewhere . . . ah . . . *non compos mentis,* as it were?"

"That's exactly what I'm afraid of," the Bishop said firmly.

Lord Darcy looked thoughtful for a moment, then glanced silently at His Royal Highness, the Duke.

"I want you to make a thorough investigation, Lord Darcy," said the Duke. "Be as discreet as possible. We want no scandal. If there is anything wrong with my lord of Cherbourg's mind, we will have the best care taken, of course. But we must find him first." He glanced at the clock on the wall. "There is a train for Cherbourg in forty-one minutes. You will accompany My Lord Bishop."

Lord Darcy rose smoothly from his chair. "I'll just have

time to pack, Your Highness." He bowed to the Bishop. "Your servant, my lord." He turned and walked out the door, closing it behind him.

But instead of heading immediately for his own apartments, he waited quietly outside the door, just to one side. He had caught Duke Richard's look.

Within, he heard voices.

"My Lord Marquis," said the Duke, "would you see that My Lord Bishop gets some refreshment? If your lordship will excuse me, I have some urgent work to attend to. A report on this matter must be dispatched immediately to the King my brother."

"Of course, Your Highness; of course."

"I will have a carriage waiting for you and Lord Darcy. I will see you again before you leave, my lord. And now, excuse me."

He came out of the room, saw Lord Darcy waiting, and motioned toward another room nearby. Lord Darcy followed him in. The Duke closed the door firmly and then said, in a low voice:

"This may be worse than it appears at first glance, Darcy. De Cherbourg was working with one of His Majesty's personal agents trying to trace down the ring of Polish *agents provocateurs* operating in Cherbourg. If he's actually had a mental breakdown and they've got hold of him, there will be the Devil to pay."

Lord Darcy knew the seriousness of the affair. The Kings of Poland had been ambitious for the past half century. Having annexed all of the Russian territory they could—as far as Minsk to the north and Kiev to the south—the Poles now sought to work their way westwards, toward the borders of the Empire. For several centuries, the Germanic states had acted as buffers between the powerful Kingdom of Poland and the even more powerful Empire. In theory, the Germanic states, as part of the old Holy Roman Empire, owed fealty to the Emperor—but no Anglo-French King had tried to enforce that fealty for centuries. The Germanic states were, in fact, holding their independence because of the tug-of-war between Poland and the Empire. If the troops of King Casimir IX tried to march into Bavaria, for instance, Bavaria would scream for Imperial help and would get it. On the other hand, if King John IV tried to tax so much as a single sovereign out of Bavaria, and sent troops in to collect it, Bavaria would scream just as loudly for Polish aid. As long as the balance of power remained, the Germanies were safe.

Actually, King John had no desire to bring the Germanies into the Empire forcibly. That kind of aggression hadn't been Imperial policy for a good long time. With hardly any trouble at all, an Imperial army could take over Lombardy or northern Spain. But with the whole New World as Imperial domain, there was no need to add more of Europe. Aggression against her peaceful neighbors was unthinkable in this day and age.

As long as Poland had been moving eastward, Imperial policy had been to allow her to go her way while the Empire expanded into the New World. But that eastward expansion had ground to a halt.

King Casimir was now having trouble with those Russians he had already conquered. To hold his quasi-empire together, he had to keep the threat of external enemies always before the eyes of his subjects, but he dared not push any farther into Russia. The Russian states had formed a loose coalition during the last generation, and the King of Poland, Sigismund III, had backed down. If the Russians ever really united, they would be a formidable enemy.

That left the Germanic states to the west and Roumeleia to the south. Casimir had no desire to tangle with Roumeleia, but he had plans for the Germanic states.

The wealth of the Empire, the basis of its smoothly expanding economy, was the New World. The importation of cotton, tobacco, and sugar—to say nothing of the gold that had been found in the southern continent—was the backbone of the Imperial economy. The King's subjects were well-fed, well-clothed, well-housed, and happy. But if the shipping were to be blocked for any considerable length of time, there would be trouble.

The Polish Navy didn't stand a chance against the Imperial Navy. No Polish fleet could get through the North Sea without running into trouble with either the Imperial Navy or that of the Empire's Scandinavian allies. The North Sea was Imperial-Scandinavian property, jointly patrolled, and no armed ship was allowed to pass. Polish merchantmen were allowed to come and go freely—after they had been

boarded to make sure that they carried no guns. Bottled up
in the Baltic, the Polish Navy was helpless, and it wasn't
big enough or good enough to fight its way out. They'd tried
it once, back in '39, and had been blasted out of the water.
King Casimir wouldn't try that again.

He had managed to buy a few Spanish and Sicilian ships
and have them outfitted as privateers, but they were merely
annoying, not menacing. If caught, they were treated as
pirates—either sunk or captured and their crews hanged—
and the Imperial Government didn't even bother to protest
to the King of Poland.

But King Casimir evidently had something else up his royal
sleeve. Something was happening that had both the Lords
of the Admiralty and the Maritime Lords on edge. Ships
leaving Imperial ports—Le Havre, Cherbourg, Liverpool,
London, and so on—occasionally disappeared. They were
simply never heard from again. They never got to New
England at all. And the number was more than could be
accounted for either by weather or piracy.

That was bad enough, but to make things worse, rumors
had been spreading around the waterfronts of the Empire.
Primarily the rumors exaggerated the dangers of sailing the
Atlantic. The word was beginning to spread that the mid-
Atlantic was a dangerous area—far more dangerous than the
waters around Europe. A sailor worth his salt cared very
little for the threats of weather; give a British or a French
sailor a seaworthy ship and a skipper he trusted, and he'd
head into the teeth of any storm. But the threat of evil spirits
and black magic was something else again.

Do what they would, scientific researchers simply could not
educate the common man to understand the intricacies and
limitations of modern scientific sorcery. The superstitions of
a hundred thousand years still clung to the minds of ninety-
nine per cent of the human race, even in a modern, advanced
civilization like the Empire. How does one explain that only
a small percentage of the population is capable of performing magic? How to explain that all the incantations in the
official grimoires won't help a person who doesn't have the
Talent? How to explain that, even with the Talent, years of
training are normally required before it can be used efficiently,
predictably, and with power? People had been told again and
again, but deep in their hearts they believed otherwise.

Not one person in ten who was suspected of having the Evil Eye really had it, but sorcerers and priests were continually being asked for counteragents. And only God knew how many people wore utterly useless medallions, charms, and anti-hex shields prepared by quacks who hadn't the Talent to make the spells effective. There is an odd quirk in the human mind that makes a fearful man prefer to go quietly to a wicked-looking, gnarled "witch" for a counter-charm than to a respectable licensed sorcerer or an accredited priest of the Church. Deep inside, the majority of people had the sneaking suspicion that evil was more powerful than good and that evil could be counteracted only by more evil. Almost none of them would believe what scientific magical research had shown—that the practice of black magic was, in the long run, more destructive to the mind of the practitioner than to his victims.

So it wasn't difficult to spread the rumor that there was Something Evil in the Atlantic—and, as a result, more and more sailors were becoming leery of shipping aboard a vessel that was bound for the New World.

And the Imperial Government was absolutely certain that the story was being deliberately spread by agents of King Casimir IX.

Two things had to be done: The disappearances must cease, and the rumors must be stopped. And my lord the Marquis of Cherbourg had been working toward those ends when he had disappeared. The question of how deeply Polish agents were involved in that disappearance was an important one.

"You will contact His Majesty's agent as soon as possible," said Duke Richard. "Since there may be black magic involved, take Master Sean along—incognito. If a sorcerer suddenly shows up, they—whoever they may be—might take cover. They might even do something drastic to de Cherbourg."

"I will exercise the utmost care, Your Highness," said Lord Darcy.

The train pulled into Cherbourg Station with a hiss and a blast of steam that made a great cloud of fog in the chill air. Then the wind picked up the cloud and blew it to wisps before anyone had stepped from the carriages. The passengers hugged their coats and cloaks closely about them as they came out. There was a light dusting of snow on the ground and on the platform, but the air was clear and the low winter sun shone brightly, if coldly, in the sky.

The Bishop had made a call on the teleson to Cherbourg Castle before leaving Rouen, and there was a carriage waiting for the three men—one of the newer models with pneumatic tires and spring suspension, bearing the Cherbourg arms on the doors, and drawn by two pairs of fine greys. The footmen opened the near door and the Bishop climbed in, followed by Lord Darcy and a short, chubby man who wore the clothing of a gentleman's gentleman. Lord Darcy's luggage was put on the rack atop the carriage, but a small bag carried by the "gentleman's gentleman" remained firmly in the grasp of his broad fist.

Master Sean O Lochlainn, Sorcerer, had no intention of letting go of his professional equipment. He had grumbled enough about not being permitted to carry his symbol-decorated carpetbag, and had spent nearly twenty minutes casting protective spells around the black leather suitcase that Lord Darcy had insisted he carry.

The footman closed the door of the carriage and swung himself aboard. The four greys started off at a brisk trot through the streets of Cherbourg toward the Castle, which lay across the city, near the sea.

Partly to keep My Lord Bishop's mind off his brother's troubles and partly to keep from being overheard while they were on the train, Lord Darcy and the Bishop had tacitly agreed to keep their conversation on subjects other than the investigation at hand. Master Sean had merely sat quietly by, trying to look like a valet—at which he succeeded very well.

Once inside the carriage, however, the conversation seemed to die away. My lord the Bishop settled himself into the cushions and gazed silently out of the window. Master Sean leaned back, folded his hands over his paunch and closed his eyes. Lord Darcy, like my lord the Bishop, looked out the window. He had only been in Cherbourg twice before, and was not as familiar with the city as he would like to be. It would be worth his time to study the route the carriage was taking.

It was not until they came to the waterfront itself, turned, and moved down the Rue de Mer toward the towers of Castle Cherbourg in the distance, that Lord Darcy saw anything that particularly interested him.

There were, he thought, entirely too many ships tied up at the docks, and there seemed to be a great deal of goods waiting on the wharves to be loaded. On the other hand, there did not seem to be as many men working as the apparent volume of shipping would warrant.

Crews scared off by the "Atlantic Curse," Lord Darcy thought. He looked at the men loafing around in clumps, talking softly but, he thought, rather angrily. *Obviously sailors; out of work by their own choice and resenting their own fears. Probably trying to get jobs as longshoremen and being shut out by the Longshoremen's Guild.*

Normally, he knew, sailors were considered as an auxiliary of the Longshoremen's Guild, just as longshoremen were considered as an auxiliary of the Seamen's Guild. If a sailor decided to spend a little time on land, he could usually get work as a longshoreman; if a longshoreman decided to go to sea, he could usually find a berth somewhere. But with ships unable to find crews, there were fewer longshoremen finding work loading vessels. With regular members of the Longshoremen's Guild unable to find work, it was hardly odd that the Guild would be unable to find work for the frightened seamen who had caused that very shortage.

The unemployment, in turn, threw an added burden on the Privy Purse of the Marquis of Cherbourg, since, by ancient law, it was obligatory upon the lord to take care of his men and their families in times of trouble. Thus far, the drain was not too great, since it was spread out evenly over the Empire; my lord of Cherbourg could apply to the Duke of Normandy for aid under the same law, and His Royal Highness could, in turn, apply to His Imperial Majesty, John IV, King and Emperor of England, France, Scotland, Ireland, New England and New France, Defender of the Faith, et cetera.

And the funds of the Imperial Privy Purse came from all over the Empire.

Still, if the thing became widespread, the economy of the Empire stood in danger of complete collapse.

There had not been a complete cessation of activity on the waterfront, Lord Darcy was relieved to notice. Aside from those ships that were making the Mediterranean and African runs, there were still ships that had apparently found crews for the Atlantic run to the northern continent of New England and the southern continent of New France.

One great ship, the *Pride of Calais*, showed quite a bit of activity; bales of goods were being loaded over the side amid much shouting of orders. Close by, Lord Darcy could see a sling full of wine casks being lifted aboard, each cask bearing the words: *Ordwin Vayne, Vintner*, and a sorcerer's symbol burnt into the wood, showing that the wine was protected against souring for the duration of the trip. Most of the wine, Lord Darcy knew, was for the crew; by law each sailor was allowed the equivalent of a bottle a day, and, besides, the excellence of the New World wines was such that it did not pay to import the beverage from Europe.

Further on, Lord Darcy saw other ships that he knew were making the Atlantic run loading goods aboard. Evidently the "Atlantic Curse" had not yet frightened the guts out of all of the Empire's seamen.

We'll come through, Lord Darcy thought. *In spite of everything the King of Poland can do, we'll come through. We always have.*

He did not think: *We always will.* Empires and societies, he knew, died and were replaced by others. The Roman Empire had died to be replaced by hordes of barbarians who had gradually evolved the feudal society, which had, in turn, evolved the modern system. It was, certainly, possible that the eight-hundred-year-old Empire that had been established by Henry II in the Twelfth Century might some day collapse as the Roman Empire had—but it had already existed nearly twice as long, and there were no threatening hordes of barbarians to overrun it nor were there any signs of internal dissent strong enough to disrupt it. The Empire was still stable and still evolving.

Most of that stability and evolution was due to the House of Plantagenet, the House which had been founded by Henry II after the death of King Stephen. Old Henry had brought the greater part of France under the sway of the King of England. His son, Richard the Lion-Hearted, had neglected England during the first ten years of his reign, but, after his narrow escape from death from the bolt of a crossbowman at the Siege of Chaluz, he had settled down to controlling the Empire with a firm hand and a wise brain. He had no children, but his nephew, Arthur, the son of King Richard's dead brother, Geoffrey, had become like a son to him. Arthur had fought with the King against the treacheries of Prince John, Richard's younger brother and the only other claimant to the throne. Prince John's death in 1216 left Arthur as the only heir, and, upon old Richard's death in 1219, Arthur, at thirty-two, had succeeded to the Throne of England. In popular legend, King Arthur was often confused with the earlier King Arthur of Camelot—and for good reason. The monarch who was known even today as Good King Arthur had resolved to rule his realm in the same chivalric manner—partly inspired by the legends of the ancient Brittanic leader, and partly because of his own inherent abilities.

Since then, the Plantagenet line had gone through nearly eight centuries of trial and tribulation; of blood, sweat, toil, and tears; of resisting the enemies of the Empire by sword, fire, and consummate diplomacy to hold the realm together and to expand it.

The Empire had endured. And the Empire would continue to endure only so long as every subject realized that it could not endure if the entire burden were left to the King alone. *The Empire expects every man to do his duty.*

And Lord Darcy's duty, at this moment, was greater than the simple duty of finding out what had happened to my lord the Marquis of Cherbourg. The problem ran much deeper than that.

His thoughts were interrupted by the voice of the Bishop.

"There's the tower of the Great Keep ahead, Lord Darcy. We'll be there soon."

It was actually several more minutes before the carriage-and-four drew up before the main entrance of Castle Cherbourg. The door was opened by a footman, and three men climbed out, Master Sean still clutching his suitcase.

My Lady Elaine, Marquise de Cherbourg, stood in her salon above the Great Hall, staring out the window at the Channel. She could see the icy waves splashing and dancing and rolling with almost hypnotic effect, but she saw them without thinking about them.

Where are you, Hugh? she thought. *Come back to me,*

Hugh. I need you. I never knew how much I'd need you.
Then there seemed to be a blank as her mind rested. Nothing came through but the roll of the waves.

Then there was the noise of an opening door behind her. She turned quickly, her long velvet skirts swirling around her like thick syrup. "Yes?" Her voice seemed oddly far away in her ears.

"You rang, my lady." It was Sir Gwiliam, the seneschal.

My Lady Elaine tried to focus her thoughts. "Oh," she said after a moment. "Oh, yes." She waved toward the refreshment table, upon which stood a decanter of Oporto, a decanter of Xerez, and an empty decanter. "Brandy. The brandy hasn't been refilled. Bring some of the Saint Coeurlandt Michele '46."

"The Saint Coeurlandt Michele '46, my lady?" Sir Gwiliam blinked slightly. "But my lord de Cherbourg would not—"

She turned to face him directly. "My lord of Cherbourg would most certainly not deny his lady his best Champagne brandy at a time like this, Sieur Gwiliam!" she snapped, using the local pronunciation instead of standard Anglo-French, thus employing a mild and unanswerable epithet. "Must I fetch it myself?"

Sir Gwiliam's face paled a little, but his expression did not change. "No, my lady. Your wish is my command."

"Very well. I thank you, Sir Gwiliam." She turned back to the window. Behind her, she heard the door open and close.

Then she turned, walked over to the refreshment table, and looked at the glass she had emptied only a few minutes before.

Empty, she thought. *Like my life. Can I refill it?*

She lifted the decanter of Xerez, took out the stopple, and, with exaggerated care, refilled her glass. Brandy was better, but until Sir Gwiliam brought the brandy there was nothing to drink but the sweet wines. She wondered vaguely why she had insisted on the best and finest brandy in Hugh's cellar. There was no need for it. Any brandy would have done, even the *Aqua Sancta* '60, a foul distillate. She knew that by now her palate was so anesthetized that she could not tell the difference.

But where was the brandy? Somewhere. Yes. Sir Gwiliam.

Angrily, almost without thinking, she began to jerk at the bellpull. Once. Pause. Once. Pause. Once . . .

She was still ringing when the door opened.

"Yes, my lady?"

She turned angrily—then froze.

Lord Seiger frightened her. He always had.

"I rang for Sir Gwiliam, my lord," she said, with as much dignity as she could summon.

Lord Seiger was a big man who had about him the icy coldness of the Norse home from which his ancestors had come. His hair was so blond as to be almost silver, and his eyes were a pale iceberg blue. The Marquise could not recall ever having seen him smile. His handsome face was always placid and expressionless. She realized with a small chill that she would be more afraid of Lord Seiger's smile than of his normal calm expression.

"I rang for Sir Gwiliam," my lady repeated.

"Indeed, my lady," said Lord Seiger, "but since Sir Gwiliam seemed not to answer, I felt it my duty to respond. You rang for him a few minutes ago. Now you are ringing again. May I help?"

"No . . . No . . ." What could she say?

He came into the room, closing the door behind him. Even twenty-five feet away, My Lady Elaine fancied she could feel the chill from him. She could do nothing as he approached. She couldn't find her voice. He was tall and cold and blondly handsome—and had no more sexuality than a toad. Less—for a toad must at least have attraction for another toad—and a toad was at least a living thing. My lady was not attracted to the man, and he hardly seemed living.

He came toward her like a battleship—twenty feet— fifteen . . .

She gasped and gestured toward the refreshment table. "Would you pour some wine, my lord? I'd like a glass of the . . . the Xerez."

It was as though the battleship had been turned in its course, she thought. His course toward her veered by thirty degrees as he angled toward the table.

"Xerez, my lady? Indeed. I shall be most happy."

With precise, strong hands, he emptied the last of the decanter into a goblet. "There is less than a glassful, my lady," he said, looking at her with expressionless blue eyes. "Would my lady care for the Oporto instead?"

"No . . . No, just the Xerez, my lord, just the Xerez." She swallowed. "Would you care for anything yourself?"

"I never drink, my lady." He handed her the partially filled glass.

It was all she could do to take the glass from his hand, and it struck her as odd that his fingers, when she touched them, seemed as warm as anyone else's.

"Does my lady really feel that it is necessary to drink so much?" Lord Seiger asked. "For the last four days . . ."

My lady's hand shook, but all she could say was: "My nerves, my lord. My nerves." She handed back the glass, empty.

Since she had not asked for more, Lord Seiger merely held the glass and looked at her. "I am here to protect you, my lady. It is my duty. Only your enemies have anything to fear from me."

Somehow, she knew that what he said was true, but—

"Please. A glass of Oporto, my lord."

"Yes, my lady."

He was refilling her glass when the door opened.

It was Sir Gwiliam, bearing a bottle of brandy. "My lady, my lord, the carriage has arrived."

Lord Seiger looked at him expressionlessly, then turned the same face on My Lady Elaine. "The Duke's Investigators. Shall we meet them here, my lady?"

"Yes. Yes, my lord, of course. Yes." Her eyes were on the brandy.

The meeting between Lord Darcy and My Lady Elaine was brief and meaningless. Lord Darcy had no objection to the aroma of fine brandy, but he preferred it fresh rather than secondhand. Her recital of what had happened during the days immediately preceding the disappearance of the Marquis was not significantly different from that of the Bishop.

The coldly handsome Lord Seiger, who had been introduced as secretary to the Marquis, knew nothing. He had not been present during any of the alleged attacks.

My lady the Marquise finally excused herself, pleading a headache. Lord Darcy noted that the brandy bottle went with her.

"My Lord Seiger," he said, "her ladyship seems indisposed.

Whom does that leave in charge of the castle for the moment?"

"The servants and household are in the charge of Sir Gwiliam de Bracy, the seneschal. The guard is in the charge of Captain Sir Androu Duglasse. I am not My Lord Marquis' Privy Secretary; I am merely aiding him in cataloguing some books."

"I see. Very well. I should like to speak to Sir Gwiliam and Sir Androu."

Lord Seiger stood up, walked over to the bellpull and signaled. "Sir Gwiliam will be here shortly," he said. "I shall fetch Sir Androu myself." He bowed. "If you will excuse me, my lords."

When he had gone, Lord Darcy said: "An impressive looking man. Dangerous, too, I should say—in the right circumstances."

"Seems a decent sort," said My Lord Bishop. "A bit restrained . . . er . . . stuffy, one might say. Not much sense of humor, but sense of humor isn't everything." He cleared his throat and then went on. "I must apologize for my sister-in-law's behavior. She's overwrought. You won't be needing me for these interrogations, and I really ought to see after her."

"Of course, my lord; I quite understand," Lord Darcy said smoothly.

My Lord Bishop had hardly gone when the door opened again and Sir Gwiliam came in. "Your lordship rang?"

"Will you be seated, Sir Gwiliam?" Lord Darcy gestured toward a chair. "We are here, as you know, to investigate the disappearance of my lord of Cherbourg. This is my man, Sean, who assists me. All you say here will be treated as confidential."

"I shall be happy to co-operate, your lordship," said Sir Gwiliam, seating himself.

"I am well aware, Sir Gwiliam," Lord Darcy began, "that you have told what you know to My Lord Bishop, but, tiresome as it may be, I shall have to hear the whole thing again. If you will be so good as to begin at the beginning, Sir Gwiliam . . ."

The seneschal dutifully began his story. Lord Darcy and Master Sean listened to it for the third time and found that it differed only in viewpoint, not in essentials. But the difference in viewpoint was important. Like My Lord Bishop, Sir Gwiliam told his story as though he were not directly involved.

"Did you actually ever see one of these attacks?" Lord Darcy asked.

Sir Gwiliam blinked. "Why . . . no. No, your lordship, I did not. But they were reported to me in detail by several of the servants."

"I see. What about the night of the disappearance? When did you last see My Lord Marquis?"

"Fairly early in the evening, your lordship. With my lord's permission, I went into the city about five o'clock for an evening of cards with friends. We played until rather late—two or two-thirty in the morning. My host, Master Ordwin Vayne, a well-to-do wine merchant in the city, of course insisted that I spend the night. That is not unusual, since the castle gates are locked at ten and it is rather troublesome to have a guard unlock them. I returned to the castle, then, at about ten in the morning, at which time my lady informed me of the disappearance of My Lord Marquis."

Lord Darcy nodded. That checked with what Lady Elaine had said. Shortly after Sir Gwiliam had left, she had retired early, pleading a slight cold. She had been the last to see the Marquis of Cherbourg.

"Thank you, sir seneschal," Lord Darcy said. "I should like to speak to the servants later. There is—"

He was interrupted by the opening of the door. It was Lord Seiger, followed by a large, heavy-set, mustached man with dark hair and a scowling look.

As Sir Gwiliam rose, Lord Darcy said: "Thank you for your help, Sir Gwiliam. That will be all for now."

"Thank you, your lordship; I am most anxious to help."

As the seneschal left, Lord Seiger brought the mustached man into the room. "My lord, this is Sir Androu Duglasse, Captain of the Marquis' Own Guard. Captain, Lord Darcy, Chief Investigator for His Highness the Duke."

The fierce-looking soldier bowed. "I am at your service, m' lord."

"Thank you. Sit down, captain."

Lord Seiger retreated through the door, leaving the captain with Lord Darcy and Master Sean.

"I hope I can be of some help, y' lordship," the captain said.

"I think you can, captain," Lord Darcy said. "No one saw my lord the Marquis leave the castle, I understand. I presume you have questioned your guards."

"I have, y' lordship. We didn't know m' lord was missing until next morning, when m' lady spoke to me. I checked with the men who were on duty that night. The only one to leave after five was Sir Gwiliam, at five oh two, according to the book."

"And the secret passage?" Lord Darcy asked. He had made it a point to study the plans of every castle in the Empire by going over the drawings in the Royal Archives.

The captain nodded. "There is one. Used during times of siege in the old days. It's kept locked and barred nowadays."

"And guarded?" Lord Darcy asked.

Captain Sir Androu chuckled. "Yes, y' lordship. Most hated post in the Guard. Tunnel ends up in a sewer, d'ye see. We send a man out there for mild infractions of the rules. Straightens him out to spend a few nights with the smell and the rats, guarding an iron door that hasn't been opened for years and couldn't be opened from the outside without a bomb—or from the inside, either, since it's rusted shut. We inspect at irregular intervals to make sure the man's on his toes."

"I see. You made a thorough search of the castle?"

"Yes. I was afraid he might have come down with another of those fainting spells he's had lately. We looked everywhere he could have been. He was nowhere to be found, y' lordship. Nowhere. He must have got out somewhere."

"Well, we shall have to—" Lord Darcy was interrupted by a rap on the door.

Master Sean, dutifully playing his part, opened it. "Yes, your lordship?"

It was Lord Seiger at the door. "Would you tell Lord Darcy that Henri Vert, Chief Master-at-Arms of the City of Cherbourg, would like to speak to him?"

For a fraction of a second, Lord Darcy was both surprised and irritated. How had the Chief Master-at-Arms known he was here? Then he saw what the answer must be.

"Tell him to come in, Sean," said Lord Darcy.

Chief Henri was a heavy-set, tough-looking man in his

early fifties who had the air and bearing of a stolid fighter. He bowed. "Lord Darcy. May I speak to your lordship alone?" He spoke Anglo-French with a punctilious precision that showed it was not his natural way of speaking. He had done his best to remove the accent of the local *patois*, but his effort to speak properly was noticeable.

"Certainly, Chief Henri. Will you excuse us, captain? I will discuss this problem with you later."

"Of course, your lordship."

Lord Darcy and Master Sean were left alone with Chief Henri.

"I *am* sorry to have interrupted, your lordship," said the Chief, "but His Royal Highness gave strict instructions."

"I had assumed as much, Chief Henri. Be so good as to sit down. Now—what has happened?"

"Well, your lordship," he said, glancing at Master Sean, "His Highness instructed me over the teleson to speak to no one but you." Then the Chief took a good look and did a double take. "By the Blue! Master Sean O Lochlainn! I didn't recognize you in that livery!"

The sorcerer grinned. "I make a very good valet, eh, Henri?"

"Indeed you do! Well, then, I may speak freely?"

"Certainly," said Lord Darcy. "Proceed."

"Well, then." The Chief leaned forward and spoke in a low voice. "When this thing came up, I thought of you first off. I must admit that it's beyond me. On the night of the eighth, two of my men were patrolling the waterfront district. At the corner of Rue King John II and Quai Sainte Marie, they saw a man fall. Except for a cloak, he was naked—and if your lordship remembers, that was a very cold night. By the time they got to him, he was dead."

Lord Darcy narrowed his eyes. "How had he died?"

"Skull fracture, your lordship. Somebody'd smashed in the right side of his skull. It's a wonder he could walk at all."

"I see. Proceed."

"Well, he was brought to the morgue. My men both identified him as one Paul Sarto, a man who worked around the bistros for small wages. He was also identified by the owner of the bistro where he had last worked. He seems to have been feeble-minded, willing to do manual labor for bed, board, and spending money. Needed taking care of a bit."

"Hm-m-m. We must trace him and find out why his baron had not provided for him," said Lord Darcy. "Proceed."

"Well, your lordship . . . er . . . there's more to it than that. I didn't look into the case immediately. After all, another killing on the waterfront—" He shrugged and spread his hands, palms up. "My sorcerer and my chirurgeon looked him over, made the usual tests. He was killed by a blow from a piece of oak with a square corner—perhaps a two-by-two or something like that. He was struck about ten minutes before the Armsmen found him. My chirurgeon says that only a man of tremendous vitality could have survived that long—to say nothing of the fact that he was able to walk."

"Excuse me, Henri," Master Sean interrupted. "Did your sorcerer make the FitzGibbon test for post-mortem activation?"

"Of course. First test he made, considering the wound. No, the body had not been activated after death and made to walk away from the scene of the crime. He actually died as the Armsmen watched."

"Just checking," said Master Sean.

"Well, anyway, the affair might have been dismissed as another waterfront brawl, but there were some odd things about the corpse. The cloak he was wearing was of aristocratic cut—not that of a commoner. Expensive cloth, expensive tailoring. Also, he had bathed recently—and, apparently, frequently. His toe- and fingernails were decently manicured and cut."

Lord Darcy's eyes narrowed with interest. "Hardly the condition one would expect of a common laborer, eh?"

"Exactly, my lord. So when I read the reports this morning, I went to take a look. This time of year, the weather permits keeping a body without putting a preservation spell on it."

He leaned forward, and his voice became lower and hoarser. "I only had to take one look, my lord. Then I had to take action and call Rouen. My lord, it is the Marquis of Cherbourg himself!"

Lord Darcy rode through the chilling wintry night on a borrowed horse, his dark cloak whipping around the palfrey's rump in the icy breeze. The chill was more apparent than real. A relatively warm wind had come in from the sea, bringing with it a slushy rain; the temperature of the air was above the freezing point—but not much above it. Lord Darcy had endured worse cold than this, but the damp chill seemed to creep inside his clothing, through his skin, and into his bones. He would have preferred a dry cold, even if it was much colder; at least, a dry cold didn't try to crawl into a man's cloak with him.

He had borrowed the horse from Chief Henri. It was a serviceable hack, well-trained to police work and used to the cobbled streets of Cherbourg.

The scene at the morgue, Lord Darcy thought, had been an odd one. He and Sean and Henri had stood by while the morgue attendant had rolled out the corpse. At first glance, Lord Darcy had been able to understand the consternation of the Chief Master-at-Arms.

He had only met Hugh of Cherbourg once and could hardly be called upon to make a positive identification, but if the corpse was not the Marquis to the life, the face was his in death.

The two Armsmen who had seen the man die had been asked separately, and without being told of the new identification, still said that the body was that of Paul Sarto, although they admitted he looked cleaner and better cared for than Paul ever had.

It was easy to see how the conflict of opinion came about. The Armsmen had seen the Marquis only rarely—probably only on state occasions, when he had been magnificently dressed. They could hardly be expected to identify a wandering, nearly nude man on the waterfront as their liege lord. If, in addition, that man was immediately identified in their minds with the man they had known as Paul Sarto, the identification of him as my lord the Marquis would be positively forced from their minds. On the other hand, Henri Vert, Chief Master-at-Arms of the City of Cherbourg, knew My Lord Marquis well and had never seen nor heard of Paul Sarto until after the death.

Master Sean had decided that further thaumaturgical tests could be performed upon the deceased. The local sorcerer—a mere journeyman of the Sorcerer's Guild—had explained all the tests he had performed, valiantly trying to impress a Master of the Art with his proficiency and ability.

"The weapon used was a fairly long piece of oak, Master.

According to the Kaplan-Sheinwold test, a short club could not have been used. On the other hand, oddly enough, I could find no trace of evil or malicious intent, and—"

"Precisely why I intend to perform further tests, me boy," Master Sean had said. "We haven't enough information."

"Yes, Master," the journeyman sorcerer had said, properly humbled.

Lord Darcy made the observation—which he kept to himself—that if the blow had been dealt from the front, which it appeared to have been, then the killer was either left-handed or had a vicious right-hand backswing. Which, he had to admit to himself, told him very little. The cold chill of the unheated morgue had begun to depress him unduly in the presence of the dead, so he had left that part of the investigation to Master Sean and set out on his own, borrowing a palfrey from Chief Henri for the purpose.

The winters he had spent in London had convinced him thoroughly that no man of intelligence would stay anywhere near a cold seacoast. Inland cold was fine; seacoast warmth was all right. But this—!

Although he did not know Cherbourg well, Lord Darcy had the kind of mind that could carry a map in its memory and translate that map easily into the real world that surrounded him. Even a slight inaccuracy of the map didn't bother him.

He turned his mount round a corner and saw before him a gas lamp shielded with blue glass—the sign of an outstation of the Armsmen of Cherbourg. An Armsman stood at attention outside.

As soon as he saw that he was confronted by a mounted nobleman, the Man-at-Arms came to attention. "Yes, my lord! Can I aid you, my lord?"

"Yes, Armsman, you can," Lord Darcy said as he vaulted from the saddle. He handed the reins of the horse to the Armsman. "This mount belongs to Chief Henri at headquarters." He showed his card with the ducal arms upon it. "I am Lord Darcy, Chief Investigator for His Royal Highness the Duke. Take care of the horse. I have business in this neighborhood and will return for the animal. I should like to speak to your Sergeant-at-Arms."

"Very good, my lord. The Sergeant is within, my lord."

After speaking to the sergeant, Lord Darcy went out again into the chill night.

It was still several blocks to his destination, but it would have been unwise to ride a horse all the way. He walked two blocks through the dingy streets of the neighborhood. Then, glancing about to make fairly certain he had not been followed or observed, he turned into a dark alley. Once inside, he took off his cloak and reversed it. The lining, instead of being the silk that a nobleman ordinarily wore, or the fur that would be worn in really cold weather, was a drab, worn, brown, carefully patched in one place. From a pocket, he drew a battered slouch hat of the kind normally worn by commoners in this area and adjusted it to his head after carefully mussing his hair. His boots were plain and already covered with mud. Excellent!

He relaxed his spine—normally his carriage was one of military erectness—and slowly strolled out of the other end of the alley.

He paused to light a cheap cigar and then moved on toward his destination.

"*Aaiiy?*" The blowsy-looking woman in her mid-fifties looked through the opening in the heavy door. "What might you be wanting at this hour?"

Lord Darcy gave the face his friendliest smile and answered in the *patois* she had used. "Excuse me, Lady-of-the-House, but I'm looking for my brother, Vincent Coudé. Hate to call on him so late, but—"

As he had expected, he was interrupted.

"We don't allow no one in after dark unless they's identified by one of our people."

"As you shouldn't, Lady-of-the-House," Lord Darcy agreed politely. "But I'm sure my brother Vincent will identify me. just tell him his brother Richard is here. Ey?"

She shook her head. "He ain't here. Ain't been here since last Wednesday. My girl checks the rooms every day, and he ain't been here since last Wednesday."

Wednesday! thought Lord Darcy. *Wednesday the eighth! The night the Marquis disappeared! The night the body was found only a few blocks from here!*

Lord Darcy took a silver coin from his belt pouch and held it out between the fingers of his right hand. "Would

you mind going up and taking a look? He might've come
in during the day. Might be asleep up there."

She took the coin and smiled. "Glad to; glad to. You might
be right; he might've come in. Be right back."

But she left the door locked and closed the panel.

Lord Darcy didn't care about that. He listened carefully
to her footsteps. Up the stairs. Down the hall. A knock.
Another knock.

Quickly, Lord Darcy ran to the right side of the house
and looked up. Sure enough, he saw the flicker of a lantern in one window. The Lady-of-the-House had unlocked
the door and looked in to make sure that her roomer was
not in. He ran back to the door and was waiting for her
when she came down.

She opened the door panel and said sadly: "He still ain't
here, Richard."

Lord Darcy handed her another sixth-sovereign piece.
"That's all right, Lady-of-the-House. Just tell him I was here.
I suppose he's out on business." He paused. "When is his
rent next due?"

She looked at him through suddenly narrowed eyes,
wondering whether it would be possible to cheat her
roomer's brother out of an extra week's rent. She saw his
cold eyes and decided it wouldn't.

"He's paid up to the twenty-fourth," she admitted reluctantly. "But if he ain't back by then, I'll be turning his stuff
out and getting another roomer."

"Naturally," Lord Darcy agreed. "But he'll be back. Tell
him I was here. Nothing urgent. I'll be back in a day or
so."

She smiled. "All right. Come in the daytime, if y' can,
Friend Richard. Thank y' much."

"Thank y' yourself, Lady-of-the-House," said Lord Darcy.
"A good and safe night to y'." He turned and walked away.

He walked half a block and then dodged into a dark
doorway.

So! Sir James le Lein, agent of His Majesty's Secret Service,
had not been seen since the night of the eighth. That evening
was beginning to take on a more and more sinister complexion.

He knew full well that he could have bribed the woman
to let him into Sir James' room, but the amount he would

have had to offer would have aroused suspicion. There was a better way.

It took him better than twenty minutes to find that way, but eventually he found himself on the roof of the two-story rooming house where Sir James had lived under the alias of Vincent Coudé.

The house was an old one, but the construction had been strong. Lord Darcy eased himself down the slope of the shingled roof to the rain gutters at the edge. He had to lie flat, his feet uphill toward the point of the roof, his hands braced against the rain gutter to look down over the edge toward the wall below. The room in which he had seen the glimmer of light from the woman's lantern was just below him. The window was blank and dark, but the shutters were not drawn, which was a mercy.

The question was: Was the window locked? Holding tight to the rain gutter, he eased himself down to the very edge of the roof. His body was at a thirty-degree angle, and he could feel the increased pressure of blood in his head. Cautiously, he reached down to see if he could touch the window. He could!

Just barely, but he could!

Gently, carefully, working with the tips of the fingers of one hand, he teased the window open. As was usual with these old houses, the glass panes were in two hinged panels that swung inward. He got both of them open.

So far, the rain gutter had held him. It seemed strong enough to hold plenty of weight. He slowly moved himself around until his body was parallel with the edge of the roof. Then he took a good grasp of the edge of the rain gutter and swung himself out into empty air. As he swung round, he shot his feet out toward the lower sill of the window.

Then he let go and tumbled into the room.

He crouched motionlessly for a moment. Had he been heard? The sound had seemed tremendous when his feet had struck the floor. But it was still early, and there were others moving about in the rooming house. Still, he remained unmoving for a good two minutes to make sure there would be no alarm. He was quite certain that if the Lady-of-the-House had heard anything that disturbed her, she would have rushed up the stairs. No sound. Nothing.

Then he rose to his feet and took a special device from the pocket of his cloak.

It was a fantastic device, a secret of His Majesty's Government. Powered by the little zinc-copper couples that were the only known source of such magical power, they heated a steel wire to tremendously high temperature. The thin wire glowed white-hot, shedding a yellow-white light that was almost as bright as a gas-mantle lamp. The secret lay in the magical treatment of the steel filament. Under ordinary circumstances, the wire would burn up in a blue-white flash of fire. But, properly treated by a special spell, the wire was passivated and merely glowed with heat and light instead of burning. The hot wire was centered at the focus of a parabolic reflector, and merely by shoving forward a button with his thumb, Lord Darcy had at hand a light source equal to—and indeed far superior to—an ordinary dark lantern. It was a personal instrument, since the passivation was tuned to Lord Darcy and no one else.

He thumbed the button and a beam of light sprang into existence.

The search of Sir James le Lein's room was quick and thorough. There was absolutely nothing of any interest to Lord Darcy anywhere in the room.

Naturally Sir James would have taken pains to assure that there would not be. The mere fact that the housekeeper had a key would have made Sir James wary of leaving anything about that would have looked out of place. There was nothing here that would have identified the inhabitant of the room as anyone but a common laborer.

Lord Darcy switched off his lamp and brooded for a moment in the darkness. Sir James was on a secret and dangerous mission for His Imperial Majesty, John IV. Surely there were reports, papers, and so on. Where had Sir James kept the data he collected? In his head? That was possible, but Lord Darcy didn't think it was true.

Sir James had been working with Lord Cherbourg. Both of them had vanished on the night of the eighth. That the mutual vanishing was coincidental was possible—but highly improbable. There were too many things unexplained as yet. Lord Darcy had three tentative hypotheses, all of which explained the facts as he knew them thus far, and none of which satisfied him.

It was then that his eyes fell on the flowerpot silhouetted against the dim light that filtered in from outside the darkened room. If it had been in the middle of the window sill, he undoubtedly would have smashed it when he came in; his feet had just barely cleared the sill. But it was over to one side, in a corner of the window. He walked over and looked at it carefully in the dimness. Why, he asked himself, would an agent of the King be growing an African violet?

He picked up the little flowerpot, brought it away from the window, and shone his light on it. It looked utterly usual.

With a grim smile, Lord Darcy put the pot, flower and all, into one of the capacious pockets of his cloak. Then he opened the window, eased himself over the sill, lowered himself until he was hanging only by his fingertips, and dropped the remaining ten feet to the ground, taking up the jar of landing with his knees.

Five minutes later, he had recovered his horse from the Armsman and was on his way to Castle Cherbourg.

The monastery of the Order of Saint Benedict in Cherbourg was a gloomy-looking pile of masonry occupying one corner of the great courtyard that surrounded the castle. Lord Darcy and Master Sean rang the bell at the entrance gate early on the morning of Tuesday, January 14th. They identified themselves to the doorkeeper and were invited into the Guests' Common Room to wait while Father Patrique was summoned. The monk would have to get the permission of the Lord Abbot to speak to outsiders, but that was a mere formality.

It was a relief to find that the interior of the monastery did not share the feeling of gloom with its exterior. The Common Room was quite cheerful and the winter sun shone brightly through the high windows.

After a minute or so, the inner door opened and a tall, rather pale man in Benedictine habit entered the room. He smiled pleasantly as he strode briskly across the room to take Lord Darcy's hand. "Lord Darcy, I am Father Patrique. Your servant, my lord."

"And I yours, your reverence. This is my man, Sean."

The priest turned to accept the introduction, then he paused and a gleam of humor came into his eyes. "Master

Sean, the clothing you wear is not your own. A sorcerer cannot hide his calling by donning a valet's outfit."

Master Sean smiled back. "I hadn't hoped to conceal myself from a perceptive of your Order, Reverend Sir."

Lord Darcy, too, smiled. He had rather hoped that Father Patrique would be a perceptive. The Benedictines were quite good in bringing out that particular phase of Talent if a member of their Order had it, and they prided themselves on the fact that Holy Father Benedict, their Founder in the early part of the Sixth Century, had showed that ability to a remarkable degree long before the Laws of Magic had been formulated or investigated scientifically. To such a perceptive, identity cannot be concealed without a radical change in the personality itself. Such a man is capable of perceiving, *in toto*, the personality of another; such men are invaluable as Healers, especially in cases of demonic possession and other mental diseases.

"And now, how may I help you, my lord?" the Benedictine asked pleasantly.

Lord Darcy produced his credentials and identified himself as Duke Richard's Chief Investigator.

"Quite so," said the priest. "Concerning the fact that my lord the Marquis is missing, I have no doubt."

"The walls of a monastery are not totally impenetrable, are they, Father?" Lord Darcy asked with a wry smile.

Father Patrique chuckled. "We are wide open to the sight of God and the rumors of man. Please be seated; we will not be disturbed here."

"Thank you, Father," Lord Darcy said, taking a chair. "I understand you were called to attend my lord of Cherbourg several times since last Christmas. My lady of Cherbourg and my lord the Bishop of Guernsey and Sark have told me of the nature of these attacks—that, incidentally, is why this whole affair is being kept as quiet as possible—but I would like your opinion as a Healer."

The priest shrugged his shoulders and spread his hands a little. "I should be glad to tell you what I can, my lord, but I am afraid I know almost nothing. The attacks lasted only a few minutes each time and they had vanished by the time I was able to see My Lord Marquis. By then, he was normal—if a little puzzled. He told me he had no memory of such behavior as my lady reported. He simply blanked out and then came out of it, feeling slightly disoriented and a little dizzy."

"Have you formed no diagnosis, Father?" Lord Darcy asked.

The Benedictine frowned. "There are several possible diagnoses, my lord. From my own observation, and from the symptoms reported by My Lord Marquis, I would have put it down as a mild form of epilepsy—what we call the *petit mal* type, the 'little sickness'. Contrary to popular opinion, epilepsy is not caused by demonic possession, but by some kind of organic malfunction that we know very little about.

"In *grand mal*, or 'great sickness' epilepsy, we find the seizures one normally thinks of as being connected with the disease—the convulsive 'fits' that cause the victim to completely lose control of his muscles and collapse with jerking limbs and so on. But the 'little sickness' merely causes brief loss of consciousness—sometimes so short that the victim does not even realize it. There is no collapse or convulsion; merely a blank daze lasting a few seconds or minutes."

"But you are not certain of that?" Lord Darcy asked.

The priest frowned. "No. If my lady the Marquise is telling the truth—and I see no reason why she should not, his behavior during the . . . well, call them seizures . . . his behavior during the seizures was atypical. During a typical seizure of the *petit mal* type, the victim is totally blank—staring at nothing, unable to speak or move, unable to be roused. But my lord was not that way, according to my lady. He seemed confused, bewildered, and very stupid, but he was not unconscious." He paused and frowned.

"Therefore you have other diagnoses, Father?" Lord Darcy prompted.

Father Patrique nodded thoughtfully. "Yes. Always assuming that my lady the Marquise has reported accurately, there are other possible diagnoses. But none of them quite fits, any more than the first one does."

"Such as?"

"Such as attack by psychic induction."

Master Sean nodded slowly, but there was a frown in his eyes.

"The wax-and-doll sort of thing," said Lord Darcy.

Father Patrique nodded an affirmative. "Exactly, my lord—although, as you undoubtedly know, there are far better methods than that—in practice."

"Of course," Lord Darcy said brusquely. In theory, he knew, the simulacrum method was the best method. Nothing could be more powerful than an exact duplicate, according to the Laws of Similarity. The size of the simulacrum made little difference, but the accuracy of detail did—including internal organs.

But the construction of a wax simulacrum—aside from the artistry required—entailed complications which bordered on the shadowy area of the unknown. Beeswax was more effective than mineral wax for the purpose because it was an animal product instead of a mineral one, thus increasing the similarity. But why did the addition of sal ammoniac increase the potency? Magicians simply said that sal ammoniac, saltpeter, and a few other minerals increased the similarity in some unknown way and let it go at that; sorcerers had better things to do than grub around in mineralogy.

"The trouble is," said Father Patrique, "that the psychic induction method nearly always involves physical pain or physical illness—intestinal disorders, heart trouble, or other glandular disturbances. There are no traces of such things here unless one considers the malfunction of the brain as a glandular disorder—and even so, it should be accompanied by pain."

"Then you discount that diagnosis, too?" asked Lord Darcy.

Father Patrique shook his head firmly. "I discount none of the diagnoses I have made thus far. My data are far from complete."

"You have other theories, then."

"I do, my lord. Actual demonic possession."

Lord Darcy narrowed his eyes and looked straight into the eyes of the priest. "You don't really believe that, Reverend Sir."

"No," Father Patrique admitted candidly, "I do not. As a perceptive, I have a certain amount of faith in my own ability. If more than one personality were inhabiting my lord's body, I am certain I would have perceived the . . . er . . . other personality."

Lord Darcy did not move his eyes from those of the

Benedictine. "I had assumed as much, your reverence," he said. "If it were a case of multiple personality, you would have detected it, eh?"

"I am certain I would have, my lord," Father Patrique stated positively. "If my lord of Cherbourg had been inhabited by another personality, I would have detected it, even if that other personality had been under cover." He paused, then waved a hand slightly. "You understand, Lord Darcy? Alternate personalities in a single human body, a single human brain, can hide themselves. The personality dominant at any given time conceals to the casual observer the fact that other—different—personalities are present. But the . . . the *alter egos* cannot conceal themselves from a true perceptive."

"I understand," Lord Darcy said.

"There was only one personality in the . . . the *person*, the *brain*, of the Marquis of Cherbourg at the time I examined him. And that personality was the personality of the Marquis himself."

"I see," Lord Darcy said thoughtfully. He did not doubt the priest's statement. He knew the reputation Father Patrique had among Healers. "How about drugs, Father?" he asked after a moment. "I understand that there are drugs which can alter a man's personality."

The Benedictine Healer smiled. "Certainly. Alcohol—the essence of wines and beers—will do it. There are others. Some have a temporary effect; others have no effect in single dosages—or, at least, no detectable effect—but have an accumulative effect if the drug is taken regularly. Oil of wormwood, for instance, is found in several of the more expensive liqueurs—in small quantity, of course. If you get drunk on such a liqueur, the effect is temporary and hardly distinguishable from that of alcohol alone. But if taken steadily, over a period of time, a definite personality change occurs."

Lord Darcy nodded thoughtfully, then looked at his sorcerer. "Master Sean, the phial, if you please."

The tubby little Irish sorcerer fished in a pocket with thumb and forefinger and brought forth a small stoppered glass phial a little over an inch long and half an inch in diameter. He handed it to the priest, who looked at it with curiosity. It was nearly filled with a dark amber fluid. In the fluid were little pieces of dark matter, rather like coarse-cut tobacco, which had settled to the bottom of the phial and filled perhaps a third of it.

"What is it?" Father Patrique asked.

Master Sean frowned. "That's what I'm not rightly sure of, Reverend Sir. I checked it to make certain there were no spells on it before I opened it. There weren't. So I unstoppered it and took a little whiff. Smells like brandy, with just faint overtones of something else. Naturally, I couldn't analyze it without having some notion of what it was. Without a specimen standard, I couldn't use Similarity analysis. Oh, I checked the brandy part, and that came out all right. The liquid is brandy. But I can't identify the little crumbs of stuff. His lordship had an idea that it might be a drug of some kind, and, since a Healer has all kinds of *materia medica* around, I thought perhaps we might be able to identify it."

"Certainly," the priest agreed. "I have a couple of ideas we might check right away. The fact that the material is steeped in brandy indicates either that the material decays easily or that the essence desired is soluble in brandy. That suggests several possibilities to my mind." He looked at Lord Darcy. "May I ask where you got it, my lord?"

Lord Darcy smiled. "I found it buried in a flowerpot."

Father Patrique, realizing that he had been burdened with all the information he was going to get, accepted Lord Darcy's statement with a slight shrug. "Very well, my lord; Master Sean and I will see if we can discover what this mysterious substance may be."

"Thank you, Father." Lord Darcy rose from his seat "Oh— one more thing. What do you know about Lord Seiger?"

"Very little. His lordship comes from Yorkshire . . . North Riding, if I'm not mistaken. He's been working with my lord of Cherbourg for the past several months—something to do with books, I believe. I know nothing of his family or anything like that, if that is what you mean."

"Not exactly," said Lord Darcy. "Are you his Confessor, Father? Or have you treated him as a Healer?"

The Benedictine raised his eyebrows. "No. Neither. Why?"

"Then I can ask you a question about his soul. What kind of man is he? What is the oddness I detect in him? What is it about him that frightens my lady the Marquise in spite of his impeccable behavior?" He noticed the hesitation in the priest's manner and went on before Father Patrique could answer. "This is not idle curiosity, Your Reverence. I am investigating a homicide."

The priest's eyes widened. "Not . . . ?" He stopped himself. "I see. Well, then. Granted, as a perceptive, I know certain things about Lord Seiger. He suffers from a grave illness of the soul. How these things come about, we do not know, but occasionally a person utterly lacks that part of the soul we call 'conscience', at least insofar as it applies to certain acts. We cannot think that God would fail to provide such a thing; therefore theologists ascribe the lack to an act of the Devil at some time in the early life of the child—probably prenatally and, therefore, before baptism can protect the child. Lord Seiger is such a person. A psychopathic personality. Lord Seiger was born without an ability to distinguish between 'right' and 'wrong' as we know the terms. Such a person performs a given act or refrains from performing it only according to the expediency of the moment. Certain acts which you or I would look upon with abhorrence he may even look upon as pleasurable. Lord Seiger is—basically—a homicidal psychopath."

Lord Darcy said, "I thought as much." Then he added dryly, "He is, I presume, under restraint?"

"Oh, of course; of course!" The priest looked aghast that anyone should suggest otherwise. "Naturally such a person cannot be condemned because of a congenital deficiency, but neither can he be allowed to become a danger to society." He looked at Master Sean. "You know something of *Geas* Theory, Master Sean?"

"Something," Master Sean agreed. "Not my field, of course, but I've studied a little of the theory. The symbol manipulation's a little involved for me, I'm afraid. Psychic Algebra's as far as I ever got."

"Of course. Well, Lord Darcy, to put it in layman's terms, a powerful spell is placed upon the affected person—a *geas*, it's called—which forces him to limit his activities to those which are not dangerous to his fellow man. We cannot limit him too much, of course, for it would be sinful to deprive him entirely of his free will. His sexual morals, for instance, are his own—but he cannot use force. The extent of the *geas* depends upon the condition of the individual and the treatment given by the Healer who performed the work."

"It takes an extensive and powerful knowledge of sorcery, I take it?" Lord Darcy asked.

"Oh, yes. No Healer would even attempt it until he had taken his Th.D. and then specialized under an expert for a time. And there are not many Doctors of Thaumaturgy. Since Lord Seiger is a Yorkshireman, I would venture to guess that the work was done by His Grace the Archbishop of York—a most pious and powerful Healer. I, myself, would not think of attempting such an operation."

"You can, however, tell that such an operation has been performed?"

Father Patrique smiled. "As easily as a chirurgeon can tell if an abdominal operation has been performed."

"Can a *geas* be removed? Or partially removed?"

"Of course—by one equally as skilled and powerful. But I could detect that, too. It has not been done in Lord Seiger's case."

"Can you tell what channels of freedom he has been allowed?"

"No," said the priest. "That sort of thing depends upon the fine structure of the *geas*, which is difficult to observe without extensive analysis."

"Then," said Lord Darcy, "you cannot tell me whether or not there are circumstances in which his *geas* would permit him to kill? Such as, for instance . . . er . . . self-defense?"

"No," the priest admitted. "But I will say that it is rare indeed for even such a channel as self-defense to be left open for a psychopathic killer. The *geas* in such a case would necessarily leave the decision as to what constituted 'self-defense' up to the patient. A normal person knows when 'self-defense' requires killing one's enemy, rendering him unconscious, fleeing from him, giving him a sharp retort, or merely keeping quiet. But to a psychopathic killer, a simple insult may be construed as an attack which requires 'self-defense'—which would give him permission to kill. No Healer would leave such a decision in the hands of the patient" His face grew somber. "Certainly no sane man would leave that decision to the mind of a man like Lord Seiger."

"Then you consider him safe, Father?"

The Benedictine hesitated only a moment. "Yes. Yes, I do. I do not believe him capable of committing an antisocial act such as that. The Healer took pains to make sure that Lord Seiger would be protected from most of his fellow men, too. He is almost incapable of committing any offense against propriety; his behavior is impeccable at all times; he cannot insult anyone; he is almost incapable of defending himself physically except under the greatest provocation.

"I once watched him in a fencing bout with my lord the Marquis. Lord Seiger is an expert swordsman—much better than my lord the Marquis. The Marquis was utterly unable to score a touch upon Lord Seiger's person; Lord Seiger's defense was far too good. *But*—neither could Lord Seiger score a touch upon my lord. He couldn't even try. His brilliant swordsmanship is purely and completely defensive." He paused. "You are a swordsman yourself, my lord?" It was only half a question; the priest was fairly certain that a Duke's Investigator would be able to handle any and all weapons with confidence.

He was perfectly correct. Lord Darcy nodded without answering. To be able to wield a totally defensive sword required not only excellent—superlative—swordsmanship, but the kind of iron self-control that few men possessed. In Lord Seiger's case, of course, it could hardly be called *self*-control. The control had been imposed by another.

"Then you can understand," the priest continued, "why I say that I believe he can be trusted. If his Healer found it necessary to impose so many restrictions and protections, he would most certainly not have left any channel open for Lord Seiger to make any decision for himself as to when it would be proper to kill another."

"I understand, Father. Thank you for your information. I assure you it will remain confidential."

"Thank you, my lord. If there is nothing else . . . ?"

"Nothing for the moment, Reverend Father. Thank you again."

"A pleasure, Lord Darcy. And now, Master Sean, shall we go to my laboratory?"

An hour later, Lord Darcy was sitting in the guest room which Sir Gwiliam had shown him to the day before. He was puffing at his Bavarian pipe, filled with a blend of tobacco grown in the Southern Duchies of New England, his mind working at high speed, when Master Sean entered.

"My lord," said the tubby little sorcerer with a smile, "the good Father and I have identified the substance."

"Good!" Lord Darcy gestured toward a chair. "What was it?"

Master Sean sat down. "We were lucky, my lord. His Reverence *did* have a sample of the drug. As soon as we were able to establish a similarity between our sample and his, we identified it as a mushroom known as the Devil's Throne. The fungus is dried, minced, and steeped in brandy or other spirit. The liquid is then decanted off and the minced bits are thrown away—or, sometimes, steeped a second time. In large doses, the drugged spirit results in insanity, convulsions, and rapid death. In small doses, the preliminary stages are simply mild euphoria and light intoxication. But if taken regularly, the effect is cumulative— first, a manic, hallucinatory state, then delusions of persecution and violence."

Lord Darcy's eyes narrowed. "That fits. Thank you. Now there is one more problem. I want positive identification of that corpse. My Lord Bishop is not certain that it is his brother; that may just be wishful thinking. My Lady Marquise refuses to view the body, saying that it could not possibly be her husband—and that is *definitely* wishful thinking. But *I* must know for certain. Can you make a test?'

"I can take blood from the heart of the dead man and compare it with blood from My Lord Bishop's veins, my lord."

"Ah, yes. The Jacoby transfer method," said Lord Darcy.

"Not quite, my lord. The Jacoby transfer requires at least two hearts. It is dangerous to take blood from a living heart. But the test I have in mind is equally as valid."

"I thought blood tests were unreliable between siblings."

"Well, now, as to that, my lord," Master Sean said, "in theory there is a certain very low probability that brother and sister, children of the same parents, would show completely negative results. In other words, they would have zero similarity in that test.

"Blood similarity runs in a series of steps from zero to forty-six. In a parent-child relationship, the similarity is always exactly twenty-three—in other words, the child is always related half to one parent and half to the other.

"With siblings, though, we find variations. Identical twins, for instance, register a full forty-six point similarity. Most siblings run much less, averaging twenty-three. There is a possibility of two brothers or two sisters having only one-point similarity, and, as I said, my lord, of a brother and sister having zero similarity. But the odds are on the order of one point seven nine million million to one against it. Considering the facial similarity of My Lord Bishop and My Lord Marquis, I would be willing to stake my reputation that the similarity would be substantially greater than zero—perhaps greater than twenty-three."

"Very well, Master Sean. You have not failed me yet; I do not anticipate that you ever will. Get me that data."

"Yes, my lord. I shall endeavor to give satisfaction." Master Sean left suffused with a glow of mixed determination and pride.

Lord Darcy finished his pipe and headed for the offices of Captain Sir Androu Duglasse.

The captain looked faintly indignant at Lord Darcy's question. "I searched the castle quite thoroughly, y' lordship. We looked everywhere that M' Lord Marquis could possibly have gone."

"Come, captain," Lord Darcy said mildly, "I don't mean to impugn your ability, but I dare say there are places you didn't search simply because there was no reason to think my lord of Cherbourg would have gone there."

Captain Sir Androu frowned. "Such as, my lord?"

"Such as the secret tunnel."

The captain looked suddenly blank. "Oh," he said after a moment. Then his expression changed. "But surely, y' lordship, you don't think . . ."

"I don't *know*, that's the point. My lord *did* have keys to every lock in the castle, didn't he?"

"All except to the monastery, yes. My Lord Abbot has those."

"Naturally. I think we can dismiss the monastery. Where else did you not look?"

"Well . . ." The captain hesitated thoughtfully. "I didn't bother with the strongroom, the wine cellar, or the icehouse.

I don't have the keys. Sir Gwiliam would have told me if anything was amiss."

"Sir Gwiliam has the keys, you say? Then we must find Sir Gwiliam."

Sir Gwiliam, as it turned out, was in the wine cellar. Lord Seiger informed them that, at Lady Elaine's request, he had sent the seneschal down for another bottle of brandy. Lord Darcy followed Captain Sir Androu down the winding stone steps to the cellars.

"Most of this is used as storage space," the captain said, waving a hand to indicate the vast, dim rooms around them. "All searched very carefully. The wine cellar's this way, y' lordship."

The wine-cellar door, of heavy, reinforced oak, stood slightly ajar. Sir Gwiliam, who had evidently heard their footsteps, opened it a little more and put his head out. "Who is it? Oh. Good afternoon, my lord. Good afternoon, captain. May I be of service?"

He stepped back, opening the door to let them in.

"I thank you, Sir Gwiliam," said Lord Darcy. "We come partly on business and partly on pleasure. I have noticed that my lord the Marquis keeps an excellent cellar; the wines are of the finest and the brandy is extraordinary. Saint Coeurlandt Michele '46 is difficult to come by these days."

Sir Gwiliam looked rather sad. "Yes, your lordship, it is. I fear the last two cases in existence are right here. I now have the painful duty of opening one of them." He sighed and gestured toward the table, where stood a wooden case that had been partially pried open. A glance told Lord Darcy that there was nothing in the bottles but brandy and that the leaden seals were intact.

"Don't let us disturb you, Sir Gwiliam," Lord Darcy said. "May we look around?"

"Certainly, your lordship. A pleasure." He went back to work on opening the brandy case with a pry bar.

Lord Darcy ran a practiced eye over the racks, noting labels and seals. He had not really expected that anyone would attempt to put drugs or poison into bottles; My Lady Elaine was not the only one who drank, and wholesale poisoning would be too unselective.

The wine cellar was not large, but it was well stocked

with excellent vintages. There were a couple of empty shelves in one corner, but the rest of the shelves were filled with bottles of all shapes and sizes. Over them lay patinas of dust of various thicknesses. Sir Gwiliam was careful not to bruise his wines.

"His lordship's choices, or yours, Sir Gwiliam?" Lord Darcy asked, indicating the rows of bottles.

"I am proud to say that My Lord Marquis has always entrusted the selection of wines and spirits to me, your lordship."

"I compliment both of you," Lord Darcy said. "You for your excellent taste, and his lordship for recognizing that ability in you." He paused. "However, there is more pressing business."

"How may I help you, my lord?" Having finished opening the case, he dusted off his hands and looked with a mixture of pride and sadness at the Saint Coeurlandt Michele '46. Distilled in 1846 and aged in the wood for thirty years before it was bottled, it was considered possibly the finest brandy ever made.

Quietly, Lord Darcy explained that there had been several places where Captain Sir Androu had been unable to search. "There is the possibility, you see, that he might have had a heart attack—or some sort of attack—and collapsed to the floor."

Sir Gwiliam's eyes opened wide. "And he might be there yet? God in Heaven! Come, your lordship! This way! I have been in the icehouse, and so has the chef, but no one has opened the strongroom!"

He took the lead, running, with Lord Darcy right behind him and Sir Androu in the rear. It was not far, but the cellar corridors twisted oddly and branched frequently.

The strongroom was more modern than the wine cellar; the door was of heavy steel, swung on gimbaled hinges. The walls were of stone and concrete, many feet thick.

"It's a good thing the captain is here, your lordship," the seneschal said breathlessly as the three men stopped in front of the great vault door. "It takes two keys to open it. I have one, the captain has the other. My Lord Marquis, of course, has both. Captain?"

"Yes, yes, Gwiliam; I have mine here."

There were four keyholes on each side of the wide door. Lord Darcy recognized the type of construction. Only one of the four keyholes on each side worked. A key put into the wrong hole would ring alarms. The captain would know which hole to put his own key in, and so would Sir Gwiliam—but neither knew the other's proper keyhole. The shields around the locks prevented either man from seeing which keyhole the other used. Lord Darcy could not tell, even though he watched. The shields covered the hands too well.

"Ready, captain?" Sir Gwiliam asked.

"Ready."

"Turn."

Both men turned their keys at once. The six-foot-wide door clicked inside itself and swung open when Sir Gwiliam turned a handle on his side of the door.

There was a great deal worthy of notice inside—gold and silver utensils; the jeweled coronets of the Marquis and Marquise; the great Robes of State, embroidered with gold and glittering with gems—in short, all the paraphernalia for great occasions of state. In theory, all this belonged to the Marquis; actually, it was no more his than the Imperial Crown jewels belonged to King John IV. Like the castle, it was a part of the office; it could be neither pawned nor sold.

But nowhere in the vault was there any body, dead or alive, nor any sign that there had ever been one.

"Well!" said Sir Gwiliam with a sharp exhalation. "I'm certainly glad of that! You had me worried, your lordship." There was a touch of reproach in his voice.

"I am as happy to find nothing as you are. Now let's check the icehouse."

The icehouse was in another part of the cellars and was unlocked. One of the cooks was selecting a roast. Sir Gwiliam explained that he unlocked the icehouse each morning and left the care of it with the Chief of the Kitchen, locking it again each night. A careful search of the insulated, ice-chilled room assured Lord Darcy that there was no one there who shouldn't be.

"Now we'll take a look in the tunnel," Lord Darcy said. "Have you the key, Sir Gwiliam?"

"Why . . . why, yes. But it hasn't been opened for years! Decades! Never since I've been here, at any rate."

"I have a key, myself, y' lordship," said the captain. "I just never thought of looking. Why would he go there?"

"Why, indeed? But we must look, nevertheless."

A bell rang insistently in the distance, echoing through the cellars.

"Dear me!" said Sir Gwiliam. "My lady's brandy! I quite forgot about it! Sir Androu has a key to the tunnel, my lord; would you excuse me?"

"Certainly, Sir Gwiliam. Thank you for your help."

"A pleasure, my lord." He hurried off to answer the bell.

"Did you actually expect to find My Lord Marquis in any of those places, your lordship?" asked Sir Androu. "Even if my lord had gone into one of them, would he have locked the door behind him?"

"I did not expect to find him in the wine cellar or the icehouse," Lord Darcy said, "but the strongroom presented a strong possibility. I merely wanted to see if there were any indications that he had been there. I must confess that I found none."

"To the tunnel, then," said the captain.

The entrance was concealed behind a shabby, unused cabinet. But the cabinet swung away from the steel door behind it with oiled smoothness. And when the captain took out a dull, patinaed key and opened the door, the lock turned smoothly and effortlessly.

The captain looked at his key, now brightened by abrasion where it had forced the wards, as though it were imbued with magic. "Well, I'll be cursed!" he said softly.

The door swung silently open to reveal a tunnel six feet wide and eight high. Its depths receded into utter blackness.

"A moment, m' lord," said the captain. "I'll get a lamp." He walked back down the corridor and took an oil lamp from a wall bracket.

The two of them walked down the tunnel together. On either side, the niter-stained walls gleamed whitely. The captain pointed down at the floor. "Somebody's been using this lately," he said softly.

"I had already noticed the disturbed dust and crushed crystals of niter," Lord Darcy said. "I agree with you."

"Who's been using the tunnel, then, y' lordship?"

"I am confident that my lord the Marquis of Cherbourg was one of them. His . . . er . . . confederates were here, too."

"But why? And how? No one could have got out without my guard seeing them."

"I am afraid you are right, my good captain." He smiled.
"But that doesn't mean that the guard would have reported
to you if his liege lord told him not to . . . eh?"

Sir Androu stopped suddenly and looked at Lord Darcy.
"Great God in Heaven! And I thought—!" He brought himself
up short.

"You thought *what*? Quickly, man!"

"Y' lordship, a new man enlisted in the Guard two months
ago. Came in on m' lord's recommendation. Then m' lord
reported that he misbehaved and had me put him on the
sewer detail at night. The man's been on that detail ever
since."

"Of course!" Lord Darcy said with a smile of triumph.
"He would put one of his own men on. Come, captain; I
must speak to this man."

"I . . . I'm afraid that's impossible, y' lordship. He's down
as a deserter. Disappeared from post last night. Hasn't been
seen since."

Lord Darcy said nothing. He took the lantern from the
captain and knelt down to peer closely at the footprints on
the tunnel floor.

"I should have looked more closely," he muttered, as if
to himself. "I've taken too much for granted. Ha! Two men—
carrying something heavy. And followed by a third." He stood
up. "This puts an entirely different complexion on the matter.
We must act at once. Come!" He turned and strode back
toward the castle cellar.

"But— What of the rest of the tunnel?"

"There is no need to search it," Lord Darcy said firmly.
"I can assure you that there is no one in it but ourselves.
Come along."

In the shadows of a dingy dockside warehouse a block
from the pier where the Danzig-bound vessel, *Esprit de Mer*,
was tied up, Lord Darcy stood, muffled in a long cloak.
Beside him, equally muffled in a black naval cloak, his blond
hair covered by a pulled-up cowl, stood Lord Seiger, his quite
handsome face expressionless in the dimness.

"There she is," Lord Darcy said softly. "She's the only
vessel bound for a North Sea port from Cherbourg. The

Rouen office confirms that she was sold last October to a Captain Olsen. He claims to be a Northman, but I will be willing to wager against odds that he's Polish. If not, then he is certainly in the pay of the King of Poland. The ship is still sailing under Imperial registry and flying the Imperial flag. She carries no armament, of course, but she's a fast little craft for a merchant vessel."

"And you think we will find the evidence we need aboard her?" Lord Seiger asked.

"I am almost certain of it. It will be either here or at the warehouse, and the man would be a fool to leave the stuff there now—especially when it can be shipped out aboard the *Esprit de Mer.*"

It had taken time to convince Lord Seiger that it was necessary to make this raid. But once Lord Darcy had convinced him of how much was already known and verified everything by a teleson call to Rouen, Lord Seiger was both willing and eager. There was a suppressed excitement in the man that showed only slightly in the pale blue eyes, leaving the rest of his face as placid as ever.

Other orders had had to be given. Captain Sir Androu Duglasse had sealed Castle Cherbourg; no one—no one— was to be allowed out for any reason whatever. The guard had been doubled during the emergency. Not even My Lord Bishop, My Lord Abbot, or My Lady Marquise could leave the castle. Those orders came, not from Lord Darcy, but from His Royal Highness the Duke of Normandy himself.

Lord Darcy looked at his wrist watch. "It's time, my lord," he said to Lord Seiger. "Let's move in."

"Very well, my lord," Lord Seiger agreed.

The two of them walked openly toward the pier.

At the gate that led to the pier itself, two burly-looking seamen stood lounging against the closed gate. When they saw the two cloaked men approaching, they became more alert, stepping away from the gate, toward the oncoming figures. Their hands went to the hilts of the scabbarded cutlasses at their belts.

Lord Seiger and Lord Darcy walked along the pier until they were within fifteen feet of the advancing guards, then stopped.

"What business have ye here?" asked one of the seamen.

It was Lord Darcy who spoke. His voice was low and cold. "Don't address me in that manner if you want to keep your tongue," he said in excellent Polish. "I wish to speak to your captain."

The first seaman looked blank at being addressed in a language he did not understand, but the second blanched visibly. "Let me handle this," he whispered in Anglo-French to the other. Then, in Polish:

"Your pardon, lord. My messmate here don't understand Polish. What was it you wanted, lord?"

Lord Darcy sighed in annoyance. "I thought I made myself perfectly clear. We desire to see Captain Olsen."

"Well, now, lord, he's given orders that he don't want to see no one. Strict orders, lord."

Neither of the two sailors noticed that, having moved away from the gate, they had left their rear unguarded. From the skiff that had managed to slip in under the pier under cover of darkness, four of the Marquis' Own silently lifted themselves to the deck of the pier. Neither Lord Darcy nor Lord Seiger looked at them.

"Strict orders?" Lord Darcy's voice was heavy with scorn. "I dare say your orders do not apply to Crown Prince Sigismund himself, do they?"

On cue, Lord Seiger swept the hood back from his handsome blond head.

It was extremely unlikely that either of the two sailors had ever seen Sigismund, Crown Prince of Poland—nor, if they had, that they would have recognized him when he was not dressed for a state occasion. But certainly they had heard that Prince Sigismund was blond and handsome, and that was all Lord Darcy needed. In actuality, Lord Seiger bore no other resemblance, being a good head taller than the Polish prince.

While they stood momentarily dumbfounded by this shattering revelation, arms silently encircled them, and they ceased to wonder about Crown Princes of any kind for several hours. They were rolled quietly into the shadows behind a pile of heavy bags of ballast.

"Everyone else all set?" Lord Darcy whispered to one of the Guardsmen.

"Yes, my lord."

"All right. Hold this gate. Lord Seiger, let's go on."

"I'm right with you, my lord," said Lord Seiger.

Some little distance away, at the rear door of a warehouse just off the waterfront, a heavily armed company of the Men-at-Arms of Cherbourg listened to the instructions of Chief Master-at-Arms Henri Vert.

"All right. Take your places. Seal every door. Arrest and detain anyone who tries to leave. Move out." With a rather self-important feeling, he touched the Duke's Warrant, signed by Lord Darcy as Agent for His Highness, that lay folded in his jacket pocket.

The Men-at-Arms faded into the dimness, moving silently to their assigned posts. With Chief Henri remained six Sergeants-at-Arms and Master Sean O Lochlainn, Sorcerer.

"All right, Sean," said Chief Henri, "go ahead."

"Give us a little light from your dark lantern, Henri," said Master Sean, kneeling to peer at the lock of the door. He set his black suitcase on the stone pavement and quietly set his corthainn-wood magician's staff against the wall beside the door. The Sergeants-at-Arms watched the tubby little sorcerer with respect.

"Ho*ho*," Master Sean said, peering at the lock. "A simple lock. But there's a heavy bar across it on the inside. Take a little work, but not much time." He opened his suitcase to take out two small phials of powder and a thin laurel-wood wand.

The Armsmen watched in silence as the sorcerer muttered his spells and blew tiny puffs of powder into the lock. Then Master Sean pointed his wand at the lock and twirled it counterclockwise slowly. There was a faint sliding noise and a *snick!* of metal as the lock unlocked itself.

Then he drew the wand across the door a foot above the lock. This time, something heavy slid quietly on the other side of the door.

With an almost inaudible sigh, the door swung open an inch or so.

Master Sean stepped aside and allowed the sergeants and their chief to enter the room. Meanwhile, he took a small device from his pocket and checked it again. It was a cylinder of glass two inches in diameter and half an inch high, half full of liquid. On the surface of the liquid floated a tiny sliver of oak that would have been difficult to see if the top of the glass box had not been a powerful magnifying

lens. The whole thing looked a little like a pocket compass—
which, in a sense, it was.

The tiny sliver of oak had been recovered from the
scalp of the slain man in the morgue, and now, thanks
to Master Sean's thaumaturgical art, the little sliver
pointed unerringly toward the piece of wood whence it
had come.

Master Sean nodded in satisfaction. As Lord Darcy had
surmised, the weapon was still in the warehouse. He glanced
up at the lights in the windows of the top floor of the
warehouse. Not only the weapon, but some of the plotters
were still here.

He smiled grimly and followed the Armsmen in, his
corthainn-wood staff grasped firmly in one hand and his
suitcase in the other.

Lord Darcy stood with Lord Seiger on one of the lower
decks of the *Esprit de Mer* and looked around. "So far, so
good," he said in a low voice. "Piracy has its advantages,
my lord."

"Indeed it does, my lord," Lord Seiger replied in the same
tone.

Down a nearby ladder, his feet clad in soft-soled boots,
came Captain Sir Androu, commander of the Marquis' Own.
"So far, so good, m' lords," he whispered, not realizing that
he was repeating Lord Darcy's sentiments. "We have the
crew. All sleeping like children."

"All the crew?" Lord Darcy asked.

"Well, m' lord, all we could find so far. Some of 'em are
still on shore leave. Not due back 'til dawn. Otherwise, I
fancy this ship would have pulled out long before this. No
way to get word to the men, though, eh?"

"I have been hoping so," Lord Darcy agreed. "But the fact
remains that we really don't know how many are left aboard.
How about the bridge?"

"The Second Officer was on duty, m' lord. We have him."

"Captain's cabin?"

"Empty, m' lord."

"First Officer's?"

"Also empty, m' lord. Might be both ashore."

"Possibly." There was a distinct possibility, Lord Darcy
knew, that both the captain and the first officer were still

at the warehouse—in which case, they would be picked up by Chief Henri and his men.

"Very well. Let's keep moving down. We still haven't found what we're looking for." *And there will be one Hell of an international incident if we don't find it*, Lord Darcy told himself. *His Slavonic Majesty's Government will demand all sorts of indemnities, and Lady Darcy's little boy will find himself fighting the aborigines in the jungles of New France.*

But he wasn't really terribly worried; his intuition backed up his logic in telling him that he was right.

Nevertheless, he mentally breathed a deep sigh of relief when he and Lord Seiger found what they were looking for some five or six minutes later.

There were four iron-barred cells on the deck just above the lowest cargo hold. They faced each other, two and two, across a narrow passageway. Two bosuns blocked the passageway.

Lord Darcy looked down the tweendecks hatch and saw them. He had gone down the ladders silently, peeking carefully below before attempting to descend, and his caution had paid off. Neither of the bosuns saw him. They were leaning casually against the opposite bulkheads of the passageway, talking in very low voices.

There was no way to come upon them by stealth, but neither had a weapon in hand, and there was nothing to retreat behind for either of them.

Should he, Lord Darcy wondered, wait for reinforcements? Sir Androu already had his hands full for the moment, and Lord Seiger would not, of course, be of any use. The man was utterly incapable of physical violence.

He lifted himself from the prone position from which he had been peeking over the hatch edge to look below, and whispered to Lord Seiger. "They have cutlasses. Can you hold your own against one of them if trouble comes?"

For answer, Lord Seiger smoothly and silently drew his rapier. "Against both of them if necessary, my lord," he whispered back.

"I don't think it will be necessary, but there's no need taking chances at this stage of the game." He paused. Then he drew a five-shot .42 caliber handgun from his belt holster. "I'll cover them with this."

Lord Seiger nodded and said nothing.

"Stay here," he whispered to Lord Seiger. "Don't come down the stairs . . . sorry, the *ladder* . . . until I call."

"Very well, my lord."

Lord Darcy walked silently up the ladder that led to the deck above. Then he came down again, letting his footfalls be heard.

He even whistled softly but audibly as he did so—an old Polish air he happened to know.

Then, without breaking his stride, he went on down the second ladder. He held his handgun in his right hand, concealed beneath his cloak.

His tactics paid off beautifully. The bosuns heard him coming and assumed that he must be someone who was authorized to be aboard the ship. They stopped their conversation and assumed an attitude of attention. They put their hands on the hilts of their cutlasses, but only as a matter of form. They saw the boots, then the legs, then the lower torso of the man coming down the ladder. And still they suspected nothing. An enemy would have tried to take them by surprise, wouldn't he?

Yes.

And he did.

Halfway down the steps, Lord Darcy dropped to a crouch and his pistol was suddenly staring both of them in the face.

"If either of you moves," said Lord Darcy calmly, "I will shoot him through the brain. Get your hands off those blade hilts and don't move otherwise. Fine. Now turn around. *V-e-r-r-ry slowly.*"

The men obeyed wordlessly. Lord Darcy's powerful hand came down twice in a deft neck-chop, and both men dropped to the floor unconscious.

"Come on down, my lord," said Lord Darcy. "There will be no need for swordplay."

Lord Seiger descended the ladder in silence, his sword sheathed.

There were two cell doors on either side of the passageway; the cells themselves had been built to discipline crewmen or to imprison sailors or passengers who were accused of crime on the high seas while the ship was in passage. The first cell on the right had a dim light glowing within it. The yellowish light gleamed through the small barred window in the door.

Both Lord Darcy and Lord Seiger walked over to the door and looked inside.

"That's what I was looking for," Lord Darcy breathed.

Within, strapped to a bunk, was a still, white-faced figure. The face was exactly similar to that of the corpse Lord Darcy had seen in the morgue.

"Are you sure it's the Marquis of Cherbourg?" Lord Seiger asked.

"I refuse to admit that there are *three* men who look that much alike," Lord Darcy whispered dryly. "Two are quite enough. Since Master Sean established that the body in the morgue was definitely *not* related to my lord of Guernsey and Sark, *this* must be the Marquis. Now, the problem will be getting the cell door open."

"*I vill open idt for you.*"

At the sound of the voice behind them, both Lord Darcy and Lord Seiger froze.

"To qvote you, Lord Darcy, 'If either of you moves, I vill shoodt him through the brain," said the voice. "Drop de gun, Lord Darcy." As Lord Darcy let his pistol drop from his hand, his mind raced.

The shock of having been trapped, such as it had been, had passed even before the voice behind him had ceased. Shock of that kind could not hold him frozen long. Nor was his the kind of mind that grew angry with itself for making a mistake. There was no time for that.

He had been trapped. Someone had been hidden in the cell across the passageway, waiting for him. A neat trap. Very well; the problem was, how to get out of that trap.

"Bot' of you step to de left," said the voice. "Move avay from de cell port. Dat's it. Fine. Open de door, Ladislas."

There were two men, both holding guns. The shorter, darker of the two stepped forward and opened the door to the cell next to that in which the still figure of the Marquis of Cherbourg lay.

"Bot' of you step inside," said the taller of the two men who had trapped the Imperial agents.

There was nothing Lord Seiger and Lord Darcy could do but obey.

"Keep you de hands high in de air. Dat's fine. Now listen

to me, and listen carefully. You t'ink you have taken dis ship. In a vay, you have. But not finally. I have you. I have de Marquis. You vill order your men off. Odervise, I vill kill all of you—vun adt a time. Understand? If I hang, I do not die alone."

Lord Darcy understood. "You want your crew back, eh, Captain Olsen? And how will you get by the Royal Navy?"

"De same vay I vill get out of Cherbourg harbor, Lord Darcy," the captain said complacently. "I vill promise release. You vill be able to go back home from Danzig. Vot goodt is any of you to us now?"

None, except as hostages, Lord Darcy thought. What had happened was quite clear. Somehow, someone had managed to signal to Captain Olsen that his ship was being taken. A signal from the bridge, perhaps. It didn't matter. Captain Olsen had not been expecting invaders, but when they had come, he had devised a neat trap. He had known where the invaders would be heading.

Up to that point, Lord Darcy knew, the Polish agents had planned to take the unconscious Marquis to Danzig. There, he would be operated on by a sorcerer and sent back to Cherbourg—apparently in good condition, but actually under the control of Polish agents. His absence would be explained by his "spells," which would no longer be in evidence. But now that Captain Olsen knew that the plot had been discovered, he had no further use for the Marquis. Nor had he any use for either Lord Darcy or Lord Seiger. Except that he could use them as hostages to get his ship to Danzig.

"What do you want, Captain Olsen?" Lord Darcy asked quietly.

"Very simply, dis: You vill order de soldiers to come below. Ve vill lock dem up. Ven my men vake up, and de rest of de crew come aboard, ve vill sail at dawn. Ven ve are ready to sail, all may go ashore except you and Lord Seiger and de Marquis. Your men vill tell de officials in Cherbourg vhat has happened and vill tell dem dat ve vill sail to Danzig unmolested. Dere, you vill be set free and sent back to Imperial territory I give you my vord."

Oddly, Lord Darcy realized that the man meant it. Lord Darcy knew that the man's word was good. But was he responsible for the reactions of the Polish officials at Danzig?

Was he responsible for the reactions of Casimir IX? No. Certainly not.

But, trapped as they were—

And then a hoarse voice came from across the passage-way, from the fourth cell.

"Seiger? Seiger?"

Lord Seiger's eyes widened. "Yes?"

Captain Olsen and First Officer Ladislas remained unmoved. The captain smiled sardonically. "Ah, yes. I forgot to mention your so-brave Sir James le Lein. He vill make an excellent hostage, too."

The hoarse voice said: "They are traitors to the King, Seiger. Do you hear me?"

"I hear you, Sir James," said Lord Seiger.

"Destroy them," said the hoarse voice.

Captain Olsen laughed. "Shut up, le Lein. You—"

But he never had time to finish.

Lord Darcy watched with unbelieving eyes as Lord Seiger's right hand darted out with blurring speed and slapped aside the captain's gun. At the same time, his left hand drew his rapier and slashed out toward the first officer.

The first officer had been covering Lord Darcy. When he saw Lord Seiger move, he swung his gun toward Lord Seiger and fired. The slug tore into the Yorkshire nobleman's side as Captain Olsen spun away and tried to bring his own weapon to bear.

By that time, Lord Darcy himself was in action. His powerful legs catapulted him toward First Officer Ladislas just as the point of Lord Seiger's rapier slashed across Ladislas' chest, making a deep cut over the ribs. Then Ladislas was slammed out into the passageway by Lord Darcy's assault.

After that, Lord Darcy had too much to do to pay any attention to what went on between Lord Seiger and Captain Olsen. Apparently oblivious to the blood gushing from the gash on his chest, Ladislas fought with steel muscles. Darcy knew his own strength, but he also knew that this opponent was of nearly equal strength. Darcy held the man's right wrist in a vise grip to keep him from bringing the pistol around. Then he smashed his head into Ladislas' jaw. The gun dropped and spun away as both men fell to the deck.

Lord Darcy brought his right fist up in a smashing blow to the first officer's throat; gagging, the first officer collapsed.

Lord Darcy pushed himself to his knees and grabbed the unconscious man by the collar, pulling him half upright.

At that second, a tongue of steel flashed by Lord Darcy's shoulder, plunged itself into Ladislas' throat, and tore sideways. The first officer died as his blood spurted fountain-like over Lord Darcy's arm.

After a moment, Lord Darcy realized that the fight was over. He turned his head.

Lord Seiger stood nearby, his sword red. Captain Olsen lay on the deck, his life's blood flowing from three wounds— two in the chest, and the third, like his first officer's, a slash across the throat.

"I had him," Lord Darcy said unevenly. "There was no need to cut his throat."

For the first time, he saw a slight smile on Lord Seiger's face.

"I had my orders, my lord," said Seiger, as his side dripped crimson.

With twelve sonorous, resounding strokes, the great Bell of the Benedictine Church of Saint Denys, in the court-yard of Castle Cherbourg, sounded the hour of midnight. Lord Darcy, freshly bathed and shaved and clad in his evening wear, stood before the fireplace in the reception room above the Great Hall and waited patiently for the bell to finish its tally. Then he turned and smiled at the young man standing beside him. "As you were saying, Your Highness?"

Richard, Duke of Normandy, smiled back. "Even royalty can't drown out a church bell, eh, my lord?" Then his face became serious again. "I was saying that we have made a clean sweep. Dunkerque, Calais, Boulogne . . . all the way down to Hendaye. By now, the English Armsmen will be picking them up in London, Liverpool, and so on. By dawn, Ireland will be clear. You've done a magnificent job, my lord, and you may rest assured that my brother the King will hear of it."

"Thank you, Your Highness, but I really—"

Lord Darcy was interrupted by the opening of the door. Lord Seiger came in, then stopped as he saw Duke Richard.

The Duke reacted instantly. "Don't bother to bow, my lord. I have been told of your wound."

Lord Seiger nevertheless managed a slight bow. "Your Highness is most gracious. But the wound is a slight one, and Father Patrique has laid his hands on it. The pain is negligible, Highness."

"I am happy to hear so." The Duke looked at Lord Darcy. "By the way . . . I am curious to know what made you suspect that Lord Seiger was a King's Agent. I didn't know, myself, until the King, my brother, sent me the information I requested."

"I must confess that I was not certain until Your Highness verified my suspicions on the teleson. But it seemed odd to me that de Cherbourg would have wanted a man of Lord Seiger's . . . ah . . . peculiar talents merely as a librarian. Then, too, Lady Elaine's attitude . . . er, your pardon, my lord—"

"Perfectly all right, my lord," said Lord Seiger expressionlessly. "I am aware that many women find my presence distasteful—although I confess I do not know why."

"Who can account for the behavior of women?" Lord Darcy said. "Your manners and behavior are impeccable. Nonetheless, My Lady Marquise found, as you say, your presence distasteful. She must have made this fact known to her husband the Marquis, eh?"

"I believe she did, my lord," said Lord Seiger.

"Very well," said Lord Darcy. "Would My Lord Marquis, who is notoriously in love with his wife, have kept a *librarian* who frightened her? No. Therefore, either Lord Seiger's purpose here was much more important—or he was blackmailing the Marquis. I chose to believe the former." He did not add that Father Patrique's information showed that it was impossible for Lord Seiger to blackmail anyone.

"My trouble lay in not knowing who was working for whom. We knew only that Sir James was masquerading as a common working man, and that he was working with My Lord Marquis. But until Your Highness got in touch with His Majesty, we knew nothing more. I was working blind until I realized that Lord Seiger—"

He stopped as he heard the door open. From outside came Master Sean's voice: "After you, my lady, my lord, Sir Gwiliam."

The Marquise de Cherbourg swept into the room, her fair face an expressionless mask. Behind her came My Lord Bishop and Sir Gwiliam, followed by Master Sean O Lochlainn.

Lady Elaine walked straight to Duke Richard. She made a small curtsy. "Your presence is an honor, Your Highness." She was quite sober.

"The honor is mine, my lady," replied the Duke.

"I have seen my lord husband. He is alive, as I knew he was. But his mind is gone. Father Patrique says he will never recover. I must know what has happened, Your Highness."

"You will have to ask Lord Darcy that, my lady," the Duke said gently. "I should like to hear the complete story myself."

My lady turned her steady gaze on the lean Englishman. "Begin at the beginning and tell me everything, my lord. I must know."

The door opened again, and Sir Androu Duglasse came in. "Good morning, Y' Highness," he said with a low bow. "Good morning, m' lady, y' lordships, Sir Gwiliam, Master Sean." His eyes went back to lady Elaine. "I've heard the news from Father Patrique, m' lady. I'm a soldier, m' lady, not a man who can speak well. I cannot tell you of the sorrow I feel."

"I thank you, Sir Captain," said my lady, "I think you have expressed it very well." Her eyes went back to Lord Darcy. "If you please, my lord . . ."

"As you command, my lady," said Lord Darcy. "Er . . . captain, I don't think that what I have to say need be known by any others than those of us here. Would you watch the door? Explain to anyone else that this is a private conference. Thank you. Then I can begin." He leaned negligently against the fireplace, where he could see everyone in the room.

"To begin with, we had a hellish plot afoot—not against just one person, but against the Empire. The 'Atlantic Curse.' Ships sailing from Imperial ports to the New World were never heard from again. Shipping was dropping off badly, not only from ship losses, but because fear kept seamen off trans-Atlantic ships. They feared magic, although, as I shall show, pure magic had nothing to do with it.

"My lord the Marquis was working with Sir James le Lein,

one of a large group of King's Agents with direct commissions to discover the cause of the 'Atlantic Curse'. His Majesty had correctly deduced that the whole thing was a Polish plot to disrupt Imperial economy.

"The plot was devilish in its simplicity. A drug, made by steeping a kind of mushroom in brandy, was being used to destroy the minds of the crews of trans-Atlantic ships. Taken in small dosages, over a period of time, the drug causes violent insanity. A ship with an insane crew cannot last long in the Atlantic.

"Sir James, working with My Lord Marquis and other agents, tried to get a lead on what was going on. My Lord Marquis, not wanting anyone in the castle to know of his activities, used the old secret tunnel that leads to the city sewers in order to meet Sir James.

"Sir James obtained a sample of the drug after he had identified the ringleader of the Polish agents. He reported to My Lord Marquis. Then, on the evening of Wednesday, the eighth of January, Sir James set out to obtain more evidence. He went to the warehouse where the ringleader had his headquarters."

Lord Darcy paused and smiled slightly. "By the by, I must say that the details of what happened in the warehouse were supplied to me by Sir James. My own deductions only gave me a part of the story.

"At any rate, Sir James obtained entry to the second floor of the warehouse. He heard voices. Silently, he went to the door of the room from which the voices came and looked in through the . . . er . . . the keyhole. It was dark in the corridor, but well-lit in the room.

"What he saw was a shock to him. Two men—a sorcerer and the ringleader himself—were there. The sorcerer was standing by a bed, weaving a spell over a third man, who lay naked on the bed. One look at the man in the bed convinced Sir James that the man was none other than the Marquis of Cherbourg himself!"

Lady Elaine touched her fingertips to her lips. "Had he been poisoned by the drug, my lord?" she asked. "Was that what had been affecting his mind?"

"The man was not your husband, my lady," Lord Darcy said gently. "He was a double, a simple-minded man in the pay of these men.

"Sir James, of course, had no way of knowing that. When he saw the Marquis in danger, he acted. Weapon in hand, he burst open the door and demanded the release of the man whom he took to be the Marquis. He told the man to get up. Seeing he was hypnotized, Sir James put his own cloak about the man's shoulders and the two of them began to back out of the room, his weapon covering the sorcerer and the ringleader.

"But there was another man in the warehouse. Sir James never saw him. This person struck him from behind as he backed out the door.

"Sir James was dazed. He dropped his weapon. The sorcerer and the ringleader jumped him. Sir James fought, but he was eventually rendered unconscious.

"In the meantime, the man whom Sir James attempted to rescue became frightened and fled. In the darkness, he tumbled down a flight of oaken stairs and fractured his skull on one of the lower steps. Hurt, dazed, and dying, he fled from the warehouse toward the only other place in Cherbourg he could call home—a bistro called the Blue Dolphin, a few blocks away. He very nearly made it. He died a block from it, in the sight of two Armsmen."

"Did they intend to use the double for some sort of impersonation of my brother?" asked the Bishop.

"In a way, my lord. I'll get to that in a moment.

"When I came here," Lord Darcy continued, "I of course knew nothing of all this. I knew only that my lord of Cherbourg was missing and that he had been working with His Majesty's Agents. Then a body was tentatively identified as his. If it *were* the Marquis, who had killed him? If it were not, what was the connection? I went to see Sir James and found that he had been missing since the same night. Again, what was the connection?

"The next clue was the identification of the drug. How could such a drug be introduced aboard ships so that almost every man would take a little each day? The taste and aroma of the brandy would be apparent in the food or water. Obviously, then, the wine rations were drugged. And only the vintner who supplied the wine could have regularly drugged the wine of ship after ship.

"A check of the Shipping Registry showed that new vintners had bought out old wineries in shipping ports throughout the Empire in the past five years. All of them, subsidized by the Poles, could underbid their competitors. They made good wine and sold it cheaper than others could sell it. They got contracts. They didn't try to poison every ship; only a few of those on the Atlantic run—just enough to start a scare while keeping suspicion from themselves.

"There was still the problem of what had happened to My Lord Marquis. He had not left the castle that night. And yet he had disappeared. But how? And why?

"There were four places that the captain had not searched. I dismissed the icehouse when I discovered that people went in and out of it all day. He could not have gone to the strongroom because the door is too wide for one man to use both keys simultaneously—which must be done to open it. Sir Gwiliam had been in and out of the wine cellar. And there were indications that the tunnel had also had visitors."

"Why should he have been in any of those places, my lord?" Sir Gwiliam asked. "Mightn't he have simply left through the tunnel?"

"Hardly likely. The tunnel guard was a King's Agent. If the Marquis had gone out that night and never returned, he would have reported the fact—not to Captain Sir Androu, but to Lord Seiger. He did not so report. Ergo, the Marquis did not leave the castle that night."

"Then what happened to him?" Sir Gwiliam asked.

"That brings us back to the double, Paul Sarto," said Lord Darcy. "Would you explain, Master Sean?"

"Well, my lady, gentle sirs," the little sorcerer began, "My Lord Darcy deduced the use of magic here. This Polish sorcerer—a piddling poor one, he is, too; when I caught him in the warehouse, he tried to cast a few spells at me and they were nothing. He ended up docile as a lamb when I gave him a dose of good Irish sorcery."

"Proceed, Master Sean," Lord Darcy said dryly.

"Beggin' your pardon, my lord. Anyway, this Polish sorcerer saw that this Paul chap was a dead ringer for My Lord Marquis and decided to use him to control My Lord Marquis—Law of Similarity, d' ye see. You know the business of sticking pins in wax dolls? Crude method of psychic induction, but effective if the similarity is great enough. And what could be more similar to a man than his double?"

"You mean they used this poor unfortunate man as a wax doll?" asked the Marquise in a hushed voice.

"That's about it, your ladyship. In order for the spells to work, though, the double would have to have very low mind power. Well, he did. So they hired him away from his old job and went to work on him. They made him bathe and wear fine clothes, and slowly took control of his mind. They told him that he was the Marquis. With that sort of similarity achieved, they hoped to control the Marquis himself just as they controlled his simulacrum."

My Lady Elaine looked horrified. "*That* caused his terrible attacks?"

"Exactly, your ladyship. When My Lord Marquis was tired or distracted, they were able to take over for a little while. A vile business no proper sorcerer would stoop to, but workable."

"But what did they do to my husband?" asked the Lady of Cherbourg.

"Well, now your ladyship," said Master Sean, "what do you suppose would happen to his lordship when his simulacrum got his skull crushed so bad that it killed the simulacrum? The shock to his lordship's mind was so great that it nearly killed him on the spot—*would* have killed him, too, if the similarity had been better established. He fell into a coma, my lady."

Lord Darcy took up the story again. "The Marquis dropped where he was. He remained in the castle until last night, when the Polish agents came to get him. They killed the King's Agent on guard, disposed of the body, came in through the tunnel, got the Marquis, and took him to their ship. When Captain Sir Androu told me that the guard had 'deserted', I knew fully what had happened. I knew that My Lord Marquis was either in the vintner's warehouse or in a ship bound for Poland. The two raids show that I was correct."

"Do you mean," said Sir Gwiliam, "that my lord lay in that chilly tunnel all that time? How horrible!"

Lord Darcy looked at the man for long seconds. "No. Not *all* that time, Sir Gwiliam. No one—especially not the Polish agents—would have known he was there. He was taken to the tunnel after he was found the next morning—in the wine cellar."

"Ridiculous!" said Sir Gwiliam, startled. "I'd have seen him!"

"Most certainly you would have," Lord Darcy agreed. "And most certainly you *did*. It must have been quite a shock to return home after the fight in the warehouse to find the Marquis unconscious on the wine cellar floor. Once I knew you were the guilty man, I knew you had given away your employer. You told me that you had played cards with Ordwin Vayne that night; therefore I knew which vintner to raid."

White-faced, Sir Gwiliam said, "I have served my lord and lady faithfully for many years. I say you lie."

"Oh?" Lord Darcy's eyes were hard. "Someone had to tell Ordwin Vayne where the Marquis was—someone who *knew* where he was. Only the Marquis, Sir Androu, and *you* had keys to the tunnel. I saw the captain's key; it was dull and filmed when I used it. The wards of the old lock left little bright scratches on it. He hadn't used it for a long time. Only *you* had a key that would let Ordwin Vayne and his men into that tunnel."

"Pah! Your reasoning is illogical! If My Lord Marquis were unconscious, someone could have taken the key off him!"

"Not if he was in the tunnel. Why would anyone go there? The tunnel door was locked, so, even, if he *were* there, a key would have to have been used to find him. But if he had fallen in the tunnel, he would still have been there when I looked. There was no reason for you or anyone else to unlock that tunnel—*until* you were looking for a place to conceal My Lord Marquis' unconscious body!"

"Why would he have gone to the wine cellar?" Sir Gwiliam snapped. "And why lock himself in?"

"He went down to check on some bottles you had in the wine cellar. Sir James' report led him to suspect you. Warehouses and wineries are subjected to rigorous inspection. Ordwin Vayne didn't want inspectors to find that he was steeping mushrooms in brandy. So the bottles were kept *here*—the safest place in Cherbourg. Who would suspect? The Marquis never went there. But he did suspect at last, and went down to check. He locked the door because he didn't want to be interrupted. No one but you could come in, and he would be warned if you put your key in the lock. While he was there, the simulacrumized Paul fell and struck his head on an oaken step. Paul died. The Marquis went comatose.

"When I arrived yesterday, you had to get rid of the evidence. So Vayne's men came and took the bottles of drug and the Marquis. If further proof is needed, I can tell you that we found the drug on the ship, in restoppered bottles containing cheap brandy and bits of mushroom. *But the bottles were labeled Saint Coeurlandt Michele '46!* Who else in Cherbourg but you would have access to such empty bottles?"

Sir Gwiliam stepped back. "Lies! All lies!"

"No!" snapped a voice from the door. "Truth! All truth!"

Lord Darcy had seen Captain Sir Androu silently open the door and let in three more men, but no one else had. Now the others turned at the sound of the voice.

Sitting in a wheelchair, looking pale but still strong, was Hugh, Marquis of Cherbourg. Behind him was Sir James le Lein. To one side stood Father Patrique.

"What Lord Darcy said is true in every particular," said my lord the Marquis in an icy voice.

Sir Gwiliam gasped and jerked his head around to look at my lady the Marquise. "You said his mind was gone!"

"A small lie—to trap a traitor." Her voice was icy.

"Sir Gwiliam de Bracy," said Sir James from behind the Marquis, "in the King's Name, I charge you with treason!"

Two things happened almost at once. Sir Gwiliam's hand started for his pocket. But by then, Lord Seiger's sword, with its curious offset hilt, was halfway from its sheath. By the time Sir Gwiliam had his pistol out, the sword had slashed through his jugular vein. Sir Gwiliam had just time to turn and fire once before he fell to the floor.

Lord Seiger stood there, looking down at Sir Gwiliam, an odd smile on his face.

For a second, no one spoke or moved. Then Father Patrique rushed over to the fallen seneschal. He was too late by far. With all his Healing power, there was nothing he could do now.

And then the Marquise walked over to Lord Seiger and took his free hand. "My lord, others may censure you for that act. I do not. That monster helped send hundreds of innocent men to insanity and death. He almost did the same for my beloved Hugh. If anything, he died too clean a death. I do not censure you, my lord. I thank you."

"I thank you, my lady. But I only did my duty." There was an odd thickness in his voice. "I had my orders, my lady."

And then, slowly, like a deflating balloon, Lord Seiger slumped to the floor.

Lord Darcy and Father Patrique realized at the same moment that Sir Gwiliam's bullet must have hit Lord Seiger, though he had shown no sign of it till then.

Lord Seiger had had no conscience, but he could not kill or even defend himself of his own accord. Sir James had been his decision-maker. Lord Seiger had been a King's Agent who would kill without qualm on order from Sir James— and was otherwise utterly harmless. The decision was never left up to him, only to Sir James.

Sir James, still staring at the fallen Lord Seiger, said: "But . . . how could he? I didn't tell him to."

"Yes, you did," Lord Darcy said wearily. "On the ship. You told him to destroy the traitors. When you called Sir Gwiliam a traitor, he acted. He had his sword halfway out before Sir Gwiliam drew that pistol. He would have killed Sir Gwiliam in cold blood if the seneschal had never moved at all. He was like a gas lamp, Sir James. You turned him on—and forgot to shut him off."

Richard, Duke of Normandy, looked down at the fallen man. Lord Seiger's face was oddly unchanged. It had rarely had any expression in life. It had none now.

"How is he, Reverend Father?" asked the Duke.

"He is dead, Your Highness."

"May the Lord have mercy on his soul," said Duke Richard.

Eight men and a woman made the Sign of the Cross in silence.

The Muddle of the Woad

Both pain and pride were sending their counterbalancing energies through the nervous system of Walter Gotobed, Master Cabinetmaker for His Grace, the Duke of Kent, as he opened the door of his workshop. The pain, like the pride, was mental in origin; in spite of his ninety-odd years, Master Walter was still blessed with strength in his wiry body and steadiness in his careful hands. With his spectacles perched properly on his large, thin, bony nose, he could still draw an accurate plan for anything from a closet to a cigar box. Come next Trinity Sunday, the twenty-fourth of May, the Year of Our Lord 1964, Master Walter would be celebrating his fiftieth anniversary of his appointment as Master Cabinetmaker to the Duke. He was now on his second Duke, the Old Duke having died in 1927, and would serve a third before long. The Dukes of Kent were long-lived, but a man who works with fine woods, absorbing the strength and the agelessness of the great trees from which they come, lives longer still.

The workshop was full of woody smells—the spiciness of cedar, the richness of oak, the warm tang of plain pine, the fruity sweetness of apple—and the early morning sunlight coming in through the windows cast gleaming highlights on the cabinets and desks and chairs and tables that filled the shop in various stages of progress. This was Master Walter's world, the atmosphere in which he worked and lived.

Behind Master Walter came three more men: Journeyman Henry Lavender and the two apprentices, Tom Wilderspin and Harry Venable. They followed the Master in, and the four of them walked purposefully toward a magnificent

111

creation in polished walnut that reposed on a bench in one corner. Two paces from it, Master Walter stopped.

"How does it look, Henry?" Master Walter asked without turning his head.

Journeyman Henry, not yet forty, but already having about him the tone of a woodcraftsman, nodded with satisfaction and said: "Very beautiful, Master Walter, very beautiful." It was honest appreciation, not flattery, that spoke.

"I think Her Grace the Duchess will be pleased, eh?" the old man said.

"More than pleased, Master. Mm-m-m. There's a bit of dust on it, even since last night. You, Tom! Get a clean rag with a little lemon oil on it and give it another polish." As Tom the 'prentice scampered off in obedience, Henry Lavender continued: "His Grace the Duke will appreciate your work, Master; it's one of the finest things you've turned out for him."

"Aye. And that's something you must remember, Henry— and something you two lads must get through your heads. It's not fancy carving that makes the beauty of wood; it's the wood itself. Carving's all right in its place, mind you; I've nothing against carving if it's properly done. But the beauty's in the wood. Something plain like this, without fanciness, without ornament, shows that wood, as wood, is a creation of God that can't be improved upon. All you can ever hope to do is bring out the beauty that God Himself put there. Here, give me that rag, young Tom; I'll put the final polish on this myself." As he moved the oily rag, with its faint lemon scent, over the broad, flat surface, Master Walter went on: "Careful craftsmanship is what does it, lads. Careful craftsmanship. Each piece joined solidly to the next, glued tightly, screws in firmly, with no gaps or spaces— that's what makes *good* work. Matching the grain, carefully choosing your pieces, planing and sanding to a perfect surface, applying your finish, wax or varnish or shellac, to a fine smoothness—that's what makes it *fine* work. And design—ah, *design—that* makes it *art!*

"All right, now, you, Tom, take the front end. Harry, you take the other. We've a stairway to climb, but you're both strong lads and it's not too heavy. Besides, a joiner and cabinetmaker must have strong muscles to do his work and the exercise will be good for the both of you."

Obediently, the 'prentices grasped the ends they had been assigned and lifted. They had carried it before and knew to a pound how much it weighed. They heaved upwards.

And the beautifully polished walnut scarcely moved.

"Here! What's the matter?" said Master Walter. "You almost dropped it!"

"It's *heavy*, Master," said Tom. "There's somethin' in it"

"Something in it? How could there be?" Master Walter reached out, lifted the lid. And almost dropped it again. "Good God!"

Then there was a stunned silence as the four men looked at the thing that lay within.

"A dead man," said journeyman Henry after a moment.

That was obvious. The corpse was certainly a corpse. The eyelids were sunken and the skin waxy. The man was thoroughly, completely dead.

To make the horror even worse, the nude body—from crown of head to tip of toe—was a deep, almost indigo, blue.

Master Walter found his breath again. His feelings of surprise and horror had vanished beneath a wave of indignation. "But he don't belong here! He's got no right! No right at all!"

"Daresay it ain't his fault, Master Walter," Journeyman Henry ventured. "He didn't get there by himself."

"No," said Master Walter, gaining control of himself. "No, of course not. But what a *peculiar* place to find a corpse!"

In spite of his own feelings, it was all Apprentice Tom could do to suppress a snigger.

What better place to find a corpse than in a coffin?

Even the most dedicated of men enjoys a holiday now and then, and Lord Darcy, Chief Criminal Investigator for His Royal Highness, Prince Richard, Duke of Normandy, was no exception. He not only enjoyed his work, but preferred it above all others. His keen mind found satisfaction in solving the kind of problems that, by the very nature of the work, were continually being brought to his attention. But he also knew that a one-track brain became stale very shortly—and besides he enjoyed letting his mind drift for a while.

Then, too, there was the pleasure of coming home to

England. France was fine. It was an important part of the Empire, and working for His Highness was pleasurable. But England was his home, and getting back to England once a year was . . . well, a relief. In spite of the fact that England and France had been one country for eight hundred years, the differences were still enough to make an Englishman feel faintly foreign in France. And, he supposed, vice-versa.

Lord Darcy stood at one side of the ballroom and surveyed the crowd. The orchestra was pausing between numbers, and the floor was full of people talking, waiting for the next dance. He took a drink from the whisky-and-water that he had been nursing along. This sort of thing, he congratulated himself, palled within two weeks, while his real work took fifty weeks to become irritating. Still, each was a relief from the other.

Baron Dartmoor was a decent sort, an excellent chess player, and a good man with a story now and then. Lady Dartmoor had a knack of picking the right people to come to a dinner or a ball. But one couldn't stay forever at Dartmoor House, and London society wasn't everything it was assumed to be by those who didn't live there.

Lord Darcy found himself thinking that it would be good to get back to Rouen on the twenty-second of May.

"Lord Darcy, do pardon me, but something has come up."

Darcy turned at the sound of the woman's voice and smiled. "Oh?"

"Will you come with me?"

"Certainly, my lady."

He followed her, but there was a nervousness in her manner, a tautness in her behavior, that told him there was something out of the ordinary here.

At the door to the library, she paused. "My lord, there is a . . . a gentleman who wishes to speak to you. In the library."

"A gentleman? Who is he, my lady?"

"I—" Lady Dartmoor drew herself up and took a breath. "I am not at liberty to say, my lord. He will introduce himself."

"I see." Lord Darcy unobtrusively put his hands behind his back and with his right hand drew a small pistol from the holster concealed by the tails of his green dress coat.

This didn't exactly have the smell of a trap, but there was no reason to be careless.

Lady Dartmoor opened the door. "Lord Darcy, S . . . sir."

"Show him in, my lady," said a voice from within.

Lord Darcy went in, his pistol still concealed behind his back and beneath his coattails. Behind him, he heard the door close.

The man was standing with his back to the door, looking out the window at the lighted streets of London. "Lord Darcy," he said without turning, "if you are the man I have been brought to believe you are, you are dangerously close to committing the capital crime of High Treason."

But Lord Darcy, after one look at that back, had reholstered his pistol and dropped to one knee. "As Your Majesty knows, I would rather die than commit treason against Your Majesty."

The man turned, and for the first time in his life Lord Darcy found himself face to face with His Imperial Majesty, John IV, King and Emperor of England, France, Scotland, Ireland, New England, New France, Defender of the Faith, et cetera.

He looked a great deal like his younger brother, Richard of Normandy—tall, blond, and handsome, like all the Plantagenets. But he was ten years older than Duke Richard, and the difference showed. The King was only a few years younger than Lord Darcy, but the lines in his face made him look older.

"Rise, my lord," said His Majesty. He smiled. "You *did* have a gun in your hand, didn't you?"

"I did, Your Majesty," Lord Darcy said, rising smoothly. "My apologies, Sire."

"Not at all. Only what I should have expected of a man of your capabilities. Please be seated. We will not be interrupted; my lady of Dartmoor will see to that. Thank you. We have a problem, Lord Darcy."

Darcy seated himself and the King took a chair facing him. "For the time being, my lord," said the King, "we shall forget rank. Don't interrupt me until I have given you all the data I have. Then you may ask questions as you will."

"Yes, Sire."

"Very well. I have a job for you, my lord. I know you

are on holiday, and it pains me to interrupt your leisure—but this needs looking into. You are aware of the activities of the so-called Holy Society of Ancient Albion."

It was a statement, not a question. Lord Darcy and every other Officer of the King's justice knew of the Society of Albion. They were more than just a secret society; they were a pagan sect which repudiated the Christian Church. They were reputed to dabble in Black Magic, they practiced a form of nature-worship, and they claimed direct organizational descent from the pre-Roman Druids. The Society, after a period of toleration during the last century, had been outlawed. Some said that it had remained in hiding during all the centuries since the triumph of Christianity and had only revealed itself during the easy-going Nineteenth Century, others said that its claim of antiquity was false, that it had been organized during the 1820s by the eccentric, perhaps slightly mad, Sir Edward Finnely. Probably both versions were partly true.

They had been outlawed because of their outspoken advocation of human sacrifice. Rejecting the Church's teaching that the Sacrifice of the Cross obviated for all time any further sacrifice of human life, the Society insisted that in times of trouble the King himself should die for the sake of his people. The evidence that William II, son of the Conqueror, had been killed "by an arrow offshot" by one of his own men for just that purpose added weight to the story of the antiquity of the Society. William Rufus, it was believed, had been a pagan himself, and had gone willingly to his death—but it was not likely that any modern Anglo-French monarch would do so.

Originally, it had been one of the tenets of their belief that the sacrificial victim must die willingly, even gladly; mere assassination would be pointless and utterly lacking in efficacy. But the increasing tension between the Empire and the Kingdom of Poland had wrought a change. This was a time of troubles, said the Society, and the King must die, will he or no. Evidence showed that such sentiments had been carefully instilled in the membership of the Society by agents of King Casimir IX himself.

"I doubt," said King John, "that the Society poses any real threat to the Imperial Government. There simply aren't that many fanatics in England. But a King is as vulnerable to a lone assassin—especially a fanatic—as any one else. I do not consider myself indispensable to the Empire; if my death would benefit the people, I would go to the block today. As it is, however, I rather feel that I should like to go on living for a time.

"My own agents, I must tell you, have infiltrated the Society successfully. Thus far, they have reported that there is no hint of any really organized attempt to do away with me. But now something new has come up.

"This morning, shortly before seven o'clock, His Grace the Duke of Kent passed away. It was not unexpected. He was only sixty-two, but his health had been failing for some time and he has been failing rapidly for the past three weeks. The best Healers were called in, but the Reverend Fathers said that when a man has resigned himself to dying there is nothing the Church can do.

"At exactly seven o'clock, the Duke's Master Cabinetmaker went into his shop to get the coffin that had been prepared for His Grace. He found it already occupied—by the body of Lord Camberton, Chief Investigator for the Duchy of Kent.

"He had been stabbed—*and his body was dyed blue!*"

Lord Darcy's eyes narrowed.

"It is not known," the King continued, "how long Lord Camberton has been dead. It is possible that a preservative spell was cast over the body. He was last seen in Kent three weeks ago, when he left for a holiday in Scotland. We don't know yet if he ever arrived, though I should get a report by teleson very shortly. Those are the facts as I know them. Are there any questions, Lord Darcy?"

"None, Sire." There was no point in asking the King questions which could be better answered in Canterbury.

"My brother Richard," said the King, "has a high regard for your abilities and has communicated to me in detail regarding you. I have full respect for his judgment, which was fully borne out by your handling of the 'Atlantic Curse' case last January. My personal agents, working for months, had got nowhere; you penetrated to the heart of the matter in two days. Therefore, I am appointing you as Special Investigator for the High Court of Chivalry." He handed Lord Darcy a document which he had produced from an inside coat pocket. "I came here incognito," he went on, "because I do not want it known that I am taking a personal interest in this case. As far as the public is to know, this was a decision by the Lord Chancellor—quite routine. I want you to go to Canterbury and find out who killed Lord Camberton and why. I have no data. I want you to get me the data I need."

"I am honored, Sire," said Lord Darcy, pocketing the commission. "Your wish is my command."

"Excellent. A train leaves for Canterbury in an hour and"— His Majesty glanced at his wrist watch—"seven minutes. Can you make it?"

"Certainly, Sire."

"Fine. I have made arrangements for you to stay at the Archbishop's Palace—that will be easier, I think, and more politic than putting you in with the Ducal family. His Grace the Archbishop knows that I am interested in this case; so does Sir Thomas Leseaux. No one else does."

Lord Darcy raised an eyebrow. "Sir Thomas Leseaux, Sire? The theoretical thaumaturgist?"

The King's smile was that of a man who has perpetrated a successful surprise. "The same, my lord. A member of the Society of Albion—and my agent."

"Perfect, Sire," said Lord Darcy with a smile of appreciation. "One would hardly suspect a scientist of his standing of being either."

"I agree. Are there any further questions, my lord?"

"No. But I have a request, Sire. Sir Thomas, I understand, is not a practicing sorcerer—"

"Correct," said the King. "A theoretician only. He is perfecting something he calls the Theory of Subjective Congruency—whatever that may mean. He works entirely with the symbology of subjective algebra and leaves others to test his theories in practice."

Lord Darcy nodded. "Exactly, Sire. He could hardly be called an expert in forensic sorcery. I should like the aid of Master Sean O Lochlainn; we work well together, he and I. He is in Rouen at the moment. May I send word for him to come to Canterbury?"

His Majesty's smile grew broader. "I am happy to say that I have anticipated your request. I have already sent a teleson message to Dover. A trusted agent has already left on a special boat to Calais. He will teleson to Rouen and the boat will be held for Master Sean at Calais to return to Dover.

From Dover, he can take the train to Canterbury. The weather is good; he should arrive some time tomorrow."

"Sire," said Lord Darcy, "as long as the Imperial Crown decorates a head like yours, the Empire cannot fail."

"Neatly worded, my lord. We thank you." His Majesty rose from his chair and Lord Darcy did likewise. His reversion to the royal first person plural indicated that they were no longer speaking as man to man, but as Sovereign to subject. "We give you carte blanche, my lord, but there must be no further contact with Us unless absolutely necessary. When you are finished, We want a complete and detailed report—for Our eyes only. Arrangements for anything you need will be made through His Grace the Archbishop."

"Very well, Your Majesty."

"You have Our leave to go, Lord Darcy."

"By Your Majesty's leave." Lord Darcy dropped to one knee. By the time he had risen, the King had turned his back and was once more staring out the window—making it unnecessary for Lord Darcy to back out of the room.

Lord Darcy turned and walked to the door. As his hand touched the door handle, the King's voice came again.

"One thing, Darcy."

Lord Darcy turned to look, but the King still had his back to him.

"Sire?"

"Watch yourself. I don't want you killed. I need men like you."

"Yes, Sire."

"Good luck, Darcy."

"Thank you, Sire."

Lord Darcy opened the door and went out, leaving the King alone with his thoughts.

Lord Darcy vaguely heard a bell. *Bon-n-n-ng. Bon-n-n-ng. Bon-n-n-ng.* Then a pause. During the pause, he drifted off again into sleep, but it was only a matter of seconds before the bell rang three more times. Lord Darcy came slightly more awake this time, but the second pause was almost enough to allow him to return to comfortable oblivion. At the third repetition of the three strokes, he recognized that the Angelus was ringing. It was six in the morning, and that meant that he had had exactly five hours sleep. During the final ringing of the nine strokes, he muttered the prayers rapidly, crossed himself, and closed his eyes again, resolving to go back to sleep until nine.

And, of course, couldn't sleep.

One eventually gets used to anything, he thought, feeling sleepily grumpy, *even great, clangy bells.* But the huge bronze monster in the bell tower of the cathedral church of Canterbury was not more than a hundred yards away in a direct line, and its sound made the very walls vibrate.

He pulled his head out of the pillows again, propped himself up to a sitting position, and looked around at the unfamiliar but pleasant bedroom which had been assigned him by His Grace the Archbishop. Then he looked out the window. At least the weather looked as if it would be fine.

He threw back the bedclothes, swung his legs over the edge of the bed, put his feet into his slippers, and then pulled the bell cord. He was just tying the cord of his crimson silk dressing gown—the one with the gold dragons embroidered on it—when the young monk opened the door. "Yes, my lord?"

"Just a pot of caffe and a little cream to match, Brother."

"Yes, my lord," the novice said.

By the time Lord Darcy had showered and shaved, the caffe was already waiting for him, and the young man in the Benedictine habit was standing by. "Anything else, my lord?"

"No, Brother; that will be all. Thank you."

"A pleasure, my lord." The novice went promptly.

That was one thing about the Benedictine novitiate, Lord Darcy reflected; it taught a young man from the lower classes how to behave like a gentleman and it taught humility to those who were gently born. There was no way of knowing whether the young man who had just come in was the son of a small farmer or a cadet of a noble family. If he hadn't been able to learn, he wouldn't have come even this far.

Lord Darcy sat down, sipped at the caffe, and thought. He had little enough information as yet. His Grace the Archbishop, a tall, widely-built, elderly man with an impressive mane of white hair and a kindly expression on his rather florid face, had had no more information than Lord Darcy had already received from the King. Via teleson,

Lord Darcy had contacted Sir Angus MacReady, Chief Investigator for His Lordship the Marquis of Edinburgh. Lord Camberton had come to Scotland, all right; but it had not been for a holiday. He had not told Sir Angus what he was doing, but he had been engaged in investigative work of some kind. Sir Angus had promised to determine what that work had been. "Aye, m' laird," he'd said, "I'll do the job masel'. I'll no say a word tae anybody, and I'll report tae ye direct."

Whether Lord Camberton's investigations in Scotland had anything to do with the reason for his being killed was an open question. The Holy Society of Ancient Albion had very little following in Scotland, and the murder had almost certainly not taken place there. Taking a human body from Edinburgh to Canterbury would be so difficult that there would have to be a tremendous advantage to having the body found in Canterbury that would outweigh the dangers of transportation. He would not ignore the possibility, Lord Darcy decided, but until evidence appeared that made it more probable, he would look for the death spot closer to Canterbury.

The local Armsmen had definitely established that Lord Camberton had not been killed in the place where he was found. The deep stab wound had, according to the chirurgeon, bled copiously when it had been inflicted, but there was no blood in the Duke's casket. Still, he would have to investigate the cabinetmaker's shop himself; the report of the Armsmen, relayed to him through My Lord Archbishop, was not enough.

There would be no point in viewing the body itself until Master Sean arrived; that blue dye job had a definitely thaumaturgical feel about it, Lord Darcy thought.

Meantime, he would stroll over to the ducal castle and ask a few questions. But first, breakfast was definitely in order.

Master Walter Gotobed bowed and touched his forehead as the gentleman entered the door of his shop. "Yes, sir. What may I do for you, sir?"

"You are Walter Gotobed, Master Cabinetmaker?" asked Lord Darcy.

"At your service, sir," said the old man politely.

"I am Lord Darcy, Special Investigator for His Majesty's

Court of Chivalry. I should like a few moments of your time, Master Walter."

"Ah, yes. Certainly, your lordship." The old man's eyes took on a pained expression. "About Lord Camberton, I've no doubt. Will you come this way, your lordship? Yes. Poor Lord Camberton, murdered like that; an awful thing, your lordship. This is my office; we won't be disturbed here, your lordship. Would you care to take this chair, your lordship? Here, just a moment, your lordship, let me dust the sawdust off it. Sawdust *do* get everywhere, your lordship. Now, what was it your lordship wanted to know?"

"Lord Camberton's body was found here in your shop, I believe?" Lord Darcy asked.

"Ah, yes, your lordship, and a terrible thing it was, too, if I may say so. A terrible thing to have happen. Found him, so we did, in His Grace's coffin. The Healers had told me there wasn't much hope for His Grace, and Her Grace, the Duchess, asked me to make a specially nice one for His Grace, which of course I did, and yesterday morning when we came in, there he was, Lord Camberton, I mean, in the coffin where he didn't ought to be. All over blue he was, your lordship, all over blue. We didn't even recognize him because of that, not at first."

"Not an edifying sight, I dare say," Lord Darcy murmured. "Tell me what happened."

Master Walter did so, with exhausting particulars.

"You have no idea how he came here?" Lord Darcy asked when the recital was finished.

"None at all, your lordship; none at all. Chief Bertram asked us the same thing, your lordship, 'How did he get in here?' But none of us knew. The windows and the doors was all locked up tight and the back door barred. The only ones as has keys is me and my journeyman, Henry Lavender, and neither of us was here at all the night before. Chief Bertram thought maybe the 'prentices had put him in there as a practical joke—that was before Chief Bertram recognized who he was and thought they'd stole it from the Chirurgeon's College or something—but the boys swear they don't know nothing about it and I believe 'em, your lordship. They're good boys and they wouldn't pull anything like that on me. I said as much to Chief Bertram."

"I see," said Lord Darcy. "Just for the record, where were you and journeyman Henry and the apprentices Sunday night?"

Master Walter jerked a thumb toward the ceiling. "Me and the boys were upstairs, your lordship. That's my home, and I have a room for my 'prentices. Goodwife Bailey comes in of a day to do the cleaning and fix the meals—my wife has been dead now these eighteen years, God rest her soul." He crossed himself unobtrusively.

"Then you can come in the shop from upstairs?"

Master Walter pointed toward the wall of his office. "That ladder goes up to my bedroom, your lordship; you can see the trapdoor. But it hasn't been used for nigh on ten years now. My legs aren't what they used to be, and I don't fancy a ladder any more. We all use the stairway on the outside of the building."

"Could someone have used the ladder without your knowing it, Master Walter?"

The old man shook his head firmly. "Not without my knowing of it, your lordship. If I was down here, I'd see 'em. If I was upstairs, I'd hear 'em; they'd have to move my bed from off the trapdoor. Besides, I'm a very light sleeper. A man don't sleep as well when he's past four-score and ten as he did when he were a young man, your lordship."

"And the bolts and bars were all in place when you came down yesterday morning?"

"Indeed they were, your lordship. All locked up tight."

"Journeyman Henry had the other key, you say. Where was he?"

"He were at home, your lordship. Henry's married, has a lovely wife—a Tolliver she were afore she married, one of Ben Tolliver's daughters. That's Master Ben, the baker. Henry and his wife live outside the gates, your lordship, and the guard would have seen him if he'd come in, which he and his wife say he didn't and I believe 'em. And Henry would have no cause to do such a thing no more than the boys would."

"Have you had protective spells put on your locks and bars?" Lord Darcy asked.

"Oh, yes, your lordship; indeed I have. Wouldn't be without 'em, your lordship. The usual kind, your lordship;

cost me a five-sovereign a year to have 'em kept up, but it's worth every bit."

"A licensed sorcerer, I trust? None of these hedge-magicians or witch-women?"

The old man looked shocked. "Oh, no, your lordship! Not I! I abides by the law, I do! Master Timothy has a license all right and proper, he do. Besides, the magic of them you mentioned is poor stuff at best. I don't believe none of the heresy about black magic being stronger nor white. That would be saying that the Devil were stronger nor God, and"—he crossed himself again—"I for one would never think such a thing."

"Of course not, Master Walter," Lord Darcy said soothingly. "You must understand that it is my duty to ask such questions. The place was all locked up tight, then?"

"Indeed, your lordship, indeed it was. Why, if it hadn't been that His Grace died in the night, Lord Camberton might have stayed there until this morning. But for that, we wouldn't have opened up the shop at all, it being a holiday and all."

"Holiday?" Lord Darcy looked at him questioningly. "What made the eighteenth of May a holiday?"

"Only in Canterbury, your lordship. Special day of thanksgiving it is. On that day in 1589—or '98, I misremember which—a band of assassins were smuggled into the castle by a traitor. Five of them there were. A plot to kill the Duke and his family, it were. But the plot were betrayed and the castle searched and all of 'em were found and taken before they could do anything. Hanged, they were, right out there in the courtyard." Master Walter pointed out the front of his shop. "Since then, on the anniversary, there's a day of thanksgiving for the saving of the Duke's life—though he died some years later, you understand. There's a special Mass said at the chapel and another at the cathedral, and the guard is turned out and there's a ceremonial searching of the castle, with all the Duke's Own Guard in full dress and a parade and a trooping of the colors and five effigies hanged in the courtyard and fireworks in the evening. Very colorful it is, your lordship."

"I'm sure it is," said Lord Darcy. Master Walter's recitation had recalled the facts of history to mind. "Was it carried out as usual yesterday?"

"Well, no, your lordship, it wasn't. The captain of the Duke's Own didn't think it would be right, what with the family in mourning and all. And My Lord Archbishop agreed. 'Twouldn't be proper to give thanks for the saving of the life of a Duke that's four centuries, nearly, in his grave with His late Grace not even *in* his grave yet. The Guard was turned out for five minutes of silence and a salute to His Grace instead."

"Of course. That would be the proper thing," Lord Darcy agreed. "You would not have come into the shop until this morning, then, if His Grace had not passed away. When did you lock the shop last before you unlocked it yesterday morning?"

"Saturday evening, your lordship. That is, *I* didn't lock it. Henry did. I was a little tired and I went upstairs early. Henry usually locks up at night"

"Was the coffin empty at that time?" Lord Darcy asked.

"Positively, your lordship. I took special pride in that coffin, if I may say so, your lordship. Special pride. I wanted to make sure there weren't no sawdust or such on the satin lining."

"I understand. And at what o'clock did you lock up Saturday evening?"

"You'd best ask Henry, your lordship. *Hennnry!*"

The journeyman appeared promptly. After the introduction, Lord Darcy repeated his question.

"I locked up at half past eight, your lordship. It were still light out. I sent the 'prentices upstairs and locked up tight."

"And no one came in here at all on Sunday?" Lord Darcy looked in turn at both men.

"No, your lordship," said Master Walter.

"Not a soul, your lordship," said Henry Lavender.

"Not a soul, perhaps," Lord Darcy said dryly. "But a body did."

Lord Darcy was waiting on the station platform when the 11:22 pulled in from Dover, and when a tubby little Irishman wearing the livery of the Duke of Normandy and carrying a large, symbol-decorated carpetbag stepped out of one of the coaches and looked around, Lord Darcy hailed him:

"Master Sean! Over here!"

"Ah! There you are, my lord! Good to see you again, my

lord. Had a good holiday, I trust? What there was of it, I mean."

"To be honest, I was beginning to become a bit bored, my good Sean. I think this little problem is just what we both need to shake the cobwebs out of our brains. Come along; I have a cab waiting for us."

Once inside the cab, Lord Darcy began speaking in a low voice calculated to just barely carry above the clatter of the horses' hoofs and the rattle of the wheels. Master Sean O Lochlainn listened carefully while Lord Darcy brought him up to date on the death of the Duke and the murder of Lord Camberton, omitting nothing except the fact that the assignment had come personally from the King himself.

"I checked the locks in the shop," he concluded. "The rear door has a simple slip bar that couldn't be opened from the outside except magically. The same with the windows. Only the front door has a key. I'll want you to check the spells; I have a feeling that those men are telling the truth about locking up, that none of them had anything to do with the murder."

"Did you get the name of the sorcerer who serviced the locks, my lord?"

"A Master Timothy Videau."

"Aye. I'll look him up in the directory." Master Sean looked thoughtful. "I don't suppose there's anything suspicious about the death of His Grace the Duke, eh, my lord?"

"I am chronically suspicious of all deaths intimately connected with a murder case, Master Sean. But first we will have a look at Lord Camberton's body. It's being held in the mortuary at the Armsmen's Headquarters."

"Would it be possible, my lord, to instruct the cab driver to stop at an apothecary's shop before we get to the mortuary? I should like to get something."

"Certainly." Lord Darcy gave instructions, and the cab pulled up before a small shop. Master Sean went in and came out a few moments later with a small jar. It appeared to be filled with dried leaves. The whole ones were shaped rather like an arrowhead.

"Druidic magic, eh, Master Sean?" Lord Darcy asked.

Master Sean looked startled for a moment, then grinned. "I ought to be used to you by now, my lord. How did you know?"

"A blue-dyed corpse brings to mind the ancient Briton's habit of dyeing himself blue when he went into battle. When you go into an apothecary's shop and purchase a jar full of the typically sagittate leaves of the woad plant, I can see that your mind is running along the same lines that mine had. You intend to use the leaves for a similarity analysis."

"Correct, my lord."

A few minutes later, the cab drew up to the front door of the Armsmen's Headquarters, and shortly afterwards Lord Darcy and Master Sean were in the morgue. An attendant stood by while the two men inspected the late Lord Camberton's earthly husk.

"He was found this way, my lord? Naked?" Master Sean asked.

"So I am told," Lord Darcy said.

Master Sean opened his symbol-covered carpetbag and began taking things out of it. He was absorbed in his task of selecting the proper material for his work when Bertram Lightly, Chief Master-at-Arms of the City of Canterbury, entered. He did not bother Master Sean; one does not trouble a sorcerer when he is working.

Chief Bertram was a round-faced, pink-skinned man with an expression that reminded one of an amiable frog. "I was told you were here, your lordship," he said softly. "I had to finish up some business in the office. Can I be of any assistance?"

"Not just at the moment, Chief Bertram, but I have no doubt that I shall need your assistance before this affair is over."

"Excuse me," said Master Sean without looking up from his work, "but did you have a chirurgeon look at the body, Chief Bertram?"

"Indeed we did, Master Sorcerer. Would you want to speak to him?"

"No. Not necessary at the moment. Just give me the gist of his findings."

"Well, Dr. Dell is of the opinion that his late lordship had been dead forty-eight to seventy-two hours—plus whatever time he was under a preservative spell, of course. Can't tell anything about that time lapse, naturally. Died of a stab wound in the back. A longish knife or a short thrust with a sword. Went in just below the left shoulder blade, between the ribs, and pierced the heart. Died within seconds."

"Did he say anything about bleeding?"

"Yes. He said there must have been quite a bit of blood from that stab. Quite a bit."

"Aye. So I should say. Look here, my lord."

Lord Darcy stepped closer.

"There was a preservative spell on the body, all right. It's gone now—worn off—but there's only traces of microorganisms on the surface. Nothing alive within. But the body was washed after the blood had coagulated, and it was dyed after it was washed. The wound is clean, and the dye is *in* the wound, as you see. Now, we'll see if that blue stuff is actually woad."

"Woad?" said Chief Bertram.

"Aye, woad," said Master Sean. "The Law of Similarity allows one to determine such things. The dye on the man may be exactly similar to the dye in the leaf, d'ye see. If it is, we get a reaction. Actually, all these come under the broad Law of Metonymy—an effect is similar to its cause, a symbol is similar to the thing symbolized. And vice versa, of course." Then he muttered something unintelligible under his breath and rubbed his thumb along the leaf of woad. "We'll see," he said softly. "We'll see." He put the leaf on the blue skin of the dead man's abdomen, then lifted it off again almost immediately. The side of the leaf that had touched the skin was blue. On the abdomen of the corpse was a white area, totally devoid of blueness, exactly the size and shape of the leaf.

"Woad," said Master Sean with complacency. "Definitely woad."

Master Sean was packing his materials away in his carpetbag. Half an hour had been sufficient to get all the data he needed. He dusted off his hands. "Ready to go, my lord?"

Lord Darcy nodded, and the two of them headed toward the door of the mortuary. Standing near the door was a smallish man in his middle fifties. He had graying hair, a lean face, mild blue eyes and a curiously hawklike nose. On the floor at his feet was a symbol-decorated carpetbag similar to Master Sean's own.

"Good day, colleague," he said in a high voice. "I am

Master Timothy Videau." Then he gave a little bow. "Good day, your lordship. I hope you don't mind, but I was interested in watching your procedure. Forensic sorcery has always interested me, although it isn't my field."

"I am Sean O Lochlainn," said the tubby little Irishman. "This is my superior, Lord Darcy."

"Yes, yes. So Chief Bertram informed me. Isn't it terrible? Lord Camberton being murdered that way, I mean."

As he talked, he fell into step with the other two men and walked with them toward the street. "I suppose you do a lot of similarity analysis in your work, Master Sean? It is a technique with which I am not at all familiar. Protective spells, avoidance spells, repairs—that's my work. Household work. Not as exciting as your work, but I like it. Gives a man a sense of satisfaction and all that. But I like to know what my colleagues are doing."

"You came down here to watch Master Sean at work, then, Master Timothy?" Lord Darcy asked in a bland voice, betraying no trace of the thoughts in his mind.

"Oh, no, your lordship. I was asked down by Chief Bertram." He looked at Master Sean and chuckled. "You'll get a laugh out of this, Master Sean. He wanted to know what it would cost to buy a preservator big enough to serve the kitchen in the Armsmen's barracks!"

Master Sean laughed softly, then said: "I dare say that when you told him he decided to stick with a good, old-fashioned icehouse. You're the local agent, then?"

"Yes. But there's not much profit in it yet, I fear. I've only sold one, and I'm not likely to sell any more. Much too expensive. I get a small commission, but the real money for me would be in the servicing. The spell has to be reinforced every six months or so."

Master Sean smiled ingratiatingly. "Sounds interesting. The spell must have an interesting structure."

Master Timothy returned the smile. "Yes, quite interesting. I'd like to discuss it with you . . ."

Master Sean's expression became more attentive.

" . . . But unfortunately Master Simon has put the whole process under a seal of secrecy."

"I was afraid of that," Master Sean said with a sigh.

"Would I be intruding if I asked what you two are talking about?" Lord Darcy asked.

"Oh, I'm sorry, my lord," Master Sean said hurriedly. "Just shop talk. Master Simon of London has invented a new principle for protecting food from spoilage. Instead of casting a spell on each individual item—such as the big vintners do with wine casks and the like—he discovered a way to cast a spell on a specially-constructed chest, so that anything put in it is safe from spoilage. The idea being that, instead of enchanting an *object*, a *space* is given the property necessary to do the same thing. But the process is still pretty expensive."

"I see," said Lord Darcy.

Master Sean caught the tone of his voice and said: "Well, we mustn't talk shop, Master Timothy. Er . . . did your lordship want me to have a look at those locks? Might be a good idea, if Master Timothy is free for an hour."

"Locks?" said Master Timothy.

Master Sean explained about the locks on the cabinet-maker's shop.

"Why, certainly, Master Sean," said Master Timothy. "I'd be glad to be of any assistance I can."

"Excellent," said Lord Darcy. "Come to My Lord Archbishop's Palace as soon as you have the data. And thank you for your assistance, Master Timothy."

"It's a pleasure to be of service, your lordship," said the hawk-nosed little sorcerer.

In a quiet sitting room in the palace, His Grace the Archbishop introduced Lord Darcy to a tall, lean man with pale features and light brown hair brushed straight back from a broad, high forehead. He had gray-blue eyes and an engaging smile.

"Lord Darcy," said the Archbishop, "may I present Sir Thomas Leseaux."

"It is a pleasure to meet your lordship," said Sir Thomas with a smile.

"The pleasure is mine," said Lord Darcy. "I have read with great interest your popularization, 'Symbolism, Mathematics, and Magic.' I am afraid your more technical work is beyond me."

"You are most kind, my lord."

"Unless you need me," said the Archbishop, "I shall leave you two gentlemen alone. I have some pressing matters at hand."

"Certainly, Your Grace," said Lord Darcy.

When the door had closed behind His Grace, Lord Darcy waved Sir Thomas to a chair. "No one knows you're meeting me here, I trust?" he said.

"Not if I can help it, my lord," said Sir Thomas. There was a wry smile on his lips and one eyebrow lifted slightly. "Aside from the fact that I might get my throat cut, I would lose my effectiveness as a double agent if the Brotherhood found that I was having an appointment with a King's Officer. I used the tunnel that goes from the crypt in the Cathedral to the Palace cellars to get here."

"You might have been seen going into the church."

"That wouldn't bother them, my lord," Sir Thomas said with a negligent flip of one hand. "Since the Society was outlawed, we're expected to dissemble. No use calling attention to oneself by staying away from church, even if we don't believe in Christianity." His smile twisted again. "After all, why not? If a man can be expected to pretend to belief in pagan Druidism, to verbally denounce the Christian faith in grubby little meetings of fanatics, then why shouldn't those pagans pretend to the Christian faith for the same reason—to cover up their real activities. The only difference is in whether one is on one side of the law or the other."

"I should think," said Lord Darcy, "that the difference would be in whether one was for or against King and Country."

"No, no." Sir Thomas shook his head briskly. "That's where you err, my lord. The Holy Society of Ancient Albion is as strongly for King and Country as you or I."

Lord Darcy reached into his belt pouch, took out a porcelain pipe and a package of tobacco, and began to fill the bowl. "Elucidate, Sir Thomas. I am eager to hear details of the Society—both operational data and theory."

"Theory, then, my lord. The Society is comprised of those who believe that these islands have a Destiny—with an upper-case D—to bring peace and contentment to all mankind. In order to do this, we must return to the practices and beliefs of the original inhabitants of the islands—the Keltic peoples who had them by right at the time of the Caesarian invasion of 55 B.C."

"*Were* the Kelts the aborigines of these islands?" Lord Darcy asked.

"My lord, bear with me," Sir Thomas said carefully. "I am trying to give you what the Society officially believes. In judging human behavior, one must go by what an individual *believes* is true—not by what is *actually* true."

Lord Darcy fired up his pipe and nodded. "I apologize. Continue."

"Thank you, my lord. These practices to which I refer are based upon a pantheistic theology. God is not just a Trinity, but an Infinity. The Christian outlook, they hold, is true but limited. God is One—true. He is more than Three in One, however; He is Infinity in One. They hold that the Christian belief in the Three Persons of God is as false—and as true—as the statement: 'There are three grains of sand on the beaches of England.' " He spread his hands. "The world is full of spirits—trees, rocks, animals, objects of all kinds—all full of . . . well, call it spirit for want of a better word. Further, each spirit is intelligent—often in ways that we can't fathom, but intelligent, nonetheless. Each is an individual, and may be anywhere on the spectrum from 'good' to 'evil.' Some are more powerful than others. Some, like dryads, are firmly linked to a specific piece of material, just as a man is linked to his body. Others are 'free spirits'—what we might call 'ghosts,' 'demons,' and 'angels.' Some—most, in fact—can be controlled; some directly, some indirectly, through other spirits. They can be appeased, bribed, and threatened.

"Now the ancient Britons knew all the secrets for appeasing these spirits—or bribing or controlling them—whatever you want. So, it appears, do the Brotherhood of Druids—the inner circle of the Society. At least, so they tell the lesser members. Most of them are of The Blood, as they call it—people from Scotland, Ireland, Wales, Brittany, the Orkneys, the Isle of Man, and so on. Pure Keltic—or so they claim. But those of Anglo-Saxon, Norman, or Frankish descent are allowed in occasionally. No others need apply.

"Don't get the idea they're not for Country, my lord. They are. We're meant to rule the world eventually. The King of the British Isles is destined to be ruler of an empire that will cover the globe. And the King himself? He's the protection, the hex shield, the counter-charm that keeps the hordes of 'bad spirits' from taking over and making life miserable for everybody. The King keeps the storms in place, prevents earthquakes, keeps pestilence and plague away, and, in general, protects his subjects from harm.

"For King and for Country, my lord—but not in exactly the way you or I think of it "

"Interesting," Lord Darcy said thoughtfully. "How do they explain away such things as the storms and frosts that *do* hit Britain?"

"Well, that's His Majesty's fault, you see," said Sir Thomas. "If the Sovereign does not comport himself properly, in other words, if he doesn't follow the Old Faith and do things by the Druidic rules, then the Evil Ones can get through the defenses."

"I see. And one of those rules is that His Majesty must allow his life to be taken any time the Brotherhood feels like it?"

"That's not quite fair, my lord," Sir Thomas said. "Not 'anytime they feel like it'—only when danger threatens. Or every seventh year, whichever comes first."

"What about other sacrifices?"

Sir Thomas frowned. "So far as I know, there have been no human deaths. But every one of their meetings involves the ritual killing of an animal of some kind. It depends upon the time of year and the purpose of the meeting, whether one animal or another is sacrificed."

"All of which is quite illegal," Lord Darcy said.

"Quite," Sir Thomas said. "My dossiers and reports are all on file with His Grace the Archbishop. As soon as we have all the evidence we need, we will be able to make a clean sweep and round up the whole lot of them. Their pernicious doctrines have gone far enough."

"You speak with some heat, Sir Thomas."

"I do. Superstition, my lord, is the cause of much of the mental confusion among the lower classes. They see what is done every day by sorcerers using scientific processes and are led to believe in every sort of foolishness because they confuse superstition with science. That's why we have hedge magicians, black wizards, witches' and warlocks' covens, and all the rest of that criminal fraternity. A person becomes ill, and instead of going to a proper Healer, he goes to a witch, who may cover a wound with moldy bread and make meaningless incantations or give a patient with heart trouble a tea brewed of foxglove or some such herb which has no symbolic relationship to his trouble at all. Oh, I tell you, my lord, this sort of thing must be stamped out!"

The theoretician had dropped his attitude of bored irony. He evidently felt quite strongly about the matter, Lord Darcy decided. Licensed Healers, of course, used various herbs and drugs on occasion, but always with scientific precision according to the Laws of Magic; for the most part, however, they relied on the Laying on of Hands, the symbol of their Healing Art. A man took his life in his hands whenever he trusted his health to anyone but a priestly Healer or took his pains and ills to anyone who operated outside the Church.

"I have no doubt of the necessity of clearing up the whole Society, Sir Thomas," said Lord Darcy, "but unless you intend to notify His Majesty the King that the time to strike is near, I fear I cannot wait for the gathering in of the net. I am looking specifically for the murderer of Lord Camberton."

Sir Thomas stood up and thrust his hands into his coat pockets while he stared moodily at a tapestry on the wall. "I've been wondering about that ever since I heard of Lord Camberton's death."

"About what?"

"About the woad dye—I presume it *was* woad, my lord?"

"It was."

"It points clearly toward the Society, then. Some of the Inner Circle have the Talent—poorly trained and misused, but a definite Talent. There is nothing more pitiful in this world, my lord, than to see the Talent misused. It is criminal!"

Lord Darcy nodded in agreement. He knew the reason for Sir Thomas' anger. The theoretician did not, himself, possess the Talent to any marked degree. He theorized; others did his laboratory work. He proposed experiments; others, trained sorcerers, carried them out. And yet Sir Thomas wished passionately that he could do his own experimenting. To see another misuse what he himself did not have, Lord Darcy thought, must be painful indeed to Sir Thomas Leseaux.

"The trouble is," Sir Thomas went on, "that I can give you no clue. I know of no plot to kill Lord Camberton. I know of no reason why the Society should want him dead. That does not mean, of course, that no such reason exists."

"He was not, then, investigating any of the activities of the Society?"

"Not that I know of. Of course, he may have been investigating the private activities of someone connected with the Society."

Lord Darcy looked thoughtfully at the smoldering tobacco in the bowl of his pipe. "And that hypothetical someone used the resources of the Society to rid himself of whatever exposure Lord Camberton might have threatened?" he suggested.

"It's possible," Sir Thomas said. "But in that case the person would have to be rather high up in the Inner Circle. And even then I doubt that they would do murder for a private reason."

"It needn't have been a private reason. Suppose Camberton had found that someone in this city was a Polish agent, but did not know he was connected with the Society. Then what?"

"It's possible," Sir Thomas repeated. He turned away from his inspection of the tapestry and faced Lord Darcy. "If that were the case, then he and other Polish agents might do away with Lord Camberton. But that gets us no further along, my lord. After months of work, I still have no evidence that any one of the Inner Circle is, in fact, a Polish agent. Further, out of the seven members of the Inner Circle, there are still at least three I cannot identify at all."

"They remain hidden?"

"In a way. At the meetings, the members wear a white gown and hood, similar to a monastic habit, while the Inner Circle wear green gowns and hoods that completely cover the head, with a pair of eyeholes cut in them. No one knows who they are, presumably. I have positively identified four of them and am fairly certain of a fifth."

"Then why did you say there were at least three you could not identify? Why the qualification?"

Sir Thomas smiled. "They are shrewd men, my lord. Seven of them always appear for the functions. But there are more than seven. Possibly as many as a dozen. At any given meeting, seven wear green and the remainder wear white. They switch around, so that those not of the Inner Circle are led to believe that Master So-and-So is not a member of the Circle because they have seen him at meetings wearing common white."

"I take it, then, that the complete membership never attends any given meeting," said Lord Darcy. "Otherwise the process of elimination would eventually give the whole trick away."

"Exactly, my lord. One is notified as to date, time, and place."

"Where do they usually take place?"

"In the woods, my lord. There are several groves nearby. Perfectly safe. There are guards posted round the meeting, ready to sound the alarm if Men-at-Arms should come. And no ordinary person would come anywhere near or say a word about it to the King's Officers; they're frightened to death of the Society."

"You say there are always seven. Why seven, I wonder?"

Sir Thomas gave a sardonic chuckle. "Superstition again, my lord. It is supposed to be a mystic number. Any apprentice sorcerer could tell them that only the number five has any universal symbolic significance."

"So I understand," said Lord Darcy. "Inanimate nature tends to avoid fiveness."

"Precisely, my lord. There are no five-sided crystals. Even the duo-decahedron, a regular solid with twelve pentagonal faces, does not occur naturally. I will not bore you with abstruse mathematics, but if my latest theorems hold true, the hypothetical 'basic building blocks' of the material universe—whatever they may be—cannot occur in aggregates of five. A universe made of such aggregates would go to pieces in a minute fraction of a second." He smiled. "Of course such 'building blocks', if they exist, must remain forever hypothetical, since they would have to be so small that no one could see them under the most powerful microscope. As well try to see a mathematical point on a mathematical line. These are symbolic abstractions which are all very well to work with, but their material existence is highly doubtful."

"I understand. But then living things—?"

"Living things show fiveness. The starfish. Many flowers. The fingers and toes of the human extremities. Five is a very potent number to work with, my lord, as witness the use of the pentacle or pentagram in many branches of thaumaturgy. Six also has its uses; the word 'hex' comes from 'hexagon', as in the Seal of Solomon. But that is because of the prevalence of the hexagon in nature, both animate and inanimate. Snowflakes, honeycombs, and so on. It hasn't the power of five, but it is useful. Seven, however, is almost worthless; its usefulness is so limited as to be nearly nil. Its use in the Book of the Apocalypse of St. John the Divine is a verbal symbology which—" He stopped abruptly with a wry smile. "Pardon me, my lord. I find that I tend to fall into a pedagogical pattern if I don't watch myself."

"Not at all. I am interested," Lord Darcy said. "The question I have in mind, however, is this: Is it possible that Lord Camberton was the victim of some bizarre sacrificial rite?"

"I . . . don't . . . know." Sir Thomas spoke slowly, thoughtfully. He frowned for a moment in thought, then said: "It's possible, I suppose. But it would indicate that Lord Camberton himself was a member of the Inner Circle."

"How so?"

"He would have had to go *willingly* to his death. Otherwise the sacrifice would be worthless. Granted, there has been an attempt of late—fomented by Polish agents—to make an exception in the case of the King. But it hasn't taken hold very strongly. Most of these people, my lord, are misguided fanatics—but they are quite sincere. To change a tenet like that is not as easy as King Casimir IX seems to think. If His Slavonic Majesty were to be told that a marriage in which the bride was forced to make her responses against her will at gunpoint was a true sacrament, he would be shocked that anyone could believe such a thing. And yet he seems to think that believers in Druidism can be manipulated into believing something non-Druidic very easily. His Slavonic Majesty is not a fool, but he has his blind spots."

"Is it possible, then," Lord Darcy asked, "that Camberton was one of the Inner Circle?"

"I really don't think he was, my lord, but it's certainly possible. Perhaps it would be of benefit to look over my written reports. My Lord Archbishop has copies of all of them."

"An excellent idea, Sir Thomas," said Lord Darcy, rising from his chair. "I want a list of known members and a list of those you suspect." He glanced at his watch. He had two

and a half hours yet before his appointment with the family of the late Duke of Kent. That should be time enough.

"This way, your lordship. Their Graces and Sir Andrew
will see you now," said the liveried footman. Lord Darcy
was escorted down a long hallway toward the room where
the family of the late Duke awaited him.

Lord Darcy had met the Duke, his wife, and his son
socially. He had not met either the daughter, Lady Anne,
or the Duchess' brother, Sir Andrew Campbell-MacDonald.

De Kent himself had been a kindly but austere, rather
humorless man, strict in morals but neither harsh nor
unforgiving. He had been respected and honored throughout the Empire and especially in his own duchy.

Margaret, Duchess of Kent, was some twenty years younger
than her husband, having married the Duke in 1944, when
she was twenty-one. She was the second child and only
daughter of the late Sir Austin Campbell-MacDonald. Viva-
cious, witty, clever, intelligent, and still a very handsome
woman, she had, for two decades, been a spark of action
and life playing before the quieter, more subdued background
of her husband. She liked gay parties, good wines, and good
food. She enjoyed dancing and riding. She was a member
of The Wardens, one of the few women members of that
famous London gambling club.

Nonetheless, no breath of scandal had ever touched her.
She had carefully avoided any situation that might cast any
suspicion of immoral behavior or wrongdoing upon either
herself or her family.

There had been two children born of the union: Lord
Quentin, nineteen, was the son and heir. Lady Anne, sixteen, was still a schoolgirl, but, according to what Lord Darcy
had heard, she was already a beautiful young lady. Both
children showed the vivaciousness of their mother, but were
quite well-behaved.

The Duchess of Kent's brother, Sir Andrew, was, by repute,
an easy-going, charming, witty man who had spent nearly
twenty-five years in New England, the northern continent
of the New World, and now, nearing sixty, he had been back
in England for some five years.

The Dowager Duchess was seated in a brocaded chair. She
was a handsome woman with a figure that maturity had

ripened but not overpadded and rich auburn hair that showed
no touch of gray. The expression on her face showed that
she had been under a strain, but her eyes were clear.

Her son, Lord Quentin, stood tall, straight and somber
by her side. Heir Apparent to the Ducal Throne of Kent,
he was already allowed to assume the courtesy titles of "Your
Grace" and "My Lord Duke", although he could not assume
control of the government unless and until his position was
confirmed by the King.

Standing a short, respectful distance away was Sir Andrew
Campbell-MacDonald.

Lord Darcy bowed. "Your Grace, Sir Andrew, I am grieved
that we should have to meet again under these circumstances. I was, as you know, long an admirer of His late
Grace."

"You are most kind, my lord," said the Dowager Duchess.

"I am further grieved," Lord Darcy continued, "that I must
come here in an official capacity as well as in a personal
capacity to pay my respects to His late Grace."

Young Lord Quentin cleared his throat a little. "No apologies are necessary, my lord. We understand your duty."

"Thank you, Your Grace. I will begin, then, by asking
when was the last time any of you saw Lord Camberton
alive."

"About three weeks ago," said Lord Quentin. "The latter
part of April. He went to Scotland for a holiday."

The Dowager Duchess nodded. "It was a Saturday. That
would have been the twenty-fifth."

"That's right," the young Duke agreed. "The twenty-fifth
of April. None of us has seen him since. Not alive, I mean.
I identified the body positively for the Chief Master-at-Arms."

"I see. Does any of you know of any reason why anyone would want to do away with Lord Camberton?"

Lord Quentin blinked. Before he could say anything, his
mother said: "Certainly not. Lord Camberton was a fine and
wonderful man."

Lord Quentin's face cleared. "Of course he was. I know
of no reason why anyone should want to take his life."

"If I may say so, my lords," said Sir Andrew, "Lord
Camberton had, I believe, turned many a malefactor over to
the mercies of the King's justice. I have heard that he was

threatened with violence on more than one such occasion, threatened by men who were sentenced to prison after their crimes were uncovered through his efforts. Is it not possible that such a person may have carried out his threat?"

"Eminently possible," Lord Darcy agreed. He had already spoken to Chief Bertram about investigations along those lines. It was routine in the investigation of the death of an Officer of the King's justice. "That may very likely be the explanation. But I am, naturally, bound to explore every avenue of investigation."

"You are not suggesting, my lord," the Dowager Duchess said coldly, "that anyone of the House of Kent was involved in this dreadful crime?"

"I suggest nothing, Your Grace," Lord Darcy replied. "It is not my place to suggest; it is my duty to discover facts. When all the facts have been brought to light, there will be no need to make suggestions or innuendoes. The truth, whatever it may be, always points in the right direction."

"Of course," said the Duchess softly. "You must forgive me, my lord; I am overwrought."

"You must forgive my sister, my lord," Sir Andrew said smoothly, "her nerves are not of the best."

"I can speak for myself, Andrew," the Dowager Duchess said, closing her eyes for a moment. "But my brother is right, Lord Darcy," she added. "I have not been well of late."

"Pray forgive me, Your Grace," Lord Darcy said gently. "I have no desire to upset you at so trying a time. I think I have no further questions at the moment. Consider my official duties to be at an end for the time being. Is there any way in which I can serve you personally?"

She closed her eyes again. "Not at the moment, my lord, though it is most kind of you to offer. Quentin?"

"Nothing at the moment," Lord Quentin repeated. "If there is any way in which you can help, my lord, rest assured that I will inform you."

"Then, with Your Graces' permission, I shall take my leave. Again, my apologies."

As he walked down the corridor that led toward the great doorway, escorted by the seneschal, Lord Darcy was suddenly confronted by a young girl who stepped out of a nearby doorway. He recognized her immediately; the resemblance to her mother was strong.

"Lord Darcy?" she said in a clear young voice. "I am Lady Anne." She offered her hand.

Lord Darcy smiled just a little and bowed. The kissing of young ladies' hands was now considered a bit old-fashioned, but Lady Anne, at sixteen, evidently felt quite grown up and wanted to show it.

But when he took her hand, he knew that was not the reason. He touched his lips to the back of her hand. "I am honored, my lady," he said as he dexterously palmed the folded paper she had held.

"I am sorry I could not welcome you, my lord," she said calmly, "but I have not been well. I have a terrible headache."

"Perfectly all right, my lady. I trust you will soon be feeling better."

"Thank you, my lord. Until then—" And she walked on past him. Lord Darcy went on without turning, but he knew that one of the three he had left in the room behind him had opened the door and observed the exchange between himself and Lady Anne.

Not until he had left the main gates of the Ducal Palace did he look at the slip of paper.

It said:

"My lord, I must speak with you. Meet me at the Cathedral, near the Shrine of St. Thomas, at six. *Please!*"

It was signed "Anne of Kent."

At five thirty, Lord Darcy was sitting in his rooms in the archiepiscopal palace listening to Master Sean make his report.

"Master Timothy and I checked the locks and bars on the cabinetmaker's shop doors and windows, just as you instructed, my lord. Good spells they are, my lord: solid, competent work. Of course, I could have opened any one of 'em myself, but it would take a sorcerer who knew his stuff. No ordinary thief could have done it, nor an amateur sorcerer."

"What condition are they in, then?" Lord Darcy asked.

"As far as Master Timothy and myself could tell, not a one of 'em had been broken. O' course, that doesn't mean that they hadn't been tampered with. Just as a good locksmith can open a lock and relock it again without leaving any trace, so a good sorcerer could have opened those spells and re-set 'em without leaving a trace. But it would take a top-flight man, my lord."

"Indeed." Lord Darcy looked thoughtful. "Have you checked the Guild Register, Sean?"

Master Sean smiled. "First thing I did, my lord. According to the Register of the Sorcerer's Guild, there is only one man in Canterbury who has the necessary skill to do the job—aside from meself, that is."

"That exception is always granted, my good Sean," said Lord Darcy with a smile. "Only one? Then obviously—"

"Exactly, my lord. Master Timothy himself."

Lord Darcy nodded with satisfaction and tapped the dottle from his pipe. "Very good. I will see you later, Master Sean. I must do a little more investigating. We need more facts."

"Where are you going to look for them, my lord?"

"In church, Master Sean; in church."

As his lordship walked out, Master Sean gazed after him in perplexity. What had he meant by that?

"Maybe," Master Sean murmured to himself, half in jest, "he's going to pray that the Almighty will tell him who did it."

The cathedral was almost empty. Two women were praying at the magnificently jeweled Shrine of St. Thomas Becket, and there were a few more people at other shrines. In spite of the late evening sun, the ancient church was dim within; the sun's rays came through the stained glass windows almost horizontally, illuminating the walls but leaving the floor in comparative darkness.

As he neared the shrine, Lord Darcy saw that one of the two kneeling women was Lady Anne. He stopped a few yards away and waited. When the girl rose from prayer, she looked around, saw Lord Darcy, and came directly toward him.

"Thank you for coming, my lord," she said in a low voice. "I'm sorry I had to meet you this way. The family thought it would be better for me not to talk to you because they think I'm being a silly hero-worshiping girl. But that's not so, really—though I *do* think you're just wonderful." She was looking up at him with wide gray eyes. "You see, my lord, I know all about you. Lady Yvonne is a schoolmate of mine. She says you're the best Investigator in the Empire."

"I try to be, my lady," Lord Darcy said. He had not spoken more than a score of words to Yvonne, daughter of the Marquis of Rouen, but evidently she had been smitten by a schoolgirl crush—and from the look in Lady Anne's eyes, the disease was contagious.

"I think the sooner you solve the murder of Lord Camberton, the better for everyone, don't you?" Lady Anne asked. "I prayed to St. Thomas to help you. He ought to know something about murders, oughtn't he?"

"I should think so, yes, my lady," Lord Darcy admitted. "Do you feel that I will need special intercession by St. Thomas to solve this problem?"

Lady Anne blinked, startled—then she saw the gleam of humor in the tall man's steel-gray eyes. She smiled back. "I don't think so, my lord, but one should never take things for granted. Besides, St. Thomas won't help you unless you really need it."

"I blush, my lady," Lord Darcy said without doing so. "I assure you there is no professional jealousy between St. Thomas and myself. Since I work in the interests of justice, Heavenly intervention often comes to my assistance, whether I ask for it or not."

Looking suddenly serious, she said: "Does Heaven never interfere with your work? In the interest of Divine Mercy, I mean?"

"Perhaps, sometimes," Lord Darcy admitted somberly. "But I should not call it 'interference'; I should call it, rather, an 'illumination of compassion'—if you follow me, my lady."

She nodded. "I think I do. Yes, I think I do. I'm glad to hear you say so, my lord."

The thought flashed through Lord Darcy's mind that Lady Anne suspected someone—someone she hoped would not be punished. But was that necessarily true? Might it not simply be compassion on her own part?

Wait and see, Lord Darcy cautioned himself. *Wait and see.*

"The reason I wanted to talk to you, my lord," Lady Anne said in a low voice, "is that I think I found a Clue."

Lord Darcy could almost hear the capital letter. "Indeed, my lady? Tell me about it."

"Well, *two* Clues, really," she said, dropping her voice still further to a conspiratorial whisper. "The first one is something I saw. I saw Lord Camberton on the night of the eleventh, last Monday, when he came back from Scotland."

"Come, this is most gratifying!" Lord Darcy's voice was a brisk whisper. "When and where, my lady?"

"At the castle, at home. It was very late—nearly midnight, for the bells struck shortly afterward. I couldn't sleep. Father was so ill, and I—" She stopped and swallowed, forcing back tears. "I was worried and couldn't sleep. I was looking out the window—my rooms are on the second floor—and I saw him come in the side entrance. There's a gas lamp there that burns all night. I saw his face clearly."

"Do you know what he did after he came in?"

"I don't know, my lord. I thought nothing of it. I stayed in my rooms and finally went to sleep."

"Did you ever see Lard Camberton alive again?"

"No, my lord. Nor dead either, if it comes to that. Was he *really* stained blue, my lord?"

"Yes, my lady, he was." He paused then: "What was the other clue, my lady?"

"Well, I don't know if it means anything. I'll leave that for you to judge. Last Monday night, when Lord Camberton came home, he was carrying a green cloak folded across his arm. I noticed it particularly because he was wearing a dark blue cloak and I wondered why he needed two cloaks."

Lord Darcy's eyes narrowed just a trifle. "And—?"

"And yesterday . . . well, I wasn't feeling very well, you understand, my lord. My Father and I were very close, my lord, and—" Again she stopped for a moment to fight back tears. "At any rate, I was just walking through the halls. I wanted to be alone for a while. I was in the West Wing. It's unused, except for guests, and there's no one there at the present time. I smelled smoke—a funny odor, not like wood or coal burning. I tracked the smell to one of the guest rooms. Someone had built a fire in the fireplace, and I thought that was odd, for yesterday was quite mild and sunny, like today. There was still smoke coming from the ashes, though they had been all stirred up. The smoke smelled like cloth burning, and I thought *that* was very odd, too, so I poked about a bit—and I found *this!*" With a flourish, she took something from the purse at her belt, holding it out to Lord Darcy between thumb and forefinger.

"I think, my lord, that one of the servants at the castle knows something about Lord Camberton's murder!"

She was holding a small piece of green cloth, burnt at the edges.

Master Sean O Lochlainn came into Lord Darcy's room bearing a large box under one arm and a beaming smile on his round Irish face. "I found some, my lord!" he said triumphantly. "One of the draper's shops had a barrel of it. Almost the same color, too."

"Will it work, then?" Lord Darcy asked.

"Aye, my lord." He set the box on the nearby table. "It'll take a bit o' doing, but we'll get the results you want. By the by, my lord, I stopped by the hospital at the abbey and spoke to the Healer who performed the autopsy on His late Grace, the Duke. The good Father and the chirurgeon who assisted both agree: His Grace died of natural causes. No traces of poison."

"Excellent! A natural death fits my hypothesis much better than a subtle murder would have." He pointed at the box that Master Sean had put on the table. "Let's have a look at this floc."

Master Sean obediently opened the box. It was filled to the brim with several pounds of fine green fuzz. "That's floc, my lord. It's finely-chopped linen, such as that bit of cloth was made of. It's just lint, is all it is. But it's the only thing that'll serve our purpose." He looked around and spotted the piece of equipment he was looking for. "Ah! I see you got the tumbling barrel."

"Yes. My Lord Archbishop was good enough to have one of his coopers make it for us."

The device was a small barrel, with a volume of perhaps a dozen gallons, with a crank at one end, and mounted in a frame so that turning the crank would cause the barrel to rotate. The other end of the barrel was fitted with a tight lid.

Master Sean went over to the closet and took out his large, symbol-decorated carpetbag. He put it on the table and began taking various objects out of it. "Now, this is quite a long process, my lord. Not the simplest thing in the world by any means. Master Timothy Videau prides himself on being able to join a rip in a piece of cloth so that the seam can't be found, but that's a simple bit of magic compared to a job like this. There, all he has to do is make use of the Law of Relevance, and the two edges of a rip in cloth have such high relevance to each other that the job's a snap.

"But this floc, d'ye see, has no direct relevance to the bit o' cloth at all. For this, we have to use the Law of Synecdoche, which says that the part is equivalent to the whole—and contrariwise. Now, let's see. Is everything dry?"

As he spoke, he worked, getting out the instruments and materials he needed for the spells he was about to cast.

It was always a pleasure for Lord Darcy to watch Master Sean at work and listen to his detailed explanations of each step. He had heard much of it countless times before, but there was always something new to be learned each time, something to be stored away in the memory for future reference. Not, of course, that Lord Darcy could make direct use of it himself; he had neither the Talent nor the inclination. But in his line of work, every bit of pertinent knowledge was useful.

"Now, you've seen, my lord," Master Sean went on, "how a bit of amber will pick up little pieces of lint or paper if you rub it with a piece of wool first, or a glass rod will do the same if you rub it with silk. Well, this is much the same process, basically, but it requires patterning and concentration of the power, d'ye see. That's the difficult part. Now, I must have absolute silence for a bit, my lord."

It took the better part of an hour for Master Sean to get the entire experiment prepared to his satisfaction. He dusted the floc and the bit of scorched cloth with powders, muttered incantations, and made symbolic designs in the air with his wand. During it all, Lord Darcy sat in utter silence. It is dangerous to disturb a magician at work.

Finally, Master Sean dumped the box of floc into the barrel and put the bit of green cloth in with the fluffy lint. He clamped the cover on and made more symbolic tracings with his wand while he spoke in a low tone.

Then he said: "Now comes the tedious part, my lord. This is pretty fine floc, but that barrel will still have to be turned for an hour and a half at least. It's a matter of probability, my lord. The damaged edges of the cloth will try to find a bit of floc that is most nearly identical to the one that was there previously. Then that bit of floc finds another that was most like the next one and so on. Now, it's a rule that the finer things are divided, the more nearly identical they become. It is theorized that if a pure substance, such as salt, were to be reduced to its ultimate particles, they'd all be identical. In a gas—but that's neither here nor there. The point is that if I had used, say, pieces of half-inch green thread, I'd have to use tons of the stuff and the tumbling would take days. I won't bore you with the mathematics of the thing. Anyhow, this will take time, so—"

Lord Darcy smiled and raised a hand. "Patience, my dear Sean. I have anticipated you." He thought of how the King had done the same to him only the day before. He pulled a bell rope.

A knock came at the door and when Lord Darcy said "Come in" a young monk clad in novice's robes entered timidly.

"Brother Daniel, I think?" said his lordship.

"Y-yes, my lord."

"Brother Daniel, this is Master Sean. Master Sean, the Novice Master informs me that Brother Daniel is guilty of a minor infraction of the rules of his Order. His punishment is to be a couple of hours of monotonous work. Since you are a licensed sorcerer, and therefore privileged, it is lawful for a lay brother to accept punishment from you if he so wills it. What say you, Brother Daniel?"

"Whatever my lord says," the youth said humbly.

"Excellent. I leave Brother Daniel to your care, Master Sean. I shall return in two hours. Will that be plenty of time?"

"Plenty, my lord. Sit down on this stool, Brother. All you have to do is turn this crank—slowly, gently, but steadily. Like this. That's it. Fine. Now, no talking. I'll see you later, my lord."

When Lord Darcy returned, he was accompanied by Sir Thomas Leseaux. Brother Daniel was thanked and dismissed from his labors.

"Are we ready, Master Sean?" Lord Darcy asked.

"Ready, indeed, my lord. Let's have a look at it, shall we?"

Lord Darcy and Sir Thomas watched with interest as Master Sean opened the end of the barrel.

The tubby little sorcerer drew on a pair of thin leather

gloves. "Can't get it damp, you see," he said as he put his hands into the end of the wooden cylinder, "nor let it touch metal. Falls apart if you do. Come out, now . . . easy . . . easy . . . ahhhhh!"

Even as he drew it out, tiny bits of floc floated away from the delicate web of cloth he held. For what he held was no longer a mass of undifferentiated floc; it had acquired texture and form. It was a long robe of rather fuzzy green linen, with an attached hood. There were eyeholes in the front of the hood so that if it were brought down over the head the wearer could still see out.

Carefully, the round little Irish sorcerer put the reconstituted robe on the table. Lord Darcy and Sir Thomas looked at it without touching it.

"No question of it," Sir Thomas said after a moment. "The original piece came from one of the costumes worn by the Seven of the Society of Albion." Then he looked at the sorcerer. "A beautiful bit of work, Master Sorcerer. I don't believe I've ever seen a finer reconstruction. Most of them fall apart if one tries to lift them. How strong is it?"

"About that of a soft tissue paper, sir. Fortunately, the weather has been dry lately. In damp weather"—he smiled—"well, it's more like damp tissue paper."

"Elegantly put, Master Sean," said Sir Thomas with a smile.

"Thank you, Sir Thomas." Master Sean whipped out a tape measure and proceeded to go over the reconstituted garment carefully, jotting down the numbers in his notebook. When he was through, he looked at Lord Darcy. "That's about it, my lord. Will we be needing it any further?"

"I think not. In itself it does not constitute evidence; besides, it would dissolve long before we could take it to court."

"That's so, my lord." He picked up the flimsy garment by the left shoulder, where the original scrap of material was located, and lowered most of the hooded cloak into the box which had held the floc. Then, still holding to the original bit of cloth with gloved thumb and forefinger, he touched the main body of the cloak with a silver wand. With startling suddenness, the material slumped into a pile

of formless lint again, leaving the original cloth scrap in
Master Sean's fingers.

"I'll file this away, my lord," he said.

Three days later, on Friday the twenty-second, Lord Darcy
found himself becoming impatient. He wrote more on the
first draft of the report which would eventually be sent to
His Majesty and reviewed what he had already written. He
didn't like it. Nothing new had come up. No new clues,
no new information of any kind. He was still waiting for
a report from Sir Angus MacReady in Edinburgh, hoping that
would clear matters up. So far, nothing.

His late Grace, the Duke of Kent had been buried on
Thursday, with My Lord Archbishop officiating at the
Requiem Mass. Half the nobility of the Empire had been
there, as had His Majesty. And Lord Darcy had induced My
Lord Archbishop to allow him to sit in choir in the sanc-
tuary so that he could watch the faces of those who came.
Those faces had told him almost nothing.

Sir Thomas Leseaux had information that showed that
either Lord Camberton himself or Sir Andrew Campbell-
MacDonald or both were very likely members of the Society of Albion. But that proved nothing; it was extremely
possible that one or both might have been agents sent in
by the Duke himself.

"The question, good Sean," he had said to the tubby little
Irish sorcerer on Thursday afternoon, "remains as it was
on Monday. Who killed Lord Camberton and why? We have
a great deal of data, but they are, thus far, unexplained data.
Why was Lord Camberton placed in the Duke's coffin? When
was he killed? Where was he between the time he was killed
and the time he was found?

"Why was Lord Camberton carrying a green costume? Was
it the same one that was burnt on Monday? If so, why did
whoever burnt it wait until Monday afternoon to destroy
it? The green habit would have fit either Lord Camberton
or Sir Andrew, both of whom are tall men. It certainly did
not belong to any of the de Kents; the tallest is Lord Quentin,
and he is a good six inches too short to have worn that
outfit without tripping all over the hem.

"I am deeply suspicious, Sean; I don't like the way the
evidence is pointing."

"I don't quite follow you, my lord," Master Sean had said.

"Attend. You have been out in the city; you have heard what people are saying. You have seen the editorials in the *Canterbury Herald*. The people are convinced that Lord Camberton was murdered by the Society of Albion. The clue of the woad was not wasted upon Goodman Jack, the proverbial average man.

"And what is the result? The members of the Society are half scared to death. Most of them are pretty harmless people, in the long run; belonging to an illegal organization gives them the naughty feeling a little boy gets when he's stealing apples. But now the Christian community is up in arms against the pagans, demanding that something be done. Not just here, but all over England, Scotland, and Wales.

"Lord Camberton wasn't killed as a sacrifice, willing or otherwise. He'd have been disposed of elsewhere—buried in the woods, most likely.

"He was killed somewhere inside the curtain wall of Castle Canterbury, and it was murder—not sacrifice. Then why the woad?"

"As a preservative spell, my lord," Master Sean had said. "The ancient Britons knew enough about symbolism to realize that the arrowhead leaves of the woad plant could be used protectively. They wore woad into battle. What they didn't know, of course, was that the protective spells don't work that way. They—"

"Would you use woad for a protective spell, as a preservative to prevent decomposition of a body?" interrupted Lord Darcy.

"Why . . . no, my lord. There are much better spells, as you know. Any woad spell would take quite a long time, and the body has to be thoroughly covered. Besides, such spells aren't very efficient."

"Then why was it used?"

"Ah! I see your point, my lord!" Master Sean's broad Irish face had suddenly come all over smiles. "Of course! The body was *meant* to be found! The woad was used to throw the blame on the Holy Society of Ancient Albion and divert suspicion from somewhere else. Or, possibly, the entire purpose of the murder was to give the Society a bad time, eh?"

"Both hypotheses have their good points, Master Sean, but we still do not have enough data. We need *facts*, my good Sean. *Facts!*"

And now, nearly twenty-four hours had passed and no new facts had come to light. Lord Darcy dipped his pen in the ink bottle and wrote down that disheartening fact.

The door opened and Master Sean came in, followed almost immediately by a young novice bearing a tray which contained the light luncheon his lordship had asked for. Lord Darcy pushed his papers to one side to indicate where the tray should be placed. Master Sean held out an envelope in one hand. "Special delivery, my lord. From Sir Angus MacReady in Edinburgh."

Lord Darcy reached eagerly for the envelope.

What happened was no one's fault, really. Three people were crowded around the table, each trying to do something, and the young novice, in trying to maneuver the tray, had to move it aside when Master Sean handed over the envelope to Lord Darcy. The corner of the tray caught the neck of the ink bottle, and that theretofore upright little container promptly toppled over on its side and disgorged its contents all over the manuscript Lord Darcy had been working on.

There was a moment of stunned silence, broken by the profuse apologies of the novice. Lord Darcy inhaled slowly, then calmly told the lad that there was no damage done, that he was certainly not at fault, and that Lord Darcy was not the least bit angry. He was thanked for bringing up the tray and dismissed.

"And don't worry about the mess, Brother," Master Sean said. "I shall clean it up myself."

When the novice had left, Lord Darcy looked ruefully at the ink-stained sheets and then at the envelope he had taken from Master Sean's fingers. "My good Sean," he said quietly, "I am not, as you know, a nervous or excitable man. If, however, this envelope does not contain good news and useful information, I shall undoubtedly throw myself on the floor in a raving convulsion of pure fury and chew holes in the rug."

"I shouldn't blame you in the least, my lord," said Master Sean, who knew perfectly well that his lordship would do no such thing. "Go sit down in the easy-chair, my lord, while I do something about this minor catastrophe."

Lord Darcy sat in the big chair near the window. Master Sean brought over the tray and put it on the small table at his lordship's elbow. Lord Darcy munched a sandwich and drank a cup of caffe while he read the report from Edinburgh.

Lord Camberton's movements in Scotland, while not exactly done in a blaze of publicity, had not been gone about furtively by any means. He had gone to certain places and asked certain questions and looked at certain records. Sir Angus had followed that trail and learned what Lord Camberton had learned, although he confessed that he had no notion of what his late lordship had intended to do with that information or what hypothesis he may have been working on or whether the information he had obtained meant anything, even to Lord Camberton.

His lordship had visited, among other places, the Public Records Office and the Church Marriage Register. He had been checking on Margaret Campbell-MacDonald, the present Dowager Duchess of Kent.

In 1941, when she was only nineteen, she had married a man named Chester Lowell, a man of most unsavory antecedents. His father had been imprisoned for a time for embezzlement and had finally drowned under mysterious circumstances. Chester's younger brother, Ian, had been arrested and tried twice on charges of practicing magic without a license, but had been released both times after a verdict of "Not Proven," and had finally gone up for six years for a confidence game which had involved illegal magic and had been released in 1959. Chester Lowell himself was a gambler of the worst sort, a man who cheated at cards and dice to keep his pockets lined.

After only three weeks of marriage, Margaret had left Chester Lowell and returned home. Evidently the loss had meant little to Lowell; he did not bother to try to get her back. Six months later, he had fled to Spain under a cloud of suspicion; the authorities in Scotland believed that he had been connected with the disappearance of six thousand sovereigns from a banking house in Glasgow. The evidence against him, however, was not strong enough to extradite him from the protection of the King of Aragon. In 1942, the Aragonese authorities reported that the "Inglés," Chester Lowell, had been shot to death in Zaragoza after an argument over a card game. The Scottish authorities sent an investigator who knew Lowell to identify the body, and the case against him was marked "Closed."

So! thought Lord Darcy, *Margaret de Kent is twice a widow.*

There had been no children born of her brief union with Lowell. In 1944, after an eight months courtship, Margaret had become the Duchess of Kent. Sir Angus MacReady did not know whether the Duke had been aware then of the previous marriage, or, indeed, whether he had ever known.

Sir Andrew Campbell-MacDonald had also had his history investigated by Lord Camberton. There was certainly nothing shady in his past; he had had a good reputation in Scotland. In 1939, he had gone to New England and had served for a time in the Imperial Legion. He had comported himself with honor in three battles against the red aborigines and had left the service with a captain's commission and an excellent record. In 1957, the small village in which he had been living was raided by the red barbarians and burnt to the ground after great carnage, and it had been believed for a time that Sir Andrew had been killed in the raid. He had returned to England in 1959, nearly penniless, his small fortune having vanished as a result of the destruction during the raid. He had been given a minor position and a pension by the Duke of Kent and had lived with his sister and brother-in-law for the past five years.

Lord Darcy put the letter aside and thoughtfully finished his caffe. He did not look at all as though he were about to have a rug-chewing fit of fury.

"The only thing missing is the magician," he said to himself. "Where is the magician in this? Or, rather, *who* is he? The only sorcerer in plain sight is Master Timothy Videau, and he does not apparently have any close connection with Lord Camberton or the Ducal Palace. Sir Thomas suspects that Sir Andrew might be a member of the Society of Albion, but that does not necessarily mean he knows anything about sorcery."

Furthermore, Lord Darcy was quite certain that Sir Andrew,

if he was a member of the Inner Circle, would not draw attention to the Society in such a blatant manner.

"Here is your report, my lord," said Master Sean.

Lord Darcy came out of his reverie to see Master Sean standing by his side with a sheaf of papers in his hand. His lordship had been vaguely aware that the tubby little Irish sorcerer had been at work at the other end of the room, and now it was obvious what he had been doing. Except for a very slight dampness, there was no trace of the ink that had been spilled across the pages, although the clear, neat curves of Lord Darcy's handwriting remained without change. It was, Lord Darcy knew, simply a matter of differentiation by intention. The handwriting had been put there with intention, with purpose, while the spilled ink had got here by accident; thus it was possible for a removal spell to differentiate between them.

"Thank you, my good Sean. As usual, your work is both quick and accurate."

"It would've taken longer if you'd been using these new indelible inks," Master Sean said depreciatively.

"Indeed?" Lord Darcy said absently as he looked over the papers in his hand.

"Aye, my lord. There's a spell cast on the ink itself to make it indelible. That makes it fine for documents and bank drafts and such things as you don't want changed, but it makes it hard as the very Devil to get off after it's been spilled. Master Timothy was telling me that it took him a good two hours to get the stain out of the carpet in the Ducal study a couple of weeks ago."

"No doubt," said Lord Darcy, still looking at his report. Then, suddenly, he seemed to freeze for a second. After a moment, he turned his head slowly and looked up at Master Sean. "Did Master Timothy mention exactly what day that was?"

"Why . . . no, my lord, he didn't."

Lord Darcy put his report aside and rose from his chair. "Come along, Master Sean. We have some important questions to ask Master Timothy Videau—very important."

"About ink, my lord?" Master Sean asked, puzzled.

"About ink, yes. And about something so expensive that he has sold only one of them in Canterbury." He took his blue cloak from the closet and draped it around his shoulders. "Come along, Master Sean."

"So," said Lord Darcy some three-quarters of an hour later, as he and Master Sean strolled through the great gate in the outer curtain wall of Castle Canterbury, "we find that the work was done on the afternoon of May 11th. Now we need one or two more tiny bits of evidence, and the lacunae in my hypothesis will be filled."

They headed straight for Master Walter Gotobed's shop.

Master Walter, Journeyman Henry Lavender informed them, was not in at the moment. He and young Tom Wilderspin had taken the cart and mule to deliver a table to a gentleman in the city.

"That is perfectly all right, Goodman Henry," Lord Darcy said. "Perhaps you can help us. Do you have any zebrawood?"

"Zebrawood, my lord? Why, I think we have a little. Don't get much call for it, my lord. It's very dear, my lord."

"Perhaps you would be so good as to find out how much you have on hand, Goodman Henry? I am particularly eager to know."

"O' course, my lord. Certainly." The journeyman joiner went back to the huge room at the rear of the shop.

As soon as he had disappeared from sight, Lord Darcy sprang to the rear door of the shop. It had a simple drop bar as a lock; there was no way to open it from the outside. Lord Darcy looked at the sawdust, shavings, and wood chips at his feet. His eye spied the one he wanted. He picked up the wood chip and then lifted the bar of the door and wedged the chip in so that it held the bar up above the two brackets that it fitted in when the door was locked. Then he took a long piece of string from his pocket and looped it over the wood chip. He opened the door and went outside, trailing the two ends of the string under the door. Then he closed the door.

Inside, Master Sean watched closely. The string, pulled by Lord Darcy from outside, tightened. Suddenly the bit of wood was jerked out from between the bar and the door. Now unsupported, the bar fell with a dull thump. The door was locked.

Quickly, Master Sean lifted the bar again, and Lord Darcy re-entered. Neither man said a word, but there was a smile of satisfaction on both their faces.

Journeyman Henry came in a few minutes later; evidently he had not heard the muffled sound of the door bar falling. "We ain't got very much zebrawood, my lord," he said dolefully. "Just scrap. Two three-foot lengths of six-by-three-eights. Leftovers from a job Master Walter done some years ago. We'd have to order it from London or Liverpool, my lord." He put the two boards on a nearby workbench. Even in their unfinished state, the alternate dark and light bands of the wood gave it distinction.

"Oh, there's quite enough there," Lord Darcy said. "What I had in mind was a tobacco humidor. Something functional—plain but elegant. No carving; I want the beauty of the wood to show."

Henry Lavender's eyes lit up. "Quite so, my lord! To be sure, my lord! What particular design did my lord have in mind?"

"I shall leave that up to you and Master Walter. It should be of about two pounds capacity."

After a few minutes, they agreed upon a price and a delivery date. Then: "Oh, by the by, Goodman Henry . . . I believe you had a slip of the memory when I questioned you last Tuesday."

"My lord?" Journeyman Henry looked startled, puzzled, and just a little frightened.

"You told me that you locked up tight on Saturday night at half past eight. You neglected to tell me that you were not alone. I put it to you that a gentleman came in just before you locked up. That he asked you for something which you fetched for him. That he went out the front door with you and stood nearby while you locked that door. Is that not so, my good Henry?"

"It's true as Gospel, my lord," said the joiner in awe. "How on Earth did you know that, my lord?"

"Because that is the only way it could have happened."

"That's just how it did happen, my lord. It were Lord Quentin, my lord. That is, the new Duke; he were Lord Quentin then. He asked me for a bit of teak to use as a paperweight. He knew we had a polished piece and he offered to buy it, so I sold it to him. But I never thought nothing wrong of it, my lord!"

"You did nothing wrong, my good Henry—except to forget to tell me that the incident had happened. It is of no consequence, but you should have mentioned it earlier."

"I humbly beg your pardon, my lord. But I didn't think nothing of it."

"Of course not. But in future, if you should be asked questions by a King's Officer, be sure to remember details. Next time, it might be more important."

"I'll remember, my lord."

"Very good. Good day to you, Goodman Henry. I shall look forward to seeing that humidor."

Outside the shop, the two men walked across the busy courtyard toward the great gate. Master Sean said: "What if he hadn't had any zebrawood, my lord? How would you have got him out of the shop?"

"I'd have asked for teak," Lord Darcy said dryly. "Now we must make a teleson call to Scotland. I think that within twenty-four hours I shall be able to make my final report."

There were six people in the room. Margaret, Dowager Duchess of Kent, looked pale and drawn but still regal, still mistress of her own drawing room. Quentin, heir to the Duchy of Kent, stood with somber face near the fireplace, his eyes hooded and watchful. Sir Andrew Campbell-MacDonald stood solemnly by the window, his hands in the pockets of his dress jacket, his legs braced a little apart. Lady Anne sat in a small, straightbacked chair near Sir Andrew. Lord Darcy and Master Sean faced them.

"Again I apologize to Your Graces for intruding upon your bereavement in this manner," Lord Darcy said, "but there is a little matter of the King's Business to be cleared up. A little matter of willful murder. On the 11th of May last, Lord Camberton returned secretly from Scotland after finding some very interesting information—information that, viewed in the proper light, could lend itself very easily to blackmail. Lord Camberton was murdered because of what he had discovered. His body was then hidden away until last Saturday night or early Sunday morning, at which time it was put in the coffin designed for His late Grace, the Duke.

"The information was more than scandalous; if used in the right way, it could be disastrous to the Ducal Family. If someone had offered proof that the first husband of Her Grace the Duchess was still living, she would no longer have any claim to her title, but would still be Margaret Lowell of Edinburgh—and her children would be illegitimate and therefore unable to claim any share in the estates or government of the Duchy of Kent."

As he spoke, the Dowager Duchess walked over to a nearby chair and quietly sat down. Her face remained impassive.

Lord Quentin did not move.

Lady Anne looked as though someone had slapped her in the face.

Sir Andrew merely shifted a little on his feet.

"Before we go any further, I should like you to meet a colleague of mine. Show him in, Master Sean."

The tubby little Irish sorcerer opened the door, and a sharp-faced, sandy-haired man stepped in.

"Ladies and gentlemen," said Lord Darcy. "I should like you to meet Plainclothes Master-at-Arms Alexander Glencannon."

Master Alexander bowed to the silent four. "Your Graces. Lady Anne. An honor, I assure ye." Then he lifted his eyes and looked straight at Sir Andrew. "Good morrow to ye, Lowell."

The man who had called himself Sir Andrew merely smiled. "Good morrow, Glencannon. So I'm trapped, am I?"

"If ye wish to put it that way, Lowell."

"Oh, I think not." With a sudden move, Lowell, the erstwhile "Sir Andrew" was behind Lady Anne's chair. One hand, still in his jacket pocket, was thrust against the girl's side. "I would hesitate to attempt to shoot it out with two of His Majesty's Officers, but if there is any trouble about this, the girl dies. You can only hang me once, you know." His voice had the coolness of a man who was used to handling desperate situations.

"Lady Anne," said Lord Darcy in a quiet voice, "do exactly as he says. *Exactly*, do you understand? So must the rest of us." Irritated as he was with himself for not anticipating what Lowell would do, he still had to think and think fast. He was not even certain that Lowell had a gun in that pocket, but he had to assume that a gun was there. He dared not do otherwise.

"Thank you, my lord," Lowell said with a twisted smile. "I trust no one will be so foolish as not to take his lordship's advice."

"What next, then?" Lord Darcy asked.

"Lady Anne and I are leaving. We are walking out the door, across the courtyard, and out the gate. Don't any of you leave here for twenty-four hours. I should be safe by then. If I am, Lady Anne will be allowed to return—unharmed. If there is any hue and cry . . . well, well, there won't be, will there?" His twisted smile widened. "Now clear away from that door. Come, Anne—let's go on a nice trip with your dear uncle."

Lady Anne rose from her chair and went out the door of the room with Lowell, who never took his eyes off the others. He closed the door. "I shouldn't like to hear that door opened before I leave," his voice said from the other side. Then footsteps echoed away down the corridor.

There was another door to the room. Lord Darcy headed for it.

Lord Quentin and the Duchess both spoke at once.

"No! Let him go!"

"He'll kill Anne, you fool!"

Lord Darcy ignored them. "Master Sean! Master Alexander! See that these people are kept quiet and that they do not leave the room until I return!" And then he was out the door.

Lord Darcy knew all the ins and outs of Castle Canterbury. He had made a practice of studying the plans to every one of the great castles of the Empire. He ran down a corridor and then went up a stone stairway, taking the steps two at a time. Up and up he went, flight after flight of stairs, heading for the battlements atop the great stone edifice.

On the roof, he paused for breath. He looked out over the battlement wall. Sixty feet below, he saw Lowell and Lady Anne, walking across the courtyard—slowly, so as to attract no attention from the crowds of people. They were scarcely a quarter of the way across.

Lord Darcy raced for the curtain wall.

Here, the wall was only six feet wide. He was protected from being seen from below by the crenelated walls on either side of the path atop the greater curtain wall. At a crouch, he ran for the tower that topped the great front gate. There was no one to stop him; no soldiers walked these battlements; the castle had not been attacked for centuries.

Inside the gate tower was the great portcullis, a vast mass of crossed iron bars that could be lowered rapidly in case of attack. It was locked into place now, besides being held up by the heavy counterweight in the deep well below the gate entrance.

Lord Darcy did not look over the wall to see where his quarry was now. He should be in front of them, and if he was, Lowell might—just might—glance up and see him. He couldn't take that chance.

He did not take the stairs. He went down the shaft that held the great chain that connected the portcullis to its counterweight, climbing down the chain hand over hand to the flagstones sixty feet beneath him.

There was no Guardsman in the chamber below during the day, for which Lord Darcy was profoundly grateful. He had no time to answer questions or to try to keep an inquisitive soldier quiet.

There were several times when he feared that his life, not Lady Anne's, would be forfeit this day. The chain was kept well oiled and in readiness, even after centuries of peace, for such was the ancient law and custom. Even with his legs wrapped around the chain and his hands gripping tightly, he slipped several times, burning his palms and thighs and calves. The chain, with its huge, eight-inch links, was as rigid as an iron bar, held taut by the great pull of the massive counterweight below.

The chain disappeared through a foot-wide hole that led to the well beneath, where the counterweight hung. Lord Darcy swung his feet wide and dropped lightly to the flagstoned floor.

Then, cautiously, he opened the heavy oak door just a crack.

Had Lowell and the girl already passed?

Of the two chains that held up the great portcullis, Lord Darcy had taken the one that would put him on the side of the gate to Lowell's left. The gun had been in Lowell's right hand, and—

They walked by the door, Lady Anne first, Lowell following slightly behind. Lord Darcy flung open the door and hurled himself across the intervening space.

His body slammed into Lowell's, hurling the man aside, pushing his gun off the girl's body, just before the gun went off with a roar.

The two men tumbled to the pavement and people scattered as they rolled over and over, fighting for possession of the firearm.

Guardsmen rushed out of their places, converging on the struggling figures.

They were too late. The gun went off a second time.

For a moment, both men lay still.

Then, slowly, Lord Darcy got to his feet, the gun in his hand.

Lowell was still conscious, but there was a widening stain of red on his left side. "I'll get you Darcy," he said in a hoarse whisper. "I'll get you if it's the last thing I do."

Lord Darcy ignored him and faced the Guardsmen who had surrounded them. "I am Lord Darcy, Investigator on a Special Commission from His Majesty's Court of Chivalry," he told them. "This man is under arrest for willful murder. Take charge of him and get a Healer quickly."

The Dowager Duchess and Lord Quentin were still waiting when Lord Darcy brought Lady Anne back to the palace.

The girl rushed into the Duchess' arms. "Oh, Mama! Mama! Lord Darcy saved my life! He's wonderful! You should have seen him!"

The Duchess looked at Lord Darcy. "I am grateful to you, my lord. You have saved my daughter's life. But you have ruined it. Ruined us all.

"No, let me speak," she said as Lord Darcy started to say something. "It has come out, now. I may as well explain.

"Yes, I thought my first husband was dead. You can imagine how I felt when he showed up again five years ago. What could I do? I had no choice. He assumed the identity of my dead brother, Andrew. No one here had ever seen either of them, so that was easy. Not even my husband the Duke knew. I could not tell him.

"Chester did not ask much. He did not try to bleed me white as most blackmailers would have. He was content with the modest position and pension my husband granted him, and he behaved himself with decorum. He—" She stopped suddenly, looking at her son, who had become pale.

"I . . . I'm sorry, Quentin," she said softly. "Truly I am. I know how you feel, but—"

Lord Quentin cut his mother short. "Do you mean, Mother, that it was Uncle An . . . *that* man who was blackmailing you?"

"Why, yes."

"And Father didn't know? No one was blackmailing Father?"

"Of course not! How could they? Who—?"

"Perhaps," said Lord Darcy quietly, "you had best tell your mother what you thought had happened on the night of May 11th."

"I heard a quarrel," Lord Quentin said, apparently in a daze. "In Father's study. There was a scuffle, a fight. It was hard to hear through the door. I knocked, but everything had become quiet. I opened the door and went in. Father was lying on the floor, unconscious. Lord Camberton was on the floor nearby—dead—a letter opener from Father's desk in his heart."

"And you found a sheaf of papers disclosing the family skeleton in Lord Camberton's hand."

"Yes."

"Further, during the struggle, a bottle of indelible ink had fallen over, and Lord Camberton's body was splashed with it."

"Yes, yes. It was all over his face. But how did you know?"

"It is my business to know these things," Lord Darcy said. "Let me tell the rest of it. You assumed immediately that Lord Camberton had been attempting to blackmail your father on the strength of the evidence he had found."

"Yes. I heard the word 'blackmail' through the door."

"So you assumed that your father had attacked Lord Camberton with the letter opener and then, because of his frail health, fallen in a swoon to the floor. You knew that you had to do something to save the family honor and save your father from the silken noose.

"You had to get rid of the body. But where? Then you remembered the preservator you had bought."

Lord Quentin nodded. "Yes. Father gave me the money. It was to have been a present for Mother. She sometimes likes a snack during the day, and we thought it would be convenient if she could have a preservator full of food in her rooms instead of having to call to the kitchen every time."

"Quite so," said Lord Darcy. "So you put Lord Camberton's body in it. Master Timothy Videau has explained to me that the spell cast upon the wooden chest keeps a preservative spell on whatever is kept within, so long as the door is closed. Lord Camberton was supposed to be in Scotland, so no one would miss him. Your father never completely recovered his senses after that night, so he said nothing.

"Actually, he probably never knew. I feel he probably collapsed when Lord Camberton, who had been sent to Scotland by your father for that purpose, confirmed the terrible blackmail secret. Lowell was there in the room, having been taken in to confront the Duke. When His Grace collapsed, Lord Camberton's attention was diverted for a moment. Lowell grabbed the letter opener and stabbed him. He knew the Duke would say nothing, but Lord Camberton's oath as a King's Officer would force him to arrest Lowell.

"Lowell, by the by, was a member of the Holy Society of Ancient Albion. Camberton had found that out, too. Lowell probably had lodgings somewhere in the city under another name, where he kept his paraphernalia. Camberton discovered it and brought along the green costume Lowell owned for proof. When Lowell talks, we will be able to find out where that secret lodging is.

"He left the room with the Duke and Lord Camberton still on the floor, taking the green robe with him. He may or may not have heard you knock, Lord Quentin. I doubt it, but it doesn't matter. How long did it take you to clean up the room, Your Grace?"

"I . . . I put Father to bed first. Then I cleaned the blood off the floor. I couldn't clean up the spilled ink, though. Then I took Lord Camberton to the cellar and put him in the preservator. We'd put it there to wait for Mother's birthday— which is next week. It was to be a surprise. It—" He stopped.

"How long were you actually in the room?" Lord Darcy repeated.

"Twenty minutes, perhaps."

"We don't know what Lowell was doing during those twenty minutes. He must have been surprised on returning to find the body gone and the room looking tidy."

"He was," said Lord Quentin. "I called Sir Bertram, our seneschal, and Father Joseph, the Healer, and we were all in Father's room when . . . *he* . . . came back. He looked surprised, all right. But I thought it was just shock at finding Father ill."

"Understandable," said Lord Darcy. "Meanwhile, you had to decide what to do with Lord Camberton's body. You couldn't leave it in that preservator forever."

"No. I thought I would get it outside, away from the castle. Let it be found a long ways away, so there would be no connection."

"But there was the matter of the blue ink-stain," Lord Darcy said. "You couldn't remove it. You knew that you would have to get Master Timothy, the sorcerer, to remove the stain from the rug, but if the corpse were found later with a similar stain, Master Timothy might be suspicious. So you covered up. Literally. You stained the body with woad."

"Yes. I thought perhaps the blame would fall on the Society of Albion and divert attention from us."

"Indeed. And it very nearly succeeded. Between the use of the preservator and the use of woad, it looked very much like the work of a sorcerer.

"But then came last Monday. It is a holiday in Canterbury, to celebrate the saving of a Duke's life in the Sixteenth Century. A part of the celebration includes a ritual searching of the castle. Lord Camberton's body would be found."

"I hadn't been able to find a way of getting it out," Lord Quentin said. "I'm not used to that sort of thing. I was becoming nervous about it, but I couldn't get it out of the courtyard without being seen."

"But you had to hide it that day. So you made sure the shop of Master Walter was unlocked on Saturday night and you put the body in the coffin, thinking it would stay there until after the ceremony, after which you could put it back in the preservator.

"Unfortunately—in several senses of the word—your father passed away early Monday morning. The body of Lord Camberton was found."

"Exactly, my lord."

"Lowell must have nearly gone into panic himself when he heard that the body had been found covered with woad. He knew it connected him—especially if anyone knew he was a member of the Society. So, that afternoon, he burnt his green robe in a fireplace, thinking to destroy any evidence that he was linked with the Society. He was not thorough enough."

The Duchess spoke again. "Well, you have found your murderer, my lord. And you have found what my son has done to try to save the honor of our family. But it was all unsuccessful in the end. Chester Lowell, my first husband, still lives. My children are illegitimate and we are penniless."

Master-at-Arms Alexander Glencannon coughed slightly. "Beggin' your pardon, Your Grace, but I'm happy to say you're wrong. I've known those thievin' Lowells for years. 'Twas I who went to Zaragoza back in '42 to identify Chester Lowell. I saw him masael', and 'twas him, richt enow. The resemblance is close, but this one happen tae be his younger brother, Ian Lowell, released from prison in 1959. He was nae a card-sharp, like his brother Chester, but he's a bad 'un, a' the same."

The Dowager Duchess could only gape.

"It was not difficult to do, Your Grace," said Lord Darcy. "Chester had undoubtedly told Ian all about his marriage to you—perhaps even the more intimate details. You had only known Chester a matter of two months. The younger brother looked much like him. How could you have been expected to tell the difference after nearly a quarter of a century? Especially since you did not even know of the existence of the younger Ian."

"Is it true? Really true? Oh, thank God!"

"It is true, Your Grace, in every particular," Lord Darcy said. "You have reason to be thankful to Him. There was no need for Ian Lowell to bleed you white, as you put it. To have done so might have made you desperate—for all he knew, desperate enough to kill him. He might have avoided that by taking money and staying out of your reach, but that was not what he wanted.

"He didn't want money, Your Grace. He wanted protection, a hiding place in such plain sight that no one would think of looking for him there. He wanted a front. He wanted camouflage.

"Actually, he is in a rather high position in the Holy Society of Ancient Albion—a rather lucrative position, since the leaders of the Society are not accountable to the membership for the way they spend the monies paid them by the members. In addition, I have reason to believe that he is in the pay of His Slavonic Majesty, Casimir of Poland— although, I suspect, under false pretenses, since he must know that it is not so easy to corrupt the beliefs of a religion as King Casimir seems to think it is. Nonetheless, Ian Lowell was not above taking Polish gold and sending highly colored reports back to His Slavonic Majesty.

"And who would suspect Sir Andrew Campbell-MacDonald, a man whose record was that of an honorable soldier and an upright gentleman, of being a Polish spy and a leader of the subversive Holy Society of Albion?

"Someone finally did, of course. We may never know what led His late Grace and Lord Camberton to suspect him, although perhaps we can get Ian Lowell to tell us. But their suspicion has at last brought about Lowell's downfall, though it cost both of them their lives."

There was a knock at the door. Lord Darcy opened it. Standing there was a priest in Benedictine habit. "Yes, Reverend Father?" Lord Darcy said.

"I am Father Joseph. You are Lord Darcy?"

"Yes, I am, Reverend Father."

"I am the Healer the guardsmen called in to take care of your prisoner. I regret to say I could do nothing, my lord. He passed away a few minutes ago from a gunshot wound."

Lord Darcy turned and looked at the Ducal Family. It was all over. The scandal need never come out, now. Why should it, since it had never really existed?

Sir Thomas Leseaux would soon finish his work. The Society of Albion would be rendered impotent as soon as its leaders were rounded up and confronted with the King's High Justice. All would be well.

"I should like to speak to the bereaved family," said Father Joseph.

"Not just now, Reverend Father," said the Dowager Duchess in a clear voice. "I would like to make my confession to you in a few minutes. Would you wait outside, please?"

The priest sensed that there was something odd in the air. "Certainly, my daughter. I will be waiting." He closed the door.

The Duchess, Lord Darcy knew, would tell all, but it would be safe under the seal of the confessional.

It was Lord Quentin who summed up their feelings.

"This," he said coldly, "will be a funeral I will really enjoy. We thank you, my lord."

"The pleasure was mine, Your Grace. Come, Master Sean; we have a Channel crossing awaiting us."

Too Many Magicians

CHAPTER 1

Commander Lord Ashley, Special Agent for His Majesty's Imperial Naval Intelligence Corps, stood in the doorway of a cheap, rented room in a lower middle-class section of town near the Imperial Naval Docks in Cherbourg. The door was open, and a man lay on the floor with a large, heavy-handled knife in his chest.

His lordship lifted his eyes from the corpse and looked around the room. It was small; not more than eight by ten feet, he thought, and the low ceiling was only a bare six inches above his head. Along the right-hand wall was a low bed. It was made up, but the wrinkles in the cheap blue bedspread indicated that someone had been sitting on it—most likely, the dead man. A cheap, wooden table stood in the far left corner with a matching chair next to it. An ancient, lumpy-looking easy chair—probably bought secondhand—stood against the left wall, nearer the door. Another wooden chair, the twin of the one at the table, stood at the foot of the bed, completing the furniture. There were no pictures hung on the green-painted walls; there were no extraneous decorations of any kind. The personality of the man who lived here had not been implanted forcibly upon the room itself, certainly.

Lord Ashley looked back down at the body. Then, cautiously, he closed the door behind him, stepped over to the supine figure, and took a good look. He lifted up one hand and felt for the pulse that should throb at the wrist of a living man. There was none. Georges Barbour was dead.

His lordship took a step back from the corpse and looked at it thoughtfully. In his lordship's belt pocket were one hundred golden sovereigns, money which had been drawn from the Special Fund to pay Goodman Georges Barbour for his services to Naval Intelligence. But Goodman Georges, My Lord Commander thought to himself, would no longer be any drain upon the Special Fund.

My lord the Commander stepped over the body and looked at the papers on the wooden table at the far corner of the room. Nothing there of importance. Nothing that would connect the man with the Imperial Naval Intelligence Corps. Nonetheless, he gathered them all together and slipped them into his coat pocket. There was always the chance that they might contain information in the form of coded writing or secret inks.

The small closet in the right-hand corner of the room, near the door, held only a change of clothing, another cheap suit like the one the dead man wore. Nothing in the pockets, nothing in the lining. The two drawers in the closet revealed nothing but suits of underwear, stockings and other miscellaneous personal property.

Again he looked at the corpse. This search would have to be reported immediately to My Lord Admiral, of course, but there were certain things that it would be better for the local Armsmen not to find.

The room had revealed nothing. Since Barbour had moved into the room only the day before, it was highly unlikely that he could have constructed, in so short a time, some secret hiding place that would escape the penetrating search of my lord the Commander. He checked the room again and found nothing.

A search of the body was equally fruitless. Barbour had, then, already dispatched whatever information he had to Zed. Very well.

Lord Ashley looked around the room once more to make absolutely certain that he had missed nothing.

Then he went out of the room again and down the hall to the narrow, dim stairway that led to the floor below. He went down the stairway briskly, almost hurriedly.

The concierge, who sat in her office just to one side of the front door, was a rather withered but still bright-eyed little woman who looked up at the tall, aristocratic Commander with a smile that was as bright as her eyes.

"Ey, sir? What may I do for ye?"

"I have some rather sad news for you, Goodwife," my lord said quietly. "One of your tenants is dead. We shall have to fetch an Armsman at once."

"Dead? Who? Ye don't mean Goodman Georges, good sir?"

"None other," said his lordship. He had told the concierge only a few minutes before that he was going up to see Barbour. "Has he had any visitors in the past half hour or so?" The body, my lord the Commander reasoned to himself, was still warm, the blood still fluid. By no stretch of the imagination could Barbour have been dead more than half an hour.

"Visitors?" The old woman blinked, obviously trying to focus her thoughts. "Other than yourself, sir, I saw no visitors. But there! I mightn't have seen him at all. I was out for a few minutes, a few minutes only. I went to the shop of Goodman Fentner, the tobacconist, for a bit of snuff, as is the only form of tobacco I uses."

Commander Lord Ashley looked sharply at her. "Exactly when did you leave and when did you come back, Goodwife? It may be of the utmost importance that the time be known."

"Why . . . why . . . it was just afore you come, good sir," the old woman said rather nervously. "As I come in, I heard the bell of St. Denys strike the three-quarter hour."

Lord Ashley looked at his own watch. It was one minute after eleven. "The man must have waited until he saw you leave; then he came up and came down again before you returned. How long were you gone?"

"Only as long as it takes to walk to the corner and back, sir. I don't like to stay too long away in the daytime when the door is open." She paused and a vaguely puzzled frown came over her face. "Who was it must have come up and gone down, sir?"

"Whoever it was," said my lord the Commander, "stabbed your tenant Georges Barbour through the heart. He was murdered, Goodwife, and that is why we must call an Armsman without delay."

The poor woman was absolutely shaken now, and Lord

Ashley realized that she would be of no use whatever in
dealing with the Armsmen. He was glad that he had asked
her about any possible visitors before he had mentioned that
the death was murder; otherwise, her valuable testimony
might have flown from her head completely.

"Sit down, Goodwife," he said in a kindly voice. "Compose yourself. There is nothing to fear. I shall take care of
summoning the Armsmen." As the old woman practically
collapsed into the shabby overstuffed chair she kept in her
office, Lord Ashley stepped to the outer door and opened
it. He had heard the noise of boys' high-pitched voices
outside, shrill with excitement over the game they were
playing.

Because of his years of Naval training, it was easy for
my lord the Commander to spot the urchin who was the
obvious leader of the little group.

"Here, my lad!" he called out. "You, lad, with the green
cap! How should you like to earn yourself a sixth-bit?"

The boy looked up, and his slightly grimy face broke into
a smile. "I would, my lord!" he said, snatching the rather
faded green cap from his head. "Very much, my lord!" He
had no notion whether the personage who had addressed
him actually was a lord or not, but the personage in question
was most certainly a gentleman, and such a person one
always addressed as "my lord" whenever there was a job
in the offing.

The other boys became suddenly silent, obviously hoping that they, too, might gain some small pecuniary advantage from this obviously affluent gentleman.

"Very well, then," said Lord Ashley briskly. "Here is a
twelfth. If you return here with an Armsman inside of five
minutes, I shall give you another like it."

"An . . . an *Armsman*, my lord?" It was obvious that he
could not conceive of any possible reason why any sane
person would want an Armsman within a thousand yards
of him.

"Yes, an Armsman," Lord Ashley said with a smile. "Tell
him that Lord Ashley, a King's Officer, desires his immediate assistance and then lead him back here. Do you
understand?"

"Yes, My Lord Ashley! A King's Officer, my lord! Yes!"

"Very good, my lad. And you others. Here is a twelfth-bit

apiece. If you come back with an Armsman within five minutes, you, too, will get another twelfth. And the first one to come back gets a sixth-bit for a bonus. Now run! Off with you!"

They scattered to the winds.

At half past two that afternoon, three men met in a comfortable, club-like room in the Admiralty Headquarters Building of His Imperial Majesty's Naval Base at Cherbourg.

Commander Lord Ashley sat tall, straight, and at ease, his slightly wavy brown hair brushed smooth, his uniform immaculate. He had changed into uniform only twenty minutes before, having been informed by the Lord Admiral that, while this was not exactly a formal meeting, civilian dress would not be as impressive as the royal blue and gold uniform of a full Commander.

Lord Ashley might not have been called handsome; his squarish face was perhaps a little too ruggedly weatherbeaten for that. But women admired him and men respected the feeling of determination that his features seemed to give. His eyes were gray-green with flecks of brown, and they had that seaman's look about them—as though Lord Ashley were always gazing at some distant horizon, inspecting it for signs of squalls.

Lord Admiral Edwy Brencourt had the same look in his blue eyes, but he was some twenty-five years older than Lord Ashley, although even at fifty-two his hair showed touches of gray only at the temples. His uniform, of the same royal blue as that of the Commander, was somewhat more rumpled, because he had been wearing it since early morning, but this effect was partially offset by the gleaming grandness of the additional gold braid that encased his sleeves and shoulders.

In comparison with all this grandeur, the black-and-silver uniform of Chief Master-at-Arms Henri Vert, head of the Department of Armsmen of Cherbourg, seemed rather plain, although it was impressive enough on most occasions. Chief Henri was a heavy-set, tough-looking man in his early fifties who had the air and bearing of a stolid fighter.

Chief Henri was the first to speak. "My lords, there is more to this killing than meets the eye. At least, I should say, a great deal more than meets *my* eye."

He spoke Anglo-French with a punctilious precision which showed that it was not his natural way of speaking. He had practiced for many years to remove the accent of the local *patois*—an accent which betrayed his humble beginnings— but his effort to speak properly was still noticeable.

He looked at My Lord Admiral. "Who was this Georges Barbour, your lordship?"

My Lord Admiral picked up the brandy decanter from the low table around which the three of them sat and carefully filled three glasses before answering the Chief's question. Then he said: "You understand, Chief Henri, that this case is complicated by the fact that it involves Naval Security. Nothing that is said in this room must go beyond it."

"Of course not, my lord," Chief Henri said. He was well aware that this area of the Admiralty offices had been carefully protected by potent and expensive guarding spells. His Majesty's Armed Forces had a special budget for obtaining the services of the most powerful experts in that field, magicians who stood high in the Sorcerer's Guild. These were far more powerful than the ordinary commercial spells which guaranteed privacy in public hotels and private homes.

Admiral Brencourt carefully replaced the glass stopple in the brandy decanter before he spoke again. "I'm afraid I must apologize to you, Chief Henri. Acting under my orders, Commander Lord Ashley has withheld information from the plainclothes Sergeant-at-Arms who questioned him about the Barbour murder this morning. That was, of course, for security reasons. But I have now authorized him to tell you the entire story. If you will, my lord . . ."

Lord Ashley tasted his brandy. Chief Henri waited respectfully for him to speak. He knew that certain things would still be omitted, that Lord Ashley had been briefed as to which details to reveal and which to conceal. Nevertheless, he knew that the story would be much richer in detail than it had been when he first heard it.

Lord Ashley lowered his glass and set it down. "Yesterday morning," he began, "Monday, October 24th, I received a special sealed packet from the Office of the Lord High Admiral in London. My orders were to deliver it to Admiral Brencourt this morning. I left London by train to Dover, thence across the Channel by special Naval courier boat to Cherbourg. By the time I arrived, it was nearly midnight."

He paused and looked candidly at Chief Henri. "I should point out here that if my orders had been marked 'Most Urgent,' I should have immediately taken pains to deliver the packet to My Lord Admiral, no matter what the hour. As it was, my orders were to deliver it to him this morning. I give you my word that that packet never left my sight, nor was it opened, between the time I received it and the time it reached the Admiral's hands."

"I can verify that," said Admiral Brencourt. "As you are aware, Chief Henri, our Admiralty sorcerers cast spells upon the envelopes and seals of such packets—spells which, while they do not insure that the packets will not be opened by unauthorized persons, *do* insure that they cannot be opened without detection."

"I understand, my lord," said the Chief Master-at-Arms. "You had your sorcerer check the packet, then." It was a statement, not a question.

"Yes," said the Admiral. "Continue, Commander."

"Thank you, my lord," said Lord Ashley. Then, addressing Chief Henri, "I spent the night at the Hotel Queen Jeanne. This morning at nine, I delivered the packet to My Lord Admiral." He glanced at the Admiral and waited.

"I opened the packet," Admiral Brencourt said immediately. "Most of what it contained is irrelevant to this case. There was, however, an enclosure which I was directed to hand over to Commander Lord Ashley. He was directed to take a certain sum of money to one Georges Barbour. That was the first that either of us had ever heard of Georges Barbour." He looked back at Lord Ashley, inviting him to take up the tale.

"According to my instructions within that sealed envelope," Ashley said, "I was to take the money immediately to Barbour, who was, it seems, a double agent, working ostensibly for His Slavonic Majesty Casimir of Poland, but in actuality working for the Naval Intelligence Service of the Imperial Navy. The money was to be delivered to Barbour between fifteen minutes of eleven and fifteen minutes after. I went to the appointed spot, spoke to the concierge, went upstairs, and found the door partially open. I rapped, and the door swung open farther. I saw Georges Barbour lying on the floor with a knife in his heart." He paused and spread his hands. "I was surprised by that development, naturally, but I had my duty to do. I removed his private papers—those on his desk—and I searched the room. The papers were turned over to the Admiral."

"You must understand, Chief Henri," said Admiral Brencourt, "that there was a possibility that some of those papers might have borne coded or secret messages. None of them did, however, and the lot will be turned over to you. Lord Ashley will describe to you where each item lay in the room."

Chief Henri looked at the Commander. "Would you mind submitting a written report, with a sketch map indicating where the papers and so on were?" He was more than a little piqued at the Navy's high-handed treatment of evidence in a murder case, but he knew there was nothing he could do about it.

"I will be happy to prepare such a report," said Lord Ashley.

"Thank you, your lordship. A question: Were the papers disarrayed in any way—scattered?"

The Commander frowned slightly in thought. "Not *scattered,* no. That is to say, they did not appear to have been thrown around haphazardly. But they were not all in one pile. I should say that they were . . . er . . . neatly disarrayed, if you follow my meaning. As though Barbour had been going through them."

"Or someone *else* had gone through them," said the Chief thoughtfully.

"Yes. That's possible, of course," the Commander agreed. "But would the killer have had time to look through Barbour's papers?"

"Suppose," the Chief said slowly, "that there was one single paper—or maybe a single set of them—that the killer was after. And suppose he knew enough to be able to recognize those papers on sight. He wouldn't have needed more than a few seconds to find them, would he?"

The Commander and the Admiral glanced at each other.

"No," said the Commander after a moment. "No, he wouldn't."

"Do you have any idea what such paper or papers might pertain to?" Chief Henri asked with deceptive casualness.

"None," said My Lord Admiral firmly. "And I give you my word that I am concealing nothing. This office was not even aware of the very existence of Georges Barbour; we have no idea what he was doing or what sort of papers he may have been handling. This was our first knowledge of him, and we have received no further word from London. Thus far, London does not, of course, even know he is dead. One day, perhaps, some sorcerer may discover a way to get teleson lines across the Channel, but until then we must rely on dispatches sent by courier."

"I see." Chief Henri rubbed his hands together rather nervously. "I trust that your lordships understand that I am bound to do my duty. A murder has been committed. It must be solved. I am bound to expend every effort to discover the identity of the killer and bring him to justice. There are certain steps which I must, by law, take."

"We quite realize that, Chief Henri," said the Lord Admiral.

The Chief finished the rest of his brandy. "At the same time, we have no desire to hamper the Navy in any way nor to disclose information publicly that may be of benefit to our country's enemies."

"Naturally," the Lord Admiral agreed.

"But this case is a difficult one," Chief Henri went on. "We know—thanks to the evidence of the concierge—the time at which the crime was committed to within ten minutes. We know that Barbour stayed in that room all night, left this morning at about five minutes of ten, and came back at approximately twenty after. Everyone else in the house had left much earlier, since they are all working folk. There was no one in the building except Barbour and the concierge. All very fine so far as it goes.

"But this case is almost clueless. We do not know Barbour. We have no notion of whom he might have known, whom he might have met, or with whom he might have had dealings. We have no idea who might have owned the very common knife with which he was killed.

"When all that is added to the international ramifications of this affair, I am forced to admit that the case is beyond me. The law is clear upon that point; I must notify the Investigation Department of His Royal Highness at Rouen."

Admiral Brencourt nodded. "That's quite clear. Certainly, anyone from His Highness' offices would be of assistance. Is there any further way in which we can help you?"

"If it is possible, My Lord Admiral, there is. Presumably

someone in London knows something about this fellow
Barbour. If it would not be a violation of security, I should
like to know as much about him as possible. I should like
very much to have more information from London."

"I shall certainly see what can be done, Chief Henri," the
Lord Admiral said. "Lord Ashley is returning to England
within the hour. The Office of the Lord High Admiral must
be informed of this development immediately, of course. I
shall send a letter requesting the information you desire."

In spite of himself, Chief Henri grinned. "By the Blue!
Lord Darcy is never wrong!"

"Darcy?" My Lord Admiral blinked. "I don't . . . Oh, yes.
I recall now. Chief Investigator for His Highness. He cleared
up that situation here in Cherbourg last year—the 'Atlantic Curse' business—didn't he?"

Chief Henri coughed delicately. "I may say that he did,
My Lord Admiral. I am not permitted to discuss details."

"Of course, of course. But why do you say that he is never
wrong?"

"Well, I have never known him to be," Chief Henri said
staunchly. "When I made my call to Rouen to inform his
lordship of the murder, he told me that he would not be
able to come immediately, that he was sending down his
second-in-command, Sir Eliot Meredith, to take charge until
he could get here. He also said that you would undoubtedly be sending a courier to London almost immediately
and he wondered if I would be so good, as he put it, to
ask My Lord Admiral if the courier could carry a special
message for him."

Lord Admiral Brencourt chuckled. "An astute gentleman,
Lord Darcy. I dare say we can see our way clear to that.
What is the nature of the message?"

"Lord Darcy's chief forensic sorcerer, Master Sean O
Lochlainn, is attending a convention in London at the Royal
Steward Arms. He would like you to convey the message
that he is to return to Normandy, to come straight here to
Cherbourg, as soon as possible."

"Certainly," the Lord Admiral said agreeably. "If you will
write the letter, Lord Ashley will deliver it upon his arrival.
The Royal Steward is not far from the Admiralty offices."

"Thank you," said Chief Henri. "The mail packet will not
leave Cherbourg until this evening, and the letter wouldn't

be delivered until late tomorrow afternoon. This will save a great deal of time. May I borrow pen and paper?"

"Certainly; here you are."

Chief Henri dipped the Admiral's pen in the inkstand and began to write.

CHAPTER 2

Sean O Lochlainn, Master Sorcerer, Fellow of the Royal Thaumaturgical Society, and Chief Forensic Sorcerer to His Royal Highness, Richard, Duke of Normandy, was excruciatingly angry and doing his best not to show it. That his attempt to do so was highly successful was due almost entirely to his years of training as an officer of the law; had his Irish blood been allowed to follow its natural bent, it would have boiled over. But above all things, a sorcerer must have control over his own emotions.

He was not angry at any person, least of all himself. He was furious with Fate, with Chance, with Coincidence—poor targets upon which to vent one's wrath even if one were to allow oneself to do so. Therefore, Master Sean channeled his ire, converted it, and allowed it to show as a pleasant smile and a pleasant manner.

But that did not keep him from thinking more about the paper he had spent six months in preparing, only to find that he had been anticipated, than in listening to what his lordship the Bishop of Winchester was saying. His eyes wandered over the crowd in the Main Exhibit Hall while the voice of the Bishop—who was a fine thaumaturgist and Healer, but a crashing bore—droned on in his right ear, keeping just enough attention on the episcopal voice to enable him to murmur "Yes, my lord," or "Indeed, my lord," at appropriate intervals.

Most of the men and women in the hall were wearing the light blue dress clothing appropriate to sorcerers and sorceresses, but there were many spots of clerical black, and several of episcopal purple. Over in one corner, four bearded Healers in rabbinical dress were conversing earnestly with the Archbishop of York, whose wispy white hair seemed to form a cloud around his purple skullcap. Over near the door, looking rather lost, was a Naval Commander in full dress uniform, complete with gold braid and a thin, narrow-bladed dress sword with a gilded hilt. Master Sean wondered briefly why a Naval officer was here. To give a paper, or as a guest?

His attention shifted to the botanical section of the exhibit. He thought he recognized the back of the man who was standing in front of a row of potted herbs.

"I wonder what *he's* doing here?" he muttered without thinking.

"Um-m-m?" said the Bishop of Winchester. "Who?"

"Oh. I beg your pardon. I thought I recognized a colleague of my master, Lord Darcy, but I couldn't be sure, since his back is turned."

"Where?" asked my lord the Bishop, turning his head.

"Over at the botanical display. Isn't that Lord Bontriomphe, Chief Investigator for London? It looks like him from here."

"Yes, I believe it is. The Marquis of London, as you may know, makes a hobby of cultivating rare and exotic herbs. Very likely he sent Bontriomphe down here to look over the displays. My lord the Marquis leaves his palace but seldom, you know. Dear me! Look at the time! Why, it's after nine! I had no idea it was so late! I must deliver an address at ten this morning, and I promised Father Quinn, my Healer, that I'd have a short session with him before that. You must excuse me, Master Sean."

"Of course, my lord. It has been most pleasant." Master Sean took the outstretched hand, bowed, and kissed the ring.

"Indeed, I found it most enlightening, Master Sean. Good day."

"Good day, my lord."

Physician, heal thyself, Master Sean thought wryly. The phrase was archaic only in that Healers no longer relied on "physick" to heal their patients. When the brilliant genius, St. Hilary Robert, worked out the laws of magic in the Fourteenth Century, the "leech" and the "physician" might have heard their death knell ringing from the bell tower of the little English monastery at Walsingham, where St. Hilary lived. Not everyone could use the laws; only those who had the Talent. But the ceremony of healing by the Laying On of Hands had, from that time on, become as reliable as it had been erratic before. However, it was still easier to see— and to remove—the speck in one's brother's eye than to see the beam in one's own. Besides, my lord of Winchester was a very old man, and the two ailments still incurable by the finest Healers were old age and death.

Master Sean looked back at the botanical display, but Lord Bontriomphe had vanished while the Bishop was taking his leave, and, look as he might, the tubby little Irish sorcerer could not locate the Chief Investigator of London anywhere in the crowd.

The Triennial Convention of Healers and Sorcerers was an event which Master Sean always looked forward to with pleasure, but this time the pleasure had soured—badly. To find that a paper, which one had been researching for three years and writing on for six months, has been almost exactly paralleled by the work of another is not conducive to overwhelming joy. Still, there was no help for it, Sean thought, and, besides, Sir James Zwinge felt as upset about it as Sean O Lochlainn did.

"Ah! Good morning, Master Sean! You slept well last night, I trust?" The brisk, rather dry voice came from Master Sean's left.

He turned quickly and gave a medium bow. "Good morning, Grand Master," he said pleasantly. "I slept reasonably well, thank you. And you?"

Master Sean had *not* slept well, and the Grand Master not only knew he hadn't but knew *why* he hadn't. But not even Master Sean O Lochlainn would argue with Sir Lyon Gandolphus Grey, K.G.L., M.S., Th.D., F.R.T.S., Grand Master of the Most Ancient and Honorable Guild of Sorcerers.

"As well as yourself," said Sir Lyon. "But at my age, one must not expect to sleep well. I should like to introduce you to a promising young man."

The Grand Master was an imposing figure, tall, thin almost to the point of emaciation, yet with an aura of strength about him, both physical and psychical. His hair was silvery gray, as was the rather long beard which he affected. His eyes were deep-set and piercing, his nose thin and aquiline, his brows bushy and overshadowing.

But Master Sean had known the Grand Master so long that his face and figure were too familiar to be remarkable. The tubby little Irish sorcerer found his eyes drawn to the young man who stood next to Sir Lyon.

The man was of average height, taller than Master Sean

but not nearly as tall as Sir Lyon Grey. The sleeves of his blue dress suit were slashed with white, denoting a Journeyman Sorcerer, instead of the silver of a Master. It was his face which drew Master Sean's attention. The skin was a dark reddish-brown, the nose broad and well shaped, the nearly black pupils of his eyes almost hidden beneath heavy lids. His mouth was pleasantly smiling and rather wide.

"Master Sean," said Sir Lyon, "may I present Journeyman Lord John Quetzal, fourth son of His Gracious Highness, the Duke of Mechicoe."

"A pleasure to meet your lordship," Master Sean said with a slight bow.

Lord John Quetzal's bow was much deeper, as befitted Journeyman to Master. "I have looked forward to this meeting, Master," he said in almost flawless Anglo-French. Master Sean could detect only the slightest trace of the accent of Mechicoe, one of the southernmost duchies of New England, not far north of the isthmus which connected the continent of New France. But then, one would expect a regional accent from a scion of the Moqtessuma family.

"Lord John Quetzal," said Sir Lyon, "has determined to take up the study of forensic sorcery, and I feel he will do admirably in that field. And now, if you will excuse me, I must see the Program Committee and check up on the agenda."

And Master Sean found himself left with Journeyman Lord John Quetzal. He gave the young man his best Irish smile. "Well, your lordship, I see that you're not only quite intelligent but that you have a powerful Talent."

The young Mechicain's face took on an expression of startled awe.

"You can tell that just by looking?" he asked in a hushed voice.

Master Sean's smile broadened. "No, I deduced it." *Lord Darcy should hear me now,* he thought.

"Deduced it? How?"

"Why, bless you," Master Sean said with a chuckle, "the introduction you got from Grand Master Sir Lyon was enough to tell me that. 'A promising young man,' he calls you. 'I feel he will do admirably,' he says. Why, Sir Lyon Grey wouldn't introduce the King himself that way, the King having no Talent to speak of. If you have impressed the

Grand Master, you come highly recommended indeed. Further, I can deduce that you're not the kind of lad who'd let praise go to his head—else the Grand Master wouldn't have said such a thing in your hearing."

Master Sean could sense that there was an embarrassed blush rising up beneath the young man's smooth mahogany skin, and quickly changed the subject. "What's been your specialty so far?"

Lord John Quetzal swallowed. "Why . . . uh . . . black magic."

Master Sean stared, shocked. He could not have been more shocked if a Healer or chirurgeon had announced that he specialized in poisoning people.

The young Mechicain aristocrat looked even more flustered for a second or two, but he regained control quickly. "I don't mean I *practice* it! Good Heavens!" He looked round as if he were afraid someone might have overheard. Satisfied that no one had, he returned his attention to Master Sean. "I don't mean I *practice* it," he repeated in a lower voice. "I've been studying it with a view to its prevention, you see. I know you haven't much of it here in Europe, but . . . well, Mechicoe isn't the same. Even after four hundred years, there are still believers in the Old Religion—especially the worship of Huitsilopochtelie, the old War God. Not in the cities, or even in most of the rural farming areas, but in the remote places of the mountains and the jungles."

"Ah, I see. What sort of a god was this Eightwhatsisname?" asked Master Sean.

"Huitsilopochtelie. The sort of god that's quite common among barbaric peoples, especially militaristic ones. Rigid discipline, extreme asceticism, voluntary privation, and sacrifice were expected of his followers. A typical Satanic exaggeration of the virtues of chastity, poverty, and obedience. Sacrifice meant cutting the hearts out of living human beings. Huitsilopochtelie was a nasty, bloody devil."

"Human sacrifice—or, at least, the advocation of it is not unknown here," Master Sean pointed out.

Lord John Quetzal nodded. "I know to what you refer. The so-called Ancient Society of Holy Albion. Their ringleaders were cleaned up in May of 1965, as I recall—or early June."

"Aye," said Master Sean, "and that hasn't got rid of all

of 'em by any means. Black magic isn't as uncommon as you might think, either. The story wasn't released to the public, but as a Journeyman o' the Guild, you may have read about the case of Laird Duncan of Duncan, back in '63."

"Oh, yes. I read your write-up of it in the *Journal*. That was in connection with the mysterious death of the late Count D'Evreux. I should have liked to have been there when Lord Darcy solved that one!" There was a light in his obsidian eyes.

"What has your interest in forensic sorcery got to do with black magic?" asked the Irish sorcerer.

"Well, as I said, there is a lot of Huitsilopochtelie worship in the remoter parts of the Duchy—in fact, it gets worse farther south; my noble cousin, the Duke of Eucatanne, is constantly troubled by it. If it were just peasant superstition, it wouldn't be so bad, but some of those people have genuine Talent, and some of the better educated among them have found ways of applying the Laws of Magic to the rites and ceremonies of Huitsilopochtelie. And always for evil purposes. It's black magic of the worst kind, and I intend to do what I can to stamp it out. They don't confine their activities to the remote places where their temples are hidden; their agents come into the villages and terrorize the peasants and into the cities to try to disrupt the Government itself. That sort of thing must be stopped, and I will see that it *is* stopped!"

"A formidable ambition—and a laudable one. Do you—"

"Ah! Master Sean!" said an oily voice from just to the left and behind Lord John Quetzal.

Master Sean had noticed the approach of Master Ewen MacAlister, hoping—in vain, as it turned out—that Master Ewen would not notice him. He had enough troubles as it was.

"Master Ewen," said Master Sean with a forced smile. Before he could introduce Lord John Quetzal, Master Ewen, who totally ignored the journeyman sorcerer, began talking.

"Heard you had a bit of a set-to with Sir James yesterday, Sean, eh? Heheh."

"Hardly a set-to. We—"

"Oh, I didn't mean a quarrel. What *were* you arguing about, though? Nobody seems to know."

"Because it is nobody's business," snapped Master Sean.

"Of course not, heheh. Of course not. Still, it must have been something hot, or the Grand Master wouldn't have broken it up."

"He didn't 'break it up', as you put it," Master Sean said through set teeth that were wreathed in a false smile. "He merely arbitrated our discussion."

"Yes. Heheh. Naturally." The lanky, sandy-haired Scot smiled toothily. "But I don't blame you for being angry at Sir James. He can be pretty stiff at times. Heheh. Cutting, I mean. Sharp-tongued, he is."

"Quite sharp-tongued," said Lord John Quetzal in agreement. "I've felt the bite of it, myself."

Master Ewen MacAlister turned and looked at the young Mechicain as if seeing him for the first time. "It is not proper," he said chillingly, "for a Journeyman to interrupt the conversation of Masters, nor for a Journeyman to criticize a Master. And one would be wise in any case not to criticize the Chief Forensic Sorcerer for the City of London."

Lord John Quetzal's face became wooden, mask-like. He gave a courteous bow. "I beg your pardon, Master. I have erred. If you will excuse me, Masters, I have an appointment. I trust I may see you again, Master Sean."

"Certainly. How about lunch? I have some things I'd like to talk over with you."

"Excellent. When?"

"Noon, sharp. In the dining room."

"I shall be there. Good day, Master Sean, Master Ewen." He turned and walked away, proudly, even a little stiffly.

"Good day, your lordship," Master Sean said to his retreating back.

Master Ewen blinked. " 'Your lordship,' you said? Who is the boy?"

"Lord John Quetzal," said Master Sean with a malicious smile, "is the son of His Gracious Highness, Netsualcoyotle, Duke of Mechicoe."

Master Ewen paled visibly. "Dear me," he said in a low voice, "I do hope he wasn't offended."

"Your ingratiating ways will eventually make you many friends in high places, *Master* Ewen. And now, if you'll excuse me, I, too, have an appointment." He walked away, leaving MacAlister staring after the Mechicain lad and worrying his lower lip with his long horsey upper teeth.

Master Ewen's snobbery, Sean thought, would keep him from ever getting anywhere, no matter how good a magician he was. A Master had a perfect right to tick off a Journeyman, but for important things, not trivial ones. On the other hand, if one does exercise that right, one shouldn't go all puddingy just because the one ticked off happens to have high-ranking relatives. Master Sean decided he needed something to take the bad taste out of his mouth.

He looked at his wrist watch. Nine twenty-two. He still had time for a cool, foamy beer before his appointment. He headed for the private saloon bar that had been reserved for the Convention members and their guests. Five minutes later, with a pint of good English beer firmly ensconced in his round Irish belly, Sean was climbing the stairs to the upper floor. Then he walked down the hall toward the room that had been assigned to Master Sir James Zwinge, Chief Forensic Sorcerer for the City of London.

At precisely half past nine, Sean rapped on the door. There was no answer, but he fancied he could hear someone moving about inside so he rapped again, more loudly.

This time, he got an answer, but certainly not the one he had been expecting.

The scream was hoarse and reverberating, and yet the words were clear enough. *"Master Sean! Help!"*

And then came another sound which Sean recognized as that of someone—or something—heavy falling to the floor of the room.

Sean grabbed the door handle and twisted. To no avail; the door was locked firmly.

Other doors, up and down the corridor, were popping open.

CHAPTER 3

At precisely 7:03 that evening, Lord Darcy, Chief Investigator for His Royal Highness, Richard of Normandy, stepped out of a cab at the front door of the immense town house of my lord the Marquis of London. In Lord

Darcy's hand was a large suitcase and in his eye was a purposeful gleam.

The soldier at the door, wearing the bright yellow uniform of the Marquis' Own Guard, asked him his business, and Lord Darcy informed the guard in a quiet, controlled voice that My Lord Marquis was expecting Lord Darcy from Rouen.

The guardsman looked at the tall, rather handsome man with the lean face and straight brown hair and wondered. In spite of the name and the city he gave as his residence, the gentleman spoke Anglo-French with a definite English accent. Then the guardsman saw the cold light that gleamed in the eyes and decided that it would be better to check with Lord Bontriomphe before he asked any questions.

Lord Bontriomphe was at the door in less than a minute, ushering Lord Darcy in.

"Darcy! We weren't expecting you," he said with an affable smile.

"No?" Lord Darcy asked with a smile that had the hardness of chilled steel about it. "Am I to presume that you expected me to receive My Lord Marquis' message and then take off on a pilgrimage to Rome?"

Lord Bontriomphe noted the controlled anger. "We expected you to call us on the teleson from Dover," he said. "We would have had a carriage meet you at the station when the train pulled in."

"My Lord Marquis," said Lord Darcy coolly, "has not indicated that he was willing to pay for any expenses; therefore I assumed that such expenses would come out of my own pocket. Weighing the cost of a teleson message against the cost of a cab made me prefer the latter."

"Um-m-m. I see. Well, come on into the office. I think we'll find My Lord Marquis waiting for us." He led Lord Darcy down the corridor, opened a door and stood aside to allow Lord Darcy to pass.

The office was not immense, but it was roomy and well appointed. There were some comfortable-looking chairs and a large one covered with expensive red Moorish leather. There was a large globe of the world on a carved stand, two or three paintings—including a reproduction of a magnificent Vandenbosch which depicted a waterfall—and a pair of large desks.

Behind one of them sat my lord the Marquis de London.

The Marquis could only be described as immense. He was absolutely corpulent, but his massive face had a remarkable sharpness of expression, and his eyes had a thoughtful, introspective look. And in spite of a weight that was better than twenty stone, there was an air of firmness about him that gave him an almost regal air.

"Good evening, my lord," he said without rising, but extending a broad, fat hand that reminded one of the flipper of a seal.

"My Lord Marquis," said Lord Darcy, gripping the hand and releasing it.

Then, before the Marquis could say anything more, Lord Darcy put one hand firmly on the desk, palm down, leaned over to look down at de London, and said: "And now, how much of this is flummery?"

"You mock me," said the Marquis heavily. "Sit down, if you please; I don't like to have to crane my neck to look up at you."

Lord Darcy took the red leather chair without taking his eyes off the Marquis.

"None of it is flummery," the Marquis said. "I admit I do not have the full roster of facts, but I feel I have enough to justify my actions. Would you care to hear Lord Bontriomphe's report?"

"I would," Lord Darcy said. He turned and looked at the second desk, behind which Lord Bontriomphe had seated himself. He was a fairly tall, rather good-looking, square-jawed man who was always well dressed and carried about him an air of competence.

"You may report, Bontriomphe," said the Marquis.

"Everything?"

"Everything. The conversation verbatim."

Lord Bontriomphe leaned back and closed his eyes for a moment. Lord Darcy prepared himself to listen closely. Bontriomphe had two things which made him of tremendous value to the Marquis of London: a flair for narrative and an eidetic memory.

Bontriomphe opened his eyes and looked at Darcy.

"At my lord's orders," he said, "I went to the Sorcerers and Healers Convention to look at the herb displays. He was especially interested in the specimens of Polish devilwort, which he—

The Marquis snorted. "Pah! That has nothing to do with the murder."

"I haven't said it did. Where was I? Oh, yes. Which he hasn't been able to grow from the seed, only from cuttings. He wanted to find out how the seed-grown plants had been cultivated.

"I went in to the Royal Steward a little after nine. The place was packed with sorcerers of every size and description and enough clergy to fill a church from altar to narthex. I had to convince a couple of guards at the door that I wasn't just some tourist who wanted to gawk at the celebrities, but I made it to the herb displays at about ten after. I took a good long look at the Polish devilwort—it seemed to be thriving well—and then took a survey of the rest of the stuff. I took some notes on a few other rarities, but that wouldn't interest you, so I'll omit the details.

"Then I wandered around and looked at the rest of the displays, just to see if there was anything interesting. I didn't meet anyone I knew, which made me just as happy, since I hadn't gone there for chitchat. That is, I didn't meet any acquaintance until nine twenty. That was when Commander Lord Ashley tapped me on the shoulder.

"I turned around, and there he was, in full dress Naval uniform, looking as uncomfortable as a Navy officer at a magicians' convention.

" 'Bontriomphe,' he said, 'how good to see you again.'

" 'Good to see you,' I said, 'and how is the Imperial Navy? Have you become a Specialist in Sorcery?'

"That was a deliberate joke. Tony does have a touch of the Talent; he has what they call 'an intermittent and diffuse precognitive ability' that has helped him out of tight spots several times, and which, incidentally, is useful to him at the gaming tables. But in general he doesn't know any more about magic than an ostrich knows about icebergs.

"He laughed a little. 'Not yet and not ever,' he said. 'I'm here on Naval business. I'm looking for a friend of yours, but I don't know what he looks like.'

" 'Who are you looking for?' I asked.

" 'Master Sean O Lochlainn. I checked at the desk and got his room number, but he isn't in.'

" 'If he's around,' I said, 'I haven't seen him. But then I haven't been looking for him.'

"I stood there and looked around, but I couldn't spot him any place in that crowd. But I did happen to spot another face I knew.

" 'If anybody knows where Master Sean is,' I said, 'it will be Grand Master Sir Lyon Grey. Come along.'

"Sir Lyon was standing over near one of the doors talking to a man who was wearing the habit of one of the Flemish orders. The monk took his leave just as Lord Ashley and I approached Sir Lyon.

" 'Good morning, Sir Lyon,' I said. 'I think you've met Commander Ashley.'

" 'Good morning, Lord Bontriomphe,' the old sorcerer said. 'Yes, Commander Ashley and I have met. In what way may I be of assistance?'

" 'I have a message for Master Sean O Lochlainn, Sir Lyon,' said Ashley. 'Have you any idea where he is?'

"The Grand Master started to answer, but whatever he was going to say was lost. A scrawny little Master Sorcerer with a nose like a spike and rather bugged-out blue eyes suddenly popped from the door nearby, his hands fluttering about like a couple of drunken moths who had mistaken his head for a candle flame. He took a fast look around, saw Sir Lyon, and made a beeline for us, still flapping his hands.

" 'Grand Master! Grand Master! I must speak to you immediately!' he said in a low, excited voice.

" 'Compose yourself, Master Netly,' the Grand Master said. 'What is it?'

"Master Netly noticed Lord Ashley and me and said: 'It's . . . uh . . . confidential, Grand Master.'

"The Grand Master bent a little and cocked his head to one side while Master Netly, who is a good foot shorter than Sir Lyon, stood on tiptoe to whisper in his ear. I couldn't catch a word of what he said, but I saw Sir Lyon's eyes open wider as the skinny little sorcerer spoke. Then his eyes shifted and he looked straight at me.

"When he straightened up, he was still looking at me. And believe me when Grand Master Sir Lyon Gandolphus Grey fixes you with those eyes of his, you have an urge to search your conscience to see what particularly odious sins you have committed lately. Fortunately, my soul was reasonably pure.

" 'Will both of you gentlemen come with me, please?' he asked, shifting his gaze to Lord Ashley. 'Something of importance has come up. If you will be so good as to follow me . . .'

"He turned and went out the door, and Ashley and I followed. As soon as we got out of the exhibition hall and into the corridor, I asked: 'What seems to be the trouble, Sir Lyon?'

" 'I am not certain yet. But apparently something has happened to Master Sir James Zwinge. We are fortunate that you, as an officer of the King's justice, are on hand.'

"Then Lord Ashley said: 'Your pardon, Sir Lyon, but the delivery of this message to Master Sean is most important.'

" 'I am aware of that,' the old boy said rather testily. 'Master Sean is already at the scene. That is why I asked you to come along.'

" 'I see. I beg your pardon, Sir Lyon.'

"We followed him up the stairs and down the upper corridor without saying anything more. Netly pattered along with us, his hands still flitting about.

"There were three men and a woman standing in the hall outside the room that the management had assigned to Zwinge. Two of the men were wearing the light-blue dress clothing of sorcerers, and so was the woman. The third man was wearing ordinary merchant-class business clothes.

"One of the sorcerers was Master Sean. The second was a tall young man wearing the white slashes of a Journeyman, a Mechicain, by the look of him. The sorceress was one of the most beautiful honey blondes I have ever had the good fortune to meet in a hotel corridor, with a full-breasted, wide-shouldered, wide-hipped, narrow-waisted body and dark-blue eyes. She was only a couple of inches shorter than I am, and she—"

"Pfui—" For the second time, the Marquis of London interrupted the report of Lord Bontriomphe. "While you may enjoy dwelling upon the beauties of women, there is no need to do it, much less to overdo it. Darcy has already met Mary, Dowager Duchess of Cumberland. Continue."

"Sorry," Lord Bontriomphe said blandly. "The third man turned out to be Goodman Lewis Bolmer, the manager of the Royal Steward Arms. He's about an inch taller than Master Sean and looks as though he had lost about fifty pounds too fast. His face and jowls sag and give him a sort of floppy look, as if he were made up of hounds' ears. He looked both worried and frightened.

"I asked what had happened as soon as I had identified myself.

"Master Sean said: 'I had an appointment with Sir James at nine thirty, I knocked on the door and no one answered. I knocked again. Then I heard a scream and a sound as of a heavy body falling. Since then, there's been nothing. The door is locked, and we can't get in.'

"I looked at Goodman Lewis. 'Have you the key?'

" 'Yes, your lordship,' he said, nodding and jiggling his jowls. 'I brought it as soon as Master Netly told me what had happened. But it won't turn the bolt. It's stuck. Spell on it, I daresay.'

" 'It's a personalized lock spell,' Master Sean said. 'I'd say that only Sir James' key will open it. But I'm afraid he may be badly injured. We'll have to get that door down.'

"If you've ever been in the Royal Steward, you know how thick those doors are. Very old fashioned oak work—the building dates back to the Seventeenth Century.

" 'Can you take the spell off, Sean?' I asked.

" 'Sure and I can,' he said. 'But it would take time. Half an hour if I'm lucky and get the psychic pattern right away. Two or three hours if I'm not lucky. That's not just an ordinary commercial spell; that's a personal job put on there by Master Sir James himself.'

"I knelt down and took a peek through the keyhole. I couldn't see anything but the far wall of the room. The keyhole is big enough, but the door is so thick that it's like looking through a tunnel. Those doors are two inches thick.

"I stood up again and turned to Goodman Lewis. 'Go get an ax. We'll have to chop through.'

"He looked as if he were about to object, but he just said, 'Yes, your lordship. Right away,' and hurried away.

"While he was gone, I asked some questions. 'What happened right after you heard the scream, Sean?'

" 'Nothing for a few seconds,' he said. 'Then my colleagues, here, came out of their rooms.'

" 'Which rooms?'

" 'Netly Dale has the room to the left of Sir James' room, and Lord John Quetzal has the room to the right, if I am not mistaken.'

"Netly clasped his hands together to keep from fluttering them and nodded. 'That's right. Absolutely correct.'

"Lord John Quetzal just nodded his head in agreement.

" 'Lord John Quetzal,' I said. The name had struck a bell. 'You are the fourth son of His Gracious Highness, De Mechicoe, I think?'

"He bowed. 'The same, my lord.'

"Then I turned to the blond vision. I didn't know who she was at the time, but she was wearing the De Cumberland arms in full on her right breast instead of just the crest on her shoulder, so I deduced—"

Lord Bontriomphe stopped his narrative again as he heard a snort from de London. "Yes, my lord?"

"It is not necessary to inform us of your deductions of the obvious," said the Marquis with heavy sarcasm. "Darcy wants facts, not the rather puerile thought processes by which you may have arrived at them."

"I sit corrected, my lord," said Lord Bontriomphe. "At any rate, I correctly identified the lady.

" 'Where is your room, Your Grace?' I asked.

" 'Just across the hall,' she said, pointing.

"The hallways in the Royal Steward are eight feet wide, and her room was directly opposite Zwinge's.

" 'Thank you,' I said. 'Now . . .' I looked at the others . . . 'Why did you all come out of your rooms? What alarmed you?'

"They all said the same thing. The scream. None of them had heard Sean knocking; the doors are too thick for that to be noticed. I know; I tried it myself later. You can hear a knock on another door only if you listen carefully. That scream must have been a hell of a loud one. The only person to hear the body drop to the floor at that time was Sean. None of the others had opened their doors yet. I couldn't establish which one of the other three came out first; none of them noticed. There was evidently too much confusion at the time.

"When the manager, Goodman Lewis, came back with the ax, I glanced at my watch. It was twenty-three minutes of ten. Approximately seven minutes had passed since Sean had knocked on the door.

"I used the ax myself. Everyone else stood back, well away from the door. I cut a good-sized area out of the center without damaging either the frame or the lock. I kept everyone else out and squeezed through the hole I'd cut.

"It was an ordinary room, twelve by fifteen, with a bathroom. Across the room were two windows, both shuttered and bolted, but the shutters had been adjusted to let in the daylight. The glass panes were closed and unbroken.

"The body of our Chief Forensic Sorcerer was almost exactly in the middle of the room, more than six feet from the door. He was lying on his left side, in a pool of fresh blood, and there was so much blood on his jacket that it was hard for me to see at first what had happened. Then I saw that there was a rip in his jacket, high up on the left side of his chest, above the heart. I opened his jacket for a look. There was a vertical stab wound in the chest at that point.

"A couple of feet away, lying in the pool of blood, near the edge, was a knife. It was a heavy-handled one, with a black onyx hilt and a solid silver blade. I've seen knives like that before, Lord Darcy, and so have you. A sorcerer's knife, used in certain spells for symbolically cutting psychic linkages or something of the sort. But they can cut physically as well as psychically.

"About halfway between the body and the door was a key, the same kind of heavy brass key that the manager had tried to open the door with. I marked the spot with one of my own keys and then tried the key on the door. It worked; it turned the bolt, but no other key would. It was Sir James' key, all right.

"I searched the body. Nothing much there—his own key ring; two golden sovereigns, three silver sovereigns, and some odd change; a notebook full of magical symbols and equations which I don't understand; an ordinary small pocket-knife; a cardfolder which contained his certificate as a Master Sorcerer, his license to practice magic—signed by the Bishop of London—his official identification as Chief Forensic Sorcerer, a card identifying him as a Fellow of the Royal Thaumaturgical Society, and a few personal cards. You can look at it all, Darcy; My Lord Marquis has it in an envelope in the wall safe.

"He had three other suits, all hanging neatly in the closet, with nothing in the pockets. There were some papers on the desk, all filled with thaumaturgical symbolism, and more like them in the wastebasket. I left them where they were. The only other thing in the room was his symbol-decorated carpetbag—the kind every sorcerer carries. I didn't try to open it or move it; it is not wise to meddle with the belongings of magicians, not even dead ones.

"The point is that there was nobody in that room but the dead man. I searched it carefully. There was no place to hide. I looked under the bed and in the closet and in the bathroom.

"Furthermore, nobody could have left by that door. It had been locked by the only key that would lock it, and that key was inside the room. Besides, there were four people in that corridor within seconds after Sir James screamed, and three of them were watching that door from that time until I cut it open.

"The windows were bolted shut from the inside. The glass and the laths in the shutters were solid. The windows look out on a small patio which is a part of the dining area. There were twelve people out there—all sorcerers—who were eating breakfast. None of them saw anything, although their attention was directed to the windows by the scream. Besides, the wall is sheer—a thirty-foot drop without ledges, handholds, or toeholds. No exit that way.

"There is no evidence that anyone went into that room or came out of it.

"By the time I had searched the room, the Chief Master-at-Arms and two of his men had arrived. You've met Chief Hennely Grayme—big, husky chap with a square face? Yes. Well, I told him to take over, to get a preservation spell cast over the body, and to touch nothing.

"Then I went back out in the hall and herded everybody out of there and into one of the empty rooms down the hall. The manager gave me the key and I told him to go on about his business.

"Commander Lord Ashley was a little impatient. He had already delivered his message to Master Sean and had to report back to the Lord Admiral's office, so I told him to go ahead. Sir Lyon, Master Sean, Master Netly, Journeyman Lord John Quetzal, and the Dowager Duchess of Cumberland all looked shocked at what they'd seen through the door, and none of them seemed to have much to say.

" 'Sir Lyon,' I said, 'that room was locked and sealed. Sir James was stabbed at a time when there was no one else in the room. What do you make of it?'

"He stroked his beard for a moment, then said: 'I understand your question. Yes, on first glance I should say that he was killed by Black Magic. But that is merely a supposition based upon the physical facts. I do not suppose you can detect it yourself, but this hotel is not at present equipped with just the ordinary commercial spells for privacy, to prevent unwarranted use of the clairvoyant Talent. Before the Convention started a special group of six sorcerers went through the entire building reinforcing those spells and adding others. They do not affect precognition, since there is no way to cast a spell into the future, but they prevent anyone from using his clairvoyant Talent to see into another's room, and they make it very difficult to understand or detect what is going on in someone else's mind. Before I can state flatly that Sir James was killed by Black Magic I should want further investigation into the facts.'

" 'There will be,' I told him. 'Next question, then: Who had reason to kill him? Had anyone quarreled with him?'

"So help me, Lord Darcy, every eye in the room turned to Master Sean. Except Master Sean's, of course.

"Naturally, I asked him what the quarrel was about.

" 'It wasn't a quarrel,' he said firmly. 'Both Sir James and I were angry, but not at each other.'

" 'Who were you angry with, then?'

" 'Not with anyone. We had both been working on a new thaumaturgical effect, and had discovered almost identical spells to produce that effect. It has happened before in the history of magic. We may have been growling and snapping at each other, but we weren't angry at anything but the coincidence.'

" 'How did the . . . er . . . discussion come about? I asked him.

" 'Chance conversation in the committee room. We fell to talking and the subject came up. We compared notes, and . . . well, there it was. What we were really arguing about was who was to present his paper first. So we called Sir Lyon over to decide the problem.'

"I looked at Sir Lyon. He nodded. 'That's correct. I decided that it would be best for them to pool their findings and present the paper jointly, under both their names, with a full explanation that the work had been done by both independently.'

" 'Tell me, Sir Lyon,' I said, 'this paper—or these papers—wouldn't be just a lot of thaumaturgical equations, would they?'

" 'Oh, no. They would have a full exposition of the effect. There would be equations, of course, but the text would be in Anglo-French. Naturally, there would be a lot of technical words, professional jargon, if you will, but—'

" 'Where is Sir James' paper, then? I asked. 'It isn't in his room.'

" 'I have it,' said Sean. 'It was agreed between Sir James and myself that I should do a first collation between the two papers, and then we'd talk the thing over this morning at nine-thirty and do a second draft of our collaboration.'

" 'When was the last time you saw Sir James?' I asked.

" 'Last evening at about ten, it was,' Sean explained. 'I went with him to his room, so he could give me his manuscript. So far as I know, that's the last anyone saw of him. He was going to do a little further work he had in mind, and he didn't want to be disturbed until half past nine.'

" 'Would he have been using a knife for that work?'

" 'Knife?' he said, looking puzzled.

" 'You know. One of those big, black-handled silver knives.'

"Oh. You mean a contact cutter. I wouldn't think so; he said he wanted to do some paper work, is all. Not any actual experimentation. Still, I suppose it's possible.'

"I said, 'Master Sean, do you mind if I take a look at Sir James' manuscript?'

"I guess that must have fired his Irish temper up. 'I don't see what that has to do with this business,' he said peevishly. 'I've been working on this thing for three years. It was bad enough that Sir James was doing the same thing, but I'm not going to let out this information until I'm ready to present it myself!'

"Then Grand Master Sir Lyon spoke. 'I cannot insist that you show those papers to the Chief Investigator, Master Sean;

I cannot ask you to reveal the process. But I feel that the subject may possibly have a bearing on the case.'

"Master Sean opened his mouth and then closed it again. After a second or so, he said: 'Well, that's already on the Program anyway. My paper was to have been called "A Method of Performing Surgery Upon Inaccessible Organs." Sir James called his "The Surgical Incision of Internal Organs Without Breaching the Abdominal Wall." ' '

"That was when Master Netly squeaked, 'You mean a method of controlling a blade within an enclosed space? Astounding!' Then he backed away from Sean a couple of steps. *'That's* what he meant when he screamed!'

"That was the first I'd heard that Master Sir James had actually screamed words. The words were—and they all agreed on it—

" *'Master Sean! Help!'* "

The Marquis of London had been sitting during the entire narration with his eyes closed, but he was not asleep. "Satisfactory," he said. Then he opened his eyes, looking at Lord Darcy. "Now," he rumbled, "you understand why I felt constrained to order the arrest of Master Sean O Lochlainn on suspicion of murder."

CHAPTER 4

Lord Darcy looked long and deeply into the eyes of My Lord Marquis, and the Marquis calmly returned that steady gaze. At last Lord Darcy said: "I see. Do you consider the evidence conclusive, then?"

"Oh, by no means," said the Marquis, patting the air with a heavy hand. "I certainly should not care to place the case before the Court of High justice with the evidence now at hand. If I had that evidence, Master Sean would have already been charged with premeditated murder, not merely with suspicion."

"I see," Lord Darcy repeated, his voice icily polite. "Am I to presume that I will be expected to find that evidence?"

The Marquis de London lifted his massive shoulders perhaps a quarter of an inch and lowered them again. "It is a matter of indifference to me. However, understanding as I do your personal interest in the case, you may certainly count upon full co-operation from this office in any investigation you may care to undertake."

"Ahh. That's the way the wind blows, is it?" said Lord Darcy. "Very well. I accept your hospitality and your co-operation. Will you release Master Sean on his own recognizance until such time as the remainder of the evidence is in?"

My Lord Marquis frowned, and for the first time there seemed to be a touch of discomfort in his manner. "You know as well as I that a man arrested for a capital crime cannot be released on his own recognizance. Such is the law; I am powerless to abrogate the King's Law."

"Of course," murmured Lord Darcy. "Of course. I trust, however, that I may speak to Master Sean?"

"Naturally. He is in the Tower, and I have given orders that he is to be made comfortable. You may see him at any time."

Lord Darcy rose to his feet. "My thanks, my lord. In that case, I shall go about my business. May I have your leave to go?"

"You have my leave, my lord. Lord Bontriomphe will see you to the door." The Marquis of London rose ponderously to his feet and walked out of his office without another word.

Lord Darcy said nothing to Lord Bontriomphe until both of them were standing at the front door. Then he said: "My Lord Marquis likes to play games, Bontriomphe."

"Hm-m-m. Yes. Yes, he does." Bontriomphe paused. "I am certain you can handle this, Darcy."

"I think so. Don't be surprised by anything."

"I shan't. Good evening, my lord."

"Good evening. I shall see you on the morrow."

Master Sean O Lochlainn, in his comfortable room in that ancient fortress known as the Tower of London, was no longer angry—not even at Fate. The emotion that filled him now was a sort of determined patience. He knew Lord Darcy would come, and he knew that his imprisonment was purely nominal.

Earlier in the afternoon, when he had found himself charged with suspicion of murder, he had felt some small pique when he was told that he would not be allowed to bring his symbol-decorated carpetbag to the Tower with him. Locking up a sorcerer is difficult enough in itself; to allow him to have the tools of his trade would be foolish indeed.

But the Tower Wardens had erred in thinking that a sorcerer was helpless without his tools. They had not taken into account a certain spell that Master Sean had long since cast upon that symbol-decorated carpetbag. The effect of that spell can be expressed simply: The tools of a sorcerer cannot long be separated from their Master against his will. And the way the spell worked in practice was thus:

The carpetbag had been locked in Master Sean's room at the Royal Steward Arms, to remain there until such time as Master Sean's ultimate disposition should be decided. That had been ordered by the Chief Master-at-Arms at the time of Master Sean's arrest. Master Sean had delivered his key to the Chief Master-at-Arms in polite submission to the majesty of the law. But there had not been any special spell on the lock of Master Sean's room, such as there had been on the late Master James Zwinge's room. Therefore, when one of the hotel servants was making her cleaning rounds at one o'clock that afternoon, she had had with her a key to Master Sean's room—a key that would work.

Quite naturally, Bridget Courville took each room as she came to it. When she came to Master Sean's room, she went in and looked around.

"All's neat," she said to herself. "Bed unmade, but of course that's the way it always is. Ah, these sorcerers are neat enough, for sure. No bottles or trash scattered about. Not drinkers, much, I think. Which it shouldn't be for a sorcerer."

She tidied up—made the bed, laid out clean towels, put in new soap bars, and did all the other little things that needed to be done.

She noticed the symbol-decorated carpetbag, of course. There was one like it in almost every room during this convention. But she paid no attention to it consciously.

Her subconscious, however, whispered to her that "it didn't ought to be here."

It can be said that Bridget Courville really didn't think about what she was doing when she picked up the bag and set it out in the hall before she locked up the room and went on to the next one.

At one fifteen, a catering servant—a young lad in his late teens whose duty it was to see that drinks and food were brought to the guests when they were ordered—saw the bag sitting in the hall. It seemed out of place. Without bothering to think about it, he picked it up and took it downstairs. He left it on the luggage rack near the front entrance and promptly forgot about it.

Hennely Grayme, Chief Master-at-Arms for the City of London, having made all the notes he could on the scene of the crime, left the hotel at five minutes of two. He stopped near the door and saw the carpetbag on the luggage rack. He noticed the initials S. O L. on the handle. Automatically, he picked it up and took it with him. When he stopped by at the Tower, he said a few words to the Chief Warder and, without mentioning it, left the carpetbag behind.

The carpetbag remained unnoticed in the anteroom of the Chief Warder's office until fifteen minutes of three. During that time, many people went in and out of that anteroom without noticing the bag; none of them were going in the right direction.

At two forty-five, the Warder in charge of the cell in which Master Sean was incarcerated saw the bag. On his way out, after reporting to the Chief Warder, he picked up the bag.

Had he been going off duty, had he been going to the Middle Tower instead of St. Thomas' Tower, he would not even have noticed the symbol-decorated carpetbag. The spell was specific. But he did pick it up, and he did carry it up the spiral staircase to Master Sean's cell.

He unlocked the door to Master Sean's cell, then knocked politely.

"Master Sean, it is I, Warder Linsy."

"Come in, me boy, come in," said Master Sean jovially.

The door opened, and when Master Sean saw the carpetbag in the Warder's hand, he suppressed a smile and said: "What can I do for you, Warder?"

"I was to come up and see what you wanted for dinner, Master," Warder Linsy said deferentially. Absently he put the bag down inside the door.

"Ah, it's of no matter to me, my good Warder," said Master Sean. "Whatever the Chief Warder orders will be good enough for me."

Warder Linsy smiled. "That's good of you, Master." Then

he lowered his voice. "Ain't none of us thinks you done it, Master Sean. We knows a sorcerer couldn't of killed a man. Not that way, I mean. Not by black magic."

"Thank you for your confidence, me boy," Master Sean said expansively. "I assure you it's not misplaced. Now, if you'll excuse me, I have some thinking to do."

"Of course, Master. Of course." And Warder Linsy closed the door, locked it carefully, and went on about his business.

Lord Darcy's trip from the Palace du Marquis to the Tower of London was uneventful. The cab clattered out of Mark Lane, swerved, and descended Tower Hill. In Water Lane, at the gate, it stopped. Lord Darcy stepped out.

A heavy, whitish fog drifted through the bars of the great iron fence and clung to the shadows of the Gothic archways. There was a fading sound of bells as the ships on the Thames moved through the mist-laden waters. The air was muggy, and a faint smell of marine decay drifted over the wall that formed one side of the fortress. Lord Darcy wrinkled his nostrils at the aroma that assailed them, and then walked over the stone bridge that led from the Middle Tower to another tower—larger and gray-black, with a few whitish stones here and there in its walls. There was another archway, then a short, straight path, and then Lord Darcy turned toward the right and entered St. Thomas' Tower.

Within a few minutes, the Warder was unlocking the door to Master Sean's cell. "Call me when you wants to leave, your lordship," he said. He left, closing the door and relocking it.

"Well, Master Sean," said Lord Darcy with a spark of humor in his gray eyes, "I trust you are enjoying this idyllic relaxation from your onerous duties, eh?"

"Hm-m-m—yes and no, my lord," said the tubby little sorcerer. He waved a hand at the small plain table on which his carpetbag sat. "I can't say I enjoy being locked up, but it has given me an opportunity to experiment and meditate."

"Indeed? Upon what?"

"Upon getting in and out of locked rooms, my lord."

"And what have you learned, my good Sean?" Lord Darcy asked.

"I've learned that the security system here is quite good, but not quite good enough. To hold *me* in, I mean. The spell on that lock took me ten minutes to solve." He picked up a small wand of gleaming brass and twirled it between thumb and forefinger. "I relocked it, of course, my lord. No need to disturb the Warder, who's a decent sort of fellow."

"I see you regained possession of your bag of equipment easily enough. Well, one could hardly expect an ordinary prison magician to compete with a Master Sorcerer of your capabilities. Now pray be seated and explain to me in detail how you came to be incarcerated in one of London's oldest landmarks. Omit no detail."

Lord Darcy did not interrupt while Master Sean told his story. He had worked with the little sorcerer for years; he knew that Sean's memory was accurate and complete.

"And then," Master Sean finished, "Lord Bontriomphe brought me here—with, I must say, sincere apologies. I can't for the life of me see why the Marquis should order me locked up, though. Surely a man of his abilities should be able to see that I had nothing to do with Sir James' death."

Lord Darcy scooped tobacco from a leathern pouch and thumbed it into the gold-worked porcelain bowl of his favorite pipe. "Of course he knows you're innocent, my dear Sean," he said crisply. "My Lord Marquis is a parsimonious man and a lazy one. Bontriomphe is an excellent investigator, but he lacks the deductive faculty in its highest form. My Lord Marquis, on the other hand, is capable of brilliant reasoning, but he is both physically and mentally indolent. He leaves his own home but rarely, and never for the purpose of criminal investigation. When he is pressured into doing so, My Lord Marquis is perfectly capable of solving some of the most intricate and complex puzzles with nothing more to work with than the verbal reports given him by Lord Bontriomphe. His mind is—brilliant." Lord Darcy lit his pipe and surrounded himself with a cloud of fragrant smoke.

"Coming from you," said Master Sean, "that's quite a compliment"

"Not at all. It is merely a statement of fact. Perhaps it runs in the blood; we are cousins, you know."

Master Sean nodded. "At least the laziness doesn't run in the blood, my lord. But why lock me up because he's lazy?"

"Lazy *and* parsimonious, my good Sean," Lord Darcy corrected the sorcerer. "Both factors apply. He has already recognized that this case is far too complex for the relatively feeble powers of Lord Bontriomphe to cope with." Lord Darcy smiled and took the pipe from his lips. "You said a moment ago that I had complimented my lord's brilliancy. If that is so, then he has, in his own way, paid the same compliment to me. He is mentally lazy; therefore, he wishes to get someone else to do the work—someone competent to solve the problem with the same facility with which he would do it himself, were he to apply his mind. He has chosen me, and I flatter myself that he would not have chosen any other man."

"That still doesn't explain why he locked me up," Master Sean said. "He could have just asked you for assistance."

Lord Darcy sighed. "You have forgotten his parsimony again, my good Sean. Were he to ask His Royal Highness of Normandy to spare my services for a short while, he would be obligated to pay my salary from his own Privy Purse. But by incarcerating you, he deprives me of my most valued assistant. He knows I would not suffer you to be imprisoned one second longer than necessary. He knows that putting you in the Tower would force me to take a leave of absence, to solve the case on my own time, thereby saving himself a pretty penny."

"Blackmail," said Master Sean.

" 'Blackmail' is perhaps too strong a word," Lord Darcy said thoughtfully, "but I will admit that no other is quite strong enough. That problem, however, will be taken care of in its own time. At the moment, we are concerned with the death of Sir James.

"Now—what about the lock on Sir James' room?"

Master Sean settled himself deeper into his chair. "Well, my lord, as you know, most commercial spells are pretty simple, especially those where more than one key has to be used, as they have in a hotel."

Lord Darcy nodded patiently. Master Sean O Lochlainn had a rather pedagogical habit of framing his explanations as though they were lectures to be used in the training of apprentice sorcerers—which was not surprising, since the tubby little master magician had at one time taught in one of the Sorcerers' Guild's schools and had written two

textbooks and several monographs upon the subject. Lord
Darcy had long ago formed the habit of listening, even
though he had heard parts of each lecture before, for there
was always something to be learned, something new to be
stored away in the memory for future reference. Lord Darcy
did not have the inborn Talent necessary to make use of
the Laws of Magic directly, but one never knows when some
esoteric bit of data might become pertinent and useful to
a criminal investigator.

"The average commercial spell uses the Law of Contagion, so that every key which touches the lock during the
casting of the spell will unlock and lock it," Master Sean
continued. "But that means a relative weakening of the spell.
An ordinary duplicate key won't work the lock, but any good
apprentice o' the Guild could break the spell if he had such
a duplicate. And any Master could break it *without* the key
in a minute or two.

"But a personal spell by a Master uses the Law of Relevance to bind the whole lock-and-key mechanism together
as a unit—one key, one lock. The spell is cast with the key
in the lock, so that the binding considers the key simply
as a detachable part of the mechanism, if you follow me,
my lord. No other key will work, either to lock or to unlock
the mechanism, even if it is so physically like the proper
key that they couldn't be told apart."

"And Master Sir James' key-and-lock had that sort of spell
on it, eh?" Lord Darcy asked.

"That it did, my lord."

"Could a Master Sorcerer have removed the spell?"

Master Sean nodded. "Aye, that he could—in half an hour.
But look what that would entail, my lord.

"The Unknown would have to stand in that corridor for
at least half an hour, maybe more, going through the proper
ritual. Anyone who came by during that time couldn't help
but notice. Certainly Master Sir James would have noticed
if he was inside the room.

"But let's say the Unknown actually does that. Now he
opens the door with an ordinary duplicate, goes inside, and
kills Master Sir James. Fine.

"Then he comes out, and casts *another* spell on the
lock-and-key—with the key in the lock, as it must be. That
takes him another half hour.

"And *then* . . ."

Master Sean held up his forefinger dramatically.

" . . . And *then—he has to get that key back into the room!*"

Master Sean spread his hands, palms upward. "I submit that it isn't possible, my lord. Not even for a magician."

Lord Darcy puffed thoughtfully at his pipe for the space of two seconds. Then he said: "Is it not theoretically possible to move an object from one point in space to another without actually traversing the space between the two points?"

"Theoretically?" Master Sean made a wry grin. "Oh, yes, my lord. *Theoretically.* The Transmutation of metals is theoretically possible, too. But, like instantaneous transportation, no one has ever done it. If anyone did solve the rites and ceremonies necessary, it would be the biggest scientific breakthrough of the Twentieth Century. It couldn't be kept quiet. It is simply beyond our present stage of science, my lord.

"And when and if it is ever done, my lord, the process will not be used for such minor things as moving a big brass key a few feet."

"Very well, then," said his lordship, "we can eliminate that."

"The trouble is," said Master Sean, "that all those heavy privacy spells make it difficult for a man to do his work properly. If it weren't for them, your job would be simple."

"My dear Sean," said Lord Darcy with a smile, "if it were not for the privacy spells used in every hotel, private home, office building, and in public structures of all kinds, my job would not be simple, it would be nonexistent.

"Although the clairvoyant Talent is no doubt a useful one, its indiscriminate use leads to so much encroachment upon personal privacy and individual rights that we must protect ourselves from it. Imagine what a clairvoyant could do in a world where such protective spells were not used. There would be no need for investigators like myself. In such a world the police would have merely to bring the case to the attention of a clairvoyant, who would immediately inform them of how the crime was committed and who had committed it.

"On the other hand, think what opportunity there would be for a corrupt government to employ such clairvoyants to spy upon private citizens for their own nefarious purposes. Or think of the opportunities for criminal blackmail.

"We must be thankful that modern privacy spells protect us from such improper uses of the Talent, even though it makes physical investigation of a crime necessary. Even as it is, I am never called upon when something happens in the countryside. If a person is killed in a field or in a forest, a journeyman sorcerer working for the local Armsmen can easily take care of the job—as easily as he finds lost children and strayed animals. It is in the cities, towns and villages where my ability to deduce facts from physical and thaumaturgical evidence makes me useful.

"It is my job to find method, motive, and opportunity." He took a small, silver, ivory-handled tool from his pocket and began tamping the ashes in his pipe. "Method, motive and opportunity," he repeated thoughtfully. "So far we have no candidates for the first two and entirely too many for the last." He returned the tamper to his pocket and the pipe to his mouth.

"Normally, my dear Sean," he continued, "when a case appears to have magical elements in it, finding the magician involved is a prime factor in the problem. You will recall the interesting behavior of Laird Duncan at Castle D'Evreux, the curious habits of the one-armed tinker at the Michaelmas Fair, the Polish sorcerer in the Atlantic Curse problem, the missing magician in the Canterbury blackmail case, and the odd affair of Lady Overleigh's solid gold chamber pot. In each case, only one sorcerer was directly involved.

"But what have we here?" Lord Darcy gestured with his pipe in the general direction of the Royal Steward Hotel. "We have nearly half the licensed sorcerers of the Empire, a collection that includes some seventy-five or eighty percent of the most powerful magicians on Earth.

"We are faced with a plenitude—indeed, a plethora—of suspects, all of whom have the ability to use black magic against Master Sir James Zwinge, and had the opportunity of doing so."

Master Sean thoughtfully massaged his round Irish nose between the thumb and forefinger of his left hand. "I can't understand why any of 'em would do it, my lord. Every Guild member knows the danger of it. *'The mental state necessary to use the Talent for black sorcery is such that it invariably destroys the user.'* That's a quote from one of the basic textbooks, my lord, and every *grimoire* contains a variation of it. How could any sorcerer *be* so stupid?"

"Why do chirurgeons occasionally become addicts of the poppy distillates?" Lord Darcy asked.

"I know, my lord; I know," Master Sean said wearily. *"One act of black magic isn't fatal; it doesn't even cause any detectable mental or moral change in many cases. But the operative word there is 'detectable.' And that's because the moral rot must already have set in before a man with the Talent would even consider practicing black magic."*

Even though it had happened before and would happen again, no member of the Guild of Sorcerers liked the idea that any single other member would resort to the perversion of his Art that constituted Black Magic.

Not that they were afraid to face it—oh, no! Face it they must, and face it they did—with a vengeance. Lord Darcy knew—although very few who were not high-ranking Masters of the Guild had that knowledge—exactly what happened to a member who was found guilty of using his Talent for evil.

Destruction!

The evil sorcerer, convicted by his own mind, convicted by the analysis of a true jury of his true Peers, convicted by those who could really understand and sympathize with his motives and reasons, was condemned to have his Talent . . .

. . . Removed.

. . . Obliterated.

. . . Destroyed.

A Committee of Executors was appointed—a group of sorcerers large enough and powerful enough to overcome the Talent-power of the guilty man.

And when they were through, the convicted man had lost nothing but his Talent. His knowledge, his memory, his morals, his sanity—all remained the same. But his ability to perform magic was gone . . . never to return.

"Meanwhile," said Lord Darcy, "we have a problem of our own. Commander Lord Ashley gave you my message?"

"Indeed he did, my lord."

"I hate having to take you away from the Convention,

my good Sean; I know what it means to you. But this is no ordinary murder; it concerns the security of the Empire."

"I know, my lord," said Master Sean, "duty is duty." But there was a touch of sadness in his voice. "I did rather want to present my paper, but it will be published in the Journal, which will be just as good."

"Hm-m-m," said Lord Darcy. "When were you scheduled to present your paper?"

"On Saturday, my lord. Master Sir James and I were going to combine our papers and present them jointly, but of course that is out of the question now. They'll have to be published separately."

"Saturday, eh?' said Lord Darcy. "Well, if we can get back to Cherbourg by tomorrow afternoon, I should say that most of the urgent work will be cleared up within twenty-four hours, say by Friday afternoon. You could take the evening boat back and be in time to present both your paper and the late Master Sir James'."

Master Sean brightened. "That's good of you, my lord! But you'll have to get me out o' this plush cell if we're to get the job done!"

"*Hah!*" Lord Darcy shot suddenly to his feet. "My dear Master Sean, *that* problem has, I think, already been solved— although it may take a little time to make the . . . er . . . proper arrangements. And now I shall bid you good night; I shall see you again tomorrow."

CHAPTER 5

The fog had thickened in the courtyard below the high, embattled walls surrounding the Tower of London, and beyond the Water Lane gate the world seemed to have disappeared into a wall of impalpable cotton wool. The gas lamps in the courtyard and above the gate seemed to be shedding their light into nothingness.

"Had you no one waitin' for you, your lordship?" asked the Sergeant Warder as he stood on the steps with Lord Darcy.

"No," Lord Darcy admitted. "I came in a cab. I must confess I failed to check with the weather prognostication. How long is the fog to last?"

"According to the chief sorcerer at the Weather Office, your lordship, it isn't due to break up until five minutes after five o'clock in the morning. It's to turn to a light drizzle, which will clear at six twelve."

"Well, I certainly can't stay here until sun-up," Lord Darcy said ruefully.

"I'll have the man at the gate see if he can't whistle you up a cab, your lordship; it's still fairly early. You can wait in the outer—" He stopped. From somewhere in the fog that choked Water Lane came the clatter of hooves and the rattle of wheels, becoming increasingly louder.

"That may be a cab, now, your lordship!" He raised his authoritative voice to a commanding bellow: *"Warder Jason! Signal that cab!"*

"Yes, Sergeant!" came a fog-muffled voice from the gate, followed immediately by the shrill *beep! beep! beep!* of a cab whistle.

"I fear we are to be disappointed, Sergeant," Lord Darcy said. "Your ears should tell you that the vehicle approaching is drawn by a pair; therefore, it is a private town-carriage, not a public cab. There is no cabman in the whole of London who would be so profligate as to use two horses where one will do."

The Sergeant Warder cocked one ear toward the sound. "Hm-m-m. Dare say you're right, your lordship. It *do* sound like a pair, now I listen closer. Still . . ."

"They are a well-trained pair," said his lordship. "Almost perfectly in step. But since two hooves cannot possibly strike the paving stones at precisely the same instant, there is a slight echo effect, clearly discernible to the trained ear."

The beeping sound of the whistle had stopped. Evidently the Warder at the gate had realized that the approaching vehicle was not a cab.

Nonetheless, the carriage could be heard to slow and stop outside the gate. After a moment, the reins snapped, and the horses started again. The carriage was turning, coming in the gate. It loomed suddenly out of the fog, seeming to coalesce into solidity out of the very substance of the rolling mist itself. It came to a halt at the curbing stone several yards away, still shadowy in the feeble yellow glow of the gas lamps.

Then a voice called out quite clearly from within it: "Lord Darcy! Is that you?"

It was plainly a feminine voice, and quite familiar, but because of the muffling effect of the fog and the distorting effect of the interior of the cab, Lord Darcy did not recognize it immediately. He knew that, standing almost directly under the gas lamp as he was, his own features stood out rather clearly at that distance.

"You have the advantage of me, my lady," he said.

There was a low laugh. "You mean you can't even read arms anymore?"

Lord Darcy had already noticed that a coat-of-arms was emblazoned on the door of the coach, but it was impossible to make it out in this light. There was no need to, however; Lord Darcy had recognized the voice upon the second hearing of it.

"Even the brilliancy of the arms of Cumberland can be dimmed beyond recognition in a London pea-soup," Lord Darcy said as he walked toward the vehicle. "Your Grace should have more than just the regulation night-lights and fog-lights if you want your arms to be recognized on a night like this."

He could see her clearly now; the beautiful face and the cloud of golden hair were only slightly dimmed by shadow and fog.

"I'm alone," she said very softly.

"Hullo, Mary," Lord Darcy said with equal softness. "What the deuce are you doing here?"

"Why, I came to fetch *you*, of course," said Mary, Dowager Duchess of Cumberland. "You dismissed your cab earlier because you didn't think about the fog coming, so now you're marooned. There isn't a cab to be had this side of St. Paul's. Get in, my dear, and let's leave this depressing prison."

Lord Darcy turned toward the Sergeant Warder, who still stood beneath the gas lamp. "Thank you for your efforts, Sergeant. I shan't need a cab. Her Grace has very kindly offered transportation."

"Very good, your lordship. Good night, your lordship. Good night, Your Grace."

They wished the Sergeant Warder a good night, Lord Darcy climbed into the carriage, and, at a word from Her Grace, the coachman snapped his reins and the carriage moved off into the swirling fog.

The Duchess pulled down the blinds and turned up the lamp in the top of the coach so that the two passengers could see each other clearly.

"You're looking well, my dear," she said.

"And you are as beautiful as ever," Lord Darcy replied. There was a mocking glint in his eyes that Her Grace of Cumberland could not quite fathom. "Where would you like to go?" she asked, trying to probe that look with her own startlingly dark-blue eyes.

"Anywhere you'd like, my sweet. We could just drive about London for a while—for however long it takes you to tell me about the important information you have regarding this morning's murder of Master Sir James Zwinge."

Her eyes widened. For a moment, she said nothing. Then: "Damn! How did you know?"

"I deduced it."

"Rot!"

"Not at all. You have a keen mind, my dear; you should be able to follow my reasoning."

Again there was a silence, this time for nearly a minute, as Mary de Cumberland looked unblinkingly at Lord Darcy, her mind working rapidly. Then she gave her head a quick shake. "You have some information I don't."

"I think not. Unless, perhaps, I know how your mind works better than you do. You have the delightful habit, my dear, of making a man feel as though he were terribly important to you—even when you have to tell small lies to do it."

She smiled. "You *are* important to me, darling. Furthermore, small lies are necessary to good manners and to diplomacy; there is no harm in them. And what, pray, does that have to do with your pretended deduction?"

"That was unworthy of you, my dear. You know I never pretend to mental abilities other than those I actually possess." His voice had an edge.

She smiled contritely and put out a hand to touch his arm. "I know. I apologize. Please explain."

Lord Darcy's smile returned. He put his hand on hers. "Apology accepted. Explanation—a simple one—as follows:

"You claimed that you had come to fetch me at the Tower.

Now, I know that, aside from myself, the Warders at the Tower, Master Sean, and two other people, no one in London knew of my whereabouts or could have learned it by other than thaumaturgical means. No one but those even knew I was in London. You are a sorceress, true, but only journeyman, and we both know you are not prescient to any degree above normal. You might have deduced that I would come immediately when I heard of Master Sean's arrest, but you could not possibly have known at exactly what time I would leave the Tower. Ergo, your arrival was a coincidence.

"However, as your coach approached the gate, you heard the Warder whistling for a cab. You would not have stopped for that; you stopped to identify yourself to the Warder so that you could enter the courtyard. Therefore, your destination must have been the Tower itself; if it were not, you would have gone on by, ignoring the whistle.

"Then you came on in and saw me. The very tone of your voice when you hailed me showed that you had not expected to see me there.

"Your reasoning powers are well above average; it was hardly the work of a mental giant, however, to deduce from the whistle and my presence in the courtyard that it was I who desired a cab. Knowing, as you do, that I am not careless by habit, you further deduced that, having but recently arrived in London, I had failed to notice the fog prediction in the *Courier,* and had dismissed the cab that brought me. Thereupon, you spoke your flattering and entirely mendacious little piece about having come to get me."

Her laugh was soft and throaty. "It wasn't a lie intended to deceive you, my dear."

"I know. You wanted me to gasp in amazement and say: 'Goodness me! How*ever* did you know I was going to be here? Have you become a seer, then?' And you would have smiled and looked wise and said: 'Oh, I have my ways.' "

She laughed again. "You know me too well, my lord. But what has all that to do with your knowing I had information about the death of Master Sir James?"

"We return to the coincidence of your arrival at the Tower," Lord Darcy said. "If you had not come for me, then what was your purpose? It must have been important, else you would not have come out on so foggy a night. And yet, the moment you see *me*, you ask me to get in, and off we go. Whatever business you had at the Tower can be conducted with me, eh? Obviously, you went to tell Master Sean something, but not something strictly personal. Ergo—" He smiled, letting the conclusion go unsaid.

"One day," said the Dowager Duchess of Cumberland, "I shall learn not to try to beat you at your own game."

"But not, I pray, too soon," said Lord Darcy. "Few people of either sex bother to exercise their intellect; it is refreshing to know a woman who does."

"Alas!" Her voice was heavy with mock tragedy. "He loves me only for my mind!"

"Mens sana in corpore sano, my dear. Now let's get back to this information you have."

"Very well," she said, looking suddenly thoughtful. "I don't know whether it means anything or not; I'll give it to you for what it's worth and let you decide whether to follow it up."

Lord Darcy nodded. "Go ahead."

"It was something I saw—and heard," said Mary de Cumberland. "At seven minutes of eight this morning—I noticed the time particularly because I had an appointment for breakfast at eight-fifteen—I left my room at the hotel." She stopped and looked directly into his eyes. "I have the room directly across the hall from Master Sir James'. Did you know that?"

"Yes."

"Very well, then. I opened the door. I heard a voice coming through the door of the room opposite. As you know, the doors at the Royal Steward are quite thick; normal conversation won't carry through. But this was a woman's voice, not high in pitch, but quite strong and quite penetrating. Her words were very clear. She said—"

"Wait." Lord Darcy lifted a hand, interrupting her. "Can you repeat the words *exactly,* Mary?"

"I can; yes," the Duchess said firmly. "She said: 'By God, Sir James! You condemn him to death! I warn you! If *he* dies, *you* die!'"

There was a pause, a silence broken only by the clatter of hooves and the soft sussuration of pneumatic tires on the street.

"And the intonation that you have just reproduced," Lord Darcy said, "is that accurate? She sounded both angry and frightened?"

"More anger than fright, but there was certainly a touch of fear."

"Very good. Then what?"

"Then there was a very faint sound—as of someone speaking in a more normal tone of voice. It was hardly audible, much less recognizable or understandable."

"It could have been Sir James speaking?"

"It could have. It could have been anyone. I assumed, of course, at the time, that it *was* Sir James—but actually it could have been anyone."

"Or even no one?"

She thought for a second. "No. No, there was someone else in that room besides her."

"How do you know?"

"Because just then the door flew open and the girl came flouncing out. She slammed it shut behind her and went on down the hall without even noticing me—or, at least, not indicating it if she had. Then whoever was still in the room put a key in the lock and locked the door. Naturally, I had not intended to be a witness to such a scene; I ignored it and went on down to breakfast."

"Who was the girl?" Lord Darcy asked.

"To my knowledge, I had never seen her before," the Duchess said, "and she was certainly the kind of girl one would not easily forget. She is a tiny creature—not five feet tall, but perfectly formed, a truly beautiful figure. Her hair is jet black and quite long, and was bound with a silver circlet in back, giving it a sort of horsetail appearance. Her face was as beautiful as the rest of her, with pixieish eyes and a rather sensuous mouth. She was wearing the costume of an apprentice—blue, with a white band at the sleeve— and that's odd, because, as you know, apprentices are allowed at the Convention only by special invitation, and such invitations are quite rare."

"It is even odder," Lord Darcy said musingly, "that an apprentice should use such speech toward a Master of the Art."

"Yes, it is," Her Grace agreed. "But, as I said, I really thought little of it at the time. After Master Sean was arrested, however, the incident came to mind again. I spent the rest of the morning and all afternoon trying to find out what I could about her."

"And yet you did not think it important enough to mention it either to Lord Bontriomphe or to the Chief Master-at-Arms?" Lord Darcy asked quietly.

"Important? Of course I thought it was important! I still do. But—mention it to the Armsmen? To what purpose, my dear? In the first place, I had no real information; at the time, I didn't even know her name. In the second place, that was an hour and a half before the murder actually took place. In the third place, if I had told either Bontriomphe or Chief Master Hennely about it, they would simply have bungled the whole thing by arresting her, too, and they would have had no more case against her than they do against Master Sean."

"And in the fourth place," Lord Darcy added, "you fancy yourself a detective. Go ahead. What did you find out?"

"Not much," she admitted. "I found her name easily enough in the Grand Register of the Convention. She's the only female apprentice listed. The name is Tia Einzig. T-I-A E-I-N-Z-I-G."

"Einzig?" Lord Darcy lifted an eyebrow. "Germanic, definitely. Possibly Prussian, which would, no doubt, make her a Polish subject.

"The name may be Prussian; she isn't," said Her Grace. "She is, however—or was—a subject of His Slavonic Majesty. She came from some little place on the eastern side of the Danube, a few hundred miles from the Adriatic coast— one of those towns with sixteen letters in its name, only three of which are vowels. K-D-J-A-something. She left in 1961 for the Grand Duchy of Venetia and lived in Belluno for about a year. Then she was in Milano for a couple of months, then went on to Torino. In 1963, she came to France, to live in Grenoble. All this came out last year, when her case was brought to Raymond's attention."

"Raymond?"

"His Grace, the Duke of Dauphine," Mary de Cumberland explained. "Naturally, a request for extradition would have to be brought to his personal attention."

"Naturally." The sardonic light had returned to Lord Darcy's eyes, and now it gleamed dangerously. "Mary."

"Yes?"

"I retract what I said about your being a woman who uses her intellect. The rational mind marshals its facts and reports them in a logical order. This is the first I have heard of any extradition proceedings."

"Oh." She flashed him a brilliant smile. "I'm sorry, my dear. I—"

He cut her off. "First, may I ask where you got this information? You certainly didn't pop off to Dauphine this afternoon and ask your old friend the Duke to let you look at the Legal Proceedings Record of the Duchy of Dauphine."

"How did you know he was an old friend?" the Dowager Duchess asked. "I don't recall ever having mentioned it to you before."

"You haven't. You are not a woman who parades the names of influential friends. Neither would you call an Imperial Governor by his Christian name alone unless you were a close friend. That is neither here nor there. I repeat: What is your source for this history of Tia Einzig?"

"Father Dominique. The Reverend Father Dominique ap Tewdwr, O.S.B., who was the Sensitive in charge of the clerical commission which the Archbishop appointed to investigate the personality of Tia Einzig. His Grace the Duke asked that the commission be appointed to make the investigation because of the charges that were made against her in Belluno, Milano, and Torino—the requests for extradition, so that she could be tried locally on the charges against her."

"What were those charges, specifically?"

"The same in all three cases. Practicing sorcery without a license, and . . ."

"And?"

"And black magic."

CHAPTER 6

Carlyle House has been the property of the Dukes of Cumberland since it was built, although it is frequently and erroneously supposed that it is a part of the heritage of the Marquisate of Carlisle by those who do not recognize that the names are similar in pronunciation but not in spelling.

Mary, Dowager Duchess of Cumberland—formerly Duchess Consort, née Lady Mary de Beaufort—had been the second wife of the widowed Duke of Cumberland. The Duke, at the time of the marriage, was in his sixties, Lady Mary in her early twenties. But no one who knew them had thought of it as a May-December marriage, not even the Duke's son and heir by his late first wife. The old Duke, though only remotely related to the Royal Family, had the typically Plantagenet vigor, handsomeness, and longevity. His golden blond hair had lightened over the years, and his face had begun to show the deepening lines of age, but he was still as good as any man twenty years his junior, and he looked and behaved no older. But even a strong and powerful man may have an accident with a horse, and His late Grace was no exception.

Mary, who had loved her husband, not only for his youthful vigor but for his mature wisdom, was a widow before she was thirty.

Her stepson, Edwin—who, upon the death of his father, followed by His Majesty's confirmation, had become the present Duke of Cumberland—was rather a dull fellow. He was perfectly competent as an Imperial Governor, but he lacked the Plantagenet spark—however diluted—that his father had had. He liked and respected his stepmother—who was only six months his junior—but he did not understand her. Her vivaciousness, her quickness of mind, and especially her touch of the Talent, made her alien to him.

An agreement had been reached. De Cumberland would take care of the duchy, remaining in Carlisle; his stepmother would be given Carlyle House for life. It was all His Grace could do for a stepmother he loved but did not in the least understand.

When Lord Darcy and the Duchess entered the front door of Carlyle House, the seneschal who held it open for them murmured, "Good evening, Your Grace, your lordship," and closed the door quickly to block out the gray tendrils of fog that seemed to want to follow them into the brightly lit hall.

"Good evening, Geffri," said Her Grace, turning so that the seneschal could help her off with her cloak. "Where is everyone?"

"My lords the Bishops of Winchester and Carlisle have

retired, Your Grace. The Benedictine Fathers have gone to St. Paul's to chant Evensong with the Chapter; they were so good as to inform me that because of the fog they will spend the night at the Chapter House with their brethren. Sir Lyon Grey is remaining at his room in the Royal Steward tonight. Master Sean O Lochlainn has sent word that he is temporarily indisposed."

"Indisposed!" The Duchess laughed. "I should think so! He will spend the night in the Tower of London, Geffri."

"So I have been informed, Your Grace," said the imperturbable seneschal. "Sir Thomas Leseaux," he continued, taking Lord Darcy's cloak, "is in the salon. My Lord John Quetzal is upstairs donning his evening attire and should be down shortly. The selection of hot dishes which Your Grace ordered has been placed upon the buffet."

"Thank you, Geffri. Oh . . . I have sent the coach to the Palace du Marquis to fetch Lord Darcy's luggage. Let's see . . . where can we put my lord?"

"I should suggest the Lily Suite, Your Grace. It adjoins the Rose Suite and has a communicating door, making it suitable for the transfer thence of Master Sean's things, if that will be suitable and convenient for his lordship."

"Perfect, Geffri," said Lord Darcy. "When my things have been taken up, let me know, will you? I have not had an opportunity to freshen up since I arrived."

"I shall see that your lordship is notified immediately."

"Very good. Thank you, Geffri."

"A pleasure, your lordship."

"Come, my lord," said the Duchess, taking his arm, "we'll go in and have a drink with Sir Thomas to take the chill of the fog out of our bones."

As the two of them walked toward the salon, Lord Darcy said: "Who are your Benedictine guests?"

"The older one is a Father Quinn, from the north of Ireland."

"Father Quinn?" Lord Darcy said musingly. "I don't believe I know him. Who is the other?"

"A Father Patrique of Cherbourg," said Her Grace. "A remarkable Sensitive and Healer. You must meet him."

"Father Patrique and I have already met," said Lord Darcy, "and I must say I agree with your evaluation. It will be a pleasure to see him again."

They went into the large, high-ceilinged room which served as both salon and dining room. At the far end of the salon, in a large easy chair, his feet outstretched to the warmth of the blaze in the great fireplace, his hand holding a partly-filled goblet, sat a tall, lean man with pale features and with light brown hair brushed straight back from a broad, high forehead.

He rose to his feet as soon as he saw his hostess and Lord Darcy approaching.

"Good evening, Your Grace. Lord Darcy! How good to see you again!" His engaging smile seemed to make his blue-gray eyes sparkle.

Lord Darcy took his outstretched hand. "Good to see *you* again, Sir Thomas! You're looking as fit as ever."

"For a scholar, you mean," said Sir Thomas with a chuckle. "Here! May I be so bold as to offer you both a splash of our gracious hostess's excellent brandy?"

"Indeed you may, Sir Thomas," said the Duchess with a smile. "I feel as though I had fog in every vertebra."

Sir Thomas went to the sideboard and extracted the glass stopple from the brandy decanter with lean, agile fingers. As he poured the clear, red-brown liquid into two thin-walled brandy goblets, he said: "I was fairly certain you would be here as soon as I heard of Master Sean's arrest, but I hardly expected you so soon."

A trace of irony came into Lord Darcy's smile. "My Lord de London was good enough to send a special messenger across the Channel to relay the news, and I was able to make good train and boat connections."

Sir Thomas handed each of the others a goblet of brandy. "Is it your intention to put your brilliant brain to work to solve this murder in order to clear Master Sean?"

Lord Darcy laughed. "Far from it. My Lord Marquis would like me to do just that, but I shan't oblige him. The case is interesting, of course, but my duty lies in Normandy. Just among the three of us—and I ask you to let it go no further until after tomorrow—I intend to get Master Sean out by presenting my cousin de London with a dilemma. For that purpose, I have gathered enough facts to force him to release Master Sean. Then the two of us shall return to Normandy."

Mary de Cumberland looked at him with an expression

that was both hurt and astonished. "You're returning and taking Master Sean with you? So soon? Shan't he be permitted to finish Convention Week?"

"I'm afraid not," Lord Darcy said. There was apology and contriteness in his manner and voice. "We have a murder of our own to solve, Sean and I. I can't reveal details, and I admit that the case is neither as spectacular nor as . . . er . . . notorious as this one, but duty is duty. If the matter can be resolved quickly, of course, Master Sean may be back before the week is out."

"But what about the paper he was to present?" the Duchess persisted.

"If it is at all possible," Lord Darcy promised firmly, "I shall see that he gets back. If nothing else, I shall see to it that he gets back Saturday to deliver his paper. That, after all, is a part of his duty as a sorcerer."

"And you'll just hand the case right back to Lord Bontriomphe, eh?" asked Sir Thomas.

"I don't need to hand it back," said Lord Darcy with a chuckle, "since I did not accept it in the first place. It's all his, and I wish him luck. He and the Marquis are perfectly capable of its solution, have no fear of that."

"Without a forensic sorcerer to aid them?" Sir Thomas said.

"They'll manage," said Lord Darcy. "The late Sir James Zwinge was not the only capable forensic sorcerer in London. Besides, it is apparent that My Lord Marquis does not feel the need for a good forensic sorcerer. As soon as the second-best one was killed, he proceeded to lock up the best one. Hardly the act of a man who was desperate for first-class thaumaturgical advice."

As the other two laughed quietly, Lord Darcy took a sip from his brandy goblet.

A door at the other end of the room opened.

"Good evening, Your Grace; good evening, gentlemen," said a warm baritone voice. "I'm terribly sorry. Have I interrupted any thing?"

Lord Darcy, too, had turned to look. The newcomer was a handsome young man in crimson and gold evening dress whose distinctive features marked him as Mechicain. This, then, was Lord John Quetzal du Moqtessuma de Mechicoe.

"Not at all, my lord," said the Duchess, "we have been

expecting you. Come in and permit me to introduce our new guest."

The introductions were made in due form, and Lord John Quetzal's heavy-lidded eyes brightened as Lord Darcy's name was spoken.

"It's a very great pleasure to meet you, my lord," he said, "though, of course, I deplore the circumstances that bring you here. I do not for a moment believe Master Sean guilty of this terrible crime."

"Thank you, my lord," Lord Darcy replied. "And I thank you for Master Sean, too." Then he added smoothly, "I did not realize that Master Sean's guilelessness was so transparently obvious that it would be utterly convincing upon such short acquaintance."

The Mechicain looked rather self-conscious. "Well, it's not exactly that. Transparent? No, I shouldn't say that Master Sean is at all transparent. It's . . . er—" He hesitated in momentary confusion.

"My Lord John Quetzal's modesty does him credit," the Duchess cut in gently. "His is a Talent rare even among sorcerers. He is a witch-smeller."

"Indeed?" Lord Darcy looked at the young man with increased interest. "I confess that I have never met a sorcerer with that ability before. You can detect, then, the presence of a practitioner of black magic, even at a distance?"

Lord John Quetzal nodded. "Yes, my lord." He seemed embarrassed, like an adolescent lad who has just been told he is very handsome by a beautiful woman.

Sir Thomas chuckled. "Naturally, Lord Darcy, he would know immediately that Master Sean does not dabble in black magic. To a witch-smeller, that would be instantly apparent." He turned his smile toward Lord John Quetzal. "When we have some free time together, I should like to discuss theory with you and see how it actually squares with practical results."

"That . . . that would be an honor and a pleasure, Sir Thomas," said the young nobleman. There was an awestruck note in his voice. "But . . . but I'm very weak in symbological theory. My math isn't exactly my strong point."

Sir Thomas laughed. "Don't worry, my lord; I promise not to smother you in analogy equations. Good Heavens, that's *work*! When I am away from my library, I do everything I can to avoid any heavy thinking."

That, Lord Darcy knew, was not true; Sir Thomas was merely putting the young man at ease. Sir Thomas Leseaux, in spite of his degree of Doctor of Thaumaturgy, was not a practicing sorcerer. He did not possess the Talent to any marked degree. He was a theoretical thaumaturgist who worked with the higher and more esoteric forms of the subjective algebrae, leaving it to others to test his theories in practice. His brilliant mind was capable of grasping symbological relationships that an ordinary sorcerer could only dimly perceive. There were very few Th.D.'s who could follow his abstruse and complex symbolic analogies through to their final conclusions; most Masters of the Art bogged down hopelessly after the first few similarities. Sir Thomas had not been so lacking in awareness as to suppose a mere Journeyman could follow his mathematics. On the other hand, he immensely enjoyed discussing the Art with practicing magicians.

"May I ask you a question, my lord?" Lord Darcy asked thoughtfully. "Even though I am not officially involved in the investigation of the murder of Sir James Zwinge, a man in my profession has a certain natural curiosity. I should like to ask you what might be considered a professional question, and"—he smiled—"if you like you may send me a bill for services rendered."

Lord John Quetzal returned the smile. "If the question requires that I invoke a spell, I shall most certainly bill you—at the usual Journeyman's rates, of course. To do otherwise would impair my standing in the Guild. But if you merely want a professional opinion, I am at your service."

"Then I shall leave the matter in your hands," said Lord Darcy. "The question is: Have you detected the presence of a black magician amongst the members of the Convention?"

There was a sudden silence, as if time itself were suspended for a moment. Both Sir Thomas and the Duchess seemed to be holding their breaths, awaiting the young Mechicain nobleman's answer.

But from Lord John Quetzal there was only a moment of hesitancy. When he spoke, his voice was firm.

"My lord, it is my ambition to study forensic sorcery under the tutelage of a Master. I have, as a matter of course, studied both law enforcement and criminal detection. May I counter your question with one of my own?"

"Certainly," said Lord Darcy.

Lord John Quetzal compressed his lips for a moment in thought before continuing. "Let us suppose that you personally knew, through the exercise of your own abilities, that a certain man was a criminal—that he had committed a particular crime. But let us further assume that, aside from your own personal knowledge, there was not one shred of proof whatever of the fact. My counter-question is: Would you denounce the man?"

"No," said Lord Darcy without hesitation. "Your point is well taken. It is nugatory to accuse a man without proof. But a word to the investigating officials, merely to give them a lead so they can discover proof if it exists, is certainly not a public accusation."

"Perhaps not," said the young sorcerer slowly. "I shall certainly take your words under advisement. But at the moment I feel that my unsupported word alone is not sufficient evidence even for that."

"That, of course, is your decision," the investigator said evenly. "But keep it in mind that if your Talent as a witch-smeller is widely known—if it is known, for instance, to someone whose very life might depend upon your silence—then I should advise you to be very careful that you are not silenced permanently."

Before Lord John Quetzal could answer, the door to the hall opened and Geffri appeared. "I trust you will pardon the intrusion, Your Grace, but I was instructed to notify his lordship as soon as his lordship's luggage had been taken to the Lily Suite."

"Oh, yes; thank you, Geffri," said Lord Darcy.

"I believe I shall put on my evening clothes, too," said Her Grace. "Will you excuse me, gentlemen? And pray don't allow my absence to delay your own supper; help yourselves from the array on the buffet."

Fifteen minutes later, Lord Darcy, having bathed and shaved, was feeling more human than he had for hours. He took one last look at himself in the full-length mirror that hung on the bedroom wall of the Lily Suite. He made minor adjustments to the silver lace at his throat and wrists, flicked an almost microscopic bit of dust from the coral satin of his dress jacket, and decided he was ready to face the company in a better humor than when he had left them.

Downstairs, the door to the salon was open, and, as he approached it, Lord Darcy could hear Sir Thomas Leseaux's voice.

"The fact remains, my lord, that Sir James is, after all, dead."

"Couldn't it have been suicide, Sir Thomas?" asked Lord John Quetzal. "Or an accident?"

It was inevitable, Lord Darcy thought. Great and brilliant men and women, whose usual conversations were in the realm of ideas, would normally shun gossip or sporting events or even crime—except in the abstract—as topics for an evening's discourse. But give them a murder—not a commonplace death in a public house brawl, nor a shooting in a robbery, nor a sordid killing in a fit of jealousy, nor an even more sordid sex crime, but an inexplicable death surrounded by mystery—give them a nice, juicy, puzzle of murder, and lo! they can speak of nothing else.

Sir Thomas Leseaux had said, less than half an hour ago, that he wanted to get Lord John Quetzal alone to discuss the theory of magic, with special emphasis on witch-smelling—and now he was saying:

"Accident or suicide? Why, as to that, I don't know, of course, but the authorities seem to be operating upon the assumption that it is murder."

"But why? I mean, what reason would anyone have for killing Master Sir James Zwinge? What is the motive?"

"A very good question," said Lord Darcy as he entered the salon. Only the two men were present. Obviously the Duchess had not yet finished dressing. "As a purely cerebral exercise, I have been pondering that question myself. But don't let me interrupt you. Pray continue your conversation whilst I sample the selection of goodies on the buffet table."

"Lord John Quetzal," said Sir Thomas, "seems to be at a loss for discovering a motive for the murder."

Lord Darcy looked at the row of copper bowls, each with its small alcohol flame flickering brightly beneath, and lifted the cover of the first. "Ah! Ham!" he said. "Very well, Sir Thomas. What about motive? Who might have wanted him dead?" He put a slice of ham on his plate and opened the next bowl.

Sir Thomas frowned. "No one that I know of," he said slowly. "He could be quite acerb at times, but he would not willingly have harmed anyone, I think."

Darcy ladled some hot cherry sauce over his ham. "You know of no threats to kill him? No violent arguments with anyone?"

"Aside from his so-called argument with Master Sean, you mean? Yes, come to think of it, there was one such. Master Ewen MacAlister said some rather bitter things about him a month ago. Master Ewen had made application to get on the Naval Research Staff, and Sir James—who had certain connections with Naval Research—recommended that Master Ewen's application not be approved."

"A revenge motive, then?" Lord Darcy poured himself a generous glass of claret and seated himself in a chair facing the other two, his tray on his lap. "I have never had the pleasure of meeting Master Ewen MacAlister, but from what Master Sean tells me, the pleasure would be doubtful. Is he the kind of man who would kill for revenge?"

"I . . . don't . . . know," said Sir Thomas slowly. "I can imagine his killing someone to prevent that person from harming him, but I hesitate to say he would bother to do so after the harm was done."

Lord Darcy made a mental note to tell Lord Bontriomphe about that in the morning. It might be wise for Bontriomphe to make inquiries to find out whether Master Ewen had made or intended to make application for some other position that Sir James Zwinge had "certain connections" with.

"Anyone else?" Darcy asked, looking down at his plate.

"No," said Sir Thomas after a moment. "No one that I know of, my lord."

"Do you know a Damoselle Tia Einzig?" Darcy asked in the same quiet tone of voice.

Sir Thomas' smile vanished. After several seconds, he said: "I know her, yes, my lord. Why?"

"She seems to have got herself charged with black magic. And it appears that Sir James was killed by black magic."

Sir Thomas' normally pale features darkened. "See here! You're not accusing Tia of this murder, are you?"

"Accuse? Not at all, Sir Thomas. I merely point out a possible connection."

"Well, there's nothing to it! Nothing, d'you understand! Tia is no more a witch than *you* are! I'll not have you making such insinuations, do you hear?"

"Do calm yourself, Sir Thomas," Darcy said mildly. "Relax.

Get a grip on your emotions. Tell yourself a joke—or think of some refreshing equation."

The color in Sir Thomas' face subsided, but he did not smile at Lord Darcy's sally. "My deepest apologies, my lord. I . . . I hardly know what to say. I'm . . . I'm not myself. It's a . . . a touchy subject, my lord."

"Think nothing of it, Sir Thomas. I had no desire to upset you, but I am not at all offended. Murder is a touchy subject when it strikes as closely as this one has. Perhaps we had best discuss something else."

"No, no, please. Not on my account, I beg you."

"My dear Sir Thomas, I insist. All evening, I have been wanting to ask Lord John Quetzal questions about Mechicoe, and you have given me the perfect excuse for doing so. Murder is my business, but if I am not engaged in solving a given crime, discussing it begins to pall. So—

"My lord, if my memory of history has not betrayed me, the first Anglo-French ships touched the shores of Mechicoe in the year 1569, and the members of that expedition were the first Europeans your ancestors had ever seen. What was the cause of the superstitious awe with which the Europeans were regarded?"

"Ah! That's an interesting thing, my lord," the young man said with enthusiasm. "First you must understand the legend or myth of Quetzalcoatle . . ."

The first few minutes were a bit awkward, but the young Mechicain's enthusiasm was so genuine that both Sir Thomas and Lord Darcy were actually caught up in the discussion, and it was going full blast when the Dowager Duchess came down. An hour after that, all four of them were still discussing Mechicoe.

Lord Darcy did not get to bed until late, and he did not get to sleep until even later.

CHAPTER 7

Lord Darcy's resolve to keep his hands off the Zwinge case, to allow—or rather force—his cousin the Marquis of London to use his own resources to solve it, was a firm one. He had no intention of getting himself involved, even

if that required that he bottle up his own intrinsic curiosity, seal the bottle, and sit on the cork. It was fortunate
that he was not forced to do that, for Lord Darcy's curiosity was capable of generating a great deal of pressure. Any
resolve, no matter how firm, can be dissipated, abolished,
negated, removed, by changing circumstances, and the circumstances were to change drastically on the following
morning.

On that morning, Thursday, Lord Darcy lay in his bed,
drowsing, his mind still in a semi-dreamy state, his thoughts
wandering. There was a quiet knock on the door of his
bedroom.

"Yes?" he said without opening his eyes.

"Your caffe, my lord, as you ordered," said a low voice.

"Just leave it in the sitting room," Lord Darcy said drowsily. "I shall be out in a few minutes."

But he wasn't. He drifted off to sleep again. He did not
hear the bedroom door open; he did not hear the nearly
silent footsteps that crossed the thick carpet from the door
to his bed.

Suddenly, someone touched his shoulder. His eyes came
open instantly, and he was wide awake.

"Mary!"

The Dowager Duchess curtsied. "Your servant, my lord.
Shall I bring your caffe in, my lord?"

Lord Darcy sat up. "Ah! Capital! A Duchess for a serving wench! Indeed, yes! Bring the caffe in immediately! Hop
to it, Your Grace!" He chuckled softly as the Duchess went
out again, a soft smile on her lips. "And by the by!" he
called after her, "Will you have My Lord Marquis polish my
boots?"

She came back in, pushing a wheeled serving cart upon
which sat a silver caffe pot, a spoon, and a single caffe cup
with saucer.

"Your boots are already polished, my lord," she said, still
keeping her voice in the proper deferential tone. "I took the
liberty, my lord, of having your lordship's clothing brushed
and pressed, and hung in the clothes cupboard in the sitting room." She poured his caffe.

"Oh, indeed?" Lord Darcy said, reaching for his cup. "All
done by a Bishop, I presume?"

"My Lord Bishop," said the Duchess, "had other, more

pressing, business. However, His Imperial Majesty the King is prepared to take you for your morning drive."

Lord Darcy paused suddenly, the cup not yet touching his lips.

Bantering is all well enough, but one must draw the line somewhere.

One does not jest about His Most Sovereign Majesty the King.

And then Lord Darcy realized that his brain was not as completely awake as he had thought. He took a sip of the caffe and then returned the cup to its saucer before he spoke again.

"Who is His Majesty's agent?" he asked quietly.

"He's waiting in the hall. Shall I bring him in?"

"Yes. Wait! What o'clock is it, anyway?"

"Just on seven."

"Ask him to wait a minute or so. I'll dress. Fetch my clothes."

Seven minutes and some odd seconds later, Lord Darcy, fully dressed in proper morning costume, opened the door to his sitting room. Mary, Dowager Duchess of Cumberland, was nowhere in sight. A short, spare, melancholy-looking man, wearing the usual blue-gray drab of a cabman, was sitting on one of the chairs. When he saw Lord Darcy, he came politely to his feet, his square cabman's hat in his hand.

"Lord Darcy?"

"The same. And you?"

From his cap, the smallish man took a silver badge engraved with the Royal Arms. Near the top a stone, polished but not faceted and looking like a quarter-inch bit of translucent gray glass, was inset in the metal.

"King's Messenger, my lord," said the man. He slid his right thumb forward and touched the stone. Immediately, it ceased to be a small lump of dull gray glass.

In the light, it gleamed with the reddish glow of a ruby!

There was no mistaking it. The stone was magically attuned to one man and one man only—the man whose touch would cause that red color to shine within it. A Royal Badge could be stolen, of course, but no thief could give that gray, drab stone its ruby glow.

The brilliant Sir Edward Elmer, Th.D., had designed that spell more than thirty years before, and no one had solved it yet; it was a perfect identification for Personal Agents of His Most Dread and Sovereign Majesty, John IV. The late Sir Edward had been Grand Master of the Sorcerers Guild, and it was accepted that he had outranked even Sir Lyon Gandolphus Grey as a sorcerer.

"Very well," said Lord Darcy. He did not ask the man's name; a King's Messenger remains anonymous. "The message?"

The Messenger bowed his head. "You are to accompany me, my lord. By His Majesty's request"

Lord Darcy frowned. "That's all?"

Again the Messenger bowed. "I have delivered His Majesty's message, my lord. I can say no more, my lord."

"I see. Will there be any objections if I come armed?"

A wide smile broke over the face of the King's Messenger. "If I may say so, my lord, it would be most expedient. His Majesty gave me a further message to your lordship, to be delivered only in case your lordship should ask that question. A message to be delivered in His Majesty's own words, my lord. If I may?"

"Proceed," said Lord Darcy.

Closing his eyes, the Messenger concentrated for a moment. When he spoke, the voice was cultured and clear; it had none of the patois of the Londoner of the lower middle class. The timbre and intonation had changed, too.

The voice was that of the King.

"My dear Darcy. The last time we met, you came armed. I should not expect a man of your caliber to break a precedent. The matter is most urgent. Come with all haste."

Lord Darcy suppressed a desire to bow low to the Messenger and say: "Immediately, Sire." The Messenger was, after all, only an instrument. He was completely trustworthy, else he would not carry a Silver Badge; even his ordinary messages were to be honored. But when he delivered a message in His Majesty's Own Voice, even he, the Messenger, did not know what he said. When he murmured the key spell to himself, the message in the Royal Voice was delivered. The Messenger had no memory of it either before or after the delivery. He had submitted willingly to the recording of that message, and he had submitted willingly to its delivery and erasure. No sorcerer on Earth could pry that information out of him once it had been delivered, since, in his mind, it no longer existed.

Before it had been delivered, of course, it could be pried out, but not from a King's Messenger. Any attempt to get such a message from the mind of a King's Messenger without authority would result in the immediate death of the Messenger—a fact which the Messenger realized and accepted as a part of his duty to Sovereign and Empire.

After a moment, the King's Messenger opened his eyes. "All right, your lordship?"

"Perfectly, my good fellow. Are you a good cabman?"

"The best in London, my lord—though I say it who shouldn't."

"Excellent! We must go without delay!"

During the ride, Lord Darcy mused upon the King's words. When he had asked the Messenger whether or not he should go armed, it had been a simple question that any Officer of His Majesty's Peace might have asked. Lord Darcy had had no notion that the Messenger was actually taking him to the Royal Presence; he had asked about arming himself purely in the interests of his official duties. And now, as a result of a perfectly ordinary question, he found himself among the small handful of men who were permitted to be armed in the Royal Presence.

Traditionally, only the Great Lords of State were permitted to remain armed in the King's presence—and they only with swords.

In so far as he knew, Lord Darcy was the only person who, in all of history, had been given Royal permission— which amounted to a command—to appear before His Majesty armed with a gun. It was a singular, a unique, honor—and Lord Darcy was well aware of it.

But those thoughts did not distract his mind for long; of far more importance at the moment was the reason for the King's message. Why should His Majesty be personally interested in an affair which, although it had its outré elements, was, after all, a rather ordinary murder? At least, on the surface of it, it seemed to have no connection with Affairs of State. However . . .

Suddenly Lord Darcy smote his forehead with the palm of his hand. "Fool!" he muttered sharply to himself. "Dolt!

Moron! Idiot! Cherbourg, of course!" This, he thought, is what comes of allowing one's emotions to be distracted by Master Sean's plight when one should have them under full control for analyzing the problem at hand. The thing was as plain as a pikestaff once a competent mind came to focus on it.

Therefore, Lord Darcy was not in the least surprised, after the cab had swept through the gates of Westminster Palace, past the armed guard who recognized the vehicle and driver immediately, to find that a Naval officer wearing the uniform of a Commander was waiting for him in the courtyard. In fact, the lack of such a person would indeed have surprised him.

The Commander opened the door of the cab, and, as Lord Darcy stepped out, the Commander said: "Lord Darcy? I am Commander Lord Ashley and your servant, my lord."

"And I yours, my lord," said Lord Darcy. "Your presence here, by the by, confirms my suspicions."

"Suspicions?" The Commander looked startled.

"That there is presumed to be a connection between the murder of a certain Georges Barbour in Cherbourg two days ago, and the murder of Master Sir James Zwinge yesterday in the Royal Steward. At least, Naval Intelligence presumes a connection."

"We are almost certain there is a connection," said Lord Ashley. "Will you come this way? There is to be a meeting in Queen Anette's Parlor immediately. Just through this door, down the hall to the stairway and— But perhaps I am taking a liberty, my lord. Do you know your way about the Palace?"

"I have made it a point, my lord, to study the floor plans of the great palaces and castles of the Empire. Queen Anette's Parlor, where the Treaty of Kobenhavn was revised and signed in 1891, is directly above the Chapel of St. Edward the Confessor—consecrated in 1633, during the reign of Edward VII. Thus, it would be up this stairway, left turn, down the hall, through the Gascon Door, right turn, fifth door on the right, easily recognizable by the fact that it still bears the gilt-and-polychromed personal arms of Anette of Flanders, consort to Harold II." Lord Darcy gave Commander Lord Ashley a broad smile. "But to answer the question as you meant it: No, I have never been in Westminster Palace before."

The Commander smiled back. "Nor have I." He chuckled. "If I may say so, I find myself somewhat taken aback by this sudden soaring into a rather rarified atmosphere. Two men whom I had never met are done in—something which happens all too frequently in Intelligence work—and then, without warning, what seemed a rather routine killing is suddenly catapulted to the importance of an Affair of State." He lowered his voice a little. "His Majesty himself will attend the meeting." They went up the stairway and turned left, toward the Gascon Door.

"Tell me," Lord Darcy said, "have you any theory?"

"As to who killed them? Polish agents, of course," the Commander said. "But if you mean do I have any theory as to who the agents may be, then—no, I don't. Could be anyone, you know. Some little shopkeeper or tradesman or something of the sort, a perfectly ordinary appearing man, is one day told by his Polish superiors, 'Go to such-and-such a place, where you will find a man named thus-and-so. Kill him.' He does it, and an hour later is back at his regular business. No connection between him and the dead man. No motive that can be linked personally to the killer. No clue of any kind." They passed through the doorway and turned right.

"I trust," said Lord Darcy with a smile, "that your pessimism is not generally shared by the Naval Intelligence Corps."

"Well, as a matter of fact," said the Commander in a slightly apologetic tone, "I believe it is. If the killers can be found, so much the better, of course, but that will be merely a by-product of the real business, you see."

"Then the Navy feels that there is something more dangerous going on than murder?" The two men stopped before the door with the gilt-and-polychrome arms that marked Queen Anette's Parlor.

"Indeed we do. The King views it with greatest consternation. He'll give you any further information."

Lord Ashley opened the ornate door, and the two men went in.

CHAPTER 8

The three men seated at the long table were immediately recognizable to Lord Darcy, although he had met only one of them before. Lord Bontriomphe was looking his usual calm, affable self.

The erect, silver-bearded old man with the piercing eyes and the magnificent blade of a nose could only be Sir Lyon Grey, in spite of the fact that he wore ordinary morning clothing instead of the formal pale-blue and silver of a Master Sorcerer.

The third man had a highly distinctive face. He appeared to be in his late forties or early fifties, although his dark, curly, slightly disarrayed hair showed only a few threads of gray, and then only when one looked closely. His forehead was high and craggy, giving his head a rather squared-off appearance; his eyes were heavy-lidded and deep-set beneath thick, bushy eyebrows; his nose was as large as Sir Lyon's, but instead of being thin and bladelike, it was wide and slightly twisted, as though it had been broken at least once and allowed to heal without the services of a Healer. His mouth was wide and straight, and the moustache above it was thick and bushy, spreading out to either side like a cat's whiskers, each hair curling separately upwards at the end. His heavy beard was full, but was cut fairly short, and was as wiry and curly as his hair, moustache, and eyebrows.

At first glance, one got the impression of forbidding ruthlessness and remorseless purpose; it required a second, closer look to see that those qualities were modified by both wisdom and humor. It was the face of a man with tremendous inner power and the ability to control and use it both wisely and well.

Lord Darcy had heard the man described, and the uniform of royal blue heavily encrusted with gold merely clinched the identification of Peter de Valera ap Smith, Lord High Admiral of the Imperial Navy, Commander of the Combined Fleets, Knight Commander of the Order of the Golden Leopard, and Chief of Staff for Naval Operations.

A fourth man, standing near the Lord High Admiral, seemed about the same age, but his hair was noticeably gray, and his features were so commonplace that they paled into insignificance in comparison. Lord Darcy did not recognize him, but the uniform he wore was that of a Naval Captain, which suggested that he was connected with Naval Intelligence.

When Commander Lord Ashley performed the necessary introductions, all of Lord Darcy's tentative identifications had proved correct, including the last; the man was Captain Percy Smollett, Chief of Naval Intelligence, European Branch.

Of the three Navy men, Lord Darcy noticed, only the Lord High Admiral wore his dress sword; he alone of the three was so permitted in the Royal Presence. Lord Darcy was suddenly intensely aware of the pistol on his right hip, concealed though it was by his morning coat.

Hardly had the introductions been completed when a door to an adjoining room opened suddenly, and a man wearing the livery of the Major Domo of the Royal Household entered.

"My lords and gentlemen!" he said firmly. "His Imperial Majesty the King!"

The six men were on their feet. As the King entered, they bowed low rather than genuflecting. This was a nice point of etiquette often misunderstood. His Majesty was dressed in the uniform of the Commander-in-Chief of the Imperial Navy. Had he worn full regalia or ordinary street clothes, a genuflection would have been in order; but in Army or Navy uniform he was wearing the *persona* of a military officer—an officer of the most exalted rank, true, but an officer, nonetheless, and no military officer rates a genuflection.

"My lords and gentlemen, please be seated," said His Majesty.

John IV, by the Grace of God, King and Emperor of England, France, Scotland, Ireland, New England, and New France; Defender of the Faith, et cetera, was the perfect model of a Plantagenet King. Tall, broad of shoulder, blue of eye, and blondly handsome, John of England was a direct descendant of Henry II, the first Plantagenet King, through Henry's grandson, King Arthur. Like his predecessors, King John IV showed all the strength, ability, and wisdom that was typical of the oldest ruling family in Europe. In no way but physically did he resemble the members of the wild, spendthrift, unstable cadet branch of the family—now fortunately extinct—which had descended from the youngest son of Henry II, the unhappy Prince John Lackland who had died in exile three years before the death of King Richard the Lion-Hearted in 1219.

The King sat at the head of the table. To his left sat, in order, the Lord High Admiral, Captain Smollett, and Lord Bontriomphe. To his right were Sir Lyon, Commander Lord Ashley, and Lord Darcy.

"My lords, gentlemen, I think we all understand the reason for this meeting, but in order to get the facts straight in our minds, I will ask My Lord High Admiral to explain what we are up against. If you will, my lord."

"Certainly, Sire." My Lord High Admiral's voice was a faintly rasping baritone which, even when it was muted, sounded as though it should be bellowing orders from the quarterdeck instead of holding a quiet discussion at Westminster Palace. He looked round the table with his piercing seaman's gaze. "This concerns a weapon," he said bluntly. "That is, *I* call it a weapon. Sir Lyon doesn't. But I'm only a Navy man, not a sorcerer. We all know that sorcery has its limitations, eh? That's why magic can't be used in warfare; if a sorcerer uses magic to destroy an enemy ship, he has to use Black Magic, and no sane sorcerer wants to do that. Besides, Black Magic isn't that effective. The Polish Royal Navy tried to use it back in '39, and our counter-spells nullified it easily. We blasted 'em out of the water with cannon while they were trying to make their spells work. But, as I understand it, this is *not* Black Magic." He looked over at the Grand Master. "Perhaps you'd better explain, Sir Lyon."

"Very well, my lord," said the Master Sorcerer. "Perhaps, to begin with, I had best make it clear to you that the line between what we call 'Black' magic and what we call 'White' magic is not as clearly defined as many people suppose. We say, for instance, that the practice of the Healing Art is White Magic, and that the use of curses to cause illness or death is Black Magic. But, one may ask, is it White Magic to cure a homicidal maniac of a broken leg so that he may go out and kill again? Or, contrariwise, is it Black Magic to curse that same maniac so that he dies and kills no more? Well, in both cases—yes. It can be so proven by the symbological mathematics of the Theory of Ethics. I won't bore you with the analogy equations themselves; suffice it to say that, in such widely diverse cases, the Theory of Ethics is quite clear.

"This is summed up in the aphorism that every first-year apprentice sorcerer knows by heart: *Black Magic is a matter of symbolism and intent.*"

Sir Lyon smiled and turned his right palm up in a gesture of admission. "So, of course, is White Magic—but it is the Black against which we must warn."

"Quite understandable," said Captain Smollett.

"I shan't go into this further," said Sir Lyon, "except to say that the Theory of Ethics *does* allow one to *interfere* with the actions of another, when that other is bent upon destruction. As a result, we have perfected the . . . er . . . 'weapon' which my lord the High Admiral has mentioned." Sir Lyon glanced round the table again, his deep-set brilliant eyes looking at each man in turn. Then he bent over and took an object from beneath the table and placed it on the polished oaken surface for all to see.

"This is it, my lords and gentlemen."

It was an odd-looking device. The main bulk was a brass cylinder eight inches in diameter and eighteen inches long. This cylinder was mounted on a short tripod which held it horizontally four inches off the table top. On one end of the cylinder, there were two handles, fitted so that the cylinder could be aimed by gripping with both hands. From the other end there projected a smaller cylinder, some three inches in diameter and ten inches long. The last four inches flared out to a diameter of six inches, making a bell-like muzzle.

Lord Bontriomphe smiled. "That's a very oddly shaped gun, Sir Lyon."

The Grand Master chuckled dryly. "Your lordship perceives, of course, that the device is *not* a gun—but, in a way, the analogy is an apt one. I cannot demonstrate its operation here, of course, but the explanation of its operation—"

"One moment, Sir Lyon." The King's voice cut in smoothly.

"Sire?" The Grand Master Sorcerer's eyebrows lifted. He had not expected His Majesty to interrupt at that point.

"Can the device be operated against a single man?" His Majesty asked.

"Of course, Sire," said Sir Lyon. "But Your Majesty must understand that it works to inhibit only a single type of operation, and we have not the facilities here to—"

"Bear with me, Sir Sorcerer," said the King. "I think we *do* have the facilities you mention. Could you use Lord Darcy as your target?"

"I could, Sire," said Sir Lyon, a speculative gleam in his deep-set eyes.

"Excellent." The King looked at Lord Darcy. "Would you consent to an experiment involving yourself, my lord?"

"Your Majesty has but to ask," said Lord Darcy.

"Very good." His Majesty held out his right hand. "Would you be so good as to give me the pistol you carry at your hip, my lord?"

It was as though a silent lightning bolt had struck every man at the table. Heads jerked round. Every eye focused in startled surprise on Lord Darcy's face. The Lord High Admiral grasped the hilt of his narrow-bladed Naval dress sword and withdrew it half an inch from its scabbard.

The shock was obvious. How *dare* any man come into the King's Sovereign Presence armed with a pistol?

"Peace, My Lord Admiral!" said the King. "My lord of Arcy comes armed by Our request and permission. Your pistol, Lord Darcy."

Coolly, Lord Darcy performed an act that would have turned the stomach of every right-thinking man in the Empire. He drew a gun in the presence of His Dread and Sovereign Majesty the King.

Then he rose, leaned across the table, and presented the pistol to the King, butt first. "As Your Majesty bids," he said calmly.

"Thank you, my lord. Ah! An excellent weapon! I have always considered the .40 caliber MacGregor to be the finest handgun yet built. Are you ready, Sir Lyon?"

Sir Lyon Grey had obviously already fathomed the King's intentions. He smiled and swiveled the gleaming metal device around so that the bell-like muzzle pointed directly at Lord Darcy. "I am ready, Sire," he said.

The King, meanwhile, had unloaded the MacGregor, taking all seven of the .40 caliber cartridges out and placing them on the table in front of him while five pairs of eyes watched him in fascination.

"My lord," said the King, looking up, "I shall ask you to ignore what Sir Lyon is doing."

"I understand, Sire," said Lord Darcy.

"Excellent, my lord." His Majesty's eyes moved upwards, along the wall opposite. "Hm-m-m. Yes. My lord, I call your attention to the stained glass in yonder window—particularly to that area which depicts King Arthur holding the scroll, the scene which symbolizes the establishment of the Most Ancient and Noble Order of the Round Table."

Lord Darcy looked at the window. "I see the section to which Your Majesty refers," he said.

"Good. That window, my lord, is a priceless work of art. Nonetheless, it offends me."

Lord Darcy looked back at the King. His Majesty pushed the unloaded pistol, and it slid across the polished surface to come to rest in front of Lord Darcy. Then he flipped a finger, and a single cartridge spun across the table to come to rest beside the gun. "I repeat, my lord," said the King, "that bit of glass offends me. Would you do me the favor of putting a bullet through it?"

"As you command, Sire," said Lord Darcy.

Had he not known that he was the subject of a scientific experiment, the scene that followed would have been one of the most humiliating in Lord Darcy's career. It was only afterwards that he realized that a single snicker or chuckle from any of the other six men at the table would have snapped his temper. For a man who normally had such magnificent control over his emotions, such an explosion of wrath would have been almost the final humiliation. But no one laughed, for which Lord Darcy was afterward deeply thankful.

The task was a simple one. Pick up the cartridge, place it in the chamber, close the lock, aim, and fire.

Lord Darcy reached for the pistol with his right hand and for the cartridge with his left. Somehow, he caught the handgun wrong, so that he gripped it upside down, with the muzzle facing him. At the same time, his fingers closed on the cartridge wrong, so that it slipped from his grasp and skittered across the table. He reached out again, grabbed at it, and it slid away. Then, angry, he slammed his palm down on it and finally caught it.

Then there was a loud clatter. In focusing his attention on the cartridge, he had allowed the pistol to slip from the grasp of his other hand.

He set his teeth and clenched his left hand around the

wayward cartridge. Then he reached out with great determination and picked up the pistol with his right hand. Fine.

Now to open the lock. His right thumb found the stud
and pushed it, but his other fingers missed their grip at that
point, and the gun was suddenly hanging from his forefinger,
swinging by the trigger guard. He tried to swing it round
so that he could grasp the butt but it slipped from his
forefinger and banged to the table top again.

Lord Darcy took a deep breath. Then, with calm deliberation, he reached out and picked up the gun. This time,
he used his left thumb to open the lock, but in doing so
he dropped the cartridge again.

The next few minutes were a nightmare. The cartridge
persisted in slipping from his grasp when he tried to pick
it up, and when he did manage to pick it up it refused to
go into the chamber. And just as it seemed about to slide
in properly, he would drop the gun again.

Lord Darcy set his teeth; the muscles in the sides of his
jaw stood out in hard relief. Moving his hands slowly and
carefully, he finally managed—after many fumbles, slips, and
errors—to get the cartridge into the chamber and close the
lock.

His feeling of relief at having achieved this was so great
that his fingers relaxed and the gun fell to the table again.
Angry, he reached out, snatched it up, aimed in the general direction of the window, and—

The gun went off with a crash, long before he had
intended it to.

King Arthur and his scroll remained serenely undamaged while the slug slammed into the stone wall two feet
away, chipping off a large flake of stone and ricochet-
ing up to the ceiling, where it buried itself in an oak
beam.

After what seemed like an interminably long silence, Sir
Lyon Gandolphus Grey said softly: "Magnificent! Your
Majesty, in all our tests, no one has ever managed to load
the gun, much less come that close to hitting the target.
We are fortunate in knowing that we shall not find many
minds so superbly disciplined—especially in the ranks of
the Polish Royal Navy."

His Majesty spun the remaining six cartridges down the
table. "Reload and reholster your weapon, my lord. Please

accept my apologies for any . . . ah . . . inconveniences this experiment may have caused."

"Not at all, Sire. It has been a most educational experience." He scooped up the six cartridges and reloaded his MacGregor with expert ease. Although the belled muzzle of the device was still pointed in his direction, Sir Lyon's hands were no longer upon the grips.

"I congratulate you, my lord," said the King. "All of us here, with the exception of Lord Bontriomphe and yourself, have seen this device in operation before. As Sir Lyon says, you are the first ever to succeed in loading a weapon while under its spell." Then he looked at Sir Lyon. "Have you anything further to add, Sir Sorcerer?"

"Nothing, Sire . . . unless there are any questions."

Lord Bontriomphe raised a hand. "One question, Sir Lyon."

"Certainly, my lord."

Lord Bontriomphe gestured toward the device. "Is this gadget one that can be operated by anyone—by any layman, I mean—or does it require a sorcerer as operator?"

Sir Lyon smiled. "Fortunately, my lord, the device cannot be operated by one without a trained Talent. It does not, however, require the services of a Master; an apprentice of three years standing can operate the device."

"Then, Sir Lyon," said Lord Darcy, cutting off whatever it was that Lord Bontriomphe had to say, "the secret of its operation is divided into two parts. Am I correct?"

"My lord," said Sir Lyon after a moment, "your lack of the Talent is a great loss to the Sorcerers Guild. As you have correctly deduced, there are two parts to the spell. The first— and most important—part is built into this device here." He pointed toward the golden-gleaming brass instrument. "The symbolism built into this . . . er . . . 'gadget' I think you called it, Lord Bontriomphe—is most important. Within this brass cylinder are the invariables—what we call the 'hardware' of the spell. But this, by itself, is of no use. It can only be used by a sorcerer who can use the proper verbal spells to activate it. These spells we call the 'software'—if you follow me, my lord."

Lord Bontriomphe nodded, grinning. "Between the two of you," he said, "you and Lord Darcy have answered my question. Do proceed, Sir Lyon."

"I think there is no need to," said Sir Lyon. "I shall turn the rest of the discussion over to the Lord High Admiral."

"I think we can all see," said the Lord High Admiral without waiting for Sir Lyon to sit down, "what this device could do to an enemy ship in the hands of a sorcerer who knew the spells. It does not prevent them from steering the ship—that, as I understand it, would be Black Magic—but any attempt to load and fire their batteries would result in chaos. We have seen what happens when *one* man attempts it. You should see what it does to a *team!* Each man is not only fumbling his own job, but is continually getting in the way of others. As I said—chaos.

"With this device, my lords and gentlemen, the Imperial Navy can keep the Slavonic Royal Navy bottled up in the Baltic for as long as necessary. Provided, of course, that *we* have it and *they* don't.

"And that, sirs, is the crux of our problem. The secret of this device must not be allowed to fall into Polish hands!"

The crux indeed! thought Lord Darcy, suppressing a smile of satisfaction. The King had already taken out his pipe and was filling it; Lord Darcy, the Lord High Admiral, and Captain Smollett had immediately reached for their own smoking equipment. But Lord Darcy was watching Captain Smollett. He could have predicted almost to the word what the Lord High Admiral's next words would be.

"We are faced, then," said my lord the High Admiral, "with a problem of espionage. Captain Smollett, the details, if you please."

"Aye, aye, my lord." The Chief of Naval Intelligence puffed solemnly on his pipe for a second. Then: "Problem's very simple, m'luds. Answer's difficult. Someone's been tryin' to sell the secret of this device to the Poles, d'you see. Here's what's happened:

"We had a double agent in Cherbourg—name's Barbour, Georges Barbour. Not Anglo-French, actually. Pole. Did damn' good work for us, though. Trustworthiness high."

Smollett took his pipe from his mouth and gestured with the stem. "Now"—he stabbed the air with the pipestem—"a few weeks ago, Barbour got a letter—anonymous, untraceable—saying that the secret of the device was for sale. Description of exterior and of effect of device quite accurate, you understand, m'luds. Very well. Barbour contacted his superior—chap known to him only by code name 'Zed'—and asked for instructions. Zed came to me; I went to My Lord High Admiral. Amongst the three of us, we set a trap."

"Your pardon, Captain Smollett," said Lord Darcy, taking advantage of a pause in the captain's narrative.

"Certainly, m'lud."

"No one knew of this trap save yourself, my lord the High Admiral, and Zed?"

"No one, m'lud," Captain Smollett said emphatically. "Absolutely no one."

"Thank you. Pardon the interruption, Captain."

"Certainly, m'lud. At any rate." He took a puff from his pipe. "At any rate, we set it up. Barbour was to make further contact. Asking price for details of secret—five thousand golden sovereigns."

And worth it, too, Lord Darcy thought to himself. One golden sovereign was worth fifty silver sovereigns, and a "twelfth-bit"—one twelfth of a silver sovereign—would buy a cup of caffe in a public house. One can buy an awesome amount of caffe for a quarter of a million silver sovereigns.

"Negotiations took time," Captain Smollett continued. "Barbour couldn't appear too eager. Look suspicious, eh? Yes. Well, 't'any rate, negotiations went on. Barbour, you must understand, was not working through Intelligence in Cherbourg. Worked through Zed. Had to be careful of contacts with us, you see. Always watched by Polish agents in Cherbourg." Captain Smollett gave a short, sharp, barking laugh. "While we watched Poles, of course. Devilish job.

"Didn't dare break Barbour's cover, d'you see; too damn' valuable a man. Now—during the negotiations, the man who was trying to sell the secret came twice to see Barbour. Barbour described him. Black hair, black beard and moustache, straight nose, fairly tall. Wore blue-tinted glasses, spoke with a hoarse, whispery voice in a Provence accent. Fairly tall. Dressed like a member of the well-to-do merchant class."

Lord Darcy caught Lord Bontriomphe's eyes, and the two investigators exchanged quick grins. The description was such that neither of the two men needed Captain Smollett's next statement.

"Obviously a disguise," said Captain Smollett.

"A question, Captain," said Lord Bontriomphe.

"Yes, m'lud?"

"This bloke made two appointments with Barbour. Since you must have known about 'em before hand, why didn't you grab him then—when he kept the appointments?"

"Couldn't, m'lud," Captain Smollett said firmly. "Not without breaking Barbour's cover. Too many Polish agents in Cherbourg keeping an eye on Barbour. *They* knew Barbour was dealing with this chap—called himself Goodman FitzJean, by the way. Any attempt to grab FitzJean would have meant that we'd've had to grab Barbour, too, d'you see. If we didn't, the Polish agents would've known that we knew about Barbour. *Not*, p'raps, that he was a double agent, but—at least—that we knew of 'im, eh? Would've broken his cover, rendered him useless to His Slavonic Majesty. Couldn't afford that, d'you see."

"You could have had this FitzJean followed after the appointments," Lord Bontriomphe pointed out.

"We *did*, m'lud," the captain said with some acerbity. "Naturally. Both times." Captain Smollett frowned in chagrin. "Unfortunately, I am forced to admit that the man eluded our agents both times." He took a deep breath. "Our Goodman FitzJean, m'luds and gentlemen, is no amateur." He looked around at each of the others. "Damn' sharp man. Don't know whether he knew he was being followed or not. But he likely suspected Polish agents following him, even if he didn't suspect Imperial agents. Managed to get away both times, and I make no apologies, m'luds."

Captain Smollett paused to take a breath, and the Lord High Admiral cut in—this time addressing His Majesty.

"With your permission, Sire, I stand behind Captain Smollett. No agent or group of agents can follow a suspect for very long if the suspect is aware that he is being followed and is trained in evasion techniques."

"I am aware of that, my lord," said King John calmly. "Please continue, Captain Smollett."

"Yes, Sire," said the captain. He cleared his throat. "As I was saying, m'luds, we failed to follow the so-called FitzJean. But Barbour had—with our connivance—baited the trap. He agreed, d'you see, that the information FitzJean had was worth the five thousand golden sovereigns. He told FitzJean that His Slavonic Majesty's Government had agreed to the price. *Provided . . ."* Captain Smollett gestured vaguely with his pipe, and cleared his throat again.

"Provided . . . ahum . . . that he prove to Barbour that he—FitzJean, that is—prove that he was a person who had access to the secret."

Captain Smollett put his pipe back in his mouth and surveyed the others with his eyes. "I trust you follow, m'luds," he said, clenching the pipe in his molars and speaking round it. "FitzJean wouldn't divulge the plans of the device without cash in hand. But how were the Polish agents to know that the secret was worth anything? Eh?"

Captain Smollett held up a finger. *"That,* m'luds, is what our double agent Barbour told FitzJean. Not the truth, of course. Barbour had to give a cover story to His Slavonic Majesty's agents. Told them, as a matter of fact, that he had contacted an Imperial Naval officer who was willing to give him the plans for the deployment of Imperial and Scandinavian ships in the North Sea and the Baltic. Price, according to what Barbour told his Polish superiors, was two hundred golden sovereigns." Captain Smollett spread his hands in a gesture of disgust. "Most they'd pay, of course, since fleet deployment can be changed rather quickly. But still useful.

"Evidently, the Poles agreed. But they wouldn't pay until they'd received the information. On the other hand, FitzJean demanded a hundred gold sovereigns just to prove that he was in earnest.

"We agreed. Barbour was to pretend that the money was coming from Poland. Said that, upon proof of FitzJean's bona fides, he'd give FitzJean a hundred sovereigns and then get the other forty-nine hundred and pay them when the details of the secret were delivered. Trouble was, FitzJean wouldn't make a definite appointment. Clever of him, you know. Kept Barbour on tenterhooks, as it were. D'you follow, m'luds?"

"I follow," said Lord Bontriomphe. "This FitzJean was actually trapped into giving away his identity for five thousand silver sovereigns. Right? But he didn't do so, did he? That is, your organization never paid the hundred gold sovereigns, did they?"

"No, m'lud," said Captain Smollett. "The hundred sovereigns were never paid." He looked across the table. "Explain, Commander," he said to Lord Ashley.

Commander Lord Ashley nodded. "Aye, sir." He looked at Lord Darcy, then at Lord Bontriomphe. "I was supposed to bring the money to him yesterday morning. He was dead when I arrived; stabbed only minutes before, evidently."

He went on to explain exactly what he had done following his examination of the body, including the conversation with Chief Henri and Lord Admiral Brencourt.

Lord Bontriomphe listened without asking questions until the commander's narrative was finished; then he looked at the Lord High Admiral and waited expectantly.

"Huhum!" The Lord High Admiral gave a rumbling chuckle. "Yes, my lords. The connection, of course. It was this: Sir James Zwinge, Master Sorcerer and Chief Forensic Sorcerer for the City of London, was also the head of our counterespionage branch—operating under the code name of 'Zed.' "

CHAPTER 9

"And now," said Lord Darcy an hour later, "I am prepared to make an arrest for the murder of Master Sir James Zwinge."

My lord the Marquis of London remained all but motionless behind his desk. Only the slight narrowing of his eyes gave any indication that he had heard what the Chief Investigator of Normandy had said.

Lord Darcy and Lord Bontriomphe had returned to de London's office immediately after His Majesty had dismissed the meeting at Westminster Palace. Lord Darcy could still hear the King's last orders: "Then we are agreed, my lords. Our civilian investigators will proceed to investigate these murders as though they were in no way connected with the Navy, as though they were merely seeking a murderer. No connection must be made between the killing of Barbour and the killing of Sir James, as far as the public is concerned. Meanwhile, the Naval Intelligence Corps will be working to uncover the other contacts of Barbour, and make a minute investigation of the reports he filed with 'Zed' and the reports 'Zed' filed with the London office. There may be more evidence than we realize in those report files.

Finally, we must all do our best to see that His Slavonic Majesty's secret agents remain at least as much in the dark as we are."

For a moment, Lord Darcy had thought that last bit of heavy sarcasm from the King had made Lord High Admiral Peter de Valera ap Smith angry. Then he had realized that the Lord High Admiral's choked expression came from a valiant and successful attempt to smother a laugh.

By Heaven, Lord Darcy had thought, *I must get to know that old pirate better.*

My lord of London had been seated behind his desk reading a book when Lord Darcy and Lord Bontriomphe had entered the office. The Marquis had picked up a thin golden bookmark, put it carefully between the pages of the book, closed the book and placed it on the desktop before him. "Good morning, my lords," he had rumbled, inclining his head perhaps an eighth of an inch. "There is a letter for you, Lord Darcy." He had pushed a white envelope across the desk with a fat forefinger. "Delivered this morning by special courier."

"Thank you," Lord Darcy had murmured politely, picking up the envelope. He had broken the seal, read the three sheets of closely written paper, refolded them, replaced them in the envelope, and smiled.

"A very informative letter from—as you no doubt noticed from the seal, My Lord Marquis—Sir Eliot Meredith, my Assistant Chief Investigator. And now, I am prepared to make an arrest for the murder of Master Sir James Zwinge."

"Indeed?" said my lord the Marquis after a moment. "You have solved the case? Without checking the evidence personally? Without questioning a witness? How extraordinarily astute—even for you, my dear cousin."

"You are hardly one to cavil at lack of personal investigation," Lord Darcy said mildly, seating himself comfortably in the red leather chair. "As for my witness, there is no need to question him any further. The information is before us; we have but to examine it.

The Marquis put his palms flat on his desktop, inhaled four pecks of air, and let it out slowly through his nose. "All right. Let's hear it."

"It is simplicity itself. So obvious, in fact, that one tends to overlook it because of the very obviousness of the killer.

Consider: A man is killed inside a locked and sealed room—in a hotel full of magicians. Naturally, we are led to believe that it is black magic. Obvious. In fact, *too* obvious. That is exactly what we are supposed to believe."

"How *was* it done, then?" asked the Marquis, becoming interested.

"Zwinge was stabbed to death right in front of the very witnesses who were there to testify that the room was locked and sealed," Lord Darcy said calmly.

My lord the Marquis closed his eyes. "I see. That's the way the wind blows, eh?" He opened his eyes again and looked at Lord Bontriomphe. Lord Bontriomphe looked back at him, steadily, expressionlessly. "Continue, Lord Darcy," the Marquis said. "I should like to hear all of it."

"As you have deduced, dear cousin," Lord Darcy continued, "only Bontriomphe could have done it. It was he who broke the door down. He was the first one in the room. He ordered the others to stay out, to stay back. Then he bent over the unconscious body of Sir James, and, concealing his actions with his own body, sank a knife into the Master Sorcerer's heart."

"How did he know Sir James would be unconscious? Why did Sir James scream? What motive did Bontriomphe have?" The three questions were deliberate, almost emotionless. "You have explanations, I presume?"

"Naturally. There are several drugs in the *materia medica* of the adept herbalist which will cause unconsciousness and coma. Bontriomphe, knowing that Sir James intended to lock himself into his room yesterday morning, managed to slip some such drug into the sorcerer's morning caffe—a simple job for an expert. After that, all he had to do was wait. Eventually, Sir James would be missed. Someone would wonder why he had not kept an appointment. Someone would check his room and find it locked. At last, someone would ask the management to see if something could be wrong. When the manager found he could not open the door, he would ask for official help. And, fortuitously, Lord Bontriomphe, Chief Investigator for My Lord Marquis of London, just happens to be right on the spot. He calls for an ax and . . ." Lord Darcy turned one hand palm up as though he were handing the Marquis the whole case on a platter, and left the sentence unfinished.

"Go on." There was a dangerous note in the Marquis' voice.

"The scream is easily explained," Lord Darcy said. "Sir James was not completely comatose. He heard Master Sean knock. Now, Sean had an appointment at that time; Sir James knew it was he at the door. Aroused by the knock, he called out: 'Master Sean! Help!' And then he collapsed back into his drugged coma. Bontriomphe, of course, could not have known that would happen, but it was certainly a stroke of luck, even though it was completely unnecessary to his plan. If there had been no scream, Sean would certainly have known something was amiss and notified the manager. After that, everything would have followed naturally."

Lord Darcy folded his arms, slumped back in the chair, rested his chin on his chest, and looked at the speechless, glowering de London from beneath his brows. "The motive is quite clear. Jealousy."

"*Pah!*" the Marquis exploded. "Now I have you! Up to now, you have been clever. But now you show that your wits are addled. A woman? *Pfui!* Lord Bontriomphe may occasionally play the fool, but he is not a fool about women. I will not go so far as to say that the woman does not live whom Lord Bontriomphe could not get if he wanted her, but I will say that his ego is such that he would have no desire for a woman who did not want him or who had rejected him for another. He would not go out of his way to snap his fingers at such a woman, much less kill because of her."

"Agreed," said Lord Darcy complacently. "I mentioned no woman. And I was not speaking of *his* jealousy."

"Of whose, then?"

"Of yours."

"Hah! This is fatuous."

"Not at all. Your hobby of herb cultivation, my lord, is one of the strongest passions of your life. You are an acknowledged expert and are proud of that fact. Zwinge, too, was an herbalist, but not quite in your league. Still, if you ever had any real rival in the field, it was Master Sir James Zwinge. Recently, Sir James succeeded in growing Polish devilwort from the seed instead of from cuttings, as is normally done. You have failed to do so. Therefore, out of pique, you asked Bontriomphe to remove your rival; he, out of loyalty, proceeded to do so. And there you have it, my lord: Method, Motive, and Opportunity. *Quod erat demonstrandum.*"

My Lord Marquis swiveled his head and glared at Lord Bontriomphe. "Are you an accessory to this imbecilic tom-foolery?"

Lord Bontriomphe shook his head once, left to right. "No, my lord. But it does look as though he has us dead to rights, doesn't it?"

"Buffoon!" the Marquis snorted. He looked back at Lord Darcy. "Very well. I know when I am being gulled as well as you do. I regret having jailed Master Sean; it was frivolous. And you are well aware that I would just as soon go to the Tower myself as to lose the services of Lord Bontriomphe for any extended length of time. Outside this building, he is my eyes and ears. I will sign an order for Master Sean's release immediately. Since you have been assigned to this case by the King, you will, of course, be remunerated from the Royal Privy Purse?"

"Beginning today, yes," said Lord Darcy. "But there is the little matter of yesterday—including cross-Channel transportation, train ticket, and cab fare."

"Done," the Marquis growled. He signed a release form, poured melted sealing wax on it, and stamped it with the seal of the Marquisate of London, all without a word. Then he heaved his massive bulk out of the chair. "Lord Bontriomphe, give my lord cousin what is owed him. Open the wall safe and take it out of petty cash. I am going upstairs to the plant rooms." He did not quite slam the door as he left.

Lord Bontriomphe looked at Lord Darcy. "Look here—you don't really think . . ."

"*Chah!* Don't be ridiculous. I know perfectly well that every word of your narrative was accurate and truthful. And the Marquis is quite aware that I know it." Lord Darcy was not one to err in a matter of judgment like that, and, as it turned out, he did not. Lord Bontriomphe's recital was correct and precise in every detail.

"Let's get to the Tower," said Lord Darcy.

Lord Bontriomphe was at his desk taking a pistol out of a drawer. "Just a second, my lord," he said, "I once resolved never to go out on a murder case unarmed. By the way, don't you think it would be best to set up an auxiliary headquarters in the Royal Steward? That way we can keep in touch with each other and with Chief Hennely's plainclothes investigators."

"An excellent idea," said Lord Darcy, "and speaking of plainclothes investigators, did you get statements from everyone concerned yesterday?"

"As many as possible, my lord. Of course, we couldn't get everyone, but I think the reports we have now are fairly complete."

"Good. Bring them along, will you? I should like to look them over on our way to the Tower. Are you ready to go?"

"Ready, my lord," said Lord Bontriomphe.

"Very well, then," said Lord Darcy. "Come, let's get Master Sean out of durance vile."

CHAPTER 10

As the official carriage, bearing the London arms, moved through the streets toward the Royal Steward Hotel, its pneumatic tires jouncing briskly on their spring suspensions as a soft accompaniment to the clopping of the horses' hooves, Sean O Lochlainn, Master Sorcerer, leaned back in the seat, clutching his symbol-decorated carpetbag to his round paunch.

"Ah, my lords," he said to the two men on the seat opposite, "a relief it is, indeed, to be free again. Twenty-four hours of sitting in the Tower is not my notion of a grand time, and you may be sure of that. Not that I object to being alone in a comfortable room for a while; any sorcerer who doesn't take a week or so off every year for a Contemplation Retreat will find his power deserting him. But when there's work to be done . . ." He paused. "My lord, you didn't get me out of the Tower by *solving* this case, did you?"

Lord Darcy laughed. "No fear, my good Sean. You haven't missed any of the excitement yet."

"His lordship," said Lord Bontriomphe, "got you out by simple but effective blackmail."

"*Counter*-blackmail, if you please," Lord Darcy corrected.

"I merely showed de London that Lord Bontriomphe could be jailed on the same sort of flimsy evidence that the Marquis used to jail you."

"Now wait a moment," said Lord Bontriomphe. "The evidence wasn't all *that* flimsy. There was certainly enough—in both cases—to permit holding a man for questioning."

"Certainly," Lord Darcy agreed. "But My Lord Marquis had no intention of questioning Master Sean. He was adhering to the letter of the law rather than to its spirit. It is a matter of family rivalry; we have, the Marquis and I, similar although not identical abilities, and therefore a basically friendly but at times emotionally charged antagonism. He would not dare have locked up an ordinary subject of His Majesty on such evidence unless he honestly believed that the suspect had actually committed the crime. Indeed, I will go further: he would never even have considered such an act."

"I'm glad to hear you say that," said Lord Bontriomphe, "since it happens to be true. But once in a while, this rivalry goes a little too far. Normally, I keep out of it, but then—"

"Permit me to correct you," Lord Darcy said with a smile. "Normally, you do *not* keep out of it. To the contrary, you are normally rigidly loyal to My Lord Marquis; you normally take *his* side, forcing me to outwit both of you—an admittedly difficult job. This time, however, you felt that imprisoning Master Sean in order to get at me was just a little too much. I am well aware that, had it been *I* who went to the Tower, the matter would have been quite different."

Lord Bontriomphe gazed dreamily at the roof of the carriage. "Now *there's* a thought," he said in a speculative tone.

"Don't think on it too hard, my lord," said Master Sean with gentle menace. "Not too hard at all, at all."

Lord Bontriomphe brought his eyes down sharply and started to say something, but his words were forever lost as the carriage slowed suddenly and the driver opened the trapdoor in the roof and said:

"The Royal Steward, my lords."

Half a minute later, the footman opened the door, and the three men got out. Lord Bontriomphe quietly slipped a couple of large coins into the footman's hand. "Wait for us, Barney. See that the carriage and horses are taken care of, and then you and Denys wait in the pub across the street. We may be quite some time, so have a few beers and relax. I'll send word if we need you."

"Very good, my lord," Goodman Barney said warmly. "Thank you."

Then Lord Bontriomphe followed Lord Darcy and Master Sean into the Royal Steward.

Lord Darcy was standing alone just inside the foyer, looking through the glass-paned doors at the crowd in the lobby.

"Where's Master Sean?" Bontriomphe asked.

"In there. I sent him on ahead. As you will observe, there are at least a dozen well-wishers and possibly two dozen who are merely curious, all of whom are crowded around Sean, congratulating him upon his release, saying they knew all along he was innocent, and pumping him for information about the murder of Sir James Zwinge. While their attention is thus distracted, my lord, you and I will make a quiet entrance and go directly to the murder room. Come."

They did not attract attention as they went in. This was Visitors' Day at the Sorcerers Convention, and the lobby was filled with folk who had come to see the displays and the sorcerers themselves. They were just two more sightseers.

At one of the display booths, a journeyman sorcerer was demonstrating a children's toy to two wide-eyed children and a fondly patronizing father. It consisted of a six-inch black wand with one white tip, five differently-colored pith balls an inch in diameter, and a foot-long board with six holes in it, five of which were ringed with colors to match the balls and the fifth one ringed with white.

"Now you'll notice, my lads," said the journeyman sorcerer, "that the balls aren't in their proper holes; the colors don't match. The object of the game is to put 'em right, you see. The rule is that you move one ball at a time, like this:" He aimed the wand at the board, which was several feet away, and one of the balls floated smoothly up and across, to drop into the extra hole. Then another moved into the vacated hole to match colors. The process was repeated until all the balls were in the proper holes. "You see? Now, I'll just mix these balls up again and let you try it, lad. Just point the white tip of the wand and think of which color ball you want to come up; then, when it's in the air, think of the color hole you want it to go to. There, now. That's it—"

It was more than just a toy, Lord Darcy knew; it was a testing and teaching device. With the spell it now had on it, anyone could do the trick; but the spell was timed to fade slowly over a period of a few months. By that time, most children were thoroughly tired of it, anyway. But if a rare child with the Talent got hold of one, his interest usually did not wane. Furthermore, he began to get the feel of the spell itself, aided by the simple ritual and ceremony of the game. If that happened, the child would still be able to do the trick a year later, though none of his un-Talented friends would. The original spell had worn off and had been replaced by the child's own simple version. A booklet went with the game which explained all that to the parents, urging them to have the child given further tests if he succeeded in preserving the activity of the toy.

At another booth, a priest in clerical black with white lace at collar and cuffs was distributing booklets describing the new building being erected at Oxford to house the Royal Thaumaturgical Laboratories at Edward's College. The display was a scale model of the proposed structure.

Directly in their path, the two men saw what looked like an ordinary door frame. An illusion sign floated in its center, translucent blue letters that said: PLEASE STEP THROUGH.

As they did, the illusion sign vanished and they could feel what seemed to be a slight wind tugging at their clothing. On the other side, another illusion sign appeared.

THANK YOU
*If you will examine your clothing,
you will see that every speck
of loose dust and lint has been removed.
This is a prototype device, still in the
experimental stage. Eventually, no
home will be without one.
Wells & Sons
Thaumaturgical Home Appliances*

"Quite a gadget," said Lord Bontriomphe. "Look; even our boots are shiny," he added as they walked through the second sign and it dissolved around them.

"Useful," Lord Darcy agreed, "but quite impracticable. Sean told me they had it at the last Convention. It makes a good advertisement for the company, but that 'no home will be without one' is visionary. Far too expensive, since the spell has to be renewed by a Master Sorcerer at least once a week. With this mob in here, they'll be lucky if they get through the day with it."

"Hm-m-m. Like that 'See London From the Air' device they had a few years back," said Bontriomphe. "Remember that?"

"I read something about it. I don't recall the details," Lord Darcy said.

"It looked quite impressive. They had a crystal ball about"—he held his hands in front of him as though he were grasping an imaginary sphere—"oh, ten inches in diameter, I guess. It was mounted on a pedestal, and you looked into it from above. It gave you the weird feeling that you were looking down from a great height, from a point just above Admiral Buckingham Hall, where the exhibit was. You could actually see people walking about, and carriages moving through the streets, as though you were up in a cathedral spire looking down. There was a magic mirror suspended a couple of hundred feet above the building, you see, which projected the scene into the crystal by psychic reflection."

"Ah, I see. Whatever happened to it? I've heard no more about it," Lord Darcy said.

"Well, right off the bat, the War Office was interested. You can imagine what sort of reconnaissance you'd have, with a magic mirror floating high over enemy lines and an observer safe behind your own lines watching everything they were doing. Anyway, the War Office thaumaturgists are still working on it, but it hasn't come to anything. In the first place, it takes three Masters to run it: One to levitate the mirror, one to keep the mirror activated, and one to keep the receiving crystal activated. And they have to be specially trained for the job and then train together as a team. In the second place, the sorcerers controlling the mirror have to be within sight of the mirror, and the plane of the surface has to be perpendicular to a radius of the crystal ball. Don't ask me why; I'm no sorcerer and I don't know a thing about the theory. At any rate, the thing hasn't been made practical for long distance transmission of images yet."

They left the lobby and started upstairs toward the late Sir James Zwinge's room.

"So far," said Lord Darcy, "aside from such things as the semaphore and the heliotelegraph—both of which require line-of-sight towers for transmission—the only practical means of long distance communication we have is the teleson. And the mathematical thaumaturgists still have not come up with a satisfactory theory to explain its functioning. Ah! I see that your Armsmen are on duty." They had reached the top of the stairway. Down the hall, directly in front of the door to the murder room were two black-clad Armsmen of the King's Peace.

"Good morning, Jeffers, Dubois," said Lord Bontriomphe as he and Lord Darcy approached the door.

The Armsmen saluted. "Good morning, my lord," said the older of the two.

"Everything all right? No disturbances?"

"None, my lord. Quiet as a tomb."

"Jeffers, " said Lord Bontriomphe with a smile, "with a wit like that, you will either rise rapidly to Master-at-Arms or you will remain a foot patrolman all your life."

"My ambition is modest, my lord," said Jeffers with a straight face. "I only wish to become a Sergeant-at-Arms. For that, I need only to be a half-wit."

"Foot patrolman," Lord Darcy said sadly. "Forever." He looked at the door to the murder room. "I see they have covered the hole in the door."

"Yes, my lord," said Jeffers. "They just tacked this panel over the hole. Otherwise, the door's untouched. Would you be wanting to look in, my lords?" He took a large, thick, heavy brass key from the pouch at his belt. "This is Sir James' key," he said. "You can open the door, but Grand Master Sir Lyon has put a spell on the room itself, my lords."

Lord Darcy took the key, fitted it into the long, narrow keyhole, turned the bolt, and opened the door. He and Lord Bontriomphe stopped at the threshold.

There was no tangible barrier at the door. There was nothing they could see or touch. But the barrier was almost palpably there, nonetheless. Lord Darcy found that he had no desire to enter the room at all. Quite the contrary; he felt a distinct aversion to the room, a sense of wanting to avoid, at all costs, going into that room for any reason whatever. There was nothing in that room that interested him, no reason at all why he should enter it. It was taboo—a forbidden place. To look from without was both necessary and desirable; to enter was neither necessary nor desirable.

Lord Darcy surveyed the room with his eyes.

Master Sir James Zwinge still lay where he had fallen, looking as though he had died only minutes before, thanks to the preservative spell which had been cast over the corpse.

Footsteps came down the hall. Lord Darcy turned to see Master Sean approaching.

"Sorry to be so long, my lord," said the sorcerer as he neared the door. He stopped at the threshold. "Now what have we here? Hm-m-m. An aversion spell, eh? Hm-m-m. And cast by a Master, too, I'll be bound. It would take quite a time to solve that one." He stood looking through the door.

"It was cast by Grand Master Sir Lyon himself," said Lord Darcy.

"Then I'll go fetch him to take it off," said Master Sean. "I wouldn't waste time trying to take it off meself."

"Pardon me, Master Sorcerer," said Armsman Jeffers deferentially, "are you Master Sean O Lochlainn?"

"That I am."

The Armsman took an envelope from an inside jacket pocket. "The Grand Master," he said, "told me to be sure and give this to you when you came, Master Sean."

Master Sean placed his symbol-decorated carpetbag on the floor, took the envelope, opened it, extracted a single sheet of paper, and read it carefully.

"Ah!" he said, his round Irish face beaming. "I see! Ingenious! I shall most certainly have to remember that one!" He looked at Lord Darcy with the smile still wreathing his face. "Sir Lyon has given me the key. He expected me to be here this morning. Now, if you'll excuse me for a few minutes—"

The tubby little Irish sorcerer knelt down and opened his carpetbag. He fished around inside and took out a gold-and-ebony wand, a small brazen bowl, an iron tripod with six-inch legs, two silver phials, and an oddly constructed flint-and-steel fire-striker.

The others stepped back respectfully. One does not disturb a magician at work.

Master Sean placed the tripod on the floor just in front of the open door and set the small brazen bowl on top of it. Then he put in a few lumps of charcoal from his carpetbag. Within two minutes, he had the coals glowing redly. Then he added a large pinch of powder from each of the two silver phials, and a dense column of aromatic blue-gray smoke arose from the small brazier. Master Sean traced a series of symbols in the air with his wand while he murmured something the others could not hear. Then he carefully folded, in an intricate and complex manner, the letter from Sir Lyon Grey. When it was properly folded, he dropped it on the coals. As it burst into flame, he traced more symbols and murmured further words.

"There," he said. "You can go in now, my lords."

The two investigators walked across the threshold. Their aversion to doing so had completely vanished. Master Sean took a small bronze lid from his carpetbag and fitted it tightly over the mouth of the little brazier.

"Just leave it there, lads," he said to the two Armsmen. "It will cool off in a few minutes. Mind you don't knock it over, now." Then he joined Lord Darcy and Lord Bontriomphe inside the murder room.

Lord Darcy closed the door and looked at it. From the inside, the damage done by Lord Bontriomphe's ax work was plainly visible. Otherwise, there was nothing unusual about the door. A rapid but thorough inspection of the doors and windows convinced Lord Darcy that Lord Bontriomphe had been absolutely right when he said the room was sealed. There were no secret panels, no trapdoors. The windows were firmly bolted, and there was no way they could have been bolted from the outside by other than magical means.

With difficulty, Lord Darcy slid back the bolt on one of the windows and opened it. It creaked gently as it swung outward.

Lord Darcy looked out the window. There was a thirty-foot drop of smooth stone beneath him. The window opened onto a small courtyard, where several chair-surrounded tables formed a part of the dining facilities of the Royal Steward Hotel.

Some of the tables were occupied. Five sorcerers, three

priests, and a bishop had all heard the window open and were looking up at him.

Lord Darcy craned his neck around and looked up. Ten feet above were the windows of the next floor. Lord Darcy pulled his head back in and closed the window.

"No one went out that way," he said firmly. "For an ordinary man to have done so would have required a rope. He would have had either to slide down thirty feet or to climb up ten feet hand over hand."

"An *ordinary* man," said Lord Bontriomphe, emphasizing the word. "But levitation is not too difficult a trick for a Master Sorcerer."

"What say you, Master Sean?" Lord Darcy asked the tubby little sorcerer.

"It could have been done that way," Master Sean admitted.

"Furthermore," said Lord Bontriomphe, "those bolts could have been thrown from the outside by magic."

"Indeed they could," Master Sean agreed.

Lord Bontriomphe looked expectantly at Lord Darcy.

"Very well," said Lord Darcy with a smile, "let us proceed to try that theory by what the geometers call, I believe, the *reductio ad absurdum*. Imagine the scene. What happens?"

He gestured toward the body on the floor. "Sir James is stabbed. Our sorcerer-murderer—if you'll pardon the double entendre—goes to the window. He opens it. Then he steps up to the sill and steps out into empty air, levitating himself as he does so. Then he closes the window and proceeds to cast a spell which slides the bolts into their sockets. When that is done, he floats off somewhere—up or down, it matters not which." He looked at Master Sean. "How long would that take?"

"Five or six minutes at the least. If he could do it at all. Levitation causes a tremendous psychic drain; the spell can only be held for a matter of minutes. In addition, you're asking him to cast a second spell while he's holding the first. A spell of the type that was cast on this room is what we call a *static* spell, my lord. It imposes a *condition*, you see. But levitating and the moving of bolts are *kinetic* spells; you have to keep them moving. To use two kinetic spells at the same time requires tremendous concentration, power, and precision. I would hesitate, myself, to try casting a window-locking spell with a thirty-foot drop beneath me. Certainly not if I were in a hurry or distracted."

"And even if it could be done, it would take five or six minutes," Lord Darcy said. "Bontriomphe, would you mind opening the *other* window? We haven't tested it yet."

The London investigator drew back the bolt and pushed the window open. It groaned audibly.

"What do you see out there?" Lord Darcy asked.

"About nine pairs of eyes staring up at me," Lord Bontriomphe said.

"Exactly. Both windows make a slight noise when they are opened. That noise is quite audible in the courtyard below. Yesterday morning, Sir James' scream was clearly audible through that window, but even if it had not been— even if Sir James had not screamed at all when he was stabbed—the killer could not have gone out through that window without being seen, much less hovered there for five or six minutes."

Lord Bontriomphe pulled the window closed again. "What if he were invisible?" he asked, looking at the little Irish sorcerer.

"The Tarnhelm Effect?" asked Master Sean. He chuckled. "My lord, regardless of what the layman may think, the Tarnhelm Effect is extremely difficult to use in practice. Besides, 'invisibility' is a layman's term. Spells using the Tarnhelm Effect are very similar in structure to the aversion spell you met at the door to this room. If a sorcerer were to cast such a spell about himself, your eyes would avoid looking directly at him. You wouldn't realize it yourself, but you would simply keep your eyes averted from him at all times. He could stand in the middle of a crowd and no one could later swear that he was there because no one would have seen him except out of the corner of the eye, if you follow me.

"Even if he were alone, you wouldn't see him because you'd never look at him. You would subconsciously assume that whatever it was you were seeing out of the corner of your eye was a cabinet or a hatrack or an umbrella stand or a lamppost—whatever was most likely under the circumstances. Your mind would explain him away as something that *ought* to be there, as a part of the normal background and therefore unnoticeable.

"But he wouldn't actually be invisible. You could see him, for instance, in a mirror or other reflecting surface simply because the spell wouldn't keep your eyes away from the mirror."

"He could cast a sight-avoidance spell on the mirror, couldn't he?" Lord Bontriomphe asked. "That's a static spell, I believe."

"Certainly," said Master Sean. "He could cast a sight-avoidance spell on every reflecting surface in the place. But a man has to look *somewhere,* and even a layman would get suspicious under circumstances like that. Besides, to anyone with even a half-trained Talent, he'd be detectable immediately.

"And even supposing he did make himself invisible outside that window, do you realize what he would have to do? Now you have him juggling three spells at once: he's levitating himself; he's making himself 'invisible'; and he's closing that window.

"No, my lord; it won't do. It just isn't humanly possible."

Lord Darcy let his gaze wander over the room. "That's settled, then. Our killer did not go out those windows either by thaumaturgical or by ordinary physical means. Therefore, we—"

"Wait a minute!" said Lord Bontriomphe, his eyes widening. He pointed a finger at Master Sean. "Look here; suppose it happened this way. The killer stabs Master Sir James. His victim screams. The killer knows that you are outside the door. He knows he can't get out through the door. The windows are out, too, for the reasons you've just given. What can he do? He uses the Tarnhelm Effect. When I come busting in here with an ax, I don't see him. As far as I'm concerned, the room is empty except for the corpse. I wouldn't be able to see him, would I? Then, when the door's open, he walks out as cool as an oyster, with nobody noticing him."

Master Sean shook his head. "*You* wouldn't notice him; that's so. But *I* would have. And so would Grand Master Sir Lyon. We were both looking in through that hole in the door, and a man can see the whole room from there—even the bathroom, when the door to it is open."

Lord Bontriomphe looked at the bathroom through the open door. "No, you can't. Take a look. Suppose he were lying down in the tub. You couldn't even see him from in here."

"True. But I distinctly recall your looking down directly into the tub. You couldn't have done that if a killer using the Tarnhelm Effect were in it."

Lord Bontriomphe frowned thoughtfully. "Yes. I did. Hm-m-m. Well, that eliminates that. He wasn't in the room, and he didn't leave the room." He looked at Lord Darcy. "What does that leave?"

"We don't know yet, my dear fellow. We need more data." He stepped over to where the body lay and knelt down, being careful not to disturb anything.

Master Sir James Zwinge had been a short, lean man, with receding gray hair and a small gray beard and moustache. He was wearing a neat, fairly expensive gentleman's suit, rather than the formal sorcerer's costume to which he was entitled. As Bontriomphe had said, it was difficult to see the stab wound at first glance. It was small, barely an inch long, and had not opened widely. It was further obscured by the blood which covered the front of the dead magician's clothing. Nearby, a black-handled, silver-bladed knife lay in the pool of blood on the floor, its gleaming blade splashed with red.

"This blood—" Lord Darcy gestured with his hand. "Are you absolutely certain, Bontriomphe, that it was fresh when you broke into this room?"

"Absolutely certain," Bontriomphe said. "It was bright red and still liquid. There was still a slight flow of blood from the wound itself. I'll admit I am not a chirurgeon, but I am certainly no amateur when it comes to knowing something about *that* particular subject. He couldn't have been dead more than a few minutes when I first saw his body."

Lord Darcy nodded. "Indeed. The condition of the blood even now, under the preservation spell, shows a certain freshness."

He gestured toward a key that lay a few feet away from the body. "Is that your key, my lord?"

Lord Bontriomphe nodded. "Yes. I put it there to mark the spot when I picked up Sir James' key."

"It is still where you put it?"

"Yes."

Lord Darcy measured the distance between the key and the door with his eye. "Four and a half feet," he murmured. He stood up. "Give me Sir James' key. Thank you. An experiment is in order."

"An experiment, my lord?" Master Sean repeated. His face brightened.

"Not of the thaumaturgical variety, my good Sean. That will come in good time." He walked over to the door and opened it, ignoring the two Armsmen who stood at attention outside. He looked down at his feet. "Master Sean, would you be so good as to remove this brazier?"

The tubby little Irish sorcerer bent over and put his hand near the brazen bowl. "It's still a little hot. I'll put it on the table." He picked up the tripod by one leg and carried it into the room.

"I don't see what you're getting at," said Lord Bontriomphe.

"Surely you have noticed the clearance between the bottom of the door and the floor?" Lord Darcy said. "Is it possible that the murderer simply stabbed Sir James, came out, locked the door behind him, and slid the key back under the door?"

Master Sean blinked. "With me standing outside the door all the time?" he said in surprise. "Why, that's impossible, me lord!"

"Once we have eliminated the impossible," Lord Darcy said calmly, "we shall be able to concentrate on the merely improbable."

He knelt down and looked at the floor beneath the door. "As you see, the space is somewhat wider than it appears to be from the inside. The carpeting does not extend under the door. Close the door, if you will, Master Sean."

The sorcerer pushed the door shut and waited patiently on the other side. Lord Darcy put the heavy brass key on the floor and attempted to push it under the door. "I thought not," he said, almost to himself. "The key is much too large and thick. It can be forced under—" He pushed hard at the key. "But it wedges tight. And the thickness of the carpet would stop it on the other side." He pulled the key out. "Open the door again, Master Sean."

The door swung inward. "Observe," Lord Darcy continued, "how the attempt to push it under has scored the wood at that point. It would be impossible even to make the attempt without leaving traces, much less—" He paused, cutting off his own words abruptly. "What is this?" he said, leaning over to peer more closely at a spot on the carpet inside the room.

"What's *what?*" asked Lord Bontriomphe.

Lord Darcy ignored him. He was looking at a spot on the carpet near the right-hand doorpost, on the side away from the hinges, and approximately eight inches in from the edge of the carpet itself.

"May I borrow your magnifying glass, Master Sean?" Lord Darcy said without looking up.

"Certainly." Master Sean went over to the table, opened his symbol-decorated carpetbag, took out a large bone-handled lens, and handed it to his lordship.

"What is it?" he asked, echoing Lord Bontriomphe's question. He knelt down to look, as Lord Darcy continued to study a small spot on the carpet without answering.

The mark, Master Sean saw, was a dark stain in the shape of a half circle, with the straight side running parallel to the door and the arc curving in toward the interior of the room. It was small, about half the size of a man's thumbnail.

"Is it blood?" asked Master Sean.

"It is difficult to tell on this dark green carpet," said Lord Darcy. "It might be blood; it might be some other dark substance. Whatever it is, it has soaked into the fibers of the pile, although not down to the backing. Interesting." He stood up.

"May I?" said Lord Bontriomphe, holding out his hand for the glass.

"Certainly." He handed over the lens, and while the London investigator knelt to look at the stain, Lord Darcy said to Master Sean: "I would be much obliged, my dear Sean, if you would make a similarity test on that stain. I should like to know if it is blood, and, if so, whether it is Sir James' blood." He narrowed his eyes thoughtfully. "And while you're at it, do a thorough check of the bloodstain around the body. I should like to be certain that all of the blood is actually Sir James Zwinge's."

"Very good, my lord. Would you want any other tests besides the usual ones?"

"Yes. First: Was there, *in fact,* anyone at all in this room when Sir James Zwinge died? Second: If there was any black magical effect directed at this room, of what sort was it?"

"I shall endeavor to give satisfaction, my lord," Master Sean said doubtfully, "but it won't be easy."

Lord Bontriomphe rose to his feet and handed Master Sean the magnifying glass. "What would be difficult about it?" he asked. "I know those tests aren't exactly routine, but I've seen journeyman sorcerers perform them."

"My dear Bontriomphe," said Lord Darcy, "consider the circumstances. If, as we assume, this act of murder was committed by a magician, then he was most certainly a master magician. Knowing, as he must have, that this hotel abounds in master magicians, he would have taken every precaution to cover his tracks and hide his identity—precautions that no ordinary criminal would ever think of and could not take even if he *had* thought of them. Since Master Sir James was killed rather early yesterday morning, it is likely that the murderer had all of the preceding night for the casting of his spells. Can we, then, expect Master Sean to unravel in a few moments what another master may have taken all night to accomplish?"

He put his hand into an inside jacket pocket and took out the envelope which de London had handed him earlier. "Besides, I have further evidence that the killer or killers are quite capable of covering their tracks. This morning's communication from Sir Eliot Meredith, my Chief Assistant, is a report of what he has thus far discovered in regard to the murder of the double agent Georges Barbour in Cherbourg. It contains two apparently conflicting pieces of information." He looked at Master Sean.

"My good Sean. Would you give me your professional opinion of the journeyman who is the forensic sorcerer for Chief Master-at-Arms Henri Vert in Cherbourg?"

"Goodman Juseppy?" Master Sean pursed his lips, then said: "Competent, I should say; quite competent. He's not a Master, of course, but—"

"Would you consider him capable of bungling the two tests which I have just asked you to perform?"

"We are all capable of error, my lord. But . . . no. In an ordinary case, I should say that Goodman Juseppy's testimony as to his results would be quite reliable."

"In an ordinary case. Just so. But what if he were pitted against the machinations of a Master Sorcerer?"

Master Sean shrugged. "Then it's certainly possible that his results might be in error. Goodman Juseppy simply isn't of that caliber."

"Then that may account for the conflicting evidence," Lord Darcy said. "I hesitate to say definitely that it does, but it may."

"All right," said Lord Bontriomphe impatiently, "just what is this conflicting evidence?"

"According to Goodman Juseppy's official report, there was no one in Barbour's room at the time he was killed. Furthermore, there had not been anyone but himself in the room for several hours before."

"Very well," said Lord Bontriomphe, "but where is the conflict?"

"The second test," said Lord Darcy calmly. "Goodman Juseppy could detect no trace whatever of black magic— or, indeed, of any kind of sorcery at all."

In the silence that followed, Lord Darcy returned the envelope to his jacket pocket.

Master Sean O Lochlainn sighed. "Well, my lords, I'll perform the tests. However, I should like to call in another sorcerer to help. That way—"

"No!" Lord Darcy interrupted firmly. "Under no circumstances! As of this moment, Master Sean, you are the only sorcerer in this world in whom I can unhesitatingly place complete trust."

The little Irish sorcerer turned, took a deep breath, and looked up into Lord Darcy's eyes. "My lord," he said in a low, solemn voice, "in all humility I wish to point out that while yours is undoubtedly the finest deductive mind upon the face of this Earth, *I* am a Master Sorcerer." He paused. "We have worked together for a long time, my lord. During that time I have used sorcery to discover the facts, and you have taken those facts and made a cogent case of them. You cannot do the one, my lord, and I cannot do the other. Thus far there has been a tacit agreement between us, my lord, that I do not attempt to do your job, and you do not attempt to do mine. Has that agreement been abrogated?"

Lord Darcy was silent for a moment, trying to put his thoughts into words. Then, in a startlingly similar low voice, he said: "Master Sean, I should like to express my most humble apologies. I am an expert in my field. You are an expert on sorcery and sorcerers. Let it be so. The agreement has *not* been abrogated—nor, I trust, shall it ever be."

He paused for a moment, then, after a deep breath, said, in a more normal tone of voice, "Of course, Master Sean. You may choose any kind of consultation you wish."

During the moment of tension between the two friends, Lord Bontriomphe had quietly turned away, walked over to the corpse, and looked down at it without actually seeing it.

"Well, my lord—" There was just the slightest touch of embarrassment in Master Sean's voice. He cleared his throat and began again. "Well, my lord, it wasn't exactly consultation I was thinking of. What I really need is a good assistant. With your permission, I should like to ask Lord John Quetzal to help me. He's only a journeyman, but he wants to become a forensic sorcerer and the experience will be good for him."

"Of course, Master Sean, an excellent choice I should say. Now let me see—" He looked across at the body again. "I shan't disturb the evidence any more than is necessary. Those ceremonial knives are all constructed to the same pattern, are they not?"

"Yes, my lord. Every sorcerer must make his own, with his own hands, but they are built to rigid specifications. That's one of the things an apprentice has to learn right off, to build his own tools. You can't use another man's tools in this business, nor tools made by an ordinary craftsman. It's the making of them that attunes them to the individual who uses them. They must be generally similar and individually different."

"So I understand. Would you permit me to examine your own, so that I need not disturb Sir James'?"

"Of course." He got the knife from his carpetbag and handed it to his lordship. "Mind you don't cut yourself; that blade is razor sharp."

Lord Darcy eased the onyx-handled knife from its black couirbouilli sheath. The gleaming blade was a perfect isosceles triangle, five inches from handguard to point and two inches wide at the handguard. Lord Darcy turned it and looked at the base of the pommel. "This is your monogram and symbol. I presume Sir James' knife is identified in the same way?"

"Yes, my lord."

"Would you mind looking at that knife and telling me whether you can positively identify it as his?"

"Oh, that's the first thing I looked at. Many's the time I've seen it, and it's his knife, all right."

"Excellent. That accounts for its being here." He slid the deadly-looking blade back into its sheath and handed it back to the little sorcerer.

"That blade is pure silver, Master Sean?" Lord Bontriomphe asked.

"Pure silver, my lord."

"Tell me: how do you keep a razor edge on anything that soft?"

Master Sean smiled broadly. "Well, I'll admit it's a hard job getting the edge on it in the first place. It has to be finished with jeweler's rouge and very soft kidskin. But it's only used as a symbolical knife, d'ye see. We never actually cut anything material with it, so it never needs to be sharpened again if a man's careful."

"But if you never cut anything with it," said Lord Bontriomphe, "then why sharpen it at all? Wouldn't it work as well if its edges were as dull as, say, a letter opener?"

Master Sean gave the London investigator a rather pained look. "My lord," he said with infinite patience, "this is a symbol of a *sharp* knife. I also have a slightly different one with blunt edges; it is a symbol for a *dull* knife. Your lordship should realize that, for many purposes, the best symbol for a thing is the thing itself."

Lord Bontriomphe grinned and raised one hand, palm outward. "Sorry, Master Sorcerer; my apologies. But please don't give me any lectures on advanced symbolic theory. I never could get it through my head."

"Is there anything else you wanted to look at, Bontriomphe?" Lord Darcy asked briskly. "If not, I suggest we be on our way, and permit Master Sean to go about his work. We will instruct the guards at the door that you are not to be disturbed, Master Sean. When you have finished, notify Chief Master-at-Arms Hennely Grayme that we should like an autopsy performed upon the body immediately. And I should appreciate it very much if you would go to the morgue and personally supervise the chirurgeon's work."

"Very well. I'll see to it. I'll get the report to My Lord Marquis' office as soon as possible."

"Excellent. Come, Bontriomphe; there is work to be done."

CHAPTER 11

As Lord Bontriomphe gave instructions to the Armsmen outside the late Master Sir James Zwinge's room, Lord Darcy walked across the hall to the door facing the murder room and rapped briskly on it at a point just above the keyhole.

"Are you decent, Your Grace?"

There was a muffled flurry of movement inside, and the door flew open. "Lord Darcy!" said the Dowager Duchess of Cumberland, flashing him a brilliant smile. "You startled me, my lord."

Lord Darcy pitched his own voice low enough so that the Armsmen and Lord Bontriomphe could not hear. "There is an old adage to the effect that people who listen at keyholes often hear things that startle them."

Raising his voice to a normal speaking tone, he went on. "I should like to speak to Your Grace privately for a moment, if I may."

"Certainly, my lord." She stepped back to let him in the room, and he closed the door behind him.

"What is it?" she asked.

"A few quick questions, Mary. I need your help."

"I thought you were going back to Cherbourg as soon as you got Master Sean out of the Tower."

"Circumstances have changed," he cut in. "Bontriomphe and I are working together on the case. But never mind that now. When you told me about the Damoselle Tia last night, the one thing you failed to mention was her connection with Sir Thomas Leseaux."

Her Grace's blue eyes widened. "But—aside from the fact that he was among those who recommended her for apprenticeship in the Guild, I don't know of any connection. Why?"

Lord Darcy frowned in thought. "Unless I am very much

mistaken, the connection goes a great deal deeper than that. Sir Thomas is in love with the girl—or thinks he is. He is also afraid that she might be mixed up in something illegal, something criminal—and he is afraid to admit the possibility to himself."

"Criminal? Do you mean Black Magic or . . ." she hesitated, "the actual murder of Sir James?"

"I don't know. It might be either or both—or something completely different. But I am not so much interested in what Sir Thomas suspects as I am in what the girl was and is actually doing that may be connected with the murder. At the same time, I do not want her to know that she is suspected in any way. Therefore, I would rather not question her myself. She has already undergone the routine questioning by a plainclothes Sergeant-at-Arms; to subject her to any further questioning would indicate that we have singled her out for special treatment. So far, she does not know that she was seen leaving Sir James' room, and I am not ready for her to know yet."

"You want me to question her, then?" asked the Duchess, her eyes almost sparkling with animation.

"Precisely. I know you, Mary; you are going to snoop anyway, and I would prefer that all the snoopers in this case have their activities co-ordinated as much as possible. So your job will be the Damoselle Tia. Question her—but not directly. Use indirectness and subtlety. Get to know her; gain her confidence if you can. Certainly there would be nothing suspicious about the two of you discussing the murder. I dare say everyone in the hotel is discussing it."

She laughed. "Discussing it? Haven't you felt the psychic tension in this place?"

"To a certain extent, but not, obviously, to the degree that you can sense it."

"Well, it's there, all right. There have been enough protective spells cast, enough amulets charged, enough charms and counter-charms worked in the past twenty-four hours to ward off a full phalanx of the Legions of Hell." Her smile faded. "They're not only talking about it, my dear; they're doing something about it. The Guild is a damn sight more disturbed than it would appear upon the surface. There is a Black Sorcerer around with enough power to kill Master Sir James Zwinge. That's enough to make a Master edgy;

what do you think it's doing to us journeymen? We've got to find him—and yet the counter-spells in this hotel have obfuscated any trace of the kind of evil malignancy that should be hanging like swamp fog over the place. It has all of us in a tizzy."

"I shouldn't wonder," Lord Darcy said. "But at least that will allow you to bring up the subject at any time without arousing suspicion."

"True. But there's another factor we'll have to consider. It will soon be all over the place, if it isn't already, that you are working on this case, and it is certainly no secret that you and I are friends. If the Damoselle Tia knows that, *she* may try to pump *me* for information."

"Let her try, my dear. Find out what kind of information she's looking for. If she just asks questions that would be normal under the circumstances, that tells us one thing. If the questions seem a little too urgent or a trifle off-key, that tells us another. But don't give her any information except what is common knowledge. Tell her that I am reticent, that I am dull, that I am a bore—anything you like, so long as you make it clear to her that I tell you nothing.

"And try to keep a close watch on the girl, if you can do it without being too conspicuous about it.

"Will you do that for me, Mary?"

"I'll do my best, my lord."

"Excellent. Lord Bontriomphe and I will be setting up a temporary headquarters here in the hotel. There will be a Sergeant-at-Arms on duty there at all times. If you have any messages for me, let him know, or leave a sealed envelope with my name on it."

"Very well," said Her Grace, "I'll take the job. Be on about your snooping, and I shall be on about mine."

Lord Bontriomphe was waiting patiently in the hall outside. "Where now?" he asked.

"Down to see the General Manager, Goodman Lewie," said Lord Darcy. "We may as well make arrangements for our temporary headquarters." They walked on down the hall. "Do you have three good Sergeants-at-Arms to spare for this duty, so we can have someone there twenty-four hours a day?"

"Easily," Lord Bontriomphe said. "Plainclothes or uniformed?"

"Uniformed, by all means. Everyone will know they are Armsmen anyway, and Armsmen in uniform will draw attention away from any plainclothes operatives we may need to use."

"Right. I'll arrange it with Chief Hennely."

Downstairs at the desk, Lord Bontriomphe asked to speak to Goodman Lewie Bolmer. The clerk disappeared and returned a minute later and said: "Goodman Lewie asks if you would be so good as to come back to his office, my lords."

The two investigators followed the clerk back to an office at the rear of the registration desk. Lewie Bolmer stood up as they were shown in.

The general manager looked haggard. Except for the dark pouches beneath his eyes, his saggy face looked pale and sallow, as though the folds and bags of translucent skin that made up his face were filled with soft suet instead of flesh. His smile seemed genuine, but it was as tired as the rest of him.

"Good afternoon, your lordships," he said. "How may I help you?"

Lord Bontriomphe introduced Lord Darcy, and then explained their need for a temporary headquarters.

"I think . . . yes, we have just the thing," said the manager after a moment's thought. "I can put you in the night manager's office. He can double up with the afternoon manager if . . . uh . . . when he comes back to work. I'll clean out his desk and . . . uh . . . put his stuff in the other office. It's a fairly good-sized office—just a little smaller than this one. Will that do?"

"We'd like to take a look at it, if we may," said Bontriomphe.

"Certainly. If your lordships will come this way—"

He led them to a corridor that ran from the lobby to the rear of the building, just to one side of the registration desk. There were two doors leading off it to the right, just a few yards from the lobby. Further back, more doors led off on either side. Goodman Lewie opened the second of the two doors.

The first one is the afternoon manager's office," he explained. "This is what I had in mind, your lordships." He waved his hand in a gesture that took in the fifteen-by-fifteen room.

"It looks fine to me," said Lord Bontriomphe. "What do you think, Darcy?"

"Perfectly satisfactory, I should say." He looked down the corridor toward the rear of the building. "Where does this corridor lead, Goodman Lewie?"

"Those are the service rooms back there, your lordship. Lumber rooms, furniture repair workshop, laundry, janitors' supplies—that sort of thing. The door at the far end is the back entrance. It opens into Potsmoke Alley, which is an extension of Upper Swandham Lane."

"Can it be opened from the outside?"

"Only with a key. It has a night lock on it. Anyone could go out, but one needs a key to get back in."

"I have an idea," said Lord Bontriomphe. "We can station an Armsman back there to make sure no unauthorized person comes in, then we'll unlock the door. That way, the Armsmen can come and go as necessary without tromping through your lobby and disturbing your guests. Would that be all right?"

"Of course, your lordship!"

"Good. I'll have a Sergeant-at-Arms down here to take charge of the office."

"Very well, your lordship. I'll have the desk cleared out. Will there be anything else?"

"Yes," said Lord Darcy. "One other thing. Yesterday, the hotel was closed to all except members of the Healers' and Sorcerers' Convention, was it not?"

"And their guests, yes. Only those who had business here were allowed in. The doormen had explicit orders about that."

"I see. Is any record kept?"

"Oh, yes. There is a register book kept at the door at all times. Not today, of course, since this is Visitor's Day, but during those times when the Convention is closed."

"I should like to see it, if I may," Lord Darcy said.

"You certainly may, your lordship. Shall we return to my office? I'll fetch the register book for you."

A minute or so later, the three men were looking at a clothbound register book which lay open on Bolmer's desk.

"That's the page for Wednesday," Lewie Bolmer said. "From midnight to midnight."

Lord Darcy and Lord Bontriomphe looked down the list.

There were four columns, marked *Time Arrived, Name, Business,* and *Time Departed.*

There were not many entries; the first one was for half past six, when a man from the Royal Postal Service had delivered the mail; he had left again at 6:35. At twelve minutes of nine Commander Lord Ashley had arrived, giving as his business "Official message for Master Sorcerer Sean O Lochlainn." He had left at 9:55. At two minutes after nine, Lord Bontriomphe had come in, on "Personal business of the Marquis de London." No time of departure was noted. The next entry was for 9:51. It simply said "Chief Master-at-Arms Hennely Grayme, and four Men-at-Arms. On the King's Business."

"No help there," said Lord Bontriomphe. "But then, I didn't expect there would be."

Lord Darcy grinned. "What kind of entry were you expecting? '9:20 a.m.; Master Sorcerer Lucifer S. Beelzebub. Business: To murder Master Sir James Zwinge. Exit time: 9:31' I suppose?"

"That would have been helpful," admitted Lord Bontriomphe.

"I notice there's no exit time down for you or for the Armsmen." He looked up at Goodman Lewie. "Why is that?"

The hotel manager was stifling a yawn. "Eh? What, your lordship? The time of leaving? Well, there were so many Armsmen in and out that I simply gave the doormen orders to allow any Officer of the King's Peace to come and go as he pleased." He stifled another yawn. "Pardon me. Lack of sleep. My night manager, who has the midnight-to-nine shift, didn't show up for work last night, so I had to take over."

"Perfectly all right," said Lord Darcy, still looking at the register book. There were more entries in the afternoon, mostly merchants and manufacturers who used sorcery or employed sorcerers in the course of their business. One entry caught his eye.

"What's this?" he said, tapping it with his finger.

Lord Bontriomphe read it aloud: " '2:54; Commander Lord Ashley; official business with Manager Bolmer.' No exit time marked."

"Wuh . . . well, your lordships, there were several Navy men in and out. Official business, you know."

"Official business? Why did they want to talk to you?" Darcy asked.

"Not to me. To . . . to Paul Nichols, my night manager."

"About what?"

"I . . . I'm not at liberty to say, your lordship. Strict instructions from the Admiralty. In the King's Name."

"I see," said Lord Darcy in a hard voice. "Thank you, Goodman Lewie. There will be a Sergeant-at-Arms around later to take over that office. Come on, Bontriomphe." He turned and strode out of the office, with Lord Bontriomphe at his heels.

They were halfway across the lobby, threading their way through the crowded exhibits, before Lord Bontriomphe spoke. "Do I detect blood in your eye?"

"Damn right you do," snapped Darcy. "How far is the Admiralty Office from here?"

"Ten minutes if we walk, or we can take the coach and get there in three."

"The coach, by all means," said Lord Darcy.

Barney, the footman, was standing near the coach, which was drawn up alongside the curb a few yards from the front door of the Royal Steward.

"Barney," Lord Bontriomphe shouted. "Where's Denys?"

"Still in the pub, my lord," the footman called back.

"Get ready to go, I'll fetch him." He ran across the street to the pub and was out again thirty seconds later with the coachman running alongside him.

"To the Admiralty Office!" Lord Bontriomphe ordered as Denys climbed into his seat. "As fast as you can." He climbed inside with Lord Darcy.

"So Smollett is holding out on us," he said, as the coach started forward with a jerk.

"He knows something we don't, that's for certain," said Lord Darcy.

"Keep in mind that those orders to keep quiet were given to Bolmer yesterday, before the King ordered us to work together."

"True," said Lord Darcy, "but considering the fact that the Navy is all in a pother about a man who has suddenly turned up missing, and that Goodman Lewie Bolmer shows by his behavior that he is convinced that his night manager will not return, doesn't it seem odd to you that neither Smollett nor Ashley mentioned it to us this morning?"

"More than odd," Lord Bontriomphe agreed. "That's what I said: Smollett is holding out on us. You want to hold him while I poke him in the eye, or the other way around?"

"Neither," said Lord Darcy. "We'll each take an arm and twist."

CHAPTER 12

Lord Bontriomphe had not misjudged the time very much; it was less than four minutes later when Darcy and Bontriomphe climbed out of the coach in front of the big, bulky, old building that housed the Admiralty offices of the Imperial Navy. They went up the steps and through the wide doors into a large anteroom that was almost the size of a hotel lobby. They were heading toward a desk marked *Information* when Lord Darcy suddenly spotted a familiar figure.

"There's our pigeon," he murmured to Lord Bontriomphe, then raised his voice:

"Ah, Commander Ashley."

Lord Ashley turned, recognized them, and gave them an affable smile. "Good afternoon, my lords. Can I do anything for you?"

"I certainly hope so," said Lord Darcy.

Lord Ashley's smile disappeared. "What's the trouble? Has anything happened?"

"I don't know. That's what I want you to tell me. Why is the Navy so interested in a certain Paul Nichols, the night manager at the Royal Steward?"

Lord Ashley blinked. "Didn't Captain Smollett tell you?"

"Sure he did," said Lord Bontriomphe. "He told us all about it. But we forgot. That's why we're here asking questions."

Commander Lord Ashley ignored the London investigator's sarcasm. There was a vaguely troubled look in his seaman's eyes. Abruptly he came to a decision. "That information will have to come from Captain Smollett. I'll take you to his office. May I tell him that you have come to get the information directly from him?"

"So," said Lord Darcy with a dry smile, "Captain Smollett prefers that his subordinates keep silent, eh?"

Lord Ashley grinned lopsidedly. "I have my orders. And there are good reasons for them. The Naval Intelligence Corps, after all, does not make a habit of broadcasting its information to the four winds."

"I'm aware of that," said Lord Darcy, "and I am not suggesting that the corps acquire such habits. Nonetheless, His Majesty's instructions were, I think, explicit."

"I'm certain it was merely an oversight on the captain's part. This affair has the whole Intelligence Corps in an uproar, and Captain Smollett and his staff, as I told you this morning, do not have any high hopes that the killers will be found."

"And frankly don't much care, I presume," said Lord Darcy.

"I wouldn't go so far as to say that, my lord; it is simply that we don't feel that the tracking down of hired Polish assassins is our job. We're not equipped for it. Our job is the impossible one of finding out everything that King Casimir's Navy is up to and keeping him from finding out anything at all about ours. You people are equipped and trained to catch murderers, and we—very rightly, I think—leave the job in your hands."

"We can't do it without the pertinent information," said Lord Darcy, "and that's what we're here to get."

"Well, I don't know whether the information is pertinent or not, but come along; I'll take you to Captain Smollett."

The two investigators followed the commander down a corridor, up a flight of stairs, and down another corridor toward the rear of the building.

There was a middle-aged petty officer sitting behind a desk in the outer office who looked up from his work as the three men entered. He did not even bother to look at the two civilians.

"Yes, My Lord Commander?" he said.

"Would you tell Captain Smollett that Lord Darcy and Lord Bontriomphe are here to see him. He will know what their business is."

"Aye, my lord." The petty officer got up from behind the desk, went into an inner office, and came out again a minute or so later. "Compliments of the captain, my lords. He would like to see all three of you in his office immediately."

There are three ways of doing things, Lord Darcy thought to himself, *the right way, the wrong way, and the Navy way.*

Captain Smollett was standing behind his desk when they went into the room, a pipe clenched firmly between his teeth, his gray-fringed bald head gleaming in the afternoon sunlight that streamed through the windows at his back.

"Good afternoon, m'luds," he said briskly. "Didn't expect to see you again so soon. Trust you have some information for me."

"I was rather hoping you had some information for us, Captain," Lord Darcy said.

Smollett's eyebrows lifted. "Eh? Not much, I'm afraid," he said, speaking through his teeth and around his pipestem. "Nothing new has happened since this morning. That's why I was hoping that you had some information."

"It is not new information I want, Captain Smollett. By now, indeed, it may be rather stale.

"Yesterday afternoon at 2:54 your agent, Commander Lord Ashley, returned to the Royal Steward Hotel. After that, several other of your agents came and went. The General Manager, Goodman Lewie Bolmer, has informed us that he is under strict instructions from the Navy, in the King's Name, to give information to no one, including, presumably, duly authorized Officers of the King's Peace, operating under a special warrant which also permits them to act and speak in the King's Name.

"I could have forced the information from him but he was acting in good faith and he had enough troubles as it is. I felt that you could give me all the information he has and a great deal more besides. We met My Lord Commander downstairs, but doubtless he, too, is under orders, so, as with Goodman Lewie, it would not be worth my time to pry the information out of him when I can get it from you.

"This much we know: Goodman Paul Nichols, the night manager, failed to show up for work at midnight last night. This, apparently, is important; and yet, your agents were asking questions about him some nine hours before. What we want to know is why. I shall not ask you why we were not given this information this morning; I shall merely ask that we be given it now."

Captain Smollett was silent for the space of several seconds, his cold gray eyes looking with unblinking directness into Darcy's own. "Um," he said finally, "I suppose I deserve that. Should have mentioned it this morning. I admit it. Thing is, it just isn't in your jurisdiction—that is, normally it wouldn't be. We have men looking everywhere for Nichols, but he hasn't done a thing we can prove."

"What do you think he's done?"

"Stolen something," said Captain Smollett. "Trouble is, we can't prove the thing we think he's stolen ever existed. And if it did exist, we're not certain of its value."

"Very mysterious," said Lord Bontriomphe. "At least, to me. Does this have a beginning somewhere?"

"Hm-m-m. Beg your pardon. Don't mean to sound mysterious. Here, will you be seated? Brandy on the table over there. Pour them some brandy, Commander. Make yourselves comfortable. It's a rather longish story."

He sat down behind his desk, reached out toward a pile of file folders, and took an envelope out of the top one.

"Here's the picture: Zwinge was a busy man. Had a great many things to keep an eye on. Being Chief Forensic Sorcerer for the City of London would be a full-time job for an ordinary man." He looked at Lord Bontriomphe. "Be frank, m'lud. Did you ever suspect that he was working for the Naval Intelligence Corps?"

"Never," Bontriomphe admitted, "though Heaven knows he worked hard enough. He was always busy, and he was one of those men who think that anything more than five hours sleep a night is an indication of sloth. Tell me, Captain, did My Lord Marquis know?"

"He was never told," said Captain Smollett. "Zwinge did say that he suspected that My Lord de London was aware of his Navy work, but if so he never mentioned it."

"He wouldn't," said Lord Bontriomphe.

"No, of course not. At any rate, Zwinge had a great many irons in the fire. More things going on in Europe than just this one affair, I can assure you. Nonetheless, he felt it necessary to go to this Healers and Sorcerers Convention. Look odd if he didn't, he said, what with his being right here in London and all. But of course he kept right on working, even there."

"That is undoubtedly why he put the special spell on the lock of his hotel room," said Lord Darcy.

"No doubt, no doubt," agreed Captain Smollett. "At any

rate, yesterday morning he sent this letter to me by messenger from the hotel." He handed the envelope to Lord Darcy. "You'll notice it is stamped 7:45 A.M."

Lord Darcy looked at the outside of the envelope. It was addressed to Captain Percy Smollett and was marked "Personal." Darcy opened it and took out the single sheet of paper. "This is in code," said Lord Darcy.

"Of course," said Captain Smollett. He took another sheet from the file and handed it over. "Here is the clear," he said. Lord Darcy read the message aloud:

" 'Sir: I have a special packet for you containing information of the utmost importance which I have just received. It is impossible for me to leave the hotel at this time, and I do not wish to entrust this information to a common messenger. Accordingly, I have given the envelope with my seal upon it to the hotel manager, Goodman Paul Nichols. He has placed it in the hotel safe and has been instructed to hand it over to your courier.' "

The note was signed with the single letter "Z."

Lord Darcy handed the papers back to the captain. "I see, Captain. Pray continue."

"As I said, the message arrived at 7:45. It was placed on my desk with the rest of my morning mail. Now—I didn't arrive here at the office until a few minutes before ten. Hadn't had time to even glance at my mail when Commander Ashley came in, bringing the news from Cherbourg that Barbour had been murdered—which was bad enough—and the further intelligence that Master Sir James had been stabbed to death only half an hour before. Since you already know of the importance we've attached to this affair, you'll understand that for the next few hours I was a very busy man. Didn't have a chance to look at my mail until well after two o'clock. When I decoded the letter, I sent Ashley, here, over to fetch the packet." He looked at the Commander. "You'd better take it from there, Commander. I'm sure Lord Darcy prefers to get his facts as directly as possible."

"Aye, sir." He turned to face Lord Darcy. "I went directly to the hotel and asked to see Goodman Lewie, and told him that Sir James had left an envelope addressed to Captain Smollett in the safe, to be delivered to the Navy.

"He said he knew nothing of it, and I told him that it had been left with Goodman Paul.

"He informed me that Goodman Paul had made no mention of it when he went off duty at nine, but he agreed to open the safe and get the envelope out.

"I was standing by him when he opened the safe. It's a small one and there wasn't much inside it. Certainly there was no envelope addressed to Captain Smollett, nor any sign that there had ever been one. Bolmer swore that he had not opened the safe that morning, and both of the desk clerks substantiated that. Bolmer and his two assistant managers are the only ones who know the combination, and the security spell only allows the assistant managers to open the safe during the time they are on duty, that is, from three P.M. till midnight for the afternoon manager and from midnight to nine A.M. for the night manager."

Lord Darcy nodded. "That does rather narrow it down to Goodman Paul. Only he could have removed that packet from the safe."

"My thought exactly," said Commander Lord Ashley. "Naturally, I insisted upon speaking to Paul Nichols immediately, and asked for his home address. It turns out that he lived there in the hotel; he has a room up on the top floor. Bolmer took me up and I knocked on Nichols' door, got no answer, and Bolmer let us in with a pass key. Nichols wasn't in. His bed was made and certainly didn't look as though it had been slept in. Bolmer said that was odd because usually Nichols goes out to have a bite to eat after he gets off work, then comes back to the hotel and sleeps until around six o'clock."

"Did you find out whether Nichols took advantage of the hotel's maid service?" Lord Darcy asked.

The Commander nodded. "He did. Nichols quite often went out of an evening, and the maid had orders to make up his room between 7:30 and 8:30. I looked the room over and checked through his things. He didn't seem to have packed anything. His suitcase, empty, was in the closet, and Bolmer said that as far as he knew it was the only suitcase Nichols owned."

"That's the advantage of being a counterspy," said Lord Bontriomphe with a sigh. "If an officer of the King's Peace tried searching a man's room without a warrant he'd find himself in the Court of the King's Bench trying to explain to My Lord justice how he had come to make such a mistake."

"Well, I didn't really search the place," Ashley said. "I was just taking a look around."

"So," said Lord Darcy, "you found that Nichols was not there and apparently had not been to bed since the bed was made on the previous evening."

"Right. I questioned some of the hotel servants. No one had seen him come back from his breakfast—or perhaps for him it was supper—so I instructed Bolmer to say nothing but to let us know as soon as Nichols returned. Then I came back here and reported to Captain Smollett."

Lord Darcy nodded and looked back at the captain.

"Been looking for him ever since. Sent men over to the hotel, to wait for him to come to work at midnight; he didn't show up. Still no sign of him. Not a trace."

"You suspect then," said Lord Darcy, "that the disappearance of the packet and the disappearance of Nichols are linked. I agree with you. The contents of that envelope would have been in code, would they not, Captain?"

"Yes indeed. And not the simple code used for that note, either. Furthermore, Zwinge always used ink and paper with a special spell on it. If an unauthorized person broke the seal, the writing would vanish before he could get the paper out of the envelope."

"Obviously, then, Nichols did not remove it from the safe, read it over, and decide that it was valuable on the spur of the moment."

"Obviously not," agreed Captain Smollett. "Furthermore, Zwinge was no fool. Wouldn't have given it to Nichols unless he trusted him. Also, since the envelope had that protective spell on it, the only way to read the contents would be to get it to a magician who is clever enough and powerful enough to analyze and nullify Master Sir James Zwinge's spell."

"Do you have any idea what sort of information might have been in that envelope, Captain Smollett?" Lord Darcy asked.

"None. None whatsoever. Can't have been terribly urgent— that is, not requiring immediate action—or Zwinge would have brought it here himself, in spite of everything. But it was certainly important enough to drive King Casimir's agents to murder to get it."

"How do you think this ties in with the murder of Barbour, then? And with the Navy's new secret weapon?"

The captain scowled and puffed at his pipe for a few seconds. "Now there we're on shaky ground. Obviously it was discovered that Barbour was a double agent; otherwise he wouldn't have been killed."

"I agree with you there," said Lord Darcy.

"Very well. But that leaves us several possible speculations about FitzJean and about the Poles' knowledge of the confusion projector.

"If, as we hope, they know nothing of the device, then they knew nothing about FitzJean except the purely mendacious material which Barbour had passed on to them. When they discovered he was a double agent, they simply killed him and ignored FitzJean. Information on fleet disposition isn't worth taking any great pains over.

"However, I am afraid that we would be unrealistically optimistic to put any faith in the notion that the Polish Government is entirely unaware of the existence of the confusion projector.

"Much more likely, they are sparing no effort to find out what it is and how it works—which would still indicate that they know nothing whatever about FitzJean. If they did, they would certainly not have killed Barbour until they could get their hands on FitzJean—which, of course, they may have done. Or again they may already have the secret and not give two hoots in Hell about FitzJean.

"And finally, there is the possibility that FitzJean was himself a Polish agent sent in to test Barbour. When they discovered that Barbour's output to them differed drastically from what they knew the input to be, his death warrant was sealed."

Captain Smollett spread his hands. "But these are mere speculations; they tell us nothing. Important thing right now's to get our hands on Paul Nichols. Would have given you this before, but, as I said, there's actually nothing we can hold Nichols on. Can't prove that envelope ever existed, much less that he stole it. So how could we turn the matter over to Officers of the King's Justice?"

"My dear Captain, you should study something besides Admiralty law. Fleeing the scene of a crime is always enough evidence to warrant asking for a man's arrest and detention for questioning. Now the first question any investigator asks himself is: Where would the suspect go? To the Polish Embassy?"

Smollett shook his head. "No. There's a twenty-four hour watch on everyone entering or leaving the Polish Embassy."

"Exactly. I know that. So do the Poles. But the local headquarters for this Polish espionage ring is somewhere in the City. Where?"

"Wish I knew," said the captain. "Give half a year's pay for that information. We have reason to believe that there are at least three separate rings operating here in London, each unknown to the others, or at least known only to a select few. We know some of the agents, of course. We keep an eye on 'em; I've had my men watching every known agent in London for the past eighteen hours. So far, no news. But what we do *not* know is where any of their headquarters might be. Hate to admit it, but it's true. We have no hint, no suggestion, no clue of any kind."

"Then the only way to find Nichols," Lord Darcy said, "is to comb London for him. And that requires legwork. While your men are searching for him covertly, Lord Bontriomphe and the Armsmen of London can be looking for him for questioning on the charge of fleeing the scene of a crime."

Bontriomphe nodded. "We can have a net out for him within an hour. If we find anything, Captain, I'll let you know immediately."

"Very good, m'lud."

"I'd better get started on it," Bontriomphe said, getting to his feet. "The quicker the better. If you need to contact me for any reason, Captain, send word to the Royal Steward. We have set up our headquarters there; there will be a Sergeant-at-Arms on duty at all times, and I shall be checking in there regularly."

"Excellent. Thank you, m'lud."

"I shall see you later, gentlemen. Good day." Lord Bontriomphe walked out the door as if he were pleased at the prospect of finally having something he could sink his teeth into.

"As for me, Captain," said Lord Darcy, "I should like to ask your indulgence in what I know may be a touchy matter."

"What might that be?"

"I should like to have a look at your secret files, most especially at the letters from Barbour concerning FitzJean and the confusion projector."

"M'lud," said Captain Smollett with a wintery smile, "any Intelligence organization is justly jealous of its secret files and our Corps is no exception. Until now, these files have been classified *Most Secret*. Barbour's existence as a double agent was known only to the high echelons of the Admiralty. But you've taken me to task once for withholding information. Won't happen again. I shall have the pertinent files brought in so that both you and Commander Ashley can study them. And may I ask *your* indulgence?"

"Certainly, Captain, what is it?"

"With your permission, I'd like to make Commander Lord Ashley the liaison officer between the civilian investigators and the Navy. To be more specific, between you and me. He knows the Navy, he knows Intelligence work, and he knows something about criminal investigation. He was in the Naval C.I.D. before he was transferred to this Corps. His orders will be to assist you in every possible way. You agree, m'lud?"

"Of course, Captain. A splendid idea."

"Very well, Commander; those are your orders then."

"Aye, aye, Captain." He smiled at Lord Darcy. "I'll keep out from underfoot as much as possible, my lord."

"That's settled, then," said Captain Smollett, getting to his feet. "Now I'll go get those files."

Master Sean O Lochlainn stood near the closed door of the murder room and surveyed its entire contents. Then he turned to Journeyman Sorcerer Lord John Quetzal who stood next to him. "Now, d'ye understand what we have to be careful of? We are not yet ready to take the preservative spell off the body, so we have to be careful that none of the spells that we're working with inside the room interfere with it. D'ye understand?"

Lord John Quetzal nodded. "Yes, Master, I think I do."

Master Sean smiled at him. "I think you do, too, my lad. You followed through on the blood tests beautifully." He paused. "By the by, d'ye think you could do them by yourself next time, should you happen to be called upon to perform them?"

Lord John Quetzal glanced sideways at the little sorcerer. "The blood tests? Yes, Master Sorcerer, I think I could," he said firmly.

"Ah, good." Master Sean nodded with satisfaction. *"But"*— he raised a warning finger—"this next one's a little tougher.

"We're dealing here with psychic shock. Now, whenever a man's hurt, or when he dies, there's psychic shock—unless, of course, he just fades away in his sleep or something like that.

"But *here* we're talking about violence."

"I understand," said Lord John Quetzal.

"All right. Now, you're going to be my thurifer. The ingredients are laid out on the table. Now I'll ask *you* to prepare the thurible, seeing as how it's you that's got to use it."

"Very well, Master," said the young Mechicain nobleman, with the tiniest trace of uneasiness in his voice.

On the table near the door sat the instrument which Master Sean had taken from his symbol-decorated carpet-bag. It was a brazen pot with a perforated brazen cap, which, when assembled, would swing from the end of a clutch of chains some three feet long. Now, it was open, on the table.

Lord John Quetzal took several tools from his own car-petbag. Under the watchful eye and sharp ear of Master Sean O Lochlainn, the young sorcerer prepared the contents of the thurible.

After placing the brazen pot on an iron tripod, he fired up several lumps of charcoal in the bottom of it. Then, from the row of jars and bottles which had been lined up on the table, he took various ingredients and put them into his special golden mixing bowl, using a small golden spoon. With his own pencil-sized golden wand, he cast a spell over each ingredient as he added it, stirring it into the mixture.

There was frankincense and sweet balsam, samonyl and fenogreek, turmeric and taelesin, sandalwood and cedarwood, and four other lesser known but even more powerful ingredients—added in a precise order, each with its unique and individual spell.

And when he had finished the mixing, and cast the final spell, the journeyman sorcerer lifted his head and turned his dark eyes to the tubby little Master.

Sean O Lochlainn nodded his head. "Very well done. *Very*

well done." He smiled. "Now I'll not ask you if you know what you've done. It's a habit of mine to assume that a student lacks knowledge. Being, as it were, a student meself, I know how much knowledge I lack. And besides," he chuckled, "as Lord Darcy would tell you, I'm a man who's fond of lecturing.

"The spell we're about to perform is a dynamic spell, and must be warded off by a dynamic spell—which means that in order to protect the body I'll have to be working while you are censing the room. D'ye understand, my lad?"

"I do, Master."

"Very well. Now, when you place that mixture into the thurible, there will be given off a smoke, which is composed of many different kinds of small particles. Because of the spell you've cast on them, these particles will tend to be attracted to, and adhere to, the walls and the furniture in this room in a particular manner.

"They will form what we call hologram patterns upon the surfaces they touch. Each of the different kinds of smoke particles forms its own pattern according to the psychic influences which have been impressed upon those surfaces. And by understanding the totality of those patterns we may identify definitely those psychic impressions."

He folded his arms on his chest, looked up at the tall young Mechicain, and gave him his best Irish grin. "Ah, lad, you're the kind of student a man looks for. You listen when the old master talks, and you don't get bored by what you already know, because you're waiting for more information."

Again, that almost invisible flush colored John Quetzal's dark skin. "Yes, Master Sean," he said carefully, "I have learned pattern theory."

"Aye—pattern *theory* you've learned. But you're wise enough to admit that you know only theory, not practice." He nodded his head in satisfaction. "You'll make a fine forensic sorcerer, lad. A *fine* forensic sorcerer!" Then his smile twisted slightly. "That is, you have the right attitude, me lad. Now we'll see if you have the technique."

He turned away from Lord John Quetzal and looked again at the walls. "If you do this thing right, Lord John Quetzal, there will be, upon those walls, patterns in smoke particles, each individual pattern distinguished by the spell cast on the various substances, and the hologram patterns distinguished by the combination of those spells. No man without the Talent will see anything but slightly smudgy walls—if that. You and I will see the patterns, and I'll do my best to show you how to interpret them."

He turned again.

"Are you ready, my lad?"

Lord John Quetzal set his lips. "I'm ready, Master."

"Very well, then."

Master Sean took two wands from his symbol-decorated carpetbag, walked over to the corpse which lay near the edge of the desk, and stood over it. "I'm ready, lad. Go ahead. Watch your spells."

The young Mechicain blew gently on the lumps of charcoal in the bottom of the thurible until they flared red-orange, then, his lips muttering a special spell, he poured the aromatic contents of the golden cup over the glowing coals. Immediately a dense cloud of white smoke rose toward the ceiling. Lord John Quetzal quickly fitted the perforated cap down over the bowl, locked it in place, and picked up the thurible by its clutch of chains. His left hand held the end of the chains, his right hand held them about halfway down, allowing the thurible to swing free. He moved over to the nearest wall, swinging the censer in a long arc, allowing the dense smoke to drift toward it.

He moved along the wall step by step, swinging the thurible rhythmically, his lips moving in time with it, and the dense smoke drifted along the walls and billowed upwards, spreading a clinging, heavy fragrance through the room.

While his assistant performed the censing, the Master Sorcerer stood immobile over the body, a long wand of glittering crystal in each hand, his arms flung wide to provide the psychic umbrella which would protect the corpse from being affected by the magical ritual that John Quetzal was enacting.

The Irish sorcerer's pose did not seem strained. There was an aura of strength about him; he seemed taller, somehow; and his thick torso had an appearance of hardness about it. The light from the gas lamp glittered and flickered in the depths of the two crystal wands, flashing sparkling rainbows about the room.

The smoke from the censer avoided the area under Master

Sean's control. It billowed in great clouds, but there seemed to be an invisible force that kept that portion of the room totally clear of the tiny particles. Those microscopic bits of fragrant ash moved toward walls, furniture and ceiling, each clinging in its individual way—but none came near the powerful figure of the Master Sorcerer who shielded one area of evidence from their effect.

Three times, the young sorcerer made the circuit of the room with his swinging thurible, and except for that one specially protected area, the air grew dimly blue with smoke.

Then, while Master Sean still remained unmoving, he went back to the table, placed the hot, smoking thurible on the iron tripod, removed the perforated cap, and replaced it with a solid cap which cut off the flow of smoke and smothered the burning coals.

From his own symbol-decorated carpetbag, he took a silver wand with a knoblike thickening at one end. Grasping it by the other end, he turned and traced symbols in the air toward each wall in turn.

As he did so, the fog of smoke moved even more strongly toward the walls, and the air quickly cleared.

After a moment, Lord John Quetzal softly said: "It is finished, Master."

Master Sean looked around the room, lowered his arms, walked over and put the two crystal wands back in his carpetbag. Then he surveyed the room once more.

"A fine job, my lad," he said. "Indeed a fine job. Now, can you tell me what happened here?"

Lord John Quetzal looked. Although both sorcerers were using their eyes, it was not their eyes with which they saw. To a man without the Talent, the psychic patterns wrought by the acts which had taken place within the room, and brought out by the censing process, would have been totally invisible. To a man with the Talent they were quite clear.

But while Lord John Quetzal could perceive the patterns, he had not yet had enough training to interpret them. Master Sean sensed his hesitation. "Go ahead, lad," he said. "Rely on your hunches. Make a guess. 'Tis the only way you can check on your perceptions, and thereby progress from supposition to certainty."

"Well," Lord John Quetzal began uncertainly, "it looks

like—" He stopped, then said: "But of course that's ridiculous. It just couldn't be that way."

Master Sean let out his breath in an exasperated manner. "Oh, lad, lad! You're trying to second-guess yourself. You're trying to make a *logical* interpretation before you've subjectively absorbed the data. Now I'll ask you again. What does it seem to you happened?"

Lord John Quetzal took another look. This time he pivoted slowly, turning a full three hundred and sixty degrees, taking in every bit of his surroundings. Then, carefully, he said: "There was no one else in this room but Sir James . . ." He hesitated.

"That's correct, absolutely correct," said Master Sean. "Go on. You still haven't said what it is that looks paradoxical."

Lord John Quetzal said, in a faintly puzzled voice, "Master, it looks to me as though Sir James Zwinge were killed twice. Several minutes—perhaps as much as half an hour—intervened between the murders."

Master Sean smiled and nodded. "You almost have it, lad. I think the results of the autopsy will bear you out. But you haven't analyzed the full significance of what is there." He made a broad sweeping gesture with his arm. "Take a good look at what the patterns show. There are two strong patterns superimposed chronologically. Two successive psychic shocks occurred while our late colleague was alone in this room. And, as you've pointed out, they were separated in time by half an hour. The first, d'you see, was when he was *killed;* the second occurred when he *died.*"

CHAPTER 13

The broad doors that led from the lobby of the Royal Steward Hotel to the main ballroom were closed but not locked. There was no sign upon the door that said *Convention Members Only;* at a Sorcerers Convention such signs were unnecessary. The spell on those doors was such that none of the lay visitors who were so eagerly thronging to the displays in the lobby would ever have thought of entering them—or, if the thought did occur to them, it would be dismissed in a matter of seconds.

Sir Thomas Leseaux and the Dowager Duchess of Cumberland pushed through the swinging doors. A few feet inside the ballroom Lady de Cumberland stopped and took a deep breath.

"Trouble, Your Grace?"

"Good Heavens, what a mob!" said Mary de Cumberland. "I feel as though they're breathing up all the fresh air in London."

The ballroom presented a picture that was both peaceful and relaxed in comparison with the lobby. The room was almost the same size but contained only a tenth as many people. And instead of the kaleidoscopic variety of color in the costumes displayed in the lobby, the costumes in the ballroom were of a few basic colors. There was the dominating pale blue of the Sorcerers, modified by the stark black-and-white of the priestly Healers, and the additional touch of episcopal purple. The dark rabbinical dress of the occasional Jewish Healer was hardly distinguishable from that of a priest, but an occasional flash of bright color showed the presence of a very few *Hakime*, Healers who were part of the entourages of various Ambassadors from the Islamic countries.

"Visitors Day," said Sir Thomas, "is simply something we must put up with, Your Grace. The people have a right to know what the Guild is doing; the Guild has the duty to inform the people."

Mary turned her bright blue eyes up to Sir Thomas' face. "My dear Sir Thomas, there are many acts that human beings must perform which are utterly necessary. That does not necessarily mean that they are enjoyable. Now, where is this lovely creature of yours?"

"A moment, Your Grace, let me look." Sir Thomas, who was a good two inches taller than the average, surveyed the ballroom. "Ah, there she is. Come, Your Grace."

The Dowager Duchess followed Sir Thomas across the floor. The Damoselle Tia was surrounded by a group of young, handsome journeymen. Mary of Cumberland smiled to herself. It was obvious that the young journeymen were not discussing the Art with the beautiful apprentice. Her 'prentice's smock was plain pale blue, and was not designed to be alluring, but on the Damoselle Tia . . .

And then the Dowager Duchess noticed something that

had escaped her attention before: the Damoselle Tia was wearing arms which declared her to be an apprentice of His Grace, Charles Archbishop of York.

To Mary of Cumberland, the Damoselle Tia appeared somewhat taller than she had when the Duchess saw her leaving Master Sir James' room on the previous morning. Then she saw the reason. Tia was wearing shoes of fashion that had arisen in the southern part of the Polish Hegemony and had not yet been accepted in the fashion centers either of Poland or of the Empire. They were like ordinary slippers except that the toes came to a point and the heels were lifted above the floor by a spike some two-and-a-half inches long. *Good Heavens,* thought Mary to herself, *how can a woman wear such high heels without ruining her feet?*

Was it, she wondered, some psychological quirk? Tia was a tiny girl, a good inch less than five feet tall without those outré heels, and a good foot shorter than the Dowager Duchess of Cumberland. Did she wear those heels simply to increase her physical height?

No, Mary decided; Tia had too much self-assurance, too much confidence in her own abilities, to need the false prop of those little stilts. She wore them simply because they were the fashion she had become used to. They were "native costume," nothing more.

"Excuse me," said Sir Thomas Leseaux, pushing his way through the crowd that surrounded Tia. Every one of the journeymen looked thrice at Sir Thomas. Their first look told them that he did not wear the blue of a sorcerer. *A layman, then?* Their second look encompassed the ribbons on his left breast which proclaimed him a Doctor of Thaumaturgy and a Fellow of the Royal Thaumaturgical Society. *No, not a layman.* Their third look took in his unmistakable features, which identified him immediately as the brilliant theoretical sorcerer whose portrait was known to every apprentice of a week's standing. They stepped back, fading away from Tia in awe at the appearance of Sir Thomas.

Tia had noticed that the handsome young sorcerers who were paying court to her seemed to be vanishing, and she looked up to discover the cause of the dispersion. Mary de

Cumberland noticed that Tia's eyes lit up and a smile came to her pixieish face when she saw the tall figure of Sir Thomas Leseaux.

Well, well, she thought, *so Tia reciprocates Sir Thomas' feelings.* She remembered that Lord Darcy had said "Sir Thomas is in love with the girl—or thinks he is." But Lord Darcy was not a Sensitive. Since she herself was sensitive to a minor degree, she knew that there was no question about the feeling between the two.

Before Sir Thomas could speak the Damoselle Tia bowed her head. "Good afternoon, Sir Thomas."

"Good afternoon, Tia. I'm sorry to have dispersed your court.

"Your Grace," continued Sir Thomas, "may I present to you the Damoselle Tia. Tia, I should like you to know my friend, Mary, Duchess of Cumberland."

Tia curtsied. "It is an honor to meet Your Grace."

Then Sir Thomas looked at his watch and said, "Good Heavens! It's time for the meeting of the Royal Thaumaturgical Society." He gave both women a quick, brief smile. "I trust you ladies will forgive me. I shall see you later on."

Mary de Cumberland's smile was only partly directed toward Tia. The rest of it was self-congratulatory. Lord Darcy, she thought, would approve of her timing; by carefully checking the meeting time of the R.T.S., she had obtained an introduction by Sir Thomas and his immediate disappearance thereafter.

"Tia," she said, "have you tasted our English beer? Or our French wines?"

The girl's eyes sparkled. "The wines, yes, Your Grace. English beer? No." She hesitated. "I have heard they compare well with German beers."

Her Grace sniffed. "My dear Tia, that is like saying that claret compares with vinegar." She grinned. "Come on, let's get out of this solemn conclave and I'll introduce you to English beer."

The Sword Room of the Royal Steward was, like the lobby, thronged with visitors. In one of its booths, the Dowager Duchess of Cumberland lifted the chilled pewter mug.

"Tia, my dear," she said, "there are many drinks in this world. There are wines for the gourmet, there are whiskies and brandies for the men, there are sweet cordials for the women, and there are milk and lemonade for children—but for good friendly drinking, there is nothing that can compare with the honest beer of England."

Tia picked up her own mug and touched it to Mary's. "Your Grace," she said, "with an introduction like that, the brew of England shall be given its every opportunity."

She drank, draining half the mug. Then she looked at Mary with her sparkling pixie eyes. "It is good, Your Grace!"

"Better than our French wines?" asked Mary, setting down her own mug half empty.

Tia laughed. "Right now, much better, Your Grace; I was thirsty."

Mary smiled back at her. "You're quite right, my dear. Wine is for the palate—beer is for the thirst."

Tia drank again from her mug. "You know, Your Grace, where I come from, it would be terribly presumptuous for a girl of my class even to sit down in the presence of a duchess, much less to sit down and have a beer with her in a public house."

"Fiddle!" said Mary de Cumberland. "I'm not a Peer of the Realm; I'm as much a commoner as you are."

Tia shook her head with a soft laugh. "It would make no difference, Your Grace. *Anyone* with a title is considered infinitely far above a common person like myself—at least, in the province of Banat, which, I confess, is all of the Polish Hegemony I have ever seen. So when I hear the title 'Duchess', I automatically give a start."

"I noticed," said Mary, "and I point out to you that anyone who aspires to a degree in Sorcery had better learn to handle symbols better than that."

"I know," the girl said softly. "I intend to try very hard, Your Grace."

"I'm sure you will, my dear." Then, changing the subject quickly: "Tell me, where did you learn Anglo-French? You speak it beautifully."

"My accent is terrible," Tia objected.

"Not at all! If you want to hear how the language *can* be butchered, you should hear some of our Londoners. Whoever taught you did very well."

"My Uncle Neapeler, my father's brother, taught me," Tia said. "He is a merchant who spent a part of his youth in the Angevin Empire. And Sir Thomas has been helping me a great deal—correcting my speech and teaching me the proper manners, according to the way things are done here."

The Duchess nodded and then gave Tia a quick smile. "Speaking of Sir Thomas—I hope his title doesn't make you frightened of him."

The sparkle returned to Tia's eyes. "Frightened of Sir Thomas? Oh, Your Grace, *no!* He's been so good to me. Much better than I deserve, I'm sure.

"But, then, everyone has been so good to me since I came here. Everyone. Nowhere does one find the friendliness, the *good*ness that one finds in the realm of His Majesty King John."

"Not even in Italy?" the Dowager Duchess asked casually.

Tia's expression darkened. "They might have hanged me in Italy."

"Hanged you? My dear, what on earth for?"

After a moment's silence, the girl said: "It's no secret, I suppose. I was charged with practicing the Black Art in Italy."

The Dowager Duchess of Cumberland nodded gravely. "Yes. Go on. What happened?"

"Your Grace, I have never been able to stand by and watch people suffer. I think it is because I watched both my parents die when I was very young—within a few months of each other. I wanted so very much for them both to live, and there was nothing I could do. I was—helpless to do anything for them. All children experience that terrible feeling of helplessness at times, Your Grace—but this was a very special thing." There was a heavy somberness in her dark eyes.

Mary de Cumberland said nothing, but her sympathy was apparent.

"I was brought up by Uncle Neapeler—a kind and wondrous man. He has the Healing Talent, too, you see, but it is untrained." Tia was looking back down at her beer mug, running one tiny, dainty finger around and around its rim. "He had no opportunity to train it. He might never have known that he possessed it if he had not spent so many years of his life in the Angevin Empire, where such things are searched out. He found that I had it, and taught me all he knew—which was small enough.

"In the Slavonic States, a man's right to become a Healer is judged by his political connections and by his ability to pay. And the right to have the services of a trained Healer is judged in the same way. Uncle Neapeler is—*was*—a merchant, a hard man of business. But he was never rich except in comparison to the villagers, and he was politically suspect because of the time he had spent in the Imperial domains.

"He used his Talent, untrained as it was, to help the villagers and the peasants when they were ill. They all knew they could rely on him for help, no matter who they were, and they loved him for it. He brought me up in that tradition, Your Grace."

She stopped, compressed her lips, and took another drink from her mug. "Then—something happened. The Count's officers . . ." She stopped again. "I don't want to talk about that," she said after a moment. "I . . . I got away. To Italy. And there were sick people there. People who needed help. I helped them, and they gave me food and shelter. I had no money to support myself. I had nothing after . . . but never mind. The poor helped me, for the help I could give them. For the children.

"But those who did not know called it Black Magic.

"First in Belluno. Then in Milano. Then in Torino. Each time, the whisper went around that I was practicing the Black Art. And each time, I had to go on. Finally, I had to flee the Italian States altogether.

"I got across the Imperial border and went to Grenoble. I thought I would be safe. I thought I could get a job of some kind—apprentice myself as a lady's personal maid, perhaps, since it is an honored profession. But the Grand Duke of Piemonte had sent word ahead, and I was arrested by the Armsmen in Grenoble.

"I was frightened. I had broken no Imperial law, but the Piemontese wanted to extradite me. I was brought before my lord the Marquis of Grenoble, who heard my plea and turned the case over to the Court of Justice of His Grace the Duke of Dauphine. I was afraid they would just hand me over to the Piemontese authorities as soon as they heard the charge. Why should anyone listen to a nobody?"

"Things just aren't done that way under the King's justice," said the Dowager Duchess.

"I know," said Tia. "I found that out. I was turned over to a special ecclesiastical commission for examination." She drank again from the mug and then looked straight into Mary of Cumberland's eyes. "The commission cleared me," she said. "I had practiced magic without a license, that was true. But they said that that was not an extraditable offense under the law. And the Sensitives of the commission found that I had not practiced Black Magic in my healing. They warned me, however, that I must not practice magic in the Empire without a license to do so.

"Father Dominique, the head of the commission, told me that a Talent such as mine should be trained. He introduced me to Sir Thomas, who was lecturing at a seminar for Master Sorcerers in Grenoble, and Sir Thomas brought me to England and introduced me to His Grace the Archbishop of York.

"Do you know the Archbishop, Your Grace? He is a saint, a perfect saint."

"I'm sure he'd be embarrassed to hear you say so," said the Duchess with a smile, "but just between us, I agree with you. He is a marvelous Sensitive. And obviously"—she gestured toward the archiepiscopal arms on Tia's shoulder— "His Grace's decision was favorable. Quite favorable, I should say."

Tia nodded. "Yes. It was through the recommendation of His Grace that I was accepted as an apprentice of the Guild."

Mary de Cumberland could sense the aura of dark foreboding that hung like a pall around the girl. "Well, now that your future is assured," she said warmly, "you have nothing to worry about."

"No," said Tia with a little smile. "No. Nothing to worry about." But there was bleakness in her eyes, and the pall of darkness did not dissipate.

At that moment, the waiter reappeared and coughed politely. "Your pardon, Your Grace." He looked at Tia. "Your pardon, Damoselle. Are you Apprentice Sorcerer Tia . . . uh . . . Einzig?" He hit the final g a little too hard.

Tia smiled up at him. "Yes, I am. What is it?"

"Well, Damoselle, there's a man at the bar who would like to speak to you. He says you'll know him."

"Really?" Tia did not turn to look. She raised an eyebrow. "Which one?"

The waiter did not turn, either. He kept his voice low. "The chap at the bar, Damoselle, on the third stool from the right; the merchant in the mauve jacket."

Casually, Tia shifted her eyes toward the bar. So did the Dowager Duchess. She saw a dark man with bristling eyebrows, a heavy drooping moustache, and deep-set eyes that darted about like a ferret's. The jacket he wore was of the oddly-cut "Douglas style," which was a strong indication that he was a Manxman, since the style was very little favored except on the Isle of Man.

She heard Tia gasp, "I . . . I'll speak to him. Would you excuse me, Your Grace?"

"Of course, my dear. Waiter, would you refill our mugs?"

Mary watched as Tia rose and walked over to the bar. She could see the stranger's face and Tia's back, but in the hash of emotion that was washing back and forth through the room, it was impossible to interpret Tia's emotions. As for the stranger, there was no way for her to catch his words. His face seemed immobile, his lips seemed hardly to move, and what movements they did make were covered by the heavy moustache. The entire conversation took less than two minutes. Then the stranger bowed his head to Tia, rose, and walked out of the Sword Room.

Tia stood where she was for perhaps another thirty seconds. Then she turned and came back to the booth where the Dowager Duchess of Cumberland waited. On her face was a look which Mary could only interpret as grim joy.

"Excuse me, Your Grace," she said. "A friend. We had not seen each other for some time." She sat down and picked up her tankard.

Then she said suddenly, "Pardon me, Your Grace. What o'clock is it?"

Mary looked at the watch on her wrist "Twelve after six."

"Oh, dear," said Tia, "Sir Thomas told me specifically that I should wear evening costume after six."

Mary laughed. "He's right, of course. We should both have changed before this."

Tia leaned forward. "Your Grace," she said confidingly, "I must admit something. I'm not used to Angevin styles. Sir Thomas was good enough to buy me some evening dresses, and there is one in particular I have never worn before. I should like to wear it tonight, but"—her voice sank even lower—"I don't know how to wear the thing properly. Would Your Grace be so good as to come up and help me with it?"

"Surely, my dear," Mary said with a laugh, "under one condition."

"What's that, Your Grace?"

"The dress I have to wear normally requires a battalion of assistants to get it on. Do you think you can substitute for a battalion?"

The statement was untrue; the Duchess was perfectly capable of dressing herself, but Lord Darcy had asked her to keep an eye on this girl and, even though she was not certain that it was still necessary, she would obey his orders.

"I can certainly try, Your Grace," said Tia, smiling. "My room is two flights up."

"Good, we'll go up and strap you into your finery, then go down one flight and strap me into mine. Between the two of us we'll have every sorcerer in the place groveling at our feet."

The Duchess signed the bill that the waiter presented, and the two women left the Sword Room.

Tia turned the key in the door to her room. She pushed open the door and stopped. On the floor, just beyond the door, was an envelope. She picked it up and smiled at the Duchess. "Excuse me, Your Grace," she said, "the dress I was telling you about is in the closet over there. I would like Your Grace to give me your opinion on it. It's the blue one."

Mary walked over to the closet, opened it, and looked at the array of dresses, but before she could say anything she heard Tia's voice behind her. She could not understand the words of the girl's short expletive, but she could feel the anger in them. Slowly she turned around and said, "What seems to be the trouble?"

"Trouble?" the girl's eyes flashed fire. Her right hand crumpled the envelope and then with a convulsive gesture threw it into the wastebasket nearby. "No trouble, Your Grace, no trouble at all." Her smile was forced. She walked over to the closet and looked at the dress. She stared at it without saying anything.

Mary of Cumberland stepped back. "It's a lovely dress,

Tia," she said quietly. "You'll look magnificent in it." With one lightning-like movement she reached out to the waste-basket, grabbed the piece of paper Tia had thrown away, and slipped it into her pocket. "Yes," she said, "a very beautiful dress."

Mary could sense the girl's hesitation and confusion. Something in that note had upset her, had changed her plans, and now she was trying to think of what to do next.

Tia turned, a pained look on her face. "Your Grace, I don't . . . I don't feel well. I should like to lie down for a few minutes." For a moment, Mary de Cumberland thought she should offer her services as a Healer. Then she real-ized that that would simply add to the confusion. Tia had no headache. She simply wanted to get rid of her guest. There was nothing Mary could do.

"Of course, my dear. I understand. I shall," she smiled, realizing she was repeating Sir Thomas' words, "see you later on, then. Good evening, my dear."

She went out into the hall and heard the door close behind her. *What now?* she thought. There was no way of intrud-ing on Tia without making her intrusion obvious. What to do next?

She went down the stairs. Halfway down she took out the note that had been under Tia's door, the note she had retrieved from the wastebasket. She opened it and looked at it.

It was in a language she could not identify. Not a single word of it was understandable. The only thing that stood out was a number that was easily recognizable.

7:00.

Nothing else was comprehensible.

CHAPTER 14

Lord Darcy leaned back in the hard, straight-backed chair that apparently epitomized Admiralty furniture and stretched his back muscles. "Ahhh-h-h . . ." he exhaled audibly. He felt as though weariness had settled into every cell of his body.

Then he leaned forward again, closed the folder on the

table in front of him, and looked across the table at Lord Ashley.

"Doesn't tell us much, does it, my lord?"

Lord Ashley shook his head. "No, my lord. None of them do. The mysterious FitzJean remains as mysterious as ever."

Lord Darcy pushed the folder away from him. "Agreed." He drummed his fingers on the tabletop. "We have no clue from Barbour as to FitzJean's identity. The Admiralty staff at Cherbourg Naval Base did not even know of Barbour's existence. Unless something unexpected turns up, we will get no further information about FitzJean from that end."

"Do you see any clues at this end, my lord?"

"Well, look at the data." Lord Darcy gestured toward the pile of folders. "Only three men, presumably, know how to build and how to activate the confusion projector: Sir Lyon Grey, Sir Thomas Leseaux, and the late Sir James Zwinge. Of course, it is possible that that information was stolen from them, but let us explore the first possibility that suggests itself: Could it have been one of them?"

The Commander frowned. "It's hard to imagine that such respected and trusted men could betray the Empire."

"Indeed," said Lord Darcy. "It is difficult to imagine why *any* highly-placed officer could betray the Empire. But it has happened before, and we must consider the possibility.

"What about Sir Thomas, for instance? He worked out the theory and the mathematics for this device. What about Sir Lyon, or Sir James? They collaborated on working out the thaumaturgical engineering technique which made the device a working reality.

"If you had to pick one of the three, my lord, which would it be?"

The Commander leaned back in his chair and looked up, away from the low-hanging gas lamp, at the shadowed beams of the high ceiling.

"Well," he said after a moment, "first off, I'd eliminate Sir Thomas. Since the basic discovery was his, it would have been much simpler all around for him to have sold it directly to His Slavonic Majesty's Government in the first place, if he needed money that badly."

"Agreed," said Lord Darcy tonelessly.

"Sir Lyon," Commander Ashley continued, "has plenty of money in his own right. I don't say that a quarter of a million silver sovereigns would mean nothing to him, but it hardly seems enough to entice a man in his position to commit treason."

"Agreed," Lord Darcy repeated.

"Sir James?" Ashley paused. "I don't know. Certainly he was not a wealthy man."

He stared at the ceiling for another twenty seconds, then lowered his head and looked at Darcy. "Here's a suggestion for you, my lord. I don't know how good it is, but we can try it for size."

"Proceed," said Lord Darcy. "I should be grateful for any light you may shed upon the subject."

"All right; suppose that Zwinge and Barbour were in this together. Naturally, to cover themselves, they would have to invent the mysterious FitzJean. No one ever saw FitzJean and Barbour together. Our agents saw him enter Barbour's place, and they saw him leave it. He came from nowhere and vanished into nowhere. What could be simpler than for Barbour himself to impersonate this mysterious being? Barbour, after all, actually did have contacts with Polish agents."

"Barbour wasn't Zwinge's only contact," Lord Darcy pointed out. "Why not use one of the others, and quietly sell the secret without all this play-acting?"

The Commander put his hand on the table, palm up. "What would happen if he did? As soon as the Royal Polish Navy was equipped with this device, we would find it out. We would know that one of those three men had sold it. Our first suspicion would naturally fall on Zwinge, because, of the three, only he was known to have had any contacts with Polish agents.

"After all, an ordinary man with a secret to sell can't simply say to himself, 'Well, I guess I'll just dot out and peddle it to a Polish agent.' Polish agents aren't that easy to find."

"True," Lord Darcy said thoughtfully. "It is difficult to sell something if you don't know how to get in contact with your customers. Pray continue."

"Very well then. In order to divert suspicion from himself, he sets up this little playlet with Barbour. Everyone is looking for the mysterious FitzJean. A trap is laid for him. Meanwhile, Barbour is actually dealing with the Poles, giving them the same story about FitzJean."

"How was the playlet to end, then?" Lord Darcy asked.

"Well, let's see. The secret is given to the Poles. The Poles pay off Barbour. I imagine Zwinge would have found some excuse to be there at the same time. I doubt if he would have trusted Barbour with five thousand golden sovereigns.

"The trap for the mysterious FitzJean fails, of course, since there is no FitzJean, and—after we find that the Polish Navy has the confusion projector—Zwinge's excuse is: 'FitzJean must have become suspicious of Barbour and peddled the secret elsewhere.'

"Zwinge may have intended to pay off Barbour, to split the money with him, or he may have intended to kill him. We can't know which."

"Interesting," said Lord Darcy. "There is certainly nothing impossible about just such a plan having been conceived, but, if so, the plan did not come off. What, then, are your theories as to what actually *did* happen?"

"Personally," said the Commander, "I believe that the Poles discovered that Barbour was working for Zed, and that Zed was Sir James. Now then, if my hypothesis is anywhere close to the truth, there are at least two possible explanations for what happened.

"One: The Poles decided that the whole business about the confusion projector was mere bait for some kind of trap, a hoax cooked up for some reason by Sir James; so they sent out agents to eliminate both.

"Or, two: They had reason to believe that Sir James actually was a traitor and was ready to negotiate with them. They would know that Sir James wouldn't give the plans and specifications for the device to Barbour unless all the arrangements were made. But they would also know that he would have had to have those plans in a place where he could lay his hands on them quickly. He must have had them already drawn up and hidden somewhere; he could hardly have expected to be able to sit down and draw them from memory at the snap of a finger.

"So, while one group of agents is dealing with Barbour in Cherbourg, another is watching Zwinge in London. Arrangements for the payoff are made in Cherbourg, and Barbour sends this information to Zwinge. Zwinge, not knowing he is being watched by Polish agents, fetches the plans to send them to Barbour. But now, the Poles know where those plans are because Zwinge has taken them from their hiding place. They send orders to Cherbourg to dispose of Barbour, and the agents here kill Zwinge and grab the plans, thereby saving themselves five thousand golden sovereigns."

"I must admit," said Lord Darcy slowly, "that my lack of knowledge of international intelligence networks has hampered me. That theory would never have occurred to me. What about the actual mechanism of Sir James' murder? How did the Polish agents actually go about killing him?"

Commander Lord Ashley shrugged eloquently. "Now there you have me, my lord. My knowledge of black magic is nil, and, in spite of Captain Smollett's statement of my qualifications, I am forced to admit that my experience in the Naval C.I.D. never included a murder investigation."

Lord Darcy laughed. "Well, that is honest enough, anyway. I hope this investigation will allow you to see how we poor benighted civilians go about it. What o'clock is it?" He looked at the watch at his wrist. "Heavens! It's after six. I thought the Admiralty closed at six o'clock."

The Commander grinned. "I daresay Captain Smollett left word for us not to be disturbed."

"Of course," said Lord Darcy. "All right. Let's put these folders back in their files and go to the hotel. I want to ask Sir Lyon Grey some questions if we can get hold of him, and also I should like to speak to His Grace the Archbishop of York. We need to know more about a girl named Tia Einzig."

"Tia Einzig?" Lord Ashley blinked. The name was totally new to him.

"I'll tell you what little I know about her on the way over to the hotel. Will the Admiralty have transportation for us? Or will we have to find a cab?"

"I'm afraid the Admiralty coaches are all locked up at six, my lord," said the Commander. "We'll have to take a cab—if we can find one."

"If not, we can walk," said Lord Darcy. "It's not as if the Royal Steward were halfway across the city."

A few minutes later, they walked down the darkened corridors of the Admiralty offices. In the lobby, an armed Petty Officer let them out through the front door. "Awfully foggy out tonight, my lords," he said. "Trust you have a good ride. Captain Smollett left orders that a coach be waiting for you."

"Let us thank God for small favors," said Lord Darcy.

The fog was even heavier than it had been the night before. At the curb, barely visible in the dim glow of the gas lamp above the doors of the Admiralty Building, stood a coach bearing the Admiralty arms. The two men went down the steps to the curb. Commander Lord Ashley said:

"Petty Officer Hosquins, is that you?"

"Yes, My Lord Commander," came a voice from the driver's seat, "Captain Smollett told us to wait for you."

"Excellent. Take us to the Royal Steward, then." And the two men climbed into the coach.

It took longer to make the trip than it had earlier that afternoon. Most of the visitors, anticipating the fog, had gone home. Lord Darcy and Lord Ashley found the lobby almost deserted. A man wearing the silver-slashed blue of a Master Sorcerer was looking at one of the displays. Lord Darcy and Lord Ashley went over to him and Lord Darcy tapped him on the shoulder.

"Your pardon, Master Sorcerer," he said formally. "I am Lord Darcy, special investigator under a King's Warrant, and I would appreciate it if you could tell me where I might find Sir Lyon Gandolphus Grey."

The master sorcerer turned, an obsequious smile on his face. "Ah, Lord Darcy," he said. "It is indeed a pleasure to meet your lordship. I am Master Ewen MacAlister. My very good friend Master Sean O Lochlainn has told me a great deal about you, your lordship." Then his face fell in sudden gloom. "I am sorry to say, your lordship, that Grand Master Sir Lyon is unavailable at the moment. He is attending a Special Executive Session of the top officers of the Royal Thaumaturgical Society and the Sorcerers Guild. Can I do anything else to help your lordships?"

Lord Darcy refrained from pointing out that thus far he had done nothing at all to help their lordships. "Ah, that is too bad. But no matter. Tell me, is His Grace the Archbishop of York also attending that meeting?"

"Oh no, your lordship. His Grace is not a member of the Executive Committee. His ecclesiastical ties are much too onerous to permit him to take on the added burden. As a matter of fact, I saw His Grace only a few moments ago. He is taking his evening tea in the restaurant—in the Buckler Room, your lordship."

He lifted his hand and took a quick glance at his wristwatch. "Yes, that was only a few minutes ago, your lordships. His Grace should still be there.

"Tell me, is there anything else I can do to help your lordships?" Before either of them could answer, he went on, "Can I do anything that will aid you in apprehending the fiendish criminal who perpetrated the heinous murder of"— he suddenly looked very sad—"our good friend Master Sir James? A deplorable thing. Is your lordship prepared to make an arrest?"

"We shall do our best, Master Ewen," said Lord Darcy briskly. "We thank you for your information. Good evening, Master Ewen, and thank you again."

He and Lord Ashley turned and walked toward the restaurant, leaving Master Ewen MacAlister looking blankly after them.

"Master Ewen MacAlister, eh?" said Lord Ashley. "Oily little bastard, isn't he?"

"I should have known him, from Master Sean's description, even if he had not introduced himself."

"Is there any possibility, my lord," Lord Ashley said thoughtfully, "that Master Ewen is involved in the matter?"

Lord Darcy took two more steps before he answered the question. "I shall be honest with you," he said then. "Although I have no evidence, I feel it highly probable that Master Ewen MacAlister is one of the prime movers in the mystery which surrounds Sir James' death."

Lord Ashley looked surprised. "You didn't seem disposed to question him any further."

"I have read the statement he made to Lord Bontriomphe yesterday. He was in his room all that morning until ten or fifteen minutes after nine. He is not sure of the time. After that, he was down in the lobby. Master Sean corroborates a part of his testimony. The interesting thing, however, is that Master Ewen's room is on the floor above, and directly over, the room in which Sir James was killed."

"That *is* food for thought," said Ashley as they approached the door of the Buckler Room.

Lord Darcy pushed the door open and the two men went in. The courtyard outside, which had been visible that morning from Sir James' room, was now shrouded in fog, but the gas lamps gave bright illumination to the restaurant itself. The two men stopped and surveyed the room. At one table an elderly man in episcopal purple sat by himself, sipping tea.

Lord Darcy said, "That, I believe, is His Grace of York." They walked toward the table.

The Archbishop appeared to be deep in thought. He had a notebook on the table and was carefully marking down symbols upon its open pages.

"My apologies for this interruption, Your Grace," said Lord Darcy politely. "I would not willingly disturb your cogitations, but I come upon the King's Business."

The old man looked up with a smile, the light from the gas lamps making a halo of the silver hair that surrounded his purple skullcap. Without rising he extended his hand. "You do not interrupt, my lord," he said gently. "My time is yours. You are Lord Darcy from Rouen, I believe?"

"I am, Your Grace," said Lord Darcy, "and this is Commander Lord Ashley of the Imperial Naval Intelligence Corps."

"Very good," said the wise old Sensitive. "Please be seated, my lords. Thank you. You come then to discuss the problem propounded by the death of Sir James Zwinge."

"We do, Your Grace," said Lord Darcy, settling himself in his chair. His Grace of York folded his hands upon the table.

"I am at your service. Anything that may be done to clear this matter up . . ."

"Your Grace is most kind," said Lord Darcy. "I am not, as you know, a Talented man," he began, "and there are, therefore, certain data which you may possess that I do not."

"Very probably. Such as what?"

"As I understand it, it would be difficult for a sorcerer to perform a rite of Black Magic within this hotel without giving himself away. Furthermore, every sorcerer here has been examined for orthodoxy of practice and carries a license signed by his diocesan bishop attesting to that examination."

"And so your question is," the Archbishop interjected smoothly, "how is it such a person could have escaped our notice."

"Precisely."

"Very well, I shall attempt an explanation. Let us begin with the license to practice. This license is given to an individual sorcerer when, upon completing his apprenticeship, he becomes qualified, according to the rules of the Guild, to practice his Art. Each three years thereafter he is reexamined and his license renewed if he passes the qualifications. You are aware of this?"

Lord Darcy nodded. "Yes, Your Grace."

"Very well," said the Archbishop, "but what would disqualify a sorcerer? What would prevent the Church from renewing his license? Well, there are many things, but chief among them would certainly be the practice of Black Magic. Unfortunately, except for a very few peculiarly qualified Sensitives it is not possible to detect when a man has practiced what is technically known as Black Magic if the spells are minor, if the harm they have done is relatively small, if the practitioner has not been too greatly corrupted by the practice. Do you follow?"

"I think so," said Lord Darcy.

"Then," continued the Archbishop, raising a finger, "you will see how it is that a man may get away with practicing Black Magic for some time before it has such an effect upon his psyche that it becomes obvious to a Board of Examiners that he can no longer be certified as practicing orthodox sorcery.

"Now a major crime, such as murder, would, of course, instantly be detectable to a certifying commission assembled for the purpose. The sorcerer in question would be required to undergo certain tests which he would automatically fail if he had used his Art to commit so heinous a crime as murder."

He turned a hand palm upward. "But you can see that it would be impossible to give every sorcerer here such a test. The Guild must assume that a member is orthodox unless there is sufficient evidence to warrant testing his orthodoxy."

"I quite understand that," said Lord Darcy, "but I also know that you are one of the most delicate Sensitives and one of the most powerful Healers in Christendom." He looked directly into the Archbishop's eyes. "I knew Lord Seiger of Yorkshire."

His Grace's eyes showed sadness. "Ah, yes, poor Seiger. A troubled soul. I did for him what I could, and yet I knew . . . yes, I knew . . . that in spite of everything he would not live long."

"Your Grace recognized him as a psychopathic killer," said Lord Darcy. "If we have such a killer in our midst now, would he not be as easily recognizable as was Lord Seiger?"

The Archbishop's troubled eyes looked first at Lord Darcy and then at Lord Ashley. "My lords," he said carefully, "the realm of magic is not that easily divisible into stark white and deadly black, nor can human souls be so easily judged. Lord Seiger was an extreme case, and, therefore, easily perceived and easily isolated, even though he was difficult to treat. But one cannot say 'this man is capable of killing,' and 'this man has killed,' and for that reason alone isolate him from society. For these traits are not necessarily evil. The ability to kill is a necessary survival characteristic of the human animal. To do away with it by fiat would be in essence to destroy our humanity. For instance, as a Sensitive I can detect that both of you are capable of killing; further, that both of you have killed other human beings. But that does not tell me whether or not these killings were justified. We Sensitives are not angels, my lords. We do not presume to the powers of God Himself. Only when there is true, deep-seated evil intent does it become so blatantly obvious that it is instantly detectable. I find, for instance, no such evil in either of you."

There was a long moment of silence and finally Lord Darcy said, "I believe I understand. Am I correct, however, in saying that, if every sorcerer here were to be given the standard tests for orthodoxy, anyone who had committed a murder by Black Magic would be detectable through these tests?"

"Oh, indeed," said the Archbishop, "indeed. Rest assured that if the secular arm cannot discover the culprit these tests *will* be given. But"—he emphasized his point with a long, thin finger—"as yet neither the Church nor the Guild has any evidence whatever that such black sorcery has been practiced. That is why we hold off."

"I see," said Lord Darcy. "One other thing, with Your Grace's permission. What do you know of a Damoselle Tia Einzig?"

"Damoselle Tia?" the saintly old man chuckled. "Ah, there

is one, my lord, whom you may dismiss immediately from your mind if you suspect her of any complicity in this affair. In the past few months she has been examined twice by competent Boards and Examiners. She has never in her life practiced Black Magic."

"I disagree with you that that alone absolves her of complicity," said Lord Darcy. "A person could certainly be involved in a murder without having been the actual practitioner of Black Magic. Correct me if I am wrong."

The Archbishop looked thoughtful. "Well, you are right, of course. It would be possible . . . yes, yes, it *would* be possible . . . for Damoselle Tia to have committed a crime, so long as it was not the crime of Black Magic we would not necessarily have detected it." He smiled. "I assure you there is no harm in her, no harm at all."

His attention was distracted by someone who was approaching the table. Lord Darcy looked up. Mary of Cumberland was excited, but she was doing her best to keep from showing it.

"Your Grace," she said. She curtsied quickly, and then looked at Lord Darcy. "I"—she stopped and glanced at Lord Ashley and then at the Archbishop before looking back at Lord Darcy—"Is it all right to talk, my lord?"

"About your assignment?" Lord Darcy asked.

"Yes."

"We have just been discussing Tia. What new intelligence do you have for us?"

"Pray be seated, Your Grace," said the Archbishop. "I should like to hear anything you have to say about Tia."

In a low voice the Dowager Duchess of Cumberland told of her conversation with Tia Einzig, of Tia's short meeting with the man in the bar, and of the incident concerning the note in Tia's room, with an attention to detail and accuracy that not even Lord Bontriomphe could have surpassed.

"I have been looking all over for you," she finished up. "I went to the office; the Sergeant-at-Arms said he hadn't seen you. It was just lucky that I walked in here."

Lord Darcy held out his hand. "Let me see that piece of paper," he snapped. She handed it to him.

"That's why I was in such a hurry to find you. All I can read on it are the numbers."

"It is in Polish," said Lord Darcy. " 'Be at the *Dog and Hare* at seven o'clock,' " he translated. "There is no signature."

He glanced at his watch. "Three minutes of seven! Where the Devil is the *Dog and Hare*?"

"Could that be *'Hound and Hare'*?" said Lord Ashley. "That's a pub on Upper Swandham Lane. We can just make it."

"You know of no *'Dog and Hare'*? No? Then we'll have to take a chance," Lord Darcy said. He turned to the Dowager Duchess. "Mary, you've done a magnificent job. I haven't time to thank you further just now. I must leave you in the company of the Archbishop. Your Grace must excuse us. Come on, Ashley. Where is this *Hound and Hare*?"

They walked out of the Buckler Room into the lobby of the hotel. Lord Ashley gestured. "There's a corridor that runs off the lobby here and opens into Potsmoke Alley. A turn to our right puts us on Upper Swandham Lane. No more than a minute and a half."

The two men pulled their cloaks about them and put up their hoods to guard against the chill of the fog outside. Ignoring the looks of several sorcerers who wondered why two men were charging across the lobby at high speed, they went down the corridor to the rear door. A Man-at-Arms was standing by the door.

"I'm Lord Darcy," snapped the investigator. "Tell Lord Bontriomphe that we are going to the *Hound and Hare*; that we shall return as soon as possible."

CHAPTER 15

In Potsmoke Alley the fog closed about the two men, and when the rear door to the Royal Steward was closed behind them they were surrounded by darkness.

"This way," said Ashley. They turned right, feeling their way down Potsmoke Alley to the end of the block of buildings to where St. Swithin's Street crossed the narrow alley and widened it to become Upper Swandham Lane. Here there were a few gas lanterns glowing dimly in the fog, but even so it was difficult to see more than a few feet ahead.

As he and Ashley emerged from Potsmoke Alley, Lord Darcy could hear a distant *click! . . . click! . . . click! . . .* approaching through the fog to their right, on St. Swithin's Street. It sounded like someone wearing shoes with steel taps. To the left he could hear two pairs of leather-shod boots retreating, one fairly close by, the other farther down the street. Somewhere ahead, far down Upper Swandham Lane, he could hear a coach and pair clattering slowly across the cobblestones.

The two men crossed St. Swithin's Street and went down Upper Swandham Lane. "I think that's it ahead," said Lord Ashley, after a minute. "Yes. Yes, that's it."

The sign underneath the gas lantern depicted a bright blue gazehound in hot pursuit of an equally blue hare.

"All right, let's go in," said Lord Darcy. "Keep your hood up and your cloak closed. I shouldn't want anyone to see that Naval uniform. This way, we might be ordinary middle-class merchants."

"Right," said Lord Ashley, "I hope we can spot the girl. Do you know her when you see her?"

"I think so. Her Grace's description was quite detailed; there can't be many girls of her size and appearance wandering about London." He pushed open the door.

There was a long bar stretching along the full length of the wall to Darcy's left. Along the wall to his right was a series of booths that also stretched to the back of the room. In the rear there were several tables in the center of the floor, between the bar and the booths. Some men at one were playing cards, and a dart board on the back wall was responding with the *thunk! . . . thunk! . . . thunk! . . .* of darts thrown by a patron whose arm was as strong as his aim was weak.

Darcy and Ashley moved quickly to an empty spot at the bar. In spite of the number of customers the big room was not crowded.

"See anybody we know?" murmured Lord Ashley.

"Not from here," Lord Darcy said. "She could be in one of those rear booths. Or possibly she hasn't arrived yet."

"I think your second guess was correct," Ashley said. "Take a look in the mirror behind the bar."

The mirror reflected the front door perfectly, and Lord Darcy easily recognized the tiny figure and beautiful face of Tia Einzig. As she walked across the room toward the back the identification was complete in Darcy's mind. "That's the girl," he said. "Notice the high heels that Her Grace mentioned."

And, he realized, those heels also explained those clicking footsteps he had heard on St. Swithin's Street. She hadn't been more than thirty seconds behind Ashley and himself.

Tia did not look around. She walked straight toward the rear as if she knew exactly where the person she was to meet would be waiting. She went directly to the last booth, near the back door of the pub, and slid in on the far side, facing the front door.

"I wonder," said Lord Darcy, "is there somebody already in that booth? Or is she waiting for the person who sent her the note?"

"Let's just stroll back and see," said Lord Ashley.

"Good, but don't get too close. I don't want either of them to see our faces."

"We could watch the dart game," said Lord Ashley, "that might be interesting."

"Yes, let's," said Lord Darcy. They walked slowly back to the far end of the bar.

There was someone in the booth, seated directly across from Tia Einzig. It was obviously a man, but the hood of the cloak completely concealed his face, and he kept his head bent low over the table.

Lord Darcy said: "Let's move over to that table. I want to see if I can hear their conversation. But move carefully. Keep your face concealed without being obvious about it."

The nearest table was further toward the front of the room than the booth that the two men were watching. They could no longer see the hooded man at all. His back was to them now and he kept his voice low, so that, while it was audible, it was not intelligible. Tia, however, was facing them, and, as Mary de Cumberland had told Lord Darcy the previous evening, the girl's voice had abnormal carrying power, even when she did not speak loudly.

For several seconds all they could hear was the low mutter of the man's voice, then Tia said, "If you didn't want him dead, why did you kill him?" Her expression was hard and cold, with an undertone of anger.

More muttering, then Tia again: "You discovered that Zed, the much-feared head of Imperial Naval Intelligence in Europe, was actually Master Sir James Zwinge, and you mean to sit there and tell me that King Casimir's Secret Service didn't want him dead."

A couple of angry words from the hooded man.

"I'll talk any way I please," said Tia. "*You* keep a civil tongue in *your* head."

She said nothing more for nearly a minute, as she listened to the hooded man with that unchanging stony expression of cold anger on her beautiful face. Then an icy smile came across her lips.

"No, I will not," she said. "I won't ask him. Not for you, not for Poland, not for King Casimir's whole damned army!"

A short phrase from the hooded man. Tia's cold smile widened just a trifle. "No, damn you, not for *him* either. And do you know why? Because I know *now* that you *lied* to me! Because I know now that he's safe from the torture chambers of the Polish Secret Service!"

The hooded man said something more. "Signing his death warrant?" She laughed sharply, without humor. "Oh no. You've harassed me long enough. You've tried to force me to betray a country that has been good to me, and a man who loves me. I've lived in constant fear and terror because of you, but no longer. Oh, I'm going to sign a death warrant all right— yours! I'm going to blow this whole plot sky high. I'm going to tell the Imperial authorities everything I know, and I hope they hang you, you vicious, miserable little . . ."

She stopped suddenly and blinked. "What?" She blinked again.

Lord Darcy, watching Tia's face covertly from beneath his hood, saw her expression change. Where before it had been stony, now it became wooden. The cold expression became no expression at all.

The Commander suddenly reached over and grabbed Darcy's wrist.

"Watch it!" he whispered harshly. "They're going to leave by the back door!"

Lord Darcy smiled inwardly. Lord Bontriomphe had mentioned that Ashley had occasional flashes of precognition, and here was an example of it. Such flashes came to an untrained Talent in moments of personal stress.

As Ashley had predicted, Tia rose to her feet, as did the hooded man, his back still toward the watchers. The hooded man did not turn. Tia did, and the two of them walked directly out the back door, only a few feet away.

Darcy and the Commander were on their feet, heading toward the back door. Then Lord Darcy stopped, his hand on the doorknob.

"What are you waiting for?" Ashley asked.

"I want them to get far enough ahead so that they won't notice the light when I open this door."

"But we'll lose them in this fog!"

"Not with those high heels of hers. You can hear them ten yards away."

He eased the door open a trifle. "Hear that? They're moving away toward our right. What street is this?"

"This would be Old Barnegat Road," said Lord Ashley.

"All right, let's go." Lord Darcy swung open the door and the two men stepped out into the billowing fog. The steady clicking of Tia's heels was still clearly audible.

"Let's close up the distance," Lord Darcy said as they walked steadily through the shrouded darkness. "If we walk quietly, they won't notice our footsteps over the sound of hers."

The two men said nothing for several minutes as they followed the beacon of sound that came from Tia's heels. Then, in a low voice, Lord Ashley said, "You know, I didn't understand much of that conversation back at the pub but I guess I should be thankful I could understand any of it at all."

"Why?" asked Lord Darcy.

"I had rather assumed it would be in Polish. We know the Einzig girl speaks Polish and the note indicates that the man does, too."

"Quite the contrary," said Lord Darcy. "The note indicates that the man has a slight acquaintance with the Polish tongue, but hardly enough to carry on a lengthy conversation in it. The Poles differentiate between a 'hound' and a 'dog' just as we do. Yet in translating *Hound and Hare* into Polish, he used the Polish word for 'dog,' which no one who was conversant with the language would have done. And that tells us a great deal more about the man we are following."

"In what way, my lord?"

"That he is vain, pretentious, and has an overdeveloped sense of the melodramatic. He could quite as easily have written the note in Anglo-French, yet he did not. Why?"

"Perhaps because he felt that it would not be understood by anyone else who happened to see it."

"Precisely; and you have fallen into the same error he did. Only a man who is unfamiliar with a language thinks of it as a kind of secret writing. Do you think of Anglo-French as a cryptic language with which to conceal your thoughts from others?"

"Hardly," said Lord Ashley with a smile.

"But even so," Lord Darcy said softly, "only a vain, pretentious man would attempt to show off his patently poor knowledge of a language to a person whose native tongue it is."

At a corner ahead of them, the sound of Tia's heels turned again to the right. "Where are we now?" Lord Darcy asked.

"If I haven't lost my bearings, we just passed Great Harlow House; that means they turned on Thames Street, heading roughly south."

Lord Darcy wished, not for the first time, that he knew more about the geography of London. "Have you any idea where they're going?" he asked.

"Well, if we keep on this way," said Lord Ashley, "we'll pass St. Martin's Church and end up smack in the middle of Westminster Palace."

"Don't tell me they're going to see the King," said Lord Darcy. "I really don't believe I could swallow that."

"Wait, they're turning left."

"Where would that be?"

"Somerset Bridge," Lord Ashley said. "They're crossing the river. We'd better drop back a little. There are lights on the bridge."

"I think not," said Lord Darcy. "We'll take our chances."

"How much longer are they going to keep walking?" Lord Ashley muttered. "Are they out on a pleasant evening stroll to Croydon or something?"

The lights on the bridge did not hamper them in any way. They were widely spaced, and the fog was so dense, especially here over the Thames, that someone standing directly under a gas lamp could not be seen from fifteen feet away. They kept walking at a steady pace.

Suddenly the clicking stopped, somewhere near the middle of the bridge. Automatically the two men also stopped. Then they heard a single sentence, muffled but clearly intelligible: "Now climb up on the balustrade."

"Good God!" said Darcy. "Let's go!"

The two men broke into a run. Caution now was out of the question. The hooded man came suddenly into sight, through the veil of fog. He was standing near one of the gas lamps. Tia Einzig was nowhere to be seen. From the river below came the sound of a muffled splash.

At the sound of footsteps the hooded man turned, his face still hidden, shadowed from the overhead light by the hood of his cloak. He froze for a second as if deciding whether or not to run. Then he realized it was too late, that his pursuers were too close for him to escape. His right hand dived beneath his cloak and came out again with a small-sword. Its needlelike blade gleamed in the foggy light.

The Imperial Navy's training was such that Commander Lord Ashley's reaction was almost instinctive. His own narrow-bladed sword came from its scabbard and into position before the hooded man could attack.

"Take care of him!" Lord Darcy shouted. "I'll get the girl!" He was already racing across the bridge to the downstream side, opening his cloak and dropping it behind him as he ran. He vaulted to the top of the broad stone balustrade, stood for a moment, then took a long clean dive into the impenetrable blackness below.

CHAPTER 16

Commander Lord Ashley did not see Lord Darcy's dive from the bridge. His eyes had not for a second left the hooded figure that faced him in the tiny area of mist-filled light beneath the gas lamp. He felt confident, sure of himself. The way the other man had drawn his sword proclaimed him an amateur.

Then, as his opponent came in suddenly, he felt an odd surge of fear. The sword in the other man's hand seemed to flicker and vanish as it moved!

It was only by instinct and pure luck that he managed to avoid the point of the other's sword and parry the thrust with his own blade. And still his eyes could not find that slim, deadly shaft of steel. It was as if his eyes refused to focus on it, refused to look directly at it.

The next few seconds brought him close to panic as thrust after thrust narrowly missed their mark, and his own thrusts were parried easily by a blade he could not see, a blade he could not find.

Wherever he looked, it was always somewhere else, moving in hard and fast, with strikes that would have been deadly, had his own sword not somehow managed to ward them off each time. His own thrusts were parried again and again, for each time the other blade neared his own, his eyes would uncontrollably look away.

He did not need to be told that this was sorcery. It was all too apparent that he was faced with an enchanted blade in the hands of a deadly killer.

And then the Commander's own latent, untrained Talent came to the fore. It was a Talent that was rare even in the Sorcerers Guild. It was an ability to see a very short time into the future, usually only for seconds, and—very rarely—for whole minutes.

The Guild could train most men with that Talent; these were the sorcerers who predicted the weather, warned of earthquakes, and foresaw other natural phenomena that were not subject to the actions of men. But, as yet, not even the greatest thaumaturgical scientists had devised a method of training the Commander's peculiar ability. For that ability was the rarest of all—the ability to predict the results of the actions of men. And since the thaumaturgical laws of time symmetry had not yet been fathomed, that kind of Talent still could not be brought to the peak of reliability that others had been.

The Commander had occasional flashes of precognition, but he never knew when they would come nor how long he could sustain their flow. But, like any other intelligent man who has what he knows is an accurate hunch, Commander Lord Ashley was capable of acting upon it.

Quite suddenly, he realized that he had known instinctively, with each thrust, where that ensorcelled blade was going to be. The black sorcerer who sought to kill him might have trained Talent on his side, but he could not possibly cope with Commander Lord Ashley's hunches.

Once he realized that, Ashley's eyes no longer sought the enemy's blade, or the arm that held it. They watched the body of his opponent. It moved from one position to another as though posing for sketches in a beginner's textbook. But he could have kept his eyes closed and still known.

For a little while, Ashley did nothing but ward off the other's attacks, getting the feel of the black sorcerer's sword work. But he was no longer retreating.

He began to move in. Step by step he forced his opponent back. Now they were directly beneath the gas lamp again. Lord Ashley could tell that the other man was beginning to lose his confidence. His thrusts and parries were less certain. Now the panic and fear were all on the other side.

With careful deliberation, Commander Lord Ashley plotted out his own course of action. He did not want this man dead; this sorcerer and spy must be arrested, tried, and hanged, either for the actual murder of Sir James Zwinge, or for having ordered it done. There was no doubt in Lord Ashley's mind as to the guilt of this black sorcerer, but it would be folly to kill him, to take the King's justice into his own hands.

He knew, now, that it would be easy to take his opponent alive. It would require only two quick moves: a thrust between elbow and wrist to disarm the man, and then a quick blow to the side of his head with the flat of the blade to knock him senseless.

Lord Ashley made two more feints to move his opponent back and get him in just the right position to receive the final thrust. The sorcerer retreated as though he were obeying orders—which, indeed, he was: the orders of the lightning-swift sword in the Commander's hand.

Now the gas lamp was at Ashley's back, and for the first time the light fell full upon the face beneath the hood.

Lord Ashley smiled grimly as he recognized those features. Taking *this* man in would be a pleasure indeed!

Then the moment came. Ashley began his lunge toward the sorcerer's momentarily unprotected forearm.

It was at that moment that he felt his Talent desert him. He had become overconfident, and the psychic tension, which had sustained his steady flow of accurate hunches, had fallen below the critical threshold.

His left foot slipped on the fog-damp pavement of the bridge.

He tried to regain his balance but it was too late. In that moment, he could almost feel death.

But he had already thrown the fear of death so deeply into his opponent that the sorcerer did not see the opening as a chance to kill. He only saw that, for a moment, the deadly Naval sword no longer threatened him. His cloak swirled around him as he turned and ran, vanishing into the surrounding fog as though he had never been.

Lord Ashley kept himself from falling flat on his face by catching his weight on his outstretched left arm. Then he was back on his feet, and a stab of pain went through his right ankle. He could hear the running steps of the sorcerer fading into the distance, but he knew he could never catch him trying to run on a twisted ankle.

He braced himself against the balustrade for a moment and gave in to the laughter that had been welling up ever since he had seen that twisted, frightened face. The laughter was at himself, basically. To think that, for a few seconds, he had actually been deathly afraid of that obsequious little worm, Master Ewen MacAlister!

It took half a minute or so for the laughter to subside. Then he pulled a deep breath of fog-laden air into his lungs, and wiped the perspiration from his forehead with the back of his left hand. Deftly, he slid his sword back into its sheath.

It was too bad, he thought, that a spot of slippery pavement had prevented him from capturing Master Ewen, but at least the identity of the black sorcerer was now known, and Lord Darcy could—

Lord Darcy!

The haze of excitement cleared from his brain, and he limped across the bridge to the balustrade on the downstream side.

Black as pitch down there. He could see nothing.

"Darcy!" the Commander's voice rang out across the water, but the dense fog that brooded over the river seemed to distort and disperse the sound before it traveled far. There was no answer.

Twice more he called, and still there was no answer.

He heard rapid footsteps coming from his right and turned to face them, his hand on the hilt of his narrow-bladed sword.

MacAlister returning? It couldn't be! And yet . . .

Damn the fog! He felt as though he were isolated in a little world of his own, whose boundaries were a bank of cotton wool a dozen feet away, and which was surrounded by invisible beings that were nothing but disembodied footsteps.

Then he saw a glow of light, and out of the cotton wool came a friendly figure, carrying a pressure-gas lantern. Lord Ashley didn't know the big, heavy man, but the black uniform of a London Armsman made him a friend. The Armsman slowed, stopped, and put his hand on the hilt of his own smallsword. "May I ask what's going on here, sir?" he inquired politely. But his eyes were wary.

Lord Ashley carefully took his hand off the hilt of his own sword. The Armsman kept his where it was. "I heard a disturbance on the bridge, sir," he said stolidly. "A noise of swords clashing, it sounded like, sir. Then somebody from off the bridge ran past me in the fog. And just now . . ." He paused. "Were that you shouting, sir?"

It came suddenly to Lord Ashley what a forbidding figure he must be. In his long black Naval cloak, with the hood up, and his back to the lamp, his shadowed face was as invisible as MacAlister's had been. He reached up with one hand and pulled back the hood, and then pushed the cloak back over his shoulders so that the Armsman could see his uniform.

"I am Commander Lord Ashley," he said. "Yes, Armsman, there has been trouble. The man you heard running is a criminal wanted for murder."

"Murder, your lordship?" said the Armsman blankly. "Who was he?"

"I'm afraid he did not give me his name," said Lord Ashley. The statement was perfectly true, he thought, and he wanted to tell Darcy about MacAlister before he told anyone else. "The point is that a short time ago he pushed a young girl off the bridge. My companion dived in after her."

"Dived in after her? That were a foolish thing to do on a night like this. Likely we've lost two people instead of one, your lordship."

"That may well be," Lord Ashley admitted. "I've called him and he doesn't answer. But he's a powerful man, and although the chances are against his having found the girl, there's a good chance he can make it to shore by himself."

"All right, your lordship, we'll start looking for both of them right away." He took out his whistle and blew a series of shrill, high, keening notes into the murk-filled air—the "Assistance" call of the King's Armsmen. A second or two later, they heard distant whistles from both sides of the river blowing the answer: "Coming." After several more seconds, the Armsman repeated the call, to give his hearers a bearing.

"There'll be help along in a few minutes. Nothing we can do till then," the Armsman said briskly. He took a notebook from his jacket pocket. "Now, your lordship, if I might have your name again and the names of the other people involved."

The Commander repeated his own name, then he said, "The girl's name is Tia Einzig." He spelled it. "She is an important witness in a murder case, which is why the killer tried to do away with her. The man who went in after her is Lord Darcy, the—"

"Lord Darcy, did you say?" The Armsman lifted his head suddenly from the notebook. "Lord Darcy, the famous investigator from Rouen?"

"That's right," said Lord Ashley.

"The same Lord Darcy," persisted the Armsman, who seemed to want to make absolutely sure of the identification, "who came over from Normandy to help Lord Bontriomphe solve the Royal Steward Hotel Murder?"

"The same," Lord Ashley said wearily.

"And he's gone and jumped in the *river*?"

"Yes, that's what I said. He jumped in the river. He was trying to save this girl. By now he's had time to swim clear to the Nore. If we wait a little longer, he may be on his way back."

The Armsman looked miffed. "No need to get impatient, your lordship. We'll get things done as fast as we can." He put his whistle to his lips again and sent out the distress call a third time. Then, after a moment, a fourth.

Then they could hear hoofbeats clattering on the distant street and the sound changed to a hollow thunder as the horse galloped onto the bridge. They could see a glow of light approaching through the fog; the Armsman signaled with his own lantern. "Here comes the sergeant now, your lordship."

The mounted Sergeant-at-Arms was suddenly upon them, pulling his big bay gelding to a halt, as the Armsman came to attention. "What seems to be the trouble, Armsman Arthur?"

"This gentleman here, Sergeant, is Commander Lord Ashley of the Imperial Navy." Referring to his notebook, he went on to report quickly and concisely what Lord Ashley had told him. By that time, they could hear the thud of heavy boots and the clatter of hoofbeats from both ends of the bridge, as more Armsmen approached.

"All right, My Lord Commander," said the sergeant, "we'll take care of it. Likely he swam for the right bank since it's the nearer, but we'll cover both sides. Arthur, you go to the Thames Street River Patrol Station. Tell them to get their boats out, and to send a message to the other patrol stations downriver. We'll want everything covered from here to Chelsea."

"Right away, Sergeant." Armsman Arthur disappeared into the fog.

"I'd like to ask a favor if I may, Sergeant," said Lord Ashley.

"What might that be, My Lord Commander?"

"Send a horseman to the Royal Steward Hotel, if you would. Have him report exactly what happened to the Sergeant-at-Arms on duty there. Also, there is an official Admiralty coach waiting for me there, Petty Officer Hosquins in charge. Have your man tell Hosquins that Commander Lord Ashley wants him to bring the coach to Thames Street and Somerset Bridge immediately. I'm going to assume that Lord Darcy made for the right bank, and help your men search that side."

"Very good, My Lord Commander. I'll send a man right along."

Mary de Cumberland walked across the almost deserted lobby of the Royal Steward, doing her best to suppress her nervous impatience.

She felt she ought to be doing something, but what?

She would like to have talked to someone but there was no one to talk to.

Sir Lyon and Sir Thomas were still in conclave with the highest ranking sorcerers of the Empire. Master Sean was at the morgue attending to the autopsy of Sir James Zwinge. Lord Bontriomphe, according to the Sergeant-at-Arms who was on duty in the temporary office, was out prowling the city in search of a missing man named Paul Nichols. (She knew that the Sergeant-at-Arms would not have given her even that much information except that Lord Bontriomphe had told him that Her Grace of Cumberland would be bringing in information. The sergeant apparently assumed that her status in the investigation was a great deal more official than it actually was.)

And Lord Darcy was in a low dive down the street, keeping an eye on Tia.

Which left the Duchess with nothing to do.

Part way across the lobby, she turned and headed down the hall that led back to the temporary office. Maybe some information had come in. Even if none had, it was better to be talking to the sergeant than to be pointlessly pacing the hotel lobby.

If this had been a normal convention, she could have found plenty of convivial companionship in the Sword Room, but the murder had stilled the thirst of every sorcerer in the hotel. She went through the open door of the little office. "Anything new, Sergeant Peter?"

"Not a thing, Your Grace," said the Sergeant-at-Arms, rising to his feet. "Lord Bontriomphe's not back yet and neither is Lord Darcy."

"You look as though you're as bored as I am, Sergeant Do you mind if I sit down?"

"It would be an honor, Your Grace. Here, take this chair. Not too comfortable, I'm afraid. They didn't exactly give their night manager their best furniture."

They were interrupted by another Sergeant-at-Arms who walked in the door. He gave the Duchess a quick nod, said, "Evening, mum," and then addressed Sergeant Peter. "Are you in charge here, Sergeant?"

"Until Lord Bontriomphe or Lord Darcy gets back, I am. Sergeant Peter O Sechnaill."

"Sergeant Michael Coeur-Terre, River Detail. Lord Darcy

might not *be* back. Girl named Tia Einzig got pushed off
Somerset Bridge, and Lord Darcy jumped off the bridge after
her. They're putting out patrol boats and search parties on
both sides of the river from Somerset Bridge to Chelsea, but
personally I don't think there's much chance. A Commander
Lord Ashley asked us to report to you. He said Lord
Bontriomphe would want the information."

Sergeant Peter nodded. "Right," he said briskly. "I'll tell
his lordship as soon as he comes in. Anything else?"

"Yes. Do you know where an Admiralty coach is parked
around here with a Petty Officer Hosquins in charge of it?
Commander Lord Ashley says he wants it at Thames Street
and Somerset Bridge immediately. He wants transportation
for Lord Darcy when they find him, though it's my opinion that his lordship is done for."

Mary de Cumberland had already risen to her feet. Now
she said, in a very quiet voice, "He is not dead. I should
know it if he were dead."

"I beg your pardon, mum?" said Sergeant Michael.

"Nothing, Sergeant," she said calmly. "At Thames Street
and Somerset Bridge, you said? I know where the Admiralty coach is. I shall tell Petty Officer Hosquins."

Sergeant Michael noticed, for the first time, the Cumberland
arms on Mary's dress. Simultaneously, Sergeant Peter said,
"Her Grace is working with us on this case."

"That's . . . that's very good of Your Grace, I'm sure," said
Sergeant Michael.

"Not at all, Sergeant." She swept out of the room, walked
rapidly down the hall, across the lobby, and out the front
door of the Royal Steward. She hadn't the dimmest notion
of where the Admiralty coach might be parked, but this was
no time to quibble over details.

It didn't take her long to find it. It was waiting half a
block away, toward St. Swithin's Street. There was no
mistaking the Admiralty arms emblazoned on its door. The
coachman and the footman were sitting up in the driver's
seat, their greatcoats wrapped around them and a blanket
over their legs, quietly smoking their pipes and talking.

"Petty Officer Hosquins?" Mary said authoritatively. "I'm
the Duchess of Cumberland. Lord Ashley has sent word that
the coach is wanted immediately at Thames Street and
Somerset Bridge. I'm going with you." Before the footman

had even had a chance to climb down she had opened the door and was inside the coach. Petty Officer Hosquins opened the trap door in the roof and looked down at her.

"But Your Grace," he began.

"Lord Ashley," the Duchess cut in coldly, "said *'immediately.'* This is an emergency. Now, dammit, get a move on, man."

Petty Officer Hosquins blinked. "Yes, Your Grace," he said. He closed the trap. The coach moved on.

CHAPTER 17

There was a chilling shock as Lord Darcy's body cut into the inky waters of the Thames. For long seconds it seemed as if he would keep on going down until he buried himself in the mud and muck at the bottom; then he was fighting his way up again, tearing off his jacket. His head broke the surface, he took one deep breath, and then doubled over to pull off his boots.

And all the while Lord Darcy was telling himself that he was a fool—a bloody, stupid, harebrained fool. The girl had allowed herself to be pushed in without a struggle, and she had fallen without a sound. What chance was there of finding her in a world of darkness and watery death, better than a hundred yards from the nearest bank? A heaviness at his hip reminded him of something else. He could have drawn his pistol, but he would never have shot a man armed only with a sword, and the time it would have taken to force the man to drop his weapon and then turn him over to Ashley would have been precious seconds wasted. His chances of finding the girl were small now; they would have been infinitesimal if there had been any delay.

At least, he told himself, he could have drawn his gun and dropped it on the bridge as he had his cloak. Its added weight now was only a hindrance. Regretfully he drew it from its holster and consigned it forever to the muddy depths of the mighty river. He surfaced again and looked around. It was not as dark as he had thought. Dimly, he could still see the lights on the bridge.

"Tia!" he shouted. "Tia Einzig! Where are you? Can you hear me?"

She should have been borne downstream, beneath Somerset Bridge, but how far beneath the surface? Had she already taken her last gasp and filled her lungs with water?

And then he heard a noise.

There was a soft, spluttering, sobbing sound and a faint splash.

"Tia Einzig!" he shouted again. "Say something! Where are you?"

There was no answer except that faint sound again, coming from upstream, between himself and the bridge. His sprint across the bridge and his long dive had put him downstream from her, as he had hoped.

Lord Darcy swam toward the sound, his powerful arms fighting against the current of the Thames. The sound came closer, a sort of mewing sob that hardly sounded human.

And then he touched her.

She was struggling, but not much. just enough, apparently, to keep her head above water. He put his left arm around her, holding them both up with powerful strokes of his right, and her struggles stopped. Her cloak, he noticed, was gone—probably torn off when she struck the water. The whimpering sounds had ceased, and her body was completely relaxed but she was still breathing. He kept her face above water and began swimming toward the right bank, towing her through the chilling water. Thank God she was small and light, he thought. She didn't weigh more than seven stone, sopping wet.

The joke struck him as funny but he couldn't waste his breath now in laughing. *It would be like laughing at my own funeral,* he thought, and this second joke was grim enough to preclude any desire to laugh.

Where was the damned bank, anyway? How long does it take to cover a hundred-odd yards of water? He felt as though he had been swimming for hours, and the muscles of his right shoulder were beginning to feel the strain. Treading water, carefully holding the girl's head above the surface, he changed about, letting his right arm keep her up, and swimming with his left.

Hours more seemed to pass, and now there was nothing but blackness around him. The lights of the bridge had

long since faded away, and the lights on the river bank—
if there *was* any river bank!—were not yet visible.

Had he lost his bearings? Was he swimming downstream
instead of across it? There was no way of knowing; his body
was moving with the water and there was nothing visible
to judge by.

Then, as he reached out for another in a seemingly endless
series of strokes, his fingers slammed into something hard
and sent a stinging pain into his hand and wrist. He reached
out again, more carefully this time.

It was a shelf of stone, one of the steps leading down
to the water's edge from the bank above. He levered the
girl's body up onto the step, then climbed out of the water
himself. She was all right, as far as he could tell; she was
still breathing.

He realized suddenly that he was too weak and exhausted
even to climb the steps to the embankment by himself, much
less carry the girl up. But he couldn't just let her lie there
on the cold stone. He lifted her up and held her in his arms,
trying to warm her body with his, and then for a long time
he just sat there—motionless, cold, and wet, his mind almost
as blank as the endless darkness that surrounded them.

After what might have been minutes or hours of mental
and physical numbness, a slight, almost imperceptible change
in Lord Darcy's surroundings forced his sluggish mind to
function again.

What was it that was different? Something to his left.
Something he could see out of the comer of his eye. He
turned his head to look. It was nothing; just a light—a dim
glow in the distance that seemed to shift back and forth a
little and grow steadily brighter. No, not just one light, there
were two . . . three . . .

Then a voice said, "Hallooo . . . Lord Darcy! Can you hear
us, my lord?"

Lord Darcy's mind snapped into full wakefulness. The fog
must have thinned somewhat, he realized. He could tell from
the voice that they were still some distance away, but the
lights were easily visible. "Halloo," he shouted. His voice
sounded weak, even to his own ears. He tried again.
"Halloo."

"Who's that?" called the voice.

Lord Darcy grinned in spite of his weariness. "Lord Darcy here," he shouted. "You were calling me, I believe?"

Then somebody yelled: "We've found him; he's here!" Somebody else blew on a whistle. Lord Darcy felt himself beginning to shiver.

Reaction, he thought, trying to keep his teeth from chattering. *I feel weak as a kitten.* His muscles felt as though they had been jelled by the cold; the only warm spot in his body was his chest, against which he had been holding Tia. She was still breathing—quietly, regularly. But she was limp in his arms, completely relaxed; she wasn't even shivering. *That's all right*, Lord Darcy thought, *I'm shivering enough for both of us.* There were more whistles and more lights and footfalls all over the place. He wondered vaguely whether they had decided to call out the Army. And then a Man-at-Arms with a lantern was beside him, saying, "Are you all right, Lord Darcy?"

"I'm all right, just cold."

"Good Heavens, my lord, you've got the girl." He shouted up the embankment, "He's got the girl!"

But Lord Darcy hardly heard the words. The light from the man's lantern was shining directly into Tia's face, and her eyes were wide open, staring blankly, unseeingly, into nothing. He would have thought her dead, but the dead do not breathe.

There were more men around him now.

"Give his lordship more light."

"Let me help you up, my lord."

Then: "Darcy! Thank Heaven you're safe! And the girl, too! It's a miracle!"

"Hullo, Ashley," said Darcy. "Thanks for calling out the troops."

Lord Ashley grinned. "Here's your cloak. You shouldn't go around leaving things on bridges." And then he was taking off his own cloak to wrap it around Tia. He took her from Darcy's arms and carried her up the steps, carefully, tenderly.

Lord Darcy wrapped his cloak tightly around himself, but it didn't help the shivering.

"We'll have to get you some place warm, my lord, or you'll catch your death of dampness," said an Armsman.

Lord Darcy started up the steps. Then a voice from the top said, "Did you find him?"

"We found both of them, Your Grace," said another Armsman.

Darcy said, "Mary. What the deuce are you doing here?"

"As I told you last night," she said, "when you asked that same question, I came to fetch you."

"This time," Lord Darcy said, "I believe you."

When he reached the top and had climbed over the retaining wall, he saw Lord Ashley standing solidly, holding Tia in his arms. Several Armsmen were shining their lanterns on her, and Mary, not a Duchess now but a trained nurse, was looking at the girl and touching her with her Sensitive's fingers.

"How is she?" he asked. "What's the matter with her?"

"You're shivering," said Mary without looking up. "There's brandy in the coach, go get yourself some." She looked up at Lord Ashley. "Put her in the coach. We'll take her directly to Carlyle House. Father Patrique is there; she couldn't get better care in a hospital."

Two good swallows of brandy had calmed Lord Darcy's shivering. "What's the matter with her?" he asked again.

"Shock and cold, of course," she said. "There may be some internal injuries. Nothing serious. But she's under a spell, one I can't break. We'll have to get her to Father Patrique as soon as possible."

They stretched the girl out on one of the coach seats.

"Will she be all right?" asked Lord Ashley.

"I think so," said the Duchess.

Then Lord Ashley said, "Lord Darcy, may I speak to you a moment?"

"Surely; what is it?"

They stepped out of earshot of the others.

"The man on the bridge," Lord Ashley began.

"Oh, yes," said Lord Darcy. "I should have asked about him. I see you're not hurt. I hope you didn't have to kill him."

"No, I'm ashamed to say I didn't even capture him. My foot slipped on the pavement and he got away. But I got a good look at his face."

"Did you recognize him?"

"Yes. It was our oily friend, Master Ewen MacAlister."

Lord Darcy nodded. "I thought I recognized something

familiar in his voice when he told Tia to climb up on the balustrade. He had her under a spell, as Her Grace just said."

"That wasn't the only Black Magic the little swine was working," Lord Ashley said. He told Lord Darcy about the ensorcelled sword.

"Then you need not apologize for letting him escape," Darcy said. "I am thankful that you're still alive."

"So am I," said Lord Ashley. "Look here; there's not going to be room for all of us in that coach with Tia taking up one whole seat. And I shan't be needed any more tonight anyway. You two go ahead." He stepped back. "Petty Officer Hosquins," he called. "Her Grace and Lord Darcy are going to Carlyle House. One of the Armsmen will get a cab to take me home."

"Very well, My Lord Commander," answered Hosquins.

"Thank you," said Lord Darcy. "Would you do me one favor? Would you go to the Royal Steward and report everything to Lord Bontriomphe? If Master Ewen knows you recognized him, he won't show up at the hotel, of course. Tell Lord Bontriomphe to notify Sir Lyon. All right?"

"Certainly. I'll get down there right away. Good night, my lord. Good night, Your Grace," he said, raising his voice.

Lord Darcy opened the door of the coach. "To Carlyle House, Hosquins," he said, and climbed in.

It was more than an hour later before Lord Darcy really felt good again. A hot bath had taken the smell of the Thames from him, and some of the chill out of his blood. A short session with Father Patrique had removed any susceptibility to catching cold. Mary de Cumberland and the good Father had both insisted that he go to bed, so now he found himself in his silken night clothes, propped up on four or five pillows, with a couple of warm woolen blankets over his legs, a heavy shawl around his shoulders, a hot water bottle at his feet, and two bowlsful of hot, nourishing soup inside him.

The door opened and Mary de Cumberland came in, bearing a large steaming mug on a tray. "How do you feel?" she asked.

"Quite fit, really. How is Tia?"

"Father Patrique says she'll be all right. He put her to sleep. He says that she won't be able to talk to anyone until tomorrow." She put the mug down on the bedside table. "Here, this is for you."

"What is it?" Lord Darcy asked, eyeing the mug suspiciously.

"Medicine. It's good for what ails you."

"What's in it?"

"If you must know, it contains brandy, Oporto, honey, hot water, and a couple of herbs that Father Patrique prescribed."

"Humph," said Lord Darcy. "You made it sound good until you mentioned that last." He picked up the mug and sipped. "Not bad at all," he admitted.

"Do you feel strong enough to see visitors?" she asked solicitously.

"No," he said. "I'm on my deathbed. I'm in a coma. My breathing is shallow, my pulse weak and threadlike. Who wants to see me?"

"Well, Sir Thomas wanted to see you; he just wanted to thank you for saving Tia's life, but the poor man seems on the verge of collapse himself and I told him he could thank you tomorrow. Lord John Quetzal said that he could wait to speak to you until tomorrow, too. But Sir Lyon Grey arrived just a few minutes ago, and I strongly suggest that you see him."

"And where, may I ask, is Master Sean?"

"I have no doubt that he would be here, my lord, if anyone had thought to tell him of your desire for an invigorating cold bath. He is still at the morgue."

"Poor chap," said Darcy, "he's had a hard day's work."

"And what have *you* been doing?" said Her Grace. "Tatting?"

Lord Darcy ignored her. "I presume that he is making absolutely sure, one way or another, whether drugs or poisons were administered," he said thoughtfully. "I am strongly inclined to doubt that they were, but when Sean has finished with his work we shall know for certain."

"Yes," agreed Her Grace. "Will you see Sir Lyon?"

"Of course, of course. Show him in, will you?"

The Dowager Duchess of Cumberland went out and returned a minute later accompanied by the tall, stately, silver-bearded figure of Sir Lyon Gandolphus Grey. "I understand you have had quite an adventurous evening, my lord," he said gravely.

"All in the day's work for an Officer of the King's Justice, Sir Lyon. Pray be seated."

"Thank you," said Sir Lyon. Then, as the Duchess started to leave the room, "Please, Your Grace—if you would be so good as to remain? This concerns every member of the Guild, as well as the King's Officers."

"Certainly, Grand Master."

Sir Lyon looked back at Lord Darcy. "Commander Lord Ashley has informed me of his identification of Master Ewen MacAlister. He and Lord Bontriomphe have sent out word to the Armsmen all over the city to be on the watch for him. I have sent out every available Master Sorcerer in London to accompany the Armsmen, to make certain he does not use his Art to escape."

"Very good," said Lord Darcy.

"Lord Ashley's unsupported word," continued the Grand Master, "would not be sufficient in itself to bring charges against Master Ewen before the Special Executive Commission of the Guild. But it was enough to make us take immediate action to procure further evidence."

"Indeed?" said Lord Darcy with interest. "You have found this evidence, of course."

Sir Lyon nodded gravely. "We have. You are perhaps aware that a sorcerer casts certain protective and precautionary spells upon the bag in which he carries the tools of his trade?"

"I am," said Lord Darcy, remembering how easily Master Sean had regained possession of his own symbol-decorated carpetbag.

"Then you will understand why we asked Lord Bontriomphe to procure a search warrant from a magistrate immediately, and then went directly to Master Ewen's room. He, too, had put a special spell on the lock, as Sir James had done, but we solved it within fifteen minutes. Then we solved and removed the protective spells from his bag. The evidence was there—a bottle of graveyard dirt, two mummified bats, human bones, fire powder containing sulphur— and other things which no sorcerer should have in his possession without a special research permit from the Guild and special authority from the Church."

Lord Darcy nodded. " 'Black Magic is a matter of symbolism and intent,' " he quoted.

"Precisely," said Sir Lyon. "Then, in addition, I have Father Patrique's testimony concerning the black spell that Ewen cast upon Tia this evening. We have, then, my lord, quite sufficient evidence to convict him of Black Magic. Whether or not you can obtain enough evidence to convict him of his other crimes is, of course, another matter. But rest assured that the Guild will do everything in its power to help you obtain it. You have but to ask, my lord."

"I thank you, Sir Lyon. A question, merely to satisfy my curiosity: Lord Ashley told you, did he not, of the sword-play on Somerset Bridge?"

"He did."

"Am I correct in assuming that the spell Master Ewen had cast upon his own blade was in some manner a utilization of the Tarnhelm Effect?"

"It was indeed," Sir Lyon said with a rather puzzled smile. "It was astute of you to recognize it from Lord Ashley's description alone."

"Not at all," Lord Darcy said. "It is simply that Sean is an excellent teacher."

"It's more than astute, Grand Master," said the Dowager Duchess. "To me, it's irritating. I know what the Tarnhelm Effect is, of course, since I have come across mention of it in my studies, but its utilization and theory are quite beyond me."

"You should not find it irritating, but gratifying," Sir Lyon said in a firm voice. "One of the troubles with the world is that so few laymen take an interest in science. If more people were like Lord Darcy, we could eliminate the super-stitions that still cling to the minds of ninety-nine people out of a hundred." He smiled. "I realize you spoke in jest, but it behooves all of us to educate the layman whenever we can. It is only because of ignorance and superstition that hedge magicians and witches and other unlicensed practi-tioners can operate. It is only because of ignorance and superstition that so many people believe that only Black Magic can overcome Black Magic, that the only way to destroy evil is by using more evil. It is only because of ignorance and superstition that quacks and mountebanks who have no trace of the Talent can peddle their useless medallions and charms."

He sighed then, and Lord Darcy thought he looked

somehow older and wearier. "Of course, education of that kind will not eliminate the Master Ewens of this world. Modern science has given us an advantage over earlier ages, in that it has enabled us to keep our Government, our Church and our Courts more nearly uncorrupt and incorruptible than was ever before possible. But not even science is infallible. There are still quirks in the human mind that we cannot detect until it is too late, and Ewen MacAlister is a perfect example of our failure to do so."

"Sir Lyon," said Lord Darcy, "I should like to suggest that Master Ewen is more than that. In our own history, and in certain countries even today, we find organizations that attempt to hide and gloss over the wrongdoings of their own members. There was a time when the Church, the Government, and the Courts would ignore or conceal the peculations of a priest, a governor, or a judge rather than admit to the public that they were not infallible. Any group which makes a claim to infallibility must be very careful not to make any mistakes, and the mistakes that will inevitably occur must be kept secret or explained away—by lies, subterfuges and distortions. And that will eventually cause the collapse of the entire edifice. Anyone who has power in the Empire today— be it spiritual, temporal, or thaumaturgical—is trusted by the little man who has no power, precisely because he knows that we do our best to uncover the occasional Master Ewen and remove his power, rather than hiding him and pretending he does not exist. Master Ewen then becomes in himself the embodiment of the failure which may be converted to a symbol of success."

"Of course," said Sir Lyon. "But it is still unpleasant when it does happen. The last time was back in '39, when Sir Edward Elmer was Grand Master. I was on the Special Executive Commission then, and I had rather hoped it would not happen again in my lifetime. However, we shall do what must be done."

He rose. "Is there anything further I can do for you?"

"I think not, Sir Lyon, not at the moment. Thank you very much for your information.

"Oh, yes. One thing. Would you tell the sorcerers who are searching for him that if Master Ewen is taken during the night I am to be notified immediately, no matter what o'clock it is. I have several questions which I wish to put to him."

"I have already given such instructions in regard to myself," said Sir Lyon. "I shall see that you are notified. Good night, my lord. Good night, Your Grace. I shall be in my room if there is any word."

When the silvery-bearded old sorcerer had left, the Dowager Duchess said, "Well, I hope they don't catch him until morning; you need a good night's sleep. But at least this horrible mess is almost over."

"Don't be too optimistic," said Lord Darcy. "There are far too many questions which remain unanswered. As you implied, they have not yet caught Master Ewen, and Paul Nichols has managed to remain hidden wherever he is for more than thirty-six hours. We still do not have the results of Master Sean's Herculean labors. There are still too many knots in this tangled string to say that the end is in sight."

He looked down at his empty mug. "Would you mind bringing me another one of those? Without the good Father's additional flavorings this time, if you please."

"Certainly."

But when she returned, Lord Darcy was fast asleep, and the hot mug became her own nightcap instead of his.

CHAPTER 18

"I trust you are feeling fit, my lord."

The always punctilious Geffri put the caffe urn and the cup on the bedside table.

"Quite fit, Geffri; thank you," said Lord Darcy. "Ah! the caffe smells delicious. Brewed by your own hand as usual, I trust? Carlyle House is, except for my own home, the only place in the Empire where one can get one's morning caffe at exactly the right temperature and brewed to perfection."

"It is most gratifying to hear you say so, my lord," said Geffri, pouring the caffe. "By the by, I have taken the liberty, my lord, of bringing up this morning's *Courier.* There is, however, another communication which your lordship might prefer to peruse previous to perusal of the news." He produced an envelope, ten inches wide by fourteen long. Lord Darcy immediately recognized Master Sean's personal seal upon the flap.

"Master Sean," said Geffri, "arrived late last night—after your lordship had retired. He requested that I deliver this to your lordship immediately upon your lordship's awakening."

Lord Darcy took the envelope. It was quite obviously the report on the tubby little Irish sorcerer's thaumaturgical investigation and the autopsy report on the body of Sir James Zwinge.

Lord Darcy glanced at his watch on the bedside table. "Thank you, Geffri. Would you be so good as to waken Master Sean in forty-five minutes and tell him that I should like to have him join me for breakfast at ten o'clock?"

"Of course, my lord. Is there anything else, my lord?"

"Not at the moment, I think."

"It is a pleasure to serve you, my lord," said Geffri. Then he was gone.

By the time an hour had passed, Lord Darcy had read both Master Sean's report and the London *Courier*, and was awaiting the knock on the door that came at precisely ten o'clock. By that time, Lord Darcy was dressed and ready for the day's work, and the hot breakfast for two had been brought in and laid out on the table in the sitting room.

"Come in, my good Sean," Lord Darcy said. "The bacon and eggs are waiting."

The sorcerer entered with a smile on his face, but it was quite evident to Lord Darcy that the smile was rather forced.

"Good morning, my lord," he said pleasantly. "You've read my report?" He seated himself at the table.

"I have," Lord Darcy said, "but I see nothing in it to account for that dour look. We'll discuss it after breakfast. Have you seen this morning's *Courier*?"

"No, my lord, I have not." Master Sean seated himself and began to dig into the bacon and eggs. "Is there something of interest there?"

"Not particularly," said Lord Darcy. "Except for some rather flattering references to myself, and some even more flattering references to you, there is little of interest. You may peruse it at your leisure. The only offering of any consequence is the fact that there will be no fog tonight."

The next quarter of an hour was spent in relative silence. Master Sean, usually quite loquacious, seemed to have little to say.

Finally, with some irritation, Lord Darcy pushed his plate aside and said: "All pleasantries aside, Master Sean, you are not your usual ebullient self. If there is anything I should know besides what is contained in your report, I'd like to hear it."

Master Sean smiled across his caffe cup. "Oh, no, it's all there. I have nothing to add to it. Don't mean to disturb you. Perhaps I'm a bit sleepy."

Lord Darcy frowned, reached over, picked up the carefully written report and flipped it open. "Very well. I do have a question or two, merely as a matter of clarification. First, as to the wound."

"Yes, my lord?"

"According to your report, the blade entered the chest vertically, between the third and fourth ribs, making a wound some five inches deep. It nicked the wall of the pulmonic aorta and made a small gash in the heart itself, and this wound was definitely the cause of death?"

"Definitely, my lord."

"Very well." He stood up. "If you will, Master Sean, take that spoon and assume that it is a knife. Yes. Now, would you be so good as to stab me at the precise angle which would cause exactly such a wound as you discovered in Sir James' chest."

Master Sean grasped the handle of the spoon, lifted it high over his head, and brought it down slowly in a long arc to touch his lordship's chest. "Very good, Master Sean, thank you. The wound, if extended, then, would have gone well down into the bowels?"

"Well, my lord, if a bullet had entered at that angle, it would have come out the small of the back."

Lord Darcy nodded, and looked back down at the report. "And," he mused, "as could be surmised from the exterior aspect of the wound, the blade actually did slice into the ribs above and below the cut itself."

He looked up from the report. "Master Sean, if you were going to stab a man, how would you do it?"

Master Sean reversed the spoon in his hand so that his thumb was pointing toward the bowl. He moved his hand forward to touch Lord Darcy. "This way, of course, my lord."

Lord Darcy nodded. "And in that position, the flat of the knife is parallel to the ribs instead of perpendicular to them."

"Well, of course, my lord," said Master Sean. "With the blade up and down you're likely to get your blade stuck between the ribs."

"Precisely," Lord Darcy agreed. "Now, according to the autopsy report which Sir Eliot sent us yesterday from Cherbourg, Goodman Georges Barbour was stabbed in the efficient manner you have just demonstrated, and yet Sir James was stabbed in a manner which no efficient knifesman would use."

"That's true, my lord. Nobody who knew how to use a knife would come in with a high overhand stab like that."

"Why should the same man stab with two such completely different techniques?"

"If it *was* the same man, my lord."

"Very well, assuming that there were two different killers, which is the Navy's hypothesis, the blow that killed Sir James was still inefficient, was it not? Would a professional hired killer have deliberately used a thrust like that?"

Master Sean chuckled. "Well, if it were up to me to hire him, my lord, I don't think he'd pass my employment specifications."

"Neatly put," Lord Darcy said with a smile. "And by the way, did you examine the knife closely?"

"Sir James' contact cutter? I did."

"So did I, when it was on the floor of Sir James' hotel room yesterday. I should like to call your attention to the peculiar condition of that knife."

Master Sean frowned. "But . . . there was nothing peculiar about the condition of that knife."

"Precisely. That was the peculiar condition."

While Master Sean thought that over, Lord Darcy said: "Now to another matter." He sat down and turned over a page of the report. Master Sean settled himself in his chair and put the spoon back on his plate.

"You say here that Sir James died between 9:25 and 9:35, eh?"

"That's according to the chirurgical and thaumaturgical evidence. Since I meself heard him cry out at precisely half past nine—give or take half a minute—I can say that Sir James died between 9:30 and 9:35."

"Very well," Lord Darcy said. "But he was stabbed at approximately five minutes of nine. Now, as I understand it, the psychic patterns show both the time of the stabbing and the time of death." He flipped over a page of the report. "And the death thrust cut down and into the wall of the pulmonic aorta, but did not actually open that great blood vessel itself. There was a thin integument of the arterial wall still intact. The wound was, however, severe enough to cause him to fall into shock. He was mortally wounded, then, at that time."

"Well, my lord," Master Sean said. "It might not have been a mortal wound. It is possible that a good Healer, if he had arrived in time, might have saved Sir James' life."

"Because the pulmonic aorta was not actually cut into, eh?"

"That's right. If that artery had actually been severed at that time, Master Sir James would have been dead before he struck the floor. When that artery is cut open the drop in blood pressure and the loss of blood cause unconsciousness in a fraction of a second. The heart goes into fibrillation and death occurs very shortly thereafter."

Lord Darcy nodded. "I see. But the wall was not breached. It was cut almost through but not completely. Then, after lying on the floor for half an hour or better, Sir James heard your knock, which brought him out of his shock-induced stupor. He tried to lift himself from the floor, grabbing at his desk, upon which lay, among other things, his key." He paused and frowned. "Obviously his shout to you was a shout for help, and he wanted to get his key to unlock the door for you." He tapped a finger on the report. "This exertion caused the final rupture of the aorta wall. His life's blood gushed forth upon the floor, he dropped the key, and died. Is that your interpretation of it, Master Sean?"

Master Sean nodded. "That's the way it seems to me, my lord. Both the thaumaturgical and the chirurgical evidence corroborate each other."

"I agree completely, Master Sean," Lord Darcy said. He flipped over a few more pages. "No drugs or poisons, then."

"Not unless somebody used a substance that is unknown to the Official Pharmacopoeia. I performed a test for every one of 'em, and unless God Himself has repealed the Law of Similarity, Master Sir James was neither poisoned nor drugged."

Lord Darcy flipped over another page. "And the brain and

skull were both undamaged . . . no bruises . . . no fractures . . . yes." He turned to another section of the report. "Now, we come to the thaumaturgical section. According to your tests, all the blood in the room was Master Sir James'?"

"It was, my lord."

"And what of that curious half-moon stain near the door?"

"It was definitely Sir James' blood."

Lord Darcy nodded. "As I suspected," he said. "Now, according to the thaumaturgical tests, there was no one in the room except Sir James at the time he was stabbed. This corresponds to the information on Georges Barbour that we have from Cherbourg." He smiled. "Master Sean, I well understand that you can only put scientifically provable facts in a report like this, but do you have any suggestion, any guess, anything that will help me?"

"I shall try, my lord," said Master Sean slowly. "Well, as I told you yesterday, I should be able to detect the operation of a black sorcerer. As you are aware, the *ankh* is almost infallible as a detector of evil." He took a deep breath. "And now that we know the culpability of Master Ewen MacAlister, his operations should be easy to detect."

Then Master Sean pointed at the sheaf of paper in front of Lord Darcy. "But I will not—I cannot—go back on what I said there." He took another deep breath. "My lord, I can find no trace of any kind of magic—black *or* white—associated with the murder of Master Sir James Zwinge. There was no . . ."

He was interrupted by a rap on the door. "Yes," Lord Darcy said with a touch of impatience in his voice, "who is it?"

"Father Patrique," came the voice from the other side of the door.

Lord Darcy's irritation vanished. "Ah, come in, Reverend Sir."

The door opened and a tall, rather pale man in Benedictine habit entered the room. "Good morning, my lord; good morning, Master Sean," he said with a smile. "I see you are well this morning, my lord."

"In your hands, Reverend Father, how could I be otherwise? Can I be of service to you?"

"I believe you can—and be of service to yourself at the same time, if I may say so."

"In what way, Father?"

The priest looked gravely thoughtful. "Under ordinary conditions," he said carefully, "I cannot, as you know, discuss a penitent's confession with anyone. But in this case I have been specifically requested by the penitent to speak to you."

"The Damoselle Tia, I presume," said Lord Darcy.

"Of course. She has told her story twice—once to me, and once to Sir Thomas Leseaux." He looked at Master Sean, who was solemnly nodding his head up and down. "Ah, you follow me, Master Sorcerer."

"Oh, certainly, Your Reverence. The classic trilogy. Once to the Church, once to the loved one, and"—he gestured respectfully toward Lord Darcy—"once to the temporal authorities."

"Exactly," said the priest. "It will complete the Healing." He looked back at Lord Darcy, who had already risen from his chair. "I will give you no further details, my lord; it is best that you hear them for yourself. But she is well aware that it was you who saved her life last night, and you must understand that you must not depreciate your part in the matter."

"I think I understand, Reverend Father. May I ask you a couple of questions before we go in?"

"Certainly. As long as they do not require me to violate my vows, I shall answer them."

"They have merely to do with the spell that was cast over her last evening. Does she remember anything that happened after Master Ewen cast his black enchantment upon her?"

Father Patrique shook his head. "She does not. She will explain to you."

"Yes, but what bothers me, Reverend Father, is the speed and ease with which it was done. I was watching. One moment she was coherent, in full possession of her senses, the next she was an automaton, obeying his every word. I was not aware that sorcerers had such power over others."

"Oh, good Heavens, it can't be done that quickly," said Master Sean. "Not at *all*, my lord! Not even the most powerful of black sorcerers could take over another's mind just by waving his hand that way."

"Not even Satan himself can take over a human mind without some preparation, my lord," said Father Patrique. "Master Ewen must have prepared preliminary spells before that time. He would have had to, for the spell to have been as effective as it was."

"I seem to recall," said Lord Darcy, "that at the last Triennial Convention, a footpad made the foolish mistake of attacking a Master Sorcerer on the street during the last night of the Convention. The sorcerer informed the Armsmen shortly thereafter what had happened. He himself was unharmed, but the footpad was paralyzed from the neck down, completely unable to move. It was a brilliant piece of work, I admit; the spell was such that it could not be removed until the criminal made a full and complete confession of his crime—which meant, of course, that the sorcerer need not appear in Court against him. But that spell must have been cast in a matter of seconds."

"That is a somewhat different matter, my lord," said Father Patrique. "In that case, when there is evil intent on the part of the attacker, the evil itself can be reflected back upon its generator to cause the paralysis you spoke of. Any Master Sorcerer can use that as a defensive technique. But to cast a spell over a human being who has no evil intent requires the use of the sorcerer's own power; he cannot use the psychic force of his attacker, since he is not being attacked. Therefore, his own spells require much more time to be set up and to become effective."

"I see. Thank you, Father," Lord Darcy said. "That clears up the matter. Well, let's get along then and see the young lady."

"With your permission, my lord," said Master Sean, "I'll go on to the Royal Steward. Likely Lord Bontriomphe will be wanting to take a look at my report."

Lord Darcy smiled. "And likely you'd be wanting to get back to the Convention, eh?"

Master Sean grinned back. "Well, yes, my lord, I would."

"All right. I'll be along later."

Sir Thomas Leseaux, tall, lean and grim-faced, was standing outside the Gardenia Suite, which the Duchess of Cumberland had given to Tia Einzig. "Good morning, my lord," he said. "I . . . I want to thank you for what you did last night, but I know of no way to do so."

"My dear Sir Thomas, I did nothing that you would not

have done had you been there. And there is no need for the grim look."

"Grim?" Sir Thomas forced a smile. "Was I grim?"

"Of course you were grim, Sir Thomas. Why shouldn't you be? You have heard Tia's story and you are greatly afraid that I shall arrest her on a charge of espionage."

Sir Thomas blinked and said nothing.

"Come, come, my dear fellow," said Lord Darcy. "She cannot have betrayed the Empire to any great extent, else you would be as eager for her arrest as anyone. You are not a man to allow love to blind you. Further, may I remind you of the laws concerning King's Evidence. Ah, that's better, Sir Thomas, now your smile looks more genuine. And now, if you gentlemen will excuse me, I shall allow you to pace this hallway at your leisure." He opened the door and went in.

Lord Darcy walked through the sitting room of the Gardenia Suite toward the bedroom, and halfway there heard a girl's voice.

"My Lord Darcy? Is that you?"

Lord Darcy went to the bedroom door. "Yes, Damoselle, I am Lord Darcy."

She was in bed, covered by warm blankets up to her shoulders. Her lips curved in a soft smile. "You are handsome, my lord. I am very glad. I don't think I should care to owe my life to an ugly man."

"My dear Tia, so long as beauty such as yours has been saved, the beauty of he who saved it is immaterial." He walked over and sat down in the chair by her bed.

"I won't ask you how you came to be there when you were so sorely needed, my lord," she said softly. "I merely want to say again that I am glad you were."

"So am I, Damoselle. But the question, as you have said, does not concern how *I* happened to be upon that bridge, but how *you* did. Tell me about Master Ewen MacAlister."

For a moment her mouth was set in grim, hard lines; then she smiled again. "I'll have to go back a little; back to my home in Banat."

The story she told him was essentially the same as the one she had told Mary of Cumberland—with added details. Her Uncle Neapeler had been denounced for practicing his Healing Art by a business rival, and because his political sympathies were already suspect, the Secret Police of King Casimir IX had come to their home to arrest them both. But Neapeler Einzig had been prepared for just such an eventuality, and his strong—although untrained—Talent had warned him in time. Only a few minutes ahead of the dread Secret Police, they had both headed toward the Italian border. But the Secret Police, too, had sources of sorcery, and the fleeing pair had almost been caught in a trap, less than a hundred yards from the frontier. Neapeler had told his niece to run while he stood off the Secret Police.

And that was the last she had seen of him.

The story she told of her movements through Italy and of her extradition hearing in Dauphine was a familiar one to Lord Darcy, but he listened with care. Then she came to the part he had been waiting for.

"I thought I was safe when Sir Thomas brought me here to England," she said, "and then Master Ewen came to me. I didn't know who he was then; he didn't tell me his name. But he told me that Uncle Neapeler had been captured and imprisoned by the Polish Secret Police. My uncle was being treated well, he said, but his continued well-being would depend entirely upon my cooperation.

"Master Ewen told me that Sir Thomas knew the secret of a weapon that had been developed for the Angevin Imperial Navy. He didn't know what the weapon was, but the Polish Secret Service had somehow discovered its existence and knew that Sir Thomas had highly valuable information concerning it. Since he knew that Sir Thomas trusted me, he asked me to get this information for him. He threatened to torture—to kill—Uncle Neapeler unless I did as he asked." She turned her head back suddenly and looked straight at Lord Darcy. "But I didn't. You must understand that I *didn't*. Sir Thomas will tell you, I never once asked him about any of his secret work—*never!*"

Lord Darcy thought of Sir Thomas' face as he had last seen it. "I believe you, Damoselle. Go on."

"I didn't know what to do. I didn't want to tell them anything, and I didn't want to betray Sir Thomas, either. I told them that I was trying. I told them that I was work-ing my way into his confidence. I told them"—she paused for a moment, biting at her lower lip—"I told Master Ewen anything and everything I could to keep my uncle alive."

"Of course," said Lord Darcy gently. "No one can blame you for that."

"And then came the Convention," she said. "MacAlister said I had to attend, that I had to be there. I tried to stay away. I pointed out to him that even though I had been admitted to the Guild as an apprentice, the Convention does not normally accept apprentices as members. But he said that I had influence—with Sir Thomas, with His Grace the Archbishop—and that if I did not do my best to get in, he would see that I was sent one of Uncle Neapeler's fingers for every day of the Convention I missed. I had to do something, you understand that, don't you, my lord?"

"I understand," said Lord Darcy.

"Ewen MacAlister," she went on, "had warned me specifically to stay away from Master Sir James Zwinge. He said that Sir James was a top counterspy, that he was head of the Imperial Intelligence apparatus for Europe. So I thought perhaps Sir James could help me. I went to his room Wednesday morning. I met him just as he was leaving the lobby, and asked if I could speak to him. I told him that I had important information for him." She smiled a little. "He was very grouchy, but he asked me to come to his room. I told him everything—about my uncle, about Master Ewen—everything.

"And he just *sat* there!

"I told him *surely* the Imperial agents could get my uncle out of a Polish prison.

"He told me that he knew nothing about spy work, that he was merely a forensic sorcerer, working for the Marquis de London. He said he knew no way of getting my uncle out of a Polish prison or any other prison for that matter.

"I was furious. I don't really know what I said to him but it was—vicious. I wish now that I had not said it. I left his room and he locked the door after me. I may have been the last person to see Sir James Zwinge alive." Then she added hurriedly, "That is, aside from his murderer."

"Damoselle Tia," said Lord Darcy in his most gentle voice, "at this point I must tell you something, and I must ask you to reveal it to no one else until I give you leave. Agreed?"

"Agreed, of course, my lord."

"It is this. I believe that you *were* the last person to see him alive. The evidence I have thus far indicates that. But I want you to know that I do not believe you are in any way responsible for his death."

"Thank you, my lord," she said, and suddenly there were tears in her eyes.

Lord Darcy took her hand. "Come, my dear, this is a poor time to cry. Come now, no more tears."

She smiled in spite of her tears. "You're very kind, my lord."

"Oh, no, my dear Tia, I'm not kind at all. I am cruel and vicious and I have ulterior motives."

She laughed. "Most men do."

"I didn't mean it quite that way," said Lord Darcy dryly. "What I intended to convey was that I *do* have another question to ask."

She brushed tears from her eyes with one hand, and gave him her impish smile. "No ulterior motives, then. That's a shame." Then she became serious again. "What is the question?"

"Why did Master Ewen decide to kill you?" Lord Darcy was quite certain that he knew the answer, but he did not want to disclose to the girl how he knew it.

This time her smile had the same cold, vengeful quality that he had seen the night before. "Because I learned the truth," she said. "Yesterday evening I was approached by a friend of my uncle's—a Goodman Colin MacDavid—a Manxman whom I remembered from when I was a very little girl. Goodman Colin told me the truth.

"My Uncle Neapeler escaped from the trap that I told you of. Goodman Colin helped him escape, and my uncle has been working with him on the Isle of Man ever since. He is safe. But he has been in hiding all this time, because he is afraid the Poles will kill him. He thought *I* was dead—until he saw my name in the London *Courier*, in the list of those attending the Convention; then he sent Goodman Colin straight away to find me.

"But Goodman Colin also explained that when my uncle escaped he left behind evidence indicating that he had been killed. He did this to protect me. All the time Master Ewen was using my uncle's life as a weapon against me, he and the Polish Secret Police actually thought he was dead. Do you wonder that I was furious when I finally found out the truth?"

"Of course not," said Lord Darcy. "That was yesterday evening."

"Yes," she said. "Then I got a note from Master Ewen telling me to meet him in a pub called the *Hound and Hare.* Do you know of it?"

"I know where it is," said Lord Darcy. "Go on."

"I suppose I lost my temper again," she said. "I suppose I said the wrong things, just as I did with Sir James." Her eyes hardened. "But I'm not sorry for what I said to Master Ewen! I told him what I thought of him, I told him I would report everything to the Imperial authorities, I told him I wanted to see him hanged, I—" She stopped suddenly and gave Lord Darcy a puzzled frown. "I'm not quite sure what happened after that. He raised his hand," she said slowly, "and traced a symbol in the air, and . . . and after that I remember nothing, that is . . . nothing until this morning, when I woke up here and saw Father Patrique."

She reached out suddenly and grasped Lord Darcy's right hand in both of her own. "I know I have done wrong, my lord. Will I . . . will I have to appear before His Majesty's Court of High Justice?"

Lord Darcy smiled and stood up. "I rather think that you will, my dear—you will be our most important witness against Master Ewen MacAlister. I think I can assure you that you will not appear before the Court in any other capacity."

The girl was still holding Lord Darcy's hand. With a sudden movement she brought it to her lips, kissed it and then let it go.

"Thank you, my lord," she said.

"It is I who must thank you," said Lord Darcy with a bow. "If I may do you any further service, Damoselle, you have but to ask."

He went out the door of the Gardenia Suite expecting to see two men waiting for him in the hall. Instead, there were three. Father Patrique and Sir Thomas looked at him as he closed the door behind him.

"How is she?" asked Father Patrique.

"Quite well, I think." Then he glanced at the third man, a uniformed Sergeant-at-Arms.

"Sergeant Peter has news for you," Father Patrique said, "but I would not allow him to interrupt. Now, if you'll excuse me, I'll see my patient." The door closed behind him as he went into the Gardenia Suite.

Lord Darcy smiled at Sir Thomas. "All is well, my friend. Neither of you has anything to fear."

Then he looked back at the Sergeant-at-Arms. "You have information for me, Sergeant?"

"Yes, my lord. Lord Bontriomphe said it was most important. We have found Goodman Paul Nichols."

"Oh, indeed?" said Lord Darcy. "Where did you find him? Has he anything to say for himself?"

"I'm afraid not," said Sergeant Peter. "He was found in a lumber room at the hotel. And he was dead, my lord. Quite dead."

CHAPTER 19

Lord Darcy strode across the lobby of the Royal Steward Hotel, closely followed by the Sergeant-at-Arms. He went down the hallway, past the offices, toward the rear door. Sergeant Peter had already told him where the room in question was, but the information proved unnecessary, since there were two Armsmen on guard before it. It led off to the left from the narrow hallway, about halfway between the temporary headquarters office and the rear door. The room was a workshop, set up for furniture repair. There were worktables and tools around the walls, and several pieces of half-finished furniture scattered about. Toward the rear of the room was an open door, beyond which Lord Darcy could see only darkness.

Near the door stood Lord Bontriomphe and Master Sean O Lochlainn. They both looked around as Lord Darcy walked across the room toward them.

"Hullo, Darcy," said Lord Bontriomphe. "We've got another one." He gestured past the open door which, Lord Darcy now saw, opened into a small closet filled with odds and ends of wood and pieces of broken furniture. Beyond the door, just inside the closet, lay a man's body.

It was not a pleasant sight. The face was blackened and the tongue protruded. Around the throat, set deep into the flesh, was a knotted cord.

Lord Darcy looked at Lord Bontriomphe. "What happened?"

Lord Bontriomphe did not take his eyes off the corpse. "I think I shall go out and beat my head against a wall. I've been looking for this man ever since yesterday afternoon. I've combed London for him. I've asked every employee in this hotel every question I could think of." Then he looked up at Lord Darcy. "I had finally arrived at what I thought was the ridiculous conclusion that Goodman Paul Nichols had never left the hotel." He gave Lord Darcy a rather lopsided smile. "And then, half an hour ago, one of the hotel's employees, a joiner and carpenter whose job it is to keep the hotel's furniture in repair, came in here and opened that door." He gestured toward the closet. "He needed a piece of wood. He found—*that*. He came running out into the hall in a screaming fit. Fortunately I was in the office. Master Sean had just shown up, so we came back to take a look."

"He has definitely been identified as Paul Nichols?" Lord Darcy asked.

"Oh, yes, no question of that."

Lord Darcy looked at Master Sean. "There is no rest for the weary, eh, Master Sean? What do you find?"

Master Sean sighed. "Well, I won't know for sure until after the chirurgeon has performed the autopsy, but it's my opinion the man's been dead for at least forty-eight hours. There's a bruise on his right temple—hard to see because of the coagulation of the blood in the face, but it's there all right—which indicates that he was knocked unconscious before he was killed. Someone hit him on the side of the head, and then took that bit of upholsterer's cord and tightened it around his throat to strangle him."

"Forty-eight hours," said Lord Darcy thoughtfully. He looked at his watch. "That would be, give or take an hour or so, at approximately the same time Master Sir James was killed. Interesting."

"There's one thing, my lord," said Master Sean, "which you might find even more interesting." He knelt down and pointed at some bits of material lying on the corpse's shirt front. "What does that look like to you?"

Lord Darcy knelt and looked. "Sealing wax," he said softly. "Bits of blue sealing wax."

Master Sean nodded. "That's what they looked like to me, my lord."

Lord Darcy stood up. "I hate to put you through another session of such grueling work, Sean, but it must be done. I must know the time of his death, and—"

Master Sean took one more look at the dead man's shirt front, and then stood up himself. "And something more about those bits of blue sealing wax, eh, my lord?"

"Exactly."

"Well," said Lord Bontriomphe, "at least this time we know who killed him."

"Yes, I know *who* killed him, all right," Lord Darcy said. "What I don't understand is *why*."

"You mean, the motive?" Lord Bontriomphe asked.

"Oh, I know the motive. What I want to know is the motive behind the motive, if you follow me."

Lord Bontriomphe didn't.

Another half hour of meticulous investigation revealed nothing of further interest. The murder of Paul Nichols appeared to be as simple as that of Sir James had been complex. There was no locked door, no indication of Black Magic, no question as to the method of death. By the time he was finished looking the area over, Lord Darcy was convinced that his mental reconstruction of the murder was reasonably accurate. Paul Nichols had been enticed into the workshop, knocked unconscious, strangled with a handy piece of upholsterer's cord, and dumped into the small lumber room. Exactly what had happened after that was not quite as clear, but Lord Darcy felt that subsequent data would not drastically change his hypothesis.

Satisfied, Lord Darcy left the remainder of the investigation to Lord Bontriomphe and Master Sean. *Now*, he thought to himself, *what to do next?* Go to the Palace du Marquis first and pick up a gun, he decided. He had mentioned to Lord Bontriomphe that he had lost his own weapon in the Thames, and Bontriomphe had said, "I have another in my desk, a Heron .36. You can use that if you want; it's a good weapon." Lord Darcy decided that one good stiff drink would probably stand him in good stead before he took a cab to the Palace du Marquis. He went to the Sword Room and ordered a brandy and soda.

There was still a state of tension in the hotel, and the Convention seemed to have been held in abeyance. Of all the sorcerers he had seen that morning, with the exception of Master Sean himself, not one had been wearing the silver slashes of a Master. Lord Darcy saw a familiar face further down the bar, a young man who was giving his full attention to a pint of good English beer. With a slight frown, Lord Darcy picked up his glass and walked down to where the other man was sitting.

"Good morning, my lord," he said. "I should have thought you would be out on the chase."

Journeyman Sorcerer Lord John Quetzal looked up, a little startled. "Lord Darcy! I've been wanting to talk to you," he said. The smile on his face looked a little sad. "They didn't ask me to help find Master Ewen," he said. "They're afraid a journeyman couldn't hold his own against a Master."

"And you think you could?" Lord Darcy asked.

"No!" Lord John Quetzal said excitedly. "That's not the point, don't you see? Master Ewen may be a more powerful sorcerer than I am, I don't argue with that. But I don't have to face him down. If he uses magic when he's cornered, another, more powerful sorcerer can take care of him then. The point is that I can *find* Master Ewen. I can find out where he is. But nobody listens to a journeyman sorcerer."

Lord Darcy looked at him. "Now let me understand you," he said carefully. "You think you can find where Master Ewen is hiding now?"

"Not just *think*; I *know!* I am positive I can find him. When you brought the Damoselle Tia in last night, she stank to high Heaven of Black Magic." He looked apologetic. "I don't mean a real smell, you understand, not the way you'd smell tobacco smoke or"—he gestured toward Lord Darcy's glass—"brandy, or something like that."

"I understand," said Lord Darcy. "It is merely a psychic analogy to the physical sense which it most nearly resembles. That is why people with your particular kind of Talent are called witch-smellers."

"Yes, my lord; exactly. And any given act of black sorcery has its characteristic 'aroma'—a stink that identifies the sorcerer who performed it. You asked me Wednesday night if I suspected anyone, and I refused to tell you. But it was Master Ewen. I could detect the taint on him even then.

But now, with an example of his work to go on, I could smell him out anywhere in London."

He smiled rather sheepishly. "I was just sitting here trying to make up my mind whether I should go out on my own or not."

"You could detect the stink of Black Magic on the Damoselle Tia," Lord Darcy said. "How did you know that it was not she who was practicing the Black Art?"

"My lord," said Lord John Quetzal, "there is a great deal of difference between a dirty finger and a dirty finger-mark."

Lord Darcy contemplated his drink in silence for a full minute. Then he picked it up and finished it in two swallows.

"My Lord John Quetzal," he said briskly. "Lord Bontriomphe and his Armsmen are searching for Master Ewen. So are Sir Lyon and the Masters of the Guild. So are Commander Lord Ashley and the Naval Intelligence Corps. And do you know what?"

"No, my lord," said Lord John Quetzal, putting down his empty beer mug, "what?"

"You and I are going to make them all look foolish. Come with me. We must fetch a cab. First to the Palace du Marquis, and then, my lord—wherever your nose leads us."

CHAPTER 20

It took hours.

In a little pub far to the north of the river, Journeyman Sorcerer Lord John Quetzal stared blankly at a mug of beer that he had no intention of drinking.

"I think I have him, my lord," he said dully. "I think I have him."

"Very good," said Lord Darcy.

He dared say nothing further. During all this time he had followed Lord John Quetzal's leads, making marks on the map as the young Mechicain witch-smeller came ever closer to the black sorcerer who was his prey.

"It's not as easy as I thought," said Lord John Quetzal.

Lord Darcy nodded grimly. Witch-smelling—the detection of psychic evil—was not the same as clairvoyance, but even so the privacy spells in London had dimmed the young Mechicain's perceptions.

"Not easy, perhaps," he said, "but just as certain, just as sure." His lordship realized that the young journeyman had not yet perfected his innate ability to its utmost. That, of course, would come with time and further training. "Let's go through it again. Tell me the clues as you picked them up."

"Yes, my lord," said the young Mechicain. After a moment he began: "He's surrounded by those who will help him—Master Ewen is, I mean. But they will not risk their own lives for him.

"There is a tremendous amount of psychic tension surrounding him," Lord John Quetzal continued, "but it has nothing to do with him personally. They don't know that he exists."

"I understand, my lord," said Lord Darcy. "From the descriptions you have given me, it appears to me that Master Ewen is surrounded by generally un-Talented people who are attempting to use the Talent." He spread his map of London out on the table. "Now, let's see if we can get a fix." He tapped a spot on the map. "From here"—he moved his finger—"in that direction, eh?"

"Yes, my lord," said Lord John Quetzal.

"Now," Lord Darcy moved his finger further down the map. "From here"—he moved his finger again—"to there. Eh?"

"Yes."

Lord John Quetzal knew direction and magnitude, but he seemed unable to give any further information. Time after time Lord Darcy had gone through this same routine—so many times that it seemed monotonous, repetitive.

And yet, each time, more information came to the fore. At last, Lord Darcy was able to draw a circle on the map of London, and tap it with the point of his pencil.

"He is somewhere within that area. There is no other possible answer." Then he reached out and put his hand on the young journeyman's shoulder. "I know you're tired. Fatigue is the normal condition of an Investigator for the King."

Lord John Quetzal straightened his shoulders and looked up suddenly. "I know. But"—he tapped the spot that Lord

Darcy had circled—"that's quite a bit of area. I thought that I could locate him precisely, exactly." He took a deep breath. "And now I find that . . ."

"Oh, come," Lord Darcy said. "You give in too easily. We have him located; it is simply that you do not realize how closely we have surrounded our quarry. We know the general area, but we do not have the exact description of his immediate surroundings."

"But there I cannot help," Lord John Quetzal said, the dullness coming back into his voice.

"I think you can," said Lord Darcy. "I ask you to put your attention upon the symbols surrounding Master Ewen MacAlister—not his actual physical surroundings but his symbolic surroundings."

And then Lord Darcy waited.

Suddenly Lord John Quetzal looked up. "I have an intuition. I see . . ." Lord John Quetzal began again. "It is the blazon of a coat of arms, my lord: *Argent, in saltire, five fusils gules.*"

"Go on," said Lord Darcy urgently, making a rapid notation on the margin of the map.

Lord John Quetzal looked out into nothing. *"Argent,"* he said, *"in pale, three trefoils sable, the lower-most inverted."*

Lord Darcy made another note, and then put his hand very carefully on the top of the table, palm down. "I ask you to give me one more, my lord—just one more."

"Argent," said Lord John Quetzal, *"a heart gules."*

Lord Darcy leaned back in the booth, took a deep breath and said, "We have it, my lord, we have it. Thanks to you. Come, we must get back to Carlyle House."

Half an hour after that, Her Grace, Mary, the Dowager Duchess of Cumberland, was looking at the same map. "Yes, yes, of course," she said. She looked at the young Mechicain. "Of course. *Argent, in saltire, five fusils gules.*" She looked up at Lord Darcy. "The five of diamonds."

"Right," said Lord Darcy.

"And the second is the three of clubs. And the third, the ace of hearts."

"Exactly. Do you doubt now that Master Ewen is hiding there?"

She looked back down at the map. "No, of course not.

Of course he's there." She looked up at him. "You went no further, my lord?" Then she glanced at Lord John Quetzal and corrected herself. "My lords?"

"Was there any need?" Lord Darcy asked. "My Lord du Moqtessuma has assured me that if Master Ewen leaves his hiding place he shall know it. Right, my lord?"

"Right." Then he added, "That is, I cannot guarantee his future movements, but if he should go very far from there I should know it.

"One thing I do not understand," Her Grace said frankly, "is why My Lord John Quetzal did not immediately recognize the symbolism." She looked at the young Mechicain nobleman with a smile. "I do not mean this as a reflection upon your abilities. You *did* visualize the symbols— and yet you translated them in terms of heraldry rather than in terms of playing cards. Undoubtedly you could explain why, but with your permission I should like to know how Lord Darcy knew."

"It was information you did not have," Lord Darcy said with a smile. "The night before last when we were discussing Mechicoe, while you were dressing, we had a short discussion of gambling and recreation in Mechicoe. I observed that not once did Lord John Quetzal mention playing cards— from which I gathered that they are very little used."

"In Mechicoe," said Lord John Quetzal, "a deck of cards is generally considered to be a fortune-telling device, used by unlicensed wizards and black sorcerers. I am not familiar with the card deck as a gambling device, although I have heard, of course, that it can be used as such."

"Of course," said Lord Darcy. "Therefore, you translated the symbols you saw in terms of heraldry, a field of knowledge with which you are familiar. But your description is quite clear." He looked at the Duchess. "And, therefore, we came to you." He smiled. "If anyone knows the gambling clubs of London, it is you."

She looked back down at the map. "Yes," she said. "There's only one such club in that area. He must be there. It's the *Manzana de Oro*."

"Ah," said Lord Darcy. "The *Golden Apple*, eh? What do you know of it?"

"It is owned by a Moor from Granada."

"Indeed?" said Lord Darcy. "Describe him to me."

"Oh, he's an absolutely fascinating creature," said Her Grace. "He's tall—as tall as you are—and quite devilishly handsome. He has dark skin—almost black—flashing eyes, and a small pointed beard. He dresses magnificently in the Oriental fashion. There's an enormous emerald on his left ring finger, and a great ruby—or perhaps it is a spinel—in his turban. He carries at his waist a jeweled Persian dagger that is probably worth a fortune. For all I know he is an unmitigated scoundrel, but in his manners and bearing he is unquestionably a gentleman. He calls himself the Sidi al-Nasir."

Lord Darcy leaned back and laughed.

"May I ask," the Duchess said acidly, "what is so funny, my lord?"

"My apologies," said Lord Darcy, smothering his laughter. "I wasn't trying to be funny. You must credit it to our Moorish friend. 'Sidi al-Nasir' indeed! How lovely. I have a feeling I shall like this gentleman."

"Would it be too much," Her Grace said pleasantly, "for you to let us in on the joke?"

"It is the felicitous choice of name and title," Lord Darcy said. "Translating broadly, *Sidi al-Nasir* means 'My Lord the Winner.' How magnificently he has informed the upper class gamblers of London that the advantage is with the house. Yes, indeed, I think I shall like My Lord al-Nasir." He looked at the Duchess. "Do you have entry into his club?"

"You know I do," she said. "You would never have mentioned it to me otherwise."

"True," said Lord Darcy blandly. "But now that you are in on our little trap, I shall not deny you the further enjoyment of helping us close it solidly upon our quarry." He looked at Lord John Quetzal. "My lord," he said, "the quarry is cornered. We now have but to devise the trap itself."

Lord John Quetzal nodded smilingly. "Indeed, my lord. Oh, yes indeed. Now, to begin with . . ."

The night was clear. Each star in the sky above shone like a separate brilliant jewel in the black velvet of the heavens. A magnificent carriage bearing the Cumberland arms pulled up in front of the *Manzana de Oro*, the footman opened and bowed low before the polychrome and gilt door, and four people descended. The first to alight was no less than Her Grace the Dowager Duchess of Cumberland. She was followed by a tall, lean, handsome man in impeccable evening clothes. The third passenger was equally tall—a dark-faced man wearing the arms of the ducal house of Moqtessuma. All three bowed low as the fourth passenger stepped out.

His Highness the Prince of Vladistov was a short, round gentleman, with a dark, bushy, heavy beard and an eyeglass screwed into his right eye. He descended from the coach in silence with great dignity, and acknowledged his companions' bows with a patronizing tilt of his head.

Her Grace of Cumberland nodded to the brace of doormen who stood at rigid attention at either side of the entrance to the *Manzana de Oro*, and the four of them marched inside. At the inner door, Her Grace's escort spoke to the majordomo. "You may announce to My Lord al-Nasir—Her Grace, Mary, Dowager Duchess of Cumberland; Lord John Quetzal du Moqtessuma de Mechicoe; His Most Serene Highness, Jehan, Prince of Vladistov; and myself, the Lord of Arcy."

The majordomo bowed low before this magnificent company and said, "His lordship shall be so informed." Then he glanced at the Dowager Duchess. "Your pardon . . . uh . . . Your Grace vouches for these gentlemen?"

"Of course, Goodman Abdul," said Her Grace imperiously, and the party of four swept across the threshold.

Lord Darcy held back and, as Lord John Quetzal caught up with him, whispered, "Is he here?"

"He's here," said Lord John Quetzal. "I can place him within ten feet now."

"Good. Keep smiling and follow my lead. But if he moves, let me know immediately."

They followed Her Grace and the magnificently attired Prince of Vladistov into the interior.

The anteroom was large—some thirty feet broad by twenty feet deep—and gave no hint that the *Manzana de Oro* was a gambling club. The decor was Moorish, and—to Lord Darcy, who had seen Southern Spain, North Africa, and Arabia—far too Moorish. The decor was not that of a public place in the Islamic countries, but that of the *hareem*. The walls were hung with cloth-of-gold—or what passed for it;

the archways which led off it were—embroidered was the only word—embroidered with quotations from the *Qu'ran*—quotations which, while very decorative because of the Arabic script, were essentially meaningless in the context.

The floor was inlaid with Moorish tile, and exotic flowers set in brazen pots of earth were tastefully placed around the walls. In the center of the room, a golden fountain played. The water moved in fantastic patterns, always shifting, never repeating, forming weird and unusual shapes in the air. The fountain was lined with lights whose colors changed and moved with the waving patterns. The water flowed down over a series of baffles that produced a shifting musical note in the air.

Well-dressed people in evening clothes stood around exchanging pleasantries.

Her Grace turned and smiled. "Shall we go to the gaming rooms, gentle sirs?"

The Prince of Vladistov glanced at Lord Darcy. Lord Darcy said, "Of course, Your Grace."

She gestured toward one of the side doors that led off the anteroom and said, "Will you accompany me?" and led them through the arched doorway to their right. The gaming room was even more flamboyant than the anteroom. The hangings were of gold, embroidered with purple and red, decorated with scenes from ancient Islamic myth. But their beauty formed only a background to the Oriental magnificence of the room itself, and the brilliant evening dress of the people who played at the gaming tables stood out glitteringly against that background.

A number of sharp-eyed men moved unobtrusively among the gaming tables, observing the play. Lord Darcy knew they were journeymen sorcerers hired to spot any player's attempt to use a trained Talent to affect his chances. Their job was not to overcome any such magic, but merely to report it and expel the offender. The effect of any untrained Talent present in the players could be expected to cancel out.

The Prince of Vladistov smiled broadly at Lord Darcy and said, in a very low tone, "I've twigged to Master Ewen meself, my lord—thanks to Lord John Quetzal's aid. Sure and we have him now. He's in the room to the right, just beyond that arch with the purple scribblings about it."

Lord Darcy bowed. "Your Highness is most astute," he

said. "But where the Devil is Sidi al-Nasir?" It was a rhetorical question to which he did not expect an answer. Mary of Cumberland had assured him that al-Nasir invariably greeted members of the nobility when they came to his club, and yet there had been no sign of the Moor.

The Prince of Vladistov answered Lord Darcy's rhetorical question. "He seems to be in his office. We can't be sure, Lord John Quetzal and I, but we both agree that that's where he seems to be."

Lord Darcy nodded. "All right, we'll work it that way." He moved up and smiled at the Dowager Duchess of Cumberland. "Your Grace," he said very softly, "I observe that the gentleman who was at the door has followed us in."

She did not turn her head. "Goodman Abdul? Yes. By this time he is probably wondering why we have not gone to the gaming tables."

"A good question, from his point of view. We shall take advantage of it. Go over and ask him where Sidi al-Nasir is. Insist upon speaking to the Sidi. You have brought, after all, a most important guest, the Prince of the distant Russian principality of Vladistov, and you see no reason why el Sidi should not greet him as he deserves. Pour it on thick. But make sure his back is toward us."

She nodded and moved across the room toward el Sidi's minion, leaving her three companions clustered in a group around the door that was their target.

As soon as the Duchess had distracted Abdul's attention, Lord Darcy whispered, "All right. This is it. Move in."

Lord John Quetzal turned and faced the crowd, watching every movement. Lord Darcy and the Prince of Vladistov moved toward the door.

"No spell on the lock," said the short, round man with the beard. "Too many people moving in and out."

"Very good." Lord Darcy reached out, turned the knob, pulled open the door, and within the space of half a second he and his companion were inside, the door closed behind them.

Sidi al-Nasir conformed precisely to the description that the Duchess had given them. When he saw the two strangers enter his office, one hand reached for a drawer—then stopped. His black eyes looked down the equally black

muzzle of the Heron .36 that stared at him. Then they lifted
to the face of the man who carried the weapon. "With your
permission, my lord," he said coolly, "I shall put my empty
hand back on top of my desk."

"I suggest that you do so," said Lord Darcy. He glanced
at the man who sat across from Sidi al-Nasir's desk. "Good
evening, my lord. I see that you are here before me."

Commander Lord Ashley smiled calmly. "It was inevitable,"
he said in a cool, constrained voice. "I am glad to see you."
He looked toward Sidi al-Nasir. "My Lord al-Nasir," he said,
"has just proposed that I go to work for the Government
of Poland."

Lord Darcy looked at the dark-complexioned man. "Have
you now, My Lord the Winner?"

Sidi al-Nasir spread his hands on the surface of the desk
and smiled. "Ah, then you understand Arabic, most noble
lord?" he said in that language.

"While I do not, perhaps, have your liquid fluency in the
Tongue of Tongues," Lord Darcy said in return, "my poor
knowledge of the language of the Prophet is adequate for
most purposes."

Sidi al-Nasir's finely-chiseled lips wreathed in a smile. "I
am not one to contradict, most noble," he said. "But, except
that your enunciation betrays the fact that your mentor was
a subject of the Shah of Shahs, your command of the speech
of the *Qu'ran* is most flowing."

Lord Darcy allowed a half-smile to touch his lips. "It is true
that my instructor in the noble language of the Prophet of
Islam came from the Court of the Shadow of God on Earth,
the Shah of Persia, but—would you prefer that I spoke in the
debased fashion of Northwest Africa and Southern Spain?"

The sudden shift in Lord Darcy's accent made Sidi al-Nasir
blink. Then he raised his eyebrows and his smile broadened even further. "Ah, most wise one, your knowledge
betrays you. But few people of your Frankish Empire have
such a command of the Tongue of Tongues. You are, then,
the renowned Sidi of Arcy. It is indeed a pleasure to meet
you, my lord."

"I hope that events may prove that it was a pleasure
to meet you, my lord," said Lord Darcy. Then, shifting,
"But you have guests, my lord. Shall we continue in
Anglo-French?"

"Of course," said Sidi al-Nasir. He glanced at Lord Ashley. "So it was all a trap then?"

Lord Ashley nodded. "All a trap, my dear al-Nasir."

"A poor one, I think," said Sidi al-Nasir with a smile. "Poorly planned and poorly executed." He chuckled softly. "I need not even deny the truth."

"Well, we shall see," said Lord Darcy. "What is the truth?"

Sidi al-Nasir's smile did not vanish. He merely looked at Commander Lord Ashley.

Lord Ashley gave him one glance and then looked up at Lord Darcy with a smile. "Sorry to have pulled this on you. Didn't know you'd be here. We have long suspected that the *Manzana de Oro* was the headquarters of a spy ring working for His Slavonic Majesty. In order to prove our case I ran up a debt here of . . ." He looked at Sidi al-Nasir.

The Moor, still smiling, sighed. "Of some one hundred and fifty golden sovereigns, my lord. More than you could earn in a year."

Lord Ashley nodded calmly. "Exactly. And tonight you offered me two alternatives. You would either report my debt to the Admiralty, in which case—so you assumed—I would be ruined, or I could become a spy for His Slavonic Majesty."

Sidi al-Nasir's smile broadened. "That was why I said the trap was poorly laid, My Lord Commander. I deny that I made you any such offer, and you have no witnesses to prove it."

Lord Darcy, still holding his pistol level, allowed a smile to come over his own face. "My Lord al-Nasir," he said, "for your information, I shall say that I am quite confident that you *have* just made such an offer to my lord the Commander."

Sidi al-Nasir showed his white teeth in a broad smile. "Ah, my lord, *you* may be certain." He laughed. "Perhaps even *I* am certain, no? And of course Commander Lord Ashley is certain. But"—he spread his hands—"is this evidence? Would it stand up in court?" He looked suddenly very sad. "Ah, you might, of course, deport me. The evidence of My Lord Ashley may be strong enough for that. There is, certainly, enough suspicion here to force me to return to my native Spain. I must close down the *Manzana de Oro*. What a pity it will be to leave the chill and fog of London for the warmth, the color, the beauty of Granada . . ." Then he directed his smile at Lord Darcy. "But I am afraid that you cannot imprison me."

"As to that," said Lord Darcy, "possibly you are right. But we shall see."

"Is it necessary, my lord, that you keep the muzzle of that weapon pointing at me?" said Sidi al-Nasir. "I find it distinctly ungentlemanly."

"Of course, my lord," said Lord Darcy, not deviating the aim of his weapon one iota. "If you would be so good as to remove—no! no! . . . not just the gun . . . the whole drawer from your desk. There may be more than one gun in it."

Sidi al-Nasir very carefully pulled out the drawer and placed it on the desk top. "Only one, my lord, and I shouldn't think of touching it in your presence."

Lord Darcy looked at the weapon that lay by itself in the drawer. "Ah," he said, "a Toledo .39. A very good weapon, my lord. I shall see to it that it is returned to you, if the law so allows."

The Sidi al-Nasir's obsidian eyes suddenly flickered as his gaze moved across Lord Darcy's face. In that instant he realized that Darcy's information covered a great deal more territory than a mere suspicion of espionage. The Sidi knew that this trap was more dangerous than it had at first appeared.

"It is possible, my lord," he said smoothly, "that Lord Ashley's losses were due to the machinations of a certain Master Sorcerer, whom I have decided to release from my employ. The Commander's winnings up until a short time ago were considerable. The Master Sorcerer of whom I spoke may have decided to correct that. If so, of course, I am not personally responsible . . ."

"Ah," said Lord Darcy. "So Commander Lord Ashley's slight precognitive ability was overcome by Master Ewen." He addressed the Commander without taking his eyes off Sidi al-Nasir. "What did you usually play, Ashley?"

"Rouge-et-Or," said the Commander.

"I see. Then the precognition would be of little use at that game if a Master Sorcerer were working against you. If you made a bet on any given number, the sorcerer could almost always make certain that the little ivory ball did not land in the proper slot—even if he were operating from another room."

His eyes gazed directly at those of Sidi al-Nasir. "A deliberate plot, then," he said. "You tried to enlist the Commander by having your sorcerer force the game to go against him."

"We suspected something of the sort," Lord Ashley said cheerfully, "so we decided to let Sidi al-Nasir run it as he would and see what developed."

The Sidi al-Nasir shrugged, still keeping his hands well above the table. "Whatever may have happened," he said, "I assure you that this sorcerer is no longer in my employ. However, my information leads me to believe that you are rather eager to locate him. It is possible I may be of some assistance to you in your search. I might be in a position to inform you as to Master Ewen's present whereabouts. After all, we are all of us reasonable men, are we not?"

"I am afraid your information is superfluous, my lord . . ." Lord Darcy began.

At that point the door of the office was flung open and Lord John Quetzal burst in. "Look out! He's moving! He knows he's being betrayed!" he shouted.

Even as he spoke, the rear door was swinging open. Master Ewen MacAlister ran out, heading for the door that led to freedom. Only Lord John Quetzal stood between him and that door. The black sorcerer gestured with one hand toward the young Mechicain.

Lord John Quetzal threw up his hand to ward off the spell that had been cast, but his journeyman's powers were not the equal of those of a Master. His own shielding spell softened the blow, but could not completely stop it. He staggered and fell to his knees. He did not collapse, but his eyes glazed over and he remained in his kneeling position, unmoving.

But his moment of resistance, slight though it was, was enough to slow Master Ewen's flight. The bogus Prince of Vladistov was already in action. Master Sean O Lochlainn ripped off his false beard and allowed his eyeglass to drop to the floor.

Lord Darcy did not move. It took every ounce of his self-control to keep his pistol fixed firmly on the Sidi al-Nasir. The Moor also remained motionless. He did not even glance away from the muzzle of Lord Darcy's pistol.

The black sorcerer spun around to face Master Sean and

gestured with one hand, describing an intricate symbol in the air with a flourish of his fingers, his features contorted in a strained grimace.

Lord Darcy and everyone else in the room felt the psychic blast of that hastily conjured spell. Master Ewen's hours in hiding had obviously been spent in conjuring up the spells he would need to defend himself when the time came.

Master Sean O Lochlainn, toward whom the spell was directed, seemed to freeze for perhaps half a second. But he, too, had prepared himself, and he had the further advantage of having known the identity of his prey, while Master Ewen had no way of knowing—except by conjecture—who would come after him.

Master Sean's hand moved, creating a symbol in the air.

Master Ewen blinked, gritted his teeth and, from somewhere beneath his cloak, drew a long white wand.

No one else in the room, not even Lord Darcy, could move. They held their positions partly because of the psychic tension in the air around them, partly because they wanted to see the outcome of this duel between two master magicians, but primarily because the undirected corona effects of the spells themselves held them enthralled.

Except for Master Sean, no one there recognized the white wand that Master Ewen drew. But Master Sean saw it, recognized it as having been made from a human thigh bone, and in an instant had prepared a counterspell. The thighbone-wand was thrust out, and Master Ewen's lips moved malevolently.

The corona effect of the spell went beyond the immediate area. Outside in the gaming rooms, the players seemed to freeze for a moment. Then, for no apparent reason, the heavy bettors put their money on odds-on bets. One young scion of a wealthy family put fifty golden sovereigns on a bet that would have netted him a single silver sovereign if he had won.

And in al-Nasir's office, Lord John Quetzal suddenly blinked his eyes and looked away, Lord Ashley started to draw his sword, Sidi al-Nasir himself moved groggily away from his desk; and Lord Darcy's hand quivered on the grip of the Heron .36, keeping it aligned on the Sidi, but not firing.

But Master Sean had warded off the effectiveness of even

that spell, which was designed to make him take a stupid chance.

With great determination, he stalked toward Master Ewen, and his voice was hard and cold as he said, "In the Name of the Guild, Master Ewen—*yield!* Otherwise I shall not be responsible for what happens."

Master Ewen's reply contained three words—words which were furious, foul, and filthy.

Again that whitened thighbone-wand stabbed out.

And again Master Sean stood the brunt of that terrible psychic shock. Without a wand, without anything save his own hand, Master Sean made the final effective gesture of the battle.

But not the final gesture, for Master Ewen repeated himself. He stepped forward, and again jabbed with his chalk-white wand.

Then he stepped forward once more.

Another jab.

Another step.

Another jab.

Another step.

Master Sean moved to one side, watching Master Ewen.

The jabs of the black sorcerer's wand were no longer directed toward the tubby little Irish sorcerer but toward the point in space where he had been.

Master Sean took a deep breath. "I'd better catch him before he runs into the wall."

Lord Darcy did not move the muzzle of his weapon from Sidi al-Nasir. "What is he doing?" he asked.

"He's trapped in a time cycle, my lord. I've tied his thought processes in a knot. They go round and round through their contortions and end up where they started. He'll keep repeating the same useless motions again and again until I pull him out of it."

In spite of Master Ewen MacAlister's apparently thaumaturgical gestures, everyone could feel that the corona effect was gone. Whatever was going on in the repeating cycle inside Master Ewen's mind, it had no magical effect.

"How is Lord John Quetzal?" Lord Darcy asked.

"Oh, he'll be all right as soon as I release him from that daze spell."

"Magnificently done, Master Sean," said Lord Darcy. "My

Lord Ashley," he said to the Naval Commander, "will you be so good as to go to the nearest window, identify yourself, and shout for help? The place is completely surrounded by the Armsmen of London."

CHAPTER 21

Sir Frederique Bruleur, the seneschal of the Palace du Marquis, brought three cups of caffe into My Lord de London's office. The first was placed on the center of My Lord Marquis' desk, the second on the center of Lord Bontriomphe's desk, the third on the corner of Lord Bontriomphe's desk near the red leather chair where Lord Darcy was seated. Then Sir Frederique withdrew silently.

My Lord Marquis sipped at his cup, then glowered at Lord Darcy. "You insist upon this confrontation, my lord cousin?"

"Can you see any other way of getting the evidence we need?" Lord Darcy asked blandly. He had wanted to discuss the problem earlier with the Marquis of London, but the Marquis insisted that no business should be discussed during dinner.

The Marquis took another sip at his cup. "No, I suppose not," he agreed. He focused his gaze upon Lord Bontriomphe. "You now have Master Ewen locked up. Securely, I presume?"

"We have three Master Sorcerers keeping an eye on him," Lord Bontriomphe said. "Master Sean has put a spell on him that will keep him in a total daze until we get around to taking it off. I don't know what more you want."

The Marquis of London snorted. "I want to make certain he doesn't get away, of course." He glanced at the clock on the wall. "It has now been three hours since you made your arrests at the *Manzana de Oro*. If Master Ewen is still in his cell I will concede that you have him properly guarded. Now: What information did you get?"

Lord Bontriomphe turned a hand palm up. "Master Ewen admits almost everything. He knows we have him on an espionage charge; he knows that we have him on a charge of Black Magic; he knows that we have him on a charge of thaumaturgical assault and attempted murder against the person of the Damoselle Tia Einzig.

"He admits to all that, but refuses to admit to a charge of murder. Until Master Sean put him under a quieting spell, he was talking his head off—admitting everything, as long as it would not put his neck in a noose."

"*Pah!* Naturally he would attempt to save his miserable skin. Very well. What happened? I have your reports and Lord Darcy's reports. From the facts, the conclusions are obvious. What do you say?" He looked straight into Bontriomphe's eyes.

Lord Bontriomphe shrugged. "I'm not the genius around here. I'll tell you what Chief Hennely thinks. I'll give you *his* theory for what it's worth. But mind you, I don't consider that it is accurate in every detail. But Chief Master-at-Arms Hennely has discussed this with Commander Lord Ashley and with Captain Smollett, so I give you their theory for what *it's* worth."

The Marquis glanced at Lord Darcy, then looked back at Lord Bontriomphe. "Very well. Proceed."

"All right. To begin with, we needn't worry about the murder in Cherbourg. It was committed by a Polish agent detailed for the purpose, simply because they discovered that Barbour was a double agent—and our chances of finding the killer are small.

"The killer of Master Sir James is another matter. Here, we know who the killer is, and we know the tool he used.

"We know that the Damoselle Tia was being blackmailed, that Master Ewen threatened to have her uncle tortured and killed if she did not obey orders. Defying those orders, she went to Sir James Zwinge, and told him everything—including everything she knew about Master Ewen. Naturally, MacAlister had to dispose of Sir James, even though that would mean that a new head of the European Intelligence network would be appointed, and that the Poles would have to repeat all the work of discovering the identity of his successor as soon as the Navy appointed one."

He looked over at Lord Darcy. "As to *how* it was done, the important clue was that half-moon bloodstain that you pointed out to me." He looked back at the Marquis. "You see that, don't you? It was a heel print. And there was only one pair of shoes in the hotel that could have made such a print—the high-heeled shoes of Tia Einzig.

"Look at the evidence. We know, from Master Sean O

Lochlainn's report, that Master Sir James was stabbed—not at 9:30 when he screamed—but at approximately nine o'clock, half an hour before. The wound was not immediately fatal."

He glanced back at Lord Darcy. "Sir James lay there, unconscious, for half an hour—and then, when he heard Master Sean's knock, he came out of his coma long enough to shout to Master Sean for help. He lifted himself up, but this last effort finished him. He dropped and died. Do you agree?"

"Most certainly," said Lord Darcy. "It could not have happened in any other way. He was stabbed at nine—or thereabouts—but did not die until half past.

"The chirurgical evidence of the blood, and the thaumaturgical evidence of the time of psychic shock demonstrate that clearly.

"But you have yet to explain how he was stabbed inside a locked room at nine o'clock—or at any other time. The evidence shows that there was no one else in that room when he was stabbed. What is your explanation for that?"

"I hate to say it," said Lord Bontriomphe, "but it appears to me that Master Sean's testimony is faulty. With another master sorcerer at work here, the evidence could have been fudged. Here's what happened: Master Ewen, knowing that he had to get rid of the Damoselle Tia, decided to use her to get rid of Master Sir James at the same time. He put her under a spell. She talked her way into Master Sir James' room, used his own knife on him when he least suspected it, and walked out, leaving that half-moon heel print near the door."

Lord Bontriomphe leaned back in his chair. "As a matter of cold fact, if it were not for that heel print, I would say that Master Ewen put Master Sir James under a spell which forced him to stab himself with that contact cutter.

"Naturally, he would fumble the job. Even under the most powerful magic spell it is difficult to force anyone to commit suicide."

He glanced at Lord Darcy. "As you yourself noticed with the Damoselle Tia, my lord; although she was induced to jump off the bridge, she nevertheless fought to keep herself afloat after she struck the water."

"Yes, she did," Lord Darcy agreed. "Go on."

"As I said," Lord Bontriomphe continued, "if it weren't for that heel print, I would say that Sir James was forced to suicide by Black Magic." He shrugged. "That still may be possible, but I'd like to account for that heel print. So, I say that the Damoselle Tia stabbed him and walked out, and that Master Ewen used sorcery to relock the door from the room above. I don't say that she is technically guilty of murder, but certainly she was a tool in Master Ewen's hands."

The Marquis of London snorted loudly and opened his mouth to say something, but Lord Darcy held up a warning hand. "Please, my lord cousin," he said mildly. "I think it incumbent upon us to listen to the rest of Lord Bontriomphe's theories. Pray continue, my lord," he said, addressing the London investigator.

Lord Bontriomphe looked at him bitterly. "All right; so you two geniuses have worked everything out. I am just a legman; I've never claimed to be anything else. But—if you don't like those theories, here's another."

He took a deep breath and went on. "We arrested Master Sean in the first place on the rather flimsy evidence that he and Sir James had both worked out a way to manipulate a knife by thaumaturgical means. Now suppose that was done? Suppose that is the way Sir James was killed? Who could have done it?" He spread a hand.

"I won't say Sir James did—although he could have. But, to assume that he took such a roundabout way of committing suicide would be, in the words of my lord the Marquis, fatuous. To think that it happened by accident would be even more fatuous.

"Or my lord may think of another adjective; I won't quibble.

"We know that Master Sean did not do it, because it would have taken at least three quarters of an hour to prepare the spell, and, according to Grand Master Sir Lyon, there could not be more than one wall, or other material barrier, between the sorcerer and his victim—and certainly Master Sean could not have stood out in that hall, going through an intricate spell like that for half an hour or more, without being noticed. Besides, he wasn't even in that hall at that time." He waved a hand. "Forget Master Sean."

"Good of you," murmured Lord Darcy.

"Who is left? Nobody that we know of. But couldn't Master Ewen have figured out the process? After all, if two Master magicians can figure it out separately, why not a third? Or maybe he stole it; I don't know. But isn't it possible that Master Ewen forced the weapon into Master Sir James' chest?"

Lord Darcy started to say something, but this time it was the Marquis of London who interrupted.

"Great God!" he rumbled. "And it was I who trained this man!" He swiveled his massive head and looked at Lord Bontriomphe. "And pray, would you explain what happened to the weapon? Where did it disappear to?"

Lord Bontriomphe blinked, said nothing, and turned his eyes to Lord Darcy.

"Surely you see," said Lord Darcy calmly, "that the contact cutter which lay beside Sir James' body—and which, by the by, was the only edged weapon in the room—could not possibly have been the murder weapon. You *did* read the autopsy report, did you not?"

"Why, yes, but—"

"Then surely you see that a blade in the shape of an isosceles triangle—two inches wide at the base, and five inches long—could not have made a stab wound five inches deep if the cut it made was less than an inch wide.

"Even more important—as I pointed out to Master Sean earlier today—a knife of pure silver, while harder than pure gold, is softer than pure lead. Its edges would certainly have been noticeably blunted if it had cut into two ribs. And yet, the knife retained its razor edge.

"It follows that Master Sir James was not killed by his own contact cutter—further, that the weapon which killed him was not in the room in which he died."

Lord Bontriomphe stared at Lord Darcy for a long second, then he turned and looked at the Marquis of London. "All right. As I said, I didn't like those hypotheses, because they don't explain away the heel print—and now they don't explain the missing knife. So I'll stick to my original theory, with one small change: Tia brought her own knife and took it away with her."

The Marquis of London did not even bother to look up from his desk. "Most unsatisfactory, my lord," he said, "most unsatisfactory." Then he glanced at Lord Bontriomphe. "And you intend to put the blame on the Damoselle Tia? Hah! Upon what evidence?"

"Why—upon the evidence of her heel print." Lord Bontriomphe leaned forward. "It *was* Master Sir James' blood, wasn't it? And how could she have got it on her heel except after Master Sir James bled all over the middle of the floor?"

The Marquis of London looked up toward the ceiling. "Were I a lesser man," he said ponderously, "this would be more than I could bear. Your deductions would be perfectly correct, Bontriomphe—*if* that were the Damoselle Tia's heel print. But, of course, it was not."

"Whose else could it have been?" Bontriomphe snapped. "Who else could have made a half-moon print in blood like that?"

My lord the Marquis closed his eyes and, obviously addressing Lord Darcy, said: "I intend to discuss this no further. I shall be perfectly happy to preside over this evening's discussion—especially since we have obtained official permission for it. I shall return when our guests arrive." He rose and headed toward the rear door, then he stopped and turned. "In the meantime, would you be so good as to dispel Lord Bontriomphe's fantasy about the Damoselle Tia's heel print?" And then he was gone.

Lord Bontriomphe took a deep breath and held it. It seemed a good three minutes before he let it out again—slowly.

"All right," he said at last, "I told you I wasn't the genius around here. Obviously you have observed a great deal more in this case than I have. We'll do as my lord of London has agreed. We'll get them all up here and talk to them."

Then, abruptly, he slammed the flat of his hand down upon the top of his desk. "But—by *Heaven,* there's one thing I want to know before we go on with this! Why do you say that that heel print did not belong to Damoselle Tia?"

"Because, my dear Bontriomphe," said Lord Darcy carefully, "it was not a heel print." He paused.

"If it had been, the weight of the person wearing the heel would have pressed the blood down into the fiber of the rug; and yet—you will agree that it did not? That the blood touched only the top of the fibers, and soaked only a little way down?"

Lord Bontriomphe closed his eyes and let his exceptional

memory bring up a mental picture of the bloodstain. Then he opened his eyes. "All right. So I was wrong. The bloodstain was not a heel print. Then where did I make my mistake?"

"Your error lay in assuming that it was a bloodstain," said Lord Darcy.

Lord Bontriomphe's scowl grew deeper. "Don't tell me it *wasn't* a bloodstain!"

"Not exactly," said Lord Darcy. "It was only *half* a bloodstain."

CHAPTER 22

There were nine guests in the office of my lord the Marquis of London that night. Sir Frederique Bruleur had brought in enough of the yellow chairs to seat eight. Lord Bontriomphe and the Marquis sat behind their desks. Lord Darcy sat to the left of Bontriomphe's desk, in the red leather chair, which had been swiveled around to face the rest of the company. From left to right, Lord Darcy saw, in the first row, Grand Master Sir Lyon Gandolphus Grey, Mary of Cumberland, Captain Percy Smollett, and Commander Lord Ashley. And in the second row, Sir Thomas Leseaux, Lord John Quetzal, Father Patrique, and Master Sean O Lochlainn. Behind them, near the door, stood Chief Master-at-Arms Hennely Grayme, who had told Sir Frederique that he preferred to stand.

Sir Frederique had served drinks all around, then had quietly retired.

My lord the Marquis of London looked them all over once and then said: "My lords, Your Grace, gentlemen." He paused and looked them all over once again. "I will not say that it was very good of you to come. You are not here by invitation, but by fiat. Nonetheless, all but one of you have been asked merely as witnesses to help us discover the truth, and all but that one may consider themselves my guests." He paused again, took a deep breath, and let it out slowly. "It is my duty to inform you that you are all here to answer questions if they are put to you—not simply because I, as Lord of London, have requested your cooperation, but, more important, because you are here by order of our Most Dread Sovereign, His Majesty the King. Is that understood?"

Nine heads nodded silently.

"This is, then," My Lord Marquis continued, "a Court of Inquiry, presided over by myself as justice of the King's Court. Lord Bontriomphe is here as Clerk of the King's Court. This may seem irregular but it is quite in accord with the law. Is all of *that* understood?" Again, there were nine silent nods of assent. "Very well. I hardly think I need say— although by law I must—that anything anyone of you says here will be taken down by Lord Bontriomphe in writing, and may be used in evidence.

"The Reverend Father Patrique, O.B.S., is here in the official capacity of *amicus curia*, as a registered Sensitive of Holy Mother Church.

"As official Sergeant-at-Arms, we have Chief Master-at-Arms Hennely Grayme of this City.

"Presenting the case for the Crown is Lord Darcy, at present of Rouen, Chief Investigator for His Royal Highness, Prince Richard, Duke of Normandy.

"Although this Court has the power to make a recommendation, it is understood that anyone accused may appeal without prejudice, and may be represented in such Court as our Most Dread Sovereign His Majesty the King may appoint, by any counsel such accused may choose."

My Lord Marquis took another deep breath and cleared his throat. "Is all of *that* quite clear? You will answer by voice." And a ragged chorus of voices said, "Yes, my lord."

"Very well." He heaved his massive bulk up from his chair, and everyone else stood. "Will you administer the oath, Reverend Father," he said to the Benedictine. When the oath had been administered to everyone there, my lord the Marquis sat down again with a sigh of comfort. "Now, before we proceed, are there any questions?"

There were none.

The Marquis of London lifted his head a fraction of an inch and looked at Lord Darcy from beneath his brows. "Very well, my Lord Advocate. You may proceed."

Lord Darcy stood up from the red leather chair, bowed in the direction of the Court, and said, "Thank you, my Lord Justice. Do I have the Court's permission to be seated during the presentation of the Crown's case?"

"You do, my lord. Pray be seated."

"Thank you, my lord." Lord Darcy settled himself again in the red leather chair.

His eyes searched each of the nine in turn, then he said, "We are faced here with a case of treason and murder.

"Although I am aware that most of you know the facts, legally I must assume that you do not. Therefore, I shall have to discuss each of those facts in turn. You must understand that the evidence proving these facts will be produced after my preliminary presentation.

"Three days ago, shortly before eleven o'clock on the morning of Tuesday, October 25, Anno Domini One Thousand Nine Hundred and Sixty-Six, a man named Georges Barbour was stabbed to death in a cheap rooming house in Cherbourg. Evidence which will be produced before this Court will show that Goodman Georges was a double agent; that is, he was a man who, while pretending to work for the Secret Service of His Slavonic Majesty King Casimir IX, was also in the pay of our own Naval Intelligence, and was, as far as the evidence shows, loyal to the Empire. Will you testify to that, Captain Smollett?" he asked, looking at the second chair from his right.

"I will, m'lud Advocate."

"Very shortly after he was killed," Lord Darcy went on, "Commander Lord Ashley of the Naval Intelligence Corps reported the discovery of Goodman Georges' body to the Armsmen of Cherbourg. He also reported that he had been ordered to give one hundred golden sovereigns to Goodman Georges because the double agent in question needed it to pay off a certain Goodman FitzJean."

Bit by bit, item by item, Lord Darcy outlined the case to those present, omitting no detail except the precise nature and function of the confusion projector. Lord Darcy described it simply as a "highly important Naval secret."

He described the discovery of the murder of Sir James Zwinge, the attack upon the Damoselle Tia, the fight upon the bridge, the Damoselle Tia's statement, the discovery of the body of Goodman Paul Nichols, and the search for and arrest of Master Ewen MacAlister.

"The questions before this Court," Lord Darcy said, "are: Who killed those three men: And why? It is the contention of the Crown that one person, and one only, is responsible for all three deaths."

He looked over the nine faces before him, trying to assess the expressions on their faces. Not one betrayed any sign of guilt, not even the one whom Lord Darcy knew was guilty.

"I see you have a question, Captain Smollett. Would you ask it, please? No, don't bother to rise."

Captain Smollett cleared his throat. "M'lud." He paused, cleared his throat again. "Since we already have the guilty man under arrest, may I ask why this inquiry is necessary?"

"Because we do not have the guilty man under arrest, Captain. Master Ewen, no matter what his actual crimes, is not guilty of a single murder—much less a triple one."

Captain Smollett said "Um," and nothing more.

"You have before you, my lords, Your Grace, gentlemen, every bit of pertinent evidence. It is now the duty of myself as Advocate of the Crown to link up that evidence into a coherent chain. First, let us dismiss the theory that Master Ewen MacAlister was more than remotely connected with these murders. Master Ewen was, it is true, an agent of His Slavonic Majesty, working with the owner of the *Manzana de Oro*, the Sidi al-Nasir. This evidence can be produced later; let us merely accept these facts as true."

He turned to the Chief of Naval Intelligence. "Captain Smollett."

"Yes, m'lud?"

"I wish to put to you a hypothetical question, and for the sake of security let us keep it hypothetical. If . . . I say, *if* . . . you were aware of the identity of the Polish Chief of Intelligence for France and the British Isles, would you order him assassinated?"

Captain Smollett's eyes narrowed. "No, m'lud, never."

"Why not, Captain?"

"It would be stupid, m'lud. Yes. As long as we know who he is . . . uh . . . if we knew who he was . . . it would be much more to our advantage to keep an eye on him, to watch him; to see to it, in fact, that he got the information that we wanted him to have, rather than the information he wants. Also, our knowing the Chief of Polish Intelligence would lead us to his agents. It is much easier to keep the body under surveillance when one can identify the head, m'lud."

"Then would you say, Captain, that it would be very stupid of Polish Intelligence to have murdered Master Sir James Zwinge?"

"Very stupid, m'lud. Wouldn't be at all good Intelligence tactics. Not at all." For a moment, Captain Smollett blinked solemnly, digesting this new thought.

"Not even if Master Sir James had discovered that Master Ewen was working for the Poles?" Lord Darcy asked.

"Hmn-m-m. Probably not. Much better to pull Master Ewen out, move him to another post, give him a new identity."

"Thank you, Captain Smollett.

"Now. As you have seen," his words took in the entire company, "there is some question about whether Master Ewen could have committed this crime by Black Magic, and so skillfully hidden the evidence thereof that his complicity in the crime was undetectable. I put it to you, my lords, Your Grace, gentlemen, that he could not.

"Father Patrique." He looked at the Benedictine.

The priest bowed his head. "Yes, my lord?"

"You have examined Master Ewen since his arrest, Reverend Father?"

"I have, my lord."

"Is Master Ewen's Talent as strong, as powerful, as effective as that of Master Sean O Lochlainn?"

"My lord Advocate . . ." The good father then turned his attention to my lord of London. " . . . And may it please the Court . . ."

"Proceed, Reverend Sir," said my lord the Marquis.

" . . . I feel that, while my own testimony is adequate, it is not the best. In answer to your direct question, my lord, I must say that Master Ewen's Talent is weaker, far poorer, than that of Master Sean O Lochlainn.

"But I put it to you, my lords, that this is not the best evidence. Observe, if you will, the relative ease with which Master Sean conquered Master Ewen in the battle of wills at the *Manzana de Oro*. Observe how very simple it was to break the spells on Master Ewen's room lock and upon the carpetbag in which he carried his tools. I beg your pardon, my lord Advocate, if I am out of order."

"Not at all, Reverend Sir," said Lord Darcy. "But I will ask you once more. Will you testify that Master Sean's Talent is much more powerful than Master Ewen's?"

"It is, my lord."

Lord Darcy looked at Grand Master Sir Lyon Gandolphus Grey.

"Have you anything to add to this, Grand Master?"

Sir Lyon nodded. "If it please the Court, I should like to put a question to Commander Lord Ashley."

"Permission granted," rumbled de London. "Ask your question."

"My Lord Commander," said Sir Lyon. "You have described to the investigators the use by Master Ewen of the Tarnhelm Effect upon his smallsword. Would you—"

"One moment," said Lord Darcy. "I should like My Lord Commander to testify directly. If you would, Lord Ashley?"

"Of course, my lord."

Lord Darcy looked at Sir Lyon. "You want a description of the battle on Somerset Bridge, Sir Lyon?"

"Yes, if you please, my lord."

Lord Darcy looked at Lord Ashley. "If you will, My Lord Commander."

Lord Ashley described exactly the sword fight on the bridge.

Then Sir Lyon said, "With the Court's permission I should like to ask the witness a question or two."

"Granted," said My Lord de London.

"My Lord Commander," said Sir Lyon, "what kind of sword was Master Ewen using?"

"A smallsword, Grand Master. A sword with a triangular cross section—no edge—about two and a half feet in length—very sharp point."

Sir Lyon nodded. "You saw it. Then, when he began to use it, it disappeared?"

"Not exactly disappeared, Sir Lyon," Lord Ashley said. "It . . . it *flickered*. I . . . I find it difficult to explain. It is simply that I couldn't keep my eyes on it. But I knew it was there."

"Thank you, Commander," said Sir Lyon. "Now, if the Court will permit, I will give my testimony. A really powerful sorcerer, such as Master Sir James or Master Sean O Lochlainn—"

"Or yourself?" Lord Darcy asked suddenly.

Sir Lyon smiled. " . . . Or myself, if you insist, my lord Advocate. Any powerful sorcerer could have made his sword so completely invisible as to be totally undetectable."

"Thank you," said Lord Darcy. "The question I wish to put before the Court is this: Is it possible that a man of

Master Ewen's limited Talent—even though it was of Master grade—could have acted out a rite of Black Magic and then covered it up to such an extent that neither Master Sean O Lochlainn nor the combined Talents of the other Masters of the Guild at the Convention could have failed to discover what he had done?"

"Absolutely impossible, my lord," said Sir Lyon firmly.

Lord Darcy glanced back at the Benedictine priest. "What say you, Reverend Father?"

"I agree completely with Grand Master Sir Lyon," Father Patrique said quietly.

Lord Darcy turned to look at the Marquis of London. "Is there any need at this point, my lord, to call to the Court's attention the testimony of Master Sean O Lochlainn, Master Sorcerer, that he could detect no Black Magic involved in the murder of Master Sir James Zwinge?"

"You may proceed, my lord. If such evidence becomes necessary, Master Sean's testimony will be called for if and when it is needed."

"Thank you, my lord. We have"—Lord Darcy paused and looked the group over again—"then the evidence before us that Sir James Zwinge was killed by ordinary physical means. There was no Black Magic involved in the murder of Sir James Zwinge, and yet the evidence shows that he was alone in his room when he was stabbed at approximately nine o'clock and when he died half an hour later. Now, how could that be?

"I put it to you that we are far too prone to accept a magical explanation, when a simply material explanation will do."

He leaned back in his chair, but before he could say anything, Sir Thomas Leseaux raised his hand. "If I may, my lord, I should like to say that any theory of this murder which includes thaumaturgical processes would be mathematically impossible—but I do not see how a man could have been killed in the middle of a locked room by ordinary material means."

"That is why I must explain the Crown's case," said Lord Darcy. "Although, I repeat, the evidence is all before you.

"The point we have all tended to overlook is that a man need not be in the same room with another in order to kill him. There was no one else in Goodman Georges Barbour's room when he was stabbed, true—and yet he fell so near the door that it is not only quite possible but very probable that someone standing in the hall stabbed him."

"Come now," said Commander Lord Ashley, "that may be possible with Goodman Georges, but it certainly does not apply to Master Sir James."

"Oh, but it does, My Lord Commander," Lord Darcy said. "Given the proper implement, Master Sir James might easily have been stabbed from the hallway outside his room."

"But—through a locked door?" asked Lord John Quetzal.

"Why not?" asked Lord Darcy. "Locked doors are not impermeable. The doors to the rooms in the Royal Steward are very old—couple of centuries or more. Look at the size of the key required to open them. And then look at the size of the keyhole required to admit such a large, heavy key. Although the door to Sir James' room was locked, its keyhole was easily large enough to admit a one-inch wide blade."

Lord Darcy looked at Master Sean O Lochlainn. "You have a question, Master Sean?"

"That I do, my lord. I agree with you that the blade that stabbed Master Sir James came in through the keyhole. At your suggestion, I took scrapings from the keyhole and found traces of Sir James' blood. But"—he smiled a little—"if your lordship will pardon me, I suggest a demonstration of how a man could be given a high downward stab through a keyhole."

"I agree," said Lord Darcy. "First, I must direct the Court's attention to the peculiar bloodstain near the door. A full description of that bloodstain appears in the written record."

My lord the Marquis nodded. "It does. Proceed, my lord Advocate."

Lord Darcy turned and looked to his right at Lord Bontriomphe. "Would you ask Sir Frederique to bring in the door?"

Lord Bontriomphe reached behind him and pulled a cord. The rear door opened and Sir Frederique Bruleur, followed by an assistant, brought in a heavy oaken door. They placed it in the center of the room between the area of yellow chairs and the Marquis' desk, and held it upright.

"This demonstration is necessary," said Lord Darcy. "This door is exactly similar to the one on Sir James' room. It is taken from another room of the Royal Steward Hotel. Can all of you see both sides of it? Good.

"Master Sean, would you do me the favor of playing the part of your late colleague?"

"Of course, my lord."

"Excellent. Now, you will stand on"—he gestured—"*that* side of the door, so that the door handle and keyhole are on your *left*. For the purposes of this demonstration, I shall play the part of the murderer." He picked up a sheet of paper from Lord Bontriomphe's desk. "Now, let's see. Lord Ashley, might I borrow your sword?"

Without a word, Commander Ashley drew his narrow-bladed Naval sword from its sheath and presented it to Lord Darcy.

"Thank you, Commander. You have been most helpful throughout this entire investigation.

"Now, Master Sean, if you will take your place, we shall enact this small play. You must all assume that what you are about to see actually occurred, but you must not assume that the words I use were those that were actually used. There may have been slight variations."

Master Sean stood on one side of the door. Lord Darcy walked up to the other and rapped.

"Who is there?" said Master Sean.

"Special courier from the Admiralty," said Lord Darcy in a high-pitched voice that did not sound like his own.

"You were supposed to pick up the envelope at the desk," said Master Sean.

"I know, Sir James," said Lord Darcy in the same high-pitched voice, "but this is a special message from Captain Smollett."

"Oh, very well," said Master Sean, "just push it under the door."

"I am to deliver it only into your hands," said Lord Darcy, and with that he inserted the tip of the sword blade into the keyhole.

"Just push it under," said Master Sean, "and I'll take it. It will have been delivered into my hand."

"Very well, Sir James," said Lord Darcy. He knelt and, still keeping the tip of the sword blade in the keyhole, he pushed the paper underneath the door.

Master Sean, on the other side, bent over to pick it up.

And, at that point, Lord Darcy thrust forward with the sword.

There was a metallic scrape as the sword point touched Master Sean's chest.

Immediately Lord Darcy pulled the sword back. Master Sean gasped realistically, staggered back several feet, then fell to the floor. Lord Darcy pulled the paper from beneath the door and stood up.

"Master Sean," he said, "happens to be wearing an excellent shirt of chain mail—which, unfortunately, Master Sir James was not.

"You see, then, what happened. Master Sir James, bending over to pick up the proffered envelope, presented his left breast to the keyhole.

"The sword came through and stabbed him. A single drop of his blood fell—half of it falling upon the carpet, the other half upon the presumed message. The blade itself would stop the flow of blood until it was withdrawn and Master Sir James staggered back away from the door.

"He collapsed in a state of shock. His wound, though deep, was not immediately dangerous, since the blade had not severed any of the larger blood vessels, nor pierced the lung. There was some bleeding, but not a great deal. He lay there for approximately half an hour.

"The weapon had, however, cut the wall of the great pulmonic aorta to such an extent that there was only a layer of tissue keeping it intact.

"At half past nine, Master Sean, who had an appointment with him at that time, rapped on the door.

"The noise of the knocking roused Master Sir James from his stupor. He must have known that time had passed; he must have been aware that it was Master Sean at the door. Lifting himself from the floor, he grabbed at his desk, upon which were lying the key to his room and his silver-bladed contact cutter. He cried out to Master Sean for help.

"But this increased strain was too much for the thin layer of tissue which had thus far held the walls of the pulmonic aorta together. The increased pressure burst the walls of the blood vessel, spurting forth Sir James' life blood. Sir James collapsed again to the floor, dropping the knife and his key. He died within seconds."

Master Sean arose from the floor, carefully brushing off his magician's robe. Sir Frederique and his assistant removed the door.

"If it please the Court," the Irish sorcerer said, "the angle at which My Lord Darcy's thrust struck my chest would account exactly for the wound in Sir James' body."

Lord Darcy carefully put the sword he was holding on Lard Bontriomphe's desk. "You see, then," he said, "how Master James was killed, and how he died.

"Now, as to what happened:

"We must go back to the mysterious Goodman FitzJean. That Tuesday morning, he had discovered that Goodman Georges was a double agent. It became necessary to kill him. He walked up to Goodman Georges' room and knocked on the door. When Goodman Georges opened the door, FitzJean thrust forward with a knife and killed him. Naturally, there was no evidence that anyone was in the room with Georges Barbour, simply because there wasn't. FitzJean was standing in the hallway.

"Barbour had already discovered FitzJean's identity and, earlier that morning, had sent a letter to Zed—Sir James Zwinge. FitzJean, in order to keep his identity from being discovered, came here to London. Then he managed to get hold of a communication, which—so he believed—reported his identity to the Admiralty. It was, he thought, a letter to the Admiralty reporting the information from Barbour which disclosed FitzJean's identity. He immediately went up to Sir James' room, and, using that same envelope, which, of course, would identify it as an Admiralty message, tricked Sir James into bending over near the keyhole"—Lord Darcy gestured with one hand—"with the results which Master Sean and I have just displayed to you."

His eyes moved over the silent group before him. "By this time, of course, you all realize who the killer is. But, fortunately, we have further proof. You see, he failed to see the possibility of an error in his assumptions. He assumed that a letter sent by Barbour on the morning of Tuesday, October 25th, would arrive very early in the morning of Wednesday, the 26th, the following day. He further assumed that Barbour would have sent the letter to the Royal Steward Hotel, and that Barbour's letter, plus his own communication, was what was contained in the envelope addressed to the Admiralty by Sir James Zwinge.

"But, he failed to realize that Barbour might not have known that Sir James was at the Royal Steward, that indeed it was far more probable, from that point of view, for Barbour to address the letter to Sir James here at the Palace du Marquis."

He rose from his chair and walked to the desk of the Marquis. "May I have the envelope, my lord justice?" he asked.

Without a word, the Marquis de London handed Lord Darcy a pale blue envelope.

Lord Darcy looked at it. "This is postmarked Cherbourg. Tuesday October 25, is marked as the posting date, and it is marked as having been received on Wednesday morning, the 26th. It is addressed to Sir James Zwinge."

He turned back toward the group, and noted with approval that Chief Master-at-Arms Hennely Grayme had moved up directly behind one man.

"There was one peculiarity about these communications," he continued blandly. "Master Sir James had given to his agents special paper and ink, a special blue sealing wax, and a special seal. These had been magically treated so that unless the envelope was opened by either Master Sir James himself or by Captain Smollett, the paper within would be blank. Am I correct, Captain Smollett?"

"Yes, m'lud."

Lord Darcy looked at the envelope in his hand. "That is why this envelope has not been opened. Only *you* can open it, Captain, and we have reason to believe that it will disclose to you the identity of the so-called Goodman FitzJean— Sir James' murderer. Would you be so good as to open it?"

The Naval officer took the envelope, broke the blue seal, lifted the flap, and took out a sheet of paper. "Addressed to Sir James," he said. "Barbour's handwriting; I recognize it."

He did not read the entire letter. When he was halfway through, his head turned to his left. "You!" he said, in a low, angry, shocked voice.

Commander Lord Ashley rose to his feet and his right hand reached toward his sword scabbard.

And then he suddenly realized it was empty, that the sword was halfway across the room, on Lord Bontriomphe's desk. At the moment of that realization, he recognized one other thing—that there was something pressed against his back.

Chief Master-at-Arms Hennely Grayme, holding his pistol steady, said, "Don't try anything, my lord. You've killed enough as it is."

"Have you anything to say, Commander?" Lord Darcy asked.

Ashley opened his mouth, closed it, swallowed, then opened it again to speak. His eyes seemed to be focused upon something in the far distance.

"You have me, my lords," he said hoarsely. "I'm sorry I had to kill anybody, but . . . but, you would have thought me a traitor, you see. I needed the money, but I would never have betrayed the Empire. I didn't know the secret." He stopped again and put his left hand over his eyes. "I knew that Barbour was a Polish agent. I didn't know he was a double agent. I thought I could get some money from him. But I . . . I wouldn't have betrayed my King. I was just afraid someone would think I had, after that."

He stopped, took his hand down. "My lords," his voice quivered as he tried to keep it even, "I should like to make my confession to Father Patrique. After that, I should like to make my confession to the Court."

The Marquis de London nodded at Lord Darcy. He nodded back at the Marquis. "You have the Crown's permission, my lord," said Lord Darcy, "but I must ask you to leave behind your scabbard and your jacket."

Without a word, Commander Lord Ashley dropped his sword belt on the chair behind him, removed his jacket and put it on top of it.

"Chief Hennely," the Marquis de London said, "I charge you to take this man prisoner upon his own admission. Take him to the outer room, where the Reverend Father may hear his sacramental confession. You will observe the laws pertaining thereto."

"Yes, my lord," said Chief Hennely, and the three of them left the room.

"And now, my lord Advocate," said the Marquis. "Would you kindly report the full story to the Court and the witnesses present"

Lord Darcy bowed. "I shall, my lord.

"I first began to suspect Ashley when I saw that, according to the register, he had come into the hotel at 8:48 on Wednesday, giving as his business there the delivery of a message for Master Sean—and yet *he had not even attempted to locate Master Sean until 9:25,* when he spoke to Lord Bontriomphe. But that is neither here nor there, my lord. Here is what happened.

"As he told us, Ashley needed money. I will explain why in a few moments. He attempted to sell a secret he did not have and could not prove he had. Finally he was reduced to accepting a payment of one hundred golden sovereigns from Georges Barbour merely to identify himself.

"On Monday night when he arrived in Cherbourg, he went to Barbour to identify himself and was told that he would be paid the following morning. Then, Tuesday morning, Commander Ashley was told to take the hundred sovereigns to Goodman Georges.

"At that point, he panicked—not as you or I might think of panic, but cold, frightened panic, for that is the way Ashley's mind works.

"He knew that once he took the money to Barbour in his own *persona,* Barbour would recognize him. Besides, he knew that his scheme had fallen through, since Barbour was a double agent. So he went up to Barbour's room, and, when Barbour opened the door, Ashley stabbed him, using a cheap knife he had bought for the purpose.

"Then he reported the murder, assisted by the fact that the concierge of Barbour's rooming house had, fortunately for him, been out for a few minutes before Lord Ashley arrived. But he also found that, in the meantime, the information as to his identity had already been sent to Zed. Therefore, he had to cut off that information; he had to prevent it from reaching the Admiralty."

Lord Darcy took a deep breath. "In a way," he said, "you might say that I assisted him. Naturally, I did not know at that time that Ashley was a killer. Therefore, I made a request that he transmit a message to Master Sean. That enabled him to get into the Royal Steward Hotel.

"At 6:30 Wednesday morning, the mail from Cherbourg was delivered to the Royal Steward. Master Sir James picked up his at 7:00. Then, having decoded the messages he received, he went down to the desk and asked a man whom he trusted, Goodman Paul Nichols, to hold an envelope for an Admiralty courier, and at the same time he sent one of the hotel boys to the Admiralty with a message for Smollett to pick up the packet.

"Sir James returned to his room, followed by the Damoselle Tia. There followed the discussion and argument which all of you have heard of. When Tia left, Master Sir James locked his door for the last time. At 8:48 Lord Ashley arrived, ostensibly looking for Master Sean. He walked up to the registration desk and started to ask for Master Sean. But Paul Nichols immediately assumed that he was the courier from the Admiralty."

Lord Darcy gestured with an open hand. "This can't be proved, of course, but it fits in precisely. Nichols must have said something like this: 'Ah, Commander, you are the courier from the Admiralty to pick up Sir James' packet? And what could Lord Ashley do? He said, 'Yes.' He took the packet. Sir James' room number was on the outside of that envelope, and Lord Ashley went directly to that room.

"Then he and Sir James played out some version of the little act that Master Sean and I enacted."

He made a slight gesture with one hand. "And there I should like to point out a peculiar thing. Murderers are quite often—more often than we like to think—very lucky. It is quite possible that sheer luck could have allowed an ordinary person to kill Sir James in the precise manner in which he *was* killed. An ordinary person, if luck were with him, could have made that thrust through the door after having decoyed Sir James into just the right position, and the results would have been the same as they actually were.

"But that was not the way that Commander Ashley operated. The Commander has one advantage: Occasionally, in times of emotional stress, he is able to see a short time into the future.

"I call your attention again to that keyhole. The door is thick. The keyhole, though large enough to admit the blade of a Naval sword, allows very little play for it. There is no way to aim that blade except in the direction the keyhole guides it.

"Even when Sir James was maneuvered into position by the Commander's use of the letter under the door, the odds against Sir James being in precisely the right position were formidable.

"Just think of the positions it is possible to take to pull a piece of paper from under a door.

"The attitude which Sir James actually assumed is the most likely one, but would any reasonably intelligent murderer depend upon it? I think not.

"This, then, was another of the many clues which led me to identify Commander Lord Ashley as the murderer. Because of the emotional tension he was undergoing, his prophetic ability allowed him to *know*—know beyond any shadow of a doubt—precisely where Sir James would be and when he would be there. And he knew exactly what he would have to do to get Sir James into that position.

"Sir James would not allow Commander Ashley in the room; he would not unlock the door for him. Therefore, Ashley had to kill him by the only means available. And because of his touch of the Talent, he was able to do so.

"The sword went through the keyhole in a straight line. A single drop of blood fell—half of it on the carpet, the other half on the envelope.

"I think that is perfectly clear. Lord Ashley then returned the envelope to his pocket and his sword to his sheath. That is why I asked him to leave both jacket and scabbard."

He gestured toward the chair where the Commander had left his sword belt and jacket. Master Sean had already looked the jacket over.

"You were right, my lord," he said, "there's a smear on the inside of his jacket pocket, and I have no doubt that there'll be another inside the scabbard."

"Nor do I," agreed Lord Darcy. "Let me continue. At that point, Lord Ashley realized something else. He realized that one man—and *one* man only—knew that he had picked up that packet.

"I don't know exactly how Paul Nichols died, but I respectfully suggest to the Court that it was something like this:

"Commander Lord Ashley arrived back in the lobby just at 9:00 and saw Nichols leaving. The hallway toward the back door is easily visible from the lobby; he must have seen Nichols leaving his own office.

"He went back and told Nichols some kind of story, and lured him into the furniture room. A quick blow to the head and a rope around the neck"—Lord Darcy snapped his fingers—"and Goodman Paul Nichols was eliminated as a witness.

"Then, I think, panic must have struck Lord Ashley again. Standing there in that closet, over the body of a man he had just strangled, he wanted to see what was in that packet. He tore it open, scattering pieces of blue sealing wax over the body of the man he had just killed.

"And, of course, he saw nothing, for the papers came out a total blank. I presume he burnt those papers later. It would have been the intelligent thing to do.

"But he still had one more thing to do. He had to relay my message to Master Sean.

"He found Lord Bontriomphe in the lobby and—well, you all know what happened after that.

"However, I'd like to point out in passing that Lord Ashley actually *returned* to the lobby around 9:10, although he did not speak to Bontriomphe until 9:25. The obvious assumption is that he was afraid to speak to any sorcerer for fear that his emotional state would give him away, and that not until he saw Lord Bontriomphe could he find the courage to speak to anyone."

Captain Smollett raised his right hand and the golden stripes of rank at his cuff gleamed in the gaslight. "A question, m'lud, if I may." His normal hearty complexion now seemed somewhat grayed. It is not easy for the head of an Intelligence operation to discover that one of his most trusted men has betrayed him.

"Of course, Captain. What is it?"

"I think I understand what the Commander did and how he did it. What I don't understand is why. D'you have any idea, my lord?"

"Until just a few hours ago, Captain, that was the main thing that bothered me. His motive was a desire for money. As a matter of fact, a conversation I had with him yesterday at the Admiralty showed that he could only think of betrayal in terms of money. Every motive that he attributed to other possible suspects had a monetary basis.

"But, until the raid at the *Manzana de Oro* I did not understand the motive behind the motive. I did not know why he needed money so badly.

"Master Ewen MacAlister has made a full confession, and since this is merely a Court of Inquiry I can tell you what it contained without bringing him here as a witness." He paused and smiled. "At the moment, I am afraid that Master Ewen is in no condition to appear as a witness."

He placed the tips of his fingers together and looked down at the toes of his boots. "Master Sorcerer Ewen MacAlister, in the pay of the Polish Government, was working with the Sidi al-Nasir of the *Manzana de Oro* to obtain Commander Lord Ashley's services as a Polish agent by blackmailing him.

"When the wheel spins—when the card turns—when the dice tumble—a gambler feels a momentary surge of psychic tension. That is why the gambler gambles—because of the thrill. Lord Ashley's advantage was that when these surges of tension came, he was occasionally able to see what the winning play would be.

"Not often, mind you; the tension was not that great. But it gave the Commander what gamblers call an 'edge.' The odds in his favor were increased. The Commander won when he played—not always, and not spectacularly, but regularly.

"The Commander's rare ability, of course, is not detectable by the sorcerers who work in any gambling club. It cannot even be detected by a Master Sorcerer." He looked at Sir Thomas Leseaux. "Am I correct, Sir Thomas?"

The theoretical thaumaturgist nodded. "You are correct, my lord. That particular form of the Talent, since it deals with time, and since it is passive rather than active—that is, observational in nature—is undetectable. Unlike the clairvoyant, whose Talent allows him to see through space, and, occasionally, into the past, the precognitive sense, which operates into the future, is almost impossible to predict, train, or control."

Sir Thomas Leseaux shrugged slightly. "Perhaps one day a greater mathematician than I will solve the problem of the asymmetry of time. Until then . . ." He shrugged again, and left his sentence hanging.

"Thank you, Sir Thomas," said Lord Darcy. "However, it is possible for a sorcerer to thwart, under certain circumstances, the precognitive sense. Master Ewen MacAlister proceeded to act upon the gambling devices at the *Manzana de Oro* when, and only when, Commander Lord Ashley was playing.

"The Commander began to lose. Before he knew it, he was deeply in debt—and because of that he did what he did."

Lord Darcy smiled. "By the way—and this is something that Master Ewen made a great point of in his confession— I should like all of you to think for a moment of Master Ewen's position on Somerset Bridge last night, when he suddenly realized he was faced by a man who was predicting his every action. However, that is by the by.

"Actually, My Lord Commander was able to perpetrate his crimes because of fantastic good luck. He did not plot his actions; he merely acted on impulse and managed to commit one of the most baffling crimes it has ever been my good fortune to investigate.

"And then by an equally fantastic stroke of *bad* luck, he was betrayed. He is an adroit and cool man when faced with danger; he can act or he can lie with equal facility. Excellent attributes in an Intelligence agent, I must admit. But the lie he told in Sidi al-Nasir's office simply did not hold water. Yesterday afternoon, when we were looking for Paul Nichols, I asked you, Captain, if you had any notion of where he might be hiding, of where the headquarters of this Polish espionage ring might be. And you said you had no notion, none whatever.

"But, in Sidi al-Nasir's office this evening, Lord Ashley calmly admitted that he owed the Sidi some one hundred and fifty golden sovereigns, a rather large amount of money even for a Commander in His Majesty's Navy.

"His explanation to me was that Naval Intelligence had long suspected the Sidi and that he, the Commander, had contrived to get himself into debt so that Sidi al-Nasir would propose that the Commander pay the debt off by acting as an agent for His Slavonic Majesty.

"That is why I say that his luck, at that point, had turned from fantastically good to fantastically bad. In actual fact, Commander Lord Ashley had no notion that Sidi al-Nasir was in the pay of the Poles. He had got himself into debt at the *Manzana de Oro,* and the Sidi had threatened to inform you of that fact. What would you have done, Captain Smollett, if you had been so informed? Would you have cashiered the Commander?"

"Doubt it," said Smollett. "Would have had him transferred, of course. Can't have a man who gambles that way in Intelligence work. I don't object to gambling in itself, my lord; but a man should only gamble what he has—not upon his expectations."

"Exactly," said Lord Darcy. "I quite understand. There would, however, have been a black mark upon his record? He would have had little chance to rise above his present rank?"

"Little chance, my lord? I should say none whatever. Couldn't give a man Captain's stripes with a mark like that against him."

Lord Darcy nodded. "Of course not. And Ashley knew that. He had to do something to pay off Sidi al-Nasir. So he concocted this fantastic scheme to pry money out of a man whom he knew to be a Polish agent. As His Grace the Archbishop of York remarked to me yesterday, there is no evil in this man. There is, as you can see, only desperation. I think we can believe his statement that he would not willingly betray King and Country.

"Had Sidi al-Nasir made his proposition to My Lord Commander two weeks ago, or even only a week ago, none of this would have happened. It is my personal opinion that if al-Nasir had asked Lord Ashley to pay off his debt by betraying his country before tonight, his lordship's facile mind would have come up with the same lie that he told me this evening, except, Captain Smollett, that he would have told it to you.

"What would you have said if—say, a week ago—the Commander had come to you and told you that, by deliberately going into debt, he had trapped the head of the local Polish spy ring into betraying himself? That he, Commander Ashley, had been asked to become a double agent and could now become—if the term is proper—a triple agent? Be honest, Captain, what would you have said?"

Captain Smollett looked at his knees for what seemed a long time. The others in the room seemed to be holding their breaths, waiting. When Captain Smollett raised his eyes it was to look at the Marquis de London rather than at Lord Darcy. "If it please the Court, my lord," he said slowly. There was pain in his eyes. "I am forced to admit that had things come about the way Lord Darcy has just outlined them, I should have believed Commander Lord Ashley's story. I should very likely have recommended him for promotion."

At that moment, the door opened, and Father Patrique came in. He was followed by Commander Lord Ashley, whose face was pale and whose wrists were encased in padded shackles. In the rear came the watchful-eyed Chief Master-at-Arms Hennely Grayme, his pistol holstered, but his hand ready.

"My Lord justice," the priest said gravely, "it is my duty to request the attention of the Court."

"The Court recognizes the Reverend Father Patrique as *amicus curia*," the Marquis rumbled.

"My Lord justice," the good Father said, "My Lord Ashley, a Commander of the Imperial Navy of Our Most Dread Sovereign the King, wishes, of his own free will, to make a statement and deposition before this Court."

The Marquis de London glanced once at Lord Bontriomphe, who was taking down everything in his notebook, then back at Lord Ashley.

"You may proceed," he said.

CHAPTER 23

Forty minutes later, Lord Bontriomphe looked over his shorthand notes and nodded thoughtfully. "That winds it up," he said. "That covers everything."

Commander Lord Ashley was gone, to be escorted to the Tower by Chief Hennely and a squad of Armsmen. The Court of Inquiry had been officially adjourned.

My lord the Marquis surveyed the room and then looked at Lord Darcy. "Except for a few minor details in what was said, you gave us the story of Ashley's activities quite accurately. Satisfactory. I might say, *most* satisfactory." He looked around at the others, "Does anyone have any questions?"

"I have a question," said Sir Lyon Gandolphus Grey. He looked at Lord Darcy. "If I may, my lord, I should like to know why you were sure that there was no direct link between Master Ewen MacAlister and Commander Lord Ashley."

Lord Darcy smiled. "I couldn't be absolutely certain, of course, Sir Lyon. But it seemed most probable. Master Ewen was doing his best to get the Damoselle Tia to worm the secret out of Sir Thomas Leseaux. Would he have tried so hard if he had known that Lord Ashley was willing to sell it? Or, rather, claimed he had it to sell? That would have been much simpler than trying to get a stubborn child to betray everything she loved."

"But how did you know she wasn't a willing spy?" Sir Thomas asked.

"There were several reasons," said Lord Darcy. "Of course, ecclesiastical commissions had twice given her a clean bill, but there were other indications. She had gone to Sir James and argued with him, and that was hardly the behavior of a spy. A spy would have acted immediately, not argued and walked out. And a well-trained spy does not—as Tia did— throw a note from one of her fellow agents into a waste-basket and forget about it. Also—while there was the possibility that the conversation in the *Hound and Hare* might have been an act put on for my benefit—the subsequent attempt to do away with her was a strong indication that it was not. Therefore, she had, as she said then, actually intended to tell everything to the King's Officers."

The Dowager Duchess of Cumberland said: "Ironic, isn't it, that while all the Armsmen of London and half the Imperial Navy have been struggling to discover one man's identity, that letter was actually here all the time, in that envelope."

Lord Darcy reached out for the blue envelope on Lord Bontriomphe's desk, where Captain Smollett had placed it. He held it up. "You mean this?" he asked rather apologetically. "I am afraid it wouldn't have done us much good to look for that information here."

"Why not?" the Dowager Duchess frowned. "Because of the spells?"

"Oh, no," said Lord Darcy. "Because of the fact that this envelope and its contents did not exist until an hour or so ago.

"The handwriting, while a passable imitation of Georges Barbour's, is actually my own. I had a chance to study Barbour's hand thoroughly yesterday afternoon at the Admiralty Office.

"You see, I wanted Ashley's confession. We actually had very little evidence. I knew *what* he had done, and *how* he had done it, by reasoned deduction. There is, of course, the evidence of the blood in his jacket pocket and in his sword sheath, but we couldn't count on its being there. We needed more than that.

"So—this letter came into being. After all, you see, Ashley couldn't have been *certain* that the information from Barbour had been sent to the hotel. Since I knew that he had opened the envelope from the hotel at his first opportunity, I also knew that what he found were blank sheets of paper. He had no way of being sure that those sheets had contained the information that was so dangerous to him.

"The letter was a necessary deception, I think—and if you will cast your mind back, Captain Smollett, you will recall that I did not once tell you that the letter had actually come from Barbour."

"So you didn't," said Captain Smollett. "So you didn't."

"Well, my lords, Your Grace, gentlemen," the Marquis de London said, "this has been a rather strenuous night. I suggest we can make the best use of what is left of it by getting some sleep."

The eight guests left the Palace du Marquis in a body. With the exception of Captain Smollett, they were all headed for Carlyle House.

There had been still another guest present, Lord Darcy knew, a guest who would remain behind until the others had left.

Behind the Vandenbosch reproduction in My Lord Marquis' office was a sliding panel, and beyond that a small alcove. When the panel was open, anyone sitting in that darkened alcove could see through the cloth of the painting and observe and hear everything that took place.

Only the Marquis, Lord Bontriomphe, and Lord Darcy had known that someone had been in that alcove during the official inquiry which had resulted in the arrest of a killer, but it was not until some two months later, in Rouen, that Lord Darcy heard anything further from that hidden observer.

A package was delivered to Lord Darcy's residence by a King's Messenger. It was not a large package, but it was fairly heavy. There was a note with it which read:

My Lord Darcy:
Again we are indebted to you for your brilliant work

*in the protection of Our Realm. We understand that you
were so unfortunate as to lose the valuable .40 caliber
MacGregor which you so obligingly used for the demonstration at Westminster.*

*Since we deem it fitting that any weapon of this
kind worn in Our presence should be Our gift, We are
sending you this package.*

*We would have you understand however, that it is
not a purely ceremonial weapon, but is to be used in
the course of your duties. If We hear that it is hanging on the wall of your trophy room in a golden frame,
or other such foolishness, We will personally come over
there and take it away from you.*

JIVR

Inside the box lay what was probably MacGregor's finest creation: a handcrafted, man-stopping, .40 caliber handgun. The gold and enamel work on it made it as beautiful
as it was deadly. On both sides of the butt, in hard enamel,
were Lord Darcy's personal arms: *Ermine, on a fess gules,
a lion passant gardant or.* In the golden tracery work surrounding the shield were the lions of England and the lilies of France.

PART TWO

A Stretch of the Imagination

Late afternoon is not a usual time for suicide, but in Lord Arlen's case, it appeared that his death could hardly be attributable to any other cause.

Lord Arlen was the owner and head of one of the most important publishing houses in Normandy, Mayard House. Its editorial offices occupied the whole of a rather large building located in the heart of the Old City, not too far from the Cathedral of St. Ouen. On the day of the Vigil of the Feast of St. Edward the Confessor, Thursday, October 12, 1972, Lord Arlen was in his private office, sound asleep. He was accustomed to taking a nap at that time, and staff were well aware of it, so they moved quietly and spoke in low tones and only when necessary. No one had gone in or out of his office for nearly an hour.

At five minutes past four, three members of staff— Damoselle Barbara, and Goodmen Wober and Andray—heard an odd thump and further strange noises through the thick door of the private office. They all hesitated and looked at each other. They felt that something was wrong, but not one of them quite dared to open that door, fearing Lord Arlen's temper.

Within thirty seconds, Sir Stefan Imbry came charging into the room. "What's happened?" he barked. "I was in the library. Heard a noise. Chair falling, I think. Now it sounds as though my lord is being sick at his stomach." He didn't pause as he spoke, but went straight to the door of the inner office. The staff members felt a momentary sense of relief; only Chief Editor Sir Stefan would dare break in on Lord Arlen.

He flung open the door and stopped suddenly. "Good God!" he said in a strangled voice. Then, to staff, "Quickly! Help me!"

Lord Arlen was hanging by his neck from a rope that had been thrown over a massive wooden beam. He was still twitching. Below his feet was an overturned chair.

He was still just barely alive when they took him down, but his larynx had been crushed, and he died before medical aid or a Healer could be summoned.

Lord Darcy, Chief Criminal Investigator for His Royal Highness, Richard, Duke of Normandy, looked down at the small and rather pitiful body that lay on the office couch. Lord Arlen had been a short man—five-four—and weighed nine stone. In death, he no longer showed the driving, fanatical, and—at times—almost hysterical energy that had made him one of the most feared and respected men in his field. Now he looked like a boy in his teens.

Dr. Pateley, the Chirurgeon, had finished his examination of the body and looked up at Lord Darcy. "Master Sean and I can give you more accurate information after the autopsy, my lord, but I'd say he's been dead between half an hour and forty-five minutes." He smoothed his gray hair and adjusted his pince-nez glasses. "That fits in with the time your office was notified, my lord."

"Indeed it does," murmured Lord Darcy. "Master Sean? How goes it?"

Master Sean O Lochlainn, Chief Forensic Sorcerer to His Highness, was busy with a small golden wand which had a curious spiral pattern inscribed upon its gleaming surface. It is not wise to interrupt a magician while he is working, but Lord Darcy sensed that the tubby little Irish sorcerer had finished his work and was merely musing.

He was right. Master Sean turned, a half smile on his round face. "Well, me lord, I haven't had time for a complete analysis, but the facts stand out very clearly." He twirled the wand in his fingers. "There was no one else in the room at the time he died, me lord, and hadn't been for an hour. Time of death was fourteen minutes after four, give or take a minute. The time of the psychic shock of the hanging itself was five after. No evil influence in the room; no sign of Black Magic."

"Thank you, my good Sean," Lord Darcy said, his eyes focused upon the overhead beam. "As always, your evidence is invaluable."

His lordship turned to the fourth man in the room, Master-at-Arms Gwiliam de Lisles, a large, beefy, tough-looking man with huge black mustaches and the mind of a keen investigator.

"Master Gwiliam," Lord Darcy said, "would you have one of your men fetch me a ladder that can reach that beam?" He gestured upward.

"Immediately, my lord."

Two uniformed Men-at-Arms were given instructions, and the ladder was brought. Lord Darcy, with a powerful magnifying lens in his hand, climbed up the ladder to the heavy beam, ten feet above the floor, two and a half feet below the ceiling.

The rope which had hanged Lord Arlen was still in place, and Lord Darcy examined the beam and the rope itself very carefully.

Master Sean, staring upward with his blue Irish eyes, said: "May I ask what it is you might be looking for, me lord?"

"As you see," Lord Darcy said, still scrutinizing the wood, "the rope goes up over the beam, here, and is held firmly at the far end, tied to the pipe that runs just below the window behind the desk. It might be possible that Lord Arlen was strangled, the rope put about his neck, and hauled up to the position in which he was found. In that case, the friction of the rope against the wood would displace the fibers of both in an upward and backward direction. But—" He sighed and began climbing back down the ladder. "But no. The evidence is that he actually did drop from the end of that rope and was hanged."

"Would there have been time, my lord," Master Gwiliam asked, "to have hauled him up like that?"

"Possibly not, my dear Master Gwiliam, but every bit of evidence must be checked. If the fibers had showed friction the other direction, we might have been forced to recheck the timing."

"Thank you, my lord," said the plainclothes Master-at-Arms.

Lord Darcy went over to check the other end of the rope.

There was only one window in the office. Lord Arlen had liked dimness and quiet in his office, and one window was enough for him. It was directly behind his desk, and opened into a three-foot-wide air shaft that let in hardly any light, even at high noon. For illumination, his lordship had depended upon the usual gaslights, even in the daytime. They were all alight, but Lord Darcy, being his usual suspicious self, had sniffed the air for any signs of raw gas. There were none. Gas had nothing to do with the problem.

The window itself was of the usual double-hung type. To provide air flow, the upper lite was open about three inches. It was a high, narrow window, and the top of the casing was nine feet above the floor. The bottom pane was open about eight inches, and the end of the rope ran through it to tie to an exterior pipe about six inches from the bottom of the sill. It slanted up to the beam near the ceiling, and dropped to its fatal end.

A careful examination showed that the window had not been opened any farther than it was now; the whole apparatus had been varnished at least twice, and the varnish in the joints and cracks had almost sealed the window lites in place. That window hadn't been opened fully for years.

"Eight inches at the bottom and three inches at the top," Lord Darcy said thoughtfully. "Hardly enough room for a man to crawl through. And, aside from the door, there are no other ways in or out of this room." He looked at Master Sean. "None?"

"None, me lord," said the round little Irish sorcerer. "Master Gwiliam and meself have checked that over thoroughly. There's no hidden passages, no secret panels. Nothing of the like." He paused a moment, then said: "But there's no gloom."

Lord Darcy's gray eyes narrowed. "No gloom, Master Sean? Pray elucidate."

"Well, me lord, in a suicide's room, there is always a sense of gloom, of deep depression, permeating the walls. The kind of mental state a man has to be in to do away with himself nearly always leaves that kind of psychic impression. But there's no trace of that here."

"Indeed?" His lordship made a mental note. His gray eyes surveyed the room once more. "Very well. Cast a preservative spell over the body, Master Sean; I shall go out and get information from the witnesses."

"As you say, me lord," said Master Sean.

Lord Darcy headed for the library. "Come with me, Master Gwiliam," he said as he opened the door. The big Master-at-Arms followed.

In the library, five people were waiting, guarded by two husky Men-at-Arms wearing the black-and-silver uniforms of Keepers of the King's Peace. Three of the five were staff: the brown-haired, dark-eyed Damoselle Barbara; the round-faced, balding Goodman Wober; the lanky, near-sighted Goodman Andray. The fourth was Chief Editor Sir Stefan Imbry, a powerful, six-foot-four giant of a man. The fifth—a bull-like brute with a hard, handsome face— was one that Lord Darcy did not know.

Sir Stefan came to his feet. "My lord, may I ask why we are being held here? I have a dinner engagement, and these others wish to go home. Why should His Royal Highness the Duke send your lordship to investigate such a routine business, anyway?"

"It's the law," said Lord Darcy, "as you, Sir Stefan, should well know. When a member of the aristocracy dies by violence—whether intentional, accidental, or self-inflicted— it is mandatory that I enter the case. As for why you are being held here: I am an Officer of the King's Justice."

Sir Stefan paled a trifle.

Not out of fear, but out of profound respect. His Majesty, John IV, by the Grace of God, King and Emperor of England, France, Scotland, Ireland, New England and New France, King of the Romans and Emperor of the Holy Roman Empire, Defender of the Faith, was the latest of the long line of Plantagenet kings who had ruled the Anglo-French Empire since the time of Henry II.

The reminder that Lord Darcy was a Royal Officer cooled even Sir Stefan Imbry's ire.

"Of course, my lord," he said in a controlled voice. "I was merely asking for information."

"And that is all I am doing, Sir Stefan," Lord Darcy said gently. "I am collecting information." He gestured. "My duty."

"Certainly, certainly," Imbry said hurriedly, and rather abashedly. "No offense intended." Imbry was used to giving orders around Mayard House, but he knew when to defer to a superior.

"And none taken," Lord Darcy said. "Now, as to information, who is this gentleman?" He indicated the fifth member of the waiting group, the heavily muscled, hard-faced, handsome man with the dark, curly hair.

Sir Stefan Imbry made the formal introduction as the man in question stood up. "My Lord Darcy, may I present Goodman Ernesto Norman, one of our finest authors. Goodman Ernesto, Lord Darcy, Chief Investigator for His Royal Highness."

Ernesto looked at Lord Darcy with smoldering brown eyes and gave a medium bow. "An honor, your lordship."

"The honor is mine," said Lord Darcy. "I have read several of your books. One day, if you are of a mind, I should like to discuss them with you."

"A pleasure, your lordship," Goodman Ernesto said as he sat down. But there was an undertone of surliness in his voice.

Lord Darcy looked about the huge room. It was richly appointed and spacious; the walls beneath an eighteen-foot ceiling were lined with well-filled bookcases ten feet high. Above the bookcases, the walls were decorated with swords, battleaxes, maces, and shields of various designs. Several helms sat upright on the top of the bookcases. Flanking the door were two suits of sixteenth-century armor, each holding in one gauntlet a fifteen-foot cavalry lance. The window draperies were heavy dark green velvet; the gas lamps were intricately shaped and gold plated.

The pause to survey the room was filled with silence. Lord Darcy had firmly established his authority.

He looked at Sir Stefan. "I know that you have gone through this several times already, but I must ask you to repeat it again—" He glanced briefly at the other four. "—all of you."

Master-at-Arms Gwiliam, standing near the door, unobtrusively took out his notebook to record the entire conversation in shorthand.

Sir Stefan Imbry looked grim and said: "I don't see the reason for such fuss over a suicide, my lord, but it seems—"

"It *was* not *suicide!*" Damoselle Barbara's voice seemed to snap through the air.

Sir Stefan jerked his head around and looked at her angrily, but before he could speak, Lord Darcy said: "Let her speak, Sir Stefan!" Then, more softly: "Upon what do you base that statement, Damoselle?"

There were tears in her eyes, and she looked extraordinarily beautiful as she said, in a soft voice: "No material evidence. Nothing concrete that I could prove. But—as is well known—I have been My Lord Arlen's mistress for over a year. I know him. He would never have killed himself."

"I see," Lord Darcy said. "Do you have the Talent, Damoselle?"

"To a slight degree," she said calmly. "I have been tested for it. My Talent is above normal, but not markedly so."

"I understand," Lord Darcy said. "Then you have no evidence to give except your knowledge of his late lordship and your intuition?"

"None, my lord," she said in a subdued voice.

"Very well. I thank you, Damoselle Barbara. And now, Sir Stefan, if you will continue with your recitation."

Sir Stefan had calmed down, but Lord Darcy noticed that Ernesto Norman had given the Damoselle Barbara a suppressed glare of hatred.

Jealousy, Lord Darcy thought. *Hard jealousy. A stupid reaction. The man needs a Healer.*

Sir Stefan, looming tall and strong, began his story for the third time.

"At approximately half-past two . . ."

At approximately half-past two, Lord Arlen had come in from having luncheon at the Mayson du Shah and ignored a spiteful look from the Damoselle Barbara. She had been brought up in the north of England by rather straitlaced parents and did not understand that it was perfectly permissible for a gentleman to go to the Mayson du Shah for nothing but luncheon. She was used to the more staid English gentlemen's clubs of York or Carlisle.

"Where's Sir Stefan?" he snapped at Goodman Andray.

"Not come back from lunch yet, my lord," Andray said.

"Any other business waiting?"

"Goodman Ernesto is waiting for you, my lord. In the library."

"Ernesto Norman? He can wait. I'll let you know. Send Sir Stefan in as soon as he comes back."

Lord Arlen had stalked into his office.

At half-past two, he had bellowed sharply: "Barbara!"

She had, according to her testimony, said "Yes, my lord," and rushed into the inner office. He had, she said, been seated behind his desk. It was an impressive desk, some seven feet long by three feet wide. Behind it, Lord Arlen seemed impressively tall as he sat in his chair—for the very simple reason that his chair was elevated an extra six inches, and he had a six-inch-high footstool hidden beneath the desk. Anyone who sat in the guest chair, unless he was exceedingly tall, had to look up at Lord Arlen.

The Damoselle Barbara had, she said, gone into the office and stood at attention, as was proper, and said: "You called, my lord?"

Without looking up from the manuscript he was reading, he said, "Yes, my love, I did. Send in Ernesto."

"Yes, my lord." And she had gone to fetch the waiting author.

Goodman Ernesto Norman had been waiting in the library. Notified by the Damoselle Barbara that Lord Arlen would see him, he had strode angrily out, down the hall, and around to his lordship's office, and had walked in without knocking, slamming the door behind him.

Norman's testimony was: "I was ready to strangle the little jerk, my lord. Or slap him silly. Whichever was the handiest. I'd just read the galley proofs of my latest novel, *A Knight of the Armies.* The beak-faced little name-of-a-dog had *butchered* it! I told him I wouldn't have it published that way. He told me that he'd bought the rights and I had nothing to say about it. We exchanged words, I lost the argument, and I walked out."

The staff admitted that they had heard sharp voices, but none of them had heard any of the words.

Goodman Ernesto had slammed out of the inner office at fifteen minutes of three.

Sir Stefan Imbry had walked into the outer office as Norman had stormed out of the inner. The two ignored each other as Norman went on out.

"What the devil's eating him?" Sir Stefan had asked.

"Don't know, Sir Stefan," Goodman Wober had said.

"His lordship asked you to report immediately you came in, sir."

Sir Stefan's testimony was that he had gone immediately into the office, where Lord Arlen was drinking caffe—which had been brought to him by Goodman Andray a few minutes before.

"It was just a short business conference, my lord," Sir Stefan said. "I was given instructions to the format of three books we will be publishing. Entirely routine stuff, but if you want the details, my lord . . ."

"Later, perhaps. Pray continue."

"I left his office at a minute or two after three. He always naps from three to four. I went to the Art Department to check on some book illustrations, then came in here to the library to do some research, checking some of the points in a book on magic we're publishing in the spring."

"A scholarly work?" Lord Darcy asked.

"It is. *Psychologistics* by Sir Thomas Leseaux, Th.D."

"Ah! An excellent man. Master Sean will be eager to obtain a copy."

Sir Stefan nodded. "The firm will be happy to supply him with two copies. Perhaps—" His eyes brightened. "Perhaps Master Sean would consent to review it for the Rouen *Times*?"

"He might, if you approached him properly," Lord Darcy murmured. Then, more briskly: "You were here in the library, then, sir, when Lord Arlen was hanged?"

"I was, my lord."

"May I ask, then, how it was that you were apprised of the fact?" Lord Darcy was fairly certain that he knew the answer to the question, but he wanted to hear Sir Stefan's answer. "You were in the outer office, apparently, within seconds after the—ah—unfortunate incident. How did you know of it?"

"I heard the noise, my lord," said Sir Stefan. He pointed toward a window on the north, shrouded with green velvet. As he pointed, he rose to his feet. "That window, my lord, opens directly to the air shaft."

He went over and moved the curtains aside. "As you see."

The air shaft outside the window was three feet wide. A yard away was the window of Lord Arlen's office. The window itself was partially open at top and bottom, as his lordship had noted previously. So was the library window. Lord Darcy tested it. Unlike the window in Lord Arlen's office, the lites slid up and down easily; they had not been varnished over.

"Master Sean?" Lord Darcy called in a normal conversational tone.

The Irish sorcerer's round face appeared from between the closed curtains on the other side. "Aye, me lord?"

"All going well?"

"Quite well, me lord."

"Very good. Carry on."

Lord Darcy drew the curtains to, turned, and faced the others in the flickering gaslight. "Very well, Sir Stefan; that explains that. One more question."

"Yes, my lord?"

"Why was it that when you rushed in to Lord Arlen's office and found him hanging—you did not cut him down? A simple flick of a pocketknife would have released the strangling tension of the rope around his throat, would it not? Instead, *you untied the knot. Why?*"

It was the Damoselle Barbara who answered. "You didn't know, my lord?"

Lord Darcy had expected that all eyes would have gone to Sir Stefan; instead, they had come to him. He recovered quickly.

"Elucidate, Damoselle," he said calmly.

"Lord Arlen was deathly afraid of sharp instruments," the girl said. "It was an obsession with him. He never went to the Art Department, for instance, because of the razor-sharp instruments they use for making paste-ups, and that sort of thing."

Lord Darcy's eyes narrowed. "He was, I believe, smooth-shaven?"

"Smooth, yes," she answered calmly. "Shaven, no. His barber used a depilatory wax which pulled the hairs out by the roots. It was painful, but he preferred it to being approached by a razor. He would not permit anyone near him to even carry a knife. We all obeyed."

"Not even a letter opener?" Lord Darcy asked.

"Not even a letter opener," she said. She gestured toward the walls above the bookcases that lined the room. "Look at those ancient weapons. Not one of them has an edge or a sharp point. Does that answer your question about Sir Stefan's cutting down My Lord Arlen?"

"Quite adequately, Damoselle," said Lord Darcy with a slight bow.

Great God! he thought. *They all seem a little mad, and their late employer was the maddest of them all.*

Seven o'clock. Nearly three hours had passed since Lord Arlen had died. Outside, the sky was dark and clouded, and the air held an autumn chill. Inside, in Lord Arlen's office, the gas lamps and the fireplace gave the room a summery warmth. The body of Lord Arlen, covered by a blanket and a preservative spell, rested silently.

Sean O Lochlainn, Master Sorcerer, stood in the soft gaslight and eyed the end of the fatal rope. Behind him, respectfully silent, stood Lord Darcy, Dr. Pateley, and Master-at-Arms Gwiliam.

After a moment, Master Sean bent over, opened his large, symbol-decorated carpetbag, and took out several items, including a silver-tipped ebon wand.

"There's no difficulty here, my lord," Master Sean said. "The psychic shock of sudden death has charged the hemp quite strongly." Master Sean liked to lecture, and when he assumed his pedagogical manner, his brogue faded to paleness. "The Law of Relevance is involved here; scientifically speaking, we have here a psychic force field which, given the proper impetus, will tend to return to its former state."

Then his wand moved in intricate curves, and his lips formed certain ritual syllables.

Gently, gracefully, the rope began to move. As if an unseen hand were guiding it, the hempen twist made itself into a loop. Quickly, smoothly, it tied itself. For half a second, it hung in the air, an almost perfect circle. Then, suddenly, it drooped limply.

"There you are, my lord," said Master Sean with a gesture.

Lord Darcy walked over and looked at the looped and knotted rope without touching it. "Interesting. A simple slip knot, not a hangman's knot." Without looking up, he added: "Master Gwiliam, may I borrow your measuring tape?"

The burly Master-at-Arms unclipped his tape measure from his belt and handed it to his lordship.

Lord Darcy measured the distance from the floor to the noose. Then he measured the overturned chair from the leg to the seat. Then, with all due reverence, he measured the corpse from heel to neck.

Finally, he said: "Dr. Pateley, you are the lightest of us, I think. What is your weight?"

"Ten stone, my lord," said the chirurgeon. "Perhaps a pound or two under."

"You'll do, Doctor. Grab hold of that rope and put your weight on it."

Dr. Pateley blinked. "My lord?"

"Take hold of the rope above the noose and lift your feet off the floor. That's it." He measured again. "Less than a quarter of an inch of stretch. That's negligible. You may let go now, Doctor. Thank, you."

Lord Darcy handed Master-at-Arms Gwiliam his tape measure back.

Lord Darcy tilted his head back and looked up at the overhead beam which held the rope. "A singularly foolish thing to do," he said, almost to himself.

"That's true, my lord," said Master Gwiliam. "I've always considered suicide to be a very foolish act. Besides, as someone once said, 'It's so *per*manent.' "

"I am not speaking of suicide, but of murder, my good Master-at-Arms. And it is equally permanent."

"Murder, me lord?" Master Sean O Lochlainn raised his eyebrows. "Well, if you say so. It's glad I am that I am not in the detective business."

"But you are, my dear Sean," Lord Darcy said with some surprise.

Master Sean grinned and shook his round Irish head. "No, me lord. I am a sorcerer. I'm a technician who digs up facts that ordinary observation wouldn't discover. But all the clues in the world don't help a man if he can't put them together to form a coherent whole. And that is your touch of the Talent, my lord."

"*I?*" Lord Darcy looked even more surprised. "I have no Talent, Sean. I'm no thaumaturge."

"Now, come, me lord. You have that touch of the Talent that all the really great detectives of history have had—the ability to leap from an unwarranted assumption to a foregone conclusion without covering the distance between the two. You then know where to look for the clues that will justify your conclusion. You knew it was murder two hours ago, and you knew who did it."

"Well, of course! Those two points were obvious from the start. The question was not 'Who did it?' but 'How was it done?'" His lordship smiled broadly. "And now, naturally, the answer to that last question is plain as a pikestaff!"

"How are you so certain it was murder, my lord?" asked Master Gwiliam.

"For one thing, the measurements we have just made show that the late Lord Arlen's feet were seventeen inches off the ground when he was hanged. The seat of the chair is but eighteen inches from the floor. If—I say if—he had put up that noose and then kicked the chair away, he would have dropped one inch. He would have been strangled, surely, no question of that. But you have seen the cruel marks of that deeply imbedded rope in the throat of his late lordship, and you have heard Dr. Pateley testify that the larynx was crushed. By the by, Doctor, was the neck broken?"

"No, my lord," said the chirurgeon. "Badly dislocated—stretched, as it were—but not broken."

"He was a light man," Lord Darcy continued. "Nine stone. A drop of one inch could not have done all that damage." He looked at Master Sean. "Therefore, you see, it didn't happen that way. All that was necessary was to use one's imagination to see how it might have happened, and then check the evidence to see if it did happen that way. The final step is to check the evidence to make sure it could not have happened any other way. Having done that, we shall be ready to make our arrest."

Fifteen minutes later, Lord Darcy, Master Sean, and Master Gwiliam entered the library, where four Men-at-Arms held the five suspects under guard. Master Sean, his symbol-decorated carpetbag in hand, stopped at the door, flanked by the pair of standing suits of armor with their fifteen-foot spears.

Sir Stefan Imbry, who had been reading a book, let it drop to the floor and stood up. "How much longer has this got to go on, Lord Darcy?" he asked angrily.

"Only a few minutes, Sir Stefan. We have nearly completed

our investigation." All the eyes in the room, except for Master Sean's, were on his lordship.

Sir Stefan sighed. "Good. I'm glad it's over with, my lord. There will have to be a Coroner's Inquest, of course. I do hope the jury will be kind enough to bring in a verdict of 'Suicide while of unsound mind.' "

"I do not," said Lord Darcy. "It is my fond belief that they will decide that it was an act of premeditated murder and that they pray the Court of the King's High justice to try Sir Stefan Imbry for the crime."

Sir Stefan paled. "Are you mad?"

"Only at times. And this is not one of them."

The Damoselle Barbara gasped and said: "But Sir Stefan was nowhere near the office at the time!"

"Oh, but he was, Damoselle. He was here, in this room, alone, scarcely a dozen feet from where Lord Arlen was hanged. The whole procedure was quite simple. He went into Lord Arlen's office and slipped a drug into Lord Arlen's caffe. It is one of the more powerful, quick acting drugs. Within a few minutes, his lordship was unconscious. He affixed the rope to the pipe outside the window, threw the other end over the beam, and tied that end around Lord Arlen's neck in a slip knot."

"But the little snot wasn't hanged till an hour later," Goodman Ernesto Norman interrupted.

"True. Let me finish. Sir Stefan then put the unfortunate Lord Arlen's unconscious body *up on that beam.*"

"Just a minute, your lordship," Goodman Ernesto interrupted again. "I have no love for Sir Stefan particularly, but, tall as he is, he couldn't have lifted Lord Arlen ten feet in the air, even if he stood on the chair. And there was no ladder in the office."

"An acute observation, Goodman Ernesto. But you failed to take into account the fact that there was another chair in the room. Lord Arlen's desk chair is a full twenty-four inches high, as opposed to the normal eighteen."

"An extra six inches?" Ernesto Norman shook his head. "Still wouldn't have done it. He'd need at least another six—" He stopped suddenly. His eyes widened. "The foot-stool!"

"Exactly," Lord Darcy said. "Put that on top of the chair, and you have your needed six inches. I could almost do it myself, and Sir Stefan is taller than I. And nine stone is no great load for a strong man to lift."

"Even supposing I had done all that," said Sir Stefan through ashen lips, but with a controlled voice, "what am I supposed to have done next?"

"Why, my dear fellow, you left the office—after replacing the desk chair and footstool behind the desk. And after quietly putting the guest chair on its side. Then you went out and did what you told us you did, knowing that no one would disturb Lord Arlen after three o'clock."

"But we heard the chair fall at four!" the Damoselle Barbara said in a hushed voice.

"No. By your own testimony, you heard a thump. But it was Sir Stefan's statement that he heard the chair fall that influenced your thinking. The thump you heard was the sound of the beam when the shock of Lord Arlen's body, dropping nearly four feet, slammed that rope against the wood."

The Damoselle Barbara closed her eyes and shuddered. The other two members of staff just sat silently and stared.

"You waited for an hour, Sir Stefan. Then, at four o'clock, you—"

Lord Darcy stopped as he got a signal from Master Sean. "Yes, Master Sean?"

"This one, me lord. Definite." He jerked a thumb toward the suit of armor standing to the left of the door.

"That completes the investigation," Lord Darcy said with a hard smile. "You, Sir Stefan, took that fifteen-foot spear, which—like every other weapon in here—has no edge or point, and used it to push Lord Arlen's body off the beam. Then you put the spear back in the gauntlet of the empty armor and went running to the office. You knew it would take some time to untie the knot, and you knew that by that time Arlen would be dead.

"But the whole thing was incredibly stupid. You were up against a dilemma. The problem was the length of the rope. If he dropped too far, his neck would break, and that would be inconsistent with an eighteen-inch chair. But if he only dropped far enough to strangle himself, his feet would have been higher off the floor than the seat of the chair. So you tried a middle road. But the stupid thing was that you did not see that the physical evidence could not, in any case, be reconciled."

Lord Darcy turned to Master Gwiliam. "Master-at-Arms Gwiliam de Lisle, I, as an Officer of the King's justice, request that you, as an Officer of the King's Peace, arrest this man upon suspicion of murder."

As the Men-at-Arms took the broken Sir Stefan off, the shocked Damoselle Barbara said: "But *why*, my lord? Why did he do it?"

"I checked at the Records Office on Lord Arlen's will before I came here," Lord Darcy told her. "He left half his interest in the firm to you, and half to Sir Stefan. He wanted control. Now you will get it all."

The Damoselle Barbara began to cry.

But Lord Darcy noticed that Goodman Ernesto Norman had a half smile on his face, as though he were thinking, *Now I can get my novel published the way I wrote it.*

Lord Darcy sighed. "Come, Master Sean. We have an appointment for dinner, and the hour grows late."

A Matter of Gravity

The death of My Lord Jillbert, Count de la Vexin was nothing if not spectacular.

His lordship lived and worked in Castle Gisors, which towers over the town of the same name, the capital of the County of the Vexin in the eastern part of the Duchy of Normandy. The basic structure of the ancient fortress has been there since the Eleventh Century although it has been added to and partly rebuilt since.

De la Vexin had succeeded to the County Seat in 1951, and had governed the Vexin wisely and well. He had a son, a daughter, and a hobby.

It was a combination of all these that killed him.

On the night of April 11, 1974, after attending the Mass of Holy Thursday, My Lord of the Vexin ascended the helical stairway that wound itself around the inside of the Red Tower, followed by two trusted sergeants of the Count's Own Guard—who were, in turn, followed by a four-man squad of ordinary guardsmen.

This was My Lord Count's regular procedure when he went to his *sanctum sanctorum* on the top floor of the Red Tower. When he went up there, eighty feet above the flagstoned courtyard, he wanted no interruptions while he attended to his avocation.

At one minute of ten, he entered his private rooms, leaving his guardsmen outside. No one but himself had been authorized to enter the uppermost room of the Red Tower in twenty years.

He dropped the heavy bar after locking the door, completely sealing the room.

Only two people saw him alive again, and then only for a matter of seconds.

Across the wide, flagstoned courtyard from the Red Tower stood St. Martin's Hall, a new addition built in the early Sixteenth Century, as its Ricardian style attested. Its great mullioned windows cast a warm, yellowed light on the courtyard outside; the hall was brightly illuminated from within, and would remain so all night, for there was a vigil at the Altar of Repose in the Lady Chapel.

Inside, a small fire crackled in the enormous fireplace— just enough blaze to take the slight chill from the air of a pleasant spring evening. On the mantelpiece, a large clock swung its pendulum as the minute hand moved inexorably upward to mark the hour of ten.

Lord Gisors, the only son of de la Vexin, poured himself another glass of Xerez. Of average height, his blocky, not unhandsome face was almost a younger replica of his father's, except that he had his mother's near-black hair and dark brown eyes instead of the brown-and-blue combination of his father. He turned from the sideboard, still holding the unstoppered decanter. "Care for another, my dear?"

The girl seated in the big easy chair in front of the fireplace smiled. "Please." With her right hand, she held out her glass, while her left brushed the long fair hair back from her brow. *She looks beautiful,* his lordship thought.

Lord Gisors poured, then walked back to the sideboard with the decanter. As he put the glass stopple back in, he began: "You mustn't think badly of My Lord father, Madelaine, even though he is a bit testy at times. He—"

"I know," she interrupted. "I know. He thinks only of the County. Never of individuals."

Frowning slightly, his lordship came back with his glass and sat down in another easy chair near her. "But he does think of individuals, my love. He must think of every individual in the Vexin—as I must when I succeed to the County Seat. He has to take the long view and the broad view, naturally, but he *is* concerned about individuals."

She sipped at her glass of wine, then looked up at him with solemn gray eyes. "Does his concern for individuals include you? Or me? He knows we love each other, but he forbids our marriage, and insists that you marry Lady Evelynne de Saint-Brieuc—in spite of the fact that you do not love her nor she you. Is that concern for the individual or simply the desire to make an advantageous political marriage for you?"

Lord Gisors closed his eyes and held his tongue for a moment. The two of them had been over and over this ground many times; there was nothing new here. He had explained many times that, whereas My Lord the Count could forbid a marriage, he could not force one. Gisors had even reiterated time and again that he could appeal his case for marriage to His Royal Highness of Normandy, and, if that failed, to His Imperial Majesty—but that he would not do so out of deference to his father. His head seemed to ache at the monotony of "time and again."

He had not, of course, mentioned his own plans for marrying Madelaine without all the rigamarole. She might very likely rebel at the notion.

He opened his eyes again. "Be patient, my darling. I can assure you that he will—"

"—Come round to your way of thinking?" she cut in. "Never! The only time the Count de la Vexin will give his consent to our marriage will be when *you* are Count de la Vexin! Your father—"

"*Quiet!*" Lord Gisors said in an imperative undertone. "*My sister.*"

At the far end of the hall, the door to the Lady Chapel had opened and closed. The woman walking toward them with a rather solemn smile on her face was carefully removing her chapel veil as she came down the wide carpeting to the fireplace. She nodded silently to each of them, then said: "Your watch, My Lord brother. Ten to eleven, remember?"

Lord Gisors finished his wine and stood up with a smile. "Of course, My Lady Beverly. *'Can you not spend one hour with me?'* The Gospel according to Matthew." Tomorrow would be the Friday of the Crucifixion; this, the night before, would be symbolically spent in the Garden of Gethsemane with Our Lord. Gisors looked at the clock. It was the last second before ten.

"*'Father, my hour has come,'* St. John—" Gisors began. The pendulum swung down.

The clock struck the first note.

"What the devil was that?" Lord Gisors yelled.

Outside, there had been a horrendous scream.

In the courtyard itself, a minute or so earlier, two militiamen of the Count's Own had been standing near the wall of St. Martin's Hall. One was the man at post, the other the Sergeant-of-the-Guard, who was making his evening rounds. They exchanged the usual military courtesies. The guardsman reported the state of his post as being quiet; the sergeant thanked him in the proper military manner. Then he said, with a grin: "It's better doing night duty in April than in March, eh, Jaime?"

Guardsman Jaime grinned back. "At least I'm not freezing my nose off, Sergeant Andray." His eyes shifted upward as he saw a gleam of light from the corner of his eye. "Here comes My Lord Count."

Sergeant Andray turned his head to follow Jaime's gaze. He knew that Jaime did not mean that My Lord the Count was actually approaching the post, merely that his lordship was going into his private room at the top of the Red Tower. It was an occurrence both of them were used to. The Count was irregular in his visits to his private workshop, but his behavior each time was predictable. He made his presence known to those in the courtyard below by the light of his flickering torch showing through the lozenged window as he approached it from the door of his laboratory.

Then, as he stood on the desk in front of the window to light the gas jet just above the lintel, the flame of the torch rose, lifting out of sight above the window, leaving only a half-halo of light beneath.

Then the routine changed drastically.

Instead of the warm glow of the gaslight, there was an odd, moving flare of white light that seemed to chase itself around the room for a second or two.

Then, suddenly and violently, the leaded, lozenged window burst asunder, splattering glass through the air. Through that shattered window came the twisting figure of My Lord de la Vexin, a scream tearing from his throat as he somersaulted eighty feet to the stone pavement below, his small torch still in his hand, trailing a comet's tail of flame and sparks.

The Count and the courtyard met with fatal violence, and the sudden silence was punctuated only by the tinkling rain of shards of glass still falling from the ruined window above.

At 12:44 that evening, Jaque Toile, Chief Master-at-Arms for the city of Gisors, was waiting at the railroad station with two Sergeants-at-Arms as the train from Rouen pulled into the station.

Chief Jaque's hard eyes scanned the late-night passengers as they alighted from the first-class coaches. There were few of them, and the Chief quickly spotted the trio he was looking for. "Let's go," he said to the sergeants. "That's them."

The three Officers of the King's Peace moved in.

The three men who were their target stepped out of the coach and waited. The first was a tall, brown-haired, handsome man with lean features, wearing the evening dress of an aristocrat; the second was shorter and muscularly tubby wearing the working dress of a sorcerer, the third was a rather elderly, dried-up-looking fellow with gray hair, who wore pince-nez and the evening dress of a gentleman. On the shoulders of the latter two was embroidered the badge of the Duke of Normandy.

Chief Jaque walked up to the aristocratic-looking gentleman. "My Lord Darcy?"

Lord Darcy, Chief Investigator for His Royal Highness the Duke of Normandy, nodded. "I am. Chief Jaque Toile, I believe?"

"Yes, m'lord."

"My colleagues," said Lord Darcy by way of introduction, "Sean O Lochlainn, Master Sorcerer, Chief Forensic Sorcerer for His Royal Highness; Doctor James Pateley, Chief Forensic Chirurgeon."

The Chief Master-at-Arms acknowledged the introductions, then: "Sergeants Paul and Bertram, m'lord. We have an official carriage waiting, m'lord."

Four minutes later, the carriage was rolling toward Castle Gisors, its coil spring suspension and pneumatic tires making the ride comfortable in spite of the cobblestone streets. After what seemed a long silence, Lord Darcy's voice came smoothly.

"You seem pensive, my dear Chief."

"What? Oh. Yes. Sorry, m'lord. Just thinking."

"That was painfully apparent. May I inquire as to the subject of your thoughts?"

"Don't like cases like this," said Chief Jaque. "Not equipped for 'em. Ghosts, demons, black magic, that sort of thing. I'm not a scientist; I'm a peace officer."

Master Sean's blue eyes lit up with interest "Ghosts? Demons? Black magic?"

"One moment," Lord Darcy said. "Let us be systematic. The only information we received at Rouen was that de la Vexin has fallen to his death. No details were given us via teleson. Just what did happen, Chief Jaque?"

The Chief Master-at-Arms explained what had happened as pieced together from the reports of the guardsmen on duty, just prior to My Lord de la Vexin's death.

"No question he was dead," the Chief said. "Skull smashed. Neck broken. Guard Sergeant Andray called for an extension fire ladder. Only way to get up into that room. Sent the guard from the courtyard up the stairs to notify the two men on duty at his lordship's door."

"They hadn't known?" Lord Darcy asked.

Chief Jaque shook his head. "Door's too thick. Too thick to break down in a short time, even. Need an ax. That's why Andray went up the ladder. Climbed in the window and went over to unbar the door. By that time, the door guards were alerted. That's where the funny part comes in."

"Indeed?" murmured Lord Darcy. "Funny in what way?"

"Nobody in the room. Doesn't make sense."

Master Sean thumbed his chin thoughtfully. "If that's the case, Chief Jaque, then he wasn't pushed, eh? Might it be that it was purely an accident? That when he got up on that desk to light the gaslamp, something slipped and he fell accidentally through the window and to his death?"

The Chief Master-at-Arms shook his head. "Not very likely, Master Sorcerer; body was eighteen feet from the wall. Glass spattered even farther." He shook his head again. "Didn't just fall. Not possible. He was pushed."

Dr. Pateley took his pince-nez from his thin nose and looked at them as he polished them with a fine linen handkerchief. "Or *jumped*, perhaps?" he asked in his diffident voice.

The Chief glanced at him sharply. *"Jumped?* You mean suicide?"

"Not necessarily," said the chirurgeon. He glanced up at Lord Darcy. "There are many reasons why a man might jump—eh, my lord?"

Lord Darcy held back a smile. "Indeed, Doctor. Most astute of you." He looked at Chief Jaque. "Could he have jumped, Chief?"

"Could have. Doesn't make sense, though. Man doesn't commit suicide by jumping through a closed window. Doesn't make sense. A suicide who decides to jump opens the window first. Doesn't just take a flying leap through a pane of glass."

"That's not the point I had in mind," said Dr. Pateley, replacing his glasses carefully. "What if he were trying to get away from something?"

Chief Jaque's eyes widened. "I knew it! Demons!"

Twenty-five minutes later, Master Sean was saying: "Well, me lord, whatever it was that killed My Lord de la Vexin, it was certainly none of Chief Jaque's 'demons,' nor any other form of projected psychic elemental."

Dr. Pateley frowned. "A what?"

"Elemental, my dear Doctor. A projected psychic manifestation symbolized by the four elementary states of matter: solid, liquid, gas, and plasma. Or earth, water, air, and fire, as they used to call them."

Along with Lord Darcy, Master Sean and the chirurgeon were standing in the room in the Red Tower from which the late Count had been ejected so forcibly. Master Sean had prowled round the room with his eyes half closed, his golden *crux ansata* in his right hand, probing everywhere. Then the round little Irish sorcerer had made his pronouncement.

Lord Darcy had not wasted his time in watching Master Sean; he had seen that process too many times to be interested in it. Instead, his keen gray eyes had been carefully surveying the room.

It was a fairly large room, covering the entire top floor of the Fourteenth Century tower except for the small landing at the head of the stairs. The landing was closed off by a heavy, padded walnut door.

Having noted that, Lord Darcy looked at the rest of the large room.

It was square, some twenty by twenty feet, the tower having been built in the old Norman style. There was only the one window in the room; the rest of the walls were covered with shelving and cabinets. Along the length of the west wall ran a shelf some thirty-two inches deep and three feet from the floor: it was obviously used as a worktable, for it was littered with various kinds of glassware, oddly-shaped pieces of wood and metal, a couple of balances and other paraphernalia. The shelves above it contained rows of bottles and jars, each neatly labeled, containing liquids, powders, and crystals of various kinds.

On the south wall, flanking the shattered window, were two sections of shelving full of books. Half the east wall was filled with books, the other half with cabinets. There were more shelves and cabinets flanking the door of the north wall.

Because of the slight breeze that came in chillingly through the broken window, the gas flame in the sconce above it flickered and danced, casting weird shadows over the room and making glittering highlights on the glassware.

The Count's writing desk was set directly beneath the big window, its top flush with the sill. Lord Darcy walked over to the desk, leaned over it and looked down through the smashed window. There had been no unusual evidence there. My Lord the Count had, from all indications, died of a broken neck and a crushed skull although the autopsy might tell more. A search of the body had revealed nothing of any consequence—but Lord Darcy now carried the key to the late Count's ultra-private chamber in his pocket.

Below Chief Jaque and his men were carefully lifting the body from a glittering field of broken glass and putting it into the special carriage of the local chirurgeon. The autopsy would be performed in the morning by Master Sean and Dr. Pateley.

Lord Darcy leaned back and looked up at the gas flame above the window. The Count de la Vexin had come in with his torch, as usual. Climbed up on his desk as usual. Turned on the gas, as usual. Lit the gas with his torch, as usual. Then—

What?

"Spooky-looking place, eh, me lord?" Master Sean said.

His lordship turned round, putting his back to the window.

"Gloomy, at any rate, my dear Sean. Are there no other gas jets in this room? Ah, yes; I see them. Two on each of the other walls. Evidently the pipes were lengthened when the shelving was put in." He took out his pipe lighter. "Let's see if we can't shed a little more light on the subject." He went around the room carefully and lit the other six lamps. Even inside their glass chimneys, they tended to flicker; the room was better illuminated, but the shadows still danced.

"Ah! And an old-fashioned oil chandelier," Lord Darcy said, looking up. It was a brass globe some fifteen inches in diameter with a ring at the bottom and a wick with a glass chimney on top, suspended by a web of chains and a pulley system that allowed it to be pulled down for refueling and lighting. Even standing on tiptoe, Lord Darcy couldn't reach the ring.

He looked around quickly then went to the door and opened it. "Corporal, is there a hook to lower that oil lamp?"

"Blessed if I know, my lord," said the Corporal of the Guard. "His lordship never used it, the lamp, I mean. Hasn't been used as long as I know. Doubt if it has any oil in it, even, my lord."

"I see. Thank you." He closed the door again. "Well, so much for additional illumination. Hm-m-m. Dr. Pateley, you measured the body; how tall was My Lord Count?"

"Five feet six, my lord."

"That accounts for it, then."

"Accounts for what, my lord?"

"There are seven gas jets in this room. Six of them are some seven and a half feet from the floor; the seventh, over the window, is nine feet from the floor. Why did he habitually light that one first? Because it is only six and a half feet from the desk top, and he could reach it."

"Then how did he reach the others if he needed more light?" Dr. Pateley asked, adjusting his pince-nez.

Master Sean grinned, but said nothing.

Lord Darcy sighed. "My dear chirurgeon, I honestly think you never look at anything but human bodies, ill, dying, or dead. What do you see over there?" He pointed to the northeast corner of the room.

Dr. Pateley turned. "Oh. A ladder." He looked rather embarrassed. "Certainly. Of course."

"Had it not been here," Lord Darcy said, "I would be quite astonished. How else would he get to his books and . . ."

His voice trailed off. His eyes were still on the ladder. "Hm-m-m. Interesting." He went over to the ladder, tested it, then climbed up it to the ceiling. He bent his head back to look at the ceiling carefully. "Aha. This was the old watchtower." He pushed up with one hand, then with both. Overhead, a two-and-a-half-foot panel swung back on protesting hinges. Lord Darcy climbed on up and hoisted himself through the opening.

He looked around the roof of the tower, which was surrounded by crenellated walls. Then he came back down, closing the panel.

"Nothing up there, apparently, but I'll have to come back by daylight to check again, more thoroughly."

Then, without another word, he moved silently around the room, looking intently at everything but touching nothing. He looked up at the ceiling. "Heavy brass hooks," he murmured. "Why? Oh, of course. To suspend various pieces of his apparatus. Very good."

He had covered almost all the room before he finally came across something that really piqued his interest. He was standing near the door, his eyes searching the floor, when he said: "Aha! And what might this be?"

He knelt down, looked down at the object carefully, then picked it up between thumb and forefinger.

"It looks," said Master Sean, "like a four-inch piece of half-inch cotton rope, me lord. Very dirty, too."

His Lordship smiled dryly. "That appears to be exactly what it is, my good Sean. Interesting." He examined it closely.

"I would be obliged, my lord," said Master Sean in a semi-formal manner, "if you would explain why it is so interesting."

Dr. Pateley merely blinked behind his pince-nez and said nothing.

"You have noticed, my dear Sean," Lord Darcy said, "how immaculately clean this laboratory is. It is well dusted, well cleaned. Everything seems to be in its place. There are no papers scattered about. There are no messy areas. The place is as neat and as well-kept as a cavalry officer's sabre." He made a sweeping gesture to take in the whole room.

"It is, me lord, but—" Master Sean began.

"Then what, may I ask," His Lordship continued, "is a short piece of dirty rope doing on the floor?"

"I don't know, me lord." Master Sean was honestly puzzled. "What is its significance?"

Lord Darcy's smile broadened. "I haven't the foggiest notion in the world, Master Sean. But I have no doubt that there is *some* significance. What it is will await upon further information."

Another dozen minutes of inspection revealed nothing further to Lord Darcy's scrutiny. "Very well," he said, "we'll leave the rest of this until the morrow, when the light's better. Now let us go down and discuss this affair with those concerned. We'll get little sleep tonight, I fear."

Master Sean cleared his throat apologetically. "My lord, the good chirurgeon and I, not being qualified for interrogating witnesses, had best occupy our time with the autopsy. Eh?"

"Eh? Oh, certainly, if you wish. Yes, of course." This, Lord Darcy thought, is what comes of assuming that others, even one's closest associates, have the same interests as oneself.

Within St. Martin's Hall, the clock on the mantelpiece solemnly struck the quarter-hour. It was fifteen minutes after two on the morning of Good Friday, 12 April 1974.

The Reverend Father Villiers stood near the fireplace, looking up at Lord Darcy. He was not tall—five-six or so— but his lean, compact body had an aura of physical strength about it. He was quick and accurate in his movements, but never seemed jerky or nervous. There was a calm awareness in him that showed spiritual strength as well. He was, Lord Darcy judged, in his forties, with only a faint touch of gray in his hair and mustache. The fine character lines in his handsome face showed strength, kindliness, and a sense of humor. But at the moment he was not smiling: there was a feeling of tragedy in his eyes.

"They are all in the Chapel, my lord," he was saying in his brisk, pleasant, low tenor. "Lord Gisors, Lady Beverly, the Damoselle Madelaine, and Sir Roderique MacKenzie."

"Who are the latter pair, Reverend Sir?" Lord Darcy asked.

"Sir Roderique is Captain of the Count's Own Guard. The Damoselle Madelaine is his daughter."

"I shall not disturb them, Reverend Father," Lord Darcy said. "To seek solace before our Sacramental Lord on His Altar of Repose on this night is the sacrosanct right of every Christian, and should not be abrogated save in dire emergency."

"You don't consider murder an emergency?"

"Before its commission, yes. Not after. What makes you think it was murder, Reverend Father?"

The priest smiled a little. "It wasn't suicide. I spoke to him shortly before he went over to the Red Tower: as a Sensitive, I'd have picked up any suicidal emotions easily. And it could hardly have been an accident; if he'd merely lost his balance and fallen, he'd have landed at the foot of the wall, not eighteen or twenty feet away."

"Eighteen," murmured Lord Darcy.

"*Ergo*—murder," Father Villiers said.

"I agree, Reverend Father," Lord Darcy said. "The theory has been advanced that My Lord Count saw some sort of apparition which so frightened him that he leaped to his death through a closed window rather than face it. What is your opinion?"

"That would be Chief Jaque." The priest shook his head. "Hardly. His late lordship would not even have sensed the presence of a true psychic apparition, and a phony—a piece of trickery—would have neither fooled nor frightened him."

"He couldn't have perceived a true psychic apparition?"

Father Villiers shook his head once more. "He was an example of that truly rare case, the psychically blind."

Ever since St. Hilary of Walsingham had formulated his analog equations on the Laws of Magic in the late Thirteenth Century, scientific sorcerers had realized that those laws could not be used by everyone. Some had the Talent and some did not. It was no more to be expected that everyone could be a sorcerer or healer or sensitive than to expect everyone to be a musician, a sculptor, or a chirurgeon.

But the inability to play a violin does not mean an inability to enjoy—or *not* enjoy—someone else's playing. One does not have to be a musician to perceive that music exists.

Unless one is tone-deaf.

To use another analogy: There are a few—very few—men

and women who are *totally* color-blind. They are not just slightly crippled, like those who cannot distinguish between red and green; they see all things in shades of gray. To them, the world is colorless. It is difficult for such a person to understand why or how three identical objects, all the same shade of gray, can be identified by someone else as "red," "blue," and "green." To the totally color-blind, those words are without referents and are meaningless.

"His late lordship," the priest said, "had an early desire to go into the priesthood, to forgo his right to the County Seat in favor of his younger brother. He could not do so, of course. An un-Talented, psychically blind man would be as useless to the Church as a color-blind man would be to the Artists' Guild."

Naturally, Lord Darcy thought, that would not exclude the late de la Vexin from an executive position in His Imperial Majesty's Government. One doesn't need magical Talent to run a County effectively.

For over eight centuries, since the time of Henry II, the Anglo-French Empire had held its own and expanded. The Great Reform, during the reign of Richard the Great, in the late Fifteenth Century, had put the Empire on a solid working basis, using psychic science to establish a society that had been both stable and progressive for nearly half a millennium.

"Where is My Lord the late Count's younger brother?" Lord Darcy asked.

"Captain Lord Louis is with the New England Fleet," Father Villiers said. "At present, I believe, stationed at Port Holy Cross on the coast of Mechicoe."

Well, that eliminates him *as a suspect,* Lord Darcy told himself. "Tell me, Reverend Father," he said aloud, "do you know anything about the laboratory his late lordship maintained on the top floor of the Red Tower?"

"A laboratory? Is that what it is? No, I didn't know. He went up there regularly, but I have no idea what he did up there. I assumed it was some harmless hobby. Wasn't it?"

"It may have been," Lord Darcy admitted. "I have no reason to believe otherwise. Have you ever been in that room?"

"No; never. Nor, to my knowledge, has anyone else but the Count. Why?"

"Because," Lord Darcy said thoughtfully, "it is a very odd laboratory. And yet there is no doubt that it *is* some kind of laboratory for scientific research."

Father Villiers touched the cross at his breast. "Odd? How?" Then he dropped his hand and chuckled. "No. Not Black Magic, of course. He didn't believe in magic at all—black, white, purple, green, red, or rainbow. He was a Materialist."

"Oh?"

"An outgrowth of his psychic blindness, you see," the priest explained. "He wanted to be a priest. He was refused. Therefore, he rejected the basis for his refusal. He refused to believe that anything which he could not detect with his own senses existed. He set out to prove the basic tenet of Materialism: 'All phenomena in the Universe can be explained as a result of nonliving forces reacting with nonliving matter.' "

"Yes," said Lord Darcy. "A philosophy which I, as a living being, find difficult to understand, to say nothing of accepting. So that is the purpose of his laboratory—to bring the scientific method to bear on the Theory of Materialism."

"So it would appear, my lord," said Father Villiers. "Of course, I have not seen his late lordship's laboratory, but—"

"Who has?" Lord Darcy asked.

The priest shook his head. "No one that I know of. No one."

Lord Darcy glanced at his watch. "Is there anyone else in the Chapel besides the family, Reverend Sir?"

"Several. There is an outer door through which the occupants within the walls can come in directly from the courtyard. And there are four of the Sisters from the convent."

"Then I could slip in unnoticed for an hour of devotion before the Blessed Sacrament at the Altar of Repose?"

"Most assuredly, my lord; there are people coming and going all the time. But I suggest you use the public entrance; if you use the family entrance, someone is sure to notice."

"Thank you, Reverend Father. At what hour will you celebrate the Mass of the Presanctified?"

"The service begins at eight o'clock."

"And how do I get to this outside door? Through that door and turn to my left, I believe?"

"Exactly, my lord."

Three minutes later, Lord Darcy was kneeling in the back of the Chapel, facing the magnificently flowered Altar of Repose, his eyes on the veiled ciborium that stood at its center.

An hour and a quarter after that, he was sound asleep in the room which had been assigned him by the seneschal.

After the abrupt liturgical finale of the Mass of the Presanctified at a little past ten on Good Friday morning, Lord Darcy and Master Sean stood waiting outside the family entrance of the Chapel. Dr. Pateley had excused himself immediately; he had volunteered to help one of the local men to prepare the late Count's body for the funeral. "Put things back the way we found 'em, my lord," was the way he worded it.

Darcy and the stout little Irish sorcerer had placed themselves at the back of the congregation and had come out ahead of the family who were in their reserved pew at the front.

"I trust," murmured his lordship very softly, "that Almighty God has reserved a special place of punishment for people who commit murder during Holy Week."

"Aye, me lord; I know what you mean," Master Sean whispered. "Meself, I enjoy the Three Hours of Sermon on Good Friday—especially by a really good preacher, which Father Villiers is reputed to be. But—'business before pleasure.'" He paused, then went on in the same low tone. "D'you expect to clear up the case soon?"

"Before the day is out, I think."

Master Sean looked startled. "You know who did it then?" He kept his voice down.

"*Who?* Of course. That should be plain. But I need more data on *how* and *why*."

Master Sean blinked. "But you haven't even questioned anyone yet, my lord."

"No need to hurry for that. But my case is as yet incomplete."

Master Sean shook his head and chuckled. "Your touch of the Talent, me lord."

"You know, my dear Sean, you have almost convinced me that I *do* have a touch of the Talent. How did you put it?"

"Like all great detectives, my lord, you have the ability to leap from an unjustified assumption to a foregone conclusion without passing through the distance between. Then you back up and fill in." He paused again. "Well, then, who—"

"*Ssst!* Here they come."

Three people had come out of the Chapel: Lord Gisors, Lady Beverly, and the Damoselle Madelaine MacKenzie.

Master Sean's lips barely moved and his voice was barely audible as he said: "Wonder where the rest of the Clan MacKenzie went, me lord?"

"We'll ask." Both of them knew that Captain Sir Roderique MacKenzie and his son, Sergeant Andray, had been sitting in the family pew with the others.

The three came up the hallway toward the big fireplace in St. Martin's Hall, where Lord Darcy and Master Sean were waiting.

Lord Darcy stepped forward and bowed. "My Lord de la Vexin."

The young man looked startled. "No. My fa—" He stopped. It was the first time anyone had ever addressed him as "Lord de la Vexin." Of course it was only a courtesy title; he would not be the Count of the Vexin until his title had been validated by the King.

Lord Darcy, seeing the young man's confusion, went on: "I am Lord Darcy, my lord. This is Master Sean. We appreciate the invitation to breakfast that was conveyed to us by your seneschal."

The new Lord de la Vexin had recovered his composure. "Ah, yes, I am pleased to meet you, my lord. This is my sister, Lady Beverly, and the Damoselle Madelaine. Come; breakfast should be ready for us immediately." He led the way.

The breakfast was delicious, not sumptuous: small, exquisitely poached *quinelles de poisson*; portions of eggs Boucher; hot cross buns; milk and caffe.

Captain Roderique and Sergeant Andray made their appearance a few minutes before the meal began, followed almost immediately by Father Villiers.

Conversation during breakfast consisted only of small talk, allowing Lord Darcy to observe the others of the party without being obtrusive about it.

De la Vexin still seemed dazed, as though his mind were somewhere else, only partly pulled back by conversation. The Damoselle Madelaine, blond and beautiful, behaved with decorum, but there was a bright, anticipatory gleam in her eyes that Lord Darcy did not care for. Lady Beverly, some ten years older than her brother, her dark hair faintly tinged with gray at the temples, looked as though she had been born a widow—or a cloistered nun; she was quiet, soft-spoken, and self-effacing, but underneath Lord Darcy detected a firmness and intelligence kept in abeyance. Captain Sir Roderique MacKenzie was perhaps an inch taller than Lord Darcy—lean, with an upright, square-shouldered posture, a thick light brown mustache and beard, and a taciturn manner typical of the Franco-Scot. His son was a great deal like him, except that he was smooth-shaven and his hair was lighter, though not as blond as that of his sister Madelaine. Both had an air about them that was not quite either that of the military or that of the Keepers of the King's Peace, but partook of both. They were Guardsmen and showed it.

Father Villiers seemed preoccupied, and Lord Darcy could understand why. The symbolic death of the Lord Jesus and the actual death of the Lord de la Vexin were too closely juxtaposed for the good Father's own spiritual comfort. Being a priest is not an easy life-game to play.

After breakfast, a fruit compote of Spanish oranges was served, followed by more caffe.

The late Count's son cleared his throat. "My lords, ladies, gentlemen," he began. He paused for a moment and swallowed. "Several of you have addressed me as 'de la Vexin.' I would prefer, until this matter is cleared up, to retain my title of Gisors. Uh—if you please." Another pause. He looked at Lord Darcy. "You came here to question us, my lord?"

Lord Darcy looked utterly guileless. "Not really, Lord Gisors. However, if you should care to discuss the death of his lordship, it might clear up some of the mysterious circumstances surrounding it. I know that none of you were in that room at the time of the—ah—incident. I am not looking for alibis. But have any of you any conjectures? How did the late Count de la Vexin die?"

Silence fell like a psychic fog, heavy and damp.

Each looked at the others to speak first, and nobody spoke.

"Well," Lord Darcy said after a time, "let's attack it from another direction. Sergeant Andray, of all the people here, you were apparently the only eyewitness. What was your impression of what happened?"

The sergeant blinked, sat up a little straighter, and cleared his throat nervously. "Well, your lordship, at a few minutes before ten o'clock, Guardsman Jaime and I were—"

"No, no, Sergeant," Lord Darcy interrupted gently. "Having read the deposition you and Jaime gave to Chief Jaque, I am fully conversant with what you saw. I want to know your theories about the cause of what you saw."

After a pause, Sergeant Andray said, "It looked to me as if he'd *jumped* through the window, your lordship. But I have no idea why he would do such a thing."

"You saw nothing that might have made him jump?"

Sergeant Andray frowned. "The only thing was that ball of light. Jaime and I mentioned it in my report."

"Yes. 'A ball of yellowish-white light that seemed to dance all over the room for a few seconds, then dropped to the floor and vanished,' you said. Is that right?"

"I should have said, 'dropped *toward* the floor,' your lordship. I couldn't have seen it actually hit the floor. Not from that angle."

"Very good, Sergeant! I wondered if you would correct that minor discrepancy, and you have done so to my satisfaction." Lord Darcy thought for a moment. "Now. You then went over to the body, examined it, and determined to your satisfaction that his lordship was dead. Did you touch him?"

"Only his wrist, to try to find a pulse. There was none, and the angle of his head . . ." He stopped.

"I quite understand. Meanwhile, you had sent Guardsman Jaime for the fire wagon. When it came, you used the extension ladder to go up and unlock the door, to let the other guardsmen in. Was the gaslight still on?"

"No. It had been blown out. I shut off the gas, and then went over and opened the door. There was enough light from the yard-lamps for me to see by."

"And you found nothing odd or out of the way?"

"Nothing and nobody, your lordship," the sergeant said firmly. "Nor did any of the other guardsmen."

"That's straightforward enough. You searched the room then?"

"Not really searched it. We looked around to see if there was anyone there, using hand torches. But there's no place to hide in that room. We had called the Armsmen; when they came, they looked more carefully. Nothing."

"Very well. Now, when I arrived, that gaslight over the window was lit. Who lit it?"

"Chief Master-at-Arms Jaque Toile, your lordship."

"I see. Thank you, Sergeant." He looked at the others, one at a time. Their silence seemed interminable. "Lady Beverly, have you anything to add to this discussion?"

Lady Beverly looked at Father Villiers with her calm eyes.

The priest was looking at her. "My advice is to speak, my child. We must get to the bottom of this"

I see, Lord Darcy thought. *There is something here that has been discussed in the confessional. The Reverend Father* cannot *speak—but he can advise* her *to.*

Lady Beverly looked back to Lord Darcy. "You want a theory, my lord? Very well." There was a terrible sadness in her voice. "His late lordship, my father, was punished by God for his unbelief. Father Villiers has told me that this could not be so, but"—she closed her eyes—"I greatly fear that it is."

"How so, my lady?" Darcy asked gently.

"He was a Materialist. He was psychically blind. He denied that others had the God-given gift of the Sight and the Talent. He said it was all pretense, all hogwash. He was closed off to all emotion."

She was no longer looking *at* Lord Darcy, she was looking through and beyond him, as though her eyes were focused somewhere on a far horizon.

"He was not an evil man," she continued without shifting her gaze, "but he was sinful." Suddenly her eyes flickered, and she was looking directly into Lord Darcy's gray eyes. "Do you know that he forbade a wedding between my brother and the Damoselle Madelaine because he could not see the love between them? He wanted Gisors to marry Evelynne de Saint-Brieuc."

Darcy's eyes moved rapidly to Lord Gisors and Madelaine MacKenzie. "No, I did not know that. How many did?"

It was Captain Sir Roderique who spoke. "We all did,

my lord. He made a point of it. The Count forbade it, and I forbade it. But legally I had no right to forbid my daughter."

"But why did he—"

Lord Darcy's question was cut off abruptly by Lady Beverly. "Politics, my lord. And because he could not see true love. So God punished him for his obstinacy. May I be excused, my lord? I would hear the Three Hours."

Quickly, Father Villiers said: "Would you excuse us both, my lord?"

"Certainly, Reverend Sir, Lady Beverly," Lord Darcy said, rising. His eyes watched them in silence as they left the room.

Half past noon.

Lord Darcy and Master Sean stood in the courtyard below the Red Tower gazing at a small sea of broken glass surrounded by a ring of Armsmen and Guardsmen.

"Well, my dear Sean, what did you think of our little breakfast conversation?"

"Fascinating, me lord," said the sorcerer. "I think I'm beginning to see where you're going. Lady Beverly's mind is not exactly straight, is it?"

"Let's put it that she seems to have some weird ideas about God," Lord Darcy said. "Are you ready for this experiment, Master Sean?"

"I am, me lord."

"Don't you need an anchor man for this sort of thing?"

Master Sean nodded. "Of course, me lord. Chief Jaque is bringing Journeyman Emile, forensic sorcerer for the County. I met him last night; he's a good man: he'll be a Master one day.

"Actually, me lord, the spells are quite simple. According to the Law of Contiguity, any piece of a structure remains a part of the structure. We can return it to the last state in which it was still a part of the contiguous whole—completely, if necessary, but you only want to return it to the point *after* the fracture but *before* the dispersal. Doing it isn't difficult; it's holding it in place afterwards. That's why I need an anchor man."

"I'll take my measurements and make my observations as quickly as possible," Lord Darcy promised. "Ah! There they are!"

Master Sean followed his lordship's gaze toward the main gate of the courtyard. Then, very solemnly, he said: "Ah, yes. One man is wearing the black-and-silver uniform of a Chief Master-at-Arms; the other is wearing the working garb of a Journeyman Sorcerer. By which I deduce that they are *not* a squad of Imperial Marines."

"Astute of you, my dear Sean: keep working at it. You will become an expert detective on the same day that I become a Master Sorcerer. Chief Jaque and I will go up to the tower room while you and Journeyman Emile work here. Carry on."

Lord Darcy toiled up eight flights of stairs, past several offices, vaguely wishing he were in the castle at Evreux, where the Countess D'Evreux's late brother had installed a steam-powered elevator. *No fool he,* Lord Darcy thought.

At the top landing, an Armsman and a Guardsman came immediately to attention as his lordship appeared. He nodded at them. "Good afternoon." With thumb and forefinger he probed his left-hand waistcoat pocket. Then he probed the other. "Is that room locked?" he asked.

The Armsman tested it. "Yes, your lordship."

"I seem to have mislaid the key. Is there another?"

"There is a duplicate, your lordship," said the Guardsman, "but it's locked up in Captain Sir Roderique's office. I'll fetch it for you, if you like; it's only two floors down."

"No. No need." Lord Darcy produced the key from his right-hand waistcoat pocket. "I've found it. Thank you, anyway, Guardsman. Chief Jaque will be up in a few minutes."

He unlocked the door, opened it, went in, and closed the door behind him.

Some three minutes later, when Chief Jaque opened the door, he said: "Looking for something, my lord?"

Lord Darcy was on his knees, searching a cupboard, moving things aside, taking things out. "Yes, my dear Chief; I am looking for the wherewithal to hang a murderer. At first, I thought it more likely it would be in one of the high cupboards, but they contain nothing but glassware. So I decided it must be—ah!" He pulled his head back out of the cupboard and straightened up, still on his knees. From his fingers dangled a six-foot length of ordinary-looking cotton rope.

"Bit scanty to hang a man," Chief Jaque said dubiously.

"For this murderer, it will be quite adequate," said Lord Darcy, standing up. He looked closely at the rope. "If only it—"

He was interrupted by a halloo from below. He went to the shattered remains of the window and looked down. "Yes, Master Sean?" he called.

"We're ready to begin, me lord," the round little Irish sorcerer shouted up. "Please stand back."

In the courtyard, Armsmen and Guardsmen stood in a large circle, facing outward from the center, surrounding the fragments from the broken window. Journeyman Emile, a short, lean man with a Parisian accent, had carefully chalked a pale blue line around the area, drawing it three inches behind the bootheels of the surrounding guard.

"It is that I am ready, Master," he said in his atrocious patois. "Excellent," said Master Sean. "Get the field set up and hold it. I will give you all the strength I can."

"But yes, Master." He opened his symbol-decorated carpetbag—similar to in general, but differing from in detail, Master Sean's own—and took out two mirror-polished silvery wands which were so deeply incised with symbol engraving that they glittered in the early afternoon sunlight. "For the Cattell Effect, it is that it is necessary for the silver, no?"

"It is," agreed Master Sean. "You will be handling the static spells while I take care of the kinetic. Are you ready?"

"I am prepared," Journeyman Emile said. "Proceed." He took his stance just inside the blue-chalked circle, facing the Red Tower and held up his wands in a ninety-degree V.

Master Sean took an insufflator from his own carpetbag and filled it with a previously-charged powder. Then moving carefully around the circle, he puffed out clouds of the powder, which settled gently to the courtyard floor, touching each fragment of glass with at least one grain of the powder.

When he had completed the circle, Master Sean stood in front of Journeyman Emile. He put the insufflator back in his carpetbag and took out a short, eighteen-inch wand of pale yellow crystal, with which he inscribed a symbol in the air.

The Cattell Effect began to manifest itself.

Slowly at first, then more rapidly, the fragments from the shattered window began to move.

Like a reverse cascade in slow motion, they lifted and gathered themselves together, a myriad of sparkling shards moving upward, fountaining glitteringly toward the empty window casement eighty feet above. There was a tinkling like fairy bells as occasional fragments struck each other on the way up as they had struck on the way down.

Only the superb discipline of the Armsmen and Guardsmen kept them from turning to see.

Up, up, went the bits and pieces, like sharp-edged raindrops falling toward the sky.

At the empty opening, they coalesced and came together to form a window—that was not quite a window. It bulged.

Inside the late Count's upper room, Lord Darcy watched the flying fragments return whence they had come. When the stasis was achieved, Lord Darcy glanced at the Chief Master-at-Arms.

"Come, my dear Jaque; we must not tax our sorcerers more than necessary." He walked over to the window, followed by the Chief Armsman.

The lozenged window was neither a shattered wreckage nor a complete whole. It bulged outward curiously, each piece almost touching its neighbor, but not fitted closely to it. The leading between the lozenges was stretched and twisted outward, as if the whole window had been punched from within by a gigantic fist and had stopped stretching at the last moment

"Not quite sure I understand this," said Chief Jaque.

"This is the way the window was a fraction of a second after his lordship, the late Count, struck it. At that time, it was pushed outward and broken, but the fragments had yet to scatter. I direct your attention to the central portion of the window."

The Chief Master-at-Arms took in the scene with keen eyes. "See what you mean. Like a mold, a casting. There's the chin—the chest—the belly—the knees."

"Exactly. Now try to get yourself into a position such that you would make an impression like that," Lord Darcy said.

The Chief grinned. "Don't need to. Obvious. Calves bent back at the knees. Head bent back so the chin hit first. Chest and belly hit first." He narrowed his eyes. "Didn't jump out: didn't fall out. Pushed from behind—violently."

"Precisely so. Excellent, Chief Jaque. Now let us make our measurements as rapidly and as accurately as possible," Lord Darcy said, "being careful not to touch that inherently unstable structure. If we do, we're likely to get badly-cut hands when the whole thing collapses."

Below, in the courtyard, an unmoving tableau presented itself. Armsmen and Guardsmen stood at parade rest, while the two sorcerers stood like unmoving statues, their eyes and minds on the window above, their wands held precisely and confidently.

Minute after minute went by, and the strain was beginning to tell. Then Lord Darcy's voice came: "Anytime you're ready, Master Sean!"

Without moving, Master Sean said sharply, "Sergeant! Get your men well back! Move 'em!"

The Sergeant-at-Arms called out orders, and both Armsmen and Guardsmen rapidly moved back toward the main gate. Then they turned to watch.

The magicians released control. The powerful forces which had held up the glass shards no longer obtained, and gravity took over. There was an avalanche, a waterfall of sparkling shards. They slid and tumbled down the stone wall with a great and joyous noise and subsided into a heap at the foot of the Red Tower.

The display had not been as spectacular as the reconstruction of the window had been, but it was quite satisfactory to the Armsmen and Guardsmen.

A few minutes later, Master Sean toiled his way up the stairs and entered the late Count's laboratory.

"Ah! Master Sean," said Lord Darcy, "where is Journeyman Emile?"

The Irish sorcerer's smile was a little wan. "He's headed home, me lord. That's exhaustin' work, and he hasn't trained for it as I have."

"I trust you conveyed to him my compliments. That was a marvelous piece of work the two of you did."

"Thank you, me lord. I gave Journeyman Emile my personal compliments and assured him of yours. Did you get what you wanted, me lord?"

"I did, indeed. There is but one more thing. A simple test, but I'm sure it will be most enlightening. First, I will call your attention to those two five-gallon carboys which Chief Jaque and I have just discovered in one of the lower cupboards."

The carboys, which had been lifted up to the worktable, stood side by side, labels showing. One of them, with scarcely half an inch of pale yellowish liquid in it, was labeled *Concentrated Aqueous Spirit of Niter*. The other, half full of a clear oily-looking liquid, was *Concentrated Oil of Vitriol*.

"I suppose you knew you'd find 'em, me lord?" Master Sean said.

"I didn't *know*; I merely suspected. But their presence certainly strengthens my case. Do they suggest anything to you?"

Master Sean shrugged. "I know what they are, me lord, but I'm not a specialist in the Khemic Arts."

"Nor am I." Lord Darcy took out his pipe and thumbed tobacco into it. "But an Officer of the King's justice should be widely read enough to be a jack-of-all-trades, at least in theory. Do you know what happens when a mixture of those acids is added to common cotton?"

"No—wait." Master Sean frowned, then shook his head. "I've read it somewhere, but—the details won't come."

"You get nitrated cotton," Lord Darcy said.

Chief Jaque coughed delicately. "Well, what does *that* do, your lordship?"

"I think I can show you," his lordship said with a rather mysterious smile. From his wallet, he took the four-inch piece of blackened rope he had found near the door the evening before. Then he picked up the six-foot piece of clean rope he had found half an hour before. Using his sharp pocketknife, he cut a small piece from the end of each and put them on the lab table about eighteen inches from each other. "Chief Jaque, take these long pieces and put them on the desk, well away from here. I shouldn't want to lose *all* my evidence. Thank you. Now watch."

He lit each bit with his pipe lighter. They both flared in a sudden hissing burst of yellow-white flame and were gone, leaving no trace. Lord Darcy calmly lit his pipe.

Master Sean's eyes lit up. "Aaa-hah!"

Chief Jaque said: "The demon!"

"Precisely, my dear Chief. Now we must go down and talk to the rest of the *dramatic personae.*"

As they went back down the stairs, Master Sean said: "But why was the short piece covered with dirt, me lord?"

"Not dirt, my dear Sean; lampblack."

"Lampblack? But why?"

"To render it invisible, of course."

"You are not preaching the Three Hours, Reverend Father?" Lord Darcy asked with a raised eyebrow.

"No, my lord," Father Villiers replied. "I am just a little too upset. Besides, I thought my presence here might be required. Father Dubois very kindly agreed to come over from the monastery and take my place."

Clouds had come, shortly after noon, to obliterate the bright morning sun, and a damp chill had enveloped the castle. The chill was being offset by the fire in the great fireplace in St. Martin's Hall, but to the ten people seated on sofas and chairs around the fireplace, there seemed to be a different sort of chill in the huge room.

The three MacKenzies, father, son, and daughter, sat together on one sofa, saying nothing, their eyes moving around, but always coming back to Lord Darcy. Lady Beverly sat alone near the fire, her eyes watching the flames unseeingly. Master Sean and Dr. Pateley were talking in very low tones on the opposite side of the fireplace. Chief Jaque stood stolidly in front of the mullioned window, watching the entire room without seeming to do so.

On the mantelpiece, the big clock swung its pendulum with muffled clicks.

Lord Gisors rose from his seat and came toward the sideboard where Lord Darcy and Father Villiers were talking.

"Excuse me, Lord Darcy, Father." He paused and cleared his throat a little, then looked at the priest. "We're all a little nervous, Reverend Sir. I know it's Good Friday, but would it be wrong to—er—to ask if anyone wants a glass of Xerez?"

"Of course not, my son. We are all suffering with Our Lord this day, and may suffer more, but I do not think He would frown upon our use of a stiff dose of medicinal palliative. Certainly Our Lord did not. According to St. John, He said, 'I thirst,' and they held up to Him a sponge soaked in wine. After He had received it, He said, 'It is accomplished.' " Father Villiers stopped.

" 'And gave up His spirit,' " Lord Gisors quoted glumly.

"Exactly," said the priest firmly. "But by Easter Day His spirit had returned, and the only casualty among the faithful that weekend was Judas. I'll have a brandy, myself."

Only Lady Beverly and Chief Jaque refused refreshment—each for a different reason. When the drinks were about half gone, Lord Darcy walked casually to the fireplace and faced them all.

"We have a vexing problem before us. We must show how the late Count de la Vexin met his death. With the cooperation of all of you, I think we can do it. First, we have to dispense with the notion that there was any Black Magic involved in the death of his lordship. Master Sean?"

The Irishman rolled Xerez around on his tongue and swallowed before answering. "Me lords, ladies, and gentlemen, having thoroughly given the situation every scientific test, I would be willing to state in His Majesty's Court of Justice that by whatever means his lordship the Count was killed, there was no trace of any magic, black or white, involved. Not in any capacity by anyone."

Lady Beverly's eyes blazed suddenly. "By no *human* agency, I suppose you mean?" Her voice was low, intense.

"Aye, me lady," Master Sean agreed.

"But what of the punishment of God? Or the evil works of Satan?"

A silence hung in the air. After a moment, Master Sean said: "I think I'll let the Reverend Father answer that one."

Father Villiers steepled his fingers. "My child, God punishes transgressors in many ways—usually through the purgatorial torture of conscience, or, if the conscience is weak, by the reaction of the sinner's fellow men to his evildoing. The Devil, in hope that the sinner may die before he has a chance to repent, may use various methods of driving them to self-destruction.

"But you cannot ascribe an act like this to *both* God and Satan. There is, furthermore, no evidence whatever that your late father was so great a sinner that God would have resorted to such drastic punishment, nor that the Devil feared of his lordship's relenting in the near future of such minor sins as he may have committed.

"In any case, *neither God nor the Devil disposes of a man by grabbing him by the scruff of the neck and the seat of the pants and throwing him through a window!* Execution by defenestration, my child, is a peculiarly human act."

Lady Beverly bowed her head and said nothing. Again a moment of silence, broken by Lord Darcy.

"My Lord Gisors, assuming that your father was killed by purely physical means, can you suggest how it might have been done?"

Lord Gisors, who had been at the sidetable pouring himself another drink, turned slowly around. "Yes, Lord Darcy. I can," he said thoughtfully.

Lord Darcy raised his left eyebrow again. "Indeed? Pray elucidate, my lord."

Lord Gisors lifted his right index finger. "My father was pushed out that window. Correct?" His voice was shaking a little.

"Correct," Lord Darcy acknowledged.

"Then, by God, somebody had to push him out! I don't know who, I don't know how! But there had to be someone in there to do it!" He took another swallow of his drink and then went on in a somewhat calmer voice. "Look at it this way. Someone was in there waiting for him. My father came in, walked toward the window, got up on his desk, and that someone, whoever he was, ran up behind him and pushed him out. I don't know who or why, but that's what *had* to have happened! You're the Duke's Investigator. You find out what happened and who did it. But don't try to put it on any of us, my lord, because none of us was anywhere near that room when it happened!"

He finished his drink in one swallow and poured another.

Lord Darcy spoke quietly. "Assuming your hypothesis is true, my lord, how did the killer get into the room, and how did he get out?" Without waiting, for an answer from Lord Gisors, Lord Darcy looked at Captain Sir Roderique. "Have you any suggestions, Sir Roderique?"

The old Guardsman scowled. "I don't know. The laboratory was locked at all times, and always guarded when his lordship was in there. But it wasn't especially guarded when Lord Jillbert was gone. He didn't go in often—not more than once or twice a week. The room wasn't particularly guarded the rest of the time. Anyone with a key could have got in. Someone could have stolen the key from My Lord de la Vexin and had a duplicate made."

"Highly unlikely," Lord Darcy said. "His lordship wanted no one in that room but himself. On the other hand, my dear Captain, you have a duplicate."

Roderique's face seemed to turn purple. He came suddenly to his feet, looking down at Lord Darcy. "Are you accusing *me*?"

Darcy lifted a hand, palm outward. "Not yet, my dear Captain; perhaps not ever. Let us continue with our discussion without permitting our emotions to boil over." The Captain of the Guard sat down slowly without taking his eyes from Lord Darcy's face.

"I assure you, my lord," the captain said, "that no other duplicate has ever been made from the key in my possession and that the key has never been out of my possession."

"I believe you, Captain; I never said that any duplicate was made from *your* key. But let us make an hypothesis.

"Let us assume," Lord Darcy continued, "that the killer *did* have a duplicate key. Very well. What happened then?" He looked at Sergeant Andray. "Give us your opinion, Sergeant."

Andray frowned as though concentration on the problem was just a little beyond his capabilities. His handsome features seemed to be unsure of themselves. "Well—uh—well, my lord, this is—I mean—well, if it were me—" He licked his lips again and looked at his wineglass. "Well, now, my lord, supposing there were someone hidden inside the room, waiting for My Lord Count. Hm-m-m. His lordship comes in and climbs up on the desk. Then the killer would have run forward and pushed him out. Yes. That's the only way it could have happened, isn't it?"

"Then how did he get out of the room afterward, Sergeant? You have told us that there was no one in the room when you went in through the window, and that the

Guardsmen outside found no one in the room after you let them in. The room was under guard all that time, was it not?"

"Yes, my lord, it was."

"Then how did the killer get out?"

The sergeant blinked. "Well, my lord, the only other way out is through the trapdoor to the roof. He might have gone out that way."

Lord Darcy shook his head slowly. "Impossible. I looked at that rooftop carefully this morning. There is no sign that anyone has been up there for some time. Besides, how would he get down? The tower was surrounded by Guardsmen who would have seen anyone trying to go down ninety feet on a rope, and there is hardly any other way. At any rate, he would have been seen. And he could hardly have come down the stairs; the interior was full of the Guard." His lordship's eyes shifted suddenly. "Do you have any suggestions, Damoselle Madelaine?"

She looked up at him with her round blue eyes. "No, my lord. I know nothing about such things. It still seems like magic to me."

More silence.

Well, that's enough of this, Lord Darcy thought. *Now we go on to the final phase.*

"Does anyone else have a suggestion?" Apparently, no one did. "Very well, then; perhaps you would like to know my theory of how the killer—a very solid and human killer—got in and out of that room without being seen. Better than merely telling you, I shall demonstrate. Shall we repair to the late Count's *sanctum sanctorum?* Come."

There was a peculiar mixture of reluctance and avidity in the general feeling of those present, but they rose without objection and followed Lord Darcy across the courtyard to the Red Tower and up the long stairway to the late Count's room.

"Now," said Lord Darcy after they were all in the room, "I want all of you to obey my instructions exactly. Otherwise, someone is likely to get hurt. I am sorry there are no chairs in this room—evidently My Lord de la Vexin liked to work on his feet—so you will have to stand. Be so good as to stand over against the east wall. That's it. Thank you."

He took the five-inch brass key from his waistcoat pocket, then went over to the door and closed it. "The door was locked, so." Click. "And barred, so." *Thump.*

He repocketed the key and turned to face the others. "There, now. That's approximately the way things were after Lord de la Vexin locked himself in his laboratory for the last time. Except, of course, for the condition of that ruined window." He gestured toward the casement, empty now save for broken shards of glass and leading around the edges.

He looked all around the room side to side and up and down. "No, it still isn't right, is it? Well, that can soon be adjusted properly. Firstly, we'll need to get that unused oil lamp down. Yonder ladder is a full two feet short to reach a ten-foot beam. There are no chairs or stools. A thorough search has shown that the long-handled hook which is the usual accouterment for such a lamp is nowhere in the room. Dear me! What shall we do?"

Most of the others were looking at Lord Darcy as though he had suddenly become simple-minded, but Master Sean smiled inwardly. He knew that his lordship's blithering was to a purpose.

"Well! What have we here?" Lord Darcy was looking at the brass key in his hand as if he had never seen it before. "Hm-m-m, the end which engages the lock wards should make an excellent hook. Let us see."

Standing directly beneath the brass globe, he jumped up and accurately hooked the brass ring with the key. Then he lowered the big lamp down.

"What is this? It comes down quite easily! It balances the counterweight to a nicety. How odd! Can it be that it is not empty after all?" He took off the glass chimney, put it on the worktable of the east wall, went back and took out the wickholder. "Bless my soul! It is quite brimfull of fuel."

He screwed the wickholder back in and lowered the whole lamp to the fullest extent of the pulley chain. It was hardly more than an inch off the floor. Then he grabbed the chain firmly with both hands and lifted. The lamp came up off the floor, but the chain above Lord Darcy's hands went limp and did not move upward. "Ah! The ratchet lock works perfectly. The counterweight cannot raise the lamp unless one pulls the chain down a little bit and then releases it slowly. Excellent." He lowered the lamp back down.

"Now comes the difficult part. That lamp is quite heavy." Lord Darcy smiled. "But, fortunately, we can use the ladder for this." He brought the ladder over to the locked and barred door, bracing it against the wall over the lintel. Then his audience watched in stunned silence as he picked up the heavy lamp, carried it over to the ladder, climbed up, and hooked the chain over one of the apparatus hooks that the Count had fastened at many places in the ceiling.

"There, now," he said, descending the ladder. He looked up at the resulting configuration. The lamp chain now stretched almost horizontally from its supporting beam to the heavy hook in the ceiling over the door. "You will notice," said his lordship, "that the supporting beam for the lamp is not in the exact center of the room. It is two feet nearer the window than it is to the door. The center of the beam is eleven feet from the door, nine feet from the window."

"What *are* you talking about?" Lady Beverly burst out suddenly. "What has all this to do with—"

"If you please, my lady!" Lord Darcy cut her off sharply. Then, more calmly, "Restrain yourself, I pray. All will become clear when I have finished."

Good Lord, he thought to himself, *it should be plain to the veriest dunce . . .*

Aloud, he said, "We are not through yet: The rope, Master Sean."

Without a word, Master Sean O Lochlainn opened his big symbol-decorated carpetbag and took from it a coil of cotton rope; he gave it to Lord Darcy.

"This is plain, ordinary cotton rope," his lordship said. "But it is not quite long enough. The other bit of rope, if you please, my dear Sean."

The sorcerer handed him another foot-long piece of rope that looked exactly like the coil he already held.

Using a fisherman's knot, Lord Darcy tied the two together.

He climbed up on the late Count's desk and tied the end of the rope to another hook above the gaslight—the end with the tied-on extra piece. Then he turned and threw the coil of rope across the room to the foot of the ladder. He went back across the room and climbed the ladder again, taking with him the other end of the rope.

Working carefully he tied the rope to the chain link just

above the lamp, then taking the chain off the hook he looped the rope over the hook so that it supported the lamp.

He climbed back down the ladder and pointed. "As you see, the lamp is now supported solely by the rope, which is fastened at the hook above the gaslamp over the window, stretches across the room, and is looped over the hook above the door to support the weight."

By this time they all understood. There was tension in the room.

"I said," continued Lord Darcy, "that the rope I have used is ordinary cotton. So it is, except for that last additional foot which is tied above the gaslamp. That last foot is not ordinary cotton, but of specially treated cotton which is called nitred or nitrated cotton. It burns extremely rapidly. In the original death trap the entire rope was made of that substance, but there was not enough left for me to use in this demonstration.

"As you will notice, the end which supports the lamp is several inches too long after the knot was tied. The person who set this trap very tidily cut off the excess and then failed to pick up the discarded end. Well, we all make mistakes, don't we?"

Lord Darcy stood dramatically in the center of the room. "I want you all to imagine what it was like in this room last night. Dark—or nearly so. There is only the dim illumination from the courtyard lamps below." He picked up an unlit torch from the workbench a few feet away, then went to the door.

"My Lord Count has just come in. He has closed, locked, and barred the door. He has a torch in his hand." Lord Darcy lit the torch with his pipe lighter.

"Now, he walks across the room, to light the gaslamp above the window, as is his wont." Lord Darcy acted out his words.

"He climbs up on his desk. He turns on the gas valve. He lifts his torch to light the gas."

The gas jet shot a yellow flame several inches high. It touched the nitrated cotton rope above it. The rope flared into hissing flame.

Lord Darcy leaped aside and bounced to the floor, well away from the desk.

On the opposite side of the room, the heavy lamp was

suddenly released from its hold. Like some airborne jug-
gernaut, it swung ponderously along the arc of its chain.
At the bottom of that arc, it grazed the floor with the brass
ring. Then it swung up and—as anyone could see—would
have smashed the window, had it still been there. Then it
swung back.

Everyone in the room watched the lamp pendulum back
and forth dragging the cotton rope behind it. The nitrated
section had long since vanished in flame.

Lord Darcy stood on the east side of the room with the
pendulum scything the air between himself and the others.

"Thus you see how the late Count de la Vexin came to
his death. The arc this thing cuts would have struck him
just below the shoulder-blades. Naturally, it would not have
swung so long as now, having been considerably slowed
by its impact with the Count's body." He walked over,
grabbed the chain and fought the pendulum to a standstill.

They all stared fascinated at the deadly weight which now
swung in a modest two-inch wobble.

The young Lord Gisors lifted his head with a jerk and
stared straight into Lord Darcy's eyes. "Surely my father
would have seen that white rope, Darcy."

"Not if it were covered with lampblack—which it was."

Lord Gisors narrowed his eyes. "Oh, fine. So that's the
end of it, eh? With the lamp hanging there, almost touching the floor. Then—*will you explain how it got back up
to where it belongs?*"

"Certainly," said Lord Darcy.

He walked over to the lamp, removed the length of cotton
rope, pulled gently on the chain to unlock the ratchet, and
eased the lamp up. After it left his outstretched hand it
moved on up quietly to its accustomed place.

"Like that," said Lord Darcy blandly. "Except, of course,
that the glass chimney was replaced first. And the rope did
not need to be removed since it had all been burnt up."

Before anyone else could speak, Father Villiers said: "Just
a moment my lord. If someone had done that, he would
have had to have been in this room—seconds after the death.
But there is no way in or out of this room except the door—
which was guarded—and the door to the roof, which you
have said was not used. There is no other way in or out
of this room."

Lord Darcy smiled. "Oh, but there is, Reverend Father."

The priest looked blank.

"The way My Lord de la Vexin took," Lord Darcy said gently.

Surely they understand now, Lord Darcy thought. He broke the silence by saying: "The lamp was down. There was no one in this room. Then someone climbed in through the window via the fire ladder, raised the lamp again and—

"*Chief Jaque!*" Lord Darcy shouted.

But he was a fraction of a second too late.

Sergeant Andray had drawn a concealed sidearm. Chief Jaque was just a little too late getting his own gun out.

There was the sudden ear-shattering shock of a heavy-caliber pistol firing in a closed room and Chief Jaque went down with a bullet in him.

Lord Darcy's hand darted toward the pistol at his own hip but before it could clear the holster Captain Sir Roderique leaped toward his son.

"*You fool! You—*" His voice was agonized.

He grabbed the sergeant's wrist, twisted it up.

There came a second shattering blast.

Sir Roderique fell backwards; the bullet had gone in under his chin and taken the top of his head off.

Sergeant Andray screamed.

Then he spun around, leaped to the top of the desk, and flung himself out the window, still screaming.

The scream lasted just a bit over two seconds before Sergeant Andray was permanently silenced by the courtyard below.

The celebrations of Holy Saturday were over, Easter Season had officially begun. The bells were still ringing in the tower of the Cathedral of St. Ouen in the city of Rouen, the capital of the Duchy of Normandy.

His Royal Highness, Richard, Duke of Normandy leaned back in his chair and smiled across the cozy fireplace at his Chief Investigator. Both of them were holding warming glasses of fine Champagne brandy.

His Highness had just finished reading Lord Darcy's report

"I see, my lord," he said. "After the trap had been set and triggered—after the late de la Vexin had been propelled through the window to his death—Sergeant Andray went up the fire ladder alone, raised the lamp back to its usual position and then opened the barred door to allow in the other Guardsmen. The fox concealing himself among the hounds."

"Precisely, Your Highness. And you see the motive."

His Highness the Duke, younger brother of His Imperial Majesty, King John IV, was blond, blue-eyed, and handsome, like all the Plantagenets, but at this moment there was a faint frown upon his forehead.

"The motive was obvious from the beginning, my lord," he said. "I can see that Sergeant Andray wanted to get rid of My Lord de la Vexin in order to clear the way for a marriage which would be beneficial to his sister—and, of course, to the rest of the family. But your written report is incomplete." He tapped the sheaf of papers in his hand.

"I fear, Your Highness," Lord Darcy said carefully, "that it must remain forever incomplete."

Prince Richard leaned back and sighed. "Very well, Darcy. Give it to me orally. Off the record, as usual."

"As you command, Your Highness," Lord Darcy said, refilling his glass.

"Young Andray must be blamed for the murder. The evidence I have can go no further, now that both he and his father are dead. Chief Jaque, who will easily recover from the bullet wound in his shoulder, has no more evidence than I have.

"Captain Sir Roderique will be buried with military honors, since eyewitnesses can and will say that he tried to stop his son from shooting me. Further hypotheses now would merely raise a discussion that could never be resolved.

"But it was not Sergeant Andray who set the trap. Only Captain Sir Roderique had access to the key that unlocked the laboratory. Only he could have gone up there and set the death trap that killed the late Count."

"Then why," the Prince asked, "did he try to stop his son?"

"Because, Your Highness," Lord Darcy replied, "he did not think I had enough evidence to convict. He was trying to stop young Andray from making a fool of himself by giving the whole thing away. Andray had panicked—which I had hoped he would, but not, I must admit, to that extent.

"He killed his father, who had plotted the whole thing,

and seeing what he had done, went into a suicidal hysteria which resulted in his death. I am sorry for that, Your Highness."

"Not your fault, Darcy. What about the Damoselle Madelaine?"

Lord Darcy sipped at his brandy. "She was the prime mover, of course. She instigated the whole thing—subtly. No way to prove it. But Lord Gisors sees through her now. He will wed the lady his father quite properly chose for him."

"I see," said the Prince. "You told him the truth?"

"I spoke to him, Your Highness," Lord Darcy said. "But he already knew the truth."

"Then the matter is settled." His Highness straightened up in his chair. "Now, about those notebooks you brought back with you. What do they mean?"

"They are the late Count's scientific-materialistic notes on his researches for the past twenty years, Your Highness. They present two decades of hard research."

"But—really, Darcy. Research on Materialism? Of what use could they possibly be?"

"Your Highness, the Laws of Magic tell us how the mind of man can influence the material universe. But the universe is more than the mind of man can possibly encompass. The mind of God may keep the planets and the stars in their courses, but, if so, then He has laws by which He abides."

Lord Darcy finished his brandy. "There are more things in this universe than the mind of man, Your Highness, and there are laws which govern them. Someday, those notebooks may be invaluable."

The Bitter End

1

Master Sean O Lochlainn was not overly fond of the city of Paris. It was a crowded, noisy river port with delusions of grandeur brought on by memories of ancient glory.

That it had been the seat of the ancient Capetian Kings of France, there could be no denying; that the last of the Capets had been killed in 1215 by Richard the Lion-Hearted and that more than seven and a half centuries had rolled past since then were equally true facts, but Parisians would have denied both if they could.

One of the very few places Master Sean felt comfortable in all that vast city was here, in the International Bar of the Hotel Cosmopolitain. He was wearing ordinary gentleman's traveling clothes, not the silver-slashed blue that would proclaim him a Master Sorcerer, nor the insignia that would identify him as the Chief Forensic Sorcerer for Prince Richard, Duke of Normandy.

It was four o'clock of a pleasant October evening, and the shifts were just changing in the International Bar, a barman and two waiters going off duty and being replaced by their evening counterparts. It meant a lull in service for a minute or so, but Master Sean didn't mind; he still had a good half-pint of beer in his mug, and the stout little Irish magician was not a fast drinker.

It was not the best beer in the world; in the Anglo-French Empire, the English made the best beer, and the Normans the second best. There were some excellent wines available here, but Master Sean usually drank wine only with meals. Distilled spirits he drank only on the rarest of occasions. Beer was his tipple, and this stuff wasn't really *bad*, it just wasn't as good as he preferred. He sighed and took another healthy swig.

He had time to kill and no place else to kill it. He had to catch the 6:05 train west for the ninety-odd mile trip to Rouen, which gave him two more hours of nothing to do.

On the floor at his feet was his symbol-decorated carpet-bag, which contained not only the tools of his profession but, now, the thaumaturgical evidence in the Zellerman-Blair case, which he had come specifically to Paris to get from his colleague, the Chief Forensic Sorcerer for His Grace, the Duke D'Isle. Anyone noticing that carpetbag closely would immediately recognize Master Sean as a sorcerer, but that was all right; he was not exactly traveling incognito, anyway.

"Would ye be ready for having another one, sir?"

Master Sean lifted his eyes from his nearly empty mug and pushed it across the bar with a smile. "I would indeed," he said to the barman. "And might that be the lilt of County Meath I'm hearing in your voice?"

The barman worked the pump. "It would," he said, returning the smile. "Would yours be the north of Mayo?"

"Close you are," said Master Sean. "Sligo it is."

There were not many people in the International. Six people at the bar besides Master Sean, and a dozen more seated at the booths and tables. The place wouldn't be really busy for an hour or so yet. The barman decided he had a few minutes for a friendly chat with a fellow Irishman.

He was wrong.

One of the waiters moved up quickly. "Murtaugh, come here," he said in an urgent undertone. "There's something funny."

Murtaugh frowned. "What?"

The waiter glanced round with warning eyes. "Come."

The barman shrugged, came out from behind the bar, and followed the waiter over to a booth in the far corner. Master Sean, as curious as the next man if not more so, turned round on his barstool to watch.

The room was not brightly lit, and the booth was partly in shadow, but the sorcerer's keen blue eyes saw most of the detail.

There was a well-dressed man sitting alone in the booth. He was in the corner of the booth, against the wall, and his head was bent down, as though he were looking intently at the newspaper which his hands held on the table before him. To his right was a drinking glass which was either completely empty or nearly so; it was hard to tell from where Master Sean sat.

The man neither moved nor spoke when the barman addressed him. The barman touched one of his hands to attract his attention. Still nothing.

Master Sean's common sense told him to stay out of this. It was none of his business. It was out of his jurisdiction. He had a train to catch. He had— He had an insatiable curiosity.

A magician's senses and perceptions are more highly developed, more highly trained, and more sensitive than those of the ordinary man. Otherwise, he would not be a magician. Master Sean's common sense told him to stay out of this, but his other senses told him that the man was dead and that this was possibly more complex than appeared on the surface.

Before the barman and the waiter could further disturb anything on or near the booth, Master Sean grabbed his carpetbag and walked quickly and unobtrusively over to the booth.

But he found that he had underestimated the sagacity and quickness of mind of his fellow Irishman. Barman Murtaugh was saying: "No, we don't touch him, John-Pierre. You go out and fetch an Armsman and a Healer. I'm pretty sure the feller's dead, but fetch a Healer all the same. Now move." As the waiter moved, Murtaugh's eye caught sight of Master Sean. "Please go back to your seat, sir," he said. "The old gent here's been taken a bit ill, and I've sent for a Healer."

Master Sean already had his identification out. "I understand. I don't think anyone else has noticed. The both of us could stand here while John-Pierre's gone, but that might attract attention, were you to be from your post so long. On the other hand, I can stand here and pretend to be talking to him, and no one will be the wiser. Meantime, you can get back to the bar and take careful notice if anyone shows any unusual interest in what's going on at this booth."

Murtaugh handed the identification papers back to Master
Sean and made up his mind. "I'll keep me eye out, Master Sorcerer." And headed back to his station.

2

The uniformed Men-at-Arms had arrived, made their
preliminary investigation, and sealed off the bar. There were
several indignant patrons, but they were soon quieted down.

The Healer, a Brother Paul, checked over the body, and,
after several thoughtful minutes, said: "It could be several
things—heart attack, internal hemorrhage, drugs, alcohol. I'd
have to get a chirurgeon to do an autopsy before I'd take
an oath on any of them."

"How long would you say he'd been dead, Brother Paul?"

"At least half an hour, Master Sean. Perhaps as much as
an hour. Call it forty-five minutes and you'd not be far off.
Funny how he just sat there without falling over or anything, isn't it?"

Master Sean wished he had some official standing; he'd
have his instruments out in half a minute and get some facts.
"It's an old schoolboy's trick," he replied to the Healer's
remark. "Surely you've done it yourself. You feel yourself
getting sleepy, so you prop yourself up at your desk in such
a way that you don't fall over—as he's done in the corner, there. Then you put your forearms on the desktop—
in this case, tabletop—and put your reading material between
them, so that it looks natural. Then you let your head go
forward. If you've done it properly, you can go right to sleep
and look as if you're reading unless somebody notices you're
not turning pages. Or gets at the right angle to see whether
your eyes are closed."

"That suggests he felt the drowsiness coming on," said
Brother Paul.

Master Sean nodded. "He'd not likely react that way to
a heart attack. If a man's that full of alcohol, he usually
doesn't have enough control or presence of mind to pull
it off properly. A drunk just puts his head on his forearms
and goes to sleep. How about internal hemorrhage?"

"It's possible. If the bleeding weren't too rapid, he'd begin to feel drowsy and might decide a little nap would be just the thing," Brother Paul agreed. "Certain drugs, of course, would have the same effect."

Around them, Men-at-Arms were taking statements from the patrons of the International Bar.

At that moment, the front door opened, and a smoothly-dressed, rather handsome man with a dapper little mustache entered, accompanied by another Man-at-Arms. He stopped just inside the door, looked all around, and then said: "Good evening, my sirs. I have the honor to be Plainclothes Sergeant-at-Arms Cougair Chasseur. I am in charge of this case. Where is the body?"

"This way, my sergeant," said one of the Men-at-Arms, and led the newcomer over toward Master Sean and Brother Paul. The Healer was wearing the habit of his Order, so Sergeant Cougair said, "It is that you are the Healer who was called?"

The Healer bowed his head slightly. "Brother Paul, of the Hospital of St. Luke-by-the-Seine."

"Very good." The sergeant looked at Master Sean. "And you, my sir?"

The stout little Irish sorcerer carefully took out his identification, and with it the special card issued by the local Chief Forensic Sorcerer. Sergeant Cougair looked them over. He smiled. "Ah, yes. It is that you work with Lord Darcy of Rouen, is it not?"

"It is," said Master Sean.

"It is that it is a very great pleasure to meet you, my sir, a very great pleasure, indeed!" he bubbled. Then his smile faded and he looked rather dubious. "But is it not that you are a little out of your jurisdiction?"

"I am," Master Sean agreed. The atrocious Parisian manner of mangling the Anglo-French language had always set his teeth on edge, and the fellow's manner didn't help much. "I was merely being of some small assistance until you arrived. I have no further interest in the case." When talking to a Parisian, Master Sean's brogue vanished almost without a trace.

The sergeant's face brightened again. "Of course. But naturally. Now let us see what we have here." He turned his attention toward the corpse. "Without a doubt, dead. Of what did he die, Brother Paul?"

"Hard to tell, Sergeant. Master Sean and I agree that the two most likely causes of death are internal hemorrhage—possibly of the cerebral area, more likely of the abdomen. And, second, the administration of some kind of drug."

"Drug? You mean a poison?"

Brother Paul shrugged. "Whether a given substance is a drug or a poison depends pretty much on the amount given, the method by which it was given, and the intent of its use. Any drug can be a poison, and, I suppose, vice versa."

"It is that it killed him, is it not?"

"We of the Healing profession, Sergeant, use the word 'poison' in a technical sense, just as you do the word 'murder.' All homicides are not murder. Death caused by the accidental administration of an overdose of a drug is not poisoning any more than death by misadventure is murder."

"Ah, I see. A nice distinction," the sergeant said, looking enlightened. "What, then, of suicide?"

"There, if the intent was deliberate suicide, then it was intent to kill. That makes it poisoning."

"Most comprehensible. Very well, then; if we assume poisoning in your technical sense, is it that it is murder or suicide?"

"Why, as to that, Sergeant Cougair," Brother Paul said blandly, "I fear that is your area of expertise, not mine."

Master Sean had listened to all this in utter silence. He had no further interest in the case. Hadn't he said so himself?

But Sergeant Cougair turned to him. "Is it that I may ask you a technical question, Master Sean?"

"Certainly."

"Is it that it is at all possible that the deceased was killed by Black Magic?"

For what seemed like a long second, there was no sound in the room except for the murmur of voices from the patrons of the bar and the Armsmen who were questioning them. The question, Master Sean knew, was loaded—but with what?

He shook his head decisively. "Not possibly. If Brother Paul's estimate of the time of death is correct—and I tend to agree with him—then I was in this room when it happened. There is no way a death-dealing act of Black Magic could have been perpetrated against the deceased without my knowing it."

"Ah. I presumed not," the sergeant said. "I presumed that had you known of such you would have mentioned it immediately. But it was my duty to ask, you comprehend."

"Of course."

Then he turned to the Armsman who had been standing unobtrusively nearby, taking down everything in a notebook. "Is it that the body has been searched?"

"But no, my sergeant. We awaited your coming."

"Then we shall do so immediately. No. Wait. Has anyone identified the deceased?"

"But no, my sergeant. The barman and the two waiters claim never to have seen him before. Nor do any of the patrons admit to any knowledge of him."

"They have looked at him thoroughly?"

"But yes, my sergeant. We marched them by while Brother Paul held up the head for one to view."

"And none of them knew him. Incredible! Well, to work. Let us examine his person and discover what we may."

Before they could move the body out of the booth, however, a uniformed Sergeant-at-Arms came in through the door, spotted Sergeant Cougair, and hurried over. "A word with you, Chasseur?"

"Yes." The two of them walked to one side and talked for perhaps a minute in low tones. Even Master Sean's sharp sense of hearing could not make out the words. Psychically, all he could get was disappointment, frustration, and irritation on the part of Sergeant Cougair.

The uniformed sergeant departed and Sergeant Cougair came slowly, thoughtfully back to where Master Sean and the others were waiting.

"A disaster," he murmured. "Most unfortunate."

"What seems to be the trouble?" Master Sean asked.

"Alas! A family entire have been wiped out by gas. The illuminating gas, you comprehend. A most important family they were, too—not titled, but wealthy. All dead."

"A disaster, indeed," Master Sean agreed.

"What? The deaths? Oh, yes; that, certainly. But that was not the disaster to which I referred."

"Oh?" Master Sean blinked.

"But no. I referred to the fact that foul play is suspected in the deaths of the Duval family, and our entire thaumaturgical staff has been called upon to aid in the apprehension

of the perpetrators of this heinous crime. I have no forensic sorcerer to aid me in my work. My case is considered
of importance so small that I cannot get even an apprentice for some hours yet. Delay! My God, the delay! And
meanwhile, one's prime piece of evidence slowly but most
surely decomposes before one's veritable eyes!"

Master Sean glanced at his watch. Five after five. He
sighed. "Why, as to that, my dear sergeant, I'll cast a
preservative spell over the body if you want. No problem."

The sergeant's eyes lit up. "By the Blue! How marvelous! I will at once take you up upon your offer!"

"Very good. But clear the rest of these folk out of here.
I don't want a bunch of undisciplined civilians gawping at
me while I do my work."

"But I cannot let them go, Master Sorcerer!" the sergeant
protested. "They are material witnesses!"

"I didn't say to let 'em go," Master Sean said tiredly. "I
doubt if the Grand Ballroom of this hotel is being used this
early in the evening. Get hold of the manager. Your men
can keep them in there for a while."

"Admirable! I shall see that it is done."

3

Four men stood quietly in the echoing silence of an
otherwise empty barroom. Three of them were Plainclothes
Sergeant-at-Arms Cougair Chasseur and two of his Men-at-
Arms. The fourth was Master Sorcerer Sean O Lochlainn.
Brother Paul had, somewhat regretfully, returned to his duties
at the hospital; having certified that the deceased was,
indeed, deceased, he was no longer needed.

Master Sean looked down at the body. The Armsmen had
shoved a couple of tables together and reverently laid the
corpse upon them as a sort of makeshift bier. They had
carefully undressed it, and, even more carefully, Master Sean
had examined the late unknown. He was, the sorcerer judged,
a robust man in his middle fifties. The body was scarred
in several places; five of them looked like saber wounds
which had been neatly stitched by a chirurgeon, four others came in pairs, front and back, each pair apparently made

by a single bullet. The rest were the sort of cuts and scrapes any active adult might accumulate. All of them were years old. Master Sean marked the location of each on a series of special charts which he always carried in his symbol-decorated carpetbag.

Moles, warts, discolorations, all were carefully and duly noted.

There were no fresh wounds of any kind, anywhere on the body.

None of this preliminary work was necessary for a preservation spell. That sort of thing was usually left for the autopsy room. But Master Sean was curious. When a man dies of mysterious causes practically in your lap, as it were, even the most uncurious of men would be interested, and Master Sean, both by nature and by training, was more inquisitive than most.

When the superficial examination was over, Master Sean took from his symbol-decorated carpetbag a featureless, eighteen-inch, ebon wand, half an inch in diameter.

That wand was not a glossy black. It was not even a dull, flat black. It was a fathomless black, like the endless night between the stars. It did not merely fail to reflect the light that fell upon it, it seemed to absorb light as though it were somehow *reaching* for it.

Under the precise control of Master Sean's right hand and fingers and arm, that wand began to weave an intricate pattern of symbols, series after series of them, above and around the dead man.

Those watching could sense, rather than see, that within and through the body, filling its every cell to the outermost layer of skin and hardly half a hairsbreadth beyond, a psychic field, generated and formed by the master sorcerer's mind and will, began to form.

There was no visible change in the body as that eighteen-inch rod of light-absorbing night wove its fantastic spell, but every man there *knew* that the spell was having its effect.

When it was finished, the ebon wand slowed and stopped.

After a moment, Master Sean said, matter-of-factly: "There, now; he'll last as long as you need him to." And he put his wand away.

"Thank you, Master Sean," Sergeant Cougair said simply.

Then, before he said another word, he took a couple of tablecloths from other tables and covered the body.

"I have seen that done many times, Master Sorcerer," the sergeant said then, "although never so quickly nor so gracefully. It has always seemed to me as a miracle."

"No such thing," said Master Sean rather testily. "I'm a thaumaturgist, not a miracle-worker. 'Tis simply a matter of applied science."

"Is it that I may ask what precisely happens?"

Sergeant Cougair did not know it, then or ever, but he had touched one of Master Sean's few weak spots. Master Sean O Lochlainn *loved* to lecture, to explain things.

"Well, now, that's very simple, Sergeant Cougair," he said expansively. "As you may know, matter is made up of tiny little particles, so small that they could never be seen under the most powerful microscope. Indeed, it has been estimated that a single ounce of the lightest of 'em would contain some seventeen million million million million of 'em. This theory of small particles was propounded first by a Greek philosopher named Demokritos about twenty-four hundred years ago. He called those particles 'atoms' and so do we, in his honor. His hypothesis has been confirmed by thaumaturgical theory and by certain experiments done by men learned in the Khemic Art."

"I comprehend," said the sergeant, looking as though he really did.

"Very well, then; these atoms are always full of energy; they vibrate and buzz about, which helps in their Khemic activity."

"Ah!" the sergeant, with a light in his eyes. "I comprehend! Is it that it is your spell which causes the cessation of all this—this 'buzzing about', as you call it?"

"Good Heavens, *no!*" Master Sean fairly snapped. "Why if I were to do such a thing as that, the body would freeze solid in an instant, and everything about it would likely burst into flame!"

"My God." The sergeant was instantly sobered by the thought of this phenomenon. "Continue, if you please."

"I will. Now, pay attention. These atoms react with each other to form conglomerates, and these conglomerates can react to form other conglomerates, and so on. All substances are composed of conglomerates of atoms, d'ye see. They react because each conglomerate is seeking a condition which will impose the least strain upon itself."

"A most natural desire," Sergeant Cougair commented.

"Exactly so. Now, then, in a living human being, these processes take place under conditions controlled by the life force, so that the food we eat and the air we breathe are converted into the energy and the substances we need. But these processes do not stop when the life force has departed; simply, they are no longer controlled. The body no longer has any resistance to microorganisms and fungi. The body decays.

"Even without microorganisms or fungi, these activities continue uncontrolled. That's why meat hung in a butcher's ice house becomes tender as it ages; the flesh digests itself, so to speak.

"Now, what a preservative spell does is make those atomic conglomerates *satisfied*. They wish to remain at their present energy levels, to maintain the *status quo* at the time the spell was cast. They are *satisfied*."

"It is that it kills the microorganisms, is it not?" the sergeant asked.

"Oh, aye. They can't survive under any such conditions as that."

Sergeant Cougair gave a slight shudder. "I shudder," he said, suiting words to action, "to think what it would do to a living man."

Master Sean grinned. "Nothing. Absolutely nothing. The life force of more highly organized beings resists the spell easily. Why, if yonder gentleman has a tapeworm, I assure you the worm is alive. He may be getting pretty hungry, but I assure you the spell didn't kill him.

"The spell you see, is very unstable. It's a static spell, and so bleeds off in time, anyway, but—oh, too much heat, for instance, would break the spell. The conglomerates would be dissatisfied again."

"Such as in the tropics?"

"It rarely gets that hot, even in the tropics. But a very hot bath, say—almost hot enough to scald—would do the job."

Sergeant Cougair raised his hands, palms out. "I assure you, Master Sorcerer, I have no desire to give a corpse a hot bath—or any other kind." Then, more briskly: "And now let us discover what we may in and about the clothing."

There was the usual assortment of keys, a pipe, tobacco pouch, pipe lighter, coins in the amount of a sovereign and a half, forty-two sovereigns in banknotes, a fountain pen, and a brand-new notebook containing nothing but empty pages. The identification folder contained cards and papers showing that the bearer was Andray Vandermeer, a retired Senior Captain of the Imperial Legion. That, thought Master Sean, would account for the scars.

His present address was No. 117 Rue Queen Helga, Paris. An Armsman was instructed to go there and discover what he could. "If there is a wife, a child, or other relative, break the news gently. You do not know the manner of his death. It may have been a heart attack. You comprehend?"

"But yes, my sergeant."

"Positive identification can wait until we have arrived him at the morgue. Go."

The Armsman went.

"And now for *this* small object," the sergeant continued. He was holding an eight-ounce brown glass bottle full of liquid. "It has upon it the label of Veblin & Son, Pharmaceutical Herbalists. It contains, according to the same label, 'Tincture of Cinchona Bark'—now what would that be?"

"An alcoholic solution of vegetable alkaloids from a certain tree of New France," Master Sean said promptly.

"A poison?"

"Or a drug," Master Sean said. "Remember what Brother Paul said."

"Ah, certainly. But it may have been what killed him. If so, it was suicide, for we found it in his own coat pocket."

"What killed him didn't come from that bottle," Master Sean pointed out dryly. "It's still full, and the seal of the stopper is unbroken."

"What? Oh. You are quite right. But perhaps there is another bottle. Lewie, go into the Grand Ballroom and tell Armand to have all the suspects searched. Bring John-Jack back with you, and we will search this barroom."

"But yes, my sergeant." And off he went, leaving Master Sean alone with Sergeant Cougair.

"Sergeant," the stout little Irish sorcerer said carefully, "I would not presume to tell you your business, but while all this searching is going on, you might find out more about that medicine if you checked with the pharmacist who filled the prescription, and with the Healer who issued it. The stuff is taken for the cure of malaria, one of the few diseases a Healer cannot handle without such aids."

"That will be done in due time, Master Sean," said the sergeant.

"Why not now? Veblin & Son is just across the arcade in this very hotel."

Sergeant Cougair jerked his head down and looked again at the bottle in his hand. "So it is! But yes! You are correct! I thank you for calling it to my attention."

"Think nothing of it." Master Sean looked at his wristwatch. "And now, if you'll pardon me, I fear I must say goodbye. If I don't hurry, I shall miss my train."

The sergeant looked at him in astonishment. "But most certainly you shall miss your train, Master Sorcerer! You are a material witness and a suspect in a murder case. You cannot leave the city."

"I?" Master Sean was even more astonished. "*I?*"

"Certainly. It is an axiom of mine that the least likely suspect is the one most likely to have done it. Besides, I shall need you for the autopsy, to determine whether or not murder *has* been done."

Master Sean could only stare at him.

There were no words to be found for the occasion.

4

It is not wise to meddle in the affairs of wizards, for reasons well known to the *cognoscenti*, and when Master Sir Aubrey Burnes, Chief Forensic Sorcerer for His Grace the Duke D'Isle, heard what Sergeant-at-Arms Cougair Chasseur had done, he definitely felt it was meddling.

Master Sir Aubrey did not hear about it from Master Sean. That stout little Irish sorcerer was perfectly capable of washing his own linen, but he had had to make a teleson call to Lord Darcy in Rouen to explain why he had missed his train, and he had used the official Armsmen's teleson to do it. And the grapevine is almost as efficient as the teleson.

That Chasseur was well within his rights to have detained Master Sean is not debatable; whether he should have exercised those rights is moot.

Having decided that it was partly his own fault for sticking his nose into the case in the first place, and still beset by curiosity in the second place, Master Sean decided that he might as well go ahead with the autopsy and with the similarity analysis of the contents of the bottle and the dregs in the glass.

He didn't do the actual operation himself, of course; that was not his area of competence. The actual work was done by a husky young chirurgeon from Gascony who looked more like a butcher's helper than a chirurgeon, but whose fingers and brain were both nimble and accurate.

By half past seven, the body had been all sewn up nicely, and was ready to be claimed by the wife—if and when she actually identified it as being that of S/Cpt Andray Vandermeer, LL., Ret. The Armsman who had been sent to No. 117 Rue Queen Helga reported that a servant had informed him that Goodwife Vandermeer was out shopping and was not expected to return until about eight.

Master Sean, meanwhile, pondered the data he had at hand.

The tentatively-identified Vandermeer had most certainly died of an overdose of some as yet unidentified drug. A similarity analysis showed that it was the same drug as that found in the dregs at the bottom of the glass found on the table near him. The prescription drug bottle had contained exactly what the label said it did, and was most certainly *not* the alkaloid that had killed Vandermeer.

Master Sean looked over the notes he had made during the autopsy. The internal condition of the body . . . the liver . . . the kidneys . . . those lesions on the brain. . . .

The whole picture rang a very small bell somewhere in the recesses of Master Sean's memory, but he couldn't quite bring up the data. He'd never *seen* a body in just this condition before, of that he was sure. No, it was something he had read or been told. But what? Where?

The beefy young chirurgeon rose from his desk across the room and came over to where Master Sean was sitting. He had a sheaf of papers in his hand. "Here's my report, Master Sorcerer," he said politely. "If there's anything you'd like to add or change . . ." He let the sentence trail off and handed the magician the papers.

Master Sean read the report carefully, then shook his head. "No changes, Doctor Ambro, and the only thing I'd like to add is the name of the poison. Unfortunately, I can't as yet." He smiled up at the younger man. "By the bye, I should like to compliment you on your skill and dexterity with a scalpel. I've never seen a neater job. There are some pathologists who feel that just because the—er—patient is dead, any old hack work will do."

"Well, Master," the chiruurgeon said, "I feel that if a man lets himself get sloppy with the dead, he'll soon get sloppy with the living. It generates bad habits. I owe a great deal to the Healing Art, and I feel that as a technician I should do my best to repay that debt. If it weren't for a great Healer, I wouldn't be a chirurgeon at all."

"Oh? How's that, Dr. Ambro?" Master Sean was curious.

Dr. Ambro grinned. "As a lad, I had my heart set on being a chirurgeon. I felt it was a useful and rewarding trade. Then I found I wasn't cut out for it—no pun intended."

"Really?" Master Sean raised an eyebrow. "You seem singularly apt at the work to me."

Dr. Ambro chuckled. "I couldn't stand the smell. I couldn't even operate on the practice cadavers. Fresh blood nauseated me. Opening the abdominal cavity was even worse. And the dead? Forget it. And it *was* the smell. Nothing else. I couldn't even stand the odor of a raw steak or side of pork."

"Ah, I see," said Master Sean. "An unusual phenomenon, but by no means unique. Pray continue."

"Nothing much to tell, Master. A fine old Healer, Father Debrett of Pouillon, cast a mild spell on me. Now I find the scent pleasant enough—rather like roses and lilies, if you follow me."

"Oh, certainly. A well-known procedure," the sorcerer said. "Well, I'm glad it was done; it would have been a shame to let your skill be wasted."

"Thank you, Master Sean; thank you very much."

There was a knock on the office door, and it opened. A massive, totally bald head with a smiling face and bushy black eyebrows appeared around the door. "Hullo, chaps. May I come in?" the intruder asked in a pleasant baritone.

"My dear Sir Aubrey!" said Master Sean. "Of course! Do come in!"

Master Sir Aubrey Burnes, Chief Forensic Sorcerer for His Grace D'Isle, came the rest of the way into the room. He stood perhaps a hair under six feet, and was massive, not fat. He had been wrestling champion for Oxford University in 1953 and '54, and had kept himself in trim ever since.

"I didn't know if anyone connected with this office would be welcome," he said. "I'm frightfully sorry about all this, Master Sean."

"Come, come," said Master Sean. "Not your fault, my dear fellow. How has your gas poisoning case come out so far?"

"The Duvals? Sad case. Two brothers and their wives having a little party. Got a little drunk out, I'm afraid. The two men brought a keg of beer up from the cellar at one point, banged it against a gas line. Cracked the line. The servants had all been told off to go to the other wing and leave them alone, you see. By the time they had drunk a good part of the keg, plus assorted other inebriating beverages, the room was full of gas. They were too blotto to notice. By the time the servants smelled the gas and took alarm, it was too late. We're bringing in the bodies for autopsies to clinch the evidence, so Dr. Ambro will have more work to do, but there's really no question about what happened. Death due to misadventure." His smile came back: "How's your case doing?"

Master Sean told him, then added: "But I wish you wouldn't call it *my* case. Your Sergeant Cougair can have it."

"That consummate ass!" Master Sir Aubrey said with a scowl. "Well, well, what's done is done. The thing to do is for us to find out who did it and clear the thing up. I wish Lord Varney were here; our Chief Investigator's the man for this sort of thing. Unfortunately, he's laid up in hospital, as I told you earlier today."

Master Sean nodded. "Aye. How's he coming, by the bye?"

"Well as could be expected. He's a good investigator, but I don't think I'll go mountain climbing when I'm his age."

"No, nor I," Master Sean agreed. "Not even at my age. The African elephants may have crossed the Alps with Hannibal, but Irish elephants like meself stay on level ground."

Master Sir Aubrey chuckled. "And English elephants the same."

"Elephants?" said a voice from the door. "What is it that the elephants have to do with the case?"

It was Sergeant-at-Arms Cougair Chasseur.

"Nothing whatever, Sergeant," Master Sir Aubrey said coldly. "We were not discussing your case."

"No, indeed," Master Sean said smoothly. "We were discussing the case, two years ago, of the elephant theft from the Maharajah of Rajasthan in Jodhpur."

"Someone stole an elephant?" the sergeant asked in some surprise.

"Eight of them," said Master Sean. "Eight white elephants."

"My God! And how is it they were recovered?"

"They never were," Master Sean said solemnly. "They vanished utterly, without a trace."

"It seems hardly possible," Sergeant Cougair said in awe. Then his eyes narrowed and he glanced at Sir Aubrey, then back to Master Sean. "The solution is most obvious to the deductive mind. The elephants were stolen by a sorcerer. You may depend upon it."

"I wish," said Master Sir Aubrey, "that we could have assigned you the case."

"But of course," the sergeant agreed. "I dare say I should have found them easily. Elephants are very large, are they not? Not easily concealed. Well, it is of no consequence. I have a case at present to solve."

"How are you doing so far?" Master Sean asked.

"Indeed, I shall tell all," said the sergeant, "but first, is it that it is permitted that I ask the results of the autopsy? Is it that it is indeed a case of poisoning?"

"It is," said Master Sean, and proceeded to give the results of his labors.

Sergeant Cougair scowled. "Then it is indeed murder. No bottle or paper or box that could have contained the poison has been found. It has disappeared as if by—" His narrowed eyes glanced covertly at Master Sean. "—as if by magic." He let his eyes relax and looked down at his hands. "It is sad that we do not know what the poison was."

"I'm working on it," said Master Sean dryly.

"Most of a certainty," the sergeant said agreeably. "Now, as I promised, I shall tell you how we have progressed ourselves.

"We have thus far found no motive whatever. The

twenty-two customers who were in the establishment have been released to their businesses or homes, but forbidden to leave the city. I have a list of them here, should you care to peruse it. The two waiters and the barman we are keeping for a while, since it is apparent that it is more likely that one of them poisoned the drink than any other. Equally, we have apprehended for questioning the two waiters who were on duty before the changing of the shift at four of the clock. We are still looking for the barman; he is a bachelor and has not yet returned home.

"We have questioned the Goodman Jorj Veblin, who is the 'Son' of Veblin & Son, and he has deposed that the Senior Captain Vandermeer has appeared at his establishment every Tuesday for the past three months with a prescription from the Reverend Father Pierre St. Armand, Healer, for a week's supply of the medicine.

"We spoke to the Father Pierre, a venerable old gentleman, who deposes that the said Senior Captain Vandermeer did, indeed, suffer from the malaria, as you conjectured. He appears to have obtained this disease while serving with the Imperial Legion in the Duchy of Mechicoe, upon the northern continent of the New World, New England."

Master Sean sighed. He needed no one to tell him that Mechicoe was in New England, nor that New England was the northern continent of the western hemisphere. Next the sergeant would be explaining that the square of seven was forty-nine.

There was a short silence, broken at last by Master Sir Aubrey. "Well? What else?"

The sergeant spread his hands and shrugged. "Alas! I greatly fear me, Master Sorcerer, that that is all the information we have obtained so far."

"Who benefits by his death?" Master Sean asked.

"So far as we have determined, his wife only. He has no children of record. But there was no woman in the barroom during that time."

"She might have disguised herself," said the Irish sorcerer.

"It is possible, but we have a description of her. She is young—not yet thirty—with very long black hair, very tanned skin, and dark eyes. She is adjudged very beautiful, with a slim waist and a full figure—a *very* full figure. Such a one would be difficult to conceal; it has been a warm day, so she could not have worn a cloak without attracting attention. Still, we shall, of course, check her every move during the afternoon. She is reported to be shopping. If so, we can find out where and at what times, do you comprehend."

"She might have paid someone to do it for her," Master Sean pointed out.

"Again, it is possible, but it has been my experience that a paid assassin does not poison his victims. The knife, the club, the pistol are his tools. Or, for some of the more clever, the accidental-seeming death. Poison is more the tool of the amateur."

Master Sean had to admit to himself that, for once, Sergeant Cougair was very likely right.

"The problem is," Sergeant Cougair continued, "that *anyone* could have done it. Distract a man's attention but for a few seconds, and the drink is poisoned. Our sole hope, I fear me much, is to find the poison container, for which we are even now searching diligently." He looked at his wristwatch. "I go now to search out the whereabouts of Cambray, the missing barman. It was, after all, he who mixed the deceased his drink, and perhaps he has information for us. With God, my sirs." And he left.

Master Sean stared at the door that had closed behind the sergeant for two full seconds before he said: "Now let me see. Cambray, the barman, poisons Vandermeer, goes off duty, drops the poison container into the Seine, takes the 4:22 to Bordeaux, and can be in Spain in the morning, safely away from extradition. But *he* may merely be able to give information, while *I* am a suspect. I admire his reasoning powers for their depth and complexity. No merely intelligent man could reason in that manner."

"I told you he was a consummate ass," said Master Sir Aubrey.

5

Sergeant Cougair had been right about another thing: The late Senior Captain's wife was beautiful, and had a *very* lush figure. In addition, she stood no more than five feet tall.

No, Master Sean thought, it would not be possible for her to go into a bar and not be noticed, no matter what she was wearing.

There was another possibility, however. Did the woman have the Talent? If so, there were several ways she could have gone into that bar without attracting attention. The Tarnhelm Effect, for one. It did not, as popularly supposed, render a person invisible; it was merely a specialized form of avoidance spell. Anyone using the Tarnhelm Effect remained unnoticed because no one else looked in that direction; they would avoid the person with their eyes; they would look anywhere except at that person.

Mary Vandermeer had come in with three other people to identify the body: the late Senior Captain's manservant, Humfrey; the pharmacist, Jorj Veblin; and the Healer, Father Pierre. Humfrey was an old Vandermeer family retainer; he had helped bring up the child who was to become Senior Captain Andray. His old face was lined with worry wrinkles, as though the job had been far from easy.

Master Pharmacist Jorj Veblin was a competent-looking man in his early thirties, with regular, rather pleasant features and mousy brown hair which he brushed straight back and kept cut somewhat shorter than the current style.

Father Pierre looked, as the cant phrase had it, "ninety years older than Methuselah." He was taller than Master Sean, but very thin and frail-looking. His face had few wrinkles, and a benign smile, but the skin was tightly drawn over the facial bones, and the few white hairs on his skull looked like an aura in the gaslight.

One by one, separately, they were led into the room where the dead man lay. One by one, separately, they identified him as Andray Vandermeer.

Old Humfrey had tears in his eyes. "Bad, very bad. The Captain had a good many years in him yet, he did."

Goodwife Mary choked up and could say nothing but: "That's him. That's Andray."

Master Jorj looked both grim and sad. "Yes, that's Captain Andray. Poor fellow." He shook his head sadly.

Father Pierre looked long and carefully. "Yes, that's poor Andray." he said at last. Then, turning to Master Sean: "Has he been given the last rites?"

"He has not, Father," the sorcerer said. "And there is no

thaumaturgical reason why he should not be given them. We have all the evidence of that kind we need."

Senior Captain Andray Vandermeer was given the last rites of Holy Mother Church. The wife, the valet, the pharmacist, and two Armsmen were present at the ceremony. Master Sean and Master Sir Aubrey were in another room, constructing a subtle trap.

Perhaps "subtle" isn't exactly the right word, but no other will quite do. In form, it was about as subtle as coming up behind a person who is pretending deafness and shouting "*Boo!*" in his ear. But in practice, it was such that only one person would be aware that anything out of the ordinary had happened, and then only if that person possessed the Talent.

The spell itself is simple and harmless. As Master Sean had once put it to Lord Darcy: "Imagine a room full of people, each one with a different kind of noisemaker— a rattle, a drum, a horn, a ball of stiff paper to crackle, a hissing through the teeth, every sort of distracting noise you can imagine. What would you do if you had to think?"

"Put my fingers in my ears, I should imagine," Lord Darcy had replied.

"Exactly, me lord. And there's not a Talented person alive who wouldn't do the psychic equivalent of just that, if that distraction spell were cast on him. A person with little or no Talent just becomes distracted and loses his train of thought. He hasn't the least notion that it came from outside his own mind. A person with a good, but untrained Talent will recognize the spell for what it is, but won't know what to do about it. A Person with a trained Talent will block it instantly."

"Can't the response be feigned?" his lordship had asked.

"It can, me lord, but only after the initial blocking. In order to think out a lie, a false reaction, you need at least a fraction of a second of peace. Which you can't get without putting up the block, d'ye see."

"How could that be detected by a sorcerer who's putting out all that mind noise?" Lord Darcy had wanted to know.

"He couldn't," Master Sean had explained. "That's why it takes two to spring the trap. One to say *Boo!* and the other to see if the victim jumps."

This time, Master Sir Aubrey would cast the quick-shock spell, and Master Sean would watch the victim.

"Fat lot of good it did us," Master Sir Aubrey said half an hour later. "I noticed no reaction from any of the three." They had not tested Father Pierre; there was no question about a Healer having the Talent.

"Master Jorj and Goodman Humfrey haven't got a trace of the Talent," Master Sean said. "The young woman has a definite touch of it, but it's undisciplined and untrained. If there's any magic involved in this killing, we haven't uncovered it, and we haven't found a magician, either."

Master Sir Aubrey looked at the wall clock. "Fifteen of nine. You should have been in Rouen by now."

Master Sean scowled. "And now I can just twiddle my thumbs. There's nothing left for me to do. Except think. I wish I could remember what there is about that poison. . . ."

"See here, old friend," said Master Sir Aubrey, running a palm over his smooth pate, "we've got a room upstairs, with bed and bath, for important visitors. You are a visitor, and you are the Chief Forensic Sorcerer for Normandy. You are, *ergo et ipso facto*, qualified to use that room. A good shower will make you feel better. Or have a tub, if you like."

"My dear Sir Aubrey," said Master Sean with a smile wreathing his face, "you have made yourself a deal. Let's see this room."

The big sorcerer led him up a flight of stairs to a narrow corridor on the upper story. He took a key from his key ring and unlocked a door.

The room was small, but comfortable, like those of a good country inn, with the added attraction of an adjoining bath.

"I couldn't ask for better," Master Sean said. "Fortunately, I always carry a change of underclothes in me carpetbag."

He put his symbol-decorated carpetbag on the bed, opened it, and rummaged around until he came up with the underclothes. "Socks? Socks? Ah, yes, here they are."

Master Sir Aubrey was looking at the bag, using more senses than just his eyes. "Interesting anti-tampering spell you've got on your bag," he said. "Don't think I've ever come across one with quite those frequencies and textures. What's the effect, if I may ask? I detect the paralysis component, but . . . hmmm . . ."

"A little invention of me own," said Master Sean, a bit smugly. "Anybody opens it but meself, he immediately closes it again, then sits down next to it and does nothing. He's in a semi-paralytic trance, d'ye see. If anybody else comes along before I get there, the man who tried to open me bag will jump up and down and gibber like a monkey. That attracts attention. Anyone seeing a fellow behave like that in the vicinity of a sorcerer's bag will know immediately there's something wrong."

Master Sir Aubrey laughed. "I *like* it! I won't ask you for the specs on the spell; I'll try to work out one of my own."

"Be glad to give 'em to you," Master Sean said.

"No, no; more fun to work it out myself."

"Whatever you say. Look, I'll freshen meself up, and I'll see you in, say, half an hour. Is there somewhere we can get a bite to eat? I haven't had a morsel since noon."

"Do you like German food?"

"With German beer?"

"With German beer."

"Love it."

"Good," said Master Sir Aubrey. "I know a fine place. I'll be waiting downstairs. Here's the key to this room. You can leave your bag here, if you like. Just shove it under the bed and lock the door. I'll post notice that the room is yours, and nobody but a fool would disturb it."

"Right," said Master Sean. "I'll see you at—say, twenty past nine?"

6

The *Kolnerschnitzel* at Hochstetter's was delicious, and the Westphalian beer was cool and tangy. In fact, the beer was so good that, after packing away the *Kolnerschnitzel*, the two magicians had another stein.

"Ahhh!" said Master Sean, patting himself three inches below his solar plexus. "That's just what I needed. I feel so good that I'm not even angry with Sergeant Cougair any more."

"Speaking of whom," said Master Sir Aubrey, "the sergeant came into the office while you were bathing. I didn't want to bother you with anything until you'd eaten."

"Oh? Is it something that should bother me?" Master Sean asked.

"Not particularly. More data. I just didn't want you to be trying to piece everything together until you had a cold beer in your hand and enough fuel inside you to power your brain."

"I see. What was it?"

"He finally found the barman who went off duty at four this afternoon. Fellow named Cambray. He knew the deceased by sight and name. Seems the Captain came in every week, had a few drinks and left."

Master Sean nodded. "I see. Came in every week to get his prescription filled and then had a few snorts at the bar before going home."

"Precisely. Regular as clockwork, it seems. Now, here's the peculiar thing: he always ordered the same drink, which is not peculiar in itself, but what he drank was a Mechicain liqueur called *Popocotapetl*. It's not much called for, and it's rather expensive, since it's imported from across the Atlantic."

Master Sean nodded. "I've tasted it. A former pupil of mine, Master Lord John Quetzal, gave me a few drinks from a bottle his father, the Duke of Mechicoe sent him. It's a semi-sweet liqueur made from some cactus, I think."

"This wasn't semi-sweet," said Master Sir Aubrey.

"No?"

"No. Sergeant Cougair impounded the bottle—the only bottle they had, by the way—and tasted it, the idiot. He reports that the drop on his fingertip was as bitter as potash."

Suddenly several things came together in Master Sean's mind. "*Coyotl* weed!" he snapped.

The other sorcerer blinked. "What?"

"*Coyotl* weed," the Irish sorcerer said more calmly. "I was told about it by Lord John Quetzal while he was studying forensic sorcery under me. It's an alkaloid extract of the weed, actually. Been used as a poison in Mechicoe for centuries. Lord John Quetzal said it has no pharmaceutical uses, at all. I doubt if we could get a sample of the stuff to do a similarity analysis with. The Mechicains used to use it for poisoning rats, but since they've got trained sorcerers now to handle that problem, the stuff has been declared illegal except for research purposes. So someone put it in the bottle of *Popocotapetl*, eh?"

"Yes, and that makes the whole case crazier than ever," Master Sir Aubrey said. "It could have been put in there at *any* time previous to the murder—days before, even. And it would have killed anybody who drank it. *Anybody*, not just Captain Andray Vandermeer."

Master Sean said: "We might be dealing with a psychotic individual. Or, possibly, someone who wants to ruin the reputation of the International Bar or the Cosmopolitain Hotel. Your Sergeant Cougair has his work cut out for him."

"Oh, the sergeant has his theories," Master Sir Aubrey said dryly. "You see, since the barmen and waiters all agree that nobody came behind the bar except for themselves, then whoever put the poison in the bottle must have been invisible. According to the sergeant, I mean. And that means a sorcerer, and that means you."

"*Me?*" Master Sean managed to keep his voice under control—barely.

"'Least Likely Person Theory,' he calls it," the big magician continued. "But I think it's more than that. This case really has him baffled. He can't understand what happened— can't see how the trick was done. The more data he comes up with, the more mysterious it gets, and the more confused *he* gets. Not his type of case, really."

"What *is* his type of case?" Master Sean asked. "Nursery riddles?"

"No." Master Sir Aubrey chuckled. "Nothing that complicated. Street killings, bar killings, brawls, that sort of thing. The knife drawn in anger, the sudden smash of a club. Such things are usually pretty much open-and-shut. But this one is beyond his mental equipment. And instead of admitting it, he's trying to bull it through. If it weren't for your presence there, he'd probably have already rushed off and arrested the widow as the *most* likely suspect."

"What's my presence got to do with it?" Master Sean said irritatedly.

"To him," said the English sorcerer, "if there's no obvious answer at hand, then there's sorcery afoot. And you're the sorcerer. He still can't find that bottle of poison, and he thinks you magicked it away somehow."

With great care, Master Sean lifted his beerstein and drained it slowly without stopping. He put it down. "I will not," he said calmly, "let that blithering jackass upset me digestion. Let's get back to the station and see what new developments have come about, if any."

They paid their bill and strolled leisurely the quarter-mile back to the Armsmen's station, discussing several subjects that had nothing to do with the murder case.

It was twenty-five of eleven when they went into Master Sir Aubrey's office.

Lord Darcy was waiting for them.

7

Lord Darcy, Chief Investigator for His Royal Highness, Richard, Duke of Normandy, looked up from the book he was reading and took his pipe from his mouth. "I trust you gentlemen had a good meal," he said in a mild voice.

"Me lord!" Master Sean's voice showed a touch of surprise. "When did you get in?"

"Fifteen minutes ago, my dear Sean," said Lord Darcy, with a wry smile on his handsome face. "When you informed me that the Parisian authorities had you in open arrest, I took the next train east. We have to have that evidence on the Zellerman-Blair case in court on the morrow. How are you, Master Sir Aubrey?"

"As well as could be expected, my lord. And you?"

"Well, but impatient. Whom do I see to get Master Sean released on his own recognizance?"

"Justice Duprey keeps late hours. When he hears Master Sean's side of the case, against Sergeant Cougair's, he'll release Sean on the instant. But *you'll* have to bring the motion; *I* can't, naturally, since I'd be going against the . . ."

"I understand," Lord Darcy cut in. "Nor could Master Sean without representation. Very well; we'll have this Cougair and Master Sean up before the Justice as soon as possible. The problem is that nobody around here has seen Sergeant Cougair for the past hour, and nobody seems to know where he is. Naturally, he'll have to appear to tell his side of the story or the Justice won't hear it."

"Oh, I'm sure he's around somewhere," Master Sir Aubrey said. "Wait a little. When's your train back to Rouen?"

"There's a slow one at two-five," Lord Darcy said. "We'll

have to be on it. The express doesn't leave until five-twenty, and it will get us in very late for a six o'clock court.

"However, I'm sure we can make it. Would it be asking too much for you two to tell me what this farrago is all about?"

"Aye," said a voice from the door. " 'Tis a story Ah'd like tae be hearing', masel'!"

The tall, lean, well-muscled man in the doorway looked rumpled. His black-and-silver uniform was neat enough, but his thick thatch of dark, curly hair looked as if it hadn't seen a comb for weeks, his firm, dimpled jaw was bluely unshaven, and his deepset, piercing blue eyes looked rather bloodshot beneath their shaggy brows.

All three of the men in the room immediately recognized Darryl Mac Robert, Chief Master-at-Arms for the City of Paris. They gave him a ragged chorus of: "Good evening, Chief Darryl."

Chief Darryl grinned but shook his head. "Nae; 'tisna that. Ah was oop a' the nicht last nicht wi' the Pemberton robbery; nae sleep this mornin' because o' the Neinboller swindlin' case; oop a' the afternoon wi' the Duval gassing. Ah try tae get soom sleep o' the evenin', and Ah find that a routine death in a bar has snowballed as if it were rollin' down the Matterhorn. Nae, lads, 'tis nae a guid evenin'. But 'tis guid tae see yer lairdship."

"I quite sympathize with you," said Lord Darcy. "Well, do come in and sit down, my dear Chief. Master Sean, would you begin at the beginning and proceed therefrom to the present?"

"Glad to, me lord."

The telling of it took nearly three quarters of an hour, but every detail, every nuance had been told when Master Sean was through. When it was over, Lord Darcy thoughtfully smoked his pipe in silence. Chief Darryl looked grim. "It looks," he said, "as if we hae us a madman loose i' the City."

Lord Darcy took his pipestem from his mouth. "I disagree, Chief Darryl. This was a carefully planned and carefully executed murder aimed solely at one man: Senior Captain Andray Vandermeer."

"D'ye ken who did it, then?"

"The evidence we have all points in one direction. If my

theory is correct, we only need a little more data, and the thing will be quite clear."

"Then let's *get* it, mon! Ah need the sleep!"

"Well, it's hardly my place to tell your Sergeant Cougair how to conduct his own case," Lord Darcy replied carefully.

"As o' this moment, Ah'm takin' charge o' the case masel'," Chief Darryl said firmly. He looked at Master Sean. "And ye'll nae have to take Chasseur before the Justice. He'll drop the charges."

"I'm afraid, however," Lord Darcy said, "that we shall have to trouble the Justice after all. We need two search warrants."

"Ah'll get 'em. For what places?"

"One for the residence of the late Captain Andray, and another for the pharmacy of Veblin & Son."

Chief Darryl was making notes on a pad he had taken from his uniform belt. "Wha' are we tae search for, yer lairdship?"

"A bottle of *Popocotapetl* that hasn't been opened, and a bottle of poison that has."

Chief Darryl murmured to himself as he wrote. "Liqueur at Andray's home. Poison at pharmacy."

"No, no!" his lordship said sharply. "There will undoubtedly be a few bottles of the liqueur at Andray's home, and there are poisons galore in any pharmacy. No, it's the other way round; liqueur at pharmacy, poison at Andray's."

"Verra well, me laird. Anything else?"

"Find out who sold the *Popocotapetl* to the International Bar, and pick him up. I want the man who made the delivery, not the merchant, unless they are one and the same."

"Och, aye. Anything else?"

"One more thing. Bring in Mary Vandermeer, Jorj Veblin, and, following Sergeant Cougair's theory of the Least Likely Suspect, I fear you must bring in Father Pierre."

"Surely *he* couldn't have had anything to do with this murder, me lord!" Master Sean said in astonishment.

"I assure you, my dear Sean," Lord Darcy said solemnly, "that without Father Pierre's Talent, this murder could never have happened—at least, not in this way."

"Ah'll get some men on it," Chief Darryl said heavily.

8

Midnight. Three men stood in the thaumaturgical laboratory at Armsmen's Headquarters.

Chief Darryl put two bottles on the lab table. "There they are, just as ye said, yer lairdship. Item—" He picked up a pint-sized, stoppered brown glass bottle. "—a bottle found in a closet in Goodwife Mary Vandermeer's bedroom. Three-quarters empty, it is." He put it down and picked up the other, a tall quart bottle full of golden yellow liquid. "Item, a bottle of *Popocotapetl*, seal unbroken." He put it down. "And we got the woman and Veblin in holdin' cells. You wanted to see Father Pierre and the spirits man?"

"Not just yet. I want to be sure that what is in that brown bottle is what killed Vandermeer. Will you make a similarity analysis, Master Sean?"

"Aye, me lord, I'll have to go up and get me bag."

"No need," said Master Sir Aubrey, coming in through the door. He held Master Sean's symbol-decorated carpet-bag in one hand. "I took the liberty of fetching it myself."

"Ah, fine. Thank you. If ye'll excuse me, gentlemen, I'll get about me work."

Lord Darcy and Master Sir Aubrey followed Chief Darryl out of the lab, down the hall, and into the Chief's office.

"Sit ye doon gentle sirs," he said with a wave toward a couple of chairs. He planted himself firmly behind his desk. "Ah'd like tae know, ma laird, why ye eliminated the barmen as suspects, if ye dinna mind."

"Because the bottle itself was poisoned," Lord Darcy said promptly. "If a barman wants to poison a customer, he can put the stuff in just one drink. He wouldn't have to poison a whole bottle of good liquor."

"But suppose he were a madman who didn't care who he killed?" Master Sir Aubrey asked. "If he wanted to kill a lot of people, wouldn't poisoning the bottle be easiest?"

"Possibly. But in that case, he'd poison a bottle of brandy or ouiskie, something that was called for regularly, not a rare liqueur that's little called for and very expensive. And certainly he would have chosen another poison than the *coyotl*-weed extract. No, that poison was intended for

Vandermeer and none other. He was the only customer they had who drank *Popocotapetl*."

"But, ma laird," the Chief objected, "anyone could ha' coom intae the International and ordered the stuff. Some Mechicain micht hae come in, for instance."

"True," Lord Darcy said, "but he would be in very little danger of being poisoned. Consider: one usually sips a semi-sweet liqueur, especially an expensive one. One doesn't just knock it back against the tonsils as if it were cheap apple brandy. One sip of that stuff, and the customer would spit it out and complain loudly to the barman. It's a very bitter substance."

There was a pause. Suddenly, Master Sir Aubrey said: "Then why, in God's name, did *Vandermeer* drink it?"

"Aha! That's precisely the question I asked myself," said Lord Darcy. "Why should—"

He was interrupted by the entrance of Master Sean. "No doubt about it, me laird," he said firmly, "that's the stuff that killed the Captain."

"Excellent. We progress. Chief Darryl, will you have one of your men bring in Father Pierre?"

Father Pierre, looking benign but somewhat puzzled, was led in by a uniformed Armsman a minute later. Chief Darryl said: "Ah'm sorry to have inconvenienced ye, Reverend Sir, but we hae a most heinous crime tae clear oop."

"Oh, that's all right, I assure you, Chief Darryl," the old priest said. "I am happy to be of any assistance that I may."

Master Sean was mildly pleased to hear that the priest's Parisian accent had been smoothed and made less harsh by time, travel, and education.

"Verra well, Reverend Sir. Ah thank ye. Lord Darcy here would like tae ask ye a question or two."

"Of course." Father Pierre turned his soft eyes on the Chief Investigator. "What is it, my lord?"

"You were treating the late Captain Andray for malaria, I believe, Father?" Lord Darcy asked.

"Yes, I was, my lord."

"Do you know where he contracted the disease?"

"In Mechicoe, while he was serving with the Imperial Legion."

"And you were treating him with an herbal prescription?"

"Yes, my lord. Tincture of Cinchona. It is a specific for the disease."

"How did you get him to take it regularly, Father? It's a rather bitter drug, is it not?"

"Oh, yes. Very bitter." The priest glanced at Master Sean and Master Sir Aubrey. "You sorcerers are acquainted with the spell, I am sure. It's a matter of shifting modes of sensory perception."

"Aye," said Master Sean. "I was talking to a man a few hours ago who had had his sense of smell subtly altered so that an otherwise nauseous smell would smell sweet to him."

"Just so." Father Pierre looked back at Lord Darcy. "I cast a similar spell over the Captain, so that the bitterness would register as sweetness, you see. Mixed with a little lemon juice and water, a spoonful of the tincture became quite a pleasant drink—to him."

"Would that apply to just the tincture, or to anything bitter?" Lord Darcy asked.

"Oh, anything that was bitter would taste sweet to him. No getting around that. I'd warned him of it. He was not to accept anything as being sweet unless he knew for a fact that it *was* sweet, unless he knew that it actually contained sugar or honey. He was a very careful man, was Captain Andray."

"A lesson one learns in the Legion," murmured Lord Darcy. "Thank you very much, Father. I think that's all for now. Thank you again."

When the Healer had gone, Lord Darcy looked at the others. "You see? Of all the many people who might have come into that bar and ordered *Popocotapetl*, only Captain Andray Vandermeer would have sat there and quietly sipped that bitter potion without raising a fuss. He knew the liqueur was supposed to be sweet, and never noticed the *coyotl* extract."

"But why use a bitter poison like that?" Chief Darryl asked. "Wouldna it ha' been easier to use something more palatable?"

Lord Darcy shook his head. "That poison has one very important quality. Master Sean, you said it was used as a rat poison. Why?"

"Because it's painless," Master Sean said. "It puts the

victim quietly to sleep before it kills. Rats are pretty smart creatures; if they know a bait is poisoned, they'll avoid it, and they know if it kills a few friends in agony. For some reason, the bitter taste don't bother 'em if the stuff is mixed with bran and a goodly dollop of sugar-cane syrup."

"And how did the poison get i' the bottle i' the first place?" the Chief Master-at-Arms asked.

"That worried me, too, for a few moments," Lord Darcy admitted. "How could an unauthorized person get behind the bar, poison a bottle of expensive liqueur, and leave, without being seen? The International never closes, so it couldn't have been a burglary job. Obviously, then, the bottle, when it was brought into the bar, *was already poisoned!*" He waited while they absorbed that, then said, "Chief, will you have the liquor man brought in?"

The man who delivered potable spirits to the International Bar was a rotund, red-faced man named Baker who looked as though he smiled a lot when he was not caught up in the hands of the law.

"Master Sean," Lord Darcy whispered to the sorcerer, "would you go fetch that bottle of *Popocotapetl?*"

Master Sean nodded and left without a word.

Again Chief Darryl went through the preliminaries and then turned the questioning over to Lord Darcy.

"Goodman Baker," his lordship began, "I understand you make deliveries of spirits regularly to the Cosmopolitain Hotel."

"That I do, my lord." Baker spoke Anglo-French with as pronounced an English accent as Lord Darcy did, but it was pure middle-class London.

"To what other establishments do you deliver besides the International Bar?"

"Well, my lord, of the usual drinkin' spirits, that's the only place."

"You say 'the usual drinking spirits.' What other kind do you deal in?"

"Well, there's the high-proof clear spirits, what I delivers to the pharmacy of Veblin & Son. They uses 'em to make medicines, d'yer see. And they also takes the special medicinal brandy."

"I thought as much. Now, I want you to think hard—*very* hard—about my next question. Did anyone at Veblin

& Son order anything out of the ordinary in the past few months?"

"Don't have to think too hard on that one, yer lordship," Baker said with a self-satisfied air. "He bought—young Master Jorj, that is—he bought a quart of that Mechicain stuff, the Popey-cottypetal. Very dear it is, yer lordship, and as we being the only importers of it in Paris, I remembered his buying of it."

"And when was this?" Lord Darcy asked.

"Four weeks ago Friday last."

"And when was the last time you made a delivery to Veblin & Son?"

"Friday last."

"How very gratifying," Lord Darcy murmured with a pleased smile. "And did you deliver a bottle of *Popocotapetl* to the International Bar on that day?"

"I did, my lord. I suppose they told you that."

"As a matter of fact, they did not. I deduced it. I shall make a further deduction: that you always and invariably make your deliveries to Veblin & Son *before* you make your deliveries to the International."

"Why, that's true as Gospel, my lord! I always park my delivery wagon to the rear of the hotel and my helper holds the horses while I takes the deliveries in on a hand cart. From the rear door, the first place you comes to is the pharmacy, so I makes my delivery there first."

"Bringing your hand cart in with you, I presume?"

"Oh, indeed, my lord. Leave it out in the corridor, and likely there'd be a bottle or two missing when I came out."

"And you carry the delivery into the rear of the pharmacy, leaving the hand cart in the front room?"

"I do. Master Jorj keeps an eye on it for me. He'd not steal from it himself, nor let anyone else do so."

"I dare say not," Lord Darcy agreed. "Then you go on to the International and deliver their orders."

"I do, my lord."

By this time, Master Sean had returned with the bottle of *Popocotapetl*. Lord Darcy extended a hand, and the little Irish sorcerer handed him the bottle. Lord Darcy put it on the desk in front of Baker. "Is this the bottle you sold to Master Jorj Veblin four weeks ago Friday last?"

Baker looked at the bottle. "Well, now. I couldn't swear

as to that, my lord. Them bottles are all pretty much alike, and . . ."

Suddenly he picked up the bottle and looked more closely at it. "Wait a minute, my Lord. This ain't the bottle I sold him."

"How do you know?"

Baker pointed at some small figures written on the label. "The date's wrong, my Lord. This is from the shipment we received from Mechicoe two weeks ago."

"That's a stroke of luck!" said Lord Darcy. "Master Sean, bring in the bottle we found in the bar."

Master Sean returned within a minute, bearing the poisoned bottle. Lord Darcy took it, and without letting it out of his hands, showed the label to Baker. "What about this bottle?"

"Well now, I can't positively identify it as being the one I sold to Master Jorj, but it's got the proper date on it."

"Very well. Thank you very much for your help, Goodman. You may go home now."

When Baker had gone, Lord Darcy picked up his pipe and lighter, and puffed the pipe alight before speaking. "And there you have it, gentlemen. I daresay, Chief Darryl, that a little probing into the activities of Mary Vandermeer and Jorj Veblin over the past several months will reveal a greater intimacy between them than has heretofore been suspected. Vandermeer was much older than his wife, and it may be that she decided to dispose of him in favor of a younger man—Veblin, to be exact. If the Captain was like most Legion officers, he left her a small, but comfortable, fortune."

I'm afraid I don't quite see the whole picture," said Master Sir Aubrey. "Exactly what happened?"

"Very well. Some years ago Captain Andray married his present wife—rather, widow—who was a woman of Mechicain descent. He probably married her over there. At any rate, he brought her with him when he retired. And she brought with her a bottle of a *coyotl* extract. We can't be certain why, at this time; perhaps she was planning his murder even then.

"Exactly how she met Veblin, and how they made their arrangements, is something you'll have to get your men to dig out. Chief Darryl, but that's routine legwork."

"But how did ye know 'twas them?"

"Who else knew that he was under a Healer's spell that would make bitter things taste sweet? He undoubtedly told his wife, and the pharmacist would certainly guess it.

"At any rate, she gave Veblin the poison. She knew of the Captain's taste for *Popocotapetl*, and so informed Veblin. Veblin thereupon bought a bottle of the stuff, laced it with poison, and waited until Baker delivered a fresh bottle to the International Bar. Then, while Baker was unloading the medicinal spirits in the back room, Veblin switched bottles so that the poisoned bottle was delivered to the bar. Then it was simply a matter of waiting until the following Tuesday—today—" He glanced at the clock. "Yesterday," he corrected himself, "the Captain comes in, orders his drink as usual, and that's that."

"But why did he keep the good bottle after the switch?" Master Sean asked. "Why not get rid of it?"

"Because he knew that eventually the investigators would find the poison in the bottle and check with the importers. They would inform us, as they did, that he had bought a bottle. It was his intention to say, 'Oh, yes, I did, and I still have it.' He didn't know that importers of spirits put the date on the goods when they are received."

"It seems tae me," said Chief Darryl, "that a pharmacist would have plenty of poisons on hand withoot havin' tae use a special import frae Mechicoe."

"That's just the point," said Lord Darcy. "If he had used any of the normal pharmaceuticals, any competent forensic sorcerer could have identified whatever poison he used, which would increase his chances of being found out. He was hoping that there wouldn't be a man in Europe who could identify *coyotl* extract. Any other questions?"

Chief Darryl thought for a moment, then shook his head. "That aboot covers it, ma laird. Since we know how it was done and who did it, the rest is simple." He looked up at the clock at the wall. "Where the De'il is Sergeant Cougair? Ah hae a few words to say to that wee mon."

"Why, as to that," Master Sir Aubrey said, almost offhandedly, "the last time I saw him was in the upstairs bedroom."

Chief Darryl shot to his feet. "What the Hell is he doin' oop there?"

"Sitting. Just sitting."

"Armsman Stefan!" bellowed the Chief Master-at-Arms. The

door to the corridor popped open, and a Man-at-Arms stuck his head in.

"But yes, my Chief?"

"Go oop the stair tae the visitor's bedroom and fetch me Sergeant Cougair Chasseur."

"But yes, my Chief!" The door closed.

Master Sean looked at Master Sir Aubrey. Master Sir Aubrey looked at the ceiling. Lord Darcy looked puzzled.

Man-at-Arms Stefan returned. It was obvious from the contortions of his face that he was attempting to control a giggle. "My Chief, it is apparent that the Sergeant Cougair has taken leave of his senses. When one speaks to him, he leaps up and down and gibbers like the monkey."

"He does?" Chief Darryl headed toward the door. "We'll see aboot this. Coom wi' me!"

In half a minute, there were loud voices and laughter coming down the stairwell.

Master Sean sighed and opened his carpetbag. He took from it a small four-inch wand made from a twig of the hyssop plant. "I'll go up and remove the spell," he said. "You didn't by any chance tell him the poison bottle was in me carpetbag, did you, Master Sir Aubrey?"

"Of course not," the sorcerer said indignantly. "Quite the contrary. I absolutely forbade him to look there at all."

Master Sean left. Lord Darcy said nothing; he had the Zellerman-Blair case to worry about, and he had no wish to meddle in the affairs of wizards.

PART THREE

The Ipswich Phial

The pair-drawn brougham moved briskly along the Old Shore Road, moving westward a few miles from the little village of St.-Matthew's-Church, in the direction of Cherbourg.

The driver, a stocky man with a sleepy smile on his broad face, was well bundled up in a gray driving cloak, and the hood of his cowl was pulled up over his head and covered with a wide-brimmed slouch hat. Even in early June, on a sunshiny day, the Normandy coast can be chilly in the early morning, especially with a stiff wind blowing.

"Stop here, Danglars," said a voice behind him. "This looks like a good place for a walk along the beach."

"Yus, mistress." He reined in the horses, bringing the brougham to an easy stop. "You sure it's safe down there, Mistress Jizelle?" he asked, looking to his right, where the Channel stretched across to the north, toward England.

"The tide is out, is it not?" she asked briskly.

Danglars looked at his wristwatch. "Yus. Just at the ebb now."

"Very well. Wait for me here. I may return here, or I may walk on. If I go far, I will signal you from down the road."

"Yus, mistress."

She nodded once, sharply, then strode off toward the beach.

She was a tall, not unhandsome woman, who appeared to be in late middle age. Her gray-silver hair was cut rather shorter than the usual, but was beautifully arranged. Her costume was that of an upper-middle-class Anglo-French woman on a walking tour, but it was more in the British style than the Norman: well-burnished knee-high boots; a Scottish woolen skirt, the hem of which just brushed the boot-tops; a matching jacket; and a soft sweater of white wool that covered her from waist to chin. She wore no hat. She carried herself with the brisk, no-nonsense air of a woman who knows what she is and who she is, and will brook no argument from anyone about it.

Mistress Jizelle de Ville found a pathway down to the beach. There was a low cliff, varying from fifteen to twenty feet high, which separated the upper downs from the beach itself, but there were slopes and washes here and there which could be maneuvered. The cliff itself was the ultimate high-tide mark, but only during great storms did the sea ever come up that high; the normal high tide never came within fifteen yards of the base of the cliff, and the intervening space was covered with soft, dry sand which was difficult to walk in. Mistress Jizelle crossed the dry sand to the damper, more solidly packed area, and began walking westward.

It was a beautiful morning, in spite of the slight chill; just the sort of morning one would choose for a brisk, healthful walk along a pleasant beach. Mistress Jizelle was a woman who liked exercise and long walks, and she was a great admirer of scenic beauty. To her right, the rushing wind made scudding whitecaps of the ebbing tide and brought the "smell of the sea"—an odor never found on the open expanse of the sea itself, for it is composed of the aroma of the sea things which dwell in the tidal basins and the shallow coastal waters and the faint smell of the decomposition of dead and dying things beached by the rhythmic ebb and flow of tide and wave.

Overhead, the floating gulls gave their plaintive, almost catlike cries as they soared in search of the rich sustenance that the sea and shore gave them.

Not until she had walked nearly a hundred yards along the beach did Mistress Jizelle see anything out of the ordinary. When she did, she stopped and looked at it carefully. Ahead and to her left, some eight or nine yards from the base of the cliff, a man lay sprawled in the dry sand, twenty feet or so above the high-tide line.

After a moment, she walked toward the man, carefully and cautiously. He was certainly not dressed for bathing;

he was wearing the evening dress of a gentleman. She walked up to the edge of the damp sand and stopped again, looking at the man carefully.

Then she saw something that made the hairs on the back of her neck rise.

Danglars was sitting placidly in the driver's seat of the brougham, smoking his clay pipe, when he saw the approaching trio. He eyed them carefully as they came toward the carriage. Two young men and an older one, all dressed in the work clothes typical of a Norman farmer. The eldest waved a hand and said something Danglars couldn't hear over the sound of the waves and the wind. Then they came close enough to be audible, and the eldest said: "Allo! Got dee any trouble here?"

Danglars shook his head. "Nup."

The farmer ignored that. "Me an' m'boys saw dee stop up here, an' thought mayap we could help. Name's Champtier. Samel Champtier. Dese two a my tads, Evrit an' Lorin. If dou hass need a aid, we do what we can."

Danglars nodded slowly, then took his pipe from his mouth. "Good o' ya, Goodman Samel. Grace to ya. But I got no problem. Mistress wanted to walk along the beach. Likes that sort of thing. We head on pretty soon."

Samel cleared his throat. "Hass dou broke dy fast, dou an' d' miss-lady? Wife fixin' breakfast now. Mayap we bring du somewhat?"

Danglars took another puff and sighed. Norman farmers were good, kindly folk, but sometimes they overdid it. "Broke fast, Goodman Samel. Grace to ya. Mistress comes back, we got to be gettin' on. Again, grace to ya."

"Caffe, then," Samel said decisively. He turned to the elder son. "Evrit! Go tell dy mama for a pot a caffe an' two mugs! Run it, now!"

Evrit took off like a turpentined ostrich.

Danglars cast his eyes toward heaven.

Mistress Jizelle swallowed and again looked closely at the dead man. There was a pistol in his right hand and an ugly hole in his right temple. There was blood all over the sand around his head. And there was no question about his being dead.

She looked up and down the beach while she rather dazedly brushed at her skirt with the palms of her hands. Then, bracing her shoulders, Mistress Jizelle turned herself about and walked back the way she had come, paralleling her own footprints. There were no others on the beach.

Three men were talking to Danglars, and Danglars did not seem to be agitated about it. Determinedly, she strode onward.

Not until she was within fifteen feet of the brougham did Danglars deign to notice her. Then he tugged his forelock and smiled his sleepy smile. "Greeting, mistress. Have a nice walk?" He had a mug of caffe in one hand. He gestured with the other. "Goodman Samel and his boys, mistress, from the near farm. Brought a pot o' caffe."

The three farmers were tugging at their forelocks, too.

"I appreciate that," she said. "Very much. But I fear we have an emergency to attend to. Come with me, all of you."

Danglars widened his eyes. "Emergency, mistress?"

"That's what I said, wasn't it? Now, all of you follow me, and I shall show you what I mean."

"But, mistress—" Danglars began.

"Follow me," she said imperatively.

Danglars got down from the brougham. He had no choice but to follow with the others.

Mistress Jizelle led them across the sparse grass to the edge of the cliff that overlooked the place where the dead man lay.

"Now look down there. There is a dead man down there. He has, I think, been shot to death. I am not much acquainted with such things, but that is what it looks like to me."

The four knelt and looked at the body below. There was silence for a moment, then Samel said, rather formally: "Dou be right, mistress. Dead he be."

"Who is he, goodman?" she asked.

Samel stood up slowly and brushed his trousers with calloused hands. "Don't rightly know, mistress." He looked at his two sons, who were still staring down with fascination. "Who be he, tads?"

They stood up, brushing their trousers as their father had. Evrit, the elder, spoke. "Don't know, Papa. Ee not from hereabout." He nudged his younger brother with an elbow. "Lorin?"

Lorin shook his head, looking at his father.

"Well, that does not matter for the moment," Mistress Jizelle said firmly. "There is Imperial Law to follow in such cases as this, and we must do so. Danglars, get in the brougham and return to—"

"But, Mistress Jizelle," Danglars cut in, "I can't—"

"You must do exactly as I tell you, Danglars," she said forcefully. "It is most important. Go back to St.-Matthew's-Church and notify the Rector. Then go on to Caen and notify the Armsmen. Goodman Samel and his boys will wait here with me and make sure nobody disturbs anything. Do you understand?"

"Yus, mistress. Perfec'ly." And off he went.

She turned to Samel. "Goodman, can you spare some time? I am sure you have work to do, but I shouldn't like to be left here alone."

Samel smiled. "Mornin' chores all done, mistress. Eldest tad, Orval, can take care of all for a couple hours. Don't fret." He looked at the younger boy. "Lorin, go dou an' tell dy mama an' dy brother what happen, but nobody else. An' say dey tell nobody. Hear?"

Lorin nodded and ran.

"And bring dou back somewat to eat!" Evrit yelled after him.

Samel looked worried. "Mistress?"

"Yes, Goodman Samel?"

"Hass dou noticed somewat funny about d' man dere?"

"Funny?" She raised an eyebrow.

"Yea, mistress." He pointed down. "All round him, sand. Smooth. No footprints but dine own, an' dey come nowhere near him. Fresh dead, but—how he get dere?"

Five days later, Sir James le Lein, Special Agent of His Majesty's Secret Service, was seated in a comfortable chair in the study-like office of Lord Darcy, Chief Investigator for His Royal Highness, Richard, Duke of Normandy.

"And I still don't know where the Ipswich Phial is, Darcy," he was saying with some exasperation. "And neither do they."

Outside the open window, sounds of street traffic—the susurration of rubber-tired wheels on pavement, the clopping of horses' hooves, the footsteps and voices of a thousand people, and the myriad of other small noises that make up the song of a city—were wafted up from six floors below.

Lord Darcy leaned back in the chair behind his broad desk and held up a hand.

"Hold it, Sir James. You're leaping far ahead of yourself. I presume that by 'they' you mean the *Serka*—the Polish Secret Service. But what is this Phial, anyway?"

"I can't tell you for two reasons. First, you have no need to know. Second, neither do I, so I couldn't tell you if I wanted. Physically, it's a golden cylinder the size of your thumb, stoppered at one end with a golden stopper, which is sealed over with soft gold. Other than that, I know nothing but the code name: The Ipswich Phial."

Sean O Lochlainn, Master Sorcerer, who had been sitting quietly in another chair with his hands folded over his stomach, his eyes half closed, and his ears wide open, said: "I'd give a pretty penny to know who assigned that code name; sure and I'd have him sacked for incompetence."

"Oh?" said Sir James. "Why?"

Master Sean opened his eyes fully. "If the Poles don't know that the Ipswich Laboratories in Suffolk, under Master Sir Greer Davidson, is devoted to secret research in magic, then they are so incredibly stupid that we need not worry about them at all. With a name like 'Ipswich Phial' on it, the *Serka* would *have* to investigate, if they heard about it."

"Maybe it's just a red herring designed to attract their attention while something else is going on," said Lord Darcy.

"Maybe," Master Sean admitted, "but if so, me lord, it's rather dear. What Sir James has just described is an auric-stabilized psychic shield. What would you put in such a container? Some Khemic concoction, like an explosive or a poison? Or a secret message? That'd be incompetence compounded, like writing your grocery list on vellum in gold. Conspicuous consumption."

"I see," said Lord Darcy. He looked at Sir James. "What makes you think the *Serka* hasn't got it already?"

"If they had it," Sir James said, "they'd have cut and run. And they haven't; they're still swarming all over the place. There must be a dozen agents there."

"I presume that your own men are all over the place, too?"

"We're trying to keep them covered," Sir James said.

"Then they know you don't have the Phial, either."

"Probably."

Lord Darcy sighed and began filling his silver-chased porcelain pipe. "You say the dead man is Noel Standish." He tapped a sheaf of papers with his pipestem. "These say he was identified as a man named Bourke. You say it was murder. These say that the court of His Majesty's Coroner was ready to call it suicide until you put pressure on to keep the decision open. I have the vague feeling, James, that I am being used. I should like to point out that I am Chief Criminal Investigator for the Duke of Normandy, not— repeat: *not*—an agent of His Majesty's Secret Service."

"A crime has been committed," Sir James pointed out. "It is your duty to investigate it."

Lord Darcy calmly puffed his pipe alight. "James, James." His lean, handsome face was utterly impassive as he blew out a long plume of smoke. "You know perfectly well I am not obliged to investigate every homicide in the Duchy. Neither Standish nor Bourke was a member of the aristocracy. I don't *have* to investigate this mess unless and until I get a direct order from either His Highness the Duke or His Majesty the King. Come on, James—convince me."

Master Sean did not smile, although it was somewhat of a strain to keep his face straight. The stout little Irish sorcerer knew perfectly well that his lordship was bluffing. Lord Darcy could no more resist a case like this than a bee can resist clover blossoms. But Sir James did not know that. He did know that by bringing the case before his superiors, he could eventually get an order from the King, but by then the whole thing would likely be over.

"What do you want, Darcy?" the King's Agent asked.

"Information," his lordship said flatly. "You want me to go down to St.-Matthew's-Church and create a diversion while you and your men do your work. Fine. But I will not play the part of a dupe. I damn well want to know what's going on. I want the whole story."

Sir James thought it over for ten or fifteen seconds, then said: "All right, my lord. I'll give it to you straight."

For centuries, the Kings of Poland had been expanding, in an ebb-and-flow fashion, the borders of their territories, primarily toward the east and south. In the south, they had been stopped by the Osmanlis. In the east, the last bite had been taken in the early 1930s, when the Ukraine was swallowed. King Casimir IX came to the throne in 1937 at the age of twenty, and two years later had plunged his country into a highly unsuccessful war with the Empire and her Scandinavian allies, and any further thought of expansion to the east was stopped by the threat of the unification of the Russian States.

Poland was now, quite literally, surrounded by enemies who hated her and neighbors who feared her. Casimir should have taken a few years to consolidate and conciliate, but it was apparent that the memory of his father and his own self-image as a conqueror were too strong for him. Knowing that any attempt to march his armies into the German buffer states that lay between his own western border and the eastern border of the Empire would be suicidal as things stood, Casimir decided to use his strongest non-military weapon: the *Serka.*

The nickname comes from a phrase meaning roughly: "The King's Right Arm." For financial purposes, it is listed in the books as the Ministry of Security Control, making it sound as if it were a division of the King's Government. It is not; none of His Slavonic Majesty's ministers or advisors know anything about, or have any control over, its operation. It is composed of fanatically loyal men and women who have taken a solemn vow of obedience to the King himself, *not* to the Government. The *Serka* is responsible to no one but the King's Person.

It is composed of two main branches: The Secret Police (domestic), and the Secret Service (foreign). This separation, however, is far from rigid. An agent of one branch may at any time be assigned to the other.

The *Serka* is probably the most powerful, most ruthless instrument of government on the face of the Earth today. Its agents, many of them Talented sorcerers, infest every country in Europe, most especially the Anglo-French Empire.

Now, it is an historical fact that Plantagenet Kings do not take kindly to invasion of their domain by foreign sovereigns; for eight centuries they have successfully resisted such intrusive impudence.

There is a saying in Europe: "He who borrows from a Plantagenet may repay without interest; he who steals from a Plantagenet will repay at ruinous rates."

His present Majesty, John IV—by the Grace of God, King of England, Ireland, Scotland, and France; Emperor of the Romans and Germans; Premier Chief of the Moqtessumid Clan; Son of the Sun; Count of Anjou and Maine; Prince Donator of the Sovereign Order of St. John of Jerusalem; Sovereign of the Most Ancient Order of the Round Table, of the Order of the Leopard, of the Order of the Lily, of the Order of the Three Crowns, and of the Order of St. Andrew; Lord and Protector of the Western Continents of New England and New France; Defender of the Faith—was no exception to that rule.

Unlike his medieval predecessors, however, King John had no desire to increase Imperial holdings in Europe. The last Plantagenet to add to the Imperial domain in Europe was Harold I, who signed the original Treaty of Kobnhavn in 1420. The Empire was essentially frozen within its boundaries for more than a century until, during the reign of John III, the discovery of the continents of the Western Hemisphere opened a whole new world for Anglo-French explorers.

John IV no longer thought of European expansion, but he deeply resented the invasion of his realm by Polish *Serka* agents. Therefore, the theft of a small golden phial from the Ipswich Laboratories had provoked instant reaction from the King and from His Majesty's Secret Service.

"The man who actually stole it," Sir James explained, "is irrelevant. He was merely a shrewd biscuit who accidentally had a chance to get his hands on the Phial. Just how is immaterial, but rest assured that that hole has been plugged. The man saw an opportunity and grabbed it. He wasn't a Polish agent, but he knew how to get hold of one, and a deal was made."

"How much time did it take him to deal, after the Phial was stolen?" Lord Darcy asked.

"Three days, my lord. Sir Greer found it was missing within two hours of its being stolen, and notified us straight away. It was patently obvious who had taken it, but it took us three days to trace him down. As I said, he was a shrewd biscuit.

"By the time we'd found him, he'd made his deal and had the money. We were less than half an hour too late. A *Serka* agent already had the Phial and was gone.

"Fortunately, the thief was just that—a thief, not a real *Serka* agent. When he'd been caught, he freely told us everything he knew. That, plus other information received, convinced us our quarry was on a train for Portsmouth. We got hold of Noel Standish at the Portsmouth office by teleson, but . . ."

The plans of men do not necessarily coincide with those of the Universe. A three-minute delay in a traffic jam had ended with Noel Standish at the slip, watching the Cherbourg boat sliding out toward the Channel, with forty feet between himself and the vessel.

Two hours later, he was standing at the bow of H.I.M.S. *Dart,* staring southward into the darkness, listening to the rushing of the Channel waters against the hull of the fast cutter. Standish was not in a good mood.

In the first place, the teleson message had caught him just as he was about to go out to dine with friends at the Bellefontaine, and he had had no chance to change; he felt silly as hell standing on the deck of a Navy cutter in full evening dress. Further, it had taken better than an hour to convince the Commanding Admiral at the Portsmouth Naval Docks that the use of a cutter was imperative—and then only at the cost of a teleson connection to London.

There was but one gem in these otherwise bleak surroundings: Standish had a firm psychic lock on his quarry.

He had already had a verbal description from London. *Young man, early to middle twenties. Five feet nine. Slender, but well-muscled. Thick, dark brown hair. Smooth shaven. Brown eyes. Well formed brows. Face handsome, almost pretty. Well-dressed. Conservative dark green coat, puce waistcoat, gold-brown trousers. Carrying a dark olive attaché case.*

And he had clearly seen the quarry standing on the deck of the cross-Channel boat as it had pulled out of Portsmouth, heading for Cherbourg.

Standish had a touch of the Talent. His own name for a rather specialized ability was "the Game of Hide and Seek," wherein Standish did both the hiding and the seeking. Once he got a lock on someone he could follow him anywhere. Further, Standish became psychically invisible to his quarry;

even a Master Sorcerer would never notice him as long as Standish took care not to be located visually. Detection range, however, was only a matter of miles, and the man in the puce waistcoat, Standish knew, was at the limit of that range.

Someone tapped Standish on the shoulder. "Excuse me, sir—"

Standish jerked round nervously. *"What? What?"*

The young officer lifted his eyebrows, taken aback by the sudden reaction. This Standish fellow seemed to have every nerve on edge. "Begging your pardon, sir, but the Captain would have a word with you. Follow me, please."

Senior Lieutenant Malloix, commanding H.I.M.S. *Dart*, wearing his royal blue uniform, was waiting in his cabin with a glass of brandy in each hand. He gave one to Standish while the junior officer quietly disappeared. "Come in, Standish. Sit and relax. You've been staring off the starboard bow ever since we cast off, and that's no good. Won't get us there any the faster, you know."

Standish took the glass and forced a smile. "I know, Captain. Thanks." He sipped. "Still, do you think we'll make it?"

The captain frowned, sat down, and waved Standish to a chair while he said: "Hard to say, frankly. We're using all the power we have, but the sea and the wind don't always do what we'd like 'em to. There's not a damn thing we can do about it, so breathe deep and see what comes, eh?"

"Right you are, Captain." He took another swallow of brandy. "How good a bearing do we have on her?"

S/Lt Malloix patted the air with a hand. "Not to worry. Lieutenant Seamus Mac Lean, our navigator, has a journeyman's rating in the Sorcerer's Guild, and this sort of thing is his specialty. The packet boat is two degrees off to starboard and, at our present speed, forty-one minutes ahead of us. That's the good news."

"And the bad news?"

Malloix shrugged. "Wind variation. We haven't gained on her in fifteen minutes. Cheer up. Pour yourself another brandy."

Standish cheered up and drank more brandy, but it availed him nothing. The *Dart* pulled into the dock at Cherbourg one minute late, in spite of all she could do.

Nevertheless, Goodman Puce-Weskit was less than a hundred yards away as Standish ran down the gangplank of the *Dart,* and the distance rapidly closed as he walked briskly toward his quarry, following his psychic compass that pointed unerringly toward Puce-Weskit.

He was hoping that Puce-Weskit was still carrying the Phial; if he wasn't, if he had passed it on to some unknown person aboard the packet, the whole thing was blown. The thing would be in Krakowa before the month was out.

He tried not to think about that.

The only thing to do was follow his quarry until there came a chance to waylay and search him.

He had already given a letter to the captain of the *Dart,* to be delivered as soon as possible to a certain address on the Rue Queen Brigid, explaining to the agent in charge of the Cherbourg office what was going on. The trouble was, Standish was not carrying a tracer attuned to the Cherbourg office; there was no way to get in touch with them, and he didn't dare leave Puce-Weskit. He couldn't even set up a rendezvous, since he had no idea where Puce-Weskit would lead him.

And, naturally, when one needed an Armsman, there wasn't one in sight.

Twenty minutes later, Puce-Weskit turned on to the Rue Queen Brigid.

Don't tell me he's headed for the Service office, Standish thought. *My dear Puce-Weskit, surely you jest.*

No fear. A dozen squares from the Secret Service office, Goodman Puce-Weskit turned and went into a caffe-house called the Aden. There, he stopped.

Standish had been following on the opposite side of the street, so there was less chance of his being spotted. Dodging the early morning traffic, narrowly avoiding the lead horse of a beer lorry, he crossed the Rue Queen Brigid to the Aden.

Puce-Weskit was some forty feet away, toward the rear of the caffe-house. Could he be passing the Phial on to some confederate?

Standish was considering what to do next when the decision was made for him. He straightened up with a snap as his quarry suddenly began to move southward at a relatively high rate of speed.

He ran into the Aden. And saw his mistake.

The rear wall was only thirty feet away. Puce-Weskit had gone through the rear door, and had been standing *behind* the Aden!

He went right on through the large room, out the back door. There was a small alleyway there, but the man standing a few feet away was most certainly not his quarry.

"Quick!" Standish said breathlessly. "The man in the puce waist coat! Where did he go?"

The man looked a little flustered. "Why—uh—I don't know, sir. As soon as his horse was brought—"

"Horse? Where did he get a horse?"

"Why, he left it in the proprietor's charge three or four days ago. Four days ago. Paid in advance for the keeping of it. He asked it to be fetched, then he went. I don't know where."

"Where can I rent a horse?" Standish snapped.

"The proprietor—"

"Take me to him immediately!"

"And that," said Sir James le Lein, "is the last trace we were able to uncover until he reported in at Caen two days later. We wouldn't even know that much if one of our men hadn't been having breakfast at the Aden. He recognized Standish, of course, but didn't say anything to him, for obvious reasons."

Lord Darcy nodded. "And he turns up dead the following morning near St.-Matthew's-Church. Any conjecture on what he may have been doing during those two days?"

"It seems fairly clear. The proprietor of the Aden told us that our quarry—call him Bourke—had his saddlebags packed with food packets in protective-spell wrappers, enough for a three, maybe four-day trip. You know the Old Shore Road that runs southeast from Cherbourg to the Vire, crosses the river, then goes westward, over the Orne, and loops around to Harfleur?"

"Of course," Lord Darcy said.

"Well, then, you know it's mostly farming country, with only a few scattered villages, and no teleson connections. We think Bourke took that road, and that Standish followed him. We think Bourke was headed for Caen."

Master Sean lifted an eyebrow. "Then why not take the train? 'Twould be a great deal easier and faster, Sir James."

Sir James smiled. "It would be. But not safer. The trouble with public transportation is that you're essentially trapped on it. When you're fleeing, you want as much freedom of choice as possible. Once you're aboard a public conveyance, you're pretty much constrained to stay on it until it stops, and that isn't under your control."

"Aye, that's clear," said Master Sean. He looked thoughtful. "This psychic lock-on you mentioned—you're sure Standish used it on Bourke?"

"Not absolutely certain, of course," Sir James admitted. "But he certainly had that Talent; he was tested by a board of Masters from your own Guild. Whether he used it or not at that particular time, I can only conjecture, but I think it's a pretty solid assumption."

Lord Darcy carefully watched a column of pipesmoke rise toward the ceiling and said nothing.

"I'll agree with you," Master Sean said. "There's no doubt in me mind he did just that, and I'll not say he was wrong to do so. *De mortuis non disputandum est.* I just wonder if he knew how to handle it."

"How do you mean?" Sir James asked.

"Well, let's suppose a man could make himself perfectly transparent—'invisible,' in other words. The poor lad would have to be very careful, eh? In soft ground or in snow, he'll leave footprints; in a crowd, he may brush up against someone. Can you imagine what it would be like if you grabbed such a man? There you've got an armful of air that feels fleshy, smells sweaty, sounds excited, and would taste salty if you cared to try the experiment. You'll admit that such an object would be suspect?"

"Well, yes," Sir James admitted, "but—"

"Sir James," Master Sean continued, "you have no idea how conspicuous a psychically invisible person can be in the wrong circumstances. There he stands, visible to the eye, sensible to the touch, audible to the ear, and all the rest— *but there's nobody home!*

"The point I'm making, Sir James, is this: How competent was Noel Standish at handling his ability?"

Sir James opened his mouth, shut it, and frowned. After a second, he said: "When you put it that way, Master Sean, I must admit I don't know. But he handled it successfully for twelve years."

"And failed once," said Master Sean. "Fatally."

"Now hold, my dear Sean," Lord Darcy said suddenly. "We have no evidence that he failed in that way. That he allowed himself to be killed is a matter of cold fact; that he did so in that way is pure conjecture. Let's not leap to totally unwarranted conclusions."

"Aye, me lord. Sorry."

Lord Darcy focused his gray eyes on Sir James. "Then I have not been called in merely to create a diversion, eh?"

Sir James blinked. "I beg your pardon, my lord?"

"I mean," said his lordship patiently, "that you actually want me to solve the problem of 'who killed Noel Standish?'"

"Of course! Didn't I make that clear?"

"Not very." Lord Darcy picked up the papers again. "Now let's get a few things straight. How did the body come to be identified as Bourke, and where is the real Bourke? Or whoever he was."

"The man Standish was following checked into the Green Seagull Inn under that name," Sir James said. "He'd used the same name in England. He was a great deal like Standish in height, weight, and coloring. He disappeared that night, and we've found no trace of him since."

Lord Darcy nodded thoughtfully. "It figures. Young gentleman arrives at village inn. Body of young gentleman found next morning. Since there is only one young gentleman in plain sight, they are the same young gentleman. Identifying a total stranger is a chancy thing at best."

"Exactly. That's why I held up my own identification."

"I understand. Now, exactly how did you happen to be in St.-Matthew's-Church that night?" Lord Darcy asked.

"Well, as soon as Standish was fairly certain that his quarry had settled down at the Green Seagull, he rode for Caen and sent a message to my office, here in Rouen. I took the first train, but by the time I got there, they were both missing."

"Yes." Lord Darcy sighed. "Well, I suppose we'd best be getting down there. I'll have to ask His Royal Highness to order me to, so you may as well come along with me and explain the whole thing all over again to Duke Richard."

Sir James looked pained. "I suppose so. We want to get there as soon as possible, or the whole situation will become impossible. Their silly Midsummer Fair starts the day after tomorrow, and there are strangers showing up already."

Lord Darcy closed his eyes. "That's all we need. Complications."

Master Sean went to the door of the office. "I'll have Ciardi pack our bags, me lord. Looks like a long stay."

The little village of St.-Matthew's-Church was transforming itself. The Fair proper was to be held in a huge field outside of town, and the tents were already collecting on the meadow. There was, of course, no room in the village itself for people to stay; certainly the little Green Seagull couldn't hold a hundredth of them. But a respectable tent-city had been erected in another big field, and there was plenty of parking space for horse-wagons and the like.

In the village, the storefronts were draped with bright bunting, and the shopkeepers were busy marking up all the prices. Both pubs had been stocking up on extra potables for weeks. For nine days, the village would be full of strangers going about their hectic business, disrupting the peace of the local inhabitants, bringing with them a strange sort of excitement. Then they would go, leaving behind acres of ugly rubbish and bushels of beautiful cash.

In the meanwhile, a glorious time would be had by all.

Lord Darcy cantered his horse along the River Road up from Caen and entered St.-Matthew's-Church at noon on that bright sunshiny day, dressed in the sort of riding clothes a well-to-do merchant might wear. He wasn't exactly incognito, but he didn't want to attract attention, either. Casually, he made his way through the already gathering throngs toward the huge old church dedicated to St. Matthew, which had given the village its name. He guided his mount over to the local muffin square, where the array of hitching posts stood, tethered his horse, and walked over to the church.

The Reverend Father Arthur Lyon, Rector of the Church of St. Matthew, and, *ipso facto*, Rector of St.-Matthew's-Church, was a broad-shouldered man in his fifties who stood a good two inches taller than six feet. His bald head was fringed with silvery hair, and his authoritative, pleasant face was usually smiling. He was sitting behind his desk in his office.

There came a rap at his office door. A middle-aged woman came in quickly and said: "Sorry to bodder dee, Fahder, but dere's a Lord Darcy to see dee."

"Show him in, Goodwife Anna."

Lord Darcy entered Father Art's office to find the priest waiting with outstretched hand. "It's been some time, my lord," he said with a broad smile. "Good to see you again."

"I may say the same. How have you been, old friend?"

"Not bad. Pray, sit down. May I offer you a drink?"

"Not just now, Father." He took the proffered seat. "I understand you have a bit of a problem here."

Father Art leaned back in his chair and folded his hands behind his head. "Ahh, yes. The so-called suicide. Bourke." He chuckled. "I thought higher authority would be in on that, sooner or later."

"Why do you say 'so-called suicide,' Father?"

"Because I know people, my lord. If a man's going to shoot himself, he doesn't go out to a lonely beach for it. If he goes to a beach, it's to drown himself. A walk into the sea. I don't say a man has never shot himself by the seaside, but it's so rare that when it happens I get suspicious."

"I agree," Lord Darcy said. He had known Arthur Lyon for some years, and knew that the man was an absolutely dedicated servant of his God and his King. His career had been unusual. During the '39 war, he had risen to the rank of Sergeant-Major in the Eighteenth Infantry. Afterwards, he had become an Officer of the King's Peace, and had retired as a Chief Master-at-Arms before taking up his vocation as a priest. He had shown himself to be not only a top-grade priest, but also a man with the Talent as a brilliant Healer, and had been admitted, with honors, to the Order of St. Luke.

"Old friend," Lord Darcy said, "I need your help. What I am about to tell you is most confidential; I will have to ask you to disclose none of it without official permission."

Father Art took his hands from behind his head and leaned forward with a gleam in his eyes. "As if it were under the Seal of the Confessional, my lord. Go ahead."

It took better than half an hour for Lord Darcy to give the good father the whole story as he knew it. Father Art had leaned back in his chair again with his hands locked behind his head, smiling seraphically at the ceiling. "Ah, yes, my lord. Utterly fascinating. I remember Friday, sixth June, very well. Yes, very well indeed." He continued to smile at the ceiling.

Lord Darcy closed his right eye and cocked his left eyebrow. "I trust you intend to tell me what incident stamped that day so indelibly on your mind."

"Certainly, my lord. I was just reveling in having made a deduction. When I tell my story, I dare say you'll make the same deduction." He brought his gaze down from the ceiling and his hands from behind his head. "You might say it began late Thursday night. Because of a sick call which had kept me up most of the previous night, I went to bed quite early Thursday evening. And, naturally, I woke up a little before midnight and couldn't get back to sleep. I decided I might as well make use of the time, so I did some paper work for a while and then went into the church to say the morning office before the altar. Then I decided to take a walk in the churchyard. I often do that; it's a pleasant place to meditate.

"There was no moon that night," the priest continued, "but the sky was cloudless and clear. It was about two hours before dawn. It was quite dark, naturally, but I know my way about those tombstones pretty well by now. I'd been out there perhaps a quarter of an hour when the stars went out."

Lord Darcy seemed to freeze for a full second. "When the *what?*"

"When the stars went out," Father Art repeated. "One moment, there they were, in their accustomed constellations— I was looking at Cygnus in particular—and the next moment the sky was black all over. Everywhere. All at once."

"I see," said Lord Darcy.

"Well, *I* couldn't," the priest said, flashing a smile. "It was black as the Pit. For a second or two, I confess, I was almost panicky. It's a weird feeling when the stars go out."

"I dare say," Lord Darcy murmured.

"But," the Father continued, "as a Sensitive, I knew that there was no threat close by, and, after a minute, I got my bearings again. I could have come back to the church, but I decided to wait for a while, just to find out what would happen next. I don't know how long I stood there. It seemed like an hour, but it was probably less than fifteen minutes. Then the stars came back on the same way they'd gone out—all at once, all over the sky."

"No dimming out?" Lord Darcy asked. "No slow brightening back on?"

"None, my lord. *Blink:* off. *Blink:* on."

"Not a sea fog, then."

"Impossible. No sea fog could move that fast."

Lord Darcy focused his eyes on a foot-high statue of St. Matthew that stood in a niche in the wall and stared at the Apostle without actually seeing him.

After a minute, Lord Darcy said: "I left Master Sean in Caen to make a final check of the body. He should be here within the hour. I'll talk to him, but . . ." His voice trailed off.

Father Art nodded. "Our speculation certainly needs to be confirmed, my lord, but I think we're on the right track. Now, how else can I help?"

"Oh, yes. That." Lord Darcy grinned. "Your revelation of the extinguished stars almost made me forget why I came to talk to you in the first place. What I'd like you to do, Father, is talk to the people that were at the Green Seagull on the afternoon and late evening of the fifth. I'm a stranger, and I probably wouldn't get much out of them—certainly not as much as you can. I want to know the whole pattern of comings and goings. I don't have to tell an old Armsman like yourself what to look for. Will you do it?"

Father Art's smile came back. "With pleasure, my lord."

"There's one other thing. Can you put up Master Sean and myself for a few days? There is, alas, no room at the inn."

Father Art's peal of laughter seemed to rock the bell tower.

Master Sean O Lochlainn had always been partial to mules. "The mule," he was fond of saying, "is as much smarter than a horse as a raven is smarter than a falcon. Neither a raven nor a mule will go charging into combat just because some human tells him to." Thus it was that the sorcerer came riding toward St.-Matthew's-Church, clad in plain brown, seated in a rather worn saddle, on the back of a very fine mule. He looked quite pleased with himself.

The River Road had plenty of traffic on it; half the population of the duchy seemed to be converging on the little coastal village of St.-Matthew's-Church. So Master Sean was mildly surprised to see someone headed toward him, but that feeling vanished when he saw that the approaching horseman was Lord Darcy.

"Not headed back to Caen, are you, me lord?" he asked when Lord Darcy came within speaking distance.

"Not at all, my dear Sean; I rode out to meet you. Let's take the cutoff road to the west; it's a shortcut that bypasses the village and takes us to the Old Shore Road, near where the body was found." He wheeled his horse around and rode beside Master Sean's mule. Together, they cantered briskly toward the Old Shore Road.

"Now," Lord Darcy said, "what did you find out at Caen?"

"Conflicting evidence, me lord; conflicting evidence. At least as far as the suicide theory is concerned. There was evidence at the cliff edge that he had fallen or been pushed over and tumbled down along the face of the cliff. But he was found twenty-five feet from the base of the cliff. He had two broken ribs and a badly sprained right wrist—to say nothing of several bad bruises. All of these had been inflicted some hours before death."

Lord Darcy gave a rather bitter chuckle. "Which leaves us with two possibilities. *Primus:* Goodman Standish stands on the edge of the cliff, shoots himself through the head, tumbles to the sand below, crawls twenty-five feet, and takes some hours to die of a wound that was obviously instantly fatal. Or, *secundus:* He falls off the cliff, crawls the twenty-five feet, does nothing for a few hours, then decides to shoot himself. I find the second hypothesis only slightly more likely than the first. That his right wrist was sprained badly is a fact that tops it all off. Not suicide, no, not suicide." Lord Darcy grinned. "That leaves accident or murder. Which hypothesis do you prefer, my dear Sean?"

Master Sean frowned deeply, as if he were in the awful throes of concentration. Then his face brightened as if revelation had come. "I have it, me lord! He was accidentally murdered!"

Lord Darcy laughed. "Excellent! Now, having cleared that up, there is further evidence that I have not given you yet."

He told Master Sean about Father Art's singular experience with the vanishing stars.

When he had finished, the two rode in silence for a minute or two. Then Master Sean said softly: "So *that's* what it is."

There was an Armsman standing off the road at the site of the death, and another seated, who stood up as Lord Darcy and Master Sean approached. The two riders dismounted and walked their mounts up to where the Armsmen were standing.

"I am sorry, gentlemen," said the first Armsman with an air of authority, "but this area is off bounds, by order of His Royal Highness the Duke of Normandy."

"Very good; I am happy to hear it," said his lordship, taking out his identification. "I am Lord Darcy; this is Master Sorcerer Sean O Lochlainn."

"Yes, my lord," said the Armsman. "Sorry I didn't recognize you."

"No problem. This is where the body was found?"

"Yes, my lord. Just below this cliff, here. Would you like to take a look, my lord?"

"Indeed I would. Thank you."

Lord Darcy, under the respectful eyes of the two Armsmen, minutely examined the area around the cliff edge. Master Sean stayed with him, trying to see everything his lordship saw.

"Everything's a week old," Lord Darcy muttered bitterly. "Look at that grass, there. A week ago, I could have told you how many men were scuffing it up; today, I only know that it was more than two. I don't suppose there's any way of reconstructing it, my dear Sean?"

"No, me lord. I am a magician, not a miracle worker."

"Thought not. Look at the edge of this cliff. He fell, certainly. But was he pushed? Or thrown? No way of telling. Wind and weather have done their work too well. To quote my cousin de London: *'Pfui!'*"

"Yes, me lord."

"Well, let's go down to the beach and take a look from below." That operation entailed walking fifty yards or so down the cliff edge to a steep draw which they could clamber down, then back again to where Standish had died.

There was a pleasant breeze from landward that brought the smell of growing crops. A dozen yards away, three gulls squabbled raucously over the remains of some dead sea-thing.

Lord Darcy was still in a bitter mood. "Nothing, damn it. *Nothing*. Footprints all washed away long ago. Or blown away by the wind. Damn, damn, *damn!* All we have to go by is the testimony of eyewitnesses, which is notoriously unreliable."

"You don't believe 'em, me lord?" Master Sean asked.

Lord Darcy was silent for several seconds. Then, in a calmer voice, he said: "Yes. Oddly enough, I do. I think the testimony of those farmers was absolutely accurate. They saw what they saw, and they reported what they saw. But they did not—they *could* not have seen everything!"

One of the Armsmen on the cliff above said: "That's the spot, right there, my lord. Near that flat rock." He pointed.

But Lord Darcy did not even look at the indicated spot. He had looked up when the Armsman spoke, and was staring at something on the cliff face about two feet below the Armsman's boot toes.

Master Sean followed his lordship's gaze and spotted the area immediately. "Looks like someone's been carving his initials, me lord."

"Indeed. How do you make them out?"

"Looks like S . . . S . . . O. Who do we know with the initials SSO?"

"Nobody connected with this case so far. The letters may have been up there for some time. But . . ."

"Aye, me lord," said Master Sean. "I see what you mean. I'll do a time check on them. Do you want 'em preserved?"

"Unless they're more than a week old, yes. By the by, did Standish have a knife on him when he was found?"

"Not so far as I know, me lord. Wasn't mentioned in the reports."

"Hmmm." Lord Darcy began prowling around the whole area, reminding Master Sean of nothing so much as a leopard in search of his evening meal. He finally ended up at the base of the cliff, just below where the glyphs had been carved into the clay wall. He went down on his knees and began digging.

"It has to be here somewhere," he murmured.

"Might I ask what you're looking for, me lord?"

"A piece of steel, my dear Sean; a piece of steel."

Master Sean put his carpetbag on the sand and opened it, taking out a thin, dark, metallic-blue wand just as Lord Darcy said: "*Aaha!*"

Master Sean, wand still in hand, said: "What is it, me lord?"

"As you see," Lord Darcy said, standing up and displaying the object in the palm of his hand. "Behold and observe, old friend: A man's pocketknife."

Master Sean smiled broadly. "Aye. I presume you'll be wanting a relationship test, me lord? Carving, cutter, and corpse?"

"Of course. No, don't put away your wand. That's your generalized metal detector, is it not?"

"Aye, me lord. It's been similarized to all things metallic."

"Good. Put this knife away for analysis, then let's go over to where the body was found. We'll see if there isn't something else to be dug up."

The Master Sorcerer pointed the wand in his right hand at the sand and moved back and forth across the area, his eyes almost closed, his left hand held above his head, fingers spread. Every time he stopped, Lord Darcy would dig into the soft sand and come up with a bit of metal—a rusty nail, a corroded brass belt-buckle, a copper twelfth-bit, a bronze farthing, and even a silver half-sovereign—all of which showed evidence of having been there for some time.

Only one of the objects was of interest to Lord Darcy: a small lump of lead. He dropped it into a waistcoat pocket and went on digging.

At last, Master Sean, having covered an area of some eight by twelve feet, said: "That's it, me lord."

Lord Darcy stood up, brushed the sand from his hands and trousers, and looked at the collection of junk he had put on the big flat rock. "Too bad we couldn't have found a sixth-bit. We'd be an even solidus ahead. No gold in the lot, either."

Master Sean chuckled. "You can't expect to find a complete set of samples from the Imperial Mint, me lord."

"I suppose not. But here—" he took the small lump of

lead from his waistcoat pocket, "—is what I expected to find. Unless I am very much mistaken, this bullet came from the .36 Heron that the late Standish carried, and is the same bullet which passed through his head. Here; check on it, will you, my good Sean?"

Master Sean put the bullet in one of the carefully insulated pockets of his capacious carpetbag, and the two men trudged back across the sand, up the slope to the top of the cliff again.

Master Sean spread himself prone and looked over the edge of the cliff. After a minute inspection of the carving in the sandy clay of the cliff face, he got up, took some equipment from his carpetbag, and lay down again to go to work. A simple cohesion spell sufficed to set the clay so that it would not crumble. Then, he deftly began to cut out the brick of hardened clay defined by the spell.

In the meantime, Lord Darcy had called the senior of the two Armsmen to one side and had asked him a question.

"No, my lord, we ain't had any trouble," the Armsman said. "We been runnin' three eight-hour shifts out here ever since the body was found, and hardly nobody's come by. The local folk all know better. Wouldn't come near it, anyway, till the whole matter's been cleared up and the site's been blessed by a priest. Course, there was that thing this morning."

"This morning?" Lord Darcy lifted an eyebrow.

"Yes, my lord." He glanced at his wristwatch. "Just after we come on duty. Just on six hours ago—eight-twelve."

"And what happened?" his lordship asked with seemingly infinite patience.

"Well, these two folk come along the beach from the east. Romany, they was. Whole tribe of 'em come into St.-Matthew's-Church fairground early this morning. These two— man and a woman, they was—come along arm in arm. Dan—that's Armsman Danel, over there—warned 'em off, but they just smiled and waved and kept coming. So Dan went down to the beach fast and blocked 'em off. They pretended they didn't speak no Anglo-French; you know how these Romany are. But Dan made it clear they wasn't to come no farther, so off they went. No trouble."

"They went back without any argument, eh?"

"Yes, my lord, they did."

"Well, no harm done there, then. Carry on, Armsman."

"Yes, my lord."

Master Sean came back from the cliff edge with a chunk of thaumaturgically-hardened clay further loading his symbol-decorated carpetbag. "Anything else, me lord?"

"I think not. Let's get some lunch."

In a tent near the fairgrounds, an agent of *Serka*, Mission Commander for this particular operation, was opening what looked on the outside like a battered, scuffed, worn, old leather suitcase. The inside was new and in the best condition, and the contents were startlingly similar to those of Master Sean's symbol-decorated carpetbag.

Out came two small wands, scarcely six inches long, of ruby-red crystal wound with oddly-spaced helices of silver wire that took exactly five turns around the ruby core. Each wand was a mirror image of the other; one helix wound to the right, the other to the left. Out came two small glass flacons, one containing a white, coarsely-ground substance, the other an amber-yellow mass of small granules. These were followed by a curiously-wrought golden candlestick some four inches high, an inch-thick candle, and a small brazier.

Like any competent sorcerer, the Commander had hands that were strong and yet capable of delicate work. The beeswax candle was being fitted into the candlestick by those hands when there came a scratching at the closed tent flap.

The Commander froze. "Yes?"

"One-three-seven comes," said a whispered voice.

The Commander relaxed. "Very well; send him in."

Seconds later, the tent flap opened, and another *Serka* agent ducked into the tent. He glanced at the thaumaturgical equipment on the table as he sat down on a stool. "It's come to that, eh?" he said.

"I'm not certain yet," said the Commander. "It may. I don't want it to. I want to avoid any entanglement with Master Sean O Lochlainn. A man with his ability and power is a man to avoid when he's on the other side."

"Your pardon, Mission Commander, but just how certain are you that the man you saw on the mule this morning was actually Master Sean?"

"Quite certain. I heard him lecture many times at the

University at Buda-Pest when I was an undergraduate there
in 'sixty-eight, 'sixty-nine, and 'seventy. He was taking his
Th.D. in theoretics and analog math. His King paid for it
from the Privy Purse, but he supplemented his income by
giving undergrad lectures."

"Would he recognize you?"

"Highly unlikely. Who pays any attention to undergraduate
students at a large university?"

The Commander waved an impatient hand. "Let's hear
your report."

"Yes, Mission Commander," Agent 137 said briskly. "I
followed the man on muleback, as you ordered. He met
another man, ahorse, coming from the village. He was tall,
lean but muscular, with handsome, rather English-looking
features. He was dressed as a merchant, but I suspected . . ."

The Commander nodded. "Lord Darcy. Obviously. Continue."

"You said they'd go to the site of the death, and when
they took the left-hand bypass I was sure of it. I left off
following and galloped on to the village, where Number 202
was waiting with the boat. We had a good westerly breeze,
so we made it to the cove before them. We anchored and
lay some two hundred yards off-shore. Number 202 did some
fishing while I watched through field glasses.

"They talked to the Armsmen atop the cliff for a while,
then went down to the beach. One of the Armsmen pointed
to where the body had been. Darcy went on talking to him
for a while. Then Darcy walked around, looking at things.
He went over to the base of the cliff and began digging.
He found something; I couldn't see what.

"Master Sean put it in his bag, then, for ten minutes or
so, he quartered the area where the body'd been, using one
of those long, blue-black metal wands—you know—"

"A metal detector," said the Commander. "Yes. Go on."

"Yes. Lord Darcy dug every time O Lochlainn pointed
something out. Dug up an awful lot of stuff. But he found
*some*thing interesting. Don't know what it was; couldn't see
it. But he stuck it in his pocket and gave it to the sorcerer
later."

"I know what it was," said the Commander in a hard
voice. "Was that the only thing that seemed to interest him?"

"Yes, as far as I could tell," said 137.

"Then what happened?"

137 shrugged. "They went back topside. Darcy talked to one of the Armsmen; the other watched the sorcerer dig a hole in the cliff face."

The Mission Commander frowned. "Dig a hole? A *hole*?"

"That's right. Lay flat on his belly, reached down a couple of feet over the edge, and dug something out. Couldn't see what it was. Left a hole about the size of a man's two fists— maybe a bit bigger."

"Damn! Why couldn't you have watched more carefully?"

Agent 137's face stiffened. "It was very difficult to see well, Mission Commander. Any closer than two hundred yards, and we would have drawn attention. Did you ever try to focus six-by field glasses from a light boat bobbing up and down on the sea?"

"Calm down. I'm not angry with you. You did well. I just wish we had better information." The Commander looked thoughtful. "That tells us something. We can forget about the beach. Order the men to stay away; they are not to go there again for any reason.

"The Phial is not there now, if it ever was. If Master Sean did not find it, it wasn't there. If he *did* find it, it is gone now, and he and Lord Darcy know where it is. And that is a problem I must consider. Now get out of here and let me think."

Agent 137 got out.

The public room at the Green Seagull, as far as population went, looked like a London railway car at the rush hour.

Amidst all the hubbub, wine and beer crossed the bar in one direction, while copper and silver crossed it in the other, making everyone happy on both sides.

In the club bar, it was somewhat quieter, but the noise from the public bar was distinctly audible. The innkeeper himself was taking care of the customers in the club bar; he took a great deal of pride in his work. Besides, the tips were larger and the work easier.

"Would dere be anyting else for dee?" he asked as he set two pints of beer on one of the tables. "Someting to munch on, mayhap?"

"Not just now, Goodman Dreyque," said Father Art. "This will do us for a while."

"Very good, Fahder. Tank dee." He went quietly away.

Lord Darcy took a deep draught of his beer and sighed. "Cool beer is a great refresher on a midsummer evening. The Green Seagull keeps an excellent cellar. Food's good, too; Master Sean and I ate here this afternoon."

"Where is Master Sean now?" the priest asked.

"In the rooms you assigned us in the Rectory, amidst his apparatus, doing lab work on some evidence we dug up." His voice became soft. "Did you find out what happened here that night?"

"Pretty much," Father Art replied in the same low tones. "There are a few things which are still a little hazy, but I think we can fill in most of those areas."

Standish's quarry had arrived at the Green Seagull late in the afternoon of the fifth, giving the name "Richard Bourke." He was carrying only an attaché case, but since he had a horse and saddle and saddlebags, they were considered surety against indebtedness.

There were only six rooms for hire in the inn, all on the upper floor of the two-storied building. Two of these were already occupied. At two-ten, the man Danglars had come in and registered for himself and his mistress, Jizelle de Ville.

"Bourke," said Father Art, "came in at five-fifteen. Nobody else at all checked in during that evening. And nobody saw a young man wearing evening clothes." He paused and smiled brightly. "How*ev*-er . . ."

"Ahhh. I knew I could depend on you, my dear Arthur. What was it?"

Still smiling seraphically, the good father raised a finger and said: "The Case of the Sexton's Cloak."

"You fascinate me. Pray elucidate."

"My sexton," said Father Art, "has an old cloak, originally made from a couple of used horse blankets, so it wasn't exactly beautiful when new. But it *is* warm. He uses it when he has to work outside in winter. In summer, he hangs it in the stable behind the church. Claims it keeps the moths out—the smell, I mean.

"On the morning of sixth June, one of the men who works here in the inn brought it over to the church, asked my sexton if it were his. It was. Want to take a wild, silly guess where it was found?" Father Art asked.

"Does the room used by Bourke face the front or the rear?"

"The rear."

"Then it was found on the cobblestones at the rear of the building."

Smiling even more broadly, Father Art gently clapped his hands together once. "Precisely, my lord."

Lord Darcy smiled back. "Let's reconstruct. Bourke went to his room before five-thirty. Right?"

"Right. One of the maids went with him, let him in, and gave him the key."

"Was he ever seen again?"

"Only once. He ordered a light meal, and it was brought up about six. That's the last time he was seen."

"Were either of the other guests in the house at the time?"

"No. The man Danglars had left about four-thirty, and hadn't returned. No one saw Mistress Jizelle leave, but the girl who turns down the beds says that both rooms were empty at six. Bourke was still there at the time."

"Hmmmm."

Lord Darcy looked into the depths of his beer. After half a minute, he said: "Reverend Father, was a stranger in an old horse-blanket cloak actually seen in this inn, or are we speculating in insubstantial mist?"

Father Art's mouth twisted in a small grimace. "Not totally insubstantial, my lord, but not strong, either. The barmaid who was on duty that night says she remembers a couple of strangers who came in, but she doesn't remember anything about them. She's not terribly bright."

Lord Darcy chuckled. "All right, then. Let's assume that Standish actually came in here in a stolen—and uncomfortably warm—cloak. How did that come about, and what happened afterwards?"

Father Art fired up his old briar and took another sip from his seidel of beer. "Well, let's see. Standish comes into the village an hour after Bourke—perhaps a little more. But he doesn't come in directly; he circles round behind the church. Why? Not to steal the cloak. How would he know it was there?" He took two puffs from his pipe, then his eyes brightened. "Of course. To tether his horse. He didn't want it seen in the public square, and knew it would be safe in the church stable." Two more puffs.

"Hmmm. He sees the cloak on the stable wall and realizes that it will serve as a disguise, covering his evening dress. He borrows it and comes here to the inn. He makes sure that Bourke is firmly in place, then goes back to his horse and hightails it for Caen to send word to Sir James. Then he comes back here to the Green Seagull. He waits until nobody's looking, then sneaks up the stairs to Bourke's room."

The priest stopped, scowled, and took a good, healthy drink from his seidel. "Some time later, he went out the window to the courtyard below, losing the cloak in the process." He shook his head. "But what happened between the time he went upstairs and the time he dropped the cloak, and what happened between then and his death, I haven't the foggiest conjecture."

"I have several," Lord Darcy said, "but they are all very, very foggy. We need more data. I have several questions." He ticked them off on his fingers. "One: Where is Bourke? Two: Who shot Standish? Three: *Why* was he shot? Four: What happened here at the inn? Five: What happened on the beach? And, finally: *Where is the Ipswich Phial?*"

Father Art lifted his seidel, drained its contents on one extended draught, set it firmly on the table, and said: "I don't know. God does."

Lord Darcy nodded. "Indeed; and one of His greatest attributes is that if you ask Him the right question in the right way, He will always give you an answer."

"You intend to pray for answers to those questions, my lord?"

"That, yes. But I have found that the best way to ask God about questions like these is to go out and dig up the data yourself."

Father Art smiled. *"Dominus vobiscum."*

"Et cum spiritu tuo," Lord Darcy responded.

"Excavemus!" said the priest.

In his room in the Rectory, Master Sean had carefully set up his apparatus on the table. Noel Standish's .36 Heron was clamped securely into a padded vise which stood at one end of the table. Three feet in front of the muzzle, the bullet which Lord Darcy had dug from the sand had been carefully placed on a small pedestal, so that it was at exactly the same height as the muzzle. He was using certain instruments to make sure that the axis of the bullet was

accurately aligned with the axis of the Heron's barrel when
a rhythmic code knock came at the door. The sorcerer went
over to the door, unbolted it, opened it, and said: "Come
in, me lord."

"I hope I didn't interrupt anything," Lord Darcy said.

"Not at all, me lord." Master Sean carefully closed and
bolted the door again. "I was just getting ready for the
ballistics test. The similarity relationship tests have already
assured me that the slug was the one that killed Standish.
There's only to see if it came from his own gun. Have you
found any further clues?"

"None," Lord Darcy admitted. "I managed to get a good
look at the guest rooms in the Green Seagull. Nothing. Flat
nothing. I have several ideas, but no evidence." Then he
gestured at the handgun. "Pray proceed with your work, I
will be most happy to wait."

"It'll only be a minute or so," Master Sean said apologetically. He went back to the table and continued his
preparations while Lord Darcy watched in silence. His lordship was well aware of the principle involved; he had seen
the test innumerable times. He recalled a lecture that Master
Sean had once given on the subject.

"You see," the sorcerer had said, "the Principle of Relevance is important here. Most of the wear on a gun is
purely mechanical. It doesn't matter *who* pulls the trigger,
you see; the erosion caused by the gases produced in the
chamber, and the wear caused by the bullet's passing through
the barrel will be the same. It's not relevant *to the gun* who
pulled the trigger or what it was fired at. But, *to the bullet* it *is* relevant which gun it was fired from and what it
hit. All this can be determined by the proper spells."

In spite of having seen it many times, Lord Darcy always
liked to watch the test because it was rather spectacular
when the test was positive. Master Sean sprinkled a small
amount of previously charged powder on both the bullet
and the gun. Then he raised his wand and said an incantation under his breath.

At the last syllable of the incantation, there was a sound
as if someone had sharply struck a cracked bell as the bullet
vanished. The .36 Heron shivered in its vise.

Master Sean let out his breath. "Just like a homing pigeon,
me lord. Gun and bullet match."

"I've often wondered why the bullet does that," Lord Darcy said.

Master Sean chuckled. "Call it an induced return-to-the-womb fixation, me lord. Was there something you wanted?"

"A couple of things." Lord Darcy walked over to his suitcase, opened it, and took out a holstered handgun. It was a precision-made .40 caliber MacGregor—a heavy man-stopper.

While he checked out the MacGregor itself, he said: "This is one. The other is a question. How long before his body was found did Standish die?"

Master Sean rubbed the side of his nose with a thick finger. "Well, the investigative sorcerer at Caen, a good journeyman, placed the time as not more than fifteen minutes before the body was discovered. My own tests showed not more than twenty-five minutes, but not even the best pre-servative spell can keep something like that from blurring after a week has passed."

Lord Darcy slid the MacGregor into its snugly-fitted hol-ster and adjusted his jacket to cover it. "In other words, there's the usual hazy area. The bruises and fractures were definitely inflicted before death?"

"Definitely, my lord. About three hours before, give or take that same fifteen minutes."

"I see. Interesting. Very interesting." He looked in the wall mirror and adjusted his neckpiece. "Have you further work to do?"

"Only the analysis on the knife," Master Sean said.

Lord Darcy turned from the mirror. "Will you fix me up with a tracer? I'm going out to stroll about the village and possibly to the fairgrounds and the tent city. I anticipate no danger, but I don't want to get lost, either."

"Very well, me lord," the sorcerer said with resignation. He opened his symbol-decorated carpetbag and took out a little wooden box. It held what looked remarkably like one-inch toothpicks, except that they were evenly cylindrical, not tapered, and they were made of ash instead of pine. He selected one and put the box back in his bag. He handed the little cylinder to Lord Darcy, who took it between the thumb and forefinger of his right hand.

Then the Master Sorcerer took a little scented oil on his right thumb from a special golden oil stock and rubbed it along the sliver of ash, from Lord Darcy's thumb to the other end. Then he grasped that end in his own right thumb and forefinger.

A quick motion of both wrists, and the ashen splinter snapped.

But, psychically and symbolically, the halves were still part of an unbroken whole. As long as each man carried his half, the two of them were specially linked.

"Thank you, my dear Sean," Lord Darcy said. "And now I shall be off to enjoy the nightlife of the teeming metropolis surrounding us."

With that, he was gone, and Master Sean returned to his work.

The sun was a fat, squashed-looking, red-orange ellipsoid seated neatly on the horizon when Lord Darcy stepped out of the gate of the churchyard. It would be gone in a few minutes. The long shadow of the church spire reached out across the village and into the fields. The colors of the flags and banners and bunting around the village were altered in value by the reddish light. The weather had been beautiful and clear all day, and would continue to be, according to the Weather Bureau predictors. It would be a fine night.

"Please, my lord—are you Lord Darcy?"

Lord Darcy had noticed the woman come out of the church, but the village square was full of people, and he had paid little attention. Now he turned his full attention on her and was pleasantly surprised. She was quite the loveliest creature he had seen in a long time.

"I am, Damoselle," he said with a smile. "But I fear you have the advantage of me."

Her own smile was timid, almost frightened. "I am named Sharolta."

Her name, her slight accent, and her clothing all proclaimed her Romany. Her long, softly dark hair and her dark eyes, her well-formed nose and her full, almost too-perfect lips, along with her magnificently lush body, accentuated by the Romany costume, proclaimed her beautiful.

"May I be of help to you, Damoselle Sharolta?"

She shook her head. "No, no. I ask nothing. But perhaps

I can be of help to you." Her smile seemed to quaver. "Can we go somewhere to talk?"

"Where, for instance?" Lord Darcy asked carefully.

"Anywhere you say, my lord. Anywhere, so long as it is private." Then she finished. "I—I mean, not *too much* private. I mean, where we can talk. You know."

"Of course. It is not yet time for Vespers; I suggest that we go into the church," Lord Darcy said.

"Yes, yes. That would be fine." She smiled. "There were not many folk in there. It should be fine."

The interior of the Church of St. Matthew was darkened, but far from being gloomy. The flickering clusters of candles around the statues and icons were like twinkling, multicolored star clusters.

Lord Darcy and the Damoselle Sharolta sat down in one of the rear pews. Most of the dozen or so people who were in the church were farther up toward the altar, praying; there was no one within earshot of the place Lord Darcy had chosen.

Lord Darcy waited in silence for the girl to speak. The Romany become silent under pressure; create a vacuum for them to fill, and the words come tumbling over each other in eloquent eagerness.

"You are the great Lord Darcy, the great Investigator," she began suddenly. "You are looking into the death of the poor Goodman Standish who was found on the beach a week ago. Is all this not so?"

Lord Darcy nodded silently.

"Well, then, there must be something wrong about that man's death, or you would not be here. So I must tell you what I know.

"A week ago, there came to our tribe a group of five men. They said they were from the tribe of Chanro—the Sword— which is in the area of Buda-Pest. Their leader, who calls himself Suv—the Needle—asked our chief for aid and sanctuary, as it is their right, and it was granted. But they are very secretive among themselves. They behave very well, mind you; I don't mean they are rude or boorish, or anything like that. But there is—how do I say it?—there is a *wrongness* about them.

"This morning, for instance. I must tell you of that. The man who calls himself Suv wanted me to walk along the beach with him. I did not want to, for I do not find him an attractive man you understand?"

Again his lordship nodded. "Of course."

"But he said he meant nothing like that. He said he wanted to walk along the sea, but he did not want to walk alone. He said he would show me all the shore life—the birds, the things in the pools, the plants. I was interested, and I thought there would be no harm, so I went.

"He was true to his word. He did not try to make love to me. It was nice for a while. He showed me the tide pools and pointed out the different kinds of things in them. One had a jellyfish." She looked up from her hands, and there was a frown on her face.

"Then we got near to that little cove where the body was found. I wanted to turn back, but he said, no, he wanted to look at it. I said I wouldn't and started back. Then he told me that if I didn't, he'd break my arm. So I went." She seemed to shiver a little under her bright dress. "When the Armsman showed up, he kept on going, pretending he didn't understand Anglo-French. Then we saw that there were two of them, the Armsmen, I mean, so we turned around and went back. Suv was very furious."

She stopped and said no more.

"My dear," he asked gently, "why does one of the Romany come to the authorities with a story like this? Do not the Romany take care of their own?"

"Yes, my lord. But these men are not Rom."

"Oh?"

"Their tent is next to mine. I have heard them talking when they think no one is listening. I do not understand it very well, but I know it when I hear it; they were speaking *Burgdeutsch*."

"I see," said Lord Darcy softly and thoughtfully. The German of Brandenburg was the court language of Poland, which suddenly made everything very interesting indeed.

"Do you suppose, Damoselle," he said, "that you could point out this Suv to me?"

She looked up at him with those great wonderful eyes and smiled. "I'm sure I could, my lord. Come; wrap your cloak about you and we shall walk through the village."

Outside the church, the darkness was relieved only by the regulation gaslamps of the various business places, and by the quarter moon hanging high in the sky, like a half-closed eye.

In the deeper darkness of the church porch, Lord Darcy, rather much to his surprise, took the girl in his arms and kissed her, with her warm cooperation. It was several wordless minutes before they went out to the street.

Master Sean woke to the six o'clock Angelus bell feeling vaguely uneasy. A quick mental focus on his half of the tracer told him that Lord Darcy was in no danger. Actually, if he had been, Sean would have wakened immediately.

But he still had that odd feeling when he went down to Mass at seven; he had trouble keeping in his mind his prayers for the intercession of St. Basil the Great, and couldn't really bring his mind to focus until the Sanctus.

After Mass, he went up to Father Art's small parlor in the rectory, where he had been asked to break his fast, and was mildly surprised to find Sir James le Lein with the priest.

"Good morning, Master Sean," Sir James said calmly. "Have you found the Phial yet?"

The sorcerer shook his head. "Not so far as I know."

Sir James munched a buttered biscuit and sipped hot black caffe. Despite his calm expression Master Sean could tell that he was worried.

"I am afraid," Sir James said carefully, "we've been outfoxed."

"How so?" Father Art asked.

"Well, either the *Serka* have got it, or they think we have it safely away from them. They seem to have given the whole thing over." He drank more caffe. "Just after midnight, every known *Serka* agent in the area eluded our men and vanished. They dropped out of sight, and we haven't spotted a single one in over eight hours. We have reason to believe that some of them went south, toward Caen; some went west, toward Cherbourg; others are heading east, toward Harfleur."

Master Sean frowned. "And you think—"

"I think they found the Ipswich Phial and one of their men is carrying it to Krakowa. Or at least across the Polish border. I rode to Caen and made more teleson calls than I've ever made in so short a time in my life. There's a net out now, and we can only hope we can find the man with the Phial. Otherwise . . ." He closed his eyes. "Otherwise, we may be faced with an overland attack by the armies of His Slavonic Majesty, through one or more of the German states. God help us."

After what seemed like a terribly long time, Master Sean said: "Sir James, is there any likelihood that Noel Standish would have used a knife on the sealed Phial?"

"I don't know. Why do you ask?"

"We found a knife near where Standish's body was discovered. My tests show gold on the knife edge."

"May I see it?" Sir James asked.

"Certainly. I'll fetch it. Excuse me a minute."

He left the parlor and went down the rather narrow hallway of the rectory. From the nearby church came the soft chime of a small bell. The eight o'clock Mass was beginning.

Master Sean opened the door of his room . . .

. . . and stood stock still, staring, for a full fifteen seconds, while his eyes and other senses took in the room.

Then, without moving, he shouted: "Sir James! Father Art! Come here! Quickly!"

Both men came running. They stopped at the door. "What's the matter?" Sir James snapped.

"Somebody," said Master Sean in an angry rumble, "has been prowlin' about in me room! And a trick like that is likely to be after gettin' me Irish up!" Master Sean's brogue varied with his mood. When he was calmly lecturing or discussing, it became almost nonexistent. But when he became angry . . .

He strode into the room for a closer look at the table which he had been using for his thaumaturgical analyses. In the center was a heap of crumbled clay. "They've destroyed me evidence! Look at that!" Master Sean pointed to the heap of crumbled clay on the table.

"And what is it, if I may ask?"

Master Sean explained about the letters that had been cut in the cliff face, and how he had taken the chunk of clay out for further examination.

"And this knife was used to cut the letters." He gestured toward the knife on the table nearby. "I haven't been able to check it against Standish's body yet."

"That's the one with the gold traces on the blade?" Sir James asked.

"It is."

"Well, it's Standish's knife, all right. I've seen it many times. I could even tell you how he got that deep cut in the ivory hilt." He looked thoughtful. "S . . . S . . . O . . ." After a moment, he shook his head. "Means nothing to me. Can't think what it might have meant to Standish."

"Means nothing to me, either," Father Art admitted.

"Well, now," said the stout little Irish sorcerer, "Standish must have been at the top of the cliff when he wrote it. What would be right side up to him would be inverted to anyone standing below. How about OSS?"

Again Sir James thought. Again he shook his head. "Still nothing, Master Sean. Father?"

The priest shook his head. "Nothing, I'm afraid."

Sir James said: "This was obviously done by a *Serka* agent. But why? And how did he get in here without your knowing it?"

Master Sean scowled. "To a sorcerer, that's obvious. First, whoever did it is an accomplished sorcerer himself, or he'd never have made it past that avoidance spell, which is keyed only to meself and to his lordship. Second, he picked exactly the right time—when I was at Mass and had me mind concentrated elsewhere so I wouldn't notice what he was up to. Were I doing it meself, I'd have started just as the Sanctus bell was rung. After that—no problem." He looked glum. "I just wasn't expecting it, that's all."

"I wish I could have seen that carving in the clay," Sir James said.

"Well, you can see the cast if they didn't—" Master Sean pulled open a desk drawer. "No, they didn't." He pulled out a thick slab of plaster. "I made this with quick-setting plaster. It's reversed, of course, but you can look at it in the mirror, over there."

Sir James took the slab, but didn't look at it immediately. His eyes were still on the heap of clay. "Do you suppose that Standish might have buried the Ipswich Phial in that clay to keep it from being found?"

Master Sean's eyes widened. "Great Heaven! It could be! With an auric-stabilized psychic shield around it, I'd not have perceived it at all!"

Sir James groaned. "That answers the question, Why?—doesn't it?"

"So it would seem," murmured Father Art.

Bleakly, Sir James held the plaster slab up to the mirror above the dresser. "SSO. No. Wait." He inverted it, and his lean face went pale. "Oh, no. God," he said softly. "Oh, please. No."

"What is it?" the priest asked. "Does OSS mean something?"

"Not OSS," Sir James said still more softly. "055. Number 055 of the *Serka*. Olga Polovski, the most beautiful and the most dangerous woman in Europe."

It was at that moment that the sun went out.

The Reverend Father Mac Kennalty had turned to the congregation and asked them to lift up their hearts to the Lord that they might properly assist at the Holy Sacrifice of the Altar, when a cloud seemed to pass over the sun, dimming the light that streamed in through the stained glass windows. Even the candles on the Altar seemed to dim a little.

He hardly noticed it; it was a common enough occurrence. Without a pause, he asked the people to give thanks to the Lord God, and continued with the Mass.

In the utter blackness of the room, three men stood for a moment in silence.

"Well, that tears it," said Sir James's voice in the darkness. There was a noticeable lack of surprise or panic in his voice.

"So you lied to his lordship," said Master Sean.

"He did indeed," said Father Art

"What do you mean?" Sir James asked testily.

"You said," Master Sean pointed out with more than a touch of acid in his voice, "that you didn't know what the Ipswich Phial is supposed to do."

"What makes you think I *do*?"

"In the first place, this darkness came as no surprise to you. In the second, you must have known what it was, because Noel Standish knew."

"I had my orders," Sir James le Lein said in a hard voice. "That's not the point now. The damned thing is being used. I—"

"Listen!" Father Art's voice cut in sharply *"Listen!"*

In the blackness, all of them heard the sweet triple tone of the Sanctus bell.

Holy . . . Holy . . . Holy . . . Lord God Sabaoth . . .

"What—?" Sir James's low voice was querulous.

"Don't you understand?" Father Art asked. "The field of suppression doesn't extend as far as the church. Father Mac Kennalty could go on with the Mass in the dark, from memory. But the congregation wouldn't be likely to. They certainly don't sound upset."

"You're right, Father," Master Sean said. "That gives us the range, doesn't it? Let's see if we can feel our way out of here, toward the church. His lordship may be in trouble."

"Follow me," said the priest. "I know this church like I know my own face. Take my hand and follow me."

Cautiously, the three men moved from the darkness toward the light. They were still heading for the stairway when the sun came on again.

Lord Darcy rode into the stableyard behind the Church of St. Matthew, where four men were waiting for him. The sexton took his horse as he dismounted, and led it away to the stable. The other three just waited, expectantly.

"I could do with a cup of caffe, heavily laced with brandy, and a plate of ham and eggs, if they're available," said Lord Darcy with a rather dreamy smile. "If not, I'll just have the caffe and brandy."

"What's happened?" Sir James blurted abruptly.

Lord Darcy patted the air with a hand. "All in good time, my dear James; all in good time. Nothing's amiss, I assure you."

"I think a breakfast such as that could be arranged," Father Art said with a smile. "Come along."

The caffe and brandy came immediately, served by Father Art in a large mug. "The ham and eggs should be along pretty quickly," the priest said.

"Excellent! You're the perfect host, Father." Lord Darcy took a bracing jolt from the mug, then fished in his waistcoat pocket with thumb and forefinger. "Oh, by the by, Sir James, here's your play-pretty." He held up a small golden tube.

Sir James took it and looked at it while Master Sean scowled at in a way that made him seem rather cross-eyed.

"The seal has been cut," Sir James said.

"Yes. By your man, Standish. I suggest you give the thing to Master Sean for resealing until you get it back to Ipswich."

Sir James gave the Phial to Master Sean. "How did you get it back from them?" the King's Agent asked.

"I didn't." Lord Darcy settled himself back in the big chair. "If you'll be patient, I'll explain. Last evening, I was approached by a young woman . . ."

His lordship repeated the entire conversation verbatim, and told them of her gestures and expressions while they were talking inside the church.

"And you went with her?" Sir James asked incredulously.

"Certainly. For two very good reasons. *Primus:* I had to find out what was behind her story. *Secundus:* I had fallen in love."

Sir James gawked. Master Sean's face became expressionless. Father Art cast his eyes toward Heaven.

Sir James found his voice first. "In *love?*" It was almost a squawk.

Lord Darcy nodded calmly. "In love. Deeply. Madly. Passionately."

Sir James shot to his feet. "Are you mad, Darcy? Don't you realize that that woman is a *Serka* agent?"

"So indeed I had surmised. Sit down, James; such outbursts are unseemly." Sir James sat down slowly. "Now pay attention," Lord Darcy continued. "Of course I knew she was a spy. If you had been listening closely when I quoted her words, you would have heard that she said I was investigating the death of *Standish.* And yet everyone here knows that the body was identified as *Bourke.* Obviously, she had recognized Standish and knew his name."

"Standish had recognized her, too," Sir James said. "Secret Agent Number 055, of *Serka.* Real name: Olga Polovski."

"Olga," Lord Darcy said, savoring the word. "That's a pretty name, isn't it?"

"Charming. Utterly enchanting. And in spite of the fact that she's a Polish agent, you love the wench?"

"I didn't say that, Sir James," said Lord Darcy. "I did not say I loved her; I said I was 'in love' with her. There is a fine distinction there, and I have had enough experience to be able to distinguish between the two states of mind. Your use of the word 'enchanting' is quite apropos, by the way. The emotion was artificially induced. The woman is a sorceress."

Master Sean suddenly snapped his fingers. *"That's* where I heard the name before! Olga Polovski! Six years ago, she was an undergraduate at the University in Buda-Pest. A good student, with high-grade Talent. No wonder you 'fell in love' with her."

Sir James narrowed his eyes. "I see. The purpose was to get information out of you. Did she succeed?"

"In a way." Lord Darcy chuckled. "I sang like a nightingale. Indeed, Darcy's *Mendacious Cantata,* sung *forte e claro,* may become one of the most acclaimed works of art of the twentieth century. Pardon me; I am euphoric."

"You have popped your parietals, my lord," Sir James said, with a slight edge to his voice. "What was the result of this baritone solo?"

"Actually, it was a duet. We alternated on the versicles and responses. The theme of my song was simply that I was a criminal investigator and nothing more. That I hadn't more than a vague notion of what His Imperial Majesty's Secret Service was up to. That, for some reason, the apprehension of this murderer was most important to the Secret Service, so their agents were hanging around to help me. That they were more hindrance than help." He paused to take another swallow of laced caffe, then continued: "And—oh, yes—that they must be going to England for more men, because, four days ago, a heavily armed group of four men took a Navy cutter from Harfleur for London."

Sir James frowned for a second, then his face lit up. "Ah, yes. You implied that we had already found the Phial and that it was safely in England."

"Precisely. And since she had not heard of that oh-so-secret departure, she was certain that it could not be a bluff. As a result, she scrubbed the entire mission. Around midnight, she excused herself for a moment and spoke to someone—I presume it was the second in command, the much-maligned Suv. Her men took off to three of the four winds."

"And she didn't?"

"Of course not. Why arouse my suspicions? Better to keep

me under observation while her men made good their escape. I left her shortly after dawn, and—"

"You were there from sunset till dawn? What took you so long?"

Lord Darcy looked pained. "My dear James, surely you don't think I could simply hand her all that misinformation in half an hour without her becoming suspicious. I had to allow her to draw it from me, bit by bit. I had to allow her to give me more information than she intended to give in order to get the story out of me. And, of course, *she* had to be very careful in order not to arouse *my* suspicions. It was, I assure you, a very delicate and time-consuming series of negotiations."

Sir James did his best not to leer. "I can well imagine."

Father Art looked out the window, solemnly puffing his pipe as though he were in deep meditation and could hear nothing.

Rather hurriedly, Master Sean said: "Then it was you who broke the clay brick I dug out of the cliff, me lord."

"It was; I'm sorry I didn't tell you, but you were at Mass, and I was in somewhat of a hurry. You see, there were only two places where the Phial could possibly be, and I looked in the less likely place first—in that lump of clay. Standish *could* have hidden it there, but I thought it unlikely. Still, I had to look. It wasn't there.

"So I got my horse and rode out to where the body was found. You see, Standish *had* to have had it with him. He opened it to get away from his pursuers. I presume Master Sean knows how the thing works, but all I know is that it renders everyone blind for a radius of about a mile and a half."

Master Sean cleared his throat. "It's akin to what's called hysterical blindness. Nothing wrong with the eyes, ye see, but the mind blocks off the visual centers of the brain. The Phial contains a charged rod attached to the stopper. When you open it and expose the rod everything goes black. That's the reason for the auric-stabilized psychic shield which forms the Phial itself."

"Things don't go black for the person holding it," said Lord Darcy. "Everything becomes a colorless gray, but you can still see."

"That's the built-in safety spell in the stopper," said the little Irish sorcerer.

"Well, where *was* the blasted thing?" Sir James asked.

"Buried in the sand, almost under that big rock where his body was found. I just had to dig till I found it." Lord Darcy looked somber. "I fear my analytical powers are deserting me; otherwise, Master Sean and I would have found it yesterday. But I relied on his metal detector to find it. And yet, Master Sean clearly told me that a psychic shield renders anything psychically invisible. He was talking about Standish, of course, but I should have seen that the same logic applied to the Ipswich Phial as well."

"If ye'd told me what ye were looking for, me lord . . ." Master Sean said gently.

Lord Darcy chuckled mirthlessly. "After all our years together, my dear Sean, we still tend to overestimate each other. I assumed you had deduced what we were looking for, though you are no detective, you assumed I knew about psychic shielding, though I am no thaumaturge."

"I still can't quite see the entire chain of events," Father Art said "Could you clarify it for us? What was Standish doing out on that beach, anyway?"

"Well, let's go back to the night before he was killed. He had been following the mysterious Bourke. When Bourke was firmly ensconced in the Green Seagull, Standish rode for Caen, notified you via teleson, then rode back. He borrowed the sexton's cloak and went over to the inn. When he saw his chance, he dodged upstairs fast and went to Bourke's room presumably to get the Phial.

"Now, you must keep in mind that all this is conjecture. I can't prove it, and I know of no way to prove it. I do not have, and cannot get, all the evidence I would need for *proof*. But all the data I *do* have leads inescapably to one line of action.

"Master Sean claims I have a touch of the Talent—the ability to leap from an unwarranted assumption to a foregone conclusion. That may be so. At any rate, I *know* what happened.

"Very well, then. Standish went into Bourke's room to arrest him. He *knew* Bourke was in that room because he was psychically locked on to Bourke.

"But when he broke into the room he was confronted by a woman—a woman he knew. The woman was just as surprised to see Standish.

"I don't know which of them recovered first, but I strongly suspect it was the woman. Number 055 is very quick on the uptake, believe me.

"But Standish was stronger. He sustained a few good bruises in the next several seconds, but he knocked her unconscious. I saw the bruise on her neck last night.

"He searched the room and found the Phial. Unfortunately, the noise had attracted two, possibly three, of her fellow *Serka* agents. He had to go out the window, losing his cloak in the process. The men followed him.

"He ran for the beach, and—"

"Wait a minute," Sir James interrupted. "You mean Bourke was actually Olga Polovski in disguise?"

"Certainly. She's a consummate actress. The idea was for Bourke to vanish completely. She knew the Secret Service would be after her, and she wanted to leave no trace. But she didn't realize that Standish was so close behind her because he was psychically invisible. That's why she was shocked when he came into her room.

"At any rate, he ran for the beach. There was no place else to go at that time of night, except for the church, and they'd have him trapped there.

"I must admit I'm very fuzzy about what happened during that chase, but remember he had ridden for two days without much rest, and he was battered a little by the blows Olga had landed. At any rate, he eventually found himself at the edge of that cliff, with *Serka* closing in around him. Remember, it was a moonless night, and there were only stars for him to see by. But at least one of the Polish agents had a lantern.

"Standish was trapped on the edge of a cliff, and he had no way to see how far down it went, nor what was at the bottom. He lay flat and kept quiet, but the others were getting close. He decided to get rid of the Phial. Better to lose it than have it fall into King Casimir's hands. He took out his knife and carved the '055' in the side of the cliff, to mark the spot and to make sure that someone else would see it if he were killed. I'm sure he intended to dig a hole and bury it there. I don't believe he was thinking too clearly by then.

"The *Serka* men were getting too close for comfort. He might be seen at any moment. So he cut the seal of the Phial and opened it. Blackout.

"Since he could see his pursuers—however dimly—and they couldn't see him, he decided to try to get past them, back to the village. If he had a time advantage, he could find a place to hide.

"He stood up.

"But as he turned, he made a misstep and fell twenty feet to the sand below." Lord Darcy paused.

Father Art, looking thoughtful, said: "He had a gun. Why didn't he use it?"

"Because they had guns, too, and he was outnumbered. He didn't want to betray his position by the muzzle flash unless he had to," Lord Darcy said. "To continue: The fall is what broke those ribs and sprained that wrist. It also very likely knocked him out for a few minutes. Not long. When he came to, he must have realized he had an advantage greater than he had thought at first. The *Serka* couldn't see the muzzle flash from his handgun. Badly hurt as he was, he waited for them."

"Admirable," said Father Art. "It's fantastic that he didn't lose the two parts of the Phial when he fell. Must have hung on for dear life."

"Standish would," said Sir James grimly. "Go on, my lord."

"Well, at that point, the *Serka* lads must have realized the same thing. They had no way of knowing how badly Standish was hurt, nor exactly where he was. He could be sneaking up on them, for all they knew. They got out of there. Slowly, of course, since they had to feel their way, but once they reached the Old Shore Road, they made better time.

"But by that time, Standish was close to passing out again. He still had to hide the Phial, so he buried it in the sand where I found it."

"Me lord," said Master Sean, "I still don't understand who killed Standish and why."

"Oh, that. Why that was patently obvious from the first. Wasn't it, Father Art?"

The good father stared at Lord Darcy. "Begging your pardon, my lord, but not to *me* it wasn't."

Lord Darcy turned his head. "Sir James?"

"No."

"Oh, dear. Well, I suppose I shall have to back up a bit, then. Consider: The Damoselle Olga, to cover her tracks, has to get rid of 'Bourke.' But if 'Bourke' disappears into nowhere, and someone else appears from nowhere, even a moron might suspect that the two were the same. So a cover must be arranged. Someone else, not connected in any way with 'Bourke,' must appear at the Green Seagull *before* 'Bourke' shows up.

"So, what happened? A coachman named Danglars shows up; a servant who registers for himself and his mistress, Jizelle de Ville. (Danglars and Suv were almost certainly the same man, by the way.) But who sees Mistress Jizelle? Nobody. *She is only a name in a register book until the next morning!*

"The original plan was to have Mistress Jizelle show up in the evening, then have Bourke show up again, and so on. The idea was to firmly establish that the two people were separate and not at all connected. The arrival and intrusion of Standish changed all that, but things worked out fairly well, nonetheless.

"It *had* to be 'Mistress Jizelle' who killed him. Look at the evidence. Standish died—correct me if I'm wrong, Master Sean—within plus or minus fifteen minutes of the time Standish was found."

Master Sean nodded.

"Naturally," his lordship continued, "we always assume a minus time. How could the person be killed *after* the body was found?

"But there was no one else around who could have killed him! A farmer and his two sons were close enough to the road during that time to see anyone who came along unless that someone had walked along the beach. But there were no footprints in that damp sand except those of 'Mistress Jizelle'!

"Picture this, if you will: Number 055, still a little groggy, and suffering from a sore neck, is told by her returning henchmen that they have lost Standish. But she is clever enough to see what must have happened. As soon as possible, she puts on her 'Mistress Jizelle' *persona* and has her lieutenant drive her out to that section of the beach. She walks down to take a look. She sees Standish.

"Standish, meanwhile, has regained his senses. He opens his eyes and sees Olga Polovski. His gun is still in his hand.

He tries to level it at her. She jumps him, in fear of her life. A struggle. The gun goes off. *Finis."*

"Wouldn't the farmers have heard the shot?" Master Sean asked.

"At that distance, with a brisk wind blowing, the sea pounding, and a cliff to baffle the sound, it would be hard to hear a pistol shot. That one was further muffled by the fact that the muzzle was against Standish's head. No, it wouldn't have been heard."

"Why did her footprints only come up to some five yards from the body?" Sir James asked. "There were no prints in the dry sand."

"Partly because she smoothed her prints out, partly because of the wind, which blew enough to cover them. She was shaken and worried, but she did take time to search the body for the Phial. Naturally, she didn't want any evidence of that search around. She went back to consult Danglars-Suv about what to do next. When she saw the farmers, there was nothing she could do but bluff it through. Which, I must say, she did magnificently."

"Indeed." Sir James le Lein looked both cold and grim. "Where is she now?"

"By now, she has taken horse and departed."

"Riding sidesaddle, no doubt." His voice was as cold as his expression. "So you let her get away. Why didn't you arrest her?"

"On what evidence? Don't be a fool, Sir James. What would you charge her with? Could you swear in His Majesty's Court of High Justice that 'Mistress Jizelle' was actually Olga Polovski? If I had tried to arrest her, I would have been a corpse by now in that Romany camp, even if I'd had the evidence. Since I did not and do not have that evidence, there would be no point.

"I would not call it a satisfactory case, no. But you have the Phial, which was what you wanted. I'm afraid the death of Noel Standish will have to be written off as enemy action during the course of a war. It was not first degree murder; it was, as Master Sean put it yesterday, a case of accidental murder."

"But—"

Lord Darcy leaned back in the chair and closed his eyes. "Drop it, Sir James. You'll get her eventually."

Then, very quietly, he began to snore.

"I'll be damned!" said Sir James. "I worked all night on my feet and found nothing. He spends all night in bed with the most beautiful woman in Europe and gets all the answers."

"It all depends on your method of approach," Master Sean said. He opened his symbol-decorated carpetbag and took out a large, heavy book.

"Oh, certainly," said Sir James bitterly. "Some work vertically, some horizontally."

Father Arthur Lyon continued to stare out the window, hearing nothing he didn't mean to hear.

"What are you looking up there, in that grimoire?" he asked Master Sean after a moment.

"*Spells, infatuation; removal of,*" said Master Sean calmly.

The Sixteen Keys

"Naval treaties with Roumeleia are all very well," said Lord Sefton, with a superior smile on his jovial, round face, "but tell me, Your Highness, doesn't it strike you as intrinsically funny that a Greek at Constantinople should sit on a golden throne, wearing the imperial purple of the Caesars, and claim to be the representative before God of the Senate and People of Rome?"

"Indeed it does, my lord," said Prince Richard, Duke of Normandy, as he poured himself a bit more brandy. "I think it even funnier that a Frenchified Viking barbarian should sit on the ancient Throne of Britain and claim exactly the same thing. But that's politics for you, isn't it?"

The florid face of Lord Sefton appeared to approach the apoplectic. He seemed about to rebuke the Prince with something like "By Heaven, sir! How *dare* you? Who do you think you are?" Then, as though he had suddenly realized who Richard of Normandy thought he was, he paled and drowned his confusion in a hurriedly swallowed brimfull glass of Oporto.

Across the table, the Lord High Admiral had roared with laughter. Then, still chuckling, he said: "Only difference is that the people of the City of Rome agree with John of England, not with Kyril of Byzantium. And have for seven centuries or thereabouts. Wasn't it King Henry III who was the first Holy Roman Emperor, Your Highness?"

The Lord High Admiral, Richard knew, was giving Lord Sefton a chance to recover himself. "That's correct," he said. "Elected in 1280. But he didn't become *King* Henry until '83, when John II died. Let's see . . . the next four Kings

541

were elected Emperor, then, after the end of the First Baltic War in 1420, when Harold I was on the Throne, the Imperial Crown was declared to be hereditary in the Anglo-French Kings and the Plantagenet line. So Richard the Great was actually the first to *inherit* the office and title."

"Well," said Lord Sefton, apparently himself again, "I don't suppose it matters much what Kyril wants to call himself. I mean, after all, does it? Long as he does his part in the Mediterranean.

"Speaking of which, I suppose we shall have to find a way to come to some understanding with the Osmanlis, too, on this."

"Oh, yes. We'll certainly have to get an agreement with the Sultan." Not for the first time that evening, Richard wondered whatever had possessed his brother the King to appoint Sefton as Secretary for Foreign Affairs. The man was not very bright; he was certainly slow on the uptake; and he had a provincial air of superiority over anyone and anything that he could classify as "foreign." Well, whatever the King's reasons, they were good ones; if there was more to this than appeared on the surface, the Royal Duke had no desire to even speculate on what it was. If John wanted him to know, he would be told. If not . . . well, that was the business of His Most Dread and Sovereign Majesty the King.

On the other hand, Peter de Valera ap Smith, Lord High Admiral of the Imperial Navy, Commander of the Combined Fleets, Knight Commander of the Order of the Golden Leopard, and Chief of Staff for Naval Operations, was a known quantity. He was a man of middle age, with dark, curly hair that showed traces of gray. His forehead was high and craggy, his eyes heavy-lidded and deep-set beneath thick, bushy eyebrows, his nose large, wide, and slightly twisted, as though it had been broken and allowed to heal without the services of a Healer. The moustache over his wide, straight mouth was thick and bushy, spreading out to either side like a cat's whiskers. The beard was full but cut short, and was as wiry and curly as his moustache. His voice, even when muted, sounded as though its slightly rasping baritone should be bellowing orders from a quarterdeck.

On first meeting the Lord High Admiral, one got the impression of forbidding ruthlessness and remorseless purpose; it required a little time to find that these qualities were modified by both wisdom and humor. He was a man with tremendous inner power and the ability to control and use it both wisely and well.

The three men were sitting around a large table in a well-appointed drawing room, waiting for a fourth man to return. It had been one of those warm late spring days when no air moves and nothing else wants to. Not oppressively hot— just warm enough to enervate and to cause attacks of acute vernal inertia. In spite of that, the four men had worked hard all day, and now, in the late evening, they were relaxing over drinks and cigars.

At least, three of them were.

"Where the Devil is Vauxhall?" Lord Sefton asked. "He's been an infernally long time about getting that leather envelope."

Prince Richard glanced at his wristwatch. "He does seem to be taking his time. Would you be a good fellow, my lord, and go see what's delaying him? It's not like Lord Vauxhall to keep people waiting."

"Certainly, Your Highness." Lord Sefton rose and left the room.

"I thought for a moment," said the Lord High Admiral with a grin, "that you were going to say it was not like Lord Vauxhall to dally, and I was going to ask in what sense you meant the word."

Duke Richard laughed. "No comment."

A few minutes later, Lord Sefton returned, looking worried. "Can't seem to find him, Your Highness," he said. "Looked everywhere. Chap seems to have disappeared."

"Everywhere?"

"Library, office, and so on. Went upstairs and checked his bedroom and bathroom. Didn't search the whole house, of course. Might be in the kitchen, getting a snack or something. Perhaps we ought to turn out the servants?"

"Not just yet, I think," said the Lord High Admiral. He was looking out the west window. "Would you come here a moment, Your Highness?"

Duke Richard walked over to the window, followed by Lord Sefton.

Lord Peter pointed out the window. "Isn't that Lord Vauxhall's summer cottage, just beyond the little grove of trees?"

"Yes. That's what he calls it," said His Highness. "It looks as though every light in the place were on. How odd." He frowned. "Lord Sefton, you stay here and wait, in case Lord Vauxhall should return. The Admiral and I will take a stroll down there and see what's going on."

The "summer cottage" was a quarter of a mile away from the main house on the Vauxhall estate. The two men took a flagstoned pathway that went down a gentle grassy slope and through the grove of trees. Halfway up the sky, a gibbous moon leered balefully at the world beneath, casting a weird silvery radiance over the landscape, making ghostly glimmerings between the shadows of the trees.

"All the lights are on, all right," said Lord Peter as they approached the small house. "All the drapes drawn back. Looks as if there were a party going on, except it's far too quiet."

"No fear," said the Duke, "if it were one of Vauxhall's parties, we'd have heard it long before now." He went up the four steps to the front door and knocked loudly. "Vauxhall! Lord Vauxhall! It is I! De Normandy!"

"Belay that, Your Highness," said the Admiral. "It won't do any good. Look here."

The Lord High Admiral was standing to one side, looking through the big window to the left of the door.

"You seem to find a great deal by looking through windows, Lord Peter," Prince Richard grumbled. But when he looked, he had nothing to say. His face seemed to freeze, and the Lord High Admiral fancied for a moment that it looked like the handsome face on the famous marble statue of Robert, Prince of Britain, who had died so tragically young in 1708.

The body of Lord Vauxhall was lying on its back in front of the fireplace, its dead, glazed eyes staring sightlessly at the ceiling overhead. In the outstretched right hand was a heavy .44 calibre MMP, the Imperial service pistol.

After what seemed a terribly long time, Prince Richard spoke. His voice, while perfectly calm, had a curiously distant quality about it. "I see the body, but are you sure it's he? Where is the Lord Vauxhall whose dashing good looks fascinated the grand ladies of half the courts of Europe?"

"It is he," the Lord High Admiral said grimly. "I knew his father when I was a boy."

For the face of the corpse was that of an old, old man. Lord Vauxhall had aged half a century in less than an hour.

Lord Darcy, Officer of the King's Justice and Chief Investigator for His Royal Highness de Normandy, was in his sitting room, firmly planted in an easy chair, wearing one of his favorite dressing gowns—the crimson silk—smoking his favorite pipe—the big, straight-stemmed meerschaum—and reading his favorite newspaper—the London *Courier*.

Outside the half-opened window, what little breeze there was brought the faint sounds of a city which had prepared itself for sleep—small, unidentifiable sounds from the streets of Rouen. In the distance, a late night omnibus rolled over the pavement, drawn by its six-horse team.

Lord Darcy reached for the nightcap Ciardi had prepared and took a long sip of the cool drink. He had only a vague idea of what Ciardi put in the thing—rum, he knew, and lime juice and Spanish orange-blossom honey, but there were other things as well. He never asked. Let Ciardi have his little secrets; the man was far too good a servant to upset by excessive indulgence in the satisfaction of one's own curiosity. Hmmm. Did he detect, perhaps, just the slightest touch of anise? Or was it . . .

His thoughts were distracted by the increased loudness of horses' hooves in the street one story below. He had been aware of their approach for some seconds now, he realized, but now they sounded as if they were going to go right by the house. Had there been only one or two, at a slow canter, he would have paid no attention, but there were at least seven horses, and they were moving quite rapidly.

Good heavens, what a din, he thought. *You'd think it was a troop of cavalry going by.* He was torn between his natural curiosity to see who these late night riders were and the feeling of lassitude and comfort that made it seem like a terrible effort to get up and go to the window.

It seemed quite clear that comfort had won over curiosity—just when the horses pulled up to a halt in front of the house. Lord Darcy was on his feet and out of his chair to the window in as close to nothing flat as was humanly possible.

By the time the imperturbable Ciardi arrived, his lordship was already dressed.

"My lord . . ." Ciardi began.

"Yes, Ciardi; I know. It really *was* a troop of cavalry."

"Yes, my lord. Lieutenant Coronel Edouin Danvers, commanding the Duke of Normandy's Own 18th Heavy Dragoons, presents his compliments. He requested me to give you this." He handed over an envelope. "He says he will wait, my lord."

Lord Darcy tore open the envelope and read the short letter.

"Ciardi, rouse Master Sean. Then rouse Gabriel and tell him to get the light carriage ready. Master Sean and I will be accompanying Coronel Danvers to Lord Vauxhall's estate—that's five miles out of the city, on the River Road toward Paris. I don't know how long we shall be there, so I'm taking my traveling case. If we need anything more, I shall send word. Did you offer the Coronel a drink?"

"Yes, my lord. He took ouiskie and water, and I left him with the decanter on the sideboard. Will there be anything else, my lord?"

"Not at the moment. I shall go down and talk to the Coronel."

Lieutenant Coronel Danvers was a spare man of medium height with a clipped, dark, military moustache and a tanned face; he looked alert and wide awake, neatly turned out in crisp field dress. He turned round from the sideboard as the tall, handsome Chief Investigator entered the downstairs receiving room.

"Evening, Lord Darcy. Get you out of bed, did I? Sorry. Orders, you know. Have a little ouiskie; fix you right up."

"No, thanks, Coronel. I see Ciardi has thoughtfully prepared the caffe service. As soon as the water's hot, I'll make a pot."

"Never drink caffe after noon, myself, my lord. Fine stuff in the morning, though. Fine stuff."

"Yes. See here, Danvers, what the devil is this all about?"

"Be damned if I know, my lord." Coronel Danvers looked genuinely surprised. "Expected *you'd* tell *me*. Thought perhaps His Highness put it all down in that letter I brought, eh? No? Well, all I was told was to fetch you and Master Sean and Dr. Pateley and Chief Master-at-Arms Donal Brennan and a Journeyman Sorcerer named Torquin Scoll and a troop of fifty horsemen." He turned back to the sideboard, added ouiskie and water to his glass, and went on: "I came for you and Master Sean, and sent Captain Broun and Senior Captain Delgardie after the others. They'll be joining us on the road."

"Wait a second," Lord Darcy said, "I'm missing data here. You weren't out at Vauxhall's with His Highness?"

"Oh, no! Rather not." He shook his massive head. "I was at home when Sir Ramsey came charging into my yard as though the Hunnish cavalry were after him to deliver those letters from His Highness. Didn't stay; said he was heading back out."

The copper kettle over the gas flame was bubbling happily now. Lord Darcy poured boiling water into the silver funnel that held freshly-ground caffe and watched as the dark liquid filtered through. "Somebody's hurt or dead," he said, more to himself than to Coronel Danvers, "and perhaps a crime's been committed. That would account for calling in Master Sean, Dr. Pateley and myself. And Chief Donal. But why fifty horsemen? And why does he need *two* magicians?"

"That's a good question, me lord," said a voice from the door. "Why does His Grace need two magicians? Who's the other one?"

The short, sturdy figure in sorcerer's robes was Master Sean O Lochlainn, Chief Forensic Sorcerer for the Duchy of Normandy.

The Coronel spoke before Lord Darcy could. "Ah! Evening, Master Sean! Got you out of bed, did I?"

" 'Fraid you did, Coronel Danvers." Master Sean stopped a yawn.

"Terribly sorry. Here, though; I'm fixing myself a bit of ouiskie and splash; let me fix you one. Best thing for you, this time of night."

"No, thanks, Coronel; I'll have some of the caffe his lordship is making. What other magician, my lord?"

"Journeyman Torquin Scoll, according to the Coronel."

"Oh. The locksman. Good man, in his field. He's a nut on locks. Absolutely dotes on 'em, me lord. Couldn't cast a simple preservative spell over a prune, he couldn't—but give him a simple padlock, and he'll have it singing the Imperial Anthem in four-part harmony in five minutes."

"Interesting," said Lord Darcy, handing Master Sean a cup of caffe. "Opens up all kinds of speculations. Far too many, in fact. For now, we'll just have to—"

He was interrupted by the entrance of the tall, lean, silver-haired Ciardi. "Your carriage is ready, my lord. I took the liberty of packing a basket of refreshments, my lord, just in case. Your traveling case is in the luggage compartment. As is yours, Master Sean, along with your instrument bag."

"Thank you, Ciardi," said Master Sean. With the obvious exception of Lord Darcy himself, Ciardi was the only man in the world that Master Sean would trust to handle the symbol-decorated carpetbag that carried the instruments and tools of his profession.

"Excellent, Ciardi," Lord Darcy said. "Shall we finish our caffe and be off, then, gentlemen?"

The Coronel downed his drink. "I'll get my men ready, my lord."

As the cavalcade moved through the gates of the Vauxhall estate some time later, Lord Darcy remarked: "Frankly, what I miss are the flags and banners, the band music and the cheering crowds."

Master Sean, seated across from him in the carriage, lifted both brows. "Beg your pardon, me lord?"

"Well, I mean, after all, my dear Sean, if we're going to have a parade, we should do it properly. The Duke's Own should be in full dress, with sabres, not field dress, with sidearms. The dozen Armsmen should be wearing full decorations. And, above all, we should be going at a leisurely, dignified pace, at high noon, not galloping along in the middle of the night, as though we were fleeing the country. No, no; I fear that, as a parade, it has left a great deal to be desired."

Master Sean grinned. "As your cousin de London would say, me lord, 'Most unsatisfactory.' "

"Precisely. Ho! We're stopping." Lord Darcy put his head out the window, looking toward the head of the column. "It's His Highness. He's talking to Coronel Danvers, gesturing all around, as if he were including the whole countryside. What the devil *is* going on? Come along, Master Sean."

Lord Darcy opened the carriage door and climbed out, followed by the stout little Irish sorcerer. He didn't bother to give any instructions to Gabriel; that tough old horse handler would know what to do.

The Chief Sergeant Major with Coronel Danvers took a small pipe from his jacket pocket and sounded *Officers Assemble,* followed by *Senior NCOs Assemble.* The Coronel and the CSM trotted their mounts out to a broad section of the lawn, and were joined by seven other dragoons.

"This night will be one the troops will remember, regardless of what happens next," Lord Darcy said with a low chuckle as he and Master Sean walked toward where His Royal Highness was now talking to Chief Master-at-Arms Donal Brennan.

"How's that, me lord?"

"They're top heavy," his lordship said. "We've got two squadrons with us. Out there, you have two lieutenants as squadron commanders and a captain as troop commander, which is all very fine. You've got two squadron sergeants and the troop first sergeant. Still fine. But, in addition, you have the regimental commander, the regimental exec, and the regimental CSM, who will be running all around trying to get something done while trying not to give any orders except to the captain in charge of the troop. The CSM can't even do that, so he'll be trying not to tell the first what to do. Oh, it will be fun, all right." He chuckled again. "It will be all right here, where the gas lamps by the driveway give plenty of light, but wait till they're milling about in those woods with nothing but a three-quarter moon overhead."

Master Sean frowned. "Why would they be milling about in the woods, me lord?"

"Searching for something or somebody. Surely you noticed that every man Jack of 'em has a search lamp slung at his saddle. Lieutenant Coronel Edouin Danvers didn't tell me everything he knew. Which is all right; we'll get it straight from His Highness now."

Prince Richard had caught sight of Lord Darcy and Master Sean. "Ah, there you are, my lord. Sorry to drag you and Master Sean out at this time of night, but there's no help for it. Where is Goodman Torquin?"

"Right here, Your Highness," said a mellow, baritone voice from somewhere behind and below Lord Darcy's head. His lordship turned round.

The man in the working dress of a journeyman Sorcerer was not over five-two, and was built like a wrestler. He was not a dwarf, merely short—although his head seemed a trifle large for the rest of him. He had a pleasantly ugly face that made Lord Darcy suspect he practiced pugilism on the side, large warm brown eyes, and, like Master Sean, he carried a symbol-decorated carpetbag in his left hand.

Introductions were made all round, including Donal Brennan, the grim-looking black-uniformed Chief Master-at-Arms of the City of Rouen.

"Let's walk down toward the summer cottage, while I explain what all this ruckus is about," said the Duke.

Briefly, but completely, he told the story. The only thing he did not mention was the contents of the "important papers" that Lord Vauxhall had been carrying when last seen. Nor did he describe the body; they would see that soon enough.

"You must understand," he concluded, "that it is vitally important that we find those papers."

"You think they are in the diplomatic case, then, Your Highness?" Lord Darcy asked.

"Fairly certain. Vauxhall took the papers with him to put them in it. He had left it on his desk in his office, and we couldn't find it anywhere."

Lord Darcy nodded. "Yes. The obvious conclusion is that the papers are in that leather envelope. I tend to agree with Your Highness."

"That's why I called out a troop of the regiment," said the Duke. "I want these grounds searched thoroughly, and cavalrymen are trained for that sort of thing. Besides, I didn't want to pull that many Armsmen out of the city. A dozen is enough to search all the buildings, and that's what *they're* trained for."

Chief Donal nodded, apparently impressed by the Duke's sagacity.

The five men heard running footsteps behind them, and they all turned to look. Running down the grassy slope in the silvery moonlight was a figure carrying a black leather bag.

"It's Dr. Pateley," said Master Sean.

"Sorry to be late, gentlemen," puffed the gray-haired chirurgeon. "Sorry, Your Highness. Unavoidable delay. Sorry." He stopped to get his breath and to adjust the pince-nez glasses which had become awry. "Where's the body?"

"That's where we're headed now, Doctor," Prince Richard said. "Come along." The men followed.

"Sister Elizabeth had to call me in," Dr. Pateley was saying in a low voice to Master Sean. "She's a midwife and Healer of the Order of St. Luke. A little unexpected post-parturition trouble. Nothing serious. Stitching job. Baby doing fine."

"Glad to hear it," murmured Master Sean.

Ahead of them, the lights gleamed from the windows of Lord Vauxhall's summer cottage. Near the door stood a bearded man in a Naval uniform of royal blue that was lavishly decorated with gold. Lord Darcy recognized him immediately, even in the moonlight.

After the introductions had been made, Lord Darcy gripped the Lord High Admiral by the arm and said, in a low voice, "Peter, you old pirate, how are you?"

"Not bad at all, Darcy. I can't say I'm much enamored over this particular situation, but otherwise everything's fine. And you?"

"The same, I'm glad to say. Shall we go inside and view the remains?"

"You can view 'em through the window until the locksman gets that door open," Lord Peter said.

Lord Darcy looked round quickly at Prince Richard. "You mean nobody's been inside that house yet?"

"No, my lord," the Duke said. "I thought it best not to break in until you came to take charge."

"I see." He looked searchingly at the Duke's calm face. Prince Richard knew what he was doing; Plantagenets always did. But if the papers were found in that house after Richard had called in the cavalry to search for them, he'd look an awful fool. That was the chance he'd have to take. Another hour's delay, if the papers were *not* in the house, might have been disastrous.

Lord Darcy looked back at the house. The windows were of the modern "picture window" type, with only narrow transoms at top and bottom to allow for air circulation— too narrow to allow a man to enter. Without the key, it would be a major smashing job to get in. Lord Darcy could see why the Prince had made the decision he had.

"Very well, then, Your Highness; let's get started. I assume Journeyman Sorcerer Torquin designed and built those locks and designed and cast the spells on them; otherwise you'd have let Master Sean do the unlocking work."

The Duke nodded. "That's right, my lord."

Master Sean said: " 'Tis a good thing Your Highness brought him. I, meself, would hate to try to unravel one o' Goodman Torquin's lock spells in less than an hour—"

"Meanin' no disrespect, Master," Torquin Scoll put in, "but would ye care to make a small wager ye can't do it in an hour and a half?"

"—without the key," Master Sean went on. "Of course, *with* the key—"

"I'll give ye the key and two hours and still bet ye a gold sovereign."

"I will not," said Master Sean firmly. "You already have more o' my gold sovereigns than I'd care to tot up. Taking lessons from you is expensive."

"You gentlemen can talk shop elsewhere," Lord Darcy said. "Right now, I want that door unlocked."

"Yes, my lord." Goodman Torquin opened his bag and knelt down to peer at the lock, looking somehow gnome-like in the moon's radiance. He took a small lamp from his bag, lit it, and went to work.

Lord Darcy went over and peered through the window. "*How* long did you say he's been dead, Your Highness?" he said, staring.

"Less than three hours," the Duke replied. "He looked bad enough when we found him. But now . . ." He turned his head away.

"If that's what I think it is," Master Sean said softly, "I'd better get in there fast with a preservative spell."

There was the approaching thud of hooves on turf. Coronel Danvers came up at a fast canter and sprang lightly from the saddle. In the distance, through the trees, Lord Darcy could see search lamps flickering like large, slow-moving fireflies.

"Your Highness." The Coronel saluted. The Prince was, after all, the Honorary Coronel of the 18th, and Lieutenant Coronel Danvers was in uniform. "I have the perimeter surrounded and the remainder of the men on search, as you ordered. Senior Captain Delgardie will report here to me, directly anything's found."

"Very good, Coronel."

"Er—Your Highness." Danvers seemed suddenly unsure of himself. "Lord Sefton—er—presents his compliments, and wishes to know when Your Highness intends to begin interrogation of the prisoners."

"Prisoners?" said the Lord High Admiral. "What's this? What prisoners?"

"His lordship means the servants," said Prince Richard with forced calmness. "They are not prisoners. I merely asked them to remain until this thing was cleared up. I left them in Lord Sefton's care. If those papers can't be found . . ." He paused and frowned slightly. "Chief Donal—"

He was cut off by Journeyman Torquin's voice. "There ye go, my lords and gentlemen."

The front door of the little cottage swung open.

"Everyone stay out until Master Sean is through," Lord Darcy said crisply.

Master Sean went in to cast the special spell which would stop the dissolution of the corpse. Everyone left him alone, as they had Goodman Torquin; nobody but a fool disturbs a magician when he is working at his Art. It was over quickly.

The other six men came into the room.

There is something about death which fascinates all human beings, and something about horror which seems even more deeply fascinating. The thing which lay on the floor in front of the big cold fireplace, illuminated brightly by the mantled gas lamps in the wall brackets, embodied both.

The big fireplace had facings of fine marble, white, mottled with pink and gold, the great mirror over the mantelpiece reflected the walls of the room, covered by smooth brocade paper that picked up the pink-and-gold motif. The woven brocade upholstery of the furniture repeated the pattern of the walls. It was a light, airy, beautiful room that did not deserve the insult which lay on the pale eggshell carpet.

The air was thick with the smell.

The Lord High Admiral was opening transoms above and below the windows. Nobody closed the door.

"Here, Your Highness! Sit down!" At the sound of Coronel Danvers' voice, Lord Darcy turned away from the thing on the floor.

Prince Richard's face had gone gray-white, and he swallowed a couple of times as the Coronel eased him into one of the big, soft chairs. "I'm all right," the Duke managed. "It—it's rather warm in here."

"Ah. Yes. It is that," Danvers agreed. "Where did Vauxhall keep his spirits? Must be . . . Ah!" He had opened a waist-high cabinet against the west wall. "Here we are! A good stiff one will brace you right up, Your Highness. Ouiskie? Or brandy?"

"Brandy, thank you."

"There you are, Your Highness. Believe I'll have a little ouiskie, myself. Shocking sight. Absolutely shocking."

Lord Darcy, seeing that the Duke was all right and in good hands, knelt beside the corpse with Master Sean and Dr. Pateley. "Whatever killed him," his lordship murmured, "it wasn't a bullet from this." He disengaged the heavy 44 MMP from the right hand of the corpse.

The Lord High Admiral was standing, looking down over Dr. Pateley's shoulder. "No. A Morley military pistol makes rather large, easily visible holes."

Lord Darcy knew Lord Peter wasn't being sardonic—just blunt. He handed the weapon to the Lord High Admiral. "Look like it's been fired to you?"

The Naval officer's strong, capable hands unloaded the handgun, field stripped it, put it back together again. "Not recently."

"Thought not. Well, well; what's this?" Lord Darcy had been searching the clothing of the late Lord Vauxhall and had come up with a small leather case which, when opened, proved to contain a series of keys, all very much alike, numbered from 1 to 16, all neatly arrayed in order and attached to the case so that each could swing free separately. "Very pretty. Wonder what it's for? He has another set of keys of various sizes on a ring; this must be something special."

"Oh, yes; that it is, my lord," said Journeyman Sorcerer Torquin Scoll. "Made that set special for his lordship, I did. His lordship was a man of rare taste, he was." A broad grin suddenly came over the little man's face. "That is to say, my lord, he enjoyed locks as much as I do, if ye see what I mean." The grin vanished. "I shall miss him. We enjoyed talkin' locks together. And workin' with 'em. Very knowledgeable he was, and clever with his hands. I shall certainly miss him."

"I'm sure." Lord Darcy looked back down at the keys during a moment of silence, then looked up again and said: "What do they fit, if I may ask?"

"Why, they're the keys to this house, your lordship."

"*This* house? *All* of them?"

The grin came back to the pleasantly ugly face. "That's right, your lordship. There's sixteen doors in this house, and every blessed one of 'em locks with a different key—from either side. Here, I'll show ye." He opened up his symbol-decorated carpetbag and brought out a thick loose-leaf notebook. After a moment of search, he selected a sheet of paper, made a small cross-mark on it, detached it carefully, and handed it to Lord Darcy. "There ye are, your lordship. That's a plan sketch I made of this house. We're right here in the receiving room, d'ye see, where I made the cross. Those slidin' doors lead into the gallery, the dinin' room, and the library. That small door over there goes to the front bedroom. All the doors 're numbered to match the keys."

"What's this 'green room' that's all glassed in?" Lord Darcy asked.

"It's a sort of a greenhouse, your lordship. Lord Vauxhall called this a summer cottage, but he used it durin' the winter, too, when he was home. That's the reason for the fireplaces. One here, one in the library, one in the dinin' room, an' those little corner fireplaces in the bedrooms."

"How many sets of keys are there?"

"Just that one, my lord. Oh, the gard'ner has duplicates for keys three and four, so's he can tend the plants, but that's all."

Lord Darcy could sense a certain depressing tension in the room. Prince Richard was staring blankly at a half-full glass of brandy; Coronel Danvers was pouring himself a drink; Lord Peter was staring out the window; Chief Donal was watching Master Sean and Dr. Pateley go over the body.

Then he realized that the momentary shock that had hit the Duke had gone, and realized, too, what His Highness was waiting for. He had given charge of the case over to Lord Darcy and was now trying to be patient. Lord Darcy walked over to where he was sitting.

"Would Your Highness care to inspect the rest of the house?" he asked quietly.

Prince Richard looked up and smiled. "I thought you'd never ask." He finished off the brandy.

"There's nothing more I can learn from the body until Master Sean and Dr. Pateley give me their findings. I can detect no sign of struggle. Apparently he walked in here with a gun in his hand and—died."

"Why the gun, I wonder?" Prince Richard said musingly. "Had he been frightened by something, do you suppose?"

"I wish I knew. He wasn't wearing a holster, so he must have picked it up from somewhere after he left you."

"Yes. He wasn't wearing a coat, so he couldn't have concealed a weapon that big. Oh. Excuse me a moment. Chief Donal?"

"Yes, Your Highness?" said the grim-looking Chief Master-at-Arms, turning away from the body to face his Duke.

"When you have finished here, go up to the main house and take charge. Keep the servants calm and don't tell them anything. They don't even know their master is dead. If one of them does, it might tell us something. And I don't want any interrogation of any kind until Lord Darcy says so."

"I'm through now, Your Highness. Got all I need. From now on, it's up to Lord Darcy." He flashed a smile which looked very uncomfortable on his face, and must have been, for it went away immediately. "Cases involving Black Magic are way over my head, anyway. Don't like 'em at all." With no further ceremony, he left.

"Well, let's see if we can find those papers," Lord Darcy said. "Might as well try the gallery first."

"Mind if I come along?" the Lord High Admiral asked.

"Of course not, my lord," the Duke said. "How about you, Coronel? Want to take the tour with us?"

Danvers frowned and glanced at his nearly empty glass. "I think not, begging Your Highness' leave; I'd best be at hand in case Delgardie or the Sergeant Major come with news."

The sliding doors were locked, and Lord Darcy had inserted the key marked "5". It turned easily—too easily. It went right on round and clicked back into place. A turn in the other direction had the same result. The bolt remained solidly in place.

"Beggin' your pardon, my lord," said Torquin Scoll, "but I guess I'll have to come along with ye. The wrong key won't even turn the cylinder; the right key will, but it won't engage the bolt unless the right man is holdin' the key. It'll be a little tricky, even for me, since these keys are tuned to his late lordship."

He took the key case, fitted No. 5 in again, closed his eyes, and turned the key carefully. Click.

"There we go, my lords, Your Highness."

The four men went into the gallery.

"Don't you have a set of these keys tuned to yourself, Goodman Torquin?" Lord Darcy inquired.

"Do, indeed, my lord; used 'em just a week ago to do the regular spell maintenance. I'd have brought 'em with me if I'd've known what was afoot. But all that Captain— whatsisname?—Broun. If that Captain Broun'd've told me where we were going. But no, he just says the Duke wants me, so I saddled up and came along."

"My apologies, Goodman Torquin," said His Highness.

"Oh, no need, Highness; no need. Not your fault. Military mind, you know. Take orders; give orders; don't explain, especially to civilians. Not your fault at all, Highness." Then he gestured with a broad sweep of a hand. "How do you like the gallery, gentle sirs?"

"Fascinating," murmured Lord Darcy. "Utterly fascinating."

The west wall was almost all glass—seven windows, six feet wide, with only narrow pillars between them. The heavy theater-type drapes which would cover them had been drawn up to the ceiling. Outside, in the darkness, one could see the occasional gleam of search lamps, the only sign that the dragoons were at work.

But that was not the vista that Lord Darcy had found fascinating.

The east wall was covered with paintings. None of them were obscene, and not all were erotic, but they all spoke of beauty, love, and romance.

"These must have run him into quite a bit of money over the years," the Lord High Admiral remarked. "Beautiful work, all of 'em. There! That's a Van Gaughn; always admired his work."

"Some of them," said the Duke, "were done especially by his late lordship's order. This one, for instance."

"That," said Lord Peter authoritatively, "is a Killgore-Spangler. I'd recognize her style anywhere."

"I also recognize the model," Lord Darcy said in a slightly dreamy voice.

"That, too," said the Lord High Admiral.

Prince Richard looked surprised. "Both of you are acquainted with Doña Isabella Maria Constanza Diaz y Carillo de la Barra?"

The Lord High Admiral burst out laughing. "Oh, yes, Your Highness. Oh, yes. Recognized her in spite of the red wig, eh, Darcy?"

"In that pose, I'd have recognized her with a sack over her head." Lord Darcy began to chuckle.

"What *is* so funny?" Prince Richard asked in a tone that held more than a touch of irritation.

"Your Highness," Lord Darcy said, "that woman is no more a Spanish noblewoman than the Coronel's horse is. That happens to be Olga Vasilovna Polovski, Number 055 of *Serka*, the Polish Secret Service. She's the most beautiful and the most dangerous woman in Europe."

"Good God!" The Prince looked shocked. "Did Vauxhall know?"

"I hope so," said Lord Darcy. "I sincerely hope so."

"Oh, he knew, all right," said Lord Peter. "He was making special reports to Naval Intelligence at the time. That's what made the whole affair so delicious."

"I can well imagine," said Lord Darcy. They walked on.

Lord Darcy cast a practiced eye over the long gallery. If someone had wanted to hide it, the eleven-by-fifteen, two-inch-thick diplomatic case could be concealed—with difficulty—in the theater drapes that hung in graceful curves above the windows. Or there might be some secret niche behind one of the paintings. But for now he would assume that it was in plain sight—or pretty much so.

Torquin the Locksman had gone on ahead to unlock doors. The three noblemen followed in his wake. The next door led into a small but comfortable bedroom. The wallpaper here had a pattern similar to that in the receiving room, but here it was pastel blue and gold. The upholstery on the two chairs and the spread on the double bed matched it. No fancy marble on the corner fireplace, however; it was of plain fieldstone, with an unfinished ruggedness that contrasted nicely with the patterned smoothness of the rest of the room.

"Wonder how old this house is?" the Lord High Admiral asked idly as they searched the room.

"Not very, in comparison to the manor house," Lord Darcy said. "That's late Robertian—1700 or thereabout."

"It's practically brand new," Prince Richard said. "Vauxhall built it himself in 1927 or '28. It's been redecorated a couple of times since, I understand, but no drastic changes. It's rather nice, I think. And the picture gallery is much more inspiring than the one up the hill. All those ghastly old ancestors staring at you."

"Your Highness ought to know," murmured Lord Darcy.

"Oh, God, yes! Have you seen that portrait of my thrice-great grandfather, Gwiliam IV? The big one that hangs in Westminster? It was painted in 1810, just two years before he died. Really grim-looking old boy at eighty. Well, that picture used to scare the devil out of me when I was a boy. I wouldn't go anywhere near it. The eyes aren't quite looking at you, you know, but you get the feeling that if the old man just shifted them a little, he'd see you straight on. At least *I* thought so. And I had the feeling that if he ever looked straight at me he would see what a wicked little boy I was, and would leap down from his frame and devour me upon the spot. Well, there's nothing in this clothespress."

"And nothing in the bathroom," said Lord Darcy.

"It's dark under this bed," the Lord High Admiral said. "Lend me your pipe lighter, Lord Darcy. Thanks. Mmmm. No. Nothing under there." He stood up and brushed off the knees of his trousers.

Lord Darcy was looking up at the skylight. "That doesn't look as though it opens."

The other two looked up. "No," said the Lord High Admiral. "Except for that narrow transom on the leeward side."

"Yes," the Duke said, pointing. "It's operated by that cord that hangs down the wall. It goes up through that pulley, there, you see."

"I suppose all of the inner rooms have skylights, Your Highness?" Lord Darcy said.

"Oh, yes, my lord. Even the library has one, as you'll see. It has no windows, since the walls are covered with bookshelves. The only other light in there would be from the glass double doors that lead into the garden." The Duke looked all around. "Well, the next stop is the service pantry."

They went out into the north wing of the L-shaped gallery, turned right, and went to the door of the service pantry. It swung open at a touch; Torquin had been there before them.

The room was, in effect, a very small kitchen. Vauxhall did not throw big dining parties here; when he wanted food served, the servants brought it down from the main house.

"Not very big," the Lord High Admiral said, "but lots of places to look." He opened the warming oven, saw nothing, closed it, and went on to the cabinets.

Lord Darcy climbed up on a little three-legged stool and began going through shelves. "Your Highness," he said, "would I be out of order if I asked just what these 'important papers' are?"

"They're the only copies, in three languages, of our new naval treaty with Roumeleia."

"Oh, *ho*. I see."

"As ambassador to the Basileus at Constantinople, Lord Vauxhall was instrumental in persuading Kyril to agree to all the terms. The Greeks, of course, control the Bosphoros and the Dardanelles, which means they have the Black Sea bottled off from the Mediterranean.

"Casimir of Poland is still trying to get around our naval blockade of the North Sea and the Baltic. By the treaty we forced on him after the '39 war, no Polish armed vessel is to pass the Fourteenth Meridian, and no Imperial armed vessel is to pass the Tenth Meridian going the other way."

"Nobody here but us Scandinavians," growled the High Admiral.

"Right," said Prince Richard. "And the treaty also permits Scandinavian or Imperial naval vessels to stop and search *any* Polish vessel between the Eighth and Fourteenth Meridians for contraband—arms and ammunition—and to seize any that's found.

"But the situation's different in the Mediterranean. The Greeks didn't like what Poland pulled during the '39 War, and took advantage of our winning it to say that no armed vessel of *any* nation—except Roumeleia, of course—would be allowed in the Sea of Marmara. But they didn't quite have guts enough to put a stop-search-and-seizure clause in that fiat.

"Emperor Kyril is ready to do that now, provided we'll back him up in the Mediterranean. The Roumeleian Navy isn't strong enough by a long sight to patrol the Black, the Marmara, *and* the Mediterranean, and they're still worried about the Osmanlis, to say nothing of North Africa. This treaty arranges for all that."

"I see," Lord Darcy said. He was silent for a moment, then: "May I ask, Your Highness, why all this sudden need for a search of King Casimir's merchant ships?"

The Lord High Admiral's chuckle was unpleasant. "May I tell him, Your Highness?"

"Certainly. The King my brother has trusted Lord Darcy with state secrets far more crucial than this one."

That was not what the Lord High Admiral had meant, but he let it pass. He said: "His Slavonic Majesty, Casimir IX, has concocted a scheme to get himself a fleet in the Atlantic. It's a lovely scheme—and it could work. In fact—*it may already have worked.* We may have caught on just a little too late for comfort."

"Three ships is hardly a fleet," the Duke objected.

"Three ships *that we know of,* Your Highness. At any rate, what has happened is this: A few years ago, Poland started expanding her merchant fleet with a new type of vessel—a little faster, a little more sturdily built. They started making them first up in the Pomeranian Bay area. Six months later, they began tooling up for them in the Black Sea—at Odessa.

"More time goes by. At some time—which we haven't nailed down yet—the game of Shells-and-Pea begins."

"The papers don't seem to be in here," the Duke interrupted. "Shall we go into the green room?"

"Yes," said Lord Darcy. "Let's see if naval treaties grow on bushes."

There were no bushes. The room, like the gallery, had two outside walls that were practically all glass. Greenery and flowers grew in pots and tubs all over the place. Nothing spectacular, but it was colorful and pleasant.

The search continued.

"Thank goodness the roses are the thornless variety," said the Lord High Admiral as he pushed leaves and blooms aside. "Where was I?"

"You were playing the Shells-and-Pea Game with Polish merchant vessels," said Lord Darcy.

"Oh, yes. Now, you must understand that these ships are all alike. We call 'em the *Mielic* class; the *Mielic* was the first one off the ways, and they're all named after small cities. And you can't tell one from the next, except for the name painted on 'em.

"Here's what happens. Let's say the *Zamosc* sails from— oh, Danzig. She stops at the Helsingør-Hälsingborg Naval Check Point for inspection, which she passes with flying colors."

"I was afraid you'd say that," murmured Lord Darcy as he peered under a long wooden bench.

"From there," Lord Peter continued remorselessly, "she continues to Antwerp. This time, *we* check her. She's clean."

"And her colors are still flying," said Lord Darcy.

"Exactly. So she works her way south. Bordeaux, San Sebastian, La Coruña, Lisbon, and finally through the Strait of Gibraltar. She does business around the Mediterranean for a while. Finally, she heads east, through the Dardanelles and the Bosphoros, into the Black Sea, and straight for Odessa. A week later—Ouch! That rose *does* have thorns! A week later, she's coming back again. The *Zamosc* goes back through the Bosphoros, the Dardanelles, the Mediterranean, the Straits of Gibraltar, and heads south again, for the coast of Africa. A few months later, here comes the *Zamosc* again, back to Bordeaux with a hold full of zebra hides or something. Then, on north and turn east again and back to Danzig, passing every inspection with utter innocence."

"Only the name has been changed to protect the guilty," Lord Darcy remarked.

"You are so right. I won't ask how you knew."

"It was obvious. Tell me: Were the crew allowed liberty at port?" The Lord High Admiral grinned through his beard. "Not likely, eh? No, they weren't. And would it surprise you to know that the hull of a *Mielic*-class vessel looks astonishingly like that of a light cruiser? I thought not."

Lord Darcy said: "I see what you mean by the Shells-and-Pea game. It means that three different ships are involved. Number One—the *Zamosc*—is a genuine merchantman. But when it gets to Odessa, there's a heavily-armored light cruiser hull that looks exactly like her, with the name *Zamosc* lettered neatly on her bow and stem. Her cargo is heavy naval guns, ready to be mounted in some shipyard in Africa. Where?"

"Abidjan, we think."

"The Ashanti, eh? Well, well. Anyhow, the second *Zamosc*, with the same officers, but a different crew, gets by the Greeks easily because they can't board and search. Off she goes to Abidjan, where the third *Zamosc*, another genuine merchantman, is waiting. Same officers; third crew. And back to Danzig as pure as the snows of Pamir. Clever. And what happens to the original *Zamosc*?"

"Why, pretty soon the *Berdichev* comes sliding down the ways. Brand new ship. Says so in her papers."

"And this has happened three times?"

"Three times that we know of," said the Lord High Admiral. "We still haven't been able to check out every one of those ships and follow their official courses, much less try to deduce their *un*official shenanigans. The point is that we have to put a stop to it immediately."

"There is evidence," Prince Richard said, "that two more will be sailing out of the Black Sea within the week. They're stepping up operations, my lord. That's why all the worry about that damned missing diplomatic case. It has already been signed by Kyril, but he won't act on it until he sees the Imperial Seal and my signature on it. There's an official letter with it from His Majesty, signed, sealed, and everything, authorizing my own signature as proxy, and all that. It was done that way because the King my brother cannot come to Normandy at this time, and it would take just enough extra time to get the thing over there and back that we would be skating too close to the edge. Two—or even one more of King Casimir's ships out of the blockade could mean more trouble than we can handle right now.

"The Napoli Express leaves Calais in—" He pushed back the lace at his cuff and looked at his wristwatch. "—five hours and twenty-one minutes. That train only runs twice a week. If we can put that treaty on it in Paris, it will be in Brindisi in less than thirty-six hours. From there to Athens by ship is another twenty-four hours. The Basileus will be there, waiting for it, and the Greek Navy will be enforcing it in another twenty-four.

"If we don't have it on that train, we're lost."

"I don't think it's as bad as all that, Your Highness," the Lord High Admiral said. "We can get it to—"

But the Duke cut him off sharply. "Don't be an optimistic fool, my lord! If we haven't found that thing by then, it will mean that somehow—I don't know how—it has come into the hands of the *Serka*.

"Kyril trusted and liked Vauxhall. With him dead, we'd find it hard going to re-negotiate the treaty. Kyril would think us fools to lose the first copy, and he'd be right. He'd likely balk at signing another. Besides, Casimir would know all about it and be taking steps to do something else."

It was not until that point that Lord Darcy realized how much on edge the Prince was. Outbursts of that kind were not like him.

"I think you need not worry yourself unduly on that score, Your Highness," he said quietly. "I believe I can guarantee that the treaty will be on the Napoli Express in the morning." He knew he was sticking his neck out, and he knew that the axe blade was sharp. But he had that feeling . . .

The Prince took a deep breath, held it for a second, then eased it out. "I am relieved to hear that, my lord. I have never known you to be wrong on something of that kind. Thank you."

Lord Darcy felt a ghostly prickle at the back of his neck. The axe had grown a bit more solid.

"Well, wherever it is," said the Lord High Admiral, "it is not here with the vegetation. I guess the library's next."

They slid aside the double doors and went in.

And stopped.

The room was wall-to-wall and floor-to-ceiling with bookshelves. And they were full of books.

"Help us, Blessed Mary," Prince Richard said earnestly. "We'll have to look behind every one of them."

"Just a moment, Your Highness; let me check something," said Lord Darcy. He went over to the doors that led back into the front room and slid them open. Master Sean was over by the fireplace, talking in low tones with Journeyman Torquin. Coronel Danvers was sipping a drink and staring moodily out the front window. There was no sign of either Dr. Pateley or the body. Three heads turned as Lord Darcy opened the doors.

"I see the clay has been removed," Lord Darcy said.

"Aye, me lord," Master Sean said. "The hearse came. The doctor went along to make arrangements for the autopsy. I made all the tests possible for now."

"Excellent. Tell me, my good Sean, how long would it take you—possibly with the assistance of your colleague—to remove all the privacy spells around here so that an ordinary clairvoyant could find what we're looking for?"

Master Sean blinked, then looked at Goodman Torquin. "Are any of these yours?"

Torquin shook his head. "Not much good at that sort of thing, Master. Locks are my specialty. I don't know who he got to renew his privacy spells."

Master Sean looked around and seemed to feel the air. "They've been here a long while, me lord. Fifty years or so—give or take ten percent. Strong; well reinforced. Complex, too. Fine, competent workmanship. Master grade, I'd say—or a specialist. Ummm." He reached down, opened his symbol-decorated carpetbag, and took out a thin silver wand with a flat, five-pointed star on the end, looking rather like a long nail with a five-pointed head. He closed his eyes and twirled it slowly between the thumb and forefinger of his right hand. "Some of the basics are even older. This house is new, but the grounds have been private property for centuries. There was a castle up on the hill where the manor house is now, but it was torn down in the Fifteenth Century. But they had good, solid privacy spells, even then. And the more modern ones are built on an old, very solid foundation."

He opened his eyes and returned the wand to his bag. "Nine hours, me lord—if I'm lucky."

Lord Darcy sighed. "Forget it. Thank you very much, Master Sean." He slid the doors shut again.

"It was a nice idea while it lasted," said the Lord High Admiral. "Let's get on with it."

"I suggest," Lord Darcy said, "that we give it a quick look

and then go on to the dining room and the other bedroom. We can come back here if we don't find it there, but we'd feel silly if we pulled out all these books and then found it in the bath of the front bedroom."

A quick search revealed nothing.

"Dining room, then," Lord Darcy said, opening the sliding doors. "Well! What have we here?"

There was a large, bare table of polished walnut, big enough to seat ten, set lengthwise in the room. At the southern end, near the door to the front room, was an open bottle of wine and an empty glass. Lord Darcy went over and looked at them carefully. *"Schwartzschlosskellar '69.* A very good Rhenish. One drink gone, and the bottle's abominably warm. Bottom of the glass still has a sticky drop or two in it."

"His last drink," said Prince Richard.

"I think so, yes. Leave them alone; we'll have Master Sean look them over later, if it becomes necessary."

They found nothing in the dining room.

The front bedroom was very like the rear one, except that the wallpaper pattern was green and silver.

"Notice the way the bedrooms are separated," Lord Peter remarked. "Only a partition between them, but you have to go through at least two other rooms to go from one to the other. Vauxhall had a fine and very subtle sense of psychology."

"That's why he became a diplomat," said the Duke.

There was no diplomatic case in the bedroom, either.

"Back to the library," muttered the Lord High Admiral.

It took them nearly an hour, even with the help of Master Sean, Goodman Torquin, and the Coronel. They found all sorts of little odds and ends about, but nothing of importance. Certainly no Roumeleian naval treaty.

"Well, Your Highness," said the Coronel, "if it's not in this house, it must be outside, eh? Just you wait, though; one of my lads will turn it up. Old Vauxhall probably dropped it somewhere between here and the manor house. That's where I set my sharpest lads to work. I know it's disappointing, though. Tell you what! Let's all have a good stiff drink. Do us no end of good after all that dusty work. What say?"

With the exception of the two sorcerers, everybody agreed with him, for once.

They were all standing around silently, holding their glasses, or staring at walls, when a knock came at the front door, followed immediately by the entrance of Lord Sefton, the Foreign Secretary.

He was perspiring, which gave an oily look to his red, jowly face. "Ah! Your Highness, my lords, gentlemen. Thought I'd find you here." He glanced quickly at the men, not knowing any of them but the Duke and the Lord High Admiral. Prince Richard made introductions.

"Just dropped down to tell Your Highness that the Armsmen have finished searching the house. Haven't found the blasted thing, so Chief Donal is having them go over it all again. Looking for secret panels and the like. I thought maybe you'd found it here."

"No such luck," Prince Richard said. He looked at Lord Darcy. "How about that, my lord? Should we look for secret panels?"

Lord Darcy shook his head. "I've looked. Wallpapered walls like this don't lend themselves to such things. There's no way to hide the cracks. Everywhere they *could* be, I checked. I'm going to go out to the gallery again and look behind the pictures, though; if there are any secret hiding places, that's where they'll be."

"Well, then, Lord Darcy," Lord Sefton said importantly, "have you determined who committed the murder?"

"Good God!" Coronel Danvers almost dropped his glass. *"Murder?* What murder?" He jerked his head around to look at Lord Darcy. "You didn't say anything about a murder. Has there been a murder? What the devil is the fellow talking about?"

"I'm sure I don't know," said Lord Darcy. "Nobody's said anything about a murder. What *are* you talking about, Lord Sefton?"

"Yes," said Prince Richard, "please explain yourself, my lord."

Lord Sefton's flabby mouth opened, closed, and opened again. "Wuh-wuh-why, Lord *Vauxhall!* I saw him through the window when you called me down! He was right there! With a gun in his hand! Looked like an Egyptian mummy!" He stopped, swallowed, then, more calmly: "Oh. Was it suicide, then?"

Lord Darcy looked at the Duke. "You know, Your Highness,

I think that might explain the gun. I believe he was thinking of it—before he died."

"I think you're right," the Duke said solemnly. "He might have thought it would be an easier way to go. Perhaps it would have been. It might have been less—painful."

Master Sean shook his head. " 'Tisn't painful, Your Highness. Except mentally. Seeing yourself go all to pieces that way. But the nervous system goes pretty fast. Numbness sets in quite rapidly toward the last."

Lord Sefton seemed ready to go to pieces himself. "Buh-buh-but what are you talking about? Chief Donal said Vauxhall'd been killed by Black Magic! Why are you all taking it so calmly? *Why?*"

"My lord, please calm yourself and sit down," Prince Richard said firmly.

"Yes, my lord, do sit down," said the Coronel. "Here, let me fetch you a glass of brandy. Straighten you right up."

Lord Sefton took the brandy with a shaking hand. "I don't understand," he said weakly.

"Perhaps Master Sean would be good enough to explain," said His Highness.

Master Sean thought for a couple of seconds, then said: "How old would you say Lord Vauxhall was, me lord?"

"Thuh-thirty. Thirty-five."

"He was over seventy," said Master Sean. Sefton said nothing. He just looked stunned.

"These days, thanks to modern healing methods," Master Sean went on, "a man can expect the Biblical three-score-and-ten as a minimum, if accident or other violence doesn't carry him off before that. Because of the tremendous psychic burdens they bear, Kings don't get much past that, but an ordinary fellow can look forward with reasonable confidence to his hundredth birthday, and a quarter of a century more is far from uncommon. We call a man in his sixties 'middle-aged', and quite rightly, too.

"But Healers and sorcerers aren't miracle-workers. We can all expect to get older; there's no cure for that. A man slows down; his reflexes aren't what they were; he gets wrinkles and gray hair and all that sort of thing. We all know it, and we expect it. And, until about a century ago—a little more—there was nothing could be done about it.

"Then, in 1848, in the early part of the reign of Gwiliam

V, two medical thaumaturgists, working independently, discovered a method for retaining the appearance and the vigor of youth. One was a Westphalian named Reinhardt von Horst; the other an Ulsterman named Duivid Shea.

"Essentially, what they discovered was a method of keeping the entire body in balance, as it were. I'll not go into the thaumaturgical terminology, but what happens, under the effect of the treatment, is that the body keeps katabolism and anabolism so perfectly balanced that each part contributes to the support of every other part. Do you see?"

Lord Sefton nodded and held his empty glass out to Coronel Danvers, who promptly refilled it along with his own.

Lord Darcy had heard Master Sean lecture on this subject before, but he enjoyed listening to Master Sean when he got into his pedagogical mood. For one thing, he lost almost all of his brogue, and for another, he always showed a new facet of any subject, no matter how many times he'd spoken on it before.

"Now, that sounds awfully good in theory, doesn't it, my lord?

"Unfortunately, it doesn't work out that way. Take the skin, for instance. It's one of the first things to go as age progresses. That's why we get wrinkles and gray hair. The skin loses its youthful elasticity and its ability to pigment hair. The heart, on the other hand, is one of the toughest organs we have. It has to be. It keeps going, day and night, year after year, with only a tiny bit of rest between beats. If a man sees his Healer regularly, the old ticker will keep going strong until the very end. It can be the last thing to go, long after the rest of the body has given up and, to all intents and purposes, died.

"But this treatment I've been talking about spreads the wearing out process all over the whole body evenly. In order to keep such things as the purely cosmetic functions of the skin going, the heart, the liver, the pancreas, and so on, all have to give up some of their own life expectancy.

"Eventually, the body reaches the point where every organ in it, every individual cell, is on the verge of death. And when they begin dying, it happens all over, with terrifying rapidity. A matter of minutes, never more than an hour. Everything goes at once. The enzymes go wild.

Connecting fibers dissolve. Resistance to microorganisms vanishes.

"Well—you saw the result. Lord Vauxhall had taken that treatment."

"*Ugh,*" Lord Sefton said. "That's horrible."

"In effect," Master Sean continued relentlessly, "what Lord Vauxhall did was trade fifty extra years of life for fifty extra years of youth. All of us who knew him suspected it, and it came as no surprise—only as a shock."

"Great God," Lord Sefton said. "A man like Vauxhall, tied in with Black Magic. Horrible."

"Well, now, as to that," said Master Sean, "it is and it isn't. Black Magic, I mean. It's not done with evil intent. No ethical thaumaturgist in the Empire would do it, but I understand it's not considered a bad exchange in some parts of Islam. Leading the sex life of an eighteen-year-old for half a century might appear to some as a good thing. Depends on your outlook, I suppose. But the end is pretty messy."

"Tell me, Master Sean," Prince Richard said, "how many treatments does it take?"

"Oh, you have to take the treatments regularly, Your Highness. It's like an addictive drug, in a way. After a certain length of time, the withdrawal symptoms are pretty bad. The whole body has been weakened, you see, and without the support of additional spells you'd go to pieces. And more slowly. If Lord Vauxhall had stopped, say, twenty-five years ago, he might have lasted a year. But it would have been a rather horrible year.

"In the long run, of course, there's nothing a sorcerer can do. I have heard that some sorcerers using the treatment have had patients collapse and die in the middle of a treatment session. I don't think I'd care for that, meself."

"Why have I never heard of this before?" Lord Sefton asked.

"It's rarely done," Master Sean said. "Few magicians *can* do it; even fewer *would* do it. And it's a devilish difficult job. Accordingly, the price is high. Very high. Only a rich man like Lord Vauxhall could afford it. And, o' course, it's not widely advertised. We'd rather it were not discussed very much, if you follow me, Lord Sefton."

"I do indeed." The Foreign Secretary drained his glass,

and then sat blinking for a minute. At last he said: "Poor old boy. Bad way to go." He forced a smile. "Damned inconvenient, too. For us, I mean. What do you suppose he did with the treaty?" He looked up at Lord Darcy.

Lord Darcy had been thumbing tobacco into what he called his "knockabout briar" and drawing it alight. He slowly blew out a cloud of smoke and said: "Well—let's reconstruct what he must have done.

"He left the table where my lords had been talking in order to get the leather diplomatic case to put the papers in. While he was gone, he received some sign that the end was near. What would that be, Master Sean?"

"Probably his hair started coming out, me lord," the stout little Irish sorcerer replied. "That's usually the first indication. Then the skin around the eyes. And a sudden feeling of lassitude and weakness."

"We can picture the scene, then," Lord Darcy went on. "I don't know how I, personally, would react if I suddenly saw myself going like that, but Vauxhall was a pretty tough-minded man and he had known what the end would be like for years. He was prepared for it, in a way. But at the moment of realization, everything else became suddenly unimportant. He didn't want others to see him; his vanity precluded that. What went through his mind?

"Lord Vauxhall's greatest conquests were made in the field of diplomacy, but many of his most pleasurable ones were made right here in this house. He had built it himself and was proud of it and happy with it. I think he wanted to see it one last time. He could die here in peace.

"I think the gun must have been in a desk drawer or the like; we can check that later, up at the manor. It's of no matter, really, except that it shows his state of mind.

"We can imagine him making his decision and coming down here. The important thing we must imagine is what he might have done with that leather-encased treaty. He had, I think, forgotten about it. There it was, under his left arm or in his left hand, and he didn't even notice it. Like a man who has shoved his spectacles up to his forehead and forgotten them."

"Why do you say his left hand, my lord?" Prince Richard asked with a frown.

"Because he was thinking about his right hand," Lord Darcy said gently. "There was a handgun in it."

The Duke nodded silently.

"Now, at some time between then and the moment of his death, he *did* notice it—and put it down somewhere. I hardly think he deliberately concealed it. He had suddenly noticed it and it was rather heavy, so he unburdened himself of it.

"He came here, poured himself a glass of wine, and—" Lord Darcy stopped.

"The wine," he said after a half minute.

"What about it?" Lord Peter asked. "Perfectly good wine, wasn't it?"

"Oh, yes. But he wouldn't drink a Rhenish warm. He wouldn't keep it in a place where it would become warm. Oh, it's warm now, but it was cool when he opened it. Had to be."

He turned away from them suddenly and looked out the front window at the wanly moonlit scene. "I can't picture it," he said, almost as if to himself. "I just can't see him coming down that slope with a bottle of wine, a gun, and a diplomatic case. Even if he left the case in the manor house, would he have gone all the way down to the cellar for a bottle? No. It would have to be picked up on the way—" He swung round and looked at the Prince.

"Were the four of you drinking wine this evening?"

"No, my lord," said Prince Richard. "Oh, there was Oporto and Xerez on the sideboard with the spirits, but nothing that would have been brought up from the wine cellar."

"Then where the devil did he get that bottle of Rhenish?"

Prince Richard put his hand over his eyes with a sudden gesture. "I forgot all about it! There's a small cellar right here. Come! I'll show you."

They all trooped after him, through the dining room, back to the service pantry. He strode over to one wall and knelt on the parquet floor. Lord Darcy saw that there was a small, finger-sized hole in one of the wooden blocks that made up the floor and mentally cursed himself for not having seen it before.

The Duke stuck his finger in the hole and lifted. A block of the wood came up. Beneath it was a heavy steel ring which lay flat until His Highness grasped it and lifted as he stood up. The ring made a handle, and a twenty-eight by twenty-eight section of the floor swung upward on hinges. Below, a ladder led down into gloom.

Lord Darcy was already getting a candle from the supply he had noticed when the room had been searched previously. He lit it with his pipe lighter, and, pipe clenched between his teeth, descended into the little wine cellar.

Once on the floor of the underground room, he lifted his candle and looked around.

"Not much here," he said after a minute. "Most of the shelves are empty. A few good reds. And, yes, seven bottles of the *Schwartzschlosskellar* '69 and a couple of dozen of the '70. Want to come down and help me look, Peter? There's a candle here in a holder—probably the one Vauxhall used. It looks fresh."

The Lord High Admiral came down the ladder as if he were on a ship.

The men above waited with what can only be called stolid impatience. After what seemed a God-awful long time, they heard:

"Well, Darcy, so much for that."

"Yes. Nothing here. Dammit, where *is* it?"

The two men came back up the ladder looking utterly dispirited.

"A fine big buildup to a big letdown," Lord Darcy said. "Sorry, Your Highness." They all went back to the front room.

Once there, Coronel Danvers went over to the liquor cabinet, finished his drink, picked up his dragoon officers' cap, adjusted it smartly on his head, turned, and saluted His Highness the Duke.

"With Your Highness's permission, I'll go out and take a look around between here and the manor house. I'm getting a bit fidgety waiting for someone else to find that package."

"Certainly, Coronel. Let me know immediately when you find it."

"I shall, Your Highness." And he went briskly out the door.

"Amazing man, the Coronel," said the Duke.

"A good officer," said the Lord High Admiral. "What he needs is to see some action. Which he may, if we don't find that treaty."

"I believe I'll go with him," said Lord Sefton. "Maybe I

can be of some help. I'm of no use hanging about here. With your permission, Your Highness?"

"Of course, my lord."

He went out, leaving Lord Darcy with the Prince, the Lord High Admiral, Master Sean, and Goodman Torquin.

"Well," Lord Darcy said with a sigh, "I suppose there's nothing for it but to look behind all the pictures in the gallery. I wish I knew what rooms Vauxhall actually went to."

"Why, he went to all of 'em, ye know," said Torquin.

Lord Darcy looked down at the small man. "He did?"

"Oh, yea. Took a complete tour of the house, he did. The locks had just been freshly serviced by myself d'ye see, so I could tell when I opened 'em. Nobody but him had been in the house since. Funny thing—he went through every door once. And only once. Unlocked the door, went through, locked it behind him. Extraordinary. Must have wanted the house left in tip-top form, eh?"

There seemed to come a great calm over Lord Darcy as he said: "Yes. Most interesting. May I see that sketch plan again?"

"Of course, my lord." Goodman Torquin took his notebook from his bag, extracted the page, and handed it over.

Lord Darcy scrutinized it carefully, then handed it back with a brief thanks. Then he wandered about the room, staring straight ahead as if he were looking at something others could not see. No one said anything. After a few minutes, he stopped suddenly and looked at Prince Richard. "I trust that the plumbing is functioning in this house, Your Highness?"

"I should think so. Like the gas, it's turned on from outside, and the servants would have made everything ready for him when they were told he was coming home."

"That's good. If you will pardon me, gentlemen?" He opened the door to the west of the fireplace and went into the front bedroom, closing the door behind him.

"He's a deep 'un, his lordship, eh, Master?" said Torquin the Locksman.

"Probably the most brilliant deductive reasoner on the face of the Earth," Master Sean said. "And possibly the most brilliant *in*ductive reasoner. I wonder what he saw in that sketch plan of yours? He saw something. I know him well."

"Let's take a look and see if we can spot it," Prince Richard said. "I think we have all the evidence he has. If he's come up with some kind of answer, we should be able to."

"As my friend Torquin, here, might say, 'Would ye care to put a gold sovereign on it?' " Master Sean said with a grin.

"No," said His Royal Highness.

The four men looked at the sketch plan.

They were still looking fruitlessly when Lord Darcy returned some minutes later. The smile on his face was beatific.

"Ah, Your Highness! You will be pleased to know that your worries are over! All is well. I predict—" He raised a fore-finger histrionically. "I predict that very soon a man you have not seen for some time will appear in this very house, coming from the legendary direction of Hell itself, bearing with him that which you seek. He and his minions will come from the darkness into the light. I have spoken!"

The Duke stared at him. "How do you know all this?"

"Aha! I have heard voices, though I could not see the speakers," Lord Darcy said mysteriously.

"What's the matter with you, Darcy?" the Prince asked wanly.

Lord Darcy spread his arms and bowed. "I am like the weather, Highness. When the weather is brisk, I am brisk; when the weather is cool, I am cool; when the weather is blustery, I am blustery. Have you noticed how balmy it is out tonight?"

"All right, my lord; you know something. What is it?" the Lord High Admiral said in quarterdeck tones.

"Indeed I do," Lord Darcy said, regaining some of his wonted composure. "Take a good look at that sketch plan, I beg you. And remember that Torquin the Locksman has stated unequivocally that Lord Vauxhall went through each and every one of the sixteen doors in this house—we're not counting bathroom doors—once and only once. Do I state the facts, my good Torquin?"

"Yea, my lord; ye do."

"Then the facts lead inescapably to one conclusion, which, in turn, leads us to the most likely place for the treaty to be. Don't you see?"

They didn't, none of them, for a minute or so.

Then Lord Darcy said quietly: "How did he get into the house?"

Torquin the Locksman looked at him in astonishment. "Through one of the outside doors, o' course. He had all the keys."

But Master Sean burst out with: "Good heavens, yes! Parity, me lord. *Parity!*"

"Exactly, me dear Sean! Parity!" Lord Darcy said.

"I don't get it," the Lord High Admiral said flatly. "What's 'parity'?"

"The ability to make pairs, yer lordship," said Master Sean. "In other words, is a number odd or even? The number of doors coming into this house is four—that's even. If he went through all four of those doors once and only once—it don't matter at all where he went between times—he'd have ended up back outside the house."

"In-out-in-out," said Prince Richard. "Why, of course he would! Then how—" He stopped and looked back at the paper.

"Would you give me a sheet of blank paper and a pencil?" Lord Darcy asked in a low aside to Torquin. The small man produced them from his bag.

"Is the route he took supposed to be of importance?" the Lord High Admiral asked.

"Not the route, no," Lord Darcy said. He had put the paper on the mantelpiece and was sketching rapidly. "There must be ten thousand different routes he could have taken and still gone through every door exactly once. No, the route's not important."

"Parity, again," said Master Sean. "It holds true for any room with an even number of doors. I see what his lordship is driving at."

"Certainly you do," Lord Darcy said. "Once I saw that he couldn't have entered from any of the outside doors, I knew that there had to be a secret entrance to this house. It fits in well with Vauxhall's romantic nature. And when I saw what the end-points of his route through this house were, I knew where to look for the hidden entrance. So I excused myself, and went to look. I didn't want to raise any false hopes in the rest of you, so I checked to make sure the treaty was there."

"You said you were going to the head," said the Lord High Admiral.

"I did not. I merely inquired after the plumbing. Your inferences were your own. At any rate, I checked, and I heard voices from—"

A voice from within the house said: "Halloo! Is someone up there?"

"Come along," Lord Darcy said. "That will be Chief Donal with good news. I left the treaty for him to find." They all went through the dining room to the service pantry. Chief Donal and two of his sergeants were climbing out of the little wine cellar.

The Chief Master-at-Arms was holding a heavy leather diplomatic case in his hands and a broad smile on his face. "We found it, Your Highness! There you are!" He had never looked less grim.

The Duke took the case and inspected its contents. "That's it, all right, Chief Donal. Congratulations. And thank you. Where was it?"

"Well, we got to looking for secret panels, Your Highness, since the first search of the house didn't yield anything. We found this old tunnel behind a dummy wine rack in the wine cellar. There used to be an old castle up on that hill, centuries ago, and the manor house was built on its foundations. This tunnel must have been an escape route for times of siege; it ended up down here, in what was woods, then. Lord Vauxhall must have deliberately built this house on top of the old tunnel exit. We followed it and came out here. The case, there, was on the floor of the tunnel, just behind another dummy wine rack that acted as a door."

"Well, thank you again, Chief Donal," the Prince said. "You can go call off your men now. We've got what we were looking for."

They all went back out to the receiving room again, and, after the Armsmen had left, Prince Richard speared Lord Darcy with an accusing eye. "'A man I haven't seen in some time'," he quasi-quoted.

"A couple of hours, at least," Lord Darcy said tranquilly.

"May I ask what is on the piece of paper you were so assiduously working on?"

"Certainly, Your Highness. Here. As you see, it is merely one of the possible routes Vauxhall could have taken. There are thousands of possibilities, but every one of them has to either start in this room and end in the service pantry or vice versa. They are the only two rooms with an odd number of doors. Since he died in this room, he had to start his tour in the service pantry. And the only other way into that room had to be through the wine cellar."

"Simple, when you know how," the Duke said. "It's getting very late. I still have to tell Coronel Danvers to call off his dragoons. Let's shut off the lights and—if you would be so good, Journeyman Torquin—lock up those four outside doors."

"And the ones to the green room, Your Highness," the small man said firmly. "Lord Vauxhall wouldn't want no gard'ner prowlin' through the house."

"Of course."

The doors were locked and the lights put out.

As Lord Darcy turned the last gascock in the front room, he looked at the spot before the fireplace where Lord Vauxhall had died.

"Obit surfeit vanitatis," he said softly.

And the darkness came.

The Napoli Express

1

His Royal Highness, Prince Richard, Duke of Normandy, seated on the edge of his bed in the Ducal Palace at Rouen, had taken off one boot and started on the other when a discreet rap came at the door.

"Yes? What is it?" There was the sound of both weariness and irritation in his voice.

"Sir Leonard, Highness. I'm afraid it's important."

Sir Leonard was the Duke's private secretary and general factotum. If he said something was important, it was. Nevertheless—

"Come in, then, but damn it, man, it's five o'clock in the morning! I've had a hard day and no sleep."

Sir Leonard knew all that, so he ignored it. He came through the door and stopped. "There is a Commander Dhuglas downstairs, Highness, with a letter from His Majesty. It is marked *Most Urgent*."

"Oh. Well, let's see it."

"The Commander was instructed to deliver it into your hands only, Highness."

"Bother," said His Highness without rancor, and put his boot back on.

By the time he got downstairs to the room where Commander Dhuglas was waiting, Prince Richard no longer looked either tired or disheveled. He was every inch a tall, blond, handsome Plantagenet, member of a proud family that had ruled the Anglo-French Empire for over eight centuries.

Commander Dhuglas, a spare man with graying hair, bowed when the Duke entered. "Your Highness."

"Good morning, Commander. I understand you have a letter from His Majesty."

"I do, Your Highness." The Naval officer handed over a large ornately-sealed envelope. "I am to wait for an answer, Your Highness."

His Highness took the letter and waved toward a nearby chair. "Sit down, Commander, while I see what this is all about."

He himself took another chair, broke the seal on the envelope and took out the letter.

At the top was the embossed seal of the Royal Arms, and, below that:

> *My dear Richard,*
> *There has been a slight change in plans. Due to unforeseen events at this end, the package you have prepared for export must go by sea instead of overland. The bearer of this letter, Commander Edwy Dhuglas, will take it and your courier to their destination aboard the vessel he commands, the White Dolphin. She's the fastest ship in the Navy, and will make the trip in plenty of time.*
>
>

All my best,
Your loving brother,
John
>

Prince Richard stared at the words. The "package" to which His Majesty referred was a freshly-negotiated and signed Naval treaty between Kyril, the Emperor at Constantinople, and King John. If the treaty could be gotten to Athens in time, Kyril would take steps immediately to close the Sea of Marmara against certain Polish "merchant" vessels—actually disguised light cruisers—which King Casimir's Navy was building in Odessa.

If those ships got out, Casimir of Poland would have Naval forces in the Mediterranean and the Atlantic for the first time in forty years. There were three of the disguised cruisers in the Black Sea now; once they got past the Dardanelles, it would be too late. They had to be trapped in the Sea of Marmara, and that meant the treaty had to be in Athens within days.

Plans had been laid, timetables set and mathematically calculated to get that treaty there with all possible haste.

And now, His Imperial Majesty, John IV, by the Grace of God King of England, France, Scotland, and Ireland; Emperor of the Romans and Germans; Premier Chief of the Moqtessumid Clan; Son of the Sun; Lord and Protector of the Western Continents of New England and New France; Defender of the Faith, had changed those plans. He had every right to do so, of course; there was no question of that. But—

Prince Richard looked at his wristwatch and then at Commander Dhuglas. "I am afraid this message from the King my brother is a little late, Commander. The item to which he refers should be leaving Paris on the Napoli Express in five minutes."

2

The long, bright red cars of the Napoli Express seemed almost eager to get into motion; the two ten-inch-wide stripes along their length—one white and one blue—almost gave the impression that they were already in motion. Far down the track ahead, nearly outside the South Paris Station, the huge engine steamed with a distant hissing.

As usual, the Express was loaded nearly full. She only made the run from Paris to Naples twice a week, and she usually had all the passengers she could handle—plus a standby waiting list.

The trouble with being a standby is that when a reservation is cancelled at the last moment, the standbys, in order of precedence, have to take the accommodations offered or give them up to the next in line.

The poshest compartments on the Napoli Express are the eight double compartments on the last car of the train, the Observation Car, which is separated from the rest of the train by the dining car. All sixteen places had been reserved, but three of them had been cancelled at the last moment. Two

of them had been filled by standbys who rather reluctantly
parted with the extra fare required, but the sixteenth place
remained empty. None of the other standbys could afford
it.

The passengers were filing aboard. One of them—a short,
stout, dark-haired, well-dressed Irishman carrying a symbol-
decorated carpetbag in one hand and a suitcase in the
other, and bearing papers which identified him as Seamus
Kilpadraeg, Master Sorcerer—watched the other passengers
carefully without seeming to do so. The man just ahead
of him in line was a wide-shouldered, thick-set man with
graying hair who announced himself as Sir Stanley Galbraith. He climbed aboard and did not look back as Master
Seamus identified himself, put down his suitcase, surren-
dered his ticket and took back his stub.

The man behind him, the last in line, was a tall, lean
gentleman with brown hair and a full, bushy brown beard.
Master Seamus had previously watched him hurrying across
the station toward the train. He carried a suitcase in one
hand and a silver-headed walking stick in the other, and
walked with a slight limp. The sorcerer heard him give his
name to the ticket officer as Goodman John Peabody.

Master Seamus knew that the limp was phony and that
the walking stick concealed a sword, but he said nothing
and did not look back as he picked up his suitcase and
boarded the train.

The small lounge at the rear of the car already contained
some five or six passengers. The rest were presumably in
their compartments. His own compartment, according to his
ticket, was Number Two, toward the front of the car. He
headed toward it, suitcase in one hand, carpetbag in the
other. He looked again at the ticket: Number Two Upper.
The lower bed was now a day couch, the upper had been
folded up into the wall and locked into place, but there were
two lockers under the lower bed marked "Upper" and
"Lower." The one marked "Upper" still had a key in its lock;
the other did not, which meant that the man who shared
his compartment had already put his luggage in, locked it
and taken the key. Master Seamus stowed his own gear away,
locked the locker and pocketed the key. Having nothing better
to do, he went back to the lounge.

The bushy-bearded man named Peabody was seated by

himself over in one corner reading the Paris *Standard*. After one glance, the sorcerer ignored him, found himself a seat, and looked casually around at the others.

They seemed a mixed lot, some tall, some short, some middle-aged, some not much over thirty. The youngest-appearing was a blond, pink-faced fellow who was standing by the bar as if impatiently awaiting a drink, although he must have known that liquor would not be served until the train was well under way.

The oldest-appearing was a white-haired gentleman in priest's garb; he had a small white mustache and beard, and smooth-shaven cheeks. He was quietly reading his breviary through a pair of gold-rimmed half-glasses.

Between those two, there seemed to be a sampling of every decade. There were only nine men in the lounge, including the sorcerer. Five others, for one reason or another, remained in their compartments. The last one almost didn't make it.

He was a plump man—not really fat, but definitely overweight—who came puffing up just as the ticket officer was about to close the door. He clutched his suitcase in one hand and his hat in the other. His sandy hair had been tousled by the warm spring wind.

"Quinte," he gasped. "Jason Quinte." He handed over his ticket, retaining the stub.

The ticket officer said, "Glad you made it, sir. That's all, then." And he closed the door.

Two minutes later, the train began to move.

3

Five minutes out of the station, a man in a bright red-and-blue uniform came into the car and asked those who were in their staterooms to please assemble in the after lounge. "The Trainmaster will be here in a moment," he informed everyone.

In due time, the Trainmaster made his appearance in the lounge. He was a man of medium height, with a fierce-looking black mustache, and when he doffed his hat, he revealed a vast expanse of bald head fringed by black hair.

His red-and-blue uniform was distinguished from the other by four broad white stripes on each sleeve.

"Gentlemen," he said with a slight bow, "I am Edmund Norton, your Trainmaster. I see by the passenger manifest that all of you are going straight through to Napoli. The timetable is printed on the little cards inside the doors of your compartments, and another one—" he gestured "—is posted over there behind the bar. Our first stop will be Lyon, where we will arrive at 12:15 this afternoon, and there will be an hour stopover. There is an excellent restaurant at the station for your lunch. We arrive at Marsaille at 6:24 and will leave at 7:20. There will be a light supper served in the dining car at nine.

"At approximately half an hour after midnight, we will cross the border from the Duchy of Provence to the Duchy of Liguria. The train will stop for ten minutes, but you need not bother yourselves with that, as no one will be allowed either on or off the train. We will arrive at Genova at 3:31 in the morning, and leave at 4:30. Breakfast will be served from 8 to 9 in the morning, and we arrive in Rome at four minutes before noon. We leave Rome at one o'clock, which will give you an hour for lunch. And we arrive at Napoli at 3:26 in the afternoon. The total time for the trip will be 34 hours and 14 minutes.

"For your convenience, the dining car will be open this morning at six. It is the next car ahead, toward the front of the train.

"Goodman Fred will take care of all of your needs, but feel free to call on me for anything at any time." Goodman Fred made a short bow.

"I must remind you, gentlemen, that smoking is not permitted in the compartments, in the corridor or in the lounge. Those of you who wish to smoke may use the observation platform at the rear of the car.

"If there are any questions, I will be glad to answer them at this time."

There were no questions. The Trainmaster bowed again. "Thank you, gentlemen. I hope you will all enjoy your trip." He replaced his hat, turned and left.

There were four tables reserved in the rear of the dining car for the occupants of the observation car. Master Sorcerer Seamus Kilpadraeg got into the dining car early, and one by one, three other men sat down with him at the table.

The tall, husky man with the receding white hair and the white, clipped, military mustache introduced himself first.

"Name's Martyn Boothroyd. Looks like we're going to be on the train together for a while, eh?" His attention was all on the sorcerer.

"So it would seem, Goodman Martyn," the stout little Irish sorcerer said affably. "Seamus Kilpadraeg I am, and pleased to meet you."

The blocky-faced man with the two-inch scar on his right cheek was Gavin Tailleur; the blond man with the big nose was Sidney Charpentier.

The waiter came, took orders, and went.

Charpentier rubbed a forefinger against the side of his imposing nose. "Pardon me, Goodman Seamus," he said in his deep, rumbling voice, "but when you came aboard, didn't I see you carrying a magician's bag?"

"You did, sir," said the sorcerer pleasantly.

Charpentier grinned, showing strong white teeth. "Thought so. Journeyman? Or should I have called you 'Master Seamus'?"

The Irishman smiled back. "Master it is, sir."

All of them were speaking rather loudly, and around them others were doing the same, trying to adjust their voice levels to compensate for the roar and rumble of the Napoli Express as she sped southwards toward Lyon.

"It's a pleasure to make your acquaintance, Master Seamus," Charpentier said. "I've always been interested in the field of magic. Sometimes wish I'd gone into it, myself. Never have made Master, though; math's way over my head."

"Oh? You've a touch of the Talent, then?" the sorcerer asked.

"A little. I've got my ticket as a Lay Healer."

The sorcerer nodded. A Lay Healer's License was good for first aid and emergency work or for assisting a qualified Healer.

The blocky-faced Tailleur tapped the scar on his cheek with his right forefinger and said, in a somewhat gravelly voice: "This would've been a damn sight worse than it is if it hadn't been for old Sharpy, here."

Boothroyd said suddenly: "There's a question I've always

wanted to ask—oops, here's breakfast." While the waiter put plates of hot food on the table, Boothroyd began again. "There's a question I've always wanted to ask. I've noticed that Healers use only their hands, with perhaps a little oil or water, but sorcerers use all kinds of paraphernalia—wands, amulets, thuribles, that sort of thing. Why is that?"

"Well, sir, for one thing, they're slightly different uses of the Talent," the sorcerer said. "A Healer is assisting in a process that naturally tends in the direction he wants it to go. The body itself has a strong tendency to heal. Further-more, the *patient* wants it to heal, except in certain cases of severe aberration, which a Healer can take care of in other ways."

"In other words," Charpentier said, "the Healer has the cooperation of both the body and the mind of the patient."

"Exactly so," the sorcerer agreed. "The Healer just greases the skids, so to speak."

"And how does that differ from what a sorcerer does?" Boothroyd asked.

"Well, most of a sorcerer's work is done with inanimate objects. No cooperation at all, d'ye see. So he has to use tools that a Healer doesn't need.

"I'll give you an analogy. Suppose you have two friends who weigh fourteen stone apiece. Suppose they're both very drunk and want to go home. But they are so drunk that they can't get home by themselves. You, who are perfectly sober, can take 'em both by the arm and lead 'em both home at the same time. It may be a bit o' trouble; it may require all your skill at handling 'em. But you can do it without help because, in the long run, they're cooperating with you. They *want* to get home.

"But suppose you had the same weight in two sandbags, and you want to get *them* to the same place at the same time. You'll get no cooperation from three hundred and ninety-two pounds of sand. So you have to use a tool to assist you. You have a great many tools, but you must pick the right one for the job. In this case, you'd use a wheel-barrow, not a screwdriver or a hammer."

"Oh, I see," said Boothroyd, "you'd say a healer's job was easier, then?"

"Not easier. Just different. Some men who could wheel twenty-eight stone of sand a mile in fifteen minutes might not be able to handle a couple of drunks at all without using physical force. It's a different approach, you see."

Master Seamus had let his eyes wander over the other men in the rear of the dining car as he talked. There were only fourteen men at breakfast. The white-haired priest was listening to two rather foppish-looking men discourse earnestly on church architecture at the next table. He couldn't hear any of the others because of the noise of the train. Only one man was missing. Apparently the bushy-bearded Goodman John Peabody had not wanted any breakfast.

4

The saba game started early.

An imposing man with a hawk nose and a full beard, completely white except for two narrow streaks of dark brown beginning at the corners of his mouth, came over to where Master Seamus was sitting in the lounge.

"Master Seamus, I'm Gwiliam Hauser. A few of us are getting up a little game and thought maybe you'd like to join us."

"I thank you for the offer, Goodman Gwiliam," the sorcerer said, "but I'm afraid I'm not much of a gambling man."

"Hardly gambling, sir. Twelfth-bit ante. Just a friendly game to pass the time."

"No, not even a friendly game of saba. But, again, I thank you."

Hauser's eyes narrowed. "May I ask why not?"

"Ah, that you may, sir, and I'll tell you. If a sorcerer gets in a saba game with men who don't have the Talent, he can only lose."

"And why is that?"

"Because if he wins, sir, there's sure to be someone at the table who will accuse him of using his Talent to cheat. Now you should see a saba game played among sorcerers, sir. That's something to watch, though likely you'd not see most of what was going on."

Hauser's eyes cleared, and a chuckle came from somewhere inside the heavy beard. "I see. Hadn't thought of it that way. Boothroyd said you might like to play, so I asked. I'll pass on your bit of wisdom to him."

Actually, it would never occur to most folk to distrust a magician, much less accuse one of cheating at cards. But a heavy loser, especially if he's been drinking, will quite often say things he regrets later. Sorcerers rarely gamble with un-Talented people unless they are close friends.

Eventually Hauser, Boothroyd, Charpentier, the plump, nearly late Jason Quinte, and one of the two fops—the tall one with the hairline mustache, who looked as though he had been pressed into his clothes—ended up at a comer table with a deck of cards and a round of drinks. The saba game was on.

The sorcerer watched the game for a while from across the room, then opened the copy of the *Journal of the Royal Thaumaturgical Society* and began to read.

At eight-fifteen, the Irish magician finished the article on "The Subjective Algebra of Kinetic Processes" and put the *Journal* down. He was tired, not having had enough sleep, and the swaying motion of the train made it difficult to keep his eyes focused on the lines of print. He closed his eyes and massaged the bridge of his nose between thumb and forefinger.

"Beg y'pardon, Master Seamus. Mind if I join you?"

The sorcerer opened his eyes and looked up.

"Not at all. Pray sit down."

The man had reddish hair, a bulbous nose, and sagging features that hung loosely on his facial bones. His smile was pleasant and his eyes sleepy-looking. "Zeisler's my name, Master Seamus. Maurice Zeisler." He extended his right hand; his left held a large glass of ouiskie and water—heavy on the ouiskie.

The two shook hands, and Zeisler eased himself into the chair to the sorcerer's left. He gestured toward the saba table.

"Damn silly game, saba. Have to remember all those cards. Miss one, play wrong, and you're down the drain for a sovereign at least. Remember 'em all, have all the luck, bluff all the others out, and you're four sovereigns ahead. I never get the luck, and I can't keep the cards straight. Vandepole can, every time. So I stand 'em all a round of drinks and let 'em play. Lose less that way."

"Very wise," murmured the sorcerer.

"Buy you a drink?"

"No, thank you, sir. It's a bit early for me. Later, perhaps."

"Certainly. Be a pleasure." He took a hefty swig from his glass and then leaned confidentially toward the sorcerer. "What I would really like to know is, *is* Vandepole cheating? He's the well-dressed chap with the hairline mustache. Is he using the Talent to influence the fall of the cards?"

The sorcerer didn't even glance at the saba table. "Are you consulting me professionally, sir?" he asked in a mild voice.

Zeisler blinked. "Well, I—"

"Because, if you are," Master Seamus continued relentlessly, "I must warn you that a Master's fees come quite high. I would suggest you consult a Journeyman Sorcerer for that sort of thing; his fees would be much lower than mine, and he'd give you the same information."

"Oh. Well. Thank you. I may do that. Thank you." He took another long pull at his drink. "Uh—by the by, do you happen to know a Master Sorcerer named Sean O Lochlainn?"

The sorcerer nodded slowly. "I've met him," he said carefully.

"Fortunate. Never met him, myself, but I've heard a great deal about him. Forensic sorcerer, you know. Interesting work. Like to meet him sometime." His eyes had wandered away from the sorcerer as he spoke, and he was gazing out the window at the French countryside flowing by.

"You're interested in magic, then?" the Irishman asked.

Zeisler's eyes came back. "Magic? Oh, no. Got no Talent at all. No, what I'm interested in is investigative work. Criminal investigation." He blinked and frowned as though trying to remember something. Then his eyes brightened and he said: "Reason I brought up Master Sean was that I met the man he works for, Lord Darcy, who's the Chief Investigator for His Royal Highness, the Duke of Normandy." He leaned forward and lowered his voice. The ouiskie was strong on his breath. "Were you at the Healers and Sorcerers Convention in London some years back, when a sorcerer named Zwinge got murdered at the Royal Steward Hotel?"

"I was there," the sorcerer said. "I remember it well."

"I imagine so, yes. Well, I was attached to the Admiralty offices at the time. Met Darcy there." He winked an eye solemnly. "Helped him crack the case, actually, but I can't say anything more about it than that." His gaze went back out the window again. "Great investigator. Absolute genius in his field. Nobody else could crack that case, but he solved it in no time. Absolute genius. Wish I had his brains." He drained his glass. "Yes, sir, I wish I had his brains." He looked at his empty glass and stood up. "Time for a refill. Get you one?"

"Not yet. Later, perhaps."

"Be right back." Zeisler headed for the bar.

He did not come back. He got into a conversation with Fred, the attendant who was mixing drinks, and forgot about Master Seamus completely, for which the stout little Irish sorcerer was extremely grateful.

He noticed John Peabody, he of the full and bushy beard, was sitting alone at the far end of the long couch, apparently still reading his newspaper, and seemingly so thoroughly engrossed in it that it would be boorish for anyone to speak to him. But the sorcerer knew that the man was keeping at least a part of his attention on the long hallway that ran forward, past the compartments.

Master Seamus looked back at the saba game. The foppishly dressed man with the hairline mustache was raking in sizeable winnings.

If Vandepole were cheating, he was doing it without the aid of the Talent, either latent or conscious; such usage of the Talent would have been easy for the sorcerer to pick up at this short range. It was possible, of course, that the man had a touch of the precognitive Talent, but that was something which the science of magic had, as yet, little data and no theory on. Someone, some day, might solve the problem of the asymmetry of time, but no one had done it yet, and even the relatively new mathematics of the subjective algebrae offered no clue.

The sorcerer shrugged and picked up his *Journal* again. What the hell, it was no business of his.

5

"*Lyon, Gentlemen!*" came Goodman Fred's voice across the lounge, fighting successfully against the noise of the train.

"Lyon in fifteen minutes! The bar will close in five minutes! Lunch will be served in the station restaurant, and we will leave at one-fifteen! It is now twelve noon!"

Fred had everyone's attention now, so he repeated the message.

Not everyone was in the lounge. After the bar was closed— Zeisler had managed to get two more during the five minutes—Fred went forward along the passageway and knocked on each compartment door. "Lyon in ten minutes! Lunch will be served in the station restaurant. We will leave for Marsaille at 1:15."

The stout little Irish sorcerer turned in his couch to look out the window at the outskirts of Lyon. It was a pleasant place, he thought. The Rhone valley was famous for its viniculture, but now the grape arbors were giving way to cottages more and more densely packed, and finally the train was in the city itself. The houses were old, most of them, but neat and well-tended. Technically, the County of Lyonnais was a part of the Duchy of Burgundy, but the folk never thought of themselves as Burgundians. The Count de Lyonnais commanded their respect far more than the Duke of Burgundy did. His Grace respected those feelings, and allowed My Lord Count as free a hand as the King's Law would permit. From the looks of the countryside, it appeared My Lord Count did a pretty good job.

"Excuse me, Master Sorcerer," said a soft, pleasant voice.

He turned away from the window. It was the elderly-looking gentleman in clerical garb. "How may I help you, Father?"

"Allow me to introduce myself; I am the Reverend Father Armand Brun. I noticed you sitting here by yourself, and I wondered if you would care to join me and some other gentlemen for lunch."

"Master Seamus Kilpadraeg at your service, Reverend Sir. I'd be most happy to join you for lunch. We have an hour, it seems."

The "other gentlemen" were standing near the bar, and were introduced in that quiet, smooth voice. Simon Lamar had thinning dark hair that one could see his scalp through, a long face and lips that were drawn into a thin line. His voice was flat, with just a touch of Yorkshire in it as he said: "I'm pleased to meet you, Master Seamus."

Arthur Mac Kay's accent was both Oxford and Oxfordshire, and was smooth and well-modulated, like an actor's. He was the other foppishly dressed man—immaculate, as though his clothes had been pressed seconds before. He had dark, thick, slightly wavy hair, luminous brown eyes surrounded by long, dark lashes, and a handsome face that matched. He was almost too pretty.

Valentine Herrick had flaming red hair, an excessively toothy smile, and a body that seemed to radiate health and strength as he shook the sorcerer's hand. "Hate to see a man eat alone, by S'n George! A meal's not a meal without company, is it?"

"Not really," the sorcerer agreed.

"Especially at these train station restaurants," said Lamar in his flat voice. "Company keeps your mind off the tasteless food."

Mac Kay smiled angelically. "Oh, come; it's not as bad as all that. Come along; you'll see."

The *Heart of Lyon* restaurant was a fairly comfortable-looking place, not more than fifty years old, but designed in the King Gwiliam IV style of the late Eighteenth Century to give it an air of stability. The decor, however, reflected a mild pun on the restaurant's name—which had probably been carefully chosen for just that reason. Over the door, three-quarters life size, legs braced apart, right hand on the pommel of a great naked sword whose point touched the lintel, left arm holding a shield bearing the lions of England, stood the helmed, mail-clad figure of King Richard the Lion-Hearted in polychromed bas-relief. The interior, too, was decorated with knights and ladies of the time of Richard I.

"Interesting motif for the decorations," Father Armand said as the waiter led the five men to a table. "And very well done, too."

"Not period, though," Lamar said flatly. "Too realistic."

"Oh, true, true," Father Armand said agreeably. "Not early Thirteenth Century style at all." He seated himself as the waiter pulled out a chair for him. "It's the painstakingly detailed realism of the late Seventeenth, which fits in very well with the style of the rest of the interior. It must have been expensive; there are very few artists nowadays who can or will do that sort of work."

"Agreed, Father," said Lamar. "Workmanship in general isn't what it used to be."

Father Armand chose to ignore that remark. "Now, you take a look up there, at Gwiliam the Marshal—at least I presume it's he; he's wearing the Marshal arms on his surcoat. I'll wager that if you climbed up there on a stepladder and looked closely, you could see the tiny rivets in every link of his mail."

Lamar raised a finger. "And that's not period, either."

Father Armand looked astonished. "Riveted link mail not period for the Thirteenth Century? Surely, sir—"

"No, no," Lamar interrupted hastily. "I meant the surcoat with the Marshal arms. Armorial bearings of that sort didn't come in till about a century later."

"You know," said Arthur Mac Kay suddenly, "I've always wondered what I'd look like in one of those outfits. Rather dashing, I think." His actor's voice contrasted strongly with Lamar's flat tones.

Valentine Herrick looked at him, smiling toothily. "Hey! Wouldn't that be great? Imagine! Charging into combat with a broadsword like that! Or rescuing a fair princess! Or slaying a dragon! Or a wicked magician!" He stopped suddenly and actually blushed. "Oops. Sorry, Master Sorcerer."

"That's all right," said Master Seamus mildly. "You may slay all the *wicked* magicians you like. Just don't make any mistakes."

That got a chuckle from everyone, even Herrick.

They looked over their menus, chose and ordered. The food, which the sorcerer thought quite good, came very quickly. Father Armand said grace, and more small talk ensued. Lamar said little about the food, but the wine was not to his exact taste.

"It's a Delacey '69, from just south of Givors. Not a bad year for the reds, but it can't compare with the Monet '69, from a lovely little place a few miles southeast of Beaune."

Mac Kay lifted his glass and seemed to address his remarks to it. "You know, I have always contended that the true connoisseur is to be pitied, for he has trained his taste to such perfection that he enjoys almost nothing. It is, I believe, a corollary of Acipenser's Law, or perhaps a theorem derived therefrom."

Herrick blinked bright blue eyes at him. "What? I don't

know what you're talking about, but, by S'n George, I think it's damn good wine." He emphasized his point by draining his glass and refilling it from the carafe.

Almost as if he had heard the pouring as a summons, Maurice Zeisler came wandering over to the table. He did not stagger, but there was a controlled precision about his walking and about his speech that indicated a necessity to concentrate in order to do either one properly. He did not sit down.

"Hullo, fellows," he said very carefully. "Did you see who's over in the corner?" There were, of course, four corners to the big room, but a slight motion of his head indicated which one he meant.

It was bushy-bearded John Peabody, eating by himself, his suitcase on the floor beside his chair.

"What about him?" asked Lamar sourly.

"Know him?"

"No. Kept pretty much to himself. Why?"

"I dunno. Seems familiar, somehow. Like I ought to know him. Can't exactly place him, though. Oh, well." And he wandered off again, back toward the bar, whence he had come.

"Condition he's in, he wouldn't recognize his own mother," muttered Lamar. "Pass the wine, please."

6

The Napoli Express crossed the Rhone at Lyon and headed southwards through the Duchy of Dauphine, toward the Duchy of Provence, following the river valley. At Avignon, it would angle away from the river, southeast toward Marsaille, but that wouldn't be until nearly five o'clock.

The Napoli Express was not a high-speed train; it was too long and too heavy. But it made up for that by making only four stops between Paris and Napoli. Five, if you counted the very short stop at the Provence-Liguria border.

In order to avoid having to cross the Maritime Alps, the train ran along the coast of the Mediterranean after leaving Marsaille, past Toulon, Canne, Nice, and Monaco to the Ligurian coast. It looped around the Gulf of Genova to the city of Genova, then stayed with the seacoast all the way to the Tiber, where it turned east to make the short side trip to Rome. There, it crossed the Tiber and headed back toward the sea, staying with the coast all the way to arrive at last at Napoli.

But that would be tomorrow afternoon. There were hundreds of miles and hours of time ahead of her yet.

Master Seamus sat on one of the chairs on the observation deck at the rear of the car and watched the Rhone Valley retreat into the distance. There were four seats on the semicircular observation deck, two on each side of the central door that led into the lounge. The two on the starboard side were occupied by the plump, sandy-haired man who had almost missed the train—Jason Quinte—and the blond, pink-faced young man whose name the sorcerer did not know. Both were smoking cigars and talking in voices that could be heard but not understood above the rush of the wind and the rumble of the wheels over the steel tracks.

Master Seamus had taken the outer of the two remaining chairs, and Father Armand, who was trying valiantly to light his pipe in the gusts that eddied about him, had taken the other. When at last the pipe was burning properly, Father Armand leaned back and relaxed.

The door slid open and a fifth man came out, thumbing tobacco into his own pipe, a stubby briar. It was Sir Stanley Galbraith, the wide-shouldered, muscular, graying man who had preceded the sorcerer aboard the train. He ignored the others and went to the high railing that surrounded the observation deck and looked into the distance. Having packed his pipe to his satisfaction, he put away his tobacco pouch and then proceeded to search himself. Finally, he turned around, scowling. The scowl vanished when he saw Father Armand's pipe.

"Ah. Begging your pardon, Reverend Sir, but could I borrow your pipe lighter? Seem to have left my own in my compartment."

"Certainly." Father Armand proffered his lighter, which Sir Stanley promptly made use of. He succeeded in an astonishingly short time and handed the lighter back. "Thank you. My name's Galbraith, Sir Stanley Galbraith."

"Father Armand Brun. I am pleased to meet you, Sir Stanley. This is Master Sorcerer Seamus Kilpadraeg."

"A pleasure, gentlemen, a pleasure." He puffed vigorously at his pipe. "There. She'll stay lit now. Good thing it isn't raining; left my weather pipe at home."

"If you need one, Sir Stanley, let me know." It was the plump Jason Quinte. He and the pink-faced youngster had stopped talking when Sir Stanley had appeared and had been listening. Sir Stanley's voice was not overly loud, but it carried well. "I have a couple of them," Quinte went on. "One of 'em never used. Glad to make you a present of it if you want it."

"No, no. Thanks all the same, but there's no bad weather predicted between here and Napoli." He looked at the sorcerer. "Isn't that right, Master Seamus?"

The sorcerer grinned. "That's what the report said, Sir Stanley, but I couldn't tell you of my own knowledge. Weather magic isn't my field."

"Oh. Sorry. You chaps do all specialize, don't you? What is your specialty, if I may ask?"

"I teach forensic sorcery."

"Ah, I see. Interesting field, no doubt." He shifted his attention as a whiff of cigar smoke came his way. "Jamieson."

The pink-faced youth took the cigar from his mouth and looked alert "Sir?"

"What the devil is that you're smoking?"

Jamieson looked down at the cigar in his hand as though he were wondering where the thing had come from and how it had got there. "A Hashtpar, sir."

"Persian tobacco; I thought so." A smile came over his tanned face. "Good Persian is very good; bad Persian—which that is—will probably rot your lungs, my boy. That particular type is cured with some sort of perfume or incense. Reminds me of a whorehouse in Abadan."

There was a sudden awkward pause as it came to the minds of all of them that there was a man of the cloth present

"Toss it overboard, Jamie," Quinte said in a rather too-loud voice. "Here, have one of mine."

Jamieson looked at the three-quarters-smoked cigar again, then flipped it over the rail. "No, thanks, Jason. I was through with it anyway. Just thought I'd try one." He looked up at Sir Stanley with a rather sheepish grin. "They were expensive, sir, so I bought one. Just to try it, you see. But you're right—they do smell like the inside of a—uh—Daoist temple."

Sir Stanley chuckled. "Some of the worst habits are the most expensive, son. But, then, so are some of the best."

"What are you smoking, Sir Stanley?" Father Armand asked quietly.

"This? It's a blend of Balik and Robertian."

"I favor a similar blend, myself. I find Balik the best of Turkish. I alternate with another blend: Balik and Couban."

Sir Stanley shook his head slowly. "Tobacco from the Duchy of Couba is much better suited for cigars, Reverend Sir. The Duchy of Robertia produces the finer pipe tobacco, I find. Of course, I'll admit it's all a matter of taste."

"Never seen Couba," said Quinte, "but I've seen the tobacco fields in Robertia. Don't know if you've ever seen the stuff grow, Father?" It was only half a question.

"Tell me about it," said Father Armand.

Robertia was a duchy on the southern coast of the northern continent of the Western Hemisphere, New England, with a seacoast on the Gulf of Mechicoe. It had been named after Robert II, since it had been founded during his reign in the early Eighteenth Century.

"It grows about so high," Quinte said, holding his hand about thirty inches off the deck. "Big, wide leaves. I don't know how it's cured; I only saw it in the fields."

He may have been going to say more, but the door leading into the lounge slid open and Trainmaster Edmund Norton stepped out, his red-and-blue uniform gleaming in the afternoon sun.

"Good afternoon, gentlemen," he said with a smile. "I hope I'm not interrupting."

"Oh, no," said Sir Stanley. "Not at all. Just chit-chat."

"I hope you gentlemen have all been comfortable, enjoying the trip, eh?"

"No complaints at all, Trainmaster. Eh, Father?"

"Oh, none at all, none at all," said Father Armand. "A very enjoyable trip so far. You run an excellent train, Trainmaster."

"Thank you, Reverend Sir." The Trainmaster cleared his throat. "Gentlemen, it is my custom at this hour to invite all my special passengers to join me in a drink—of whatever kind you prefer. Will you join me, gentlemen?"

There could, of course, be no argument with an invitation like that. The five passengers followed the Trainmaster into the lounge.

"One thing I'll say," Father Armand murmured to the sorcerer, "it's certainly quieter in here than out there."

The Trainmaster went quietly over to the table where the saba game had resumed after lunch. He had judged his time accurately.

Vandepole raked in his winnings with one hand, while he ran the forefinger of the other across his hairline mustache.

The Trainmaster said a few words, which the sorcerer did not hear over the rumble of the train. It was quieter in here, yes, but not exactly silent.

Then Trainmaster Edmund went over to the bar, where Goodman Fred stood waiting, turned to the passengers and said in a loud voice: "Gentlemen, step up and order your pleasure. Fred, I'll see what the gentlemen at the saba table will have."

A few minutes later, the Irish sorcerer was seated at the bar watching the foam on a glass of beer slosh gently from side to side with the swaying of the train. Maurice Zeisler, he thought, was going to hate himself later. The scar-faced Gavin Tailleur had gone back to his compartment to tell him that the Trainmaster was treating, but had been unable to rouse him from his—er—nap.

Master Seamus was seated at the end of the bar, near the passageway. The Trainmaster came over and stood at the end of the bar after making sure everyone who wanted one had been served a drink.

"I'll have a beer, Fred," he said to the attendant.

"Comin' right up, Trainmaster."

"I see beer's your tipple, too, Master Sorcerer," Trainmaster Edmund said as Fred put a foaming brew before him.

"Aye, Trainmaster, that it is. Wine's good with a meal, and a brandy for special occasions is fine, but for casual or even serious drinkin', I'll take beer every time."

"Well spoken. Do you like this particular brew?"

"Very much," said the sorcerer. "Norman, isn't it?"

"Yes. There's a little area in the Duchy of Normandy, up in the highlands where the Orne, the Sarthe, the Eure, the Risle, and the Mayenne all have their sources, that has the

best water in all of France. There's good beer comes from
Ireland, and there are those who prefer English beer, but
to my taste, Norman is the best, which is why I always order
it for my train."

Master Seamus, who *did* prefer English beer, but by the
merest hair, merely said: "It's very fine stuff. Very fine,
indeed." He suspected that the Trainmaster's preference might
be shaded just a little by the fact that Norman beer was
cheaper in Paris than English beer.

"Have you been getting along well with your compartment mate?" the Trainmaster asked.

"I haven't been informed who my compartment mate is,"
the sorcerer replied.

"Oh? Sorry. It's Father Armand Brun."

7

By half past four that afternoon, Master Seamus
Kilpadraeg was dozing on the rearward couch, leaning
back in the corner, his arms folded across his chest and
his chin nearly touching his sternum. Since he did not
snore, he offended no one. Father Armand had gone back
to Compartment Number Two at a quarter after three,
and, suspecting that the gentleman was tired, the sorcerer
had decided to let him have the day couch there to
himself.

The train and the saba game went on. Jason Quinte had
dropped out of the game, but his place had been taken by
the red-haired Valentine Herrick. Gavin Tailleur had taken
Sidney Charpentier's place, and now Charpentier was sitting on the forward couch, his large nose buried in a book
entitled *The Infernal Device,* an adventure novel. Sir Stanley
Galbraith and Arthur Mac Kay were at the bar with a dice
cup, playing for drinks.

Quinte and young Jamieson were back out on the observation deck with more cigars—presumably not Hashtpars this
time.

Zeisler was still snoozing, and Lamar had apparently
retired to his own compartment.

At Avignon, the train crossed the bridge that spanned the

River Durance and curved away from the Rhone toward Marsaille.

Master Seamus was roused from his doze by the sound of Simon Lamar's flat voice, but he neither opened his eyes nor lifted his head.

"Sidney," he said to Charpentier, "I need your Healing Talent."

"What's the matter? Got a headache?"

"I don't mean *I* need it. Maurice does. He's got one hell of a hangover. I've ordered some caffe from Fred, but I'd like your help. He hasn't eaten all day, and he has a headache."

"Right. I'll come along. We'll have to get some food in him at Marsaille." He rose and left with Lamar.

The sorcerer dozed off again.

8

When the Napoli Express pulled into Marsaille at twenty-four minutes after six that evening, Master Seamus had already decided that he needed exercise before he needed food. He got off the train, went through the depot, and out into the street beyond. A brisk fifteen-minute walk got his blood going again, made him feel less drowsy, and whetted his appetite. The tangy air of the Duchy of Provence, given a touch of piquancy by the breeze from the Mediterranean, was an aperitif in itself.

The *Cannebiere* restaurant—which was nowhere near the street of the same name—was crowded by the time the sorcerer got back. With apologies to both sides, the waiter seated him at a table with a middle-aged couple named Duprey. Since he was not carrying his symbol-decorated carpetbag, there was no way for them to know that he was a magician, and he saw no reason to enlighten them.

He ordered the specialty of the house, which turned out to be a delicious thick whitefish stew with lots of garlic. It went fine with a dry white wine of rather pronounced character.

The Dupreys, as the conversation brought out, were the owners of a small leather-goods shop in Versaille who had carefully saved their money to make a trip to Rome, where they would spend a week, leaving the business in the hands of their two sons, each of whom was married to a delightful wife, and one of them had two daughters and the other a son, and . . .

And so on.

The sorcerer was not bored. He liked people, and the Dupreys were a very pleasant couple. He didn't have to talk much, and they asked him no questions. Not, that is, until the caffe was served. Then: "Tell me, Goodman Seamus," said the man, "why is it that we must stop at the Ligurian border tonight?"

"To check the bill-of-lading for the freight cars, I believe," the sorcerer said. "Some Italian law about certain imports."

"You see, John-Paul," said the woman, "it is as I told you."

"Yes, Martine, but I do not see why it should be. We are not stopped at the border of Champagne or Burgundy or Dauphine or Provence. Why Liguria?" He looked back at the magician. "Are we not all a part of the same Empire?"

"Well, yes—and no," Master Seamus said thoughtfully.

"What can you mean by that, sir?" John-Paul said, looking puzzled.

"Well, the Duchies of Italy, like the Duchies of Germany, are a part of the *Holy Roman* Empire, d'ye see, which was established in A.D. 862, and King John IV is Emperor. But they are *not* a part of what is unofficially called the *Anglo-French* Empire, which technically includes only France, England, Scotland, and Ireland."

"But we all have the same Emperor, don't we?" Martine asked.

"Yes, but His Majesty's duties are different, d'ye see. The Italian States have their own Parliament, which meets in Rome, and the laws they have passed are slightly different than those of the Anglo-French Empire. Its acts are ratified, not by the Emperor directly, but by the Imperial Viceroy, Prince Roberto VII. In Italy, the Emperor reigns, but does not rule, d'ye see."

"I—I think so," John-Paul said hesitantly. "Is it the same in the Germanies? I mean, they're part of the Empire, too."

"Not quite the same. They're not as unified as the Duchies of Italy. Some of them take the title of Prince, and some would like to take the title of King, though that's forbidden by the Concordat of Magdeburg. But the general idea's the same. You might say that we're all different states, but with the same goals, under the same Emperor. We all want individual freedom, peace, prosperity, and happy homes. And the Emperor is the living symbol of those goals for all of us."

After a moment's silence, Martine said: "Goodness! That's very poetic, Goodman Seamus!"

"It still seems silly," John-Paul said doggedly, "to have to stop a train at the border between two Imperial Duchies."

Master Seamus sighed. "You should try visiting the Poles— or even the Magyars," he said. "The delay might be as much as two hours. You would have to have a passport. The train would be searched. Your luggage would be searched. Even you might be searched. And the Poles do that even when their own people are crossing their own internal borders."

"Well!" said Martine, "I certainly shan't ever go *there!*"

"No need to worry about that," said John-Paul. "Will you have more caffe, my dear?"

Master Seamus went back to the train feeling very relaxed, thankful that two very ordinary people had taken his mind off his troubles. He never saw nor heard of either of them again.

9

By eight o'clock that evening, the Napoli Express was nearly twenty-five miles out of Marsaille, headed for a rendezvous with the Ligurian border.

The saba game was in full swing again, and Master Seamus had the private feeling that, if it weren't for the fact that no one was permitted in the lounge while the train was in the station, three or four of the die-hards would never have bothered to eat.

By that time, the sorcerer found his eyelids getting heavy again. Since Father Armand was in deep conversation with two other passengers, Master Seamus decided he might as well go back to the compartment and take his turn on the day couch. He dropped off to sleep almost immediately.

The sorcerer's inward clock told him that it was ten minutes of nine when a rap sounded at the door.

"Yes? Who is it?"

"Fred, sir. Time to make up the bed, sir."

Wake up, it's time to go to sleep, the sorcerer thought glumly as he got his feet on the floor. "Certainly, Fred; come in."

"Sorry, sir, but the beds have to be made before I go off at nine. The night man doesn't have the keys, you see."

"Certainly, that's all right. I had me little nap, and I feel much better. I'll go on out to the lounge and let you work; there's hardly room in here for two of us."

"That's true, sir; thank you, sir."

There was a new man on behind the bar. As the sorcerer sat down, he put down the glass he was polishing and came over.

"May I serve you, sir?"

"Indeed you may, me lad. A beer, if you please."

"One beer; yes, sir." He took a pint mug, filled it, and served it.

There was no one else at the bar. The saba game, like the constellations in the sky, seemed unchanged. Master Seamus entertained a brief fantasy of taking this same trip a hundred years hence and seeing nothing remarkably different about that saba game. (Young Jamieson had replaced Boothroyd, but Hauser, Tailleur, Herrick and Vandepole were still at it.) Master Seamus drank his beer slowly and looked around the lounge.

Sir Stanley Galbraith and Father Armand were seated on the rearward couch, not talking to each other, but reading newspapers which they had evidently picked up in Marsaille.

Apparently, Charpentier had managed to cure Zeisler's hangover and get some food in him, for the two of them were sitting at the near table with Boothroyd and Lamar, talking in low tones. Zeisler was drinking caffe.

Mac Kay, Quinte, and Peabody were nowhere in sight.

Then Peabody, with his silver-handled stick, limped in from the passageway. He ordered ouiskie-and-splash and took it to the forward couch to sit by himself. He, too, had a newspaper, and began reading it with his touch-me-not attitude.

The sorcerer finished his beer and ordered another.

After a few minutes, Fred came back from his final duties for the day and said to the night man: "It's all yours, Tonio. Take over." And promptly left.

"No, no; I can get it. I'm closer." It was Zeisler's voice, raised just high enough for the sorcerer to hear it. His chair was nearest the bar. He got up, caffe cup in hand, and brought it over to the bar. "Another cup of caffe, Tonio."

"Yes, sir."

Zeisler smiled and nodded at Master Seamus, but said nothing. The sorcerer returned the greeting.

And then pretended not to notice what Tonio was doing. He set the cup down behind the bar, carefully poured in a good ounce of ouiskie, then filled the cup from the carafe that sat over a small alcohol lamp. It was done in such a way that the men at the table could not possibly have told that there was anything but caffe in the cup.

Zeisler had obviously tipped him well for that bit of legerdemain long before Master Seamus had come into the lounge.

Mentally, the sorcerer allowed himself a sad chuckle. Boothroyd, Lamar, and Charpentier thought they were dutifully keeping Zeisler sober, and here he was getting blotto before their very eyes. Ah, well.

Peabody put down his newspaper and came over to the bar, glass in hand. "Another ouiskie-and-splash, if you please," he said in a very low voice.

It was brought, and he returned to his seat and his newspaper. Tonio went back to polishing glasses.

Master Seamus was well into his third beer when the Trainmaster showed up. He went around and nodded and spoke to everyone, including the sorcerer. He went back to the observation deck, and Master Seamus concluded that Quinte and Mac Kay must be back there.

Trainmaster Edmund came back to the bar, took off his hat, and wiped his balding head with a handkerchief. "Warm evening. Tonio, how are your supplies holding out?"

"We'll have plenty for the rest of the evening, Trainmaster."

"Good; good. But I just checked the utility room, and we're short of towels. These men will be wanting to bathe in the morning, and we're way short. Run up to supply and get a full set. I'll watch the bar for you."

"Right away, Trainmaster." Tonio hurried without seeming to.

The Trainmaster left his cap off and stood behind the bar. He did not polish any glasses. "Another beer, Master Sorcerer?" he asked.

"No, thanks, Trainmaster. I've had me limit for a while. I think I'll stretch me legs." He got up off the barchair and turned toward the observation deck.

"How about you, sir?" the Trainmaster called to Peabody, a few feet away, in the forward couch.

Peabody nodded, got up, and brought his glass over.

As Master Seamus passed the table where Zeisler and the other three were sitting, he heard Zeisler say: "You chaps know who that bearded chap at the bar is? I do."

"Morrie, will you shut up?" said Boothroyd coldly.

Zeisler said no more.

10

"What is going on out there? A convention?" came the voice of the sorcerer's companion from the lower berth. It was a rhetorical question, so the Master Sorcerer didn't bother to answer.

It is not the loudness of a noise, nor even its unexpectedness, that wakes one up. It is the *unusual* noise that does that. And when the noise becomes *interesting*, it is difficult to go back to sleep.

The rumble and roar of the train as it moved toward Italy was actually soothing, once one got used to it. If it had only drowned out these other noises, all would have been well. But it didn't; it merely muffled them somewhat.

The sorcerer had been one of the last few to retire; only Boothroyd and Charpentier had still been in the lounge when he left to go to his compartment.

The hooded lamp had been burning low, and the gentle snores from the lower berth told him that his compartment-mate was already asleep.

He had prepared for bed and climbed in, only to find that the other man had left his newspaper on the other berth. It had been folded so that one article was uppermost, but in the dim light all he could read was the headline: NICHO-LAS JOURDAN RITES TO BE HELD IN NAPOLI. It was an obituary notice.

He put the paper on the nearby shelf and began to doze off.

Then he heard a door open and close, and footsteps moving down the passageway. *Someone going to the toilet*, he thought drowsily. No, for the footsteps went right by his own door to Compartment Number One. He heard a light rap. *Hell of a time of night to go visiting*, he thought. Actually, it wasn't all that late—only a little after ten. But everyone aboard had been up since at least four that morning, some even longer. Oh, well; no business of his.

But there were other footsteps, farther down the corridor, other doors opening and closing.

He tried to get to sleep and couldn't. Things would get quiet for a minute or two, then they would start up again. From Compartment Three, he could hear voices, but only because the partition was next to his berth. There was only the sound; he couldn't distinguish any words. Being a curious man, he shamelessly put his ear to the wall, but could still make out no words.

He tried very hard to go to sleep, but the intermittent noises continued. Footsteps. Every five minutes or so, they would go to Number One or return from there, and, of course, these were the loudest. But there were others, up and down the passageway.

There was little he could do about it. He couldn't really say they were noisy. Just irritating.

He lay there, dozing intermittently, coming up out of it every time he heard something, drifting off each time there was a lull.

After what seemed like hours, he decided there *was* something he could do about it. He could at least get up and see what was going on.

That was when his companion had said: "What's going *on* out there? A convention?"

The sorcerer made no reply, but climbed down the short ladder and grabbed his dressing gown. "I feel the call of nature," he said abruptly. He went out.

There was no one in the passageway. He walked slowly down to the toilet. No one appeared. No one stuck his head out of a door. No one even opened it a crack to peek. Nothing.

He took his time in the toilet. Five minutes. Ten.

He went back to his compartment. His slippers on the floor had been almost inaudible, and he'd been very careful about making any noise. They couldn't have heard him.

He reported what he had found to his compartment-mate.

"Well, whatever they were up to," said the other, "I am thoroughly awake now. I think I'll have a pipe before I go back to bed. Care to join me?"

When they came into the lounge, Tonio was seated on a stool behind the bar. He looked up. "Good evening, Father; good evening, Master Sorcerer. May I help you?"

"No, we're just going out for a smoke," said the sorcerer. "But I guess you've had a pretty busy evening, eh?"

"Me? Oh, no, sir. Nobody been in here for an hour and a half."

The two men went on out to the observation deck. Their conversation was interrupted a few minutes later by Tonio, who slid open the door and said: "Are you sure there's nothing I can get you gentlemen? I have to go forward to the supply car to fetch a few things for tomorrow, but I wouldn't want you to be needing anything."

"No, thanks. That'll be all right. As soon as the good Father finishes his pipe, we'll be goin' back to bed."

Twenty minutes later, they did just that, and fell asleep immediately. It was twenty minutes after midnight.

11

At 12:25, Tonio returned with his first load. During the daytime, when people were awake, it was permissible to use a handcart to trundle things through the aisles of the long train. But a sudden lurch of the train could upset a handcart and wake people up. Besides, there was much less to carry at night.

He carefully put his load of stuff away in the cabinets behind the bar, then went back to check the observation deck to see if his two gentlemen were still there. They were not. Good; everyone was asleep.

About time, too, he thought as he headed back uptrain for his second and last load. The gentlemen had certainly been having themselves some sort of party, going from one compartment to another like that. Though they hadn't made much noise, of course.

Tonio Bracelli was not a curious young man by nature, and if his gentlemen and ladies gave him no problems on the night run, he was content to leave them alone.

The train began to slow, and at thirty minutes after midnight, it came to an easy stop at the check station on the Ligurian border. The stop was only a formality, really. The Ligurian authorities had to check the bills of lading for the cargo in the freight cars at the front of the train, but there was no search or actual checking of the cargo itself. It was all bookkeeping.

Tonio picked out what he needed for the second load, and then stood talking to the Supply Master while the train was stopped. The locomotive braked easily enough to a smooth stop, but getting started again was sometimes a little jerky, and Tonio didn't want to be walking with his arms full when that happened. He'd wait until the train picked up speed.

He reached the rearmost car at 12:50, took his load of goods to the bar and stashed them as before. Then he went to do his last duty until the morning: cleaning out the bathroom.

It was a touchy job—not because it was hard work, or even unpleasant, but because one had to be so infernally *quiet*! The day man could bang around all he liked, but if the night man did so, the gentlefolk in Four and Five, on each side of the bathroom, might complain.

He went up to the utility compartment, just forward of Number One, got his equipment, went back to the bathroom, and went to work.

When he was finished, he took a final look around to make sure. All looked fine until he came to the last check.

He looked at the floor.

Strange. What were those red stains?

He had just mopped down the floor. It was still damp, but . . .

He stepped to one side and looked down.

The stains were coming from his right boot.

He sat down on the necessary, lifted his right foot, and looked at the bootsole. Red stains, almost gone, now.

Where the devil had they come from?

Tonio Bracelli, if not curious, was conscientious. After wiping the stains from his boot and checking the other to make sure there were none, he wiped the floor and went out to track down the source of those stains.

"Track" was certainly the word. He had left footprints of the stuff, whatever it was, up and down on the tan floor of the passageway. The darker tracks led uptrain. He followed them.

When he found their source, he lost his composure.

A great pool of what was obviously blood had seeped out from beneath the door of Compartment Number One.

12

The Irish sorcerer was brought out of his sleep by a banging that almost slammed him awake, and a voice that was screaming: *"Sir! Sir! Open the door! Sir! Are you all right? Sir!"*

Both of the men in Compartment Number Two were on their feet and at the door within two seconds.

But the banging was not at their door, but at the one to their right—Number One. The two men grabbed their robes and went out.

Tonio was pounding his fists on the door of Number One and shouting—almost screaming—at the top of his voice. Down the passageway, other doors were opening.

An arm reached out and a hand grabbed Tonio's shoulder. "Now, calm down, my son! What's the trouble?"

Tonio suddenly gasped and looked at the man who had laid such a firm hand on his shoulder. "Oh, Father! Look! Look at this!" He stepped back and pointed at the blood at his feet. "He doesn't answer! What should I do, Father?"

"The first thing to do, my son, is go get the Trainmaster. You don't have the key to this door, do you? No. Then go fetch Trainmaster Edmund immediately. But mind! No noise, no shouting. Don't alarm the passengers in the other cars. This is for the Trainmaster only. Do you understand?"

"Yes, Father. Certainly." His voice was much calmer.

"Very well. Now, quickly." Then, and only then, did that strong hand release the young man's shoulder. Tonio left— hurriedly, but now obviously under control.

"Now, Master Seamus, Sir Stanley, we must be careful not to crowd round here any more than necessary."

Sir Stanley, who had come boiling out of Number Eight only half a second later than the sorcerer and his companion had come out of Number Two, turned to block the passage-way.

His voice seemed to fill the car. "All right, now. Stand away, all of you! You men get back to your quarters! Move!"

Within half a minute, the passageway was empty, except for three men. Then Sir Stanley said: "What's happened here, Father?"

"I know no more than you do, Sir Stanley. We must wait for the Trainmaster."

"I think we ought to—" Whatever it was that Sir Stanley thought they ought to do was cut off forever by the appearance of Trainmaster Edmund, who came running in from the dining car ahead, followed by Tonio, and asked almost the same question.

"What's happened here?"

The magician stepped forward. "We don't know, Train-master, but that looks like blood, and I suggest you open that door."

"Certainly, certainly." The Trainmaster keyed back the bolt of Number One.

On Lower One, Goodman John Peabody lay with his smashed head hanging over the edge, his scalp a mass of clotted blood. He was very obviously quite dead.

"I wouldn't go in there if I were you, Trainmaster," said the sorcerer, putting an arm in front of Trainmaster Edmund as he started to enter.

"What? On my own train? Why not?" He sounded indig-nant.

"With all due apologies, Trainmaster, have you ever had a murder on your train before?"

"Well, no, but—"

"Have you ever been involved in a murder investigation?"

"No, but—"

"Well, again with apologies, Trainmaster, I have. I'm a

trained forensic sorcerer. The investigators aren't going to like it if we go tramping in there, destroying clues. Do you have a chirurgeon on board?"

"Yes; the train chirurgeon, Dr. Vonner. But how do you know it's murder?"

"It's not suicide," the sorcerer said flatly. "His head was beaten repeatedly by that heavy, silver-headed walking-stick there on the floor. A man doesn't kill himself that way, and he doesn't do it accidentally. Send Tonio for the chirurgeon."

Dr. Vonner, it turned out, had had some experience with legal cases and knew what to do—and, more important, what *not* to do. He said, after examination, that not only was Peabody dead but, in his opinion, had been dead for at least an hour. Then he said that if he was needed no further, he was going back to bed. The Trainmaster let him go.

"It's nearly two hours yet to Genova," the sorcerer said. "We won't be able to notify the authorities until then. But that's all right; nobody can get off the train while it's at speed, and I can put a preservative spell over the body and an avoidance spell on the compartment."

A voice from behind the sorcerer said: "Should I not give the poor fellow the Last Rites of Holy Mother Church?"

The Irishman turned and shook his head. "No, Father. He's quite dead now, and that can wait. If there's any Black Magic involved in this killing, your work could dissipate all trace of it, destroying what might be a valuable clue."

"I see. Very well. Shall I fetch you your bag?"

"If you would be so good, Reverend Sir."

The bag was brought, and the sorcerer went about his work. The preservative spell, cast with a night-black wand, was quickly done; the body would remain in stasis until the authorities finished their investigation. The sorcerer noted down the time carefully, checking his wristwatch against that of the Trainmaster.

The avoidance spell was somewhat more involved, requiring the use of a smoking thurible and two wands, but when it was finished, no one would enter that room, or even look into it of his own free will. "You'd best relock that door, Trainmaster," said the Irish sorcerer. He looked down at the floor. "As for that stain, Tonio has already walked through it, but we'd best not have any more people do so. Would you be so good as to tell the others to stay away from this area until we get to Genova, Sir Stanley?"

"Certainly, Master Sorcerer."

"Thank you. I'll put me bag away now."

13

The sorcerer put his symbol-decorated carpetbag down on the floor while his compartment-mate closed the door behind them.

"Now that's what I call stayin' in character, me lord," said Sean O Lochlainn, Chief Forensic Sorcerer for His Royal Highness, the Duke of Normandy.

"What? Oh, you mean offering to perform the Last Rites?" Lord Darcy, the Duke's Chief Investigator, smiled. "It's what any real priest would have done, and I knew you'd get me off the hook." When he did come up out of character, he looked much younger, in spite of the disguising white hair and beard.

"Well, I did what I could, me lord. Now I suppose there's nothing for us to do but wait until we get to Genova, where the Italian authorities can straighten this out."

His lordship frowned. "I am afraid we shall have to do more than that, my dear Sean. Time is precious. We absolutely *must* get that Naval treaty to Athens in time. That means we have to be in Brindisi by ten o'clock tonight. And that means we *have* to catch that Napoli-Brindisi local, which leaves fifteen minutes after the Napoli Express gets into the station. I don't know what the Genovese authorities will do, but if they don't hold us up in Genova, they most certainly will when we reach Rome. They'll cut the car off and hold the whole lot of us until they *do* solve it. Even if we were to go through all the proper channels and prove who we are and what we're up to, it would take so long that we'd miss that train."

Now Master Sean looked worried. "What do we do if it *isn't* solved by then, in spite of everything we do?"

Lord Darcy's face became impassive. "In that case, I shall be forced to leave you. 'Father Armand Brun' would perforce disappear, evading the Roman Armsmen and becoming a fugitive—undoubtedly accused of the murder of one John Peabody. I would have to get to Brindisi by myself, under cover. It would be difficult in the extreme, for the Italians are very sharp indeed at that sort of work."

"I would be with you, me lord," Master Sean said stoutly.

Lord Darcy shook his head. "No. What would be difficult for one man would be impossible for two—especially two who had been known to have escaped together. 'Master Seamus Kilpadraeg' is a bona fide sorcerer, with bona fide papers from the Duke of Normandy and, ultimately, from the King himself. 'Father Armand' is a total phony. You can stick it out, I can't. Unless, of course, I want to explode our whole mission."

"Then me lord, we must solve the case," the magician said simply. "Where do we start?"

His lordship smiled, sighed, and sat down on the lower bed. "Now, that's more like it, my dear Sean. We start with everything we know about Peabody. When did you first notice him?"

"As I came aboard the train, me lord. I saw the walking-stick he carried. On an ordinary stick there is a decorative silver ring about two inches down from the handle. The ring on his stick was a good four inches below the silver head, the perfect length for the hilt on a sword stick. Just above the ring is an inconspicuous black stud that you press with your thumb to release the hilt from the scabbard."

Lord Darcy nodded silently. He had noticed the weapon.

"Then there was his limp," Master Sean continued. "A man with a real limp walks with the same limp all the time. He doesn't exaggerate it when he's walking slowly, then practically lose it when he's in a hurry."

"Ah! I hadn't noticed that," his lordship admitted. "It is difficult to judge the quality of a man's limp when he is trying to move about on a lurching train car, and I observed him at no other time. Very good! And what did you deduce from that?"

"That the limp was an excuse to carry the stick."

"And I dare say you are right. That he needed that stick as a weapon, or thought he would, and was not used to carrying it."

Master Sean frowned. "How so, me lord?"

"Otherwise, he would either have perfected his limp or

not used a limp at all." Lord Darcy paused, then: "Anything else?"

"Only that he carried his small suitcase to lunch with him, and that he always sat in the lounge on the first couch, where he could watch the door of his compartment," Master Sean said. "I think he was afraid someone would steal his suitcase, me lord."

"Or something in it," Lord Darcy amended.

"What would that be, me lord?"

"If we knew that, my dear Sean, we'd be a great deal closer to solving this problem than we are at this moment. We—" He stopped suddenly and put his finger to his lips. There were footsteps in the passageway again. Not as loud this time, for the men were wearing slippers instead of boots, but the doors could be heard opening and closing.

"I think the convention has started again," Lord Darcy said quietly. He walked over to the door. By the time he was easing it open, he had again donned the character of an elderly priest. He opened the door almost noiselessly.

Sir Stanley, facing down the car toward the lounge, had his back to Lord Darcy. Through the windows beyond him, the Ligurian countryside rushed by in the darkness.

"Standing guard, Sir Stanley?" Lord Darcy asked mildly.

Sir Stanley turned. "Guard? Oh, no, Father. The rest of us are going into the lounge to discuss this. Would you and Master Seamus join us?"

"I would be glad to. You, Master Sorcerer?"

Master Sean blinked, and, after a moment, said: "Certainly, Father."

14

"*Are you* absolutely *certain it was murder?*" Gwiliam Hauser's voice was harsh.

Master Sean O Lochlainn leaned back in the couch and narrowed his eyes at Hauser. "*Absolutely* certain? No, sir. Can you tell me, sir, how a man can have the whole front of his head smashed in while lying on a lower berth? *Unless* it is murder? If so, then I may reconsider my statement that I am *reasonably* certain that it was murder."

Hauser stroked his dark-streaked white beard. "I see. Thank you, Master Sorcerer." His sharp eyes looked round at the others in the lounge. "Did any of you—*any* of you—see anything at all that looked suspicious last night?"

"Or *hear* anything?" Lord Darcy added.

Hauser gave him a quick glance. "Yes. Or hear anything."

The others all looked at each other. Nobody said a word.

Finally, the too-handsome Mac Kay leaned back in his chair at the table near the bar and said: "Uh, Father, you and the Master Sorcerer had the compartment next to Peabody's. Didn't either of you hear anything?"

"Why, yes, we did," Lord Darcy said mildly. "We both remarked upon it."

All eyes in the lounge were focused on him now, with the exception of Master Sean's. The sorcerer was watching the others.

"Beginning at about twenty minutes after ten last night," Lord Darcy continued in the same mild voice, "and continuing for about an hour and a half, there was an absolute parade of footsteps up and down that passageway. There was much conversation and soft rappings at doors. There were knockings on the door of Peabody's compartment more than a dozen times. Other than that, I heard nothing out of the usual."

The three-second silence was broken by Sir Stanley. "We were just walking around, talking. Visiting, you know."

Zeisler was over at the bar, drinking caffe. Master Sean hadn't seen it this time, but he was certain Tonio had spiked the cup again. "That's right," Zeisler said in a sudden voice. "Talking. I couldn't sleep, myself. Had a nap this afternoon. Went visiting. Seems nobody else could sleep, either."

Boothroyd nodded. "I couldn't sleep, either. Noisy damn train." At that point all the others joined in—the words were different, but the agreement was there.

"And Peabody couldn't sleep either?" Lord Darcy's voice was bland.

"No, he couldn't," said Sir Stanley gruffly.

"I didn't know any of you knew the gentleman." Lord Darcy's voice was soft, his eyes mild, his manner gentle. "I did notice none of you spoke to him during the day."

"I recognized him," Zeisler said. The ouiskie wasn't slowing his brain down much. "Chap I used to know. Didn't get his name, and didn't recognize him at first, what with the beard. Didn't used to wear a beard, you see. So I went to talk to him—renew old acquaintance, you know. Bit shy at first, but we got along. He wanted to talk to the other chaps, so—" He gestured with one hand, leaving the sentence unfinished.

"I see." His lordship smiled benevolently. "Then which of you was the last to see him alive?"

Hauser looked at Jason Quinte. "Was that you, Quinte?"

"Me? No, I think it was Val."

"No, Mac talked to him after I did."

"But then Sharpie went back in, didn't you, Sharpie?"

"Yes, but I thought Simon—"

And so it went. Lord Darcy listened with a sad but benevolent smile on his face. After five minutes, it was obvious that they could not agree on who had seen Peabody last, and that not one of them wanted to own up to it.

Finally, Gavin Tailleur stood up from his seat in the rearward couch. His face was paler than usual, making the scar more conspicuous. "I don't know about the rest of you, but it's obvious *I* am not going to get any more sleep tonight. I am tired of wandering about in my nightclothes. I'm going back and put some clothes on."

Valentine Herrick, his bright red hair looking badly mussed, said: "Well, I'd like to get some sleep, myself, but . . ."

Lord Darcy, in a voice that seemed soft but still carried, said: "It doesn't much matter what we do now; we won't get any sleep after we reach Genova, and we might as well be prepared for it."

15

Master Sean wanted to talk privately with Lord Darcy. For one thing, he wanted to know why his lordship had permitted all the passengers in the car to get together to compare stories when the proper procedure would be to get them alone and ask them questions separately. Granted, here in Italy Lord Darcy had no authority to question them, and, granted, he was playing the part of a priest, but damn it! —he should have done *something*.

But no, he just sat there on the forward sofa, smiling, watching, listening, and saying very little, while the other passengers sat around and talked or drank or both.

There was quite a bit of caffe consumed, but the ouiskie, brandy, wine, and beer were not neglected, either. Master Sean and Lord Darcy stuck to caffe.

Tonio didn't seem to mind. He had to stay up all night, anyway, and at least he wasn't bored.

Just before the train reached Genova, the Trainmaster returned. He took off his hat and asked for the gentlemen's attention.

"Gentlemen, we are approaching Genova. Normally, if you happened to be awake, you could take advantage of the hour stopover to go to the restaurant or tavern, although most people sleep through this stop.

"I am afraid, however, that I shall have to insist that you all remain aboard until the authorities arrive. The doors will not be opened until they get here. I am sorry to inconvenience you in this way, but such is my duty."

There were some low mutterings among the men, but nobody said anything to contradict Trainmaster Edmund.

"Thank you, gentlemen," the Trainmaster said. "I shall do my best to see that the authorities get their work over with as promptly as possible." He returned his hat to his head and departed.

"Technically," Boothroyd said, "I suppose we're all under arrest."

"No," Hauser growled. "We are being detained for questioning. Not quite the same thing. We're only here as witnesses."

One of us isn't, Master Sean thought. And wondered how many others were thinking the same thing. But nobody said anything.

The Genovese Armsmen were surprisingly prompt. Within fifteen minutes after the train's brakes had made their last hissing sigh, a Master-at-Arms, two Sergeants-at-Arms, and four Armsmen had come aboard. All were in uniform.

This was merely the preliminary investigation. Names were taken and brief statements were written down by the Master and one of the Sergeants, apparently the only ones of the seven who spoke Anglo-French with any fluency. Master Sean and Lord Darcy both spoke Italian, but neither said anything about it. No need to volunteer information that wasn't asked for.

It was while the preliminary investigation was going on that the two Norman law officers found where each of the other twelve were billeted.

Compartment No. 3—Maurice Zeisler; Sidney Charpentier
Compartment No. 4—Martyn Boothroyd; Gavin Tailleur
Compartment No. 5—Simon Lamar; Arthur Mac Kay
Compartment No. 6—Valentine Herrick; Charles Jamieson
Compartment No. 7—Jason Quinte; Lyman Vandepole
Compartment No. 8—Sir Stanley Galbraith; Gwiliam Hauser

Number Two, of course, contained "Armand Brun" and "Seamus Kilpadraeg" and John Peabody had been alone in Number One.

The uniformed Master-at-Arms made a short, polite bow to Master Sean. Since he was armed by the sword at his side, he did not remove his hat. "Master Sorcerer, I believe it was you who so kindly put the avoidance spell and the preservation spell on the deceased one?"

"Aye, Master Armsman, I am."

"I must ask you to remove the avoidance spell, if you please. It is necessary that I inspect the body in order to determine that death has, indeed, taken place."

"Oh, certainly. Certainly. Me bag is in me compartment. Won't take but a minute."

As they went down the passageway, Master Sean saw Trainmaster Edmund standing patiently by the door of Number One, holding the key in his hand. The sorcerer knew what the Armsman's problem was. A death had been reported, but, so far, he hadn't seen any real evidence of it. Even if the Trainmaster had unlocked the door, the spell would have kept both men out, and, indeed, kept them from even looking into the compartment.

Master Sean got his symbol-decorated carpetbag out of Number Two, and told Trainmaster Edmund: "Unlock it, Trainmaster—and then let me have a little room to work."

The Trainmaster unlocked the door, but did not open it. He and the Master-at-Arms stood well back, in front of Number Three. Master Sean noticed with approval that a Man-at-Arms was standing at the far end of the passageway, in front of Number Eight, facing the lounge, blocking the way.

Himself being immune to his own avoidance spell, Master Sean looked all around the compartment. Everything was as he had left it. He looked down at the body. The blood still looked fresh, so the preservative spell had been well cast—not that the stout little Irish sorcerer had ever doubted it, but it was always best to check.

He looked down at the floor near his feet. The blood which had leaked out into the passageway was dark and dried. It had not, he noticed, been disturbed since Tonio had tromped through it. Good.

Master Sean placed his carpetbag carefully on the floor and took from it a small bronzen brazier with tripod legs. He put three lumps of willow charcoal in it, set it on the floor in the doorway, and carefully lit the charcoal. When it was hot and glowing, he took a pinch of powder from a small glass phial and dropped it on the coals. A spiral of aromatic smoke curled upwards. The magician's lips moved silently.

Then he took a four-by-four inch square of white paper from his bag and folded it in a curious and intricate manner. Murmuring softly, he dropped it on the coals, where it flared into orange flame and subsided into gray ash.

After a moment, he took a bronze lid from among his paraphernalia and fitted it to the brazier to smother the coals. He picked up the brazier by one leg and moved it aside. Then he stood up and looked at the Armsman. "There you are, Master Armsman; it's all yours." Then he gestured. "Watch the bloodstain, here, and watch that brazier. It's still hot."

The Master-at-Arms went in, looked at the remains of John Peabody and touched one wrist. He wrote in a notebook. Then he came out. "Lock it up again, Trainmaster. I can now state that a man identified as one John Peabody is dead, and that there is reason to believe that a felony has been committed."

Trainmaster Edmund looked surprised. "Is that all?"

"For now," the Armsmaster said. "Lock it up, and give me the key"

The Trainmaster locked the compartment, saying as he did so: "I can't give you a duplicate. We don't keep them around for security reasons. If a passenger loses one—" He took the key from the lock. "—we get a duplicate either from the Paris office or the Napoli office. I'll have to give you one of my master keys. And I'll want a receipt for it."

"Certainly. How many master keys do you have?"

"For this car? Two. This one, here, and one that's locked in my office forward for emergencies."

"See that it stays locked up. This key, then, is a master for this car only?"

"Oh, yes. Each car has separate lock sets. What are you doing, Master Sorcerer?" The Trainmaster looked puzzled.

Master Sean was kneeling by the door, the fingers of his right hand touching the lock, his eyes closed. "Just checking." The sorcerer stood up. "I noticed your lock spell on my own lock when I first used my key. Commercial, but very tight and well-knit. No wonder you don't keep duplicates aboard. Even an exact duplicate wouldn't work unless it was attuned to the spell. May I see that master key, Armsmaster? Thank you. Mmmmm. Yes. Thank you again." He handed the key back.

"What were you checking just now?" the Trainmaster asked.

"I wanted to see if the spell had been tampered with," Master Sean explained. "It hasn't been."

"Thank you, Master Sorcerer," the Master-at-Arms said, making a note in his notebook. "And thank you, Trainmaster. That will be all for now."

The three of them went on back to the lounge.

There was an empty space on the sofa next to Lord Darcy—who was still playing "Father Armand" to the hilt—so Master Sean walked over and sat beside him.

"How are things going, Father?" he asked in a low, conversational tone. In the relative quiet of the stationary car, it was easier to talk in soft voices without seeming to whisper.

"Interestingly," Lord Darcy murmured. "I haven't heard everything, of course, but I've been listening. They seem to be finished now."

At that moment, one of the Sergeants-at-Arms said, in Italian: "Master Armsman, here comes the Praefect."

Master Sean, like the Armsmaster, turned his head to look out the window. Then he looked quickly away.

"Our goose is cooked," he said very softly to Lord Darcy. "Look who's coming."

"I did. I don't know him."

"I do. It's Cesare Sarto. And *he* knows *me*."

16

The Roman Praefecture of Police has no exact counterpart in any other unit of the Empire. As elsewhere, every Duchy in Italy has its own organization of Armsmen which enforces the law within the boundaries of that Duchy. The Roman Praefecture is an instrumentality of the Italian Parliament to coordinate the efforts of these organizations.

The Praefects' powers are limited. Even in the Principality of Latium, where Rome is located, they have no police powers unless they have been called in by the local authorities. (Although a "citizen's arrest" by a Roman Praefect carries a great deal more weight than such an arrest by an ordinary civilian.)

They wear no uniforms; their only official identification is a card and a small golden shield with the letters SPQR above a bas-relief of the Capitoline Wolf, with a serial number and the words *Praefecture of Police* below her.

Their record for cases solved and convictions obtained is high, their record for violence low. These facts, plus the always gentlemanly or ladylike behavior of every Praefect, has made the Roman Praefecture of Police one of the most prestigious and honored bodies of criminal investigators on the face of the Earth.

In the gaslight of the train platform, Cesare Sarto waited as the Master-at-Arms came out of the car to greet him. Master Sean kept his face averted, but Lord Darcy watched carefully.

Sarto was a man of medium height with dark hair and eyes and a neatly-trimmed mustache. He was of average build, but carried himself like an athlete. There was power and speed in that well-muscled body. His face, while not exactly handsome, was strong and showed character and intelligence.

After a few minutes, he came into the car. He had a

suitcase in one hand and a notebook in the other. He put the suitcase on the floor and looked around at the fourteen passengers assembled in the lounge. They all watched him, waiting.

His eyes betrayed no flicker of recognition as they passed over Master Sean's face.

Then he said: "Gentlemen, I am Cesare Sarto, an agent of the Roman Praefecture of Police. The Chief Master-at-Arms of the city of Genova has asked me to take charge of this case—at least until we get to Rome." His Anglo-French was almost without accent.

"Technically," he continued, "this is the only way it can be handled. John Peabody was apparently murdered, but we do not yet know whether he was killed in Provence or in Liguria, and until we do, we won't know who has jurisdiction over the case.

"As of now, we must act on the assumption that Peabody died *after* this train crossed the Italian border. Therefore, this train will proceed to Rome. If we have not determined exactly what happened by then, this car will be detached and the investigation will continue. Those of you who can be exonerated beyond doubt will be allowed to go on to Napoli. The others, I fear, will have to be detained."

"Do you mean," Sir Stanley interrupted, "that you suspect one of *us*?"

"No one of you individually, sir. Not yet. But all of you collectively, yes. It surely must be obvious, sir, that since Peabody was killed in this car, someone in this car must have killed him. May I ask your name, sir?"

"Sir Stanley Galbraith," the gray-haired man said rather curtly.

Praefect Cesare looked at his notebook. "Ah, yes. Thank you, Sir Stanley." He looked around at the others. "I have here a list of your names as procured by the Master-at-Arms. In order that I may know you better, I will ask that each of you raise his hand when his name is called."

As he called off the names, it was obvious that each man's name and face were linked permanently in his memory when the hand was raised.

When he came to "Seamus Kilpadraeg," he looked the sorcerer over exactly as he had the others, then went on to the next name.

When he had finished, he said: "Now, gentlemen, I will ask you to go to your compartments and remain there until I call for you. The train will be leaving for Rome in—" He glanced at his wristwatch. "—eighteen minutes. Thank you."

Master Sean and Lord Darcy dutifully returned to their compartment.

"Praefect Cesare," Lord Darcy said, "is not only highly intelligent, but very quick-minded."

"How do you deduce that, me lord?"

"You said he knew you, and yet he showed no sign of it. Obviously, he perceived that if you were traveling under an alias, you must have a good reason for it. And, you being who you are, that the reason was probably a legitimate one. Rather than betray you in public, he decided to wait until he could talk to you privately. When he does, tell him that Father Armand is your confidant and close friend. Vouch for me, but don't reveal my identity."

"I expect him to be here within minutes."

There came a knock on the door.

Master Sean slid it open to reveal Praefect Cesare Sarto. "Come in, Praefect," the sorcerer said. "We've been expecting you."

"Oh?" Sarto raised an eyebrow. "I would like to talk to you privately, Master Seamus."

Master Sean lowered his voice almost to a whisper. "Come in, Cesare. Father Armand knows who I am."

The Praefect came in, and Master Sean slid the door shut. "Sean O Lochlainn at your service, Praefect Cesare," he said with a grin.

"Sean!" the Praefect grabbed him by both shoulders. "It's been a long time! You should write more often." He turned to Lord Darcy. "Pardon me, Padre, but I haven't seen my friend here since we took a course together at the University of Milano, five years ago. 'The Admissibility of Certain Magically Derived Evidence in Criminal Jurisprudence' it was."

"That's all right," Lord Darcy said. "I'm glad for both of you."

The Praefect looked for a moment at the slack-shouldered, white-haired, white-bearded man who peered benignly at him over gold-rimmed half-glasses. Then he looked back at Master Sean. "You say you know the Padre?"

"Intimately, for many years," Master Sean said. "Anything you have to say to me can be said in front of Father Armand in perfect confidence. You can trust him as you trust me."

"I didn't mean—" Sarto cut himself off and turned to Lord Darcy. "Reverend Sir, I did not intend to imply that one of the Sacred Clergy was not to be trusted. But this is a murder case, and they're touchy to handle. Do you know anything about criminology?"

"I have worked with criminals, and I have heard their confessions many times," Lord Darcy said with a straight face. "I think I can say I have some insight into the criminal mind."

Master Sean, with an equally straight face, said: "I think I can safely say that there are several cases that Lord Darcy might not have solved without the aid of this man here."

Praefect Cesare relaxed. "Well! That's fine, then. Sean, is it any of my business why you're traveling under an alias?"

"I'm doing a little errand for Prince Richard. It has nothing whatever to do with John Peabody, so, strictly speaking, it is none of your business. I imagine, though, that if you really had to know, His Highness would give me permission to tell you before any case came to trial."

"All right; let that rest for now. There are some other questions I must ask you."

The questions elicited the facts that neither Master Sean nor "Father Armand" had ever seen or heard of Peabody before, that neither had ever spoken to him, and that each could account for his time during the night. On being put the direct question, each gave his solemn word that he had not killed Peabody.

"Very well," the Praefect said at last, "I'll accept it as a working hypothesis that you two are innocent. Now, I have a little problem I want you to help me with."

"The murder, you mean?" Master Sean asked.

"In a way, yes. You see, it's like this: I have never handled a murder case before. My field is fraud and embezzlement. I'm an accountant, not, strictly speaking, an Armsman at all. I just happened to be in Genova, finishing up another case. I was going to go back to Rome on this train, anyway. So I got a teleson call from Rome, telling me to take over until we get there. Rome doesn't expect me to solve the case; Rome just wants me as a caretaker until the experts can take over."

He was silent for a moment, then, suddenly, a white-toothed, almost impish grin came over his face. "But the minute I recognized you, an idea occurred to me. With your experience, we just might be able to clear this up before we get to Rome! It would look good on my record if I succeed, but no black mark if I don't. I can't lose, you see. The head of the homicide division, Angelo Ratti, will be waiting for us at the station in Rome, and I'd give half a year's pay to see the look on his face if I could hand him the killer when I step off."

Master Sean gawped. Then he found words. "You mean you want us to help you nail the murderer *before* we get to Rome?"

"Exactly."

"I think that's a capital idea," said Lord Darcy.

17

The Napoli Express moved toward Rapello, on its way to Rome. In a little over an hour, it would be dawn. At four minutes of noon, the train would arrive in Rome.

First on the agenda was a search of the body and the compartment in which it lay. Peabody's suitcase was in the locker reserved for Lower One, but the key was in the lock, so there was no trouble getting it. It contained nothing extraordinary—only clothes and toilet articles. Peabody himself had been carrying nothing unusual, either—if one excepted the sword-stick. He had some loose change, a gold sovereign, two silver sovereigns, and five gold-sovereign notes. He carried some keys that probably fit his home locks or office locks. A card identified him as Commander John Wycliffe Peabody, Imperial Navy, Retired.

"I see nothing of interest there," Praefect Cesare commented.

"It's what *isn't* there that's of interest," Lord Darcy said.

The Praefect nodded. "Exactly. Where is the key to his compartment?"

"It appears to me," Lord Darcy said, "that the killer went in, killed Peabody, took the key, and locked the compartment so that the body wouldn't be found for a while."

"I agree," Cesare said.

"Then the murderer might still have the key on him," Master Sean said.

"It's possible." Praefect Cesare looked glum. "But it's far more likely that it's on or near the railroad tracks somewhere between here and Provence."

"That would certainly be the intelligent thing to do," Lord Darcy said. "Should we search for it anyway?"

"Not just yet, I think. If he kept it, he won't throw it away now. If not, we won't find it."

Lord Darcy was rather pleased with the Praefect's answer. It was the one he would have given, had he been in charge. It was rather irksome not to be in charge of the case, but at least Cesare Sarto knew what he was doing.

"The killer," the Praefect went on, "had no way of knowing that the blood from Peabody's scalp would run under the door and into the passageway. Let's assume it hadn't. When would the body have been discovered?"

"Probably not until ten o'clock this morning," Master Sean said firmly. "I've taken this train before, though not with the same crew. The day man—that's Fred, this trip—comes on at nine. He makes up the beds of those who are already awake, but he doesn't start waking people up until about ten. It might have been as late as half past ten before Peabody was found."

"I see," said Praefect Cesare. "I don't see that that gets us any forwarder just yet, but we'll keep it in mind. Now, we cannot do an autopsy on the body, of course, but I'd like a little more information on those blows and the weapon."

"I think I can oblige you, Praefect," said Master Sean.

The sorcerer carefully inspected the walking-stick with its concealed blade. "We'll do this first; it's the easier job and may give us some clue that will tell us what to do next."

From his bag, he took a neatly-folded white cerecloth and spread it over the small nearby table. "First time I've done this on a train," he muttered, half to himself. "Have to watch me balance."

The other two said nothing.

He took out a thin, three-inch, slightly concave golden

disk, a pair of tweezers, a small insufflator, and an eight-inch, metallic-looking, blue-gray wand with crystalline sapphire tips.

With the tweezers, he selected two hairs, one from the dead man and one from the silver head of the stick. He carefully laid them parallel, an inch and a half apart, on the cerecloth. Then he touched each with the wand, murmuring solemn spondees of power under his breath. Then he stood up, well away from the hairs, not breathing.

Slowly, like two tiny logs rolling toward each other, the hairs came together, still parallel.

"His hair on the stick, all right," Master Sean said. "We'll see about the blood."

The only sound in the room except the rumbling of the train was the almost inaudible movement of Sarto's pen on his notebook.

A similar incantation, this time using the little golden saucer, showed the blood to be the same.

"This one's a little more complex," Master Sean said. "Since the wounds are mostly on the forward part of the head, I'll have to turn him over and put him flat on his back. Will that be all right?" He directed the question to the Praefect.

"Certainly," Praefect Cesare said. "I have all the notes and sketches of the body's position when found. Here, I'll give you a hand."

Moving a two-hundred-pound dead body is not easy in the confines of a small compartment, but it would have been much more difficult if Master Sean's preservative spell had not prevented *rigor mortis* from setting in.

"There; that'll do. Thank you," the stout little sorcerer said. "Would either of you care to check the wounds visually?"

They would. Master Sean's powerful magnifying glass was passed from hand to hand.

"Bashed in right proper," Sarto muttered.

"Thorough job," Lord Darcy agreed. "But not efficient. Only two or three of those blows were hard enough to kill, and there must be a dozen of them. Peculiar."

"Now gentlemen," the sorcerer said, "we'll see if that stick actually was the murder weapon."

It was a crucial test. Hair and blood had been planted

before on innocent weapons. The thaumaturgical science would tell them whether or not it had happened this time.

Master Sean used the insufflator to blow a cloud of powder over both the area of the wounds and the silver knob on the stick. There was very little of the powder, and it was so fine that the excess floated away like smoke.

"Now, if you'll turn that lamp down . . ."

In the dim yellow glow of the turned-down wall lamp, almost no details could be seen. All was in shadow. Only the glittering tips of Master Sean's rapidly moving wand could be seen, glowing with a blue light of their own.

Then, abruptly, there seemed to be thousands of tiny white fireflies moving over the upper part of the dead man's face— and over the knob of the stick. There were several thin, twinkling threads of the minute sparks between face and knob.

After several seconds, Master Sean gave his wand a final snap with his wrist, and the tiny sparks vanished.

"That's it. Turn up the lights, if you please. The stick was definitely the murder weapon."

Praefect Cesare Sarto nodded slowly, looking thoughtful. "Very well. What's our next step?" He paused. "What would Lord Darcy do next?"

His lordship was standing behind and a little to the left of the Italian, and, as Master Sean looked at both of them, Darcy traced an interrogation point in the air with a forefinger.

"Why, me lord's next step," said the sorcerer as if he had known all along, "would be to question the suspects again. More thoroughly, this time." Lord Darcy held up the forefinger, and Master Sean added: "One at a time, of course."

"That sounds sensible," Sarto agreed. "And I can get away with having you two present by saying that you are Acting Forensic Sorcerer on this case and that you, Reverend Sir, are *amicus curia* as a representative of Holy Mother Church. By the way, are you a Sensitive, Father?"

"No, unfortunately, I am not."

"Pity. Well, we needn't tell them that. Let them worry. Now, what sort of questions do we ask? Give me a case of tax fraud, and I have an impressive roster of questions to ask the people involved, but I'm a little out of my element here."

"Why, as to that," Lord Darcy began . . .

18

"They are lying," Praefect Cesare said flatly, three hours later. "Each and severally, every single one of the bastards is lying."

"And not very well, either," added Master Sean.

"Well, let us see what we have here," Lord Darcy said, picking up his notes.

They were seated at the rear table in the lounge; there was no one else in the car. Segregation of the suspects had not been difficult; the Trainmaster had opened up the dining car early, and the Genovese Master-at-Arms that Sarto had brought with him was watching over it. The men had been taken from their compartments one at a time, questioned, then taken back to the dining car. That kept them from discussing the questioning with those who hadn't been questioned yet.

Tonio, the night man, had been questioned first, then told to get out of the car and stay out. He didn't mind; he knew there would be no business and no tips that morning.

The Trainmaster had arranged for caffe to be served early in the rear of the dining car, and Lord Darcy had prepared the three interrogators a pot from behind the bar.

At eight o'clock, the stewards had begun serving breakfast in the dining car. It was now nearly nine.

Rome was some three hours away.

Lord Darcy was looking over his transcript of the questioning when the Roman Praefect said: "Do you see the odd thing about this group? That they know each other?"

"Well, some of 'em know each other," Master Sean said.

"No, the Praefect is perfectly right," Lord Darcy said without looking up. "They *all* know each other—and well."

"And yet," Cesare Sarto continued, "they seem anxious that we should not know that. They are together for a purpose, and yet they say nothing about that purpose."

"Master Sean," Lord Darcy said, "obviously you did not read the Marsaille newspaper I left on your berth last night."

"No, Father. I was tired. Come to think of it, I still am. You refer to the obituary?"

"I do." Lord Darcy looked at Sarto. "Perhaps it was in the Genova papers. The funeral of a certain Nicholas Jourdan is to be held in Napoli on the morrow."

"I heard of it," Praefect Cesare said. "And I got more from the talk of my fellow officers than was in the paper. Captain Nicholas Jourdan, Imperial Navy, Retired, was supposed to have died of food poisoning, but there's evidence that it was a very cleverly arranged suicide. If it was suicide, it was probably dropped by the Neapolitan officials. We don't like to push that sort of thing if there's no crime involved because there's such a fuss afterwards about the funeral. As you well know."

"Hmm," said Lord Darcy. "I didn't know the suicide angle. Is there evidence that he was depressed?"

"I heard there was, but nobody mentioned any reason for it. Health reasons, perhaps."

"I know of another reason," Lord Darcy said. "Or, at least, a possible reason. About three years ago, Captain Jourdan retired from the Navy. It was an early retirement; he was still a young man for a Captain. Health reasons were given.

"Actually, he had a choice between forced retirement or a rather nasty court-martial.

"Apparently, he had been having a rather torrid love affair with a young Sicilian woman from Messina, and was keeping her in an apartment in Napoli. Normally, that sort of thing doesn't bother the Navy too much, but this particular young person turned out to be an agent of His Slavonic Majesty, Casimir of Poland."

"Ah*ha!* Espionage rears its ugly head," the Praefect said.

"Precisely. At the time, Captain Jourdan was commanding H.I.M.S. *Helgoland Bay* and was a very popular commander, both with his officers and his men. Obviously, the Admiralty thought well of him, too, or they shouldn't have put him in command of one of the most important battleships of the line.

"But the discovery that his mistress was a spy cast a different light on things. It turned out that they could not prove he knew she was a spy, nor that he had ever told her any Naval secrets. But the suspicion remained. He was given his choice.

"A court-martial would have ruined his career with the Navy forever, of course. They'd have found him innocent, then shipped him off to some cold little island off the southern coast of New France and left him there with nothing to do but count penguins. So, naturally, he retired.

"If, as you suggest, it was suicide, it might have been three years of despondency that accounted for it."

Praefect Cesare nodded slowly, a look of satisfaction on his face. "I should have seen it. The way these twelve men deport themselves, the way certain of them show deference to certain others . . . They are some of the officers of the *Helgoland Bay*. And so, obviously, was Peabody."

"I should say so, yes," Lord Darcy agreed.

"The trouble is," Sarto said, "we still have no motive. What we have to do is get one of them to crack. Both of you know them better than I do; which would you suggest?"

Master Sean said: "I would suggest young Jamieson. Father?"

"I agree, Master Sean. He admitted that he went back to talk to Peabody, but I had the feeling that he didn't want to, that he didn't like Peabody. Perhaps you could put some pressure on him, my dear Praefect."

Blond, pink-faced young Charles Jamieson was called in forthwith. He sat down nervously. It is not easy for a young man to be other than nervous when faced by three older, stern-faced men—a priest, a powerful sorcerer, and an agent of the dread Roman Praefecture of Police. It is worse when one is involved in a murder case.

Cesare Sarto looked grim, his mouth hard, his eyes cold. The man he had been named for, Caius Iulius, must have looked similar when faced by some badly erring young centurion more than two millennia before.

"Young man, are you aware that impeding the investigation of a major felony by lying to the investigating officer is not only punishable by civilian law, but that I can have you court-martialed by the Imperial Navy, and that you may possibly lose your commission in disgrace?"

Jamieson's pink face turned almost white. His mouth opened, but nothing came out.

"I am aware," the Praefect continued remorselessly, "that

one or more of your superiors now in the dining car may have given you orders to do what you have done, but such orders are unlawful, and, in themselves, constitute a court-martial offense."

The young man was still trying to find his voice when kindly old Father Armand broke in. "Now, Praefect, let us not be too hard on the lad. I am sure that he now sees the seriousness of his crime. Why don't you tell us all about it, my son? I'm sure the Praefect will not press charges if you help us now."

Sarto nodded slowly, but his face didn't change, as though he were yielding the point reluctantly.

"Now, my son, let's begin again. Tell us your name and rank, and about what you and your fellow officers did last night."

Jamieson's color had come back. He took a breath. "Charles James Jamieson, Lieutenant, Imperial Navy, British Royal Fleet, at present Third Supply Officer aboard His Imperial Majesty's Ship *Helgoland Bay,* sir! Uh—that is, *Father."* He had almost saluted.

"Relax, my son; I am not a Naval Officer. Go on. Begin with why you and the others are aboard this train and not at your stations."

"Well, sir, the *Hellbay* is in drydock just now, and we were all more or less on leave, you see, but we had to stay around Portsmouth. Then, a week ago, we got the news that our old Captain, who retired three years ago, had died and was being buried in Napoli, so we all got together and decided to form a party to go pay our respects. That's all there is to it, really, Father."

"Was Commander John Peabody one of your group?" the Praefect asked sharply.

"No, sir. He retired shortly after our old Captain did. Until yesterday, none of us had seen him for three years."

"Your old Captain was, I believe, the late Nicholas Jourdan?" Sarto asked.

"Yes, sir."

"Why did you dislike Commander Peabody?" the Praefect snapped.

Jamieson's face became suddenly pinker. "No particular reason, sir. I didn't like him, true, but it was just one of those things. Some people rub each other the wrong way."

"You hated him enough to kill him," Praefect Cesare said flatly.

It was as though Jamieson were prepared for that. He didn't turn a hair. "No, sir. I didn't like him, that's true. But I didn't kill him." It was as though he had rehearsed the answer.

"Who did, then?"

"It is my belief, sir, that some unknown person got aboard the train during the ten minutes we were at the Italian border, came in, killed the Commander, and left." That answer, too, sounded rehearsed.

"Very well," the Praefect said, "that's all for now. Go to your compartment and stay there until you are called."

Jamieson obeyed.

"Well, what do you think, Father?" Cesare Sarto asked.

"The same as you. He gave us some of the truth, but he's still lying." He thought for a moment. "Let's try a different tactic. We can get—"

He stopped. A man in red-and-blue uniform was coming toward them from the passageway. It was Goodman Fred, the day man.

He stopped at the table. "Excuse me, gentlemen. I have heard about the investigation, of course. The Trainmaster told me to report to you before I went on duty." He looked a little baffled. "I'm not sure what my duties would be, in the circumstances."

Before Sarto could speak, Lord Darcy said: "What would they normally be?"

"Tend the bar, and make up the beds."

"Well, there will be no need to tend bar as yet, but you may as well make up the beds."

Fred brightened. "Thank you, Father, Praefect " He went back to the passageway.

"You were saying something about trying a different tactic," Praefect Cesare prompted.

"Aye, yes," said his lordship. And explained.

19

Maurice Zeisler did not look any the better for the time since he had had his last drink. He looked haggard and old.

Sidney Charpentier was in better shape, but even he looked tired.

The two men sat in the remaining empty chairs at the rear table, facing the three inquisitors.

Master Sean said: "Goodman Sidney Charpentier, I believe you told me you were a licensed Lay Healer. May I see your license, please." It was an order, not a question. It was a Master of the Guild speaking to an apprentice.

There was reluctance, but no hesitation. "Certainly, Master." Charpentier produced the card.

Master Sean looked it over carefully. "I see. Endorsed by My Lord Bishop of Wexford. I know his lordship well. Chaplain Admiral of the Imperial Navy. What is your rank, sir?"

Zeisler's baggy eyes looked suddenly alert, but he said nothing. Charpentier said: "Senior Lieutenant, Master Seamus."

The sorcerer looked at Zeisler. "And yours?"

Zeisler looked at Charpentier with a wry grin. "Not to worry, Sharpy. Young Jamie must've told 'em. Not your fault." Then he looked at Master Sean. "Lieutenant Commander Maurice Edwy Zeisler at your service, Master Seamus."

"And I at yours, Commander. Now, we might as well get all these ranks straight. Let's begin with Sir Stanley."

The list was impressive:

> Captain Sir Stanley Galbraith
> Commander Gwiliam Hauser
> Lt. Commander Martyn Boothroyd
> Lt. Commander Gavin Tailleur
> Lt. Commander Maurice Zeisler
> Sr. Lieutenant Sidney Charpentier
> Sr. Lieutenant Simon Lamar
> Sr. Lieutenant Arthur Mac Kay
> Sr. Lieutenant Jason Quinte
> Lieutenant Lyman Vandepole
> Lieutenant Charles Jamieson

"I presume," Lord Darcy said carefully, "that if the *Helgoland Bay* were not in drydock at present, it would have been inconvenient to allow all you gentlemen to leave at one time, eh?"

Zeisler made a noise that was a blend of a cough and a laugh. "Inconvenient, Father? *Impossible.*"

"Even so," Lord Darcy continued quietly, "is it not unusual for so many of you to be away from your ship at one time? What occasioned it?"

"Captain Jourdan died," Zeisler said in a cold voice.

"Many men die," Lord Darcy said. "What made *his* death so special?" His voice was as cold as Zeisler's.

Charpentier opened his mouth to say something, but Zeisler cut him off. "Because Captain Nicholas Jourdan was one of the finest Naval officers who ever lived."

Praefect Cesare said: "So all of you were going to the Jourdan funeral—including the late Commander Peabody?"

"That's right, Praefect," Charpentier said. "But Peabody wasn't one of the original group. There were sixteen of us going; we wanted the car to ourselves, you see. But the other four couldn't make it; their leaves were suddenly cancelled. That's how Peabody, the good Father, here, and the Master Sorcerer got their berths."

"You had no idea Peabody was coming, then?"

"None. We'd none of us seen him for nearly three years," Charpentier said.

"Almost didn't recognize him," Zeisler put in. "That beard, you know. He'd grown that since we saw him last. But I recognized that sword-stick of his, and that made me look closer at the face. I recognized him. So did Commander Hauser." He chuckled. "Of course, old Hauser would."

"Why he more than anyone else?" the Praefect asked.

"He's head of Ship's Security. He used to be Peabody's immediate superior."

"Let's get back to that sword-stick," Lord Darcy said. "You say you recognized it. Did anyone else?"

Zeisler looked at Charpentier. "Did you?"

"I really didn't pay any attention until you pointed it out, Maury. Of course, we all knew he had it. Bought it in Lisbon four, five years ago. But I hadn't thought of it, or him, for three years."

"Tell us more about Peabody," Lord Darcy said. "What sort of man was he?"

Charpentier rubbed his big nose with a thick forefinger. "Decent sort. Reliable. Good officer. Wouldn't you say, Maury?"

"Oh, yes," Zeisler agreed. "Good chap to go partying with, too. I remember one time in a little Greek bar in Alexandria, we managed to put away more than a quart of *ouzo* in a couple of hours, and when a couple of Egyptian footpads tried to take us in the street, he mopped up on both of them while I was still trying to get up from their first rush. He could really hold his liquor in those days. I wonder what happened?"

"What do you mean?" Lord Darcy asked.

"Well, he only had a few drinks yesterday, but he was pretty well under the weather last night. Passed out while I was talking to him."

The Roman Praefect jumped on that. "Then you *were* the last to see him?"

Zeisler blinked. "I don't know. I think somebody else went in to see if he was all right. I don't remember who."

Praefect Cesare sighed. "Very well, gentlemen. Thank you. Go to your compartment. I will call for you later."

"Just one more question, if I may," Lord Darcy said mildly. "Commander Zeisler, you said that the late Peabody worked with Ship's Security. He was, I believe, the officer who reported Captain Jourdan's—er—liaison with a certain unsavory young woman from Messina, thereby ruining the Captain's career?" It was a shot in the dark, and Darcy knew it, but his intuition told him he was right.

Zeisler's lips firmed. He said nothing.

"Come, come, Commander; we can always check the records, you know."

"Yes," Zeisler said after a moment. "That's true."

"Thank you. That's all for now."

When they had gone, Praefect Cesare slumped down in his seat. "Well. It looks as though Praefect Angelo Ratti will have the honor of making the arrest, after all."

"You despair of solving the case already?" Lord Darcy asked.

"Oh, not at all. The case is already solved, Reverend Sir. But I cannot make an arrest."

"I'm afraid I don't follow you, my dear Praefect."

A rather sardonic twinkle came into the Italian's eyes. "Ah, then you have not seen the solution to our problem, yet? You do not see how Commander Peabody came to be the *late* Commander Peabody?"

"I'm not the investigating officer here," Lord Darcy pointed out "You are. What happened, in your view?"

"Well," Cesare said seriously, "what do we have here? We have twelve Naval officers going to the funeral of a beloved late Captain. Also, a thirteenth—the man who betrayed that same Captain and brought him to disgrace. A Judas.

"We know they are lying when they tell us that their conversations with him last night were just casual. They could have spoken to him at any time during the day, yet none of them did. They waited until night. Then each of them, one at a time, goes to see him. Why? No reason is given. They claim it was for a casual chat. At that hour of night? After every one of them had been up since early morning? A casual chat! Do you believe that, Reverend Sir?"

Lord Darcy shook his head slowly. "No. We both know better. Every one of them was—and still is—lying."

"Very well, then. What are they lying about? What are they trying to cover up? Murder, of course."

"But, by which one of 'em?" Master Sean asked.

"Don't you see?" The Praefect's voice was low and tense. "Don't you see? It was *all* of them!"

"*What?*" Master Sean stared. "But—"

"Hold, Master Sean," Lord Darcy said. "I think I see where he's going. Pray continue, Praefect Cesare."

"Certainly you see it, Father," the Praefect said. "Those men probably don't consider it murder. It was, to them, an execution after a drumhead court-martial. One of them— we don't know who—talked his way into Peabody's compartment. Then, when the opportunity presented itself, he struck. Peabody was knocked unconscious. Then, one at a time, each of the others went in and struck again. A dozen men, a dozen blows. The deed is done, and no single one of them did it. It was execution by a committee—or rather, by a jury.

"They claim they did not know Peabody was coming along. But does that hold water? Was he on this train, in this car, by coincidence? That stretches coincidence too far, I think."

"I agree," Lord Darcy said quietly. "It was no coincidence that put him on this train with the others. It was very carefully managed."

"Ah! You see, Master Sean?" Then a frown came over

Sarto's face. "It is obvious what happened, but we have no solid proof. They stick to their story too well. We need *proof*—and we have none."

"I don't think you'll get any of them to confess," Lord Darcy said. "Do you, Master Sean?"

"No," said the sorcerer. "Not a chance."

"What we need," Lord Darcy said, "is *physical* proof. And the only place we'll find that is in Compartment Number One."

"We've searched that," Praefect Cesare said.

"Then let us search it again."

20

Lord Darcy went over the body very carefully this time, his lean, strong fingers probing, feeling. He checked the lining of the jacket, his fingertips squeezing everywhere, searching for lumps or the crackle of paper. Nothing. He took off the wide belt, looking for hidden pockets. Nothing. He checked the boot heels. Nothing.

Finally he pulled off the calf-length boots themselves.

And, with a murmur of satisfaction, he withdrew an object from a flat interior pocket of the right one.

It was a flat, slightly curved silver badge engraved with the double-headed eagle of the Imperium. Set in it was what looked like a dull, translucent, grayish, cabochon-cut piece of glass. But all three men knew that if Peabody's living flesh had touched that gem, it would have glowed like a fire-ruby.

"A King's Messenger," the Praefect said softly.

No one else's touch would make that gem glow. The spell, invented by Master Sorcerer Sir Edward Elmer back in the Thirties, had never been solved, and no one knew what sorcerer at present had charge of that secret and made these badges for the King.

This particular badge would never glow again.

"Indeed," Lord Darcy said. "Now we know what Commander Peabody has been doing since he retired from the Navy, and how he managed to retire honorably at such an early age."

"I wonder if his shipmates know," Sarto said.

"Probably not," Lord Darcy said. "King's Messengers don't advertise the fact."

"No. But I don't see that identifying him as such gets us any further along."

"We haven't searched the rest of the room thoroughly yet."

Twenty minutes later, Praefect Cesare said: "Nothing. Absolutely nothing. And we've searched everywhere. What are you looking for, anyway?"

"I'm not sure," Lord Darcy admitted, "but I know it exists. Still, it might have ended up on the track with the compartment key. Hmmm." With his keen eyes, he surveyed the room carefully. Then he stopped, looking at the area just above the bed where the body lay. "Of course," he said very softly. "The upper berth."

The upper berth was folded up against the wall and locked firmly in place, making a large compartment that held mattress and bedclothes safely out of the way.

"Get Fred," Lord Darcy said. "He has a key."

Fred, indeed, had a key, and he had been using it. The beds were all made in the other compartments, the lowers changed to sofas and the uppers folded up and locked.

He couldn't understand why the gentlemen wanted that upper berth unlocked, but he didn't argue. He reached up, inserted the key, turned, and lowered the shelf until it was horizontal, all the time doing his best to keep his eyes off the thing that lay in the lower berth.

"Ahh! What have we here?" There was pleasure in Lord Darcy's voice as he picked up the large leather case from where it lay in the upper berth. Then he looked at Fred. "That'll be all for now, Fred; we'll call you when it's time to lock up again."

"Certainly, Father." He went on about his business.

Not until then did his lordship turn the seventeen-by-twelve-by-three leather envelope over. It bore the Royal Emblem, stamped in gold, just beneath the latch.

"*Uh*-oh!" said Master Sean. "More here than we thought." He looked at Lord Darcy. "Did you expect a diplomatic pouch, Father?"

"Not really. An envelope of some kind. King's Messengers usually carry messages, and this one would probably not be verbal. But this is heavy. Must weigh five or six pounds. The latch has been unlocked and not relocked. I'll wager that means *two* keys on the railroad track." He opened it and lifted out a heavy manuscript. He leafed through it

"What is it?" Cesare Sarto asked.

"A treaty. In Greek, Latin, and Anglo-French. Between Roumeleia and the Empire." There was a jerkiness in his voice.

Master Sean opened his mouth to say something and then clamped it shut.

Lord Darcy slid the manuscript back into the big leather envelope and clicked the latch shut. "This is not for our eyes, gentlemen. But now we have our evidence. I can tell you exactly how John Peabody died and prove it. You can make your arrest very soon, Praefect."

21

There were seventeen men in the observation car of the Napoli Express as she rumbled southeast, along the coast of the Tyrrhenian Sea, toward the mouth of the Tiber.

Besides the twelve Naval officers, Praefect Cesare, Master Sean, and Lord Darcy, there were also Fred, the day attendant, and Trainmaster Edmund Norton, who had been asked to attend because it was, after all, his train, and therefore his responsibility.

Praefect Cesare Sarto stood near the closed door to the observation deck at the rear of the car, looking at sixteen pairs of eyes, all focused on him. Like an actor taking his stage, the Praefect knew, not only the plot, but his lines and blocking.

Father Armand was at his left, seated at the end of the couch. Fred was behind the bar. The Trainmaster was seated at the passageway end of the bar. Master Sean was standing at the entrance to the passageway. The Navy men were all seated. The stage was set.

"Gentlemen," he began, "we have spent many hours trying to discover and sift the facts pertaining to the death of your former shipmate, Commander John Peabody. Oh, yes, Captain Sir Stanley, I know who you all are. You and your fellow officers have consistently lied to me and evaded the truth, thus delaying our solution of this deadly puzzle. But we know, now.

"First, we know that the late Commander was an official Messenger for His Imperial Majesty, John of England. Second, we know that he was the man who reported to higher authority what he knew about the late Captain Nicholas Jourdan's inamorata, certain facts which his own investigations, as a Ship's Security officer, had brought out. These facts resulted in Captain Jourdan's forced retirement, and, possibly, in his ultimate demise."

His eyes searched their faces. They were all waiting, and there was an undercurrent of hostility in their expressions.

"Third, we know how John Peabody was killed, and we know by whom it was done. Your cover-up was futile, gentlemen. Shall I tell you what happened last night?"

They waited, looking steadily at him.

"John Peabody was a man with enormous resistance to the effects of alcohol, and yet he passed out last night. Not because of the alcohol, but because someone drugged one of his drinks. Even that, he was able to fight off longer than was expected.

"Then, when Peabody was unconscious, a man carefully let himself into Peabody's compartment. He had no intent to kill; he wasn't even armed. He wanted to steal some very important papers which, as a King's Messenger, Peabody was carrying.

"But something went wrong. Peabody came out of his drugged stupor enough to realize what was going on. He made a grab for his silver-headed stick. The intruder got it first.

"Peabody was a strong man and a skillful fighter, even when drunk, as most of you know. In the struggle that ensued, the intruder used that stick as a club, striking Peabody again and again. Drugged and battered, that tough, brave man kept fighting.

"Neither of them yelled or screamed: Peabody because it was not in his nature to call for help; the intruder because he wanted no alarm.

"At last, the blows took their final toll. Peabody collapsed, his head smashed in. He was dying.

"The intruder listened. No alarm had been given. He still had time. He found the heavy diplomatic pouch in which those important documents were carried. But what could he do with them? He couldn't stop to read them there, for Tonio, the night man, might be back very soon. Also, he could not carry them away, because the pouch was far too large to conceal on his person, and if Tonio saw it, he would report it when the body was found.

"So he concealed it in the upper berth of Peabody's compartment, thinking to retrieve it later. Then he took Peabody's key, locked the compartment, tossed the key off the train, and went on about his business. He hoped he would have plenty of time, because the body should not have been found until about an hour ago.

"But Peabody, though dying, was not dead yet. Scalp wounds have a tendency to bleed profusely, and in this case, they certainly did. The blood pooled on the floor and ran out under the door.

"Tonio found the blood—and the rest you know.

"No, gentlemen, this was not a vengeance killing as we thought at first. This was done by a man whom we believe to be an agent of, or in the pay of, the *Serka*—the Polish Secret Service."

They were no longer looking at Cesare Sarto, they were looking at each other.

Sarto shook his head. "No; wrong again, gentlemen. *Only one man had the key to that upper berth last night!*" He lifted his eyes and looked at the bar.

"Trainmaster Edmund Norton," he said coldly, "you are under arrest!"

The Trainmaster was already on his feet, and he turned to run up the passageway. If he could get to the door and lock these men in—

But stout little Master Sean O Lochlainn was blocking his way.

Norton was bigger and heavier than the sorcerer, but Norton had only seconds, no time for a fight. From somewhere, he produced a six-inch knife and made an underhand thrust.

Master Sean's right hand made a single complex gesture. Norton froze, immobile for a long second.

Then, like a large red-and-blue sack of wet oatmeal, he collapsed to the deck. Master Sean took the knife from his nerveless fingers as he fell.

"I didn't want him to fall on the knife and hurt himself," he explained, almost apologetically. "He'll come around all right when I take that spell off."

The Navy men were all on their feet, facing Master Sean.

Commander Hauser fingered his streaked beard. "I didn't know a sorcerer could do anything like that," he said in a hushed, almost frightened voice.

"It can't be done at all unless a sorcerer is attacked," Master Sean explained. "All my spell did was turn his own psychic energy back on itself. Gave his nervous system a devil of a shock when the flow was forcibly reversed. It's similar to certain forms of unarmed combat, where the opponent's own force is used against him. If he doesn't attack you, there's not much you can do."

The Roman Praefect walked over to where the Trainmaster lay, took out a pair of handcuffs, and locked Norton's wrists behind his back. "Fred, you had best go get the Assistant Trainmaster; he'll have to take over now. And tell the Master-at-Arms who is waiting at the far end of the passageway to come on in. I want him to take charge of the prisoner now. Captain Sir Stanley, Commander Hauser, do you mind if I borrow Compartment Eight until we get to Rome? Good. Help me get him in there."

The Assistant Trainmaster came back with Fred, and the Praefect explained things to him. He looked rather dazed, but he took charge competently enough.

Behind the bar, Fred still looked shocked. "Here, Fred," the Praefect said, "you need some work to do. Give a drink to anyone who wants one, and have a good stiff one, yourself."

"How did you know it wasn't *me* who unlocked that upper berth last night?" Fred whispered.

"For the same reason I knew no one in the other cars on this train did it," Cesare whispered back. "The dining car was locked, and you do not have a key. Tonio did, but he had no key to the berth. Only the Trainmaster has *all* the keys to this train. Now make those drinks."

There were sixteen drinks to serve; Fred went about his work.

Boothroyd smoothed down his white hair. "Just when did the Trainmaster drug Peabody's drink, anyway?"

Master Sean took the question. "Last night, after we left

Marsaille, when Norton sent Tonio off on an errand. He told
Tonio to get some towels, but those towels wouldn't be
needed until this morning. Tonio would have had plenty of
time to get them after we retired. But Peabody was drinking, and Norton wanted to have the chance to drug him.
I've seen how easy it is for a barman to slip something into
a drink unnoticed." He did not look at Zeisler.

Sir Stanley cleared his throat. "You said we were all lying,
Praefect, that our cover-up was futile. What did you mean
by that?"

Lord Darcy had already told Sarto to take credit for
everything because "it would be unseemly for a man of the
cloth to be involved in such things." So Cesare Sarto wisely
did not mention whose deductions he was expounding.

"You know perfectly well what I mean, Captain. You and
your men did *not* go into Peabody's compartment, one at
a time, for a 'friendly chat.' You each had something specific to say to the man who turned in Captain Jourdan. Want
to tell me what it was?"

"Might as well, eh? Very well. We were pretty certain he'd
been avoiding us because he thought we hated him. We
didn't. Not his fault, you see. He did his duty when he
reported what he knew about that Sicilian woman. Any one
of us would have done the same. Right, Commander?"

"Damn right," said Commander Hauser. "Would've done
it myself. Some of us older officers told the Captain she
was no good for him from the start, but he wouldn't listen. If he was brokenhearted, it was mostly because she'd
made a proper fool of him, and no mistake."

Captain Sir Stanley took up the story again. "So that's
what we went in there for, one at a time. To tell him we
didn't hold it against him. Even Lieutenant Jamieson, eh,
my boy?"

"Aye, sir. I didn't like him, but it wasn't for that reason."

The Praefect nodded. "I believe you. But that's where the
cover-up came in. *Each and every one of you was afraid
that one of your group had killed Peabody!*"

There was silence. The silence of tacit assent.

"I watched you, listened to you," the Praefect went on.
"Each of you considered the other eleven one by one, and
came up with a verdict of 'Innocent' every time. But that
doubt remained. And you were afraid that I would find a

motive in what Peabody did three years ago. So you told me nothing. I must confess that, because of that evasion, that lying, I was suspicious at one time of all of you."

"By S'n George! Then what made you begin to suspect that Norton was guilty, sir?" asked Lieutenant Valentine Herrick.

"When it was reported to me that the Trainmaster showed up within half a minute after he had been sent for, right after Tonio found the blood. Norton had been awake since three o'clock yesterday morning: what was he still doing up, in full uniform at nearly one o'clock this morning? Why hadn't he turned things over to the Assistant Trainmaster, as usual, and gone to sleep long before? That's when I began to wonder."

Lieutenant Lyman Vandepole ran a finger over his hairline mustache. "But until you found that pouch, you couldn't be sure, could you, sir?"

"Not certain, no. But if one of you had gone in there with deliberate murder on his mind, he'd most likely have brought his own weapon. Or, if he intended to use that sword-stick, he would have used the blade, since every one of you knew it was a sword-stick. But Norton didn't, you see."

Senior Lieutenant Simon Lamar looked at "Father Armand." "With all that fighting going on next door, I'm surprised it didn't wake you up, Reverend Sir."

"I'm sure it would have," Lord Darcy said. "That is how we were able to pinpoint *when* it happened. Tonio left the car to go forward about midnight. At that time, Master Seamus and I were out on the rear platform. I was having a smoke, and he was keeping me company. We went back to our compartment at twenty after twelve. Norton didn't know we were out there, of course, but the killing must have taken place during that twenty minutes. Which means that the murder took place *before* we reached the Italian border, and Norton will have to be extradited to Provence."

Fred began serving the drinks he had mixed, but before anyone could taste his, Captain Sir Stanley Galbraith said: "A moment, gentlemen, if you please. I would like to propose a toast. Remember, we will have another funeral to attend after the one in Napoli."

When Fred had finished serving, he stood respectfully to one side, his own drink in his hand. The others rose.

"Gentlemen," said the Captain, "I give you Commander John Wycliffe Peabody, who did his duty as he saw it and died honorably in the service of his King." They drank in silence.

22

By twenty minutes after one that afternoon, the Napoli Express was twelve miles out of Rome, moving on the last leg of her journey to Napoli.

Lord Darcy and Master Sean were in their compartment, quietly relaxing after an excellent lunch.

"Me lord," said the sorcerer, "are you sure it was right to turn those copies of the treaty over to the Praefecture of Police for delivery to Imperial Naval Intelligence?"

"It was perfectly safe."

"Well, what's the use of our carrying our copies all the way to Athens, then?"

"My dear Sean, the stuff Peabody was carrying was a sham. I looked it over carefully. One of the provisions, for instance, is that a joint Anglo-French-Greek Naval base shall be established at 29° 51' North, 12° 10' East."

"What's wrong with that, me lord?"

"Nothing, except that it is in the middle of the Sahara Desert."

"Oh."

"Kyril's signature was a forgery. It was signed in Latin characters, and the Basileus reads and writes only Greek. The Greek and Latin texts do not agree with each other, nor with the Anglo-French. In one place in the Greek text, the city of Constantinople is referred to as the capital of England, while Paris is given as the capital of Greece. I could go on. The whole thing is a farrago of nonsense."

"But—*Why?*"

"One can only conjecture, of course. I believe he was a decoy. Think about it. Sixteen men all about to go to a funeral, and, at the last minute, four of them have their leaves canceled. Why? I feel the Royal touch of His Majesty's hand in there. I think it was to make certain Peabody got aboard that train with his fellow officers. It would look like a cover, as though he, too, were going to Jourdan's funeral.

"I think what happened was this: His Majesty found that the *Serka* had somehow gotten wind of our Naval treaty with Roumeleia. But they didn't know it was being signed by Prince Richard as proxy in Rouen, so they started tracing it in London. So His Majesty had this utterly nonsensical pseudo-treaty drawn up and sent it with Peabody. He was a decoy."

"Did Peabody know that?" Master Sean asked.

"Highly unlikely. If a man knows he is a decoy, he tends to act like a decoy, which ruins the illusion. No, he didn't know. Would he have fought to the death to preserve a phony document? Of course, being an honorable officer, once that pouch was locked, he would not have opened it, so he did not know its contents."

"But, me lord! If he was supposed to be a decoy, if he was supposed to lead *Serka* agents off on a wild goose chase somewhere else while you and I got the real thing safely to Athens—*why was the decoy dumped practically in our laps?*"

"I think," said his lordship with care, "that we missed connections somewhere. Other transportation may have—*must* have—been provided for us. But something must have gone awry.

"Nonetheless, my dear Sean, all will work out for the best. A murder aboard the Napoli Express will certainly hit the news services, but the story will be so confused that *Serka* won't be able to figure out what happened until too late."

"It would have been even worse confused if Cesare had come out with his conspiracy theory," the magician said. "He's a good man at his job, but he doesn't know people."

"His problem," Lord Darcy said, "is that he happens to be a master at paper work. On paper, he can spot a conspiracy two leagues away. But sentences on paper do not convey the nuances of thought that spoken words do. A conspiracy is easy to concoct if it involves only paper work, and it takes an expert to find it. But you, as a sorcerer, and I, as a criminal investigator, know that a group of human beings simply can't hold a conspiracy together that long."

"Aye, me lord," the stout little Irishman agreed. "I'm glad you stopped me. I almost told Cesare to his face that his theory was all foolishness. Why, that bunch would have given it away before they finished the job. Can you imagine Zeisler tryin' to keep his mouth shut about somethin' like that? Or young Jamieson not breaking down?"

Lord Darcy shook his head. "The whole group couldn't even hide the fact that they were doing something perfectly innocent like assuring an old comrade that they did not think ill of him. Even more ridiculous than that is the notion that any such group would pick a train to commit their murder on, a place where, to all intents and purposes, they would be trapped for hours. Those men are not stupid; they're trained Naval officers. They'd either have killed Peabody in Paris or waited until they got to Napoli. They still couldn't have held their conspiracy together, but they would have thought they had a better chance."

"Still and all," Master Sean said staunchly, "Cesare Sarto is a good investigator."

"I must agree with you there," said Lord Darcy. "He has the knack of finding answers even when you don't want him to."

"How do you mean, me lord?"

"As he and Praefect Angelo were taking Norton away, he offered his hand and thanked me. I said the usual things. I said I hoped I'd see him again. He shook his head. 'I am afraid,' he said, 'that I shall never see Father Armand Brun again. But I hope to meet Lord Darcy some day.' "

Master Sean nodded silently.

The train moved on toward Napoli.

APPENDIX

The Spell of War

The Lieutenant lay on his belly in the middle of a broad clearing in the Bavarian Forest, on the eastern side of the Danau, in a hell of warfare many miles from Dagendorf.

He was 18 years old, and his fingers, clawlike, had dug into and were holding onto the damp earth on which he lay.

Ahead of him, far out of sight beyond the trees, the Polish artillery thundered and roared. It had begun only 30 seconds before, and already it seemed as though it had been going on forever.

Next to him, lying equally flat, was Superior Sergeant Kelleigh. The sergeant was more than twice the lieutenant's age, and had seen long service in the Imperial Army.

"What do you think, sir?" he asked in a hushed voice.

The lieutenant swallowed. "Damned if I know," he said evenly. He was surprised at how calm his voice sounded. It betrayed nothing of what was inside him. "Where are those damned shells going?"

"Over our heads, sir. Hear that whistling burble?"

"I do indeed, Sergeant. Thank you."

"Pleasure, sir. Never been in an artillery barrage before, sir?"

"No, I haven't. I'm learning."

Kelleigh grinned. "We all learn, sir. You faster than most."

"Thank you again, Sergeant." The lieutenant put his field glasses to his eyes and did a quick survey of the surrounding terrain. Too many trees.

A hundred yards to their rear, the shells from the big guns

were exploding, making a syncopated counterpoint to the
roar of the artillery pieces.

"I hope Red Company got out of that," the sergeant
muttered. He was looking back toward the area where the
shells were landing. "Damn, that's good shooting!" He
touched his chest, where his bronze identification sigil rested
beneath his combat jacket. "I'd think they were using a
clairvoyant, except I believe our sorcerers are better than
theirs."

"Don't worry, Sergeant; as long as you've got your sigil
on you, you can't be seen psychically." The lieutenant was
still looking through his field glasses. "If there are any
infantry in that wood, I don't see them. I wonder if—"

Spang-ng-ng-ng!

The bullet sang off a rock not ten inches from the
lieutenant's head.

"That's the Polish infantry, sir. Let's move it."

"Right you are, Sergeant. Roll."

Staying low and moving fast, the two men performed that
maneuver known to the science of military tactics as *Getting The Hell Out.* In the 25 yards they had to move, several more bullets came close, but none hit anything but earth.

They rolled down the sharp declivity that was protecting the rest of Blue Company, and hit bottom hard enough
to take the breath from them.

The lieutenant gasped twice, then said: "Where the hell
were they firing from?"

"Damned if I know, sir. Couldn't tell."

"Well, they're out there in the woods somewhere. That's
why all the artillery shells are going over our heads."

There was no more small-arms fire, though the big guns
kept up their intermittent roar.

"We seem to be safe enough for the moment," the lieutenant said. Further down the ravine, they could see the
rest of Blue Company.

"Aye, sir." The sergeant was silent for a moment, then
said: "Been meanin' to ask you, sir, if you'll not consider
it an impertinence . . ." He paused.

"Go ahead, Sergeant. The worst I'll do is refuse to answer
if it's too personal."

"Thank you, sir. Been meanin' to ask if you were any
kin to Coronel Lord Darcy."

"He's my father," said Lieutenant Darcy.

"It's a pleasure knowin' you, sir. I remember you as a kid—I served under the coronel ten years ago. A great officer, sir."

Lieutenant Darcy suddenly found tears in his eyes. He brushed them away with a sleeve and said: "Then you're Sergeant *Brendon* Kelleigh? My father has spoken of you often. Says you're the finest NCO in His Imperial Majesty's forces. If I ever see him again, I'll tell him of your compliment. He'll be honored."

"I'm the one who's honored, sir." The sergeant's voice was a little choked. "And you'll see him again, sir. You've only been with Blue Company for a week, but I've seen enough of you in action to know you're the survivor type."

"That's as may be," said the lieutenant, "but even if I make it through this mess, I may not see him again. You were with him in Sudan, I believe."

"When he got the bullet through his chest? I was, sir."

"It clipped his heart. Now his condition is deteriorating, and the Healers can do nothing. He'll not live out the year."

After a short silence, Superior Sergeant Kelleigh said: "I'm sorry to hear that, sir. Very sorry. He was a fine officer."

The lieutenant nodded wordlessly. Then he said: "Let's move south, Sergeant, back to Blue Company. Keep low."

"Aye, sir."

They moved down the ravine.

Thirty yards or so down, the two men met Captain Rimbaud, commander of Blue Company.

"I saw you two move back," he said harshly. "What the hell happened? None of that artillery is hitting around us."

He was a big man, two inches taller than Lieutenant Darcy's six feet, and a good stone heavier. He had a blocky face and hard eyes.

"Small-arms fire, sir," the lieutenant said. "From somewhere out in those woods."

The captain's hard eyes shifted to the sergeant. "That right, Kelleigh?"

Lieutenant Darcy let his young face go wooden. He said nothing.

"Aye, sir," the sergeant said stiffly. He, too, had recognized the slight on the young lieutenant. "They're out there, sir; no question of it. First shot came within a foot of us."

Captain Rimbaud looked back at the lieutenant. "Did you see any of them?"

"No, sir." No excuses. He didn't explain about the woods. Rimbaud should be able to figure that out for himself.

The artillery was still thundering.

The captain turned and climbed carefully up the eastern slope of the ravine. A quick peek over the edge, then he slid back down. "No wonder. This slight breeze is bringing the smoke in from those cannon. You two were in the clear. I hope they choke."

"Agreed, sir," said Lieutenant Darcy.

"I think—" began the captain. He didn't finish. There was a noise and a tumble of earth and small stones, and a man came rolling down the western slope of the ravine. Both officers and the noncom had spun around and had their .44 Morleys out and ready for action before the man hit the bottom of the ravine and splashed into the water.

Then they relaxed. The man was wearing the uniform of their own outfit, the Duke of Burgundy's 18th Infantry.

As the square-jawed, tough-looking little man came to his feet, Captain Rimbaud said: "You almost got yourself shot, coming in that way, Sergeant. Who the Hell are you?"

The little sergeant threw him a salute, which the captain returned. "Junior Sergeant Sean O Lochlainn, sir, commanding what is left of Red Company." His Irish brogue was thick.

After a moment, Captain Rimbaud found his voice. *"What is* left *of Red Company?"*

"Aye, sir. The artillery got us. Wiped out the captain, the lieutenant and both senior sergeants. Out of 80 men, there's at most 15 left." He paused. "I don't know if they'll all make it here, sir. There's small-arms fire out there, too."

"Mary, Mother of God," the captain said softly. Then: "All right, let's move down. If one of their observers can get word to their artillery, there will be shells dropping in here pretty soon."

Blue Company was another 35 yards down the ravine. They were warned to watch for Red Company, and during the next few minutes 11 more of them came in. Then there were no more.

There were 75 men of Blue Company, and 12 of Red in that ravine now, all of them wondering what in Hell was going on out in those woods. For some reason, no artillery fire fell in the ravine. Either Blue and Red hadn't been spotted, or the observer couldn't get through to the guns.

While Captain Rimbaud and Sergeant Kelleigh checked out the troops, the young lieutenant sat down next to Sergeant O Lochlainn for a breathing space.

"Queer war it is," said Sean O Lochlainn. "Queer war, indeed."

Soldiers love to talk, if they have the time and opportunity. In combat, it is the only form of entertainment they have. In a hard firefight, their minds are on their precious lives, but as soon as there is a lull, and they are sure the enemy cannot hear them, they will talk. About anything. Family, wives, sweethearts, women in general, booze, beer, parties, bar fights, history, philosophy, clean and dirty jokes—

You name it, and a soldier will talk about it if he can find a buddy interested in the same subject. If he can't, he'll change the subject. But he'll talk, because it's almost the only release he has from the nervous tension of the threat of sudden dismemberment or death.

"All wars are queer, Sergeant," said Lieutenant Darcy. "What's so exceptional about this one?"

"I'd say, sir, because it is exceptionally stupid, even for a war." He glanced at the lieutenant. "Aye, sir; all wars are stupid. But this one is stupider than most. And for once, most of the stupidity is on the other side."

The lieutenant was beginning to like the stout little Irishman. "You think, then, that King Casimir is stupid?"

"Not as an overall thing, no sir," the sergeant said thoughtfully. "But His Slavonic Majesty has done a few stupid things. Wants to be a soldier, like his late father, and can't cope with it, if you see what I mean, sir."

"I do, indeed, Sergeant. Your analysis is cogent."

Sigismund III, from 1922 to 1937, had expanded the Polish Hegemony into Russia, and Poland now controlled it from Minsk to Kiev. But now the Russians showed signs of banding together, and the notion of a United Russia was one that nobody wanted to face, so Sigismund III had wisely abandoned Polish expansion toward the east. Had he remained king, it might well be that the present war would never have taken place, for that cagey old fox had known better than to attempt an attack westward against the Anglo-French Empire. But his son, Casimir IX, who had ascended the throne in 1937, knew no such wisdom. He saw the threat of the Russias and decided to move west into the Germanies, not realizing, apparently, that Charles III, by the grace of God King of England, France, Scotland and Ireland, Lord Protector of the New World, King of the Romans and the Germans, and Emperor of the Holy Roman Empire, would have to protect the Germanies. When Polish troops entered Bavaria, Prince Hermann of Bavaria had called to his liege lord for help, and King Charles had sent it.

Casimir IX wanted to be the military leader his father was, but he was simply not up to it.

Lieutenant Darcy wondered for a moment if that was the flaw in his own character. Coronel Lord Darcy had been a fine soldier and had won many honors in the field. *Am I,* the young lieutenant thought, *trying to be the soldier my father was?* Then: *Hell, no, I never wanted to be a soldier in the first place! I'm out here because the King needs me. And as soon as he doesn't need me anymore, I'm shucking this uniform and getting the Hell back home.*

"It's like Captain Rimbaud," said Sergeant O Lochlainn.

Lieutenant Darcy blinked, bringing his mind back to the conversation. "Beg your pardon, Sergeant? *What's* like Captain Rimbaud?"

"Meanin' no disrespect, sir," said the stout little Irishman, "but Captain Rimbaud's father was General Ambrose Rimbaud, of whom ye have no doubt heard, sir."

"I have," said the lieutenant. "I didn't know that Captain Rimbaud was his son."

"Oh, that he is, sir. Again meanin' no disrespect, sir, but the captain is well known throughout the battalion as a glory hunter."

"I'll reserve judgment on that, Sergeant," said the lieutenant.

"Aye, sir. I'll say no more about it."

The lieutenant edged his way up the slope of the ravine and took a quick look over the top.

He said: "Good God!" very softly.

"What is it, sir?" asked the tough little Irish sergeant.

"Take a look for yourself, Sergeant," Lieutenant Darcy said. "The place is alive with Polish soldiers."

A bullet from a Polish .28 Kosciusco rifle sang across the edge of the ravine, splattering earth over the two men. Then another.

Lieutenant Darcy slid back down the slope.

"With your permission, sir," said the stout little Irishman, "I'd just as soon not take a look now."

Lieutenant Darcy couldn't help but grin. "Excused, Sergeant. They've got us spotted." The grin faded. "There must be at least 30 of them up there in those woods. Probably more, since that smoke is obscuring a lot of them. And there must be even more, up and down the line." He frowned. "There's more smoke out there than one would think, considering how far back the artillery must be."

"I've seen it before, sir," said the Irishman. "It's more fog than smoke. On a cold, damp day like this, the smoke particles seem to make a fog condense out of the air."

The lieutenant nodded. "That accounts for the fact that the Polish infantry can stay inside that cloud and still breathe." He paused, then: "The cloud is getting denser, and it's moving this way. It will be drifting over this ravine in a minute or two. Get down to the captain and tell him what I saw. I'll stay here and make them think there's still a large force in this part of the ravine."

"Aye, sir." The sergeant moved south.

Lieutenant Darcy found an 18-inch piece of broken branch half in the rivulet that ran down the center of the ravine, and moved north about ten yards. Then he climbed up the bank again.

He took off his helmet, put it on the end of the branch, and drew his .44 Morley. Lifting the helmet with his left hand, he fired over the edge with the pistol in his right. He didn't care what his aim was; all he wanted to do was attract attention.

He did.

The bullet whanged off the crown of his helmet, knocking it off the stick into the brooklet.

Damn good shot, the lieutenant thought as he slid back down the embankment.

He retrieved his helmet. There was a shiny streak on the top but no dent. He put the helmet back on in spite of the wetness. By then, the smoky fog was drifting over the top of the ravine.

The lieutenant found himself a little jittery. *Have a smoke,* he told himself. *Relax.* The cloud over the ravine would mask the smoke from his pipe.

He took the stubby little briar from his backpack. It was already filled with tobacco, for emergencies just such as this. It took three flicks of his thumb to get his pipelighter aflame.

And then he found that his hand was shaking so badly that he could not light the pipe. He almost threw the lighter into the stream a few feet away.

He put out the flame and shoved both pipe and lighter back into his backpack.

Get hold of yourself, dammit! he thought. He was thankful that no one had seen him betray his fear that way. He was particularly thankful that Coronel Everard, the battalion commander and an old friend of his father's, hadn't seen him.

He was suddenly aware of the silence. The artillery had stopped. Now there was only the sporadic *crack!* of small-arms fire. He got to his feet and moved quickly south, toward the rest of Blue Company. The sun overhead shone sickly through the yellow-brown haze.

He almost tripped over the body that lay sprawled on the slope. The rivulet gurgled over the dead man's boots. The soldier was face-down, but the bullet hole in the small of his back showed that the slug had gone right through him. The lieutenant stepped over him, choking, and went on.

Blue Company, and what was left of Red, were up on the eastern slope of the ravine. They had scooped out toeholds in the bank in order to stay near the top, but were keeping their heads down.

Captain Rimbaud saw Lieutenant Darcy and said: "Your diversion didn't work, Darcy. They know where we are. How they can see us through this smoke, I don't know."

"Nor do I, sir. Can you see anything?"

"Not a damn thing. I can see them moving occasionally, but not for long enough to get a shot at any one of them. Have you any ideas?"

Lieutenant Darcy tried to ignore the three bodies lying at the bottom of the ravine. "Can we move farther south, sir? That would put us closer to where the rest of the battalion is."

The captain shook his head. "The terrain slopes off rather rapidly, and this ravine gets shallow and disappears. The stream flows out into a flat meadow and makes a bog of it. They'd still have us in their sights, and we'd never make it across that bog."

The lieutenant nodded. "Yes, sir. I can see that."

The troops were firing sporadically into the fog, not with the hope of hitting the occasional flitting shadow that was visible behind the rolling fogbank, but with the hope that they could keep the Polish troops back.

Sergeant Arthur Lyon, second ranking noncom of Blue Company, came running up from the right. He stood six-two, and was solidly built. He was usually smiling, and the lines in his face showed it, but there was no smile on his face now.

"Sir," he said, addressing the captain, "they're moving in to the north of us. If they get into this ravine, we'll have enfilade fire raking us."

"Mary, Mother of God," the captain said with a growl in his voice. He looked at Darcy. "Any suggestions, Lieutenant?"

The lieutenant knew this was a test. Captain Rimbaud had been testing him ever since he had joined Blue Company. "Yes, sir. Apparently, they have us outnumbered. And the cessation of the artillery fire seems ominous to me."

Rimbaud narrowed his eyes. He did not like damp-behind-the-ears lieutenants who used words like "cessation" and "ominous."

"In what way?" he asked.

"They've been lobbing those shells over the woods, sir. They hit Red Company's line and nearly wiped them out. Why haven't they shelled us? I think it's because we're too close, sir. They can't elevate their guns enough to get over those trees and drop shells on us. An observer's messenger has been sent back to tell the Poles to pull their artillery back a hundred yards so they can get at us. In that case, sir, their infantry is merely trying to scare us; they won't come down this far for fear of their own artillery."

"What would you do, Lieutenant?" Rimbaud asked.

"Do we know the characteristics of the cannon they're using, sir?" Lieutenant Darcy asked.

"The six-inch Gornicki? I don't, personally; I'm not an artilleryman."

"But our artillery officers would?"

"Certainly."

"Very well, sir," the lieutenant said decisively. "Our artillery is southwest of here. If we go to the southern end of this ravine and head back that way, we can report what we know. The Polish guns won't go back any farther than they have to in order to lob shells into us. Knowing the characteristics of the Gornicki, the artillery officers can figure out where the guns *must* be when the shells start hitting this ravine, and they can lay down a barrage on the Poles."

The captain's eyes narrowed. When he spoke, his voice was heavy with a mixture of sarcasm and scorn. "I see. On the basis of pure guesswork, you would have us *retreat?* Not while *I* am captain of this company, we won't." He turned his head to look up and eastward, though he could see nothing but the sky and the upper portions of trees. "If they haven't come here after us in exactly ten minutes, this company is going over the edge of this damned ravine and straight through them. Got that?"

"Yes, sir," said the lieutenant. Such a charge would be suicide, and the lieutenant knew it.

"Lieutenant, north of here this ravine narrows down for a few yards, then it makes a slight curve to the east. Three men could hold off anyone coming down through there. Take Sergeant Lyon and Sergeant O Lochlainn with you. Grab some rifles from the dead; they won't be needing them, and a rifle is better for that sort of work than a handgun. Don't forget to take ammo. Now, get moving. Be back here in five minutes."

Silently, the three men obeyed.

They stayed low, and as close to the eastern bank of the ravine as possible.

It was autumn now, and the dry summer had left little water running down the ravine, but it was obvious that, come spring, when the winter snows melted, the water would be much higher. What was now a trickle would become a flood.

Now, the banks were six to eight feet above the water level, but in spring the ravine would be close to full.

"The captain has a lot of nerve," Sergeant O Lochlainn said quietly. There was a touch of sarcasm in his whispered voice.

"That's not nerve," said Sergeant Lyon. "Charging through that line is idiocy."

"'Tis not what I meant, Sergeant," Sean O Lochlainn said. "What I meant was, he'd got a lot of nerve ordering me around; I didn't relinquish command of Red Company to him, but he assumes it."

"Then why did you obey?" Lyon asked.

"Habit, I guess. Habit." Sergeant O Lochlainn sounded as though he were unhappy with himself.

They came to the narrow part of the ravine. Here, the clay walls had been eroded back to uncover two huge slabs of rock, one on each side. They were almost perpendicular to the bottom, giving sheer walls seven feet high on the eastern side and nearly eight feet on the western. The gap between them was only three feet.

"I think the captain was right about this, sir," said Sergeant Lyon. "Three men with rifles can hold off anything that tries to come through there."

Lieutenant Darcy glanced at his wristwatch, then looked down the narrow corridor. It was straight for some thirty yards, then swerved northwest as the banks became clay again. "We can do it, I think," he said. "But watch out for grenades. I doubt if they have anyone who can lob a grenade that far up and over, but they might. Let's back up to that last bend. We can still pick them off if they try to come down that narrow gap, and there'll be less chance of anyone dropping a fistful of high explosive on us."

When they got into position, Lieutenant Darcy said: "If you would, Sergeant O Lochlainn, guard our rear and keep an eye on the eastern parapet, just in case the Poles try to cut us off from the rest."

"Aye, sir."

They waited. The minutes passed slowly.

"You're not a career man, are you, sir?" Sergeant Lyon asked.

"No. I saw enough of the Army when I was a boy. My father was a career man."

"Would that be the Coronel Lord Darcy that Sergeant Kelleigh always talks about?"

"Yes. Kelleigh was my father's top-kick in the old days. Are you career?"

"No, sir. When this mess is over, I'm taking my discharge as soon as I can get it."

Behind them, Sergeant O Lochlainn's voice said: "What're ye goin' to do, once ye get out, Sergeant?"

"Well, I used to think I had a call for the priesthood," Lyon said, "but I'm not sure of it, and as long as one isn't sure, one oughtn't to try it. I think I'll try out for Armsman. Being an Officer of the King's Peace is a job I think I can handle and one I *am* sure of. What about you, O Lochlainn?"

"Well, now, that's a thing I'm sure as sure of," the stout little Irishman said. "I'm going to be a Master Sorcerer."

"Indeed?" said Lieutenant Darcy. "Have you been tested for the Talent, then?"

"Why, sir, I already have me Journeyman's ticket in the Guild."

"You do? Then what the Hell are you doing in the Army? You could have got a deferment easily enough."

"So could you have, sir, I dare say. But *somebody's* got to fight this bloody war, sir. I volunteered for the same reason you did, sir." He paused. Then: "The Empire expects every man to do his duty, sir."

The lieutenant glanced at his wristwatch. Two minutes to go, and no sign of enemy activity. *Yes,* he thought, *the Empire* does *expect every man to do his duty.*

The Anglo-French Empire had already lasted longer than the ancient Roman Empire. The first Plantagenet, Henry of Anjou, had become King of England in 1154, taking the title Henry II. His son, Richard the Lion-Hearted, had become King upon the death of Henry II in 1189. Richard I had been absent from England during most of the first ten years of his reign, establishing a reputation as a fighter in the Holy Land. Even today, Islamic mothers threaten their children with *Al Rik,* a most horrendous *afreet.*

Richard had been hit by a crossbow bolt at the Siege of Chaluz in 1199, and after a long bout with infection and fever, had survived to become a wise and powerful ruler. His younger brother, John, died in exile in 1216, so when Richard died in 1219 the crown had gone to Richard's nephew, Arthur, son of Geoffrey of Brittany. Known as "Good King Arthur," he was often confused in the popular mind with King Arthur Pendragon, of ancient Kymric legend.

During Arthur's reign, St. Hilary of Walsingham had

produced his monumental works which outlined the theory and mathematics of Magic. But only those with the Talent could utilize St. Hilary's Laws of Magic.

Even today, such people were rare, and Lieutenant Darcy felt that it was a waste to allow Sean O Lochlainn to expose his God-given Talent to the sudden death that could come from combat.

Every man must do his duty, yes. But what was the duty of a Sorcerer?

"Someone cumin' from the rear," said Sergeant O Lochlainn.

"Watch ahead, Lyon," the lieutenant said sharply. He turned to see what was coming from behind.

It was Senior Sergeant Kelleigh.

"What is it, Sergeant?" the lieutenant asked.

Kelleigh swallowed. "Sir, you are in command. Captain Rimbaud is dead."

The lieutenant looked at his wristwatch. One minute left, and no one had come down that corridor. "Let's move," he said in a quiet, calm voice. "Back to the company. Keep down."

It was not true calmness, the lieutenant knew; it was numbness, overlying and masking his fear. Fear of the artillery, fear of death and dismemberment, had been suddenly supplemented by a fear that was akin to, but vastly greater than, stage fright.

He? *He?* In command?

Mary, Mother of God, pray for me!

He was younger than any other man in the outfit, and he had less combat experience than most of them. And yet the burden of command had fallen on *him.*

He knew he dared not show his inner self; he dared not crack. Not for fear of showing himself a coward, but because of what it would do to the men. In a properly trained army, when the officers are taken out of action, the noncoms can carry on. Death is expected; it may come as a shock, but not as a surprise.

But for a commander to go into a panic of fear, to show the yellow, is more demoralizing than sudden death.

A soldier, consciously or subconsciously, rightly or wrongly, always feels that his superiors know more about what is going on than he does. Therefore, if an officer cracks up, it must be because he knows something that the men don't.

And fear of the unknown can cause more despair than fear of the known.

So the fear of causing catastrophe to his troops (*his* troops!) overrode all the other fears as he led the three sergeants back to the rest of the men while the irregular *crack!* of small-arms fire punctuated the air.

The captain's body lay a few feet from the rivulet that ran down the ravine. It was covered by a blanket. Lieutenant Darcy knelt down, gently lifted the covering and looked at his late commander. There was a bullet wound in his chest, just to the left of the lower tip of the sternum.

"Went right through 'im, it did, sir," said a nearby corporal. Whittaker? Yes; Whittaker.

The lieutenant carefully turned the body on its side. The exit wound near the spine, between the fifth and sixth ribs, was larger than the entrance wound, as might be expected. From the trajectory, the lieutenant judged it must have gone right through the heart. *Probably died before he knew he'd been hit,* he thought. He replaced the blanket and stood up.

"How long do you think it will be before the Poles get their guns back in position, Sergeant?" he asked Kelleigh.

Kelleigh looked at his wristwatch. "Another five minutes is all we can depend on, sir." He looked at the lieutenant and stood expectantly, awaiting his orders. So were the other two sergeants.

Without saying anything, the lieutenant went over to where the late captain had dropped his pack. He opened it and took out the little collapsing periscope. Then he climbed up the slope of the ravine wall and eased the upper end of the periscope over the top. The captain had carried the device because regulations said he should, but he never used it because he thought it a coward's gadget. Lieutenant Darcy believed there was a difference between caution and cowardice.

After half a minute, he said: "Sergeant Kelleigh, what are the men shooting at?" Most of the foggy smoke had cleared away, and the lieutenant could see nothing but woods out there. There wasn't a Polish soldier in sight.

Kelleigh climbed up the slope and took a quick look over the top. "Why—at those Polish troops out there, sir. They're behind those trees, shootin' at us." His voice had a touch of bewilderment in it, as though he were afraid the young lieutenant had lost his reason.

The lieutenant moved up and looked over the edge. He could see them now. Some were lying prone, some standing behind trees, and now and then one would move from one tree to another in the background. He slid down a little and used the periscope again. No one. The woods were empty.

"Sergeant O Lochlainn!" he snapped.

"Aye, sir!"

"Come up here for a minute. Sergeant Kelleigh, tell the men to cease fire and get ready to move out."

"Yes, sir." He slid down and was gone.

The stout little Irish sergeant clambered up to where the lieutenant was. "Aye, sir?"

"Take a look at those woods through the periscope. Then take a look over the top. And don't think like a soldier; think like a Sorcerer."

Sergeant O Lochlainn did as he was told without saying a word until he was done. But when he brought his head down, he looked at Lieutenant Darcy. "Shades o' S'n Padraeg! You're right, sir. 'Tis an illusion. There's no troops out there. It's a psychic effect that registers on the mind, not on the eye, so it isn't visible in a mirror."

"And it's being projected through that haze?"

"Aye, sir; it's needed for a big illusion like that."

Lieutenant Darcy frowned. "We can't say there isn't *anybody* out there. Someone is shooting at us."

"Aye, sir. And a pretty good shot, too."

"Can you dispel that illusion, Sergeant?"

"No, sir; not with the equipment I've got with me. Not in a minute or two." He paused. "If we could locate the sniper—"

Lieutenant Darcy was back at the periscope. "He must have us spotted here by now. Three of us have looked over that edge, but he can't know if it's the same man or not, so—" He stopped suddenly. "I think I see him. No wonder he's so good at spotting us."

"Where, sir?"

"Up in that big tree to the northwest. About 35 feet off the ground. Here; take the periscope."

The sergeant took it and, after a moment said: "Aye, sir. I see him. I wonder if there's any more about."

"I don't think so. Have you noticed the wounds of the men who have been hit were always high on the left side of the body?"

"Now that I think of it, sir. But I thought nothing of it."

"Neither did I until I saw that those Polish troops are illusions. Then I realized that whoever was doing the shooting was high up and to the northeast. Then everything was obvious."

"That's how you knew which tree to look at, sir?"

"Yes, I—" He stopped, listening to the silence. The order to cease fire had been relayed to his troops.

Sergeant Kelleigh approached and looked up the slope at his new commander. "Sir, the troops are ready to march. We'd best get started if we're going to get out of here, sir; that artillery can start any minute now."

The lieutenant slid down the bank of the ravine. "Who are your two best riflemen, Sergeant? Your best shots."

"Corporal Whittaker and Senior Private Martinne, sir."

"Let's go. Come along, Sergeant O Lochlainn."

The remainders of Blue and Red Companies were waiting for them, packs on, rifles at the ready.

The lieutenant said "At ease" before they could come to attention, then said: "I want all of you to listen very carefully because we only have time for me to say it once. Sergeant Kelleigh, take this periscope and get up there and tell me what you see. Don't stick your head up; use the 'scope. While he's doing that, the rest of you pay attention.

"Sergeant O Lochlainn, here, has a ticket as a Journeyman Sorcerer. He and I have discovered that sorcery is being used against us. Not, I think, strictly Black Magic, eh, Sergeant?"

"Not at all, sir," said the Irishman. "An illusion is meant to confuse, but it does no direct harm. Not Black Magic at all."

"Very well, then," the lieutenant continued. "But we've been pinned down here by—"

Senior Sergeant Kelleigh came back down the slope, his eyes wide, his face white. "There's nobody up there," he said softly.

"Almost nobody. We've been pinned down by a lone

sniper. All those Polish troops we've been firing at are illusions produced by sorcery. But you can't see them in a mirror.

"The sniper is in that big tree to the northeast, about 35 feet up. Corporal Whittaker, Private Martinne, the Senior Sergeant tells me you're crack shots. Take the periscope and spot that sniper. Then both of you keep up a steady fire. Kill him if you can, but at least make sure he stays down. The rest of us are going to go over the top and head for those woods while you keep up cover fire for us. As soon as we get there, we'll all cover for you, and you come running. Everybody got all that?"

"Yes, sir," came the ragged chorus.

"Now, I want you to realize one important thing. The Poles haven't got much infantry around. If they did, they'd use them, instead of relying on one man and a set of illusions. They have damned few men to move, fire and protect those field pieces.

"So we, lads, are going through that woods and take those field pieces away from them."

Grins broke out on the soldiers' faces.

"It's going to be hard, but I want you to keep in mind that the soldiers you'll see when you get out there are only illusions. They can't hurt you. All the firing for the past quarter hour has been done by us and that sniper. Notice how quiet it is now. It has been so noisy in this ravine that we didn't realize *we* were making all the noise. But now we'll have to get out of here before the real noise starts."

Whittaker and Martinne were already up at the lip of the ravine. After a moment, the corporal said: "We've got him spotted, sir."

"Fire when ready."

The two men cut loose.

"Let's go, men," said the lieutenant.

And up and over they went.

Lieutenant Darcy, in the lead, threw a swift glance at the tall tree that held the sniper. Bullets from the rifles of Whittaker and Martinne were splashing bark off the trunk and the limb where the sniper was hiding. Good enough.

They moved fast, keeping low and spread out. It was

possible that there might be more than one sniper around, though the lieutenant didn't think so, and playing it cautiously was the order of the day.

Ahead of them, the illusory Polish infantrymen still moved about, but they no longer seemed real. They were flickering phantoms that receded and faded as the Imperial troops moved toward them.

"Where's Kelleigh goin', sir?" Sergeant O Lochlainn's voice came from a few yards to Lieutenant Darcy's left. The lieutenant took a quick glance.

Instead of going straight for the woods, Kelleigh had cut off to the left at an angle. Covered by the rifle fire from Whittaker and Martinne, he was headed straight for the sniper's tree!

"He's going to get that sniper," Lieutenant Darcy said sharply. *The damned fool!* he added to himself. He hadn't ordered Kelleigh to do that. On the other hand, he hadn't ordered him not to—simply because it hadn't occurred to him that Kelleigh would do anything like that. *And it should have,* he told himself. *It should have!*

But now was no time to say anything.

The remains of Blue and Red Companies reached the woods.

"Get down!" the lieutenant snapped. "Lay some covering fire on that tree so that Whittaker and Martinne can get over here!"

The order was obeyed, and the two men came up and over just as the Polish Gornickis exploded into thunder, launching their six-inch shells toward the ravine.

Whittaker and Martinne were only a few yards from the edge of the ravine when the first salvo exploded at the bottom of it. If the shells had landed that close on level ground, the men would have died then and there, but the walls of the ravine directed most of the blast upward. Both men were knocked flat, but they were up again and running within seconds.

Then there was the crack of a rifle shot from the sniper's tree, and Martinne fell sprawling, his left eye and temple a smashed ruin. Whittaker kept coming.

The lieutenant snapped his head around to look at the tree.

Sergeant Kelleigh was still a few yards from it. The sniper hadn't seen Kelleigh yet; he had moved around to the north side of the tree, to another branch, and had seen the two men running. One shot, and Martinne was dead.

Then the sniper saw Superior Sergeant Kelleigh. He had to make a snap decision and a snap shot. Kelleigh, obviously hit, stumbled, fell and rolled.

But he was behind that tree, and the sniper couldn't adjust his precarious position fast enough to get his rifle to bear a second time. Kelleigh, flat on his back, had his .44 MMP out and firing. Two shots.

Even as the sniper fell, Kelleigh hit him with one more shot in midair.

Seeing all this from a distance, Lieutenant Darcy gave the order to cease fire. Then: "Sergeant Lyon, you are senior NCO now. Send someone out to look at Martinne. I think he's dead, but make sure. Sergeant O Lochlainn, will you come with me?"

The thunder of the guns went on; the shells fell screaming into the ravine to spend their explosions uselessly against the clay of the walls and other, equally lifeless clay.

The lieutenant and Sergeant O Lochlainn ran northward to where Sergeant Kelleigh lay.

He was still flat on his back, eyes closed, right hand clasping his .44 Morley to his chest. It rose and fell with his chest. Beneath it, blood flowed steadily.

The lieutenant knelt down. "Kelleigh?"

The sergeant opened his eyes, focusing them unsteadily on the young face. "You know," he said distinctly.

The lieutenant nodded.

"Don't tell the coronel."

And then, very quietly, he died.

With his thumbs, the lieutenant pulled the eyelids down, held them for a few seconds. Sergeant O Lochlainn made the Sign of the Cross and murmured an almost inaudible prayer. The lieutenant made the same Sign in silence, letting the stout little Irishman's prayer do for both of them.

Then Sergeant O Lochlainn went to the body of the sniper. The Pole had fallen on his face and was very definitely dead. The Irishman opened the sniper's backpack and began rummaging through it.

"Here! What are you doing?" Lieutenant Darcy asked. Robbing the dead was not a part of civilized warfare—if such a thing existed.

"Well, sir," said Sergeant O Lochlainn without looking up from what he was doing, "this man here was a sorcerer of some small ability, and he might have the paraphernalia I need. Ah! Just the thing! Here we are!"

"What do you mean?" the lieutenant asked.

"Well, sir," the sergeant said, looking up with a grin, "if we're going to take those field pieces away from the Poles, it might be better if they're attacked by a battalion instead of the bob ends of two companies. And believe me, sir, I'm a better sorcerer than he was."

Lieutenant Darcy tried to return the grin. "I see. Very well, Sergeant; carry on."

The artillery thundered on.

Lieutenant Darcy picked up his small group of men and moved eastward with them. The soft breeze brought the smoke and stench of the thundering guns directly toward them, but it drifted slowly, and it was not dense enough to make the men cough.

There was a grim smile on Sergeant O Lochlainn's face as they neared the eastern edge of the woods. Beyond was a clear space of half a mile or so square.

Sergeants Lyon and O Lochlainn and Lieutenant Darcy lay flat on their bellies watching the battery of eight Gornickis blast away. The lieutenant watched through his field glasses for a full minute, then said: "Fifteen, maybe sixteen infantrymen with rifles. The rest are all gun crews. Range about 800 yards." He took the binoculars from his eyes and looked at the Irish sergeant. "Where do you have to be to set up our phantom battalion, Sergeant?"

"I'll have to set it up right about here, sir. But I can establish my focal point, and then get out, leaving it to operate by itself."

"Good. Because when they see your illusions coming, those gunners are going to depress their barrels and fire point blank. Can you set up the illusion so that some of them will fall when shells explode around them?"

"Nothin' to it, sir."

"Fine. The rest of us will move south to those woods flanking them. Give us ten minutes to get there before you start the phantoms moving in. Then run like Hell to get down with us before they start firing straight in here instead of over our heads. From their flank, we can enfilade them and wipe them out before they know what's happening."

"It's goin' to tear Hell out of these trees," was all the sergeant said.

The lieutenant and Sergeant Lyon led the men south through the woods and then turned eastward again, well south of the clearing where the Polish artillery blasted away.

"All right now, lads," the lieutenant said, "set your sights for 350 yards. Keep low and try to make every shot count. We won't see the phantoms, but the Poles will. We will be able to tell when they see the illusion by the way they behave; their infantry will start firing their rifles toward those trees to our left, and the gunnery crews will stop their barrage and frantically start depressing the muzzles of their pieces. As soon as their infantry begins to fire, so do we. But—mark this!—*no volleys!*

"If we all fire at once, they'll spot us. Now, I'm going to count you off and I want you to remember your number. Whatever your number is, I want you to listen for that many shots from here before you fire. After that, you may fire at will, slow and steady. We're getting low on ammo, so don't be wasteful. Got it?"

They did. The lieutenant counted them off.

For a minute or two, nothing happened. Then everything happened. There were shouts and sounds of excitement from the Polish lines. The infantrymen threw themselves prone and began firing at nothing the Imperial forces could see. The gunners began frantically spinning the wheels that would lower the aim of their guns.

The lieutenant, who had given himself no number and was therefore automatically Number Zero, took careful aim and fired. A man dropped limply and the lieutenant swallowed a sudden blockage in his throat. It was the first time he had ever deliberately fired at and killed a man.

The rest of the men, in order, began firing steadily.

Very rarely do battles go as one expects them to, but this was one of the rare ones. The Poles, to the very end, never did figure out where that death-dealing fire was coming from. The distraction of the phantoms advancing toward them in numberless hordes kept them from even thinking about their left flank. The action was over in minutes.

"Now what, sir?" asked Sergeant Lyon. "Shall we go out and take over those guns?"

"Not yet. Battalion can't be over a couple of miles south of here. Send a couple of runners. We'll wait here, just in case more Poles come. We'll be safer here in these woods than out there, standing around those field pieces. Have the runners report directly to Coronel Everard and get his orders on what to do with those things. Move."

"Yes, sir." Sergeant Lyon obeyed.

Lieutenant Darcy sat down on a nearby fallen log, took out his pipe, tamped it lightly and fired it up. Sergeant O Lochlainn came up and sat beside him. "Mind if I join you, sir?"

"Not at all. Welcome."

"Nice piece of work, sir."

"Same to you, Sergeant. I don't know what those Poles saw, but it must have been something to see. Panicked the Hell out of them. Congratulations."

"Thank you, sir." After a pause, the sergeant said: "Sir, may I ask a question? Maybe it's none of me business, and if so ye've but to tell me and I'll never think of it again."

"Go ahead, Sergeant."

"What was it Sergeant Kelleigh didn't want you to tell Coronel Everard?"

The young lieutenant frowned and puffed solemnly at his pipe for nearly half a minute before he said: "To be perfectly honest, Sergeant, I don't know of anything he would want me to keep from Coronel Everard. Not a thing."

No, he thought. *Nothing he had wanted to keep from Coronel Everard. He didn't want me to tell Coronel Darcy. And I shan't. Kelleigh made a terrible mistake, but he paid for it, and that's an end of it.*

"I see, sir," the Irishman said slowly. "He was dying and likely didn't know what he was saying. Or who he was talkin' to."

"That could be," Lieutenant Darcy said.

But he knew it wasn't so. He had known since he saw the captain's body that Kelleigh had shot him. The bullet had gone straight through, parallel to the ground, not from a high angle. And the hole had been made by a .44 Morley, not by a .28 Kosciusko.

It would have been simple. Men in a firefight don't pay

any attention to what is going on to their right or left, and what is one more shot among so many?

Kelleigh had felt that the captain's decision to charge the Polish line was suicidal, and that Darcy's planned retreat was the wiser course.

When he found that the Polish troops were an illusion, he had paid for his crime in the best way he knew how. Captain Rimbaud had been going to do the right thing for the wrong reason, and Kelleigh could no longer live with himself.

There would be no point in telling anyone. Kelleigh was dead, and the only evidence—Rimbaud's body—had been blown to bits in the first Polish salvo to hit the ravine.

But—however wrongly, Kelleigh had given Lieutenant Darcy his first command. The lieutenant would never forget that, but he would always wonder whether it had been worth it.

The Hell with it, he thought. And knocked the dottle from his pipe.